THRONE

A

FROM THE

ASHES

THRONE

A

FROM THE

ASHES

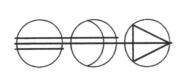

C.C. PEÑARANDA

III

LUMARIAS PRESS

Published by Lumarias Press

www.lumariaspress.com

First Edition published February 2022

Map design © 2022 by Chloe C. Peñaranda
Cover illustration © 2022 by Alice Maria Power
www.alicemariapower.com
Cover design © 2022 by Lumarias Press
Edited by Bryony Leah
www.bryonyleah.com

Identifiers
ISBN: 978-1-8382480-8-6 (eBook)
ISBN: 978-1-8382480-6-2 (paperback)
ISBN: 978-1-8382480-7-9 (hardback)

www.ccpenaranda.com

CONTENT WARNING

Contains some scenes not suitable for younger audiences. Including scenes of an explicit sexual nature, death, and violence.

DEDICATION

For you, my brave reader—dare to take the leap.

Mortus Mountains

The Dark Woods

DALRUNE

DALNIRE

Rune Desert

Galmire

Dagdune

Valleys of Fenstead

OLMSTONE

VESMIRE

Fenher

Silver Forests

FENSTEAD

CALENMOORE

East Moorlands

Esmire

South Moorlands

RHYENELLE

ELLIUM

VALGARD

Balmore

Fire Mountains

The Southern Gulf

PROLOGUE

Lilianna

L ILIANNA DIDN'T KNOW when she fell to her knees or for how long she bowed in her sorrow. She couldn't feel the ache in her bones against the cold stone of the library anymore. She couldn't feel anything in the embrace of a numbness so detached she may as well have been in another realm, another time. Perhaps if she were, her life, her dreams, would still hold the bright hope of a reality within reach. Instead, her once prosperous future had been reduced to nothing but foreboding and uncertainty.

Yet it was not for herself that her heart shattered.

Her hand moved over her still flat stomach, beginning an idle, vacant caress as she pictured the life within; the beautiful girl she carried. Even that secret had been robbed from her: the excitement of guessing, waiting to see whether she would bear a son or daughter. Regardless, she would love the child more than life itself. Protect them.

Now, every plan and joyous thought that filled her mind in the moment she confirmed her pregnancy two weeks ago required sudden, world-caving reassessment. He couldn't know.

Agalhor Ashfyre couldn't know he sired a daughter.

It was an unforgivable, dark thought that escaped in a sob from her painfully hoarse throat. She couldn't afford to think of his heart—or her own. All that mattered now was *her.*

The miracle she and Agalhor had conceived was a blessing Lilianna didn't think she would ever be granted in this life. But this child was not a gift to two doting parents who would love her endlessly; she was a death knell gripped by a twisted, sinister fate before even her first breath. If what Lilianna had discovered in the scattered texts above were true, she'd never felt such a burning determination to shield her child from it all. From the world if she had to. To protect her daughter, she would sacrifice everything.

She couldn't bear to look at the text on the Great Spirits splayed out on the desk. She had been so full of hope and wonder, in search of a solution that would bind her fate to the one she loved so they could spend an eternity or a simple length of mundane time together. Yet all it took was a second to shatter her prosperous world completely.

If she had discovered the consequences of bearing a child conceived of a Bloodline Blessed and a Descendant of Marvellas earlier, if she had known the damned fate she would be condemning the child to... perhaps she might have been more careful. She might have taken all precautions to avoid conception with Agalhor despite believing the chances were so rare they weren't worthy of concern.

Lilianna's hand circled her flat stomach. Her head bowed low. Wetness trailed her cheeks with the taunting but wondrous images that filled her mind. Their daughter. Agalhor would make the most adoring father, and she would look just like him, take after him completely. The bond they would have would be Lilianna's life's joy to watch. But in her plan to protect her child, she would be robbing them both of that irre-

A THRONE FROM THE ASHES

placeable bond. She had to cover her face with the nausea and guilt that consumed her.

Now, she had a choice to make. An awful, heart-wrenching choice that darkened her soul to think about. She couldn't afford to be selfish, couldn't afford to think from the heart. She had to protect her child.

"My love?"

Agalhor's voice rang in concern and snapped her attention upward. Lilianna jolted up, the shooting pain in both her legs confirming it had been some time since she collapsed out of utter heartbreak and disbelief. She quickly grabbed some loose parchments, shuffling them over the pages of the book she'd been reading.

As she used the desk for support while her legs regained strength and blood flow, Agalhor crossed the space. She was forced to look at him when his hand took her chin. Worry creased his forehead, and it took every ounce of her will not to break down in front of him.

He couldn't know. He wouldn't understand.

"You've been crying." His arm went around her, and she couldn't stop him when he pulled her to his chest. "Tell me what's the matter, Lili."

Lilianna didn't sob, but silent tears fell. She couldn't tell him—not without the risk of him stopping her. No one could know about the child she carried.

"I love you," she whispered, clinging to him a little tighter, savoring the feeling she didn't want to believe she had to part with.

Agalhor's hand smoothed over the hair at her nape. "And I love you. Always." He peeled her from his chest, his rough palm sliding along her jaw. "You didn't find anything in your readings today?" He meant about finding a way to break the curse of time.

Lilianna's brow pinched, and she clenched her teeth against the outpour of emotion that threatened to undo her once more. She shook her head weakly, letting him believe that was the sole reason for her upset as it had been so many times before.

"We must keep having faith, Lili," he soothed. So gentle and kind. Hopeful. Words he had spoken to her a thousand times, always the one with so much determination they would conquer time.

And she was about to tear it all away from him with what she had to do.

"Say that again," she murmured.

His hands took her face, pride and love swirling in his hazel gaze, which she held, savoring and memorizing every highlight and hue. He leaned down to touch his lips to hers—a kiss so soft and barely-there. When he pulled back, his warm smile was heartbreaking.

"Have faith we will find a way, my dear."

Her heart swelled to the point she thought it might erupt. It didn't matter—it would be left behind with him. But the word was like a song, a note of him she would carry with her for eternity. Lilianna echoed it after him as a promise, a gift he would never know he had given to their child when she left.

"Keep having…*Faythe.*"

CHAPTER 1

Zaiana

THE GENTLE, MELODIC thrum of a heartbeat did not resonate from her own chest.

Zaiana Silverfair could hear the organ singing in the human seated in the chair across the room waiting for her to make a move. Its tempo picked up with each deliberately slow step she took toward him.

Any one of the sorry-state men in the retched inn below could have been her victim for the night, but she'd been tracking this one all day. The thrill of the hunt began in the stalking. She'd followed him home, watching from the shadows as he sat down to a warm meal cooked by a seemingly loving wife, two children on either side. The sight sickened her: deceitful happiness. Zaiana was glad she had been spared from such horrid emotion. The man had left that night, heading to this very location, where she'd watched him sit down to a game of cards when he barely had enough coin to provide a sustainable meal for his family, never mind fund his reckless, foolish nighttime addiction of gambling and ale. All it had taken were a series of timed seductive looks and sultry smiles for him to forget what he'd left at home and follow her up here. She'd played this game many times—and she never lost.

It always fascinated Zaiana, the effect lust had on a man. All her human victims had been submissive to it; controlled by it. So much so they allowed themselves to be led by death in the guise of a beautiful woman.

Zaiana had glamoured herself with magick to wander the human town, rounding her ears to be accepted, not feared. If her targets stopped to think, to look with their eyes and not their cocks, they would realize she far from fit in with their species. Her beauty was her greatest weapon. Her features were too perfect, the skin on her face too porcelain and unmarked by life. Her hair was a spilled inkwell of glistening black, and her eyes—they were perhaps the most distinguishing feature that should have made them question her façade. The core of vibrant purple around her pupils against her obsidian irises was almost as bright as the lightning she could conjure from her fingertips.

Zaiana didn't care for looks. She didn't care for anything. But her looks lured her victims straight to her with no endeavor. As much as she enjoyed a chase, a fight, a *challenge*, tonight was simply to feed her guilty pleasure: to marvel over the beat of a heart, because her own was as still as stone and cold as ice.

If any of her kin knew where she was—what she was doing—she would face brutal punishment. Humans were a drug, their blood a means to strengthen the agility of her kind, nothing more. Yet Zaiana stopped feeding on them long ago.

It wasn't out of empathy. No—she wasn't capable of that emotion. She refrained from indulging on the sweetness of their life-form simply because she didn't want to depend on a feed to make her strong. She relished in the silent satisfaction she had made herself into one of the most powerful dark fae without a performance enhancer.

When Zaiana got close enough, the human man lifted his disgusting hands to touch her. She gripped his wrists before he could, slamming them against the arms of the chair he sat in, pinning them in place and leaning her head in to caress his neck with a breath. He hissed in pain but reveled in her dominance. While his mind clouded completely with desire for her body, Zaiana tuned in to the pulse of his heart. Her ability to alter its rhythm with her actions while he remained oblivious to her game was her eternal delight.

Leaning back, she lifted a hand to his chest, angling her iron-tipped middle and pointer fingers to graze their razor-sharp edges along the bare skin above his shirt. The metal guards she sported on those fingers on each hand were a gift from someone she didn't allow herself to think about anymore. They weren't just decorative jewelry or a sentimental feature; they were purposeful, a conductor of her lightning that allowed her to strike with far more precision.

Zaiana summoned a slight vibration of her bolts. It rippled delightfully through her veins to reach the end of the sharp tips she pressed over the man's heart. He tensed at the minor shock, teeth clenching and fists curling tightly around the armchair. A feline smile crept across her cheeks. She had disturbed the organ's rhythm—but she wanted more. She wanted to hear its pace quicken faster than his lust was sending it.

Fear was the ultimate trigger. Tired of the foreplay already, Zaiana released the glamour on her heritage, and the man's eyes immediately snapped to the points of her ears. He lurched back in horror, all desire to bed her winking out in an instant. Her cruel smile widened, revealing the sharp, elongated canines she hardly ever felt the need to show off. He tried to get up from his seat, but Zaiana released a stronger wave of electricity through her iron-clad fingertips that still pinched the surface of his skin. His body spasmed then fell limp when she stopped.

She tipped her head back, closing her eyes, and simply tuned in to the racing drum of terror in his chest that drowned out his desperate, pathetic pleas. It wasn't enough. It was *fast* enough, and she always relished in pushing a heart to its very limit—a pace that might drive the organ keeping the body alive to shut it down instead. With a deep breath, she rolled her shoulders back, basking in the pleasure of releasing her final glamour. Her wings. She felt them gloriously expand from each side of her spine, and she flexed, splaying them to their full length, casting a dark shadow over the man who'd turned ghostly pale, eyes bulging from his sockets.

The reek of his soiled pants hit her, and she wrinkled her nose in disgust, glancing down at the darkened patch around his crotch. She groaned in disappointment. "Now you've ruined the mood," she complained, her voice a symphonic enchantment.

The man didn't move, paralyzed by fear of the foreign species towering over him.

No one knew her kind still existed. They were believed to be long extinct, wiped out by their inferior sister race during the Dark Age. To Zaiana, their great unveiling to the world couldn't come quickly enough, and she had taken every opportunity to escape the insufferable confines beneath the Mortus Mountains that had been her prison for centuries. She would have free rein over Ungardia and beyond—when the time was right. As the masters had always taught them.

The scandalous gown she'd materialized herself in had also disappeared, and she stood in black leathers with silver accents matching the tone of her blood. The embellishments singled her out as the delegated leader of the Silverfairs, a position she'd rightfully won through strength and conquer in the Blood Trials over a century ago. Nothing was given among her kind; everything was earned.

Zaiana tucked her taloned wings in tight, bracing her hands on the arms of the chair to lean into the man again. "Your fun may have ended, but mine has just begun."

His heartbeat was delightfully erratic, blood throbbing mesmerizingly in the veins of his neck as she angled her head to watch. His breathing was short, and she knew if he didn't match it to the speed of his vital organ he would fall unconscious. Zaiana didn't want that. Lifting her pointer finger, she tore down the length of his neck with her iron claw, missing the crucial artery so he wouldn't bleed out immediately. Watching the crimson glisten and roll over his ruddy skin, she inhaled the sweet scent like finely aged wine then sent another current of electricity through his chest with her other hand. It killed the scream in his throat, but at least he was now panting hard.

"That's better," she cooed.

"P-please… I-I have a family."

Zaiana pulled back, no longer in the mood to play at those words. Her eyes flashed in a white rage while her hand shot out to his chest, braced to plunge straight through and tear out his heart. "How pathetic," she seethed, her iron claws sinking past his skin first, and he let out a choked gasp. "Using them in a bid to save your own miserable life." With more pressure, her other fingertips broke the surface, and she swallowed her dark desire upon feeling the warmth of his blood.

The man spluttered but didn't cry out.

When she couldn't hold back any longer, her whole hand reached into his chest until her fingers curled around his shuddering heart. She let out a breathless sound, the darkest, most sadistic part of her enjoying the feel of its final beats in her palm.

"Trust me, they'll be far better off without you." Zaiana retracted her arm, and with it she watched the last jolt of movement of his disconnected heart in her hand.

His body fell limp, but she didn't pay the corpse any attention as she marveled over the sticky dark crimson liquid coating her skin, dripping melodically onto the wood floor. Then, spent of her amusement and desire, she loosened her grip lazily, letting the now boring internal organ roll and thump into the pool of its own blood. The alluring scent of it overpowered the stench of urine, and she drew in a long breath.

Every time she was around exposed human blood she had to fight against past cravings; against the dark beckoning to drink. When she was young, it had never been a choice: blood was fed to them to create the strongest warriors even out of darklings. If the masters knew how long she had gone without it, she might even be killed. For disobedience or weakness—she wasn't sure what would enrage them more. Perhaps they wouldn't even believe she had won the Blood Trials, led the Silverfairs through training, and kept order and discipline of her leagues under the mountain, all without one drop of human blood in her system. That would forever remain her secret. She didn't want to depend on anything or anyone. Never again.

Zaiana looked to the dead man, a gruesome sight for anyone to find with the gaping cavity in his chest. She felt nothing. She never did. Every time she killed, she held the small, ridiculous notion that maybe she would one day feel a flicker of *something.* But it was impossible when she was a creature born without a heart; without the ability to feel remorse or empathy. She should be grateful for it. Humanity made the species weak, vulnerable, and it was their foolish love that would lose them the war to come.

She walked past the man, stopping briefly to wipe her hands on his shirt. Sliding the windowpane up, she threw the shutters open. Zaiana perched on the sill and looked up at the glittering starry sky for a few seconds of silent thought. Then she let herself fall before shooting skyward to chase the moon.

CHAPTER 2

Faythe

FAYTHE ASHFYRE HAD masterfully tuned her senses to track only two things: sapphire and steel. She ducked low, pivoting to avoid the razor's edge that swiped for her. Her hand hooked behind her back, clashing swords with Reylan when he left no pause for her to reorient herself. She caught his eye for a split second over her shoulder, and it was a small triumph to glimpse his flash of surprise. Fist clamped around the hilt, Faythe twisted smoothly, steel singing against steel. A devious smile curved her lips when it brought them face-to-face between locked blades.

"You're slowing, General." Faythe pushed off against him, and he allowed her to lead with a series of offense attacks.

"Maybe I'm just going easy on you, *Princess.*"

The title was a taunt—one that pushed her to wipe the smug look off his face. Where she was focused and calculated her steps, Reylan deflected so gracefully it was an effort not to admire the way he moved and his muscles flexed. Though parrying against her, there was an assessment in his eyes that tracked Faythe, studying her sequence—battle moves he had taught her many times over her two months in Rhyenelle.

Losing herself in combat was the best distraction Faythe knew from being homesick over her friends in High Farrow. And from the confrontation with her father, which she had actively avoided in her cowardice.

"If that helps you sleep at night." She brushed him off, stepping left, right, left, clashing steel at a new angle every time.

They darted around the ring, an exhilarating dance of danger and passion while the world around them faded away.

"Is that an offer?"

They twisted and turned. Faythe was panting, and at his words she lost focus for a split second in her incredulity. Reylan's blade halted abruptly, mere inches from her thigh.

"You're leaving your left side exposed again."

"Your tactics are spineless," she grumbled, kicking his blade and going on the offense once more.

His deep chuckle was equally as distracting. "Your right elbow is dropping."

Faythe clenched her teeth, trying to correct her error.

"You're shifting your weight too recklessly. Focus, Faythe."

"I *am* focused." Sweat beaded on her forehead. It wouldn't be long before she tunneled so far down into her lethal calm that she pushed her body to its physical limits.

"You're not." Reylan's voice was unwavering as he easily anticipated and blocked every one of her attacks. *"You're thinking of who's watching and letting fear of judgment tense your poise."*

His last sentence echoed privately in her mind. There was a strange tether that ran between Faythe and the general—one that often gave her a glimpse of his feelings and sent words so effortlessly between them. It was more than her ability; Reylan seemed able to channel back to her far easier than a loud projection of thought. Faythe had no explanation for it other than to assume it was a result of the power they'd shared in the throne room in High Farrow. She never spoke of it, but she couldn't deny the lingering bond wrapped her in a sense of *contentment*. It unnerved her, the thought that he felt it too but had yet to say anything. Perhaps he didn't want it.

Faythe's eyes flashed upward at his observation just for a second. It was enough. Reylan seized the opportunity to claim victory. A quick knock to her open left side, and she was falling. Though just as fast, a strong arm hooked around her back, saving her from the injury of sprawling to the ground. Faythe's hands lashed out on instinct, curling tightly into Reylan's shirt as he caught her.

When the maneuver had processed, Faythe exhaled hard, coming back to her full senses. Sapphire eyes claimed her entirely as she stared at him in bewilderment, their faces so close they shared breath. Those few seconds slowed despite him being quick to straighten with her. His arm didn't drop immediately. His palm flattened against her back, fingers grazing over her spine, the slow trail of his hand ending at her waist before his touch left her and she unfurled her fists. They never broke eye contact.

Faythe couldn't be sure if her heart was thundering from dwindling combat or the prickling sensation that crawled over her skin at his closeness.

There was a low shift in Reylan's voice as he said, "You're not done." His gaze flicked sideward, and Faythe's clouded mind cleared completely.

She stifled a groan, eyeing the impressive assault course she was always drilled to complete before their session was up. At first, she had insisted, wanting to advance on her agility as best she could. Now, she cursed herself for that foolish bout of determination. Her muscles protested; her breath speared her throat.

"Unless you're too tired, *Your Highness,*" Reylan chided at her hesitation.

Faythe shot him a glare then straightened and rolled her shoulders. She allowed her frown to turn to a smirk, a flare of defiance that flashed a twinkle of delight in the general's eye, before she took off. There was nothing that ignited her drive, her passion and strength, more than when she stared into the face of a threat or challenge. Adrenaline was a dangerous drug, her craving for it never curbed.

Angling her body to fall, Faythe slid against the polished floor to narrowly avoid the hook of a low bar. Then she twisted, pushing to her feet again before taking her next breath. Her mind had long trained her body to disconnect from the physical exertion in her focused state.

The freedom of movement in her new attire was glorious—an upgrade from her previous Rhyenelle fighting suit. She didn't think it were possible, but it felt even more weightless than the last and featured various concealed slots for weapons. With a flick of her wrist, a dagger snapped free, and she hurled it at the moving target that shot out for her. The dagger hit the inner circle, and the target fell backward to signal her success. There was no pause of victory; she pushed on.

Throwing her arms out for balance, Faythe stealthily walked a thin beam over a deep pit that would surely break her bones if she fell. She didn't look down. Her feet crossed over each other without hesitation. She was no stranger to the course that had become ingrained in her memory, and she was almost confident she could complete it blind-folded. *Almost*—because Reylan was a commanding pain in her ass and always changed a piece of the game every time she played. Nothing too obvious, in a test of her observation and quick adaptability.

Next was a trial of patience and calculation. Faythe stopped for a second, and in that moment, she identified Reylan's change. A cunning smile tugged at her lips as she spotted one of the five horizontally spin-ning panes was a fraction faster than the others.

Faythe had been quick to shoot down the general's suggestion that the course be adjusted to remove all real danger and tried not to be insulted by his concern. It was the danger that kept her moving, learning. To remove it would be child's play.

Faythe approached the trap, took a long breath, and let her weight become nothing as she drifted into the propellers. She was light on her feet, floating like wind, twisting like a ghost. As if she were the sixth pane, she didn't avoid them; she moved *with* them, her hands poised by her chest to better control her movements. She danced her way to the end, and when she got to the final one, she quickened her step to narrowly miss the nick of the faster spinning pane. She didn't allow herself to triumph at passing Reylan's attempt to catch her unawares. She pressed on.

Picking up speed, she eyed the ledge, knowing exactly how much momentum to build to clear the large gap ahead. A plummet into the dark space below would be to her eternal embarrassment. Her feet were silent but pushed harder against the stone the closer she got to the ledge. She waited until the last second then bent her knees, her toes pressing painfully on the harsh surface, and threw her weight into the air. Her arms reached out a fraction off skyward, and she clenched her teeth as her fingers curled awkwardly against the parallel stone fringe, the iron grip she held stinging horribly. Faythe's heart leaped in her chest when her sweat-coated palms made her grasp slip. Her feet landed against the flat of the wall, saving her face and body from kissing the stone. Not giving her hands a chance to slacken, she wasted no time in mustering every ounce of strength to hoist herself up and over the ledge.

Stamina was becoming less of a weakness, but she still detested her disadvantage in agility. She wouldn't ever be able to match the fae who surrounded her.

Faythe pushed through the rest of the course with precision before coming to her final challenge. It didn't require exuberance of energy or stealth on her feet, yet it was always the most daunting hurdle. She had run the course countless times and never completed it thanks to her damned cowardice at the last second. Faythe approached the longbow, swiftly nocking an arrow into place. The string groaned, and her arm shook—not out of feat of strength, but nerves. She brought the iron-tipped arrow up to match her line of sight then steadied her breathing and slowed her heart, which thrummed loudly in her ears. There were five targets, each progressively farther away. Her only task was to hit the first—she knew she would have zero chance of hitting the fifth, which she could barely make out with her mortal sight—yet every time she stood in this position, primed to let her arrow fly, she halted.

"Why did you stop?"

Reylan's question in her mind made her eyes flick up in answer—to King Agalhor Ashfyre of Rhyenelle, who stood poised, watching her intently from the viewing perimeter as he always did. Though the general was positioned behind her in the training hall, he knew exactly what made Faythe hesitate every time.

She couldn't be sure what it was that rattled her most about the king's presence: her embarrassment if she missed her target or disappointing him with her incompetence. Perhaps neither. She didn't know why she felt as if she had something to prove to him—to her father, who was still little more than a stranger.

When she dared to glance up again, he was gone.

Faythe's face twitched in frustration and anger. Toward herself and her own lack of conviction. She strained her arm back further, muscles aching with the strength it took to hold poise, and aimed to let loose.

An arrow soared through the open space so fast it was a blur of movement, a quick whistle slicing the silence and then a faint thud as it made its mark. Faythe's arrow slackened in her bow, and she lowered it, gaping in disbelief at the distant red fletching in the fifth and farthest target. Dead center, from what she could tell through human eyes. She whipped her head around to glare at Reylan accusingly but found him standing with arms crossed, no bow nearby. Then she caught the movement behind him.

16

"Sorry, I thought perhaps a demonstration was in order."

Strolling up to Reylan, a fae she had come to know as Kyleer suppressed a grin of amusement while dangling a longbow in his grasp. Faythe caught a glimpse of a second invading form as he was quickly joined by his brother, Izaiah. She'd met them during her first day in Rhyenelle, and over her two months in the kingdom she'd found herself effortlessly relaxed in their company. Faythe had kept close to the general as the only familiar face in these foreign lands, but she welcomed their new friendship. They were bonded companions of Reylan's, from what she'd gauged in their interactions. Both brothers were a pleasing sight and clearly immediate relatives from their matching hues of dark brown hair and striking moss-green eyes. But despite their similarities, Faythe didn't think they could appear more different. Kyleer was roguishly enticing with longer hair that waved past his nape, and he was built as broad as stone, while Izaiah was beautifully slender but strong, his hair cropped short and styled to sleek *perfection*. She'd never met two people who looked so similar and opposite at the same time. Like the sun shining in two very different seasons.

"This is a closed session," Reylan grumbled.

Faythe found it amusing watching the stern-faced general in the company of his friends. Occasionally, he let his mask slip, and it fluttered her heart—oddly—to see him loosen up every now and then. It distracted Faythe from her own sinking thoughts and feelings of being so far from High Farrow, the home she'd known her whole life.

Kyleer waved a dismissive hand at Reylan in response, which only irked the general more. Faythe bit her lip to keep from grinning.

"You didn't even hit the center," Izaiah piped up, holding out a hand for his brother's bow and reaching for a red-feathered arrow.

Kyleer scoffed but obliged.

Izaiah expertly nocked the arrow into place, lifting and releasing it in the space of a single calculated breath. Faythe turned her head back to the targets, finding the red dot in the distance to be slightly larger than before. Her mouth popped open in awe. As far as she could tell, they'd both hit dead center, but apparently, their fae sight distinguished them in accuracy.

Izaiah beamed in triumph, but Kyleer's eyes narrowed on the target. There was no warning when shadows formed around him and rolling darkness engulfed him completely. When it dispersed a few quick seconds later, Kyleer was gone.

Reylan had told Faythe of his ability before. He was a Shadowporter and could transport himself to a different location by the will of his shadows. It was Faythe's first time seeing it with her own eyes, and she was completely dumbstruck.

She didn't get the chance to question it further when Izaiah suddenly disappeared in a flash of contrasting white light, transforming into a hawk that took flight and soared above her head. He was a Shapeshifter. Faythe could only gape, eyes tracking the bird, as he flew out past the targets. With another flash of light, her eyes fell down to where he landed, and she could vaguely make out the brothers in the distance, examining—or rather, comparing—their aims. She couldn't decipher their words, but she didn't need fae sight or hearing to know they were arguing over who got the closest to hitting dead center.

Faythe did smile then, even chuckled slightly in great amusement at the childish bickering of the full-grown warrior fae. Kyleer was Reylan's second-in-command, and Izaiah his third. He was almost a century younger than his brother and the general. The obscure concept of time to a fae still baffled Faythe.

They didn't get to debate their shots for long, however, when another arrow sang past her ear—so fast she would have missed the quick blur of motion if she'd blinked. The brothers fell quiet in the distance for a moment. Two flashes of white light in contrast with clouds of black smoke, and they were back to standing next to Reylan, who had set the bow aside and now stood as serious as ever.

"Show-off," Izaiah muttered.

Reylan didn't express any humor.

"Do you ever lighten up?" Faythe gibed before she could stop herself.

Izaiah jerked a thumb toward the general. "Him? Well, there was that one time… Oh, no, not even then—"

"What about that Yulemas when—ahh, nope," Kyleer chimed in, looking deep in thought like his brother.

Faythe released a laugh. Reylan's eyes snapped to her in disgruntled warning, and she tamed her chuckle to a wide smile. Then he turned to glower at his companions as they mocked him playfully.

"Out, both of you, before I have you running training drills all week."

Izaiah rolled his eyes. "Yes, *General*," he answered with brazen sarcasm.

Faythe tensed every time they tested the lion's patience, knowing there were very few people who got away with speaking to Reylan in such a manner. But he didn't seem fazed at all by the fae. They made to leave before Kyleer turned back to her.

"That was impressive, Faythe."

"For a human?" she challenged.

Kyleer's brow curved with his mouth. "For anyone."

Faythe straightened, feeling humbly proud at the compliment, and gave a short nod in appreciation.

"If you need a break from dark and brooding over there, I can help you with your archery anytime."

"I'll keep that in mind. Thank you."

She had thought she would feel like a stranger for a long time when she first arrived in Rhyenelle, but she was relieved and over-joyed that the people and fae she'd met so far had made her feel anything but. They had welcomed her as if she'd always belonged here, and no one addressed her with any special treatment for who her father was. That part she had yet to face and hadn't even been alone with the king since coming to the mighty kingdom. It didn't stop him from routinely requesting she join him in the evenings in a place they called the Glass Garden. She knew she had to confront him at some point, but she wanted to hold onto her blissful ignorance a little longer.

When the two brothers had left, Faythe's smile fell as she met the serious eyes of Reylan.

"What are you afraid of when you pick up that bow?"

Faythe shifted on her feet at the sudden switch back to her performance on the course. She only shrugged lamely, unsure of how to put her fears into words. In truth, she didn't know why she never attempted the shot.

"You can't let your fear of failure or judgment stop you from trying. The battlefield doesn't adapt for you; a moment's hesitation can be your life, or that of another."

Instead of inspiring strength and determination as his words usually did, Faythe felt weighted with disappointment in herself—because he was right, and the thought of someone's life being in jeopardy thanks to her cowardice was a dark, helpless feeling.

He must have sensed her spiral into despair as his look softened. "Do you want to practice with your sword again? Or perhaps we should work on those close defense skills."

Faythe huffed a laugh. She had gotten better at maneuvering out of compromised positions since the first time she was so effortlessly overpowered by him. It was always what he urged her to practice most, and always what she found the hardest to grasp. She tried not to acknowledge that it wasn't out of lack of skill, but rather, having his body pressed to hers repeatedly for lengths of time scattered whatever words of guidance he spoke. Getting *out* of his hold was the last thing on her mind, and the threat of steel was insignificant.

Faythe's cheeks warmed at the memory. "I think I've had enough for today."

He wasn't at all convinced but nodded and waited for her to lead the way.

The training hall in the castle had completely stunned Faythe the first time she set foot inside. The impressively massive space was built to accommodate every skill and every practice. It was no surprise Rhyenelle's armies were famous in Ungardia when every warrior was trained to their own best abilities instead of routinely drilled in clusters. Rhyenelle spared no time or expense in accommodating everyone, resulting in legions of the finest and most diverse soldiers. It was the second thing she'd come to appreciate most about the south.

The first was their equality. Rhyenelle's capital city of Ellium didn't have just one fortitude for the royal castle and the fae; it had two, and the humans lived protected within the high walls of the outer ring. They weren't cast out to live in poverty either. They lived well and did not fear or hate the fae within the inner walls. In fact, it was more common for the two species to mingle and coexist, some even in friendship.

Neither of them spoke as they strolled the wide corridors of the castle. Faythe aimlessly admired the crimson tapestries instead, transfixed as she always was by the flaming Firebird emblem. She didn't know what it was about the element, about the mythical animal, that sparked embers inside.

Down the hall, another fae male turned the corner and began to walk toward them. His name was Malin. Reylan must have noticed Faythe tense as he took a subtle step closer.

Faythe's biggest revelation since arriving in Rhyenelle, which stunned her still, was that her father wasn't her only living blood relative. The fae in front of them was Faythe's cousin, the son of Agalhor's fallen brother who had lost his life in battle many centuries ago.

"Ah, Princess," he drawled with fake pleasantry. He was arrogant, wicked, selfish, and she'd gauged all that before he first uttered a word. Faythe was not usually one to judge before knowing someone, but Malin was the exception. He knew she didn't want to be titled—everyone had

21

been warned against it—yet he added the term every time he managed to run into her. How often that happened, she knew, was no coincidence.

"Malin," she greeted with an equally forced smile.

Before a daughter of the king was known to exist, Malin had been next in line to the throne. As far as Faythe was concerned, he still was. She didn't want it, had no plans to claim any title or standing, and not just because her half-mortal lifespan wouldn't allow for it. She simply had no desire for the crown or power. Malin wasn't convinced, however, and it was all wasted breath to try to tell him otherwise.

"I'll be going to the outer city this afternoon. I thought you might care to join me, be among your own kind after so long," he said horribly sweetly.

She couldn't deny she wanted to accept. She had been curious about Rhyenelle's human settlements since she arrived. Only, she wasn't ecstatic about the company he offered.

"She's not ready," Reylan cut in, and it was clear he disliked the prince, possibly more than she did.

Faythe's expression flexed. "I want to go," she said quickly with an edge of defense.

Reylan's eyes softened as they switched to her, and she thought she saw a hint of concern behind them. She didn't think there could be anything of concern in the human part of the city given it was shielded by a high wall. Faythe was quick to brush it off as Reylan's typical over-protective bullshit, which was a step up from the usual fae male overprotective bullshit they were all instilled with. Whatever his worry, he didn't get the chance to protest.

"Perfect!" Malin beamed. "I'll meet you in the reception hall at noon."

Faythe wanted to wipe the victorious grin off his face, but she smiled reluctantly instead, giving an answering nod before he glided past them without another word. Her face fell into a scowl the moment he did. When she glanced up at Reylan, his look was scarily calculating.

"Relax, will you? I'm not going far, and I don't need protection," she added, irked that he would object to her going at all.

Reylan crossed his arms, and Faythe mimicked him in pettiness. They stared off for a few stubborn seconds until he rolled his eyes and conceded with a long sigh.

"I'm coming with you."

Faythe didn't mind the condition. She had little desire for alone time with Malin anyway.

Her lips twitched, and she nudged him playfully, which failed to move him even a fraction. "Off-duty though. Try to enjoy yourself for once."

His own mouth fought light amusement, and he loosened his posture as they continued their walk. Faythe saw that as a small victory.

"With you and Malin in each other's company, I don't think I can be off-duty."

"He's no fool—hurting me would damage him more than anything."

Reylan smirked. "It's not you I'd be concerned for."

CHAPTER 3

Nikalias

I T WAS A strange feeling to have so many eyes on him, expecting him to uphold their expectations. To sit in the prized position he had grown so used to glancing at sideways, as hollow-minded but attentive as those who now looked at him. King Nikalias Silvergriff couldn't help but feel wrapped by the ghost of his father as he sat at the head of the council meeting, as though he were watching and weighing up his fitness to rule. Nik wore nothing upon his head, but the crown he carried bore down like solid steel.

The lords' meeting had been in full swing for nearly an hour. Nik's head swarmed with so many of the kingdom's conflicts. Each new person who spoke added to the itch crawling over his skin. He longed for escape. Yet this was his duty now. So he listened, training his mind to let go of petty issues and store away anything that actually held intellect or intrigue to be dealt with later.

Tauria sat to his right, poised and attentive to the high fae down the table. Though she objected to being here, since she never sat in on

Orlon's meetings, it felt right to have her by his side, and perhaps self-ishly, he'd only asked as her confident presence always subdued his nerves. Aside from Tauria, the disgruntled looks from the gathering of high fae, he assumed, had more to do with the bigger sway from tradition joining them on his left.

Nik held sympathy for Jakon. It couldn't be easy to be the only one of his kind seated at the head of so much scrutiny, and he didn't believe it was entirely Jakon's will to be here. When presented with the position of human emissary, as Faythe suggested, Jakon was quick to knock down the idea at first. It wasn't until only a couple of weeks ago that he decided it was worth a try—to see if he could make a difference in the town for the humans. Nik had no doubt Jakon's fiancée had great persuasion over his change of heart.

Nik turned to him when the last matter was settled. "Anything to report from the outer town?"

Jakon straightened an inch in his seat, his discomfort at the attention almost making Nik regret asking. But the human was quick to put on a confident, stoic face when the dozen other fae at the table settled their reluctant gaze on him. To Nik's admiration, his voice was unwavering as he spoke. "Galmire needs its forces reinstated. There are still people going missing. Those in Farrowhold haven't reported any more sightings of Valgard, but there are families going hungry. There's not enough food for them out there."

Jakon had already presented these issues to Nik long before now, but Nik needed the nobles to hear them too, and he had to give Jakon as much of a voice and authority during these meetings as he could if he was ever to be granted the respect he deserved. Nik had drawn his solutions for the human town and didn't need time to deliberate or reason. For the first time during the grueling meeting, his spine locked straight as he went on to address the court—a move that forewarned it would be a grave mistake to challenge what he was about to say.

"I propose we send a legion to be stationed in Galmire. If they succeed in taking that town, they are one step closer to taking the whole kingdom. I won't let that happen."

The other fae around the table mumbled their agreement—not out of consideration for the human lives, but out of fear Valgard could be advancing closer to their own doorstep if they did nothing.

"As for the humans in Farrowhold, today I announce the gates to Caius City will remain open. Indefinitely. For human and fae to pass through as they please. Goods will be distributed evenly. High Farrow would not be where it is today, would not operate and stand, without the humans outside the wall. It's about time we acknowledge that and praise those who have given you the life of luxury you are all blessed with."

A new voice sounded. "With all due respect, Your Majesty, your father—"

Nik braced his hands on the table and rose carefully from his large ornate seat. The high fae silenced himself at the movement.

"My father is no longer the king. I am."

The fae's throat bobbed as Nik pinned him firmly with his gaze. Tension weaved through the bodies. While protest twitched on the others' faces, the fae who spoke conceded, shrinking back into his seat.

Nik went on. "Human or fae, high-born or commoner, none of it matters in the grave. There is a far bigger threat at large—one that doesn't care for your immortality or wealth. Don't make an enemy out of those on our side for the shape of their ears when there may come a day when the one you believe to be *weak* may just be the one to save your life."

Nik couldn't deny personal feelings interlaced his last declaration. A twist hit his chest—as much sadness as he would allow himself to feel in Faythe's absence. While they had exchanged a few vague letters, she had yet to visit him through Nightwalking. He understood she would need time to adjust to what she faced in Rhyenelle, attempting to forge a bond with her long-lost father. Nik knew he had to be patient despite his selfish longing for her to check in. To see her, even for a moment.

Just as Nik was about to straighten and dismiss the meeting on the silence that settled, a spiteful voice carried down the table.

"If I may bring up one final concern, Your Majesty…"

Nik's eyes landed on Lord Zarrius instantly. His muscles locked at noticing his attention flash to Tauria, but he kept the ire from his face. He didn't hold any ounce of kindness for the lord he was all too acquainted with. Zarrius had been one of the lords closest to his father, a bond forged of an alignment of cruel, malicious thoughts.

Nik stayed standing, his tone hard with warning as he said, "Speak."

The arrogance that radiated from the lord was tangible, and Nik had to keep from clenching his fists, anticipating the topic that was about to be brought forth and knowing there was nothing he could do to shield Tauria from it.

"I mean no disrespect as I say this, of course, but your father knew matters of the kingdom were not to be paraded and discussed in the presence of outsiders."

Beside him, Nik could almost feel Tauria's urge to shrink back at the indirect remark, the careful shun the lord worded craftily. Though Zarrius's words were not solely directed at her; Nik had no doubt Jakon was considered an *outsider* for simply being human.

Nik put effort into keeping his voice steady. "I would not put the kingdom in jeopardy by inviting anyone here whom I believe to be disloyal."

"Allow me to be more direct." Zarrius rose, and the bold move flared Nik's dominance to near recklessness. He breathed steadily. Conflicts were bound to arise with a change of leadership. He knew this, yet he was still unprepared for it. "There are many of us who do not feel comfortable discussing High Farrow's inside matters with one from another kingdom."

Nik spared a glance at the other fae in attendance. While no one spoke out or made much movement at all, agreement was written on the harsh faces of many down the table. He had to admit, his nerves were rattled. How could he keep the peace and sway so many already against him? It was a sudden rush of uncertainty in himself, but he didn't let one ounce of it surface for the vultures who pinned him, looking for any slight reason to discredit him. Right now, Nik's reign was being tested, and it would take a great measure of time and some very careful choices to make them believe without a doubt that he was fit to wear the crown in High Farrow.

He straightened fully. "Have you reason to distrust anyone at this table, Lord Zarrius?"

The look they shared was a challenge.

"Not exactly. But the princess—"

"Queen," Nik corrected in a cool, calm tone. "If you are to address her, you will do so by proper name and title."

"And may I add"—Tauria's voice sounded, and Nik's eyes slid to her as she rose—"if you are to speak of me while I am present, you extend the curtesy of speaking *to* me?"

A wave of pride struck his chest, adding to his own confidence in the confrontation.

Tauria didn't meet his eye as she fixed her firm gaze on Zarrius. "Are we not allies, Lord Zarrius?" He opened his mouth to counter, but she continued. "Have I not spent a century at Orlon's side, entrusted by him as his ward? Have I not put the needs of High Farrow's citizens above my own in being here?"

Zarrius discredited her passionate speech instantly. "There are those who believe your time here has only been in aid of slowly gaining what you need to take back Fenstead."

"Do you speak for yourself?"

"Yes, and many others."

Nik realized he was in a dangerous position. He had never once doubted Tauria and knew with everything he had that she was true and genuine, with no cunning plan to use High Farrow to her own gain. But he was at a loss for how to convey the sentiment politically, not personally.

"I would advise you to be careful of how you speak to the king's ward, Zarrius. Do not lay accusation without merit," Nik warned.

"I lay no accusation," Zarrius said casually, but the song of his voice was taunting. "But she cannot be the King's Ward of High Farrow *and* the Queen of Fenstead."

Nik couldn't be certain where he was headed with the matter. "Then what do you suggest?"

He realized immediately his foolish words, granting Zarrius ample opportunity to lay down his favor for Tauria's fate. There was a note of cunning in the curl of his mouth, as if Nik had offered up exactly what he hoped for. The lord sat back down smoothly, subdued triumph gleaming in his eyes, making Nik's jaw lock with a flare of violence. Reluctantly, Nik sat back down too, along with Tauria.

Zarrius seized his opportunity. "Fenstead still remains overrun by Valgard. It would take far more than High Farrow's armies to take it back. Tauria Stagknight is a queen of nothing."

The rage that flashed through Nik was hot and all-consuming, made worse by feeling the ripples of Tauria's embarrassment. "Careful, Zarrius."

The lord knew he had the upper hand. Nik was king, but he was not within his rights to remove his councilmembers from power without reason and a favorable vote. Lord Zarrius was influential in High Farrow, one of the wealthiest and most respected of them all. If Nik didn't tread wisely, the lord could just as easily rally an opposition that may threaten to overthrow his rule.

"I mean no disrespect, of course. Quite the opposite, in fact." His voice sang his vision of brilliance. "I suggest we permanently instate Tauria Stagknight as the King's Ward of High Farrow. She has no kingdom, but we can perhaps gain a stronghold in two if we use her position to our advantage."

Nik hated the quickening of his heart, the fluctuation of anger, and the dread that hazed his mind.

"With Tauria as High Farrow's ward, we can offer her hand in marriage to Tarly Wolverlon. In turn, we negotiate a foothold in Olmstone, and when the time is right, we gain influence in Fenstead if we succeed in taking it back through the joining of two great armies. Perhaps Rhyenelle can be persuaded to join the cause too with their new human princess, who we all know holds ties to High Farrow as the king's previous spymaster. It may be time to call in a favor for that act of mercy from your father."

Nik was rendered speechless. Not a single element of Zarrius's proposition was even slightly appealing, yet all eyes were fixed on him to weigh up his thoughts on the cunning idea that seemed to make perfect sense. It would be a complete betrayal to those he loved, and he felt Tauria's shocked stare the loudest, as though she were begging him to meet it so he might see the plea that lay within. He couldn't, or he was sure he'd break. Nik kept his face blank as though deliberating while he sat under intense judgment. He had to be smart, in a tormenting tug-of-war with his heart and his duty. He hated what he had to say, but with the attention of his council on him, he had no choice.

"What you propose could be advantageous."

Tauria's silent outrage was like a punch to the gut. He swallowed hard, trying not to yield a reaction. Not to look at her and beg her to understand or wait for him to explain in private.

"While we remain allies, I still do not trust Varlas after his attempt to overthrow Rhyenelle. Perhaps this binding alliance could be what we need to secure influence and insight on his movements. So far, our sources have revealed silence in Olmstone, but we would be fools to assume his path of vengeance is over."

The lords nodded in agreement. When he met eyes with Zarrius, it was a conscious effort not to screw the damned consequences and wipe the smug look off his face.

"I will consider what you put forward, Lord Zarrius. For now, I believe we are done here for today."

Looks were exchanged, but it seemed only when Zarrius nodded his agreement that the others followed his lead and the room filled with chatter as they filed out. Nik's gaze lingered on Zarrius's back. He didn't trust the lord in the slightest and made a note to keep a close eye on him.

There was barely a second of silence once everyone had left before Tauria shot to her feet, furious. "You have no right!"

They weren't alone—guards still lingered around the perimeter of the council room. Nik couldn't be certain none of his guard were harboring divided allegiance. He couldn't risk his words traveling straight to Zarrius if he spoke freely, so he kept his tone calm and neutral.

"As long as you wish to remain in High Farrow under my protection, I do."

Tauria's hurt look of outrage felt like a dagger to his chest. "If selling me for the advantage of your kingdom is the condition of your *protection*, consider it my wish to be anywhere but here." She stormed from the room without a glance back, her anger billowing in the waves of her emerald gown, which flowed behind her.

Nik braced a hand on the table to rise, resisting every nerve in his body that urged him to go after her.

"I hate to agree…" Jakon's low voice was a surprise that snapped his attention back. Nik had guiltily forgotten the human was still seated. "But she's right. Is gaining power in Olmstone really worth her heart?"

No. Nothing was worth that. Caught in the conflict of heart against duty, Nik feared more than anything that he was at risk of losing both.

CHAPTER 4

Faythe

FAYTHE HAD TO admit she was a great admirer of Rhyenelle attire. While her gown flowed behind her, its asymmetrical design meant her legs had complete freedom at the front in fitted leather pants. Elegant yet practical: it seemed to be the running theme within the Kingdom of the Phoenix.

Gliding down the halls unescorted, she didn't wait for Reylan to retrieve her like a pet. She'd left her rooms after pacing their length so many times she could no longer stand the rising pressure of wild thoughts. She'd forced them back for so long, keeping herself calm and neutral in the months while she adjusted to her new surroundings, but she knew the floodgates were weakening with every new confrontation, and she was one more push away from drowning in her mess of thoughts. Evil Spirits, temple quests, and a confrontation with her father were high on the list of avoidance for now.

Faythe headed to the reception hall, where the delightful Malin would be waiting for her. The only thing urging her to suffer his company was the hope that walking among her own kind and sampling their way of life here would lift her mood. She felt Reylan's dismay creep up from behind before his tall form fell into step beside her.

"I asked you to wait for me."

Faythe didn't look at him but fought against showing her amusement on her face. "You took too long."

He only responded with a disgruntled sound.

She cast her eyes to him then and almost rolled them at the ridiculous ensemble of steel the general had equipped himself with. "I thought you said Ellium was the safest city in Ungardia," she drawled.

"It is. But sometimes danger takes on a friendly form to get through the defenses."

Even though she agreed, she didn't want to point out that his concern seemed a little excessive. In fact, *very* excessive. As if that weren't enough, she spied two more additions to Reylan's security detail down the hall.

Kyleer and Izaiah also stood armed to the teeth, in casual conversation with each other. When they spied Faythe and Reylan approaching, they straightened, Izaiah beaming from ear to ear. His smile was breathtaking paired with his dangerous elegance. Despite this, Faythe couldn't suppress her annoyance.

She paused her walk and turned to Reylan, dropping her voice low in accusation. "Is this really necessary?" It shouldn't have bothered her as much as it did, but she didn't come to the mighty kingdom to be under constant surveillance.

His face fell soft in understanding. "They'll be trailing from afar—you won't even see them." His eyes held a faint plea, and she cursed that it made *her* feel bad. She let it go.

When they caught up to the brothers, Izaiah raised a hand to his heart. "I'm trying not to be offended that you find our company so horrible, Faythe."

His playful sarcasm lifted her mood, and she released a breathy laugh, letting all her pent-up irritation dissipate with it. Being within Reylan's inner circle, among the highest-ranking and most lethal fae in Rhyenelle, Faythe thought she would feel feeble and out of place. Instead, it filled her with delightful strength, and she was humbled that they had welcomed her and didn't treat her as if she were made of glass.

Faythe held her head high as they entered into the reception hall and found Malin alone, waiting by the grand main doors. The slight twitch of his eye gave away his annoyance once he spied the fae in her company, but he plastered on a pleasant smile as always. She was glad for her companions now, if only to see Malin's stifled dismay.

"I'm eager to see what the outer city has to offer to get all these fae males so excited," Faythe said by way of greeting.

Malin cast a glance at her company. To her disappointment, he successfully kept the irritation that they wouldn't be touring the human settlement alone off his face. No doubt so he'd have the chance to voice his not-so-subtle distaste for her.

"I can't speak for all, but Ellium is home to some of the most beautiful and alluring of both species." Malin eyed her from head to toe as he spoke, and his meaning was clear: she didn't conform to his ideals.

Faythe's temper flared. Not at the insult, but at the smug gleam in his eye that she wanted desperately to claw out with her own hands. Her violent thoughts were soothed by a gentle caress from within. Faythe didn't look at Reylan but silently thanked him for keeping her from lashing out—verbally or otherwise.

Kyleer responded. "Perhaps we should go without you, Malin, so we might have a chance at drawing them in, not scaring them off."

Faythe swallowed her chuckle, struggling against the tug of her lips at the flash of ire in Malin's hazel eyes. He huffed a dismissive laugh but said nothing more as he turned and began his walk to the large ornate main doors. Faythe flashed a look of thanks to Kyleer, who gave her a side-smirk in amusement.

As soon as Faythe stepped through the great doors, she found herself breathless and awestruck as if it were her first time seeing the colossal courtyard. Rhyenelle's royal citadel was built like nothing she'd seen or imagined before. It wasn't a simple solid stone keep; the castle was a spectacular perimeter building for the vast open space in its center. Stepping past the colonnades was like being in an open colosseum. So far, she'd spent most of her time in Rhyenelle indoors, getting used to their way of life and training every moment she could to take her mind off her nerves and homesickness, so this felt wonderfully freeing.

They descended the few long stairs and began to walk across the endless courtyard. Faythe craned her neck, admiring the impressively tall castle structure around them. Glancing back, she looked up at the viewing balcony and recoiled in a hot flush at the sight of the king standing there. She quickly turned out of cowardice, and judgment crawled over her skin with every step.

"He doesn't expect anything from you," Reylan said quietly.

"I don't know what to say to him," she admitted with a drop of disappointment.

"You're here, and you're trying. He sees that. It speaks louder to him than words." His sapphires soothed her with encouragement, and Faythe was overcome by how much she needed to hear those words: the assurance that her presence in Rhyenelle wasn't a disappointment. She might have embraced him if they weren't in the company of others.

Stepping over the giant Phoenix crest branded in gold and crimson across the center courtyard, Faythe held her chin with more determination. She would overcome her fear and finally speak to Agalhor, and that notion was all the more bearable with the knowledge Reylan would be right there to build her up and console her after.

At the gates, a carriage awaited them. Ellium was an impressively large city; on foot, it would take them hours to reach the edge of the outer ring. Though, the closer they got, Faythe noticed the carriage was considerably small—certainly not big enough to accommodate the three huge warriors plus Faythe and Malin.

Stopping beside the cart, Malin answered her thoughts. "I believed it would just be you and me, Princess." He neglected to offer any larger transport.

"I prefer the skies anyway," Izaiah interjected.

Faythe turned just in time to catch the quick flare of light before the youngest brother transformed into an eagle, soaring higher and higher. When her gaze fell to meet Reylan's, his concern and irritation was far from subtle. Malin had already made himself comfortable in the cart, in no way bothered by the departure of the fae or how they planned to get to the outer ring. She offered Reylan a weak side-smile, not best pleased by the situation but needing to curb his worry.

"I'll be okay," Faythe said when it was clear he was debating finding another way there so she would not be left alone with her *beloved* cousin.

Reylan's eyes flashed to her upper thigh—specifically, to the dagger strapped there.

Faythe grinned. "Are you more concerned for his safety that I might use it, or mine that he might give me cause to?"

The corner of Reylan's mouth curled up just a little, but it was enough to relax her. *"I couldn't care less for that bastard's safety, but yours…"*

Faythe couldn't stop herself: she reached out a hand to hold his arm. His palm encased it, and a flutter passed through her chest with the contact. *"I'll see you in the outer city,"* she said. With a lingering look, her hand fell, and she turned from him to enter the carriage before her nerves rallied to stop her.

Slipping onto the bench opposite Malin, Faythe glanced sideward. Reylan was already gone. Curious to see whether he'd taken Kyleer's ability to Shadowport or Izaiah's ability to Shapeshift, she shuffled over and leaned out the open window. Instinctively, her eyes traveled skyward as if she already knew the answer. Faythe immediately spotted a white bird circling above, and she grinned wide, suppressing a chuckle.

"How you managed to bend Rhyenelle's top war commanders to your will… I'll admit, I'm impressed. You make quick work." Malin's voice was laced with the distaste he didn't bother holding back in private.

Faythe eased back into the carriage as it jolted forward. She stared at her cousin, who wore a haughty smile. Malin shared her hue of hazel hair, and his eyes almost matched the tone. He was elegantly beautiful but had a sly, manipulative look about him that made her distrust him the moment she laid eyes on him. From what she'd been warned, Malin was also a powerful Nightwalker like Agalhor who was legendary in his ability. This was the first time she'd had the displeasure of being alone with him, and he looked to be relishing in their bonding time. She knew it was only to gauge her as a possible threat to his claim of the throne. The notion seemed ridiculous, but admittedly highly amusing.

Faythe leaned back casually. "Are you jealous, Malin?"

He sneered. "Jealous of a human street rat? Hardly."

She hated that the comment stung. She kind of wanted to hurt him —everything about him said he would deserve it—but she had to be smart. "Threatened then. That you might lose your crown to a mere *human street rat.*"

It wasn't wise for her to rile someone as powerful as Malin, but short of physical violence, words were all she had. The flash of challenging fury in his eyes made her believe her words struck far deeper than a blade. To his credit, he didn't allow his anger to surface and maintained his composure.

"You may be an Ashfyre in name, but you are an insult to what the name stands for." Malin unleashed his hatred in a cool, calculated calm, as if it were fact, not opinion. When Faythe's hands curled tighter, he smirked down at her clenched fists.

"You don't know anything about me," she said pathetically.

"Do I not?" Malin's mouth turned into a crooked, goading smile as he leaned toward her with the gleam of a predator. "Faythe Ashfyre—

tragically impoverished street girl of High Farrow, trying desperately to find her place in this world. You might as well be an orphan still since you're too spineless to face your own father. You're weak, Faythe, and you will never be fit to rule; never live long enough to make an impact on anything. Your insignificant life will be short and a waste of talent." Finishing his slander of her name and existence, Malin sat back again in triumph.

Faythe's eyes burned, her rage momentarily clouded by humiliation and worthlessness. A part of her—a large, hideous part of her—agreed with him. It stirred damning thoughts in her mind, and she wanted to tell the world to burn and give up right then. She cast her eyes up to the red velvet roof of the carriage as if she would see the fleeting bright summer clouds instead, the silver bird soaring above them. Reylan had stayed with her in her darkest moments, never given up on her or seen her for her weaknesses. Faythe gripped onto his belief in her, letting it chase the shadow of uncertainty Malin tried to give life to. She would not be weak. She would not cower.

When she dropped her eyes back down, she fixed them hard on the prince. Ice sedated her fears and cooled the quick heat of embarrassment. She would not let him win. "Do you want to know what I see when I look at you, Malin?"

The prince quirked a brow, finding entertainment in her opposition.

"Fear. So expertly hidden behind false confidence. A name is just a word, another mask. Without a crown, without that claim to the Ashfyre name, who are you?" She didn't leave room for answer. "The difference between you and me is that I don't need a name or a title or a damned thing to tell me who or what I am. I didn't come here to lay claim to a throne from name alone, but I also didn't come all this way to deny my heritage. I may have come from nothing, but I will rise to everything. The greatest triumph will be having you there to bear witness as I do."

Faythe sat back but didn't relish the look of loathing that seethed on Malin's face. He was wicked, but he was no fool, and while he was armed with a sword and dagger, she was confident he wasn't unhinged or brazen enough to attack the king's daughter. Though she did picture what it would be like to face off against her cousin in a sparring ring, fair and equal in combat. The thought of plunging a dagger into his heart was darkly pleasing. Accidents happened all the time in training rings…

"Watch yourself," Malin said, so low she almost missed it.

Faythe flicked her gaze to him at the warning, but he was looking innocently out the window, his face wiped of all expression. Her spine stiffened to suppress the chill that swept over her. She would have dismissed the threat as idle, but Malin was cunning and crafty, and something about his cool demeanor made her always on edge around him. She would be a fool to ever underestimate him.

Faythe blanked him from her mind completely after the hostile conversation. She didn't expect the journey alone with him to be pleasant, but she couldn't have predicted just how bold he was. Malin had great influence within the castle, and Faythe would have to be careful not to put herself on the wrong side of the nobles in court. She had no choice but to back down and keep herself off Malin's radar as best she could.

Shuffling closer to the window, Faythe admired the city streets that brought a smile to her face. Ellium was a glorious merging of the pristine Caius City and outer town of Farrowhold. The streets were wonderful and well-kept, but not with as many dauntingly high buildings of gleaming white stone that looked too perfect to be lived in. Ellium was beautifully diverse, appealing to all walks of life. They were still within the inner ring, but Faythe had spotted several humans already, some in friendly conversation with the fae. The streets were lively with cheerful chatter, and she caught the sound of various instruments blessing the streets with joy and vibrancy.

They passed under an archway, and Faythe deduced they had entered the outer ring as the sets of rounded ears became far more frequent and pointed ears near absent altogether. It was clear they had dropped in wealth and status as the buildings saddened into hues of brown, a gut-wrenching reminder of her old hut in Farrowhold. Though, in contrast, at least the atmosphere remained positive and laughter could still be heard, unlike the dreary gloom of her former home.

Faythe let loose a sigh of relief when they finally pulled to a halt. The air in the carriage had become suffocating with the tension that thickened between her and the prince.

The door opened immediately, and Faythe didn't pause for politeness as she made to leave first. All her riled-up irritation dissipated the moment she met with familiar calming sapphires.

Reylan's hard eyes didn't hold warmth or relief; they left her to target the prince who emerged behind her. Faythe moved to stand by the general's side, wondering if he'd caught their conversation from his position in the sky. Malin wore his usual smug look and even smirked, not in the least bit fazed by the white lion's intimidation. His status protected him from any retaliation from his inferiors, and for once, that included Reylan.

Faythe narrowed her eyes on him, thinking perhaps he'd wanted Reylan to hear his slander, if only to enjoy his restrained anger knowing he couldn't do anything to defend her. It was a horribly guilty feeling to know she could be used to invoke such a reaction.

"Well, I do have business I must attend to," Malin drawled, his irritating voice snapping her back to the present. "Enjoy the town, Princess. I will meet you back here. An hour should suffice." He didn't wait for her to agree, twisting on his heel and stalking away into the masses of humans.

Faythe stared after him. It wasn't her concern what he got up to in his spare time, nor what exactly Malin's idea of business entailed in a human settlement. She despised her suspicion as she watched his back all the way until he disappeared in the throng of bodies.

"You need to be careful around him," Reylan said with a sharp edge as he matched her line of sight.

In an attempt to lighten the mood, Faythe huffed a laugh. "You should have warned me about him. It might have swayed my decision to come all this way to Rhyenelle."

"Precisely why I didn't," he muttered.

They turned and began to stroll through the streets.

"He's always had his eyes on the throne, but Rhyenelle would be damned if it ever fell to him."

Faythe felt heavy with the indirect message in his words and the burden that perhaps Reylan still hoped she would take his place. "Damned it might have to be," she answered quietly. She felt Reylan's eyes on her but was too sheepish to meet them as she couldn't stand disappointing him. She didn't leave the silence lingering for long. Spying a veranda-covered ally, her mood picked up in giddy excitement as she read the sign:

Sloan Market.

"Did you bring any money?" Faythe asked with a childish grin.

Reylan relaxed at her enthusiasm and gave a short nod.

Faythe wasted no time in heading through the maze of delightfully fragrant stalls of home-baked goods and handmade wares. It was exactly the humble setting she needed after being surrounded by so much finery and prestige. The market was bustling, but thanks to the natural deterrent of her fae companion, most humans shuffled out of their way at the sight of the stern-faced warrior. It wasn't out of fear of him, however—not like in Farrowhold—which made her feel less imposing in their joyful space.

"You could muster a smile, you know," Faythe teased, watching him scan the area, alert for the slightest possible foul play. She picked up a small pocket dagger off a table, admiring its beautifully jeweled handle.

Reylan didn't even try to act pleased.

She huffed, setting the small blade back down, ignoring the vendor's disgruntled look when she didn't make a purchase. But then she paused and decided to rise above his uptight, mood-dampening presence.

"In fact, I'll take it." She beamed at the man behind the counter, swiping it from his collection. Faythe turned to Reylan expectantly, giving a jerk of her head. While she kept a sweet smile, he rolled his eyes, reaching into his pocket to produce a silver coin.

Faythe near skipped through the stalls, making several purchases and enjoying immensely the mundane activity of shopping. Reylan trailed behind her, and when she caught sight of a particularly scandalous set of wears, Faythe smiled deviously to herself.

She was running her fingers over the luxurious, intricate lace when she realized Reylan wasn't so close behind anymore. When she turned, she had to bite her lip to keep from giggling at the fae warrior purposely averting his gaze a few feet away from the items on the stall.

"Your phony innocence is cute," she teased.

The internal conversation made him snap his head to her, and she waved him over. Reylan seemed inclined to protest, but at her pleading look he groaned faintly and made the few strides over. Faythe folded an arm, propping her chin in one hand.

"I'm thinking the white," she pondered with scrutiny. When he didn't respond, she slid her eyes to him, her smile turning into a grin. "You're blushing, General! Have you never seen a woman's lacy wears before?"

Reylan scowled at her, which only added to her growing amusement.

Faythe rolled her eyes playfully, turning to leave. "Men never do care... I don't know why we bother."

"The red."

She halted, a slow, triumphant smile tugging at her lips. She forced it down as she turned back, crossing her arms over her chest. Faythe glanced at the deep red and golden-accented lace set but didn't admit it was the one that had caught her eye in the first place.

"Is that the color you desire to see all your feminine *companions* in?"

There was a shift in his eyes, a darkening of the sapphires. They flexed slightly as if he were physically refraining from dropping his gaze to glance over her body. Faythe shivered then felt a heat creep along her cheeks at the knot that formed in her stomach, which traveled...*lower.* She dropped her arms along with all her witty remarks as she broke the stare that was becoming too intense to bear in a public space.

"I, for one, think you would look exquisite in the white, Faythe."

Faythe would have been grateful for the interruption of Izaiah's voice, except in registering his words her warm cheeks blazed. Reylan shot him a warning look, and it was scary enough that Izaiah smoothed his playful smirk immediately.

Kyleer appeared behind the general through quick clouds of black smoke. "Malin is waiting back at the carriage," he informed them. Faythe didn't fail to pick up on his distaste when he spoke the prince's name.

She slumped, enjoying her time in the town so much she didn't want to go back to court confines. And her desire to see Malin again was even less.

Reluctantly, she followed after the fae as they all turned to leave. Faythe trailed a step behind, casting her gaze over the remaining stalls. A quick gleam of light attracted her attention to a nearby jewelry stand. Faythe halted. It could have been a simple ray of sunlight breaking through the veranda cover, but it didn't beckon her to any jewel. Her feet diverted from their straight path while she fixed her gaze on the item that silently called for her to investigate. It was a basket of brass pins most wouldn't spare a second glance at, yet Faythe was driven to them while her breathing quickened the closer she got. She beheld the single expertly crafted metal pin that lay among so many others yet stood out so formidably. Her hesitant fingers reached to retrieve it. She held it up, her blood chilling.

A hollow circle divided by an upturned crescent moon, two lines overlapping its circumference. Faythe had seen it before. The flash of memory finally connected in her mind as she recalled the symbol marked above a beautiful raven-haired Spirit in the library of High Farrow.

Dakodas. The Spirit of Death and Goddess of the Moon.

"What's wrong?" Reylan's voice was steeped in concern as she stared and stared wide-eyed at the brass pin, fingers trembling under the cool metal. She couldn't respond.

Faythe looked back at the table, blanching as she sifted through the basket of brass. She fished out another: a hollow circle, three lines overlapping its circumference. There was no questioning it was Aurialis's mark. Frantic, she finally found the remaining one she felt attracted to, completing the set of three: a downward-pointing triangle within a hollow circle, a single line struck through its circumference. Faythe laid out the pins and gawked at the set of ancient Spirit symbols before her.

It couldn't be a coincidence she was seeing them now, when she had been tasked by Aurialis to seek out Dakodas's temple and stop the perilous events that could unfold if the Spirit of Death wasn't prevented from transitioning into their world. No—it wasn't chance; it was a reminder. Time was counting down and she couldn't avoid it much longer. Faythe felt nauseous at the thought of the dangerous quest, one she had yet to tell anyone about. Her time of leisure in the Kingdom of the Phoenix was coming to an end, and she still had so much to do. So much to face.

"Blood is the key to chase away foe."

Faythe snapped her eyes up to the stallkeeper, rattled by a ghostly chill at her words. Words that sounded hauntingly familiar. "What?" she breathed even though she had heard the woman clearly.

"That'll be two coppers." The woman beamed, her face turning bright.

Faythe was shaken.

The stallkeeper furrowed her brow, tilting her head in bewildered recognition. "Lilianna?"

At the mention, Faythe's heart skipped, and she backed up a step. "No, I—"

"What are you rambling on about? She hasn't—" The man who previously had his back to her behind the counter turned, eyes widening after a few seconds when they landed on Faythe. "By the Gods," he whispered. Then his voice picked up, all but shouting, "The queen has returned!"

Faythe shook her head but couldn't form any words to insist he was wholly mistaken. Attention stirred along the Sloan Market, heads turning to gawk at her, and to Faythe's horror, bodies began to flood over to where she stood. The clamor of voices rose. It was an indistinguishable hum, and Faythe flushed with dizzying heat in the crowd of humans. Her eyes flashed from face to face as they all spoke to her, but she couldn't make out their words. Some were of praise, some relief, others adoring, but none of them were directed at her—not really. The humans clustered to welcome back their long-lost queen: her mother. But she was never coming back, and Faythe wasn't her mother. She wasn't the one these people loved.

Blinking hard, she internally screamed and fought against her need to curl into herself and disappear. Her throat tightened. Someone reached out to touch her, and she jerked violently. Spinning around, Faythe had every instinct to break into a sprint and get as far away from the claustrophobic mass as possible. But she was immediately met by a wall that blocked her path. No—not a wall. It was warm, safe. Reylan.

"I've got you."

Faythe pressed her body to his and tuned in to his voice to steady her pulse before coming apart. A minute crawled so slowly, but she reeled back her panic and regained her composure. Reylan didn't release her—not until he felt her legs were no longer at risk of buckling and she stepped back.

The crowd wasn't so close anymore. When she turned, it was a great relief to find they hadn't advanced to her thanks to Kyleer and Izaiah's intimidating poise warning them to keep their distance. The repetition of her mother's name was the only thing that rang out over the chaos of voices, striking Faythe with waves of grief and guilt.

Reylan's hand on her back once again broke her from her spiral into despair. His touch willed her feet to move, and she let the buzz of voices fade away as they made haste out of the closed-in stone maze of a market. Faythe inhaled the clear air deeply when they emerged into the open square. While she paced, attempting to clear her mind as much as her lungs, Reylan stood still, his face creased with concern and troubled thoughts. He opened his mouth to speak but was cut off by a low whistle. Faythe halted, whipping her head around. At the sight of Malin, her anger momentarily blazed to drown her frantic emotions.

"I wondered if they would still remember her," he drawled in mild surprise. "Though a queen she was not. Just another *human street rat.*"

Malin tilted his head, hands stuffed into his pockets. Slowly, a sly smile curved the side of his mouth. Faythe saw red. She jolted toward him but didn't get a step closer before Reylan's arm went around her shoulders to stop her. She wanted to screw the damned consequences and take her newly purchased pocket dagger to his throat. His look of triumph spoke the true reason for his inviting her to the human town. It was not to simply be among her kind and feel welcome. No—of course not. It was a ploy to gauge her reaction should she be recognized as her mother—the people's queen, as Reylan once called her—perhaps to rattle her confidence and prove she was unfit to ever carry the weight of a crown.

Faythe's desire to submit was dominated by her need to rise; to prove him wrong. She spared a glance at Reylan, who still held her, and his arm loosened when she reassured him she would not retaliate, as pleasing as it would be. She shrugged out of his hold and stormed the few steps to the wicked prince.

All three of her fae companions circled close when she stopped in front of him. Malin didn't flinch; instead, his smile turned darkly predatory. Faythe said nothing. She looked him over—from the sleek tendrils of his hair to the polish of his boots. Slowly, deliberately. Her appraisal gained her the reaction she wanted. It was in the quick flinch of his eyes and the faint locking of his jaw, so subtle she might have missed it. Her silent assessment enraged him though he tried to mask it.

Thoughts were often betrayed by expression. Faythe held the power to delve deep into a person's mind, but she often gained exactly what she needed by being observant enough to see the true story surface on a person's face.

When her eyes trailed back up to hold his hardened stare, she wore defiance in her own expression. She didn't care if he saw it before she brushed past him. It took great restraint and a tremendous test of wills to storm away without engaging. Faythe reeled back her anger at Malin and let the ghost of panic from the mob disperse with each heavy step she took. Reylan, Kyleer, and Izaiah were close, but they left her to calm down as she marched past the carriage. There was no way in rutting damn she was suffering the journey back with her spiteful cousin.

After a minute, Reylan fell into step beside her.

"I'm not proud of my anger sometimes," she muttered, mild embarrassment surfacing from her near outburst.

"When it's justified and directed at the right source, you should be."

Faythe glanced at him and let loose a breathy laugh at his crooked smile.

"You can't let him get to you. He's threatened—and will do whatever he can—to make sure you don't become a serious candidate for the throne," he went on. "He can think whatever he wants about you, but those of us who can see are not fools to count you out so quickly."

"I'd like to squash his pompous head one day," Izaiah chimed in, flattening his palms together.

Faythe giggled at the sight. Izaiah was far more playful and laid-back than his brother and the esteemed general. She relished in his contagious humor, which was a natural deterrent to any sour mood.

Kyleer was warm and welcoming in his own way, a fiercely protective older brother to Izaiah despite them appearing the same age. Faythe had felt his fraternal love the moment she met him in Rhyenelle.

"Malin will get what's coming to him. Nether hath no fury like a pissed-off Faythe Ashfyre." Kyleer shot her a wink, but the look of pride in his eye swelled in her chest.

Faythe may have only been in the Kingdom of the Phoenix for a couple of months, but strangely, she'd never felt more at home. She couldn't be sure if it was the connection to her mother, the surprisingly welcoming fae, or Reylan—perhaps all of that. Whatever it was, she was ready to embrace anything the kingdom could throw at her.

CHAPTER 5

Zaiana

Z AIANA GLIDED WITH unfaltering confidence through the dark passages of the labyrinth under the mountain. Her home, yet it had always felt more like her prison. A cage without bars, but offering the same sparse comforts. Warped, jagged walls that she was almost certain were constantly changing. The air was tainted by the silent wails of tormented souls; scented with hopelessness and death. Walking the carved-out passages often felt like wandering through a mass grave.

While all the dark fae were forced to coexist, the exponential divide between the Silverfair and Blackfair bloodlines always put tension in the air and tested dominance. The Born competing with the Transitioned. There was no comparison in her eyes. The dark fae were brutal, merciless, and strong, but the Blackfair bloodline was particularly savage, unhinged, and arguably unsuitable to be tamed into obedience. It wasn't something Zaiana concerned herself with—they weren't under her jurisdiction as the delegated Silverfair.

Zaiana got all of a few quiet seconds before she felt a presence creep up behind her, deliberately trying to elude her senses. One corner of her mouth twitched slyly. Before he could put a hand on her shoulder, she twisted, gripping his wrist and sending a bolt of electricity through her palm. He tensed, falling to one knee before her.

Tynan grinned wickedly when she stopped her shockwaves, and he released a hard breath. "I do love it when you play dirty." His voice was a caress.

Zaiana rolled her eyes, releasing his wrist with a rough shove. Tynan Silverfair was her second-in-command...and the first pain in her ass. "You're going to have to try a little harder than that, Tynan."

"Maybe I wanted you to hear me."

She cast him a dead look when he fell into step beside her. He was tall, stunning, with roguish hair of a dirty blond. His eyes held a faint hazel that was often entrancing if one stared closely. Zaiana might have chosen him to satisfy her occasional lust, knowing he would have gladly obliged—if he desired females at all.

"You've been busy tonight," he remarked, inhaling deeply to enjoy the scent of human blood still crusted in the cracks of her scarred hands.

She ignored him. "Where are the others?" she asked with more bite than his playful reception, riding on the back of her disappointing visit to Galmire. The town was starting to bore her mindlessly. Bodies of potential targets dwindled daily with the reckless greed of the Blackfairs, who often defied orders to leave the mountain and feed sloppily. It riled her to no end despite the brutal punishment and often death that befell those who dared.

The Silverfairs were Born dark fae; the Blackfairs were *Transitioned*, once ordinary fae turned into their dark sister species. It gave them an advantage in numbers, but they lacked discipline and restraint.

Not all captured fae survived the transition attempted during the monthly full moon. Those who did either joined the ranks as a Blackfair deemed sane enough to be trained or were judged too savage for purpose and put down like dogs or used for far more brutal means.

"Acelin and Kellias are leading in the pit. I believe Drya and Selain are doing what they do best and keeping eyes in the shadows," Tynan informed her.

It was exactly where she expected each of them to be, much to her pleasure.

The five had been hand-picked by Zaiana to form her inner circle of the highest-ranking and strongest Silverfairs. Not through size or physical strength, but because each of them possessed unique attributes that made them an unshakable force to be reckoned with. Zaiana's destination had been the pit anyway—not out of want, but out of duty as an overseer. It was the time of evening the young Silverfairs and Blackfairs would be in training. As much as it was deliriously dull and frustrating to watch, Zaiana's presence as the delegate was needed to keep them in line.

Stepping into the wide, open space at least allowed her to take a deep breath of fresh air. The roof of the pit was gloriously open, giving a wonderful view of the night sky through the mountain's mouth of pointed teeth. The pit was where they trained and where any sort of socializing and fighting took place. One was almost always followed by the other, though the uncertain order of those events kept things slightly interesting.

The clang of steel and clamor of voices were enough to make Zaiana internally recoil with a severe lack of want to be there. She preferred the silence and company of stars against a black sky. Regardless of her wants, she glided with dominant poise into the space. Those who were laughing or slacking immediately straightened out of fear when they caught sight of her, turning back to their tasks with new focus in the hope she wouldn't have noticed. Still, Zaiana observed everything without trying. What she chose to make a punishable issue depended on her mood, and right now, she only desired to get the night over with and not waste breath on petty lectures.

One thing did catch her attention, however, when she glanced to the side of the hall, away from where Acelin and Kellias were preoccupied overseeing swordplay. Three young male Blackfairs surrounded one young female Silverfair in the shadow cover of the pits. One grazed wicked fingers over her wing, and she flinched back, cowering into herself, while the others laughed.

Zaiana blazed, fingertips already vibrating at the sight. She was caught between unleashing her wrath on the Blackfairs for being bold enough to dare lay hands on her and reprimanding her own who had wandered from their training. Her rage was already teetering on a razor's edge; getting to release some of it might bring relief to the storm of her mind.

The young dark fae glanced her way as she approached, taunting grins vanishing the moment they laid eyes on her. They started to back away, but Zaiana was before them, the challenge in her eyes warning against it.

"Touch her again," she said with lethal calm, "and you'll all find yourselves without hands." She summoned her lightning, allowing the purple bolts to crack over her fingers, and their eyes widened in fear. She was about to dismiss them when a wicked voice crept in, singing to her violence.

"Now, now, Zaiana, they were just having a little a fun with one curious enough to wander over. If any of them should be reminded to stay in line, it is your own."

Zaiana ground her teeth at the sound of Maverick, delegate of the Blackfairs. He sauntered over, picking aimlessly at the cuff of his leathers with an insufferable poise of arrogance. How many times had she envisioned tearing his throat out with her bare hands? She always promised to follow through one day. Perhaps when they weren't damned to live together under the abominable confines of the Mortus Mountains.

Zaiana turned from the darklings to face off with the wickedly beautiful male. The quickest way to tell the Transitioned from the Born was in their onyx eyes, a darkness that consumed whatever humanity they might have harbored as fae. Maverick was turned into a dark fae after being captured from the kingdom of Dalrune over a century ago. He was one of the most successful transitions in their history, having kept the ability of fire he was born with when so many lost theirs—and their sanity.

Maverick and Zaiana were two of the very few who possessed any magick among the dark fae. They had grown up side by side but always in competition. She bested him at many things, but he wasn't above cheating or lying to get his way—something Zaiana had no time or respect for.

They stared off in a battle of dominance, and she threw every ounce of her hatred for him into her stare. She wanted desperately to wipe the crooked smile from his face. Or make it permanent with a blade.

"Keep your rogues in line, Maverick, or I will," she warned.

To maintain any semblance of peace under the mountain, and to prevent them from destroying each other, both bloodlines had rules set by the masters to abide by. They were prohibited from fighting in malice, and certainly from killing without cause.

"Is that a threat?"

Zaiana tilted her head. "If it were, you wouldn't be asking." She felt Tynan close behind her, ready to intervene should she give the order. She never did, but as her second-in-command, it was his duty to ensure her safety at all costs. Protect her life with his own if need be. "It is merely a word of advice from one delegate to another. You'll find your little rouges aren't so useful without hands to wield a sword or wings to take flight."

Maverick's eyes twinkled in dark delight as he took a brave step forward to further close the gap between them. The pit hushed to a quiet murmur, and weapon combat ceased at the rising conflict between the delegates, though everyone wisely kept their distance. The young dark fae beside them also backed up a few strides but didn't make themselves scarce when they hadn't been granted leave to do so.

"You seem feistier than usual tonight. I'm more than happy to oblige if you're in need of…release," he taunted.

Zaiana didn't react to his attempt to degrade her. Her eyes flashed down then back up to meet his. She scoffed. "You can keep *that* disappointment for those you bribe to warm your bed." She turned to storm off, getting all of a few paces before he called back to her.

"Just as you did with Finnian?"

His words unleashed raw fury. A name and a past she'd long buried, along with his corpse. Maverick knew exactly where to strike. Tynan knew it too. His eyes darted between her and the dark fae who had made himself a target of her unhinged wrath.

Zaiana gripped the hilt of her sword at her hip. The cry of steel caressed her need for violence, and she turned to Maverick with the tamed anger of a thousand storms. "Say that name again," she dared, her voice cutting low.

Unfazed, Maverick's answering look was goading. "Even after all this time, you still let him make you weak." He sneered, shaking his head. "I can arrange for you to be reunited."

Zaiana's veins hummed, lightning shooting from her fingers to trail jagged lines of electricity over the ornate cross guard of her sword. It sparked against the polished length of dark steel to light it up with lethal volts of vibrant purple.

"Your little lightning tricks are cute." He observed the dancing bolt, tilting his head in amusement. "What would Finnian—?"

He didn't get the chance to finish. Damning the consequences, Zaiana cast out her sword hand to point directly at him, firing a powerful charge in his direction through the conduction of her steel. She didn't need the blade to fight, but she itched to cross swords with the dark demon and release the fury in her bones. Maverick pivoted to narrowly avoid her attack. Lightning blasted across the pit, crashing with an ear-splitting *boom* against the black stone wall. Coal debris crumbled, and the vibrations were felt against the ground. The sound shook the mountain.

Maverick stared at the crater she'd created in the wall with raised eyebrows. He reached for his own sword then, turning his focus on her with a predatory triumph now he'd succeeded in provoking her. For striking first, it would be her punishment to face. She knew this, but she didn't care. The need to challenge him, silence him, overshadowed all consideration of the brutal beating she would receive for breaking the utmost law.

Zaiana twisted the blade in her wrist, charged once again, and waited for him to advance. It wasn't the first time she'd faced him in combat, only it was usually planned and allowed, with strict rules to prevent a death strike. With her surfaced anger, she wasn't certain she could hold back this time. She didn't need time to size him up as opposition; she knew his style—every twitch, every habit, every flaw. Zaiana was observant and smart.

Maverick's shoulder hitched, and Zaiana effortlessly sidestepped the anticipated dart of blue flame while advancing a long step toward him. Then his foot shifted a fraction, and she ducked low in response just as the horizontal sheet of fire sliced over her head. The gap between them shortened once more. His last attempt to hit her with his pathetic tricks was easy to twist around, and when she was close enough, steel echoed against steel with the weight of her rage. The impact vibrated through every nerve in her body, awakening—then consuming.

She moved on instinct, becoming the blade that rose and fell, twisted and turned, unfaltering, unflinching. Maverick deflected, but she kept the lead and had him retreating several steps. In a foolish moment of gloating, she allowed their blades to lock.

He glared at her with sinister malice through crossed swords. "Beautifully untamed. Foolishly emotional," he remarked in an attempt to rile her further.

It worked, distracting her for long enough that she didn't realize when Maverick conjured the heat of fire without flame, scorching her palms through her connected blade.

Zaiana hissed venomously, fingers uncurling from their tight grip on the hilt. Her sword clanged to the ground. She backed up a long stride, changing stance and bringing her hands up with only her iron-clad middle and pointer fingers extended. Her ability was a discipline. It required movement, fluidity, and control to conjure and direct lightning. But she had long since mastered the dance of storms.

Maverick smirked, but she didn't take it as a sign of mockery as she noticed the faltering of his bravado in the rigidity of his poise. He sheathed his blade, taking a sloppy counter stance with balled fists. He summoned the flame to encase his knuckles.

Now it was Zaiana's turn to smirk. Then strike. She didn't give him a second to brace as she shot jagged strokes of lightning at him. She harnessed her anger, controlled her strength, and directed each bolt with precision and purpose. Maverick used all his focus to deflect and dodge, sending a few of his own lazy attacks, which exploded in beautiful, lethal fireworks of magick against her lightning. He was slowing, and Zaiana let a sly smile of victory curl up one side of her mouth. Just as she felt confident she could send the blow to finally end it, he splayed his impressive wings, shooting upward to narrowly miss the flash of lightning that erupted against the opposite wall instead. Zaiana twisted fast, a fraction away from having the blast he sent from above tear through her wings. She growled low in annoyance.

Spineless, foolish coward to retreat like that.

Debating for a quick moment whether or not to match him in the air above, she decided to track from below instead. Zaiana danced around his onslaught of fire darts but didn't strike back. Not yet. Her eyes were fixed on the insufferable black bat, her hands braced, silently charging her ability in her palms to deal her final blow. The electricity hummed delightfully at her fingertips, building in pressure, heating in anticipation. She reached deep into the storm well inside, conjuring the heights of her ability and surfacing enough to inflict serious injury, but not to kill.

No—as much as it would be her life's delight to end him once and for all, she couldn't kill him without facing execution herself. At least, not while she remained confined to the mountain under the laws of the masters. One day, she would be free, and that day, she would unleash her centuries' worth of revenge on all those who wronged her.

When the pulse of electricity trembled in her grasp, Zaiana braced her legs to absorb the kickback of her strike. Bringing her hands together at her side, she merged the currents, directing the deadly sparks along her arm, over her chest, then casting the full force of her blast through the iron tips of her fingers. Her maneuver was quick, and Maverick was too arrogant from his position in the air to clock what she had prepared. It struck him.

Maverick cried out and began to fall instantly, though not in the ungraceful, spluttering way she'd hoped for. He landed with dignity and composure. Zaiana had to credit him for his strength, if anything, to withstand such a blow. He fell to one knee, tense and shaking, while the remnants of her lightning vibrated through him. Zaiana charged once more, fingertips humming and singing to strike again.

"Enough!"

The high-pitched feminine voice that bellowed through the pit silenced everything and struck her with trepidation. Though she knew she would face punishment, Zaiana had hoped to finish the fight and have a moment to collect herself before word got back to the masters. Casting her eyes up to the stone fringe viewing platform, she instantly cursed her grave mistake when she beheld who looked down upon them.

Zaiana rarely felt even a fraction of fear, not even from Master Nephra, whose voice thundered—she could have handled the brutal beating from her. But having broken one of the utmost laws in front of their High Lord, however, justified dread gripped her still, cold heart.

CHAPTER 6

Faythe

"SO, YOU'RE SAYING you could have Shadowported with me and saved me the grueling ride with Malin?" Faythe cast Kyleer a flat look as he offered to transport her back to the castle with his ability. The wicked prince in question had passed them in his pompous carriage a while ago, whereas they were only just entering the inner ring on foot.

She declined Kyleer's offer. For one, the thought of vanishing into Spirits-know-where to end up elsewhere by his influence made her pale. That, and she'd been enjoying the leisurely stroll taking in the vibrant, bustling streets and diverse citizens of Ellium.

"I can carry one or two others at a time, depending on how far. I didn't mention it before because Malin wouldn't have stopped trying to get you alone if he didn't get his empty ramblings off his stuffed chest," he explained.

Faythe huffed a laugh.

"Besides, I knew you could handle him."

Her deviant smile fell as she glanced to her other side. While Kyleer and Izaiah strolled casually, she noticed Reylan remained tense and stared ahead, his face as straight as a die.

"Why didn't you warn me that people might still recognize my mother?" Faythe asked him quietly—not in accusation, as the adoring chants of her long-passed mother's name seemed to have struck a chord within the general too.

Reylan's look was torn. "I did fear it, but I hoped they wouldn't. I'm sorry, Faythe. I should have insisted against coming—"

Faythe shook her head to cut him off. "I wanted to come, and I'm glad we did." She offered a warm smile in an attempt to remove some of his obvious guilt. "It was just…a shock. I didn't realize how adored she was." Though it twisted a coil of dark grief to remember the people's uplifted faces and what she saw…it was hope and love. It made Faythe's chest swell with pride to know how much of an impact her mother had made in Rhyenelle to be so admired. It gave her a spark of determination to prove herself worthy of being her mother's daughter.

"She was a bright flame in this kingdom. Headstrong, fierce, loyal. Utterly human, but that didn't matter," Kyleer said solemnly. "She may have fled to High Farrow to protect you, but I believe even she knew an ember of the Phoenix was always destined to return to us." Kyleer looked to her with a gleam of pride and wonder.

Faythe's eyes burned with raw emotion at his passionate words and the loving way he spoke of her mother. Instead of succumbing to her insecurities, she gave a smile, rising a new need to be someone they should want to stake their beliefs in. Her thoughts, and perhaps even her feelings, seemed to be heard and felt by Reylan, whose face smoothed of its hard angles, the corners of his mouth upturning a fraction.

"I got some nice new things. Thank you, by the way," Faythe said to him.

"Though you forgot one thing at that last stall—"

Izaiah was prevented from finishing by a quick jab to his side by Kyleer's elbow. He looked at his brother incredulously.

"What! All I was going to say was Faythe in the white—" He cut off his own sentence this time as his eyes flashed to Reylan, and his face fell instantly. "The white pearl necklace would have looked exquisite," he reluctantly grumbled. They hadn't even passed such wears.

Faythe was caught between deep amusement and a flush of embarrassment at the topic. To distract herself, she observed the mob of pedestrian traffic they weaved through. She had one thought on her mind, which she'd wanted to confirm since she saw the wonderful diversity among the humans and fae here. "Did many from Fenstead flee to Rhyenelle after the battles?" she pondered, admiring the beauty of the golden and rich deep brown skin tones.

Reylan nodded. "Agalhor offered safe refuge to anyone who could make it here. A lot of the Fenstead natives chose to stay between Esmire and Fenher—those towns are closest to their bordering kingdom. Most of them preferred to reside in the hillsides and forestland instead of in the city. Even though Ellium offers more security, they are still highly protected by Rhyenelle forces in the towns on the outskirts."

Faythe was mesmerized by the bustling progressiveness. There was no divide here. She felt a surge of pride for Agalhor, and it thrilled her as much as terrified her to realize it wasn't only because of his selfless, generous act when their ally was in need; Faythe slowly filled with hope for herself—because she was his daughter, and for once, she didn't want to cower from that fact. Rather, she wanted to rise to it with each new honorable trait she discovered about him.

She wondered if Tauria knew how many of her people were still alive. Faythe felt warmly at ease among those she passed as she'd heard many tales from the Fenstead princess about their culture and homeland. Ellium was nothing compared to the vivid imagery Tauria had painted in Faythe's mind when she spoke devotedly of the Kingdom of the Stag and her people. It was a place Faythe could only dream of seeing for herself before it was brutally conquered. Now, she ached to think that her friend, having been in High Farrow since the battles, had no knowledge of those who sought refuge in the Kingdom of the Phoenix—their greatest allies—awaiting their queen to lead the party home one day. She tucked away her thoughts and feelings, wanting nothing more than to share what she had seen of Tauria's thriving people and inspire a bout of hope within her.

The stretch of road they walked widened, and she no longer needed to dodge clusters of bodies. They strolled casually, Faythe's eyes darting all over the city, trying to take in as much as she could since she wasn't sure when her next visit would be.

At the bottom of the intersection, two fae emerged escorting a stumbling human man. His blond curls bounced while he folded into himself, clearly intimidated by the guards on either side. Faythe's brow furrowed. She couldn't take her eyes off him and watched his back. Her breathing hitched, heart rate picking up. The man's walk struck a chord of familiarity, as did the honey color of his hair, the backpack he gripped tightly…

"Wait," Faythe meant to call out, but it barely left her lips as a whisper in her disbelief.

"What's wrong?" Reylan's voice sharpened in alarm, hand darting to the dagger at his side.

Faythe ignored him, picking up the pace as she stared and stared at the human's back, not quite believing the face her mind had already matched to the poise and disheveled hair until he turned around. "Wait!" She did call this time, and the fae guards halted upon hearing it.

The human turned. Faythe's heart stopped along with her steps. She recoiled, blinking hard to be sure she wasn't conjuring some illusion. His eyes also widened like saucers in shock then filled with relief.

"Reuben?" she choked out.

He nodded slowly then vigorously, overcome with emotion that he'd been found by a friendly face in a foreign kingdom. Reuben's shoulders slumped, his eyes glittering with tears. They both jogged the few strides and collided in each other's arms. He shook with sobs;

Faythe was too stunned to cry. She pulled back, scanning over every inch of his smooth, boyish face, which looked so familiar but foreign at the same time, as if he'd aged far more than she imagined. He was dirty and reeked of days at sea, like salt and ale. But he was unharmed.

"What in the damned Spirits are you doing here?" she breathed, incredulous. The last she'd seen her childhood friend, she was loading him as cargo on the next ship out of High Farrow…to Lakelaria. It made no sense that he was in Rhyenelle when they'd chosen the destination to keep him safe after he acted as a spy of Valgard, as they were led to believe. It was a false frontage; a masterful diversion by King Orlon. Agalhor would have checked any foreigners for treason if they tried crossing the borders, and she had no doubt the border was exactly where he was being escorted to now. Reuben didn't even know about her. About what she was or who she was.

Oh Gods. She nearly swayed at the thought of everything she had to explain to him. Though one good thing would come out of it: he would be safe here. She would damn well make sure of that.

Reuben wiped his face quickly, shrinking back when he caught a glimpse of the three intimidating fae warriors behind her. Faythe had forgotten all about them. She flashed a look at Reylan, whose hand still hovered over his blade, eyes fixed with scary intensity on the feeble threat of Reuben. Faythe resisted the urge to roll her eyes.

"He's a friend from High Farrow. I'll explain later."

Reylan's gaze snapped to hers at the internal conversation. He gave a subtle nod but didn't relax.

"I could ask you the same thing," Reuben mumbled. "But *Gods* am I glad to see you, Faythe."

The two fae guard escorts came up behind him. Reuben went rigid with fear, eyes desperate while he held her stare in a silent plea for help. They grabbed his arms, and Faythe jolted.

"Let him go."

Neither of them seemed fazed by her command. Her fingers flexed with a flare of anger.

"We've to take him in for interrogation. He'll spend a night in the cells," one of them drawled, eager to get their duty over with and clearly irked her interruption had delayed the task.

"You will let him go," she repeated, straightening confrontationally.

"On the orders of whom, girl?" The other sneered, then they both shared a mocking laugh.

Faythe's eyes flashed at the belittlement. Her hand itched to reach for her sword, which she knew wasn't at her side. With the walking armory that accompanied her, she hadn't felt the need for it on her venture into the city. Instead, her fingertips grazed the handle of the short dagger at her thigh as Reylan stepped up beside her.

"On the order of myself." His firm voice left no room for dispute. "Second to those of Faythe Ashfyre."

Snapping her head to him, Faythe's chest burst with pride. Reylan hadn't overpowered her; he'd matched her rank. More than that—he'd asserted his own power of authority as beneath hers. Faythe was conflicted with immense gratitude and a dousing of guilt, feeling she didn't have the right to the name that made the guards instantly drop their arms and offer a low bow. Not when she'd been fighting against what it stood for at every turn. She wouldn't abuse the authority she had been granted the will to use, wouldn't call upon it simply when it suited her situation. It was time to choose.

Rise or yield.

Embrace her name, claim her heritage, and fight for what could be hers...

Or submit and leave Rhyenelle no choice but to fall into the hands of the only other Ashfyre after Agalhor. Malin was cunningly selfish and pompously arrogant. She had no doubt he had it in him to rule—he was raised for it—whereas she was a far cry from the established fae royalty. But Malin was not the people's king, not beloved like Agalhor. Not like her mother. When standing in the face of such mental turmoil, Faythe realized her answer had always been there, shadowed by ugly doubt and insecurities. Facing off with the guard, she raised her chin, giving a short nod in acceptance of their apology.

Faythe wasn't born with a crown; she wasn't raised on a diet of politics and courtship. Every monarch before her had been taught from birth to know their path, crafted and molded by their ancestors past. But perhaps it was time to break that mold and find out what could become of a ruler shaped entirely of her own clay. Of heart, not expectation.

Faythe cast her eyes up to where she could spy the castle of Rhyenelle in the distance. To where the grand pillars of the building topped with the stone-carved Firebird emblem could be seen as a proud beacon for the kingdom. A sight that answered without question who she was. The crown of Rhyenelle had two heirs, but Faythe didn't fear the battle ahead to lay her rightful claim. Malin Ashfyre's hateful words would lose him the thing he valued most as every spiteful insult and belittling remark was a small offering of tinder to fuel her fire. Only when it was too late would he realize he'd inspired his own downfall.

Following the confrontation with the fae guards in the city, Faythe felt… different. She walked the halls with new purpose, feeling the crimson tapestries welcome her *home*, the Firebird emblem blazing in her wake as though even the castle was waiting for her to accept who she was; who she could be. She felt weightless and free and embraced it before the heavy weight of her decision bore down on her. The Ashfyre name she still had to prove herself worthy of.

Reuben rushed to keep up with her and her fae companions. Reylan didn't speak. He hadn't spoken a word since his declaration in the city. Faythe didn't need him to. His waves of pride had struck through her as if he'd known all along she would come to this point and had been patiently awaiting her.

At Faythe's rooms, Kyleer and Izaiah bid their goodbyes, but Reylan lingered, eyes darting between Reuben and Faythe. Her lips curled in amusement.

"Does he really look like a threat to you?"

"He came from Lakelaria. No one ever does. I helped you gain a moment with him, but he will still need to be questioned."

Faythe's smile fell, eyebrows knitting together instead. *"No, he doesn't. You don't know what he's been through. He's my friend, and I trust him,"* she said fiercely, not leaving any room for argument. But Reylan never backed down when he thought his challenge was called for. It was something Faythe greatly admired about him, and it also made him a commanding pain in her ass.

Before Reylan could counter, Reuben shuffled awkwardly, stealing their attention. His eyes shifted between Faythe and Reylan as they stared at each other with odd intensity through their internal debate. Faythe's cheeks flamed. Reuben still had no idea about her ability. She could only imagine how wild they must have looked conversing through animated looks alone.

Faythe opened the door to her rooms and motioned Reuben inside then turned back to the stern-faced general. "I'm sure you'll hear with plenty of reaction time if he tries anything," she said loosely, already anticipating he'd deign to wander close by.

To her surprise, his stiff brow eased, but his features remained sharp. "Actually, I have something I need to do. There will be guards posted along the hall. Faythe—" Reylan stopped himself, and she wanted desperately to know the end of what he had to say. He released a long breath, finishing instead with, "I'll be gone for a week."

Faythe straightened. "Gone where?" she asked, hating the sinking feeling in her stomach.

His jaw twitched in conflict as he answered, "I have duties in one of the war camps outside Ellium." The guarded look of his sapphire eyes told her it wasn't the truth.

Her chest tightened then hollowed out completely with the knowledge he would lie to her. "Well, don't hurry back on my account." The coldness in her tone hurt her as much as it did him. There was an instant twist of guilt as she realized she was only deflecting the pain he'd caused her: the worry that perhaps he didn't trust her as much as she thought he did. She turned, about to abandon him in the hallway, but his hand caught her elbow.

"Ky and Izaiah will be around for anything you need, and you don't even need to leave your rooms if you don't want to." His voice was quiet, a hint of a plea in his words.

"I can handle myself. I don't need babysitters." Without giving in to her impulse to steal a last embrace and take back her harsh words, Faythe entered her rooms, swiftly closing the door. She shut her eyes for a moment, unsure if it was her own sadness or Reylan's that momentarily coursed through her since he had yet to move from the other side of the door.

When he did walk away, Faythe was awfully disappointed in herself. He didn't owe her an explanation for his ventures. He was the sole thing that had kept her afloat on this merciless sea of new foreign customs and information. He was her guide.

"A good friend of yours?"

At Reuben's voice, Faythe snapped her eyes open, having momentarily forgotten his presence. Heat flooded her cheeks at the suggestion in his words. "Yes. Just a friend," she emphasized, pushing off the wooden door.

Stalking over to Reuben, Faythe scanned him from head to toe, taking a few seconds to fully comprehend he was really here when she thought she would never see his boyish grin and bouncing blond curls again. She shook her head in disbelief, a bemused smile curling her lips. "By the Spirits, Reuben, we have a lot to catch up on."

For the next hour, Faythe relayed her story. With the warmth of the fire, they sat immersed in conversation while she explained what had happened in detail since the moment he left them on the ship to Lakelaria. She told of the impossible, the inconceivable, and the danger that was far from over. To her surprise, Reuben absorbed everything far better than she anticipated. Nothing seemed to amaze him, and she even had to pause a few times, concerned by his lack of outward shock—about her ability, her status in Rhyenelle, and all the perilous and twisted events that had come in between, featuring their mutual friends, her new fae companions, and the new King of High Farrow.

"That's why I came back, actually," he interjected at the mention of Nik. Faythe frowned in question, and he gave a soft chuckle. "They're not cut off from current affairs, you know. In Lakelaria, I mean. When I heard there was a new king, I thought it might be safe to come back. Though I must have taken the wrong ship… *Gods*, Faythe, I can't tell you how much of a relief it is to find you here. I might be headed to my execution otherwise." While he sounded genuine, Reuben looked troubled as he watched the fire dance in the grate. He leaned forward in his seat, and Faythe copied the movement in anticipation.

"What is it like over there?" she pressed with piqued curiosity.

Conflict creased his face. He was silent for a moment, and Faythe watched him intently. She swore she caught his eyes flickering with a darkness she had never seen in him before. She studied his face, which had aged with a sharpness since she last saw him and was guarded as if he'd learned how to shield the vulnerable emotions she was used to him bearing so openly. The boy she knew was gone, replaced by a man she had yet to know. Her guilt and sadness in wondering what he'd endured didn't get the chance to take root when he spoke.

"It's wonderful. The people, the lands, the water, but—" He paused, and a flash of something dark and desolate flinched his eyes.

Faythe's back straightened with chilling unease. It were as though he

68

had traveled to some haunting memory while staring unflinchingly into the firepit. "Are you all right?"

Reuben seemed to snap out of whatever had caused his shift in mood. When he turned his head to her, the darkness winked out of his expression so fast she wondered if she'd imagined it. His features returned to their usual softness, and he smiled brightly. The sudden contrast only added to her concern.

"I was homesick. I missed you all—and my mother. How is she?"

Faythe felt her heart stop, blood going cold, and recoiled with a breath of horror. Reuben didn't know. He wouldn't have found out from across the sea that his mother had been taken, *killed* in Reuben's place when he was discovered missing. She got to her feet, breathing hard, her throat tightening, and faced away from him, a hand going over her mouth as she stalked a few paces away, trying to figure out how to break the world-shattering news. She couldn't look at him. Didn't even know if there existed the right sequence of words to explain the death of a loved one.

"She's gone, isn't she?"

Faythe twisted back, locking wide eyes on him. Reuben remained seated. His expression was grim, but his reaction was not what she expected. She mustered a solemn nod, eyes burning.

"I'm so sorry—" She choked through the lump of grief in her throat. The dagger that struck her chest was similar to when she discovered the tragedy.

Reuben rose, and when he was close enough he pulled Faythe into a comforting embrace. She returned it tightly, her body trembling with sorrowful sobs. Her friend didn't cry, and she found his lack of outward emotion odd. When she pulled back, not one tear glittered in his hard brown eyes. Faythe didn't feel right to question it. Everyone dealt with grief in their own way, and perhaps with the shock of the news he was waiting to confront his emotions in private.

Faythe was quickly coming to accept Reuben was not the same

scared young boy she'd parted with at Farrow Harbor. He'd lived a sheltered life before his expedition, and just short of a year had changed him. What he had seen, what he'd experienced—she didn't believe it was completely free of terror. Only with time would she adjust to the new person behind the friendly face, just as she knew he would have to since she had changed too. For better or worse remained to be seen.

CHAPTER 7

Tauria

S TROLLING OVER THE dusty cobbled streets, Tauria held her chin high in an attempt to cover the fact the humans' blatant stares had any effect on her. She supposed it was unusual for them to see a fae female outside the wall—perhaps it was the first time for some—but she hated feeling like a foreigner all over again in the kingdom she'd spent a century in.

Back home in Fenstead, there were no walls, no division, and humans and fae lived in perfect harmony. Fleeing to High Farrow had been a drastic contrast; so much stone acted as ramparts between those who were supposed to be of the same land. Since Nik had announced the gates were to be open indefinitely for free venture, she'd taken the opportunity to visit the town on her own.

Well, as alone as she could be as she tried to forget the two fae guards trailing behind her.

She didn't fight Nik on the matter of needing an escort. This new freedom would take the people a while to adjust to and accept, and there may be some in the human towns who might still resent her kind. She didn't blame them and knew it would take some time for the humans to see the fae as friends and allies rather than the power-hungry, selfish monsters Orlon had succeeded in making them out to be.

At the thought of Nik, her rage vibrated to the surface. She still couldn't comprehend his intention to use her as a bargaining chip in the lord's dreadful plan. She felt his contemplation of the prospect as an agonizing twist in her gut. Tauria couldn't even bear to be in the castle since the meeting a few days ago, needing time to calm down and figure out her next move. Nothing reduced her to feeling so lost and afraid more than the acknowledgment of what everyone knew to be true: that she was a monarch by name, but with no kingdom, no armies, and no crown to lead her people with.

To distract herself from her sorrow, Tauria sought companionship in a last-ditch attempt to lift her fading spirit. A part of her hoped Marlowe might be able to offer some consolation, even if it were just a humble dose of the feminine company she was missing from Faythe. She tuned in to the metronomic clank of hammer against steel long before she rounded the last corner and the blacksmiths came into view. From outside, Tauria knew Marlowe wouldn't hear her call over the loud commotion, so she took it upon herself to enter, pulling back the curtain that separated the front from the forge. A blonde head came into view, and in turn Marlowe spotted Tauria immediately, halting the next swing of her hammer midair. She grinned widely and set the tool aside.

"I was wondering how long it would take you to leave the confines of your inner city," Marlowe teased, leaning with arms crossed against the bench.

Tauria scoffed, grazing her fingers over some of the intricate tools nearby. "It does get pretty stuffy in there." At Marlowe's sympathetic gaze, she realized she wouldn't have to explain anything, figuring Jakon had already told her everything about the horrid meeting.

"I don't believe he means it," Marlowe offered carefully.

Tauria scoffed. "It sure sounded like he did. I was humiliated."

Marlowe winced. "He's in a difficult position. There will be many testing the waters with him, looking for any sign of weakness."

Tauria shook her head, unable to look at Marlowe in her flare of anger. She hadn't come out here to have the only one she considered a friend in all this side with Nik. "I won't be used for political gain."

"I don't think he would allow you to be."

"Then Jakon must not have relayed the meeting very accurately."

Marlowe released a long sigh, her small smile pitiful. "I trust he said what he had to in the moment."

"It shouldn't justify needing to put me down to silence his nobles," Tauria flared.

"Of course not," Marlowe agreed quickly. "But as he adjusts, he's bound to make mistakes, even with those he loves."

Marlowe was right, much as it didn't help to lift Tauria's sinking feelings on the matter. Her mood dropped even more knowing that as king, Nik's duty to his kingdom would always come first. She couldn't expect anything different, and upon reflection, she was hit with the damning notion that perhaps she wasn't fit to rule her own people if she couldn't understand his actions.

To sway the heavy mood, Marlowe beamed suddenly. "I have something for you." Abruptly, the blacksmith pushed off the bench. Twisting, she walked a few paces before she stumbled, bracing a hand on the bench with a sharp breath. Tauria flinched, but Marlowe cast a weak smile over her shoulder.

"Are you all right?" Tauria asked in concern, noting she had yet to straighten.

Marlowe didn't answer immediately. Her eyes vacantly searched the space in front of her, and Tauria knew then it wasn't the wood and tools of her compound she was seeing. She turned her perplexed face away, but just as Tauria was about to go to her, Marlowe righted herself, standing steady once again. She cleared her throat and continued to the back of the workshop, where she paused.

"Sometimes the visions come out of nowhere." Marlowe laughed to brush it off, but her skin had paled a shade.

Tauria dared to ask, "What are they about?"

Marlowe reached for what she had gone to retrieve. "Anything and everything," she answered through a huffed breath. Clutching the item, she paced back to Tauria. "Though they've been getting more frequent, always broken fragments that don't always make a lot of sense at first. It's becoming tiring."

Tauria couldn't imagine what such a burden would do to a person. Marlowe was brave and resilient and had never once complained about the weight of her gift. Before she could ask anything else, Marlowe lifted the item she was holding with both hands. Her smile was bright and reflected in her eyes, tactfully defusing Tauria's concern. She reluctantly dropped the subject as her eyes fell to what Marlowe held: a wooden staff but adorned with odd steel rings and far too short to fight with.

"I made this for you since you said it was your preferred weapon," she explained.

When Tauria held her look of confusion, Marlowe's mouth curved deviously. Curling her fingers around both ends, she pulled, and the wood extended with a sharp *snap* to a decent enough length for close combat. Adjusting her grip, she twisted her wrists while pulling again, and Tauria's mouth opened in awe as it came to its full size.

Marlowe smirked. "That's not even the best part." Trailing her finger down the length, the blacksmith flicked a small, concealed lever halfway down the wood, triggering the release of two razor-sharp blades on each end. She held the staff out for Tauria to take.

Tauria slowly raised a hand, and when she gripped the weapon, Marlowe released it. The light weight was pleasantly surprising. She balanced it between both hands, marveling at the unique design.

"How did you come up with this?" she breathed in disbelief.

Marlowe simply shrugged. "The extension was easy. The mechanics of the internal trigger took a few tries to figure out though."

The human before Tauria was far more than met the eye. Above her impossible gift, Marlowe's mortal mind was nothing short of brilliant.

"I thought it might come in useful when you take back your kingdom."

Tauria met Marlowe's ocean-blue eyes and was overcome with emotion. Not *if* she would take back her kingdom, but *when*. She wanted desperately for the blacksmith—and Faythe—to be alive when she did. "You have no idea what this means to me, Marlowe. Thank you," she said quietly in her surge of emotion.

"You will make a gracious queen, Tauria Stagknight—one history will remember for millennia." Marlowe's smile was warm but saddened.

Tauria held her look, *searching* those eyes that held a sea of knowledge and wonder. Truths and secrets. Fates and failures. There was encouragement and belief in them, a silent coaxing that struck something within. Were her words more than those of a loyal friend? Perhaps foresight from an oracle…?

They both snapped their heads up with alarm when one of Tauria's guards stepped past the back curtain of the compound.

"King Nikalias requests your presence, milady." He looked between them. "Both of you."

CHAPTER 8

Faythe

FAYTHE STROLLED THE castle halls with purpose but no direction. She sought out one fae in particular but had no idea where to start looking for Kyleer.

Two days since her rocky parting with Reylan and the hours were already passing far too slowly, each one watering the bud of an ache that grew in his absence. Faythe had given Reuben time to rest and adjust that morning after more hours of endless chatter and even some laughter, but still, he couldn't distract her from the nagging hollowness in her stomach. She didn't know exactly when the general would return. It had only been a couple of days, but she *missed* him.

Before she could drive herself wild within the confines of her room, she left to seek out Kyleer, intending to take him up on his offer of archery lessons to distract herself. The thought added an eager skip to her step as she scanned various hallways and peeked into a few rooms in an attempt to track him down. Her excitement was a welcome brightness, a small hope she could finally overcome her irrational fear of using the damned weapon. But so far, she'd had no luck in finding either of the Galentithe brothers.

So much for, "Kyleer and Izaiah will be around."

They were quite the opposite, though she wouldn't rat them out to their general and friend when he returned. In fact, she was glad they weren't constantly posted outside her door or trailing around her when she left her rooms as she'd feared when Reylan implied it.

Rounding the next corner, Faythe spied a set of double doors down the hall, open enough that she could peek inside. She walked toward them with extra caution, hearing faint shuffling from behind the wood. She didn't know if it was improper to invite herself in without knocking, but considering the doors were already open, Faythe decided to chance her luck in the hope it would be Kyleer or at least someone she could ask for his whereabouts. Bracing a hand on one of the doors, she slowly and silently craned her neck to look through the gap.

Her eyes widened at the sight, cheeks flaming hot, and she instinctively retreated. She'd found one brother, albeit not the one she was on the hunt for. She stayed as still as death, hoping Izaiah and his companion hadn't detected her unwelcome intrusion. His male companion, whom he was engaged in a *very* compromised position with against the far wall. The passionate kiss they shared was heated enough that Faythe felt slick with sweat over her accidental trespassing.

On her toes, Faythe was as stealthy as an assassin, retreating back the way she came. She released a long breath when she was far enough away that Izaiah wouldn't detect her presence and only hoped he was too lost in the moment to notice her there in the first place. That, she was almost confident of.

Left with only frustration, since she refused to break up Izaiah's moment to ask where his brother might be, Faythe gave up her search. She headed to the training room anyway as it was one of the few places she knew the way to unescorted. To her great relief, it was empty. No one was here to witness her failure, and perhaps she could let her arrows fly and not care if they fell short and cut through only air. Faythe rallied her confidence with each step across the great hall until she reached the rack lined with various bows and quivers filled with arrows with red fletchings. Taking a deep breath, she swiped a longbow and arrows, going over to the target range. She didn't bother to equip the quiver, setting it down in front of her instead. Taking a deep breath, she took one, nocking it into the string, but didn't yet pull and aim.

Faythe eyed the closest target, picturing her arrow protruding from it. She wouldn't try to hit any of the three specific rings on the circular plate. If she hit it at all it would be a victory. Yet the more she stared at it, the farther away the distance seemed, and her palms started to clam up. She shook her head at her own pathetic nerves. She had nothing to lose.

With a flare of determination, Faythe brought her arms up, straining to pull the arrow into position and hold the iron tip within her line of sight. Her aim wavered slightly, but she focused as best she could on the stationary target.

Then she unhooked her fingers, releasing the string's tension.

Faythe already knew her aim was sloppy and her shaky release would damage the accuracy further. The arrow was only airborne for a second, and when she heard the faint *thud* instead of the clatter against stone she relaxed her tense shoulders. It hit the very edge of the outer circle and protruded from the target at a crooked angle…but she'd hit it at least.

She huffed a laugh, shaking her head in disbelief for being so anxious about nothing. Sure, she needed *a lot* of practice to become competent, but she felt a new confidence that she could learn the weapon with the right training.

A slow, loud clap made her jolt, and she whirled around to the intruder. Kyleer wore a side-smile of satisfaction.

"So, you do know how it works."

Faythe gaped at him as he strolled over to join her. "How long have you been there?"

He simply shrugged, holding his hand out for the longbow. Faythe passed it to him without taking her eyes off him.

"I knew you were looking for me," he said and smirked at her incredulous look. "But I wanted to see if you'd attempt the shot when you thought no one was watching." Kyleer reached for an arrow, swiftly nocking it into place. He let it fly, and it hit just next to her own. "That could be the shoulder of an enemy." He didn't look at her as he went for another. Nocking then releasing, he hit the inner circle below. "That could be their leg." In a quick flash of movement, he took one final arrow and let it soar to where it hit dead center of the bullseye. "That could be him dead." Kyleer lowered the bow and turned to her. "It's not always about accuracy. If you focus too hard on trying to hit something specific, you could lose the opportunity completely in battle. Don't hesitate. Any shot could be enough to buy the most precious currency on the field." The look he assessed her with wasn't condescending, and she could see the great commander he personified in battle. "Time."

Faythe absorbed his words and the passionate tone in which he spoke. She gave a nod of understanding, casting her eyes over to the marks and imagining them as the enemy. Her adrenaline spiked knowing they wouldn't be stationary; that if she were to ever face a true battle, the red-and-white target would be racing for her. Her blood sang to life with a new flare of determination—to fight, to survive, to protect everyone in the forefront of her mind.

"I think I know why you struggle with archery," Kyleer pondered after a short pause, as if he'd answered a question that had been weighing on him. "It's a fine-tuned skill and requires diligent patience and focus."

She huffed, cutting in with, "You don't think I have patience or focus?"

He shook his head with a grin of amusement at her defensive tone.

"I've seen you train, Faythe. The sense of calm you can reel yourself into is a rare trait and will be invaluable in combat, but archery isn't something you can throw your physical being into. You can't release your anger and frustration through exertion with the swinging of a blade. But if you can find the focus to channel those emotions into the flight of an arrow while stationary…well, I believe we'll have fixed the block on your archery abilities."

Faythe blinked. Everything he said made perfect sense, and she was in awe, if slightly embarrassed he'd been silently watching her train. She would always be grateful for Reylan's mentoring. He'd taught her so much—but having someone else give an outside opinion opened her eyes to habits she needed to adjust before she could progress past more than just swordplay and agility. Kyleer was right: her anger was perhaps her biggest weakness, but she'd learned how to turn it into a strength by releasing it through the swinging of her sword.

"Why do you train so hard? As if you're preparing for a war none of us know about." Kyleer's voice stole her attention.

Her deep-set frown relaxed. To distract herself, she silently requested the bow back. Kyleer obliged, and she nocked another arrow into place. Her trembling had nothing to do with her nerves this time.

"Can't I just find interest and enjoyment in this?" she answered as casually as she could, freeing an arrow from her hold. It once again landed crookedly in the outer ring. She huffed.

"I suppose you could, but that's not the only reason, is it?" Kyleer wasn't really asking.

"The war isn't over," she pointed out.

"No, it's not. But it's been dormant for a century. What makes you so afraid it will spark again in your lifetime?"

Your lifetime.

His enlightenment to her mortality made her wince with disappointment. He didn't mention it as a weakness, but it was a cruel reminder of her numbered years in comparison to his. In comparison to all her fae friends here and in High Farrow. In a flare of anger at the wicked curse of time, Faythe brazenly snatched an arrow, aimed, and released it in the space of a breath. Her arms dropped and eyebrows rose when it hit straight this time, and almost within the second circle.

Kyleer blew out a laugh. "See? Odds are tipped in your favor when you drop the instinct to hesitate and focus your frustrations through the release."

Faythe stared at the arrow a little longer before a smile of amused disbelief creased her eyes.

Kyleer's commanding voice cut short her moment of triumph. "Your stance is still completely wrong. Try again." He was already holding an arrow out to her.

She scowled, snatching it from him.

Faythe poised herself once again to let it loose from her bow. Kyleer came around her, hands going to her waist to twist her angle slightly. His touch didn't linger for a second. Then he leveled her elbows, eyebrows creasing deeply as he moved and cocked his head, assessing her. His hand went over hers to tilt her aim, and Faythe held in a slight gasp when she noticed the crossing of raised scars, like three jagged lightning strokes, marring one of his hands and trailing past the cuff of his leathers. His slightly crooked fingers might not have been noticeable if she hadn't glanced at his unharmed hand too.

Kyleer caught her wide-eyed look, and his hands left her immediately.

"What happened?" she asked carefully, loosening the string of the bow and lowering her arms.

He wore a faint smile, but Faythe could see it. Kyleer often held a hollowness in his green irises, an agony even his genuine happiness couldn't erase. Not of any wound, perhaps not even of memory—it was like the tragedy of a lingering loneliness, the deeper kind one held when they had given up hoping it would ever be cured.

Kyleer looked at the bow in her hands expectantly, and she read the sign: he wasn't ready to open up to her. Thinking about Izaiah's permanently upbeat and playful nature, Faythe couldn't help but wonder if Kyleer had been a shield for him through their centuries of life. She strained her arm to pull back the arrow once more, and Kyleer quickly adjusted her stance again before stepping back. She released and watched in bemusement as the dart hit straight inside the inner circle.

"If you ever want to talk…" Faythe trailed off, feeling like it was a weak offer but not knowing how else to express to him that he didn't need to hide from her.

He gave a small dip of his head, full of understanding. "Likewise."

Her face fell at that. Faythe had thought she'd done a good job at suppressing the horrors that haunted her still. Nightmares that had followed her from High Farrow and plagued her with restless thoughts and sleepless nights. She hadn't told anyone, not even Reylan, though it was clear now she didn't have to.

"He's been giving you space, maybe to see if you'll open up to him first," Kyleer admitted quietly. She didn't have to ask to know he spoke of the general.

Faythe looked away, caught between embarrassment that her weakness hadn't gone unnoticed and anger that they had all been tiptoeing around the subject this whole time. Her humiliation flared in her defense. "What are you all waiting for? To see if I'll concede and run home?"

Kyleer shook his head, eyes softening as he said, "You are home."

Faythe's slowly building anger defused completely. Instead, her brow pinched as his words struck her more powerfully than she thought they would.

Kyleer walked to the wall lined with weapons, retrieving another bow before coming back and stealing an arrow from the quiver. She figured it was more to cut the somber tension than for any sort of practice. His arrow released and hit the center of the farthest target.

"Show-off," she muttered in light humor, grabbing her own arrow.

Kyleer huffed a laugh as he watched her.

Faythe let the arrow soar without much care about where it went. When she lowered her arms, she blurted, "Do you know where he is?"

His look fell in sympathy, and she hated it. Faythe thought she could stand not knowing why Reylan left days ago—more importantly, why he lied about where he was going. She shouldn't pry, and part of her felt wrong for asking someone else about his private affairs.

She shook her head. "Never mind," she muttered before he had the chance to answer. Guilt and sadness overcame her. She was no longer in the mood to practice with weaponry.

Faythe went to return her bow, but Kyleer's quiet voice halted her steps. "He's visiting…" He trailed off, hesitant. When Faythe turned back, Kyleer's eyes were creased in sorrow. Her stomach knotted. "He's visiting a grave. It's in Fenher," he explained carefully, cautious of just how much he shared with her. He knew it wasn't his place to say.

Faythe's regret over how she'd spoken to Reylan before he left twisted tighter. Her voice fell. "Why wouldn't he just tell me?"

"I'm sure he will. It's…hard for him. Reylan hasn't opened up about his past to anyone in a very long time."

"Who…?" Faythe halted her sentence, unsure if she could handle the knowledge of who Reylan had lost. She already knew he was without his parents, but this seemed far more recent.

Kyleer looked away from her, but before he did, she caught the ice-cold glaze in the forest of his irises. "We lost many people in the Battle of Fenher. Though I don't know why they call it that—it was more a slaughter of so many innocents." His fingers flexed tighter around his bow as he paced away to return it.

Faythe followed slowly, heart picking up in tempo to hear of the tragedy she felt in the notes of his voice. Something about the town he spoke of sparked a flash of memory. Then she halted her steps as she remembered.

"Fenher…" she said quietly. "It's where Varlas lost his mate."

Kyleer's hands gripped the rack tightly once he'd placed the bow back. Faythe swallowed hard, seeming to have struck a chord.

His voice was unrecognizable, so hard and detached. "He wasn't the only one." He seemed to know he'd slipped up. Not with Reylan's past, but his own. His words were tight, broken, and ice embraced her. The muscles in his large arms flexed, and his shoulder blades stiffened.

Faythe said carefully, barely louder than a whisper, "You…you had a mate?" As she spoke in past tense, her heart splintered for him.

Kyleer straightened but didn't turn to face her. She couldn't read his expression, but she opened herself up to feel his suffering. Perhaps he didn't realize he'd let the emotion slip past his guard and settle over him in a shroud of palpable anguish. It was so raw, sorrowful, and drain-ing… Faythe felt suffocated under his unfathomable grief. To lose a mate was to lose half of one's soul forever.

"Yes," he confirmed, his voice devoid of any emotion. A tremor swept through her. "Her name was Greia, and she was my mate, but we weren't…*mated.*" He turned to face her then, guarded but curious to see her reaction.

"There's a difference?"

Kyleer reached for another bow, smaller. He walked over to her and replaced her longer one with it. Faythe weighed the lighter bow.

"When we recognize our mate, it's not typically an instant love. In fact, on rare occasions, a true pairing might never find such a feeling," he explained as she followed him back to the target range. "Greia was already with another when I met her. It was during the Great Battles, and she was one of the healers who joined my legion to help with the wounded." He passed her an arrow, which Faythe took warily before nocking it to the string.

She eyed him carefully before deciding to press on when his blank expression gave little away. "What happened?"

Kyleer looked at her slackened bow expectantly. She wasn't in the mood for archery, but as he seemed unwilling to continue until she attempted the shot, she applied tension to the string, raising her arms to aim. The new bow made holding her poise a little easier. Kyleer moved around her to adjust her stance again.

"Greia was kind and selfless, and I could never understand how someone so gentle was fated to be with someone like me. But her heart already belonged to another long before she met me. It was a confusing time for her, and she insisted she needed time to sort out her thoughts." Kyleer paused, and Faythe spared him a sidelong glance, feeling the dark cogs that turned his story. "Then we went to Fenher."

She released her arrow from the shock of pain that clenched inside her chest. It hit crookedly at the bottom of the target, a near miss. Faythe didn't care and turned to him with desolate eyes.

His smile was a wince. "It was a fatal error on our part. As commanders, we led our forces away from the town where so many innocents took refuge from Olmstone and Rhyenelle. While there were many commanders on the field that day, as the leading general, Reylan always shouldered the burden of the soldiers' movement that ended in tragedy. On top of that, he lost someone very dear to him too."

Faythe swallowed hard, winded by the blow of their history. "He had a mate?" Even as she voiced it, she fought the crushing sadness in her chest for Reylan's pain.

Something conflicted crossed Kyleer's eyes as he stared at her, *studied her*, then his gaze dropped along with whatever it was he pondered in that moment. Though she found it oddly unnerving, she didn't push. Faythe waited patiently for any knowledge he was willing to share with her.

"No. But she was probably as close to a mate as one who never finds theirs could hope for. She helped ground him on a reckless path after his upbringing. She tamed him, but nothing could stop Reylan from seeing himself as the villain in everything he did. From wanting to punish himself and never finding salvation no matter how much *good* he did. Not even Farrah could silence the demons that tormented him. Not until—" Kyleer stopped himself, but before she could question it, he diverted. "He visits Fenher every year out of grief and guilt. I used to go with him, but I would always cross paths with the male who truly mourns Greia as she deserves. I didn't get the privilege of knowing her well, but if I had the chance…I think I would have fallen for her deeply. I *felt* her when she died, and my punishment for allowing that to happen is to live in the knowledge I won't ever get that chance. To know what it would have been like if she chose me."

"Ky." Faythe didn't know what to say. No words of consolation seemed enough for what he had endured. What he had lost.

"It was a long time ago," he offered somberly. Faythe figured the diverting statement was more for his own sake than hers.

"You deserve to be loved, Kyleer," she couldn't help the need to tell him when everything about him said he believed the opposite.

He gave a warm smile in appreciation, but Faythe knew it would take far more than words to get him to *feel* it. In friendship, she was dedicated to making him believe it.

Faythe doubled back to something that had grabbed her curiosity. "How do you…how do you become *mated?*"

It worked to slowly defuse the somber cloud that hung in the air. Kyleer quirked an amused brow. "It's…intimate." He paused as though deliberating whether or not it was his area to enlighten her. "The bond can be felt and strengthened without completing the *act*. We have more primal, claiming instincts than a human does. We have teeth that can puncture, and it's through the exchange of blood that the full bond is forged. It can only be broken by death."

At first, Faythe imagined it to be painful rather than intimate, but the more she thought about it, the flash of memory from High Farrow, when she'd seen those dangerous, alluring teeth Reylan bared to her— albeit in threat—a pulse of her heart shot straight down through her body. Kyleer looked to be fighting the amusement on his face, as though he knew what she was mulling over. If he knew *who* she thought of in that moment, he gave nothing away. Faythe put effort into cooling her face.

Kyleer went on. "The bond can also be rejected before the mating, but if either side rejects, that also cannot be undone. The soul will sever whatever connection was there as though its mate were dead. It's painful and can leave a permanent hollow void, but there's no lingering bond to always feel a pull to its other half even without any romantic or friendly feeling. Without the bond, one is free to be with whomever they choose."

Faythe gathered the knowledge and stored it. Even though it didn't apply to her, even though she tried not to think about the sinking feeling in her gut at that fact. "Exchanging blood doesn't sound intimate."

Another voice carried across the hall to answer. "Biting, especially between mates, is a pleasure beyond your wildest imagination, dear Faythe. And almost always performed alongside…other acts." Izaiah crept up to them, the most devious grin upturning one side of his mouth. "I should have known this is where you'd run off to."

Faythe flushed at his bold explanation of *mating*. Then the second half of his statement registered, and her already warm cheeks caught fire as she knew what he meant.

"You could have joined, you know. I'm not opposed to the idea of having a woman involved," he teased, stalking toward her with his hands stuffed casually into his finely tailored pants' pockets.

Gods have mercy. Any retorts were killed by her eternal embarrassment that he knew about her accidental trespassing on his intimate moment. Though, in her defense, it was as good as public where she'd stumbled across them.

"Sorry, I was looking for—"

"Ky, I know. And that hurts." He held a hand to his chest with a mock pout, but his eyes danced with wild amusement at her flustered unease.

Her mouth snapped shut, and she glared at him instead. She crossed her arms. "If you knew I was there, why didn't you say anything?"

His grin widened mischievously. "I was a little preoccupied."

Faythe's whole face was ablaze, and Izaiah delighted in the reaction. She refrained from snatching another arrow and aiming at him.

"Now, would you care for some real lessons? In archery…or perhaps in another skill you may feel yourself lacking in, which you witnessed today?"

Faythe gaped in disbelief, floundering for words.

"She's done for today," Kyleer cut in. She could have embraced him for it when her own response failed her.

Izaiah barked a laugh. "Your pretend innocence is adorable, Faythe." He leaned over, but she batted his hand away before he could tousle her hair.

"Get a room next time," she shot back.

His chuckles followed her as she stalked for the exit. "We did. Only, it was trespassed on by——"

"That's enough," Kyleer warned.

Izaiah didn't drop his perky attitude as he strolled to her side. "Faythe knows I'm only teasing." He waved his brother off.

While she was sure her face had flushed crimson since he'd roused her humiliation like a child, Faythe was glad for his lighthearted presence. When she looked at him, his smile was genuine, and he shot her a quick wink to ease her tension. She didn't know how much he had heard before he sauntered into the training room, but something in his look of understanding made her realize his taunting and teasing was really just a way to distract her from her heavy heart. From the subject of Reylan and the reason for his absence.

She wouldn't pry, and her disappointment in his secretiveness had dissolved completely. Whatever Reylan wanted to share about his past, she would listen. But she wouldn't press for answers she had no right to demand. Now, all she hoped was that he was safe in Fenher. And she quietly longed for his return.

CHAPTER 9

Nikalias

E VEN THE SILENCE was weighted with judgment. Nik looked over
the city from the high vantage point of his private council chamber, wondering how often his father stood in this exact spot to deliberate.
His kingdom. Everything he did now, every step he took, he couldn't help
but feel he was in the shadow of rulers far more worthy of the throne.

Jakon lingered at his back while they awaited Marlowe and Tauria.
Nik wondered if the Fenstead queen would even come. He resented
himself for how he spoke of her to his council, and as he gazed out over
his city, he wondered if that was the kind of person he had to shape
into…did he want the crown at all?

Nik's spine locked as he sensed Tauria's approach down the hall. His
relief that she had come was drowned out by the dread of looking into
her betrayed eyes. After a short knock, he called for them to enter.

He turned in time to spy the emerald of her gown flowing through
the door. Marlowe beamed wide as she headed straight to her fiancé.
Jakon's arm went around her, planting a tender kiss on her temple. Nik

had to look away—not out of discomfort, but from the dark seed of jealousy that threatened to bud at witnessing their carefree relationship. It was wrong to pluck resentment from someone else's happiness, but Nik felt the sorrow swirl in his chest that it was a blessing he didn't believe he would ever experience. Fate had other plans for him.

His eyes met Tauria's as she demanded, "Why are we here?" Her tone was as cold as her hardened gaze.

Nik had to keep his composure, not break down like a whelp before her and beg for her understanding and forgiveness in front of the humans. He had to avert his attention or he risked doing just that. "I wasn't truthful when I told the council Olmstone has been quiet," he began, focusing on Jakon's pinched brow of concern, which matched Marlowe's surprise. "I mean, I suppose it was a half-truth. There hasn't been much public movement, but their silence is perhaps because they have been working toward something far more malevolent."

"I don't like where this is going," Jakon muttered, taking a seat and pulling Marlowe down with him.

Nik reclined casually against his desk. *His father's desk,* where he had watched and learned as so many important things unfolded. Nik quickly shook the tormenting thought. "I don't expect you will. My spies don't know the specifics yet, but Varlas isn't working alone."

"Working toward what?" Tauria pressed.

"I think we all know the answer to that," Marlowe chimed in quietly. "Varlas won't stop until he's had his vengeance. It is his path, and it has been for a long time."

Nik tuned his attention in to Marlowe as she offered up the subtle foresight. Whatever she had seen regarding the Olmstone king, it was all the confirmation he needed to know Varlas was beyond reasoning. He ran his hands down his face in exasperation.

"I thought we had gotten through to him after his last attempt to ally with High Farrow forces to overthrow Rhyenelle." Nik was disappointed in himself, thinking perhaps he could have said more. Or at least seen that there was no reasoning to be had with Varlas. The signs were there, and while he'd agreed to retreat forces and maintain the alliance, his loathing of Agalhor never left his face.

"Should we warn Agalhor? If Varlas has plans to advance on Rhyenelle once again, Faythe is there." The fear that filled Jakon's eyes had riddled Nik for weeks as he'd tried to gather as much information as he could on Varlas's movements.

"So far, I don't believe there are any plans to attack. I would like to exchange words with Agalhor so he can strengthen his defenses should he try, but Varlas is no fool. He knew he couldn't overthrow Rhyenelle alone, or even allied with my father. They were relying on whatever plans they set in place with Marvellas that required the Riscillius Faythe has." Nik shook his head. "What I've gathered is that new forces have been seen moving in—those not believed to be Olmstone natives."

"Valgard?" Tauria said in disbelief.

Nik finally looked at her and wanted more than anything to console the quick flash of terror that he knew was still swirling within. He didn't need to confirm her question; it was the only possible conclusion.

"He's gone mad," Jakon muttered.

"I believe you might be right. He may have a wife and children, but I think his course was set the day his soul was severed at the death of his mate."

"If Olmstone joins with Valgard…" Tauria didn't finish her haunted statement.

"I can't be certain it is what's happening. Olmstone has strengthened its defenses to a higher scale than I believed possible with Varlas's resources alone. Some of my spies never made it back." His gut twisted at that fact. "I can't risk sending more. If Varlas suspects I'm gaining any insight into his plans, it could work gravely against us. He would have cause for war."

"It doesn't sound like he's willing to wait for a cause anyway," Jakon snapped.

Nik didn't react, knowing the human was just as fearful as he was at the thought of war; in knowing how far away their mutual dear friend was and how she was in the heart of the kingdom pinned by a vengeful king's wrath. "I'm trying to find out what I can, but it will take time. I'm not confident my words to Agalhor will be safe, as any messenger traveling by land will need to pass through Olmstone. I can't risk them being intercepted."

"So, what do we do?" Tauria asked.

Nik dropped his gaze. Out of shame, defeat. For reaching such a desperate point that he was only confiding in Tauria and the two humans for being so at a loss for what to do. He was a pitiful king.

"I'm being tested. My every action, every movement. I can't be sure who I can trust yet, as those who were close to my father are aligned in their malicious thoughts alone. That is not what I am trying to build." Nik settled his gaze on Tauria, hoping she would register his apology and understand. "They're vultures, and they're circling, looking for any reason to doubt me. I'm not such an arrogant fool to believe my position is safe. Zarrius has power, influence, and he knows it."

"What do you need from us?" Marlowe's voice was gentle.

Nik wasn't sure how to answer. He needed to get word to Agalhor. If he was also aware of what could be amassing in Olmstone, they needed their alliance to hold and to know they would band together should it become a problem. Nik wanted to be prepared to strike first if necessary, and he couldn't do so with their southern allies. If they made strategic plans, Olmstone could be attacked from both sides as it lay in between the might of High Farrow and Rhyenelle.

"I need to find a way to communicate easily with Rhyenelle," he said at last. He hated the thoughts that surfaced in his mind and wondered if Faythe would ever forgive him for what he was about to propose for her dear friends. "Traveling by land is too much of a risk. By sea is the safest course. But I also need someone I can trust."

His lingering suggestion was picked up straight away. Tauria looked to the humans just as Jakon straightened with admirable confidence.

"I'll go," he answered. Without hesitation, without considering the risks. Nik had to believe his eagerness was solely at the prospect of being reunited with Faythe.

"We'll go," Marlowe was quick to amend, a hand going over Jakon's as they exchanged a look of understanding.

"It will be dangerous. The Black Sea is notorious for pirates and harsh weather. As your friend, and for Faythe, I would never ask this of you." Nik straightened, his pained face wiped of all emotion. "But as your king, I trust you, Jakon. As my emissary you have proven your dedication and loyalty beyond doubt. You have ties here, and you have ties to the Heir of Rhyenelle. You are High Farrow's best political candidate."

Jakon rose. "We will go to Rhyenelle. But how will I get messages to you if it will take so long by sea?"

"By Nightwalking," he answered simply. "I haven't tried it before, but I believe I hold enough power to reach you in Rhyenelle. All I require is for you to gift me something of yours that holds sentiment."

"Why can't you Nightwalk to Faythe?" Tauria asked.

Nik ran a hand down his face, cursing his own negligence. "I gifted Faythe something of mine—something of value. Think of it like a token of permission. It grants her access to me from a far greater distance if she's strong enough." His implication was felt throughout the room: after all this time without hearing from her, perhaps Faythe *wasn't* strong enough in her ability. "When I gifted her the necklace, I didn't really believe she would need it. Her leave happened so fast I didn't think to ask for something in return so I could attempt to Nightwalk to her instead. Magick has bounds. Without that token of permission, she's too far away for me to reach her."

Jakon frowned in thought as if at a loss for what to hand over. Then his face smoothed as he reached to his side and pulled out a short dagger. "This was a gift from Faythe a long time ago."

Nik shook his head. "There must be something else."

"I don't have anything else." Jakon's face was pained as he extended it to him. "She would want me to give it to you, I'm sure of that."

Nik was reluctant, but he accepted it, laying it on the desk behind him. "Thank you for what you're risking for this."

Jakon offered a nod and a short smile. It did nothing to relieve the twist in his stomach at setting Faythe's friends off on a journey with perilous risks. He'd sworn to her to protect them and could only hope Faythe would forgive him for having no alternative.

"How do we track Varlas's movements?" Tauria asked.

Nik rubbed a hand down his face again as this was a key matter he had no resolution for. Even if he and Agalhor were alert, they had to find a way to get inside knowledge before they could know what they were up against. One dark, foreboding notion often chilled his thoughts: flashbacks to the haunting memory of his last conversation with his father that often stifled his ability to rest.

"I need to find a way to get eyes in Olmstone too. If they are siding with Valgard, I believe we may be up against far more than fae and steel." The atmosphere became unsettled. "I think history is indeed repeating itself and the dark fae have risen again."

Tauria gasped while Marlowe seemed to clutch Jakon's hand tighter. Her face took on a lighter pallor, but she was otherwise unsurprised.

"You are right," she confirmed, and all eyes snapped to her. "Aurialis already told us Mordecai lives. We don't know how long he's had to amass an army of dark fae."

"There can't be many. Even if he's had centuries to raise and train full-grown warriors, it would take far more time to have any force in numbers," Nik said, but the chilling look on the blacksmith's face stole all consolation from his words.

"Unless he's creating them," she explained.

Nik stood straight with the chill that shot down his spine. "Is that possible?"

Marlowe's nod was grim. "They call it the Spell of Transition. Dark and forbidden Blood Magick. I've seen things. *Nightmarish* things." Jakon drew her close as her voice dropped with terror. "It all makes sense now. Darkness is rising—in a force that could surpass the haunting tales of history."

Everyone weathered the coldness that swept the room, standing silent as they tried to process what Marlowe told them.

"If that's what Varlas is siding with…" Tauria's ghostly voice set Nik in motion. "We have to find out."

Nik nodded. "I'm working on finding a solution."

"Can you Nightwalk to your spies in Olmstone?"

His face fell as he leaned on his desk. "I could try, but it's a huge risk. My spies are being too easily snuffed out, and there's no mercy for them. When I Nightwalk, my whole mental being is projected into another's. If I'm in there when they're caught and executed—"

"You'd die too." Tauria's cracked voice was a surprise.

He nodded his confirmation, unable to bear her terror.

"Then it's not worth the risk."

"Agreed. We'll find another way," Jakon added.

Nik looked around them all, pride swelling in his chest at their fierce and protective gazes. In each of them was a warrior, not just a friend. For each other, for their kingdoms, for what was *right* in the world, they were willing to risk it all.

"Thank you," Nik said, though he wasn't sure why.

"You don't need to thank us," Jakon replied. "You may wear the crown for us all, but no kingdom was ever run by one person alone."

Their faces upturned, and Jakon's laugh was the first to break the somber stillness until they all joined in. Laughing because he was right; laughing because they weren't sure how much of the blissful sound they would get to cherish from each other.

Laughing…because it was a bright light in the darkness that had begun to descend.

CHAPTER 10

Zaiana

ZAIANA MARCHED WITH dignity and confidence behind her overseer and High Lord. Fear wasn't something she was accustomed to, but she had to admit, a slither of the wicked emotion laced her rigid spine. To keep herself calm, she imagined all the excruciating, slow, and gruesome ways she could kill Maverick. It did more than soothe her emotions about the impending confrontation with her superiors; it actually brought her a hint of joy to picture his death by her hand.

She realized now that his taunting had been purposeful, goading her into a fight to display her unhinged rage and rare lack of discipline— right in front of the High Lord. Maverick always had been wicked and relished in the petty remarks she'd long made herself immune to. That was his fun. But today, he knew which string to pull to get her to snap, hoping it would secure her a far more lethal punishment than usual.

High Lord Mordecai rarely visited them below the mountain. He preferred to reside in Valgard, a city off the coast of the mainland of

Ungardia, far away from any possible detection by the other kingdoms. He was supposed to be dead after all.

Then again, weren't they all?

Zaiana didn't understand what made Mordecai so feared and superior. He had no ability, and aside from his intimidating brute size and strength she didn't believe he possessed any more special traits than the rest of them. Hierarchy was foolish, determined by birthright instead of fitness to rule. Zaiana was not present during the conquer of Dalrune, but she had heard it was an easy steal. Their monarchs were pitiful, spineless, and had practically surrendered themselves for slaughter. Meanwhile, she had led a legion to attack Fenstead, and they had at least put up a valiant fight. Their values of peace and prosperity were their ultimate weaknesses, standing no chance against the force of her savagery.

Zaiana had fought in every great battle. Those who could glamour their dark fae heritage joined the frontlines among the fae of Valgard. It was glorious, if only because it was the sole time she got to taste any sense of freedom. Though her tether always pulled her back to the damned mountain, the Great Battles were the only few years out of her three hundred in which she had been allowed to kill, move, and decide every action for herself as one of the commanding generals. She itched to taste that freedom once again, knowing it was near, and knowing once they'd finally conquered Ungardia her freedom would be permanent. Not just from the mountain, but from every insufferable dark fae master and lord she despised.

Finally rounding the last corner into the open, cavernous council room, Zaiana halted before the long table for judgment. The other three masters were already seated, leaving Nephra to take her usual position. The grand center seat, which Zaiana was used to seeing empty, was to be occupied by High Lord Mordecai.

Zaiana straightened herself and kept her expression blank. If her stone heart could beat, she imagined it would be increasing in tempo like the effects fear had on her own victims. She could almost feel its phantom thud.

Everyone was silent while Mordecai leaned, ignorant and casual, in his throne-like chair, an elbow braced on the stone arm so he could hold his strong, angular jaw in one hand. His black, depthless eyes fixed on her. She didn't balk, staring straight back.

"Are you not going to bow?" The playful taunt in his gravelly voice made lightning prick the surface of her skin.

Reluctantly, Zaiana dropped to one knee, head falling in forced respect. He didn't deserve it. He'd done nothing for her, and she didn't consider him her king or High Lord. She did value her life, however, and voicing those treasonous thoughts would seal her painful, strung-out end.

"Better," he drawled.

Zaiana clenched her teeth.

"Your reputation precedes you." It wasn't a compliment, but the tone didn't land as an insult either. She couldn't be sure what her reputation was perceived as from one person to the next, but if it were anything short of greatness, she would feel wholly affronted. "I've heard much about your leadership and discipline. Though that is not what I witnessed mere minutes ago. Do you often give into incitement?"

"No," she ground out.

He made a curious sound. "Beautifully untamed," he remarked. Zaiana had heard those words many times—from her enemies, her lovers, the whispers in the shadows. "Do you know the consequences of striking another delegate?"

Pain. Though the methods were variable. "Yes, High Lord."

"Yet you choose to fight anyway. Why?"

Zaiana refrained from narrowing her eyes at his pointless questions. What was he trying to get her to admit?

"To defend myself."

"You attacked first."

Zaiana squared her shoulders. "Shouldn't we have the right to defend our honor, not just our bodies?"

The High Lord's mouth curled up in wicked amusement. Zaiana supposed he was beautiful in the roguish, dominant, ominous kind of way. For a dark fae brought back from the dead, he was lucky to have flesh so smooth and unmarred. She didn't know what it took to raise him, but Zaiana shuddered at the thought of the ancient and forbidden Blood Magick that would have been involved. If he bore any consequence, it lived under the surface.

Zaiana couldn't be certain the color of his blood either. He was once Born dark fae, but she wondered if his blood was now black like the Transitioned.

The full moon ritual was an event Zaiana dreaded. Out of the dozen fae captured to be turned, they were fortunate if they successfully transitioned a couple of them into the Blackfair ranks. The others… Some were so hideously disfigured from the Blood Ritual they were kept for when quick savagery might be useful on the battlefield. The rest simply died, too weak to withstand the change.

Zaiana didn't dare avert her gaze from Mordecai's, but she didn't need to as rage circulated in the air emanating from the masters at her audacity to talk back. Mordecai's eyes, however, twinkled in dark merriment.

"Yes, I think we should," he answered at last.

Zaiana didn't feel relief at his lack of reprimand. She didn't feel anything at all. Under the mountain, punishment and praise were often one and the same. Neither frightened her nor motivated her. Zaiana's achievements were all calculated steps toward her own goal and the only true desire she'd ever had. Freedom.

Mordecai stood, his tall form eclipsing the four masters still seated. Zaiana straightened her posture as he rose as if she could level with him despite his towering height. She'd never seen his wings, and had to wonder if his glamour on them was a sign he didn't trust those around him.

"I came to the mountain to choose a candidate for a very important undisclosed quest," he began, "and you were the first name that was brought to me."

She wouldn't have expected any different.

"But you were not the *only* name."

Zaiana's iron claws bit into her palms, which were clasped behind her back. "I accept any quest in your name, High Lord. I vow to lay my life for it," she said, holding back the desperation in her voice. Any chance to taste the air away from the Mortus Mountains and nearby town. Any chance to be as free as she could be while still chained by a phantom leash held by the continent's most wicked creatures.

Mordecai's cruel, taunting smile dropped her stomach with dread. "This particular task has no room for error. It is not for an undisciplined, easily provoked, or untamed dark fae with a power she cannot control."

The insult flared a deep rage within her, and she would have snapped.

But it was test.

Zaiana focused on her breathing. Counted each steady inhale. She pictured the stars that emptied her mind like the vast sky beyond. She felt the darkness of a midnight cobalt wrapping around those thoughts of recklessness and taming them into order. After her third full breath, Zaiana's anger had diffused enough not to waver her voice or tremble her hands.

"I have full control. I did not become delegate, command armies of thousands, and keep order among the Silverfairs without it," she said confidently. "I should have been the first and *only* name ever brought to you."

Mordecai's eyes glimmered, transfixed on her. Zaiana would receive penance for that hint of slander. She didn't care. Punishment would be bearable for her desire to speak the truth.

The High Lord was silent for a moment. Zaiana tried to assess the slight flickers in his expression to read what he was thinking, but he yielded nothing. The intensity in his stare should have made her bow in submission, but she stood tall, unflinching. Finally, he took a long breath after his internal deliberation.

"I am afraid I cannot take you on your words, as admirable as they are, Zaiana," he dismissed with a hint of taunting. "How about a trial?" His eyes flashed at his own brilliance as they locked on her.

Zaiana's flare to win was triggered at the mention.

"You against Maverick, but not alone. No—let's make this more entertaining, shall we? A war game of your choosing upon the trial grounds. You will each create a team with six others."

Flashbacks from a distant memory tore at an old wound as Zaiana recalled the last time she stood on those grounds—when she won the Blood Trials. She tried to push the dark images from her mind before they could rattle her confidence.

Mordecai looked away from her to glance over at the other masters, who all sat with quiet fury under their masks of passive obedience. None of them were particularly fond of her, but at least the feeling was mutual. To their great dismay and eternal hatred, Zaiana was the strongest in their ranks, which was probably why they hadn't killed her yet for the number of times she'd stepped out of line.

All four masters were Silverfairs, first or second generation from the small band of dark fae that had avoided full annihilation millennia ago. It was in this very mountain they had found escape and concealment from the fae who hunted them. Since then, they had learned to build their lives underground. Those who could glamour would seek out what they needed to survive in the nearby towns, and the once powerful and dominant species slowly faded from history. The Mortus Mountains were warded by the great Spirit Dakodas as a means to protect the last of the species. None who wandered here would ever find them, and those who dared were either killed for their blood or captured for transition.

Zaiana was unwavering in her confidence. "I will not fail, High Lord."

"I expect not." He grinned in approval.

Zaiana didn't relax. Not yet.

"Come two weeks' time, one of you will emerge triumphant and be granted the honor of the quest. I trust you very well know the rules in play for such a game. No intentional killing, no illegal weapons. But your methods, tactics, and use of abilities are unrestricted." The word "intentional" sang wonderfully.

At the dark, crooked smile that curved the corner of the High Lord's lips, Zaiana wondered if he meant for her to see the loophole in his words. Suddenly, the idea of killing Maverick didn't sound so appealing when she had someone else pushing her toward it. Whatever his motive —bloodlust perhaps—she didn't care for why Mordecai would want to witness her kill Maverick. When she took the bastard's life, it would be by her will, and hers alone.

Zaiana only gave a respectful nod in answer, thanking the Dark Spirits she'd avoided a fatal confrontation with the High Lord down here. Though, she knew better than to think she was out of the firepits with the masters. Specifically Nephra, who had been her main overseer in her three hundred years.

Mordecai came around the table, pausing next to her and almost grazing her arm. She didn't turn her head to look up at the towering force. "I look forward to seeing you in fighting action, Zaiana." His words were light, personal, and not intended for the ears of the masters.

She tightened her clenched fists in response, suppressing the electric bolts that threatened to surface in her palms. If he raised a hand to touch her...she didn't want to think of her own damning impulsive response.

Mercifully, he decided against it.

There would be many who would think her a fool not to fall at his feet, not to consider herself lucky that someone as powerful as their High Lord would take an interest in her. But it wasn't lust or desire she saw in his eyes; it was the wicked gleam of a master eyeing up his prized hound ahead of a race.

With a deep inhale, Mordecai passed her and left the council chamber without another word.

The masters also came around the long table, each of them filing out after a glare of distaste in her direction. Nephra stopped in front of her, and Zaiana braced herself as she read the fury on her face.

Master Nephra raised a hand, pouring the might of that rage into the power of her strike. The loud slap echoed as her palm connected with Zaiana's cheek, the force snapping her head painfully to the side. Zaiana absorbed the impact with clenched teeth, feeling the warm trail of her silver blood where Nephra's sharp nails cut under her cheekbone.

"You don't deserve his mercy after your disgraceful display." Nephra seethed in her face, the dark emotion of jealousy lacing her words. She was a fool for exposing her obvious resentment toward Zaiana that she'd attracted the High Lord's interest enough to be spared from punishment.

Zaiana refrained from flinching or striking back at feeling Nephra's disgusting breath so close. Nephra was a beauty. Her face had aged over the millennia, but the delicacy of youth lingered under the harshness and cruelty. Zaiana stayed still and silent. She couldn't be sure if it enraged Nephra that she couldn't invoke a reaction or satisfied her because she'd won Zaiana's obedient submission. A mixture of both, likely, as her master gave a disgruntled huff before strutting away.

Zaiana stayed still a moment longer in the empty council chamber to be sure the masters and High Lord were well out of range of crossing paths with her again. She cast her eyes up, spying the marvelous glow of the quarter moon from the opening in the mountaintop, and counted the stars, letting her mind be subdued and welcoming wandering thoughts. All creatures had desires, even one as cold, brutal, and heart-less as she. Zaiana had ended countless lives without thought, without hesitation. She was a monster of the most dangerous kind: a beast behind beauty. Yet sometimes…she wished she could be different. She wished she could care.

Zaiana stormed into the pit, eyes hard as she spotted who she was looking for. Tynan and the others came up beside her.

"Bring her," she commanded with a flick of her chin toward the young dark fae.

While Zaiana had evaded immediate punishment for her actions, she couldn't be seen as weak by everyone else. She was still the delegate of the Silverfairs, and she would be expected to punish her own for crossing over to the Blackfairs and causing the friction between both sides that had ultimately ended in Zaiana's fight. Perhaps it wasn't fair. The darkling was merely curious and had done no harm. But nothing was about fairness; it was about discipline and punishment for failure to abide by simple commands.

Zaiana didn't wait for them to retrieve whom she'd asked for. She ignored the stares of every other dark fae in the space and marched out through a side exit. She knew all five of her companions would be close behind, along with the darkling. No one spoke as her demeanor warned against it.

When they reached the privacy of their communal section—out of bounds to any but her and her five—Zaiana didn't take a seat on any of the lounge chairs around the carpeted center. She turned, straightening as Acelin and Kellias brought the young dark fae forward. Tynan came to stand beside her as her second-in-command, while the others, including Drya and Selain, stood around the darkling who awaited judgment.

Zaiana didn't immediately speak. She assessed every exterior attribute about the younger female first. To her credit, her poise didn't falter in fear. Her small, delicate face remained impassive, green eyes fixed on Zaiana. For a moment, she saw a glimpse of herself in the young dark fae before her. Black hair, just like her own, only shorter. Her wings were smaller than average and slightly crooked—not ideal for accurate flying.

At last, Zaiana said, "What is your name?"

"Amaya," she answered, unflinching.

"Did you think it was brave"—she began a short pace in front of the darkling—"to abandon your training grade and approach a group of Blackfairs?"

"No, I... They were shouting things, making fun of my wings, and I—"

"You let yourself get provoked into a situation where you were outnumbered and outmatched," Zaiana cut in harshly. "I don't stand here to reprimand you for defending yourself, but to punish you for your foolish naivety."

"I-I didn't mean to—"

"Petty insults aren't worth putting your life at risk. Words can only cut if you listen. They can only scar if you believe." Zaiana paused in front of her. Everything about the darkling was submissive. While it was what she expected, a part of her was disappointed. "Do you think I was right to challenge Maverick?"

Amaya's already pale skin turned even more chalky at the bold interrogation. "Yes."

"Why?"

Amaya paused to swallow hard. Zaiana took no pleasure in seeing the terror in her eyes that she could be wrong. She wasn't looking for the *right* response; Zaiana simply saw this as an opportunity to instill in her a method of thinking that would ensure the young fae never settled on her opinion without fair reason.

"He said something he shouldn't have. You had a right to defend—"

"*What* did he say?"

Amaya's throat bobbed. "He mentioned…he mentioned Finnian."

Zaiana tried not to flinch. Or glance down at the strip of black fabric that had remained tied to the hilt of her sword since the day she took his life—a symbol of her strength and victory for the eyes of her kin, but a dark reminder of her own foolishness to Zaiana. "It's not *what* he said that made me right in my attack. I gave him a warning, and he chose to ignore it. I attacked first because I don't make idle threats. But I would not challenge someone I can't beat. Never make the mistake of overvaluing your skills."

Amaya nodded her head firmly.

Zaiana inhaled a long breath. She already knew what she was going to do with the young dark fae, though she held rare hesitation as it could work against her if her judgment were wrong. She glanced around her circle, preparing to deliver the news of the battle they would face against Maverick.

"The High Lord came to me with an offer—a quest beyond the mountain," she began, and they all shifted, their attention piqued. "It is not a quest that was given to me. I have to earn it, take it, from Maverick, and I require six others to join me in a game on the trial ground in two weeks' time." Her eyes flashed to Tynan first, whose brows were knitted, scanning over the gathered circle. It was disappointing how long it took him to realize there had always only been five of them, excluding Zaiana, until…

"You can't be serious," he muttered at last, turning his back to the young dark fae.

Her flat look alone made him recoil.

His eyes darted between Amaya and Zaiana. "You really want to take that big a risk on this chance of freedom?" His words were careful, knowing she hated nothing more than to have her decisions challenged.

Zaiana's lips curled in a crooked smile. She kept her eyes fixed on Amaya who still seemed oblivious to the lingering suggestion in the room. "Amaya wants to be brave. Let's give her the chance to prove she's not just a naïve little darkling who doesn't know when she's out of her rank. Her punishment will be death in that arena if she fails to keep up," Zaiana explained for her sake.

Amaya's eyes widened in realization. "With all due respect—"

"You either fight or die here, where you stand," Zaiana cut in sharply, temper flaring at Amaya's boldness to object. "It is your choice."

The seed of doubt grew a bud in her gut at the young fae's obvious hesitation. Perhaps she'd made a grave mistake in choosing her as the seventh member to fight by her side, and the price of her misjudgment would be the chance in a century to have that taste of freedom. It was a relief when Amaya rolled her shoulders back, face turning fierce.

"I won't disappoint you, Zaiana."

While it satisfied her to see the flare of determination she expected from the darkling, she couldn't shake her faint uncertainty as she glanced the wary looks of her companions. She hadn't been wrong yet. Each of the five who had been by her side for over a century had never failed her, and she had never once regretted or doubted her choice of who to trust in her inner circle.

In Amaya, Zaiana saw a glimpse of her younger self and only prayed to the Dark Spirits her lack of physical strength would be compensated by the strong will and courage she believed to be there beneath the feeble surface. She chose to take confidence in her decision as six became seven once again.

CHAPTER 11

Faythe

F
AYTHE SHOT UPRIGHT, breathing so hard it stabbed her chest. Tendrils of hair clung to her forehead, and sweat dampened her nightgown. Her eyes darted around the darkness, blinking rapidly to distinguish her surroundings. Her fists gripped the sheets painfully, but the soft material brought some relief to her reeling mind—that it wasn't the cool metal bench she lay on in her nightmare. Panic had struck her heart, sending it into a frenzy. Faythe feared it would break free or shut down if she didn't calm its beats soon. She blinked hard to remember where she was and convince herself she was truly awake.

When she didn't immediately recognize her surroundings, her mind raced at the endless *terrifying* possibilities. It took an excruciatingly long minute for her human eyes to adjust to the dark. Scanning the foreign room, her memories grounded her with relief all at once.

Rhyenelle. She was in Rhyenelle. The room was still new and unfamiliar. Faythe released a long breath. Then she remembered the horrific recurring nightmare she'd just emerged from, and her eyes burned in fear and frustration.

Faythe had yet to fully admit to anyone that ever since her ordeal in High Farrow—her mental torture at the hands of the slain Captain Varis and everything that followed—the memories had haunted her in her sleep and otherwise. She had long forgotten what a full night's rest felt like. This was a familiar drain, like the one she'd suffered for decades before she was made aware of her Nightwalking.

It terrified her. She didn't think she was capable of hosting her own dreams or nightmares. Nik had enlightened her to the fact Nightwalkers didn't experience their own unconscious visions in sleep. Yet every time she gave over to the exhaustion she fought daily, Faythe skipped straight past her gold-and-white mist without even a glimpse of its glittering beauty and landed straight into the sickening relayed visions of Jakon and Marlowe's death, the captain's taunts and caresses, or worse, Caius's very real, agonizing murder.

Faythe threw back the sheets and twisted to dangle her legs off the high bed. The tips of her toes touching the chill of the wood made her shudder. *This is real.* She focused on reeling in her fast breathing and let the cool air clear her head. Her throat stung with the nausea that lapped at her. Faythe breathed, sure and steady, then dropped her head into her hands as she fought the wave of sadness. She was emotionally exhausted.

She missed her friends in High Farrow so much it became a physical pain to bear, and she was wracked with guilt that she had yet to even visit Nik through Nightwalking to check in on them all. She wasn't strong enough. Not when she couldn't get at least one full night's rest to attempt the leap between kingdoms. Faythe grasped the gold eight-point-star pendant that always hung around her neck: a gift from Nik, her one way to see him. To hear about Jakon, Marlowe, and Tauria too while they were all so far away. A tear gathered and fell straight to the floor before she realized she was crying.

Faythe was beginning to spiral into a pit of despair, letting her thoughts and frustrations collect in a storm. Before they could destroy her, she bounded to her feet in a surge of determination. She couldn't break down. She wouldn't give up before she'd given the Kingdom of the Phoenix a chance; given *herself* a chance to find out who she could be.

She knew she wasn't going to get any more sleep tonight, unable to handle the nightmare more than once in the same night without overwhelming herself with grief and guilt. Faythe slid into a robe that took the chill from her arms but did little for her bare legs in the short nightgown. She wandered into one of the adjoining rooms to her bedroom.

At first, Faythe had felt overprivileged to have been given such lavish living quarters. More lavish even than her rooms in the castle of High Farrow. She had everything she could possibly need to lock herself away in the small labyrinth and not have to leave for anything except food.

She eyed the grand pianoforte in the center of the game room and felt oddly drawn to it. She couldn't play and had never even sat in front of one before, having only seen them in High Farrow from afar. Still, Faythe slid onto the small bench, pulling back the wooden cover from the keys. The black-and-white tiles glistened beautifully under the rays of the moon that pooled in through the long balcony doors. They looked pure, untouched, and as she gazed over the long length her mind conjured silent notes, hearing faint symphonies she remembered from shows she had attended before. She suddenly envied those who could play, longing to be swept away in the wonder and magick of song.

Faythe lifted a hand, resting her fingers over the smooth, polished white tiles. She pressed down on one key then another. The notes disturbed the silence, but not in the melodic way she pined for. It was futile to even bother. In a surge of frustration, she went to slam the cover back down. Then ripples of awareness caused by a nearby presence made her halt.

It wasn't just anyone. Faythe straightened instantly, pulse skipping a beat as she scanned the room, but her brow furrowed when she couldn't spy the tall warrior form she was expecting. Her eyes skimmed out past the glass doors, and she slumped, thinking she was truly going delirious in her insomnia.

Until her eyes caught on a faintly shimmering small bird perched on the stone rail of the balcony outside. A familiar sight that filled her chest with comfort, just as it had in her most desolate hours imprisoned in High Farrow. She hadn't realized, or perhaps didn't want to admit, just how much she'd missed him in the five days of his absence.

"Are you going to sit out there all night?" she sent like a whisper.

Faythe wasn't aware Reylan had returned. She wondered if he had been in the castle long, or if he'd come straight to her. The latter thought warmed her, but her mood momentarily dipped since it was unlikely he missed her as much as she did him. Five days would be nothing to him.

Regardless, his presence lifted the internal darkness that embraced her that night, and she was glad he had decided to check in despite the late hour. She wouldn't have to suffer the rest of the long night alone.

In a quick flash of light, Reylan was standing intimidatingly tall on the balcony. He welcomed himself into the room while Faythe remained seated at the pianoforte. He halted after closing the door behind himself and quickly swept her from head to toe. Neither of them spoke. Faythe tried to focus on calming her ridiculous heartbeat at the attention that flushed her body with a desire she couldn't ignore. She pulled subconsciously at the hem of her nightgown, which felt so much shorter all of a sudden.

"You should always lock those doors," Reylan said thickly. The reprimand lacked any impact in his quiet voice of the sweetest gravel. Their eyes locked with a growing intensity while he stayed put, making no move to come closer.

"What are you doing here?" she asked, equally as hushed.

Faint creases formed around his eyes. He ignored her question to ask, "How long have you been having nightmares?"

Faythe dropped her gaze. Out of embarrassment or shame or something else entirely. Though she was sure he already knew the answer, it was a small relief to voice the dark demon she harbored. "Since everything that happened in High Farrow." To distract him from her erratic pulse, and to disguise the sound in case he could hear it, Faythe idly pressed down on the piano keys with a single finger. She felt Reylan's stare like a warm caress that shivered over her whole body while he simply watched her for a few tense, slow seconds.

Over her shallow notes, she thought she heard his sigh before he finally took some further steps into the room. Now beside her, Faythe's breath hitched at his closeness—at his hesitation, because she didn't know what he planned to do. When his hand lingered close enough to touch her shoulder…she knew what she *wanted* him to do.

To her surprise, Reylan lowered himself onto the bench next to her. Faythe tensed completely. Not out of discomfort, but from something like contentment wrapped with a hint of fear. She wanted him close, and it was an irrational thought that one wrong move could cause him to raise the steel guard she believed he had been cautiously lowering around her.

Reylan cast his glance between her and the piano, deliberating.

Faythe's eyebrows rose. "Can you play?"

Reylan looked reluctant to confess, but the confirmation was already written in his eyes. Only, it concerned Faythe that they twinkled with an essence of pain at the mention of the instrument.

"I haven't in a long time."

Seeing that it somehow triggered something dark within him, Faythe was about to close the cover, much as she really desired to ask him to recall any of the melodies he might still hold in his memory. But just as she reached up, Reylan's hands rose to rest tenderly over the black-and-white keys. He didn't look at her again. His brow set in deep reflection as he stared down at the piano.

Faythe slowed her breaths, attention darting between sapphires and his fingers as they moved to poise over specific tiles. The image of him was breathtaking. The moonlight highlighted and softened every hard angle of his face and turned his hair a glistening white. A few loose curls met the curve of his dark brow while his eyes glittered with more beauty than a night sky holding a thousand stars.

Then Reylan's fingers moved, and the night sparked to life around them. With the graceful motion of his hands, a wondrous string of notes floated from the instrument to brighten up the dark room. Faythe was awestruck, fully immersed in the beautiful symphony created by Reylan's influence. It was slow. Heartbreakingly slow. The notes rose and fell, the song dipped and weaved, and Faythe was transfixed by the powerful muscles in his tattooed forearms, which flexed while his mind translated memory to music.

Slowly, delicately, the song picked up rhythm. Notes entwined with centuries' worth of sorrow, singing the heartache of a battle-torn warrior. One who had faced war with steel, love, and his own internal monsters.

Faythe's heart pierced where she sat, eyes burning with the passion Reylan poured over the keys in front of them. Every now and then his arm would graze hers, sending a pulse of electricity through her that heightened with the song weaving through her soul. He took them out of that room, out of their world, and placed them both in a universe of endless magick and wonder. A place where no evil could touch them. Her skin prickled in the most delightful way, inspiring shivers of warmth that embraced her heart. Protected it. His fingers moved gracefully, like tranquil waves against the thrash of a storm.

When it slowed again, Faythe was near breathless. "Who taught you to play?" Her voice sounded choked with the buildup of emotion. His, hers—perhaps both—fusing in that moment she didn't care to separate them. She didn't want him to stop. Didn't want this moment to ever end.

Something in his face changed: a flash of sorrow in the twitch of his eyes at the question. Faythe wanted to retract it, but he answered before she could.

"Someone from a long time ago." His words were almost inaudible over his shallow playing, misery and heartbreak interlaced in the notes. Faythe knew the answer then, but she felt the need to ask. Wanted him to be the one to share his story with her.

"What was her name?"

Reylan stopped playing. Faythe swallowed hard, instantly guilty at the assumption and for prodding into a past she had no business knowing. Devastation stole his expression momentarily, and then he offered her a hollow smile to overshadow his grief and guilt. Faythe thought she had ruined the moment and that he'd stopped playing for good. Then he tuned his focus back into the instrument, and the song filled the empty space with wonder.

"Her name was Farrah."

That he'd chosen to share such a personal piece of himself filled Faythe's chest with bright warmth.

"I'm sorry I wasn't completely honest with you about where I went. In truth, I feared what you might think of me...once you knew the darkest parts of me—of my past and my failure."

"Nothing could make me turn away from you, Reylan."

His brow flinched as if it pained him to hear it. As if he didn't want to believe her.

Reylan's playing was soft as he took a deep breath. Faythe braced herself, anxiously anticipating, *hoping*, that he might be about to release his final guard around her; let himself be completely vulnerable and take off his armor.

"I've killed many people, Faythe. A lot of them enemies, but some out of my own darkness, and others down to my incompetence. Some of them people I deeply cared about and those who put their trust in me." Reylan missed a note, disturbing the gentle song. His teeth clenched and he stopped, hands slowly curling into fists as he refrained from bringing them down on the keys in anger. It wasn't from his error. Reylan was struggling against telling his story—partly for the dark feelings it stirred, but she thought in the way he avoided her eye that perhaps he was fearful of her judgment.

Faythe raised a hand to place it over his without thinking, taking a subtle breath to ignore the delightful sensation crawling up her arm at the contact. After a second's hesitation, his fist uncurled enough to allow her fingertips to slip into his palm.

"Don't hide from me," she pleaded quietly. "Don't put up those walls."

His eyes infused with the moon when he turned to her, the dark blue transforming into a peaceful ocean. "It's my fault she's dead," he confessed.

It tore her heart like nothing she'd felt before to see the desolate look on his face.

"It's my fault they're all dead. You caught a glimpse of it in Varlas's mind in the woods—do you remember?"

Faythe nodded, trying to hold back a tremble at the reminder of her confrontation with the Olmstone king in the woods of High Farrow. She'd seen the memory of the death of Varlas's mate, and he'd blamed the general as he rocked her lifeless body.

"It's true—it *was* my fault. Everyone who died in Fenher that day died as a result of my own incompetence as a general. Farrah was very dear to me, but that's not all."

Faythe's hand tightened over his, a silent assurance she wanted him to go on. She wanted to hear it all.

"I watched her die. Kyleer and I…we reached them on time, Farrah and Greia, but we found them with blades held to their throats. To our horror, they were soldiers we had encountered before in battle, a few who managed to escape. They killed both of them right in front of us, and I...I don't remember much of what happened after. Something darker than rage overcame me. I killed and killed to no end. I became exactly the force my uncle who raised me had honed me to be. I became death."

Faythe said nothing. The image of everything he shared brought forth what the great general beside her was capable of. Nothing about that picture frightened her. Maybe it should, but instead, a quick, hot surge of something more reckless than anger sedated her other emotions.

Faythe asked carefully, "What did your uncle do to you?" She tried to keep tethers on her building wrath from seeing his hardened expression. The faint *wince* she almost missed when Reylan spoke of him.

Reylan's jaw locked, the harshness of his face returning at the memories she'd stirred with the question. "My father was a general, close to Agalhor, and lost his life in battle. My mother lost hers soon after, when our town was invaded. I should have died that day too, but my uncle saved me. I was barely into my first century when he took me in, still a child, and I thought I owed everything to him."

Faythe's gaze traveled to his white-knuckle grip on the side of the piano, heart splintering before she even heard the turn the story was about to take.

"He trained me daily, ruthlessly and mercilessly. In me, he saw a weapon he could perfectly craft since he bore no sons of his own, only a daughter, to his cruel dismay. I became the person I hated. I became his own personal ruthless assassin carrying out his dirty work, all because I thought I owed him. I spent centuries killing. Mindlessly. If that was to be my existence, I didn't care."

The hand she held shifted as if to pull away from her, but Faythe's grip tightened to prevent it. Reylan looked down at their joined hands, and then his eyes met hers. The fear in them shook her to her bones.

"I became a monster, Faythe. A cold, heartless monster. I may not be that person anymore, but he will always live in my shadow in every step I take. It is always something I will be capable of. Killing. My uncle succeeded in making me into his perfect weapon."

Faythe held his eyes, her opinions—her *feelings*—toward him unchanged by his confession. She didn't speak as she thought over everything he said, wondering if it made her a fool not to be fearful or disgusted or even shocked. Not for what he had done. Faythe felt nothing but heartbreak and a raw, unexplainable rage. Toward the male who'd tried to break him.

"What became of your uncle?" The question clearly wasn't what he expected. What shocked her more was the soul-damning, murderous thoughts that sprinted through her mind should he confirm his uncle was still alive.

"The thing about a weapon is that it has no allegiance. Craft a lethal blade, perfect its sharpened edge, and it can kill its maker as easily as it can slay any enemy." Reylan searched her eyes for any sign she would retreat. Faythe held firm. "And that's exactly what I did. I turned on the one who made me. I killed him, and like a sword of steel and leather, I felt no remorse for it. Nor do I now. What does that say about me?"

Faythe's pause was contemplative as she stared out over the balcony at the night sky. Taking in the peaceful sight was also a means of curbing her anger toward someone who was no longer even alive. Whatever his uncle had done to make Reylan snap, she had every confidence it justified the outcome.

"It says to me that you're a survivor," she offered at last. When her gaze returned to him, Faythe was determined. Determined to get him to believe he was not his past. "You can stop trying to convince me you're the villain. We all have demons and hard choices to shoulder. Sometimes, it takes someone else to see them to realize they don't define us."

Something in his bold blue eyes changed. Liberation. However faint it was before he blinked it away.

"I trust you, Reylan. I always have."

Reylan dropped his gaze with a shake of his head. "Gods, I know you do, Faythe. I worried you shouldn't, and I considered distancing myself from you so you wouldn't trust me." Faythe didn't get to voice the string of protests that formed painfully in her throat at the thought. "Maybe it makes me selfish, but I can't. I can't stay away from you. I came back sooner than I usually would from Fenher because while I fear to no end that I might be incapable of protecting you, I can't stand the thought of your safety being in the hands of anyone else."

"Reylan." His name escaped her lips on a breath of disbelief. That her well-being had caused him such turmoil even in the safe perimeter of the castle. "I don't need protecting all the time. I can look out for myself."

Reylan stood, and as he took a few paces away Faythe was compelled to rise, drawn to copy his steps. He passed the piano, but just as she thought he was about to leave the room, he turned back to her. There was no warning when he retraced his steps all the way to where she stood. In surprise, Faythe backed up but was met with the piano behind her. Reylan halted, so close it rattled her pulse. As he leaned in, her hands reached back to brace herself, and her breathing shallowed as his fingers grazed hers. Her mind flashed between now and the first time they stood locked in this position.

Even then, that first moment in High Farrow when they were barely more than strangers, the cage of his body hadn't struck her with the fear it should. He was powerful and dangerously alluring, but she never once believed he would truly harm her. Maybe it made her a naïve fool. She didn't care.

Something sparked to life within his sapphire pools—something she believed she had seen before. It was searching, mystified, a possessive desire. His body was so close she longed to feel it pressed against hers. Reylan spoke when she came close to damning the consequences and taking that final step herself.

"I never thought I'd come across someone like you, Faythe." In his eyes was conflict. He looked over her face as though memorizing every inch or trying to figure out a puzzle. She caught his gaze lingering on her lips a second longer. "You see everything I am and know everything I've done, and yet you're still here."

"I'm not going anywhere," she promised, near breathless.

"Why?"

"Do you really have to ask?"

"Yes." It left his lips in the tone of a plea that reflected on his furrowed brow.

Faythe's heart splintered as she watched the glittering notes of vulnerability in his irises. But they were also hard, ready to raise the steel guard he wore to suppress what lay beneath from the world.

"You saw me and you heard me from the first day we met. Nothing about your past changes what I see in *you*, Reylan. I'm not going anywhere."

What moved in the atmosphere between them was electrifying and thrilling. Sapphire blazed into gold, and she felt the pull to him like the resistance of gravity. She was all too aware her robe had slid open at the top, her nightgown a dainty piece of silk exposing the curve of her breasts in the low dip. Should he look down, he'd find them pebbled and assume it was from the room's chill, not the ripples of desire that blew sand over her skin at his proximity. Her heart swelled with his words, and she'd never felt closer to him now he'd allowed her past every defense to where she knew very few had glimpsed before. Faythe was entranced by those sapphires that held her utterly at his mercy.

Just when she thought his face was inching closer, that their thoughts and desires were aligned…Reylan straightened away from her completely. Faythe blinked as awareness surrounded her once more and swallowed her disappointment. His eyes dropped. Perhaps his will was stronger than hers, or perhaps she was a pining fool for reading into signals that weren't there. Reylan was a male of honor and duty, and maybe that was what he would always see her as first and foremost. His duty to Agalhor.

"You should get some sleep."

Her desperation surfaced as she watched him start to leave. "Wait," she choked out. "I can't."

Reylan's shoulders locked as he halted.

"I've tried. I've tried to convince myself I'm in Rhyenelle, that Orlon and Varis are dead and I'm safe…" Embarrassment folded around her at the voiced weakness. "But I never really left that throne room. Even all these months later, even in another kingdom, I'm still there. Every night and sometimes in the day too. I watch my friends die; I watch my failure, my cowardice, and inability to do anything. To protect anyone. And I worry… I worry that won't ever be fixed because it's the truth." It all came pouring out of her like the release of a long-harbored confession. Faythe dared to gauge his reaction.

Reylan's expression had shifted, wiping all sadness and replacing it with something indefinable. Rage, pain, defeat—his chest rose and fell deeply with it all in his stillness. A pang of guilt hit her chest. She shouldn't have offloaded her concerns onto him. It wasn't his problem, and he seemed to have enough of his own suffering to deal with.

"Why didn't you tell me sooner?"

Faythe folded her cotton robe tighter around herself and crossed her arms against the chill. She couldn't bear the longing in his eyes, as if he thought she didn't want to confide in him. "I hoped it would pass, but it just gets worse. The nights I watch Caius…when I watch him—" Faythe swallowed hard. "It doesn't end. He dies again and again, and I'm reminded every time that I was the cause." She ground her teeth, cursing the tears that gathered and the stray drop that fell. She wiped it away angrily, staring out over the moon-kissed horizon.

"Faythe." Reylan said her name through a breath but didn't follow with anything else.

They hadn't spoken of that day in the throne room since they left for

Rhyenelle. Faythe had pushed it to the back of her mind to make room for everything new in the Kingdom of the Phoenix. She had a growing mound of emotions she stacked behind a weak barrier, constantly one wrong thought away from crushing herself with the weight of it all. Faythe trembled but couldn't be sure if it was from the cold or the risk of the dam finally breaking. With Reylan here, with her fears confronted, she was struggling now more than ever to hold it all back.

She shook her head. "It should have been me. Caius was a fighter, a dreamer. And I...I can't help anyone." The marble of grief in her throat grew painfully, to the point she feared she might stop breathing. Reylan approached her, and the moment he wordlessly pulled her into his chest...every thought and torment shattered her completely, all at once.

She wasn't consumed with tears, but rather with dry sobs. Air—there wasn't enough air, and maybe her mind was convinced she was truly drowning. She wondered in a panic if it were possible to die solely from the weight of her emotions. Reylan held her, wrapping her in a warmth she didn't think she deserved, but she grappled so desperately to find relief. When he spoke, all she tuned in to was the gentle rumble that kept her grounded and present. Her knees were weak, threatening to collapse her, but Reylan held her to him. With her ear to his chest, she felt the hard beat of his heart—a melody she wanted to memorize every note of. Faythe focused on it and let it ease the melancholic drum of her own. She savored the hard, toned safety of his body.

"Don't ever think like that," he said, voice hard. "You and Caius... your dreams aligned. He gave his life so you could carry them on; so you could seem them answered. You fought, and you survived. You deserve to live, Faythe. Live, and make every life that was taken too soon count for something. That's how we go on."

The storm that threatened to undo her was tamed as she embraced the vibrations of his voice. Faythe closed her eyes, soaking in every word, allowing him not only to calm her sadness, but to fill her with a new strength she so desperately needed. She pulled back from him, giving a weak smile, but didn't want to step away. A few seconds were suspended in time. She couldn't be sure what he was thinking behind those troubled eyes.

When Reylan released her, Faythe's shoulders fell with disappointment. He turned away before stalking through to the bedroom. She almost believed he was going to wordlessly abandon her, but she bustled in after him and watched as he made his way to the armchairs by the unlit fireplace. He took the blanket draped there and extended it to her. Faythe's anxiety lifted as she took it gratefully. She threw it over her shoulders while Reylan bent down and began snapping odd spears together.

"Are there no Firewielders in the castle?" she teased quietly, watching as embers sparked.

He smirked. "There are plenty, but I don't hang on to a collection of other people's abilities at all times in case they might be needed. It would be incredibly draining." He flashed her a crooked smile over his shoulder, and her chest warmed at the sight and the heavy weight of sadness that came so effortlessly with it.

Flashes of amber struck the wood and coals over and over until they merged enough to cast away the darkness in the firepit. Faythe stared, mesmerized by the flames that licked across the debris, forging, bonding, until a beautiful inferno filled the space. Reylan straightened then motioned his head for her to sit. She obliged, eager to feel the glorious heat.

Faythe was grateful for his company as his presence chased away the all-consuming dark thoughts that surfaced in her solitude. With Reylan here, her mind relented, just enough for her to remember there was a light in the darkness that embraced her. There was a light in *him*.

CHAPTER 12

Faythe

THERE WAS SOMETHING serene about the tango of fire. Though deadly and unpredictable, its dancing, undisciplined ribbons of flame calmed Faythe's mind as though they were the cool waves of the sea. She couldn't be sure how long had passed as she sat in silence with Reylan before his soft voice traveled over the crackle of splitting timber.

"There is one person who might have the answers to help with your nightmares." His eyes met hers, sapphire with amber tendrils. "If there's anyone who will know what you're going through and how to cure your Nightwalking…it is Agalhor."

Faythe sucked in a long breath. Of course. It made sense, and she was foolish not to have thought of it sooner. Her father, another Night-walker, who throughout his rule had likely lived centuries' worth of terrors she didn't want to imagine. Reylan was right: if there was anyone who had experienced the side effects of trauma that affected her ability, it would be him. Only, the warmth of the fire was snatched from her by the thought of the confrontation she had actively avoided since being in Rhyenelle. Reylan seemed to know it too, casting her a pitiful look.

"You have to face him at some point, and if it can help you to sleep, to be able to Nightwalk and see your friends, there won't be a better time than now," he encouraged her.

"I will—soon." Faythe mustered a smile in thanks to him and in promise to herself, though the thought rallied her nerves.

Reylan kept his eyes locked on her, irises swirling with question and wonder. "I've been waiting to ask—to let you settle in as best you can here after everything you went through," he began, and Faythe's pulse quickened in anticipation. "You brought the Temple Ruin to Rhyenelle with you. Why?"

Faythe blinked, dumbfounded that this had been playing on his mind. The Light Temple Ruin had remained sealed in the Blood Box bound by her, and she'd hidden the item under her bed. Another looming—and far deadlier—confrontation she had been avoiding in her cowardice.

"You knew it wasn't over," was all she answered, and his unchanging hard expression confirmed as much. Faythe took a long breath. She had to tell him and was at a loss for how to do so as she feared his reaction to the perilous endeavor she had to take. But as much as she wanted more than anything to exclude him from the dangerous path, the truth was she needed him. She didn't know anything about the Kingdom of Rhyenelle and would never make it across to the Niltain Isles alone. "I need to reach Dakodas's temple before the next summer solstice. It's hidden on the Niltain Isles."

Even as she rattled off the rest, it all sounded fictitious spoken aloud. She told him of the dire consequences if she failed to retrieve Dakodas's ruin from her temple before the solar eclipse on the solstice that could see the great Spirit of Death transition to their world. Faythe told him how she couldn't risk either powerful artifact falling into the hands of Marvellas, who sought the Riscillius, and ultimately Aurialis's ruin, as she puppeteered Orlon to find it within High Farrow. When she'd finished her quick relay of information, she dared a glance at Reylan. His look was scarily calculating. Firm and set. So many thoughts, strategies, and plans crossed those hard blue eyes that reflected fire. Faythe knew he had slipped into the army general persona that had seen Rhyenelle through many great battles.

"I'll send warriors or go alone—"

"No," she interjected before he wasted energy trying to find an alternative resolution. "It has to be me."

"*Why* does it have to be you?" Reylan snapped, all kindness blanketed by a protective anger that momentarily stunned her.

If Faythe were honest, she'd admit she'd cursed and shouted internally with the same damned question. Only she knew the answer—one she'd kept to herself all this time; one only Marlowe knew. Faythe couldn't hold it in any longer, not with the threats mounted against them that didn't only put her life at risk, but put the whole of Ungardia under threat if she couldn't stop the Spirits.

"There is a reason I am the only one of my kind," Faythe began quietly. She could feel Reylan's intense stare, but she chose to watch the tango of fire. "I'm an Heir of Marvellas. A direct descendant from her when she joined our world."

His confusion, shock, and bewilderment rippled like waves through her. She could have blocked him out, but she wanted to feel everything; to know how he truly felt about her sinister ties, and perhaps to soothe her terror that he wouldn't think of her any differently.

"My mother didn't flee Rhyenelle because she fell out of love with Agalhor, nor for anything so trivial or mundane. She left…because she thought she was protecting me. Aurialis seems to believe there is a prophesy that one conceived from both a Marvellas bloodline-blessed— a Nightwalker—and a direct descendant, like my mother, is the key to ending the Great Spirit-turned-fae before she can cause any more destruction." Faythe shook her head, knowing how fabricated it sounded. "We may all be doomed if it turns out to be true."

She looked at him then. His face was a shade paler than usual, brow set in a disbelieving frown. He didn't match her weak attempt at humor, and Faythe's face fell.

"If there's a possibility it is, I have to at least try, and that begins with stopping Dakodas's ascension."

It felt liberating to have someone else know everything about her, and she didn't feel in the least bit vulnerable as she laid it all out in front of Reylan: who she was, *what* she was, right down to the last dark truth. He stared her her blank-faced. She couldn't bear to let the silence settle, needing to get it over with.

"I wouldn't ask—"

"You don't need to ask." He cut her off, voice hard. "Of course I'm coming with you."

Faythe gave a weak smile in gratitude, but she was even more riddled with guilt and uncertainty that he was so quick to jump into such dangerous unknown depths with her. Without hesitation, without question.

"Spirits be damned," he muttered, and the anger on his face made her recoil in her chair. "Agalhor deserves to know... Why she left, and the danger you're in."

"I can't risk him trying to stop me—"

"He deserves to know," Reylan repeated.

Faythe swallowed hard at the coldness in his eyes and voice.

"You didn't see what her leaving did to him. It still torments him to this day. Then to find out she left with you—without even knowing of your conception..." Reylan shook his head, and she detected a hint of resentment toward her mother that made her anger flash. "I understand her wanting to protect you—believe me, I do—but she didn't give him a reason or even a goodbye, and her decision was wholly wrong. There's nothing Agalhor wouldn't have risked to keep you safe. Both of you."

Faythe's heart ached at the passion in his voice. Her mother's leaving had clearly imprinted on him too, for what it had done to his king and kingdom. "Perhaps that's what she was afraid of," Faythe said quietly.

Reylan's hard expression softened.

What she was about to say Faythe had never confided in anyone. In over a decade, she had spoken very little of her mother. Even to Jakon. "I was only nine when she was taken." Faythe dropped her eyes at the pain of the impending confession. But she wanted him to know. She wanted Reylan to know everything. "Nearly eleven years without her, and each passing year hurts like the first. Every year…suddenly, I'm that scared and alone orphaned girl on the streets of Farrowhold all over again. What hurts the most is when that day comes around…I can't ever be sure if it is the anniversary of her death, or if those who took her kept her alive and tortured her for whatever information they sought to gain. Knowing what I do now, I'm filled with even more uncertainty as to *who* took her." Faythe picked at the threads of her blanket, trying hard not to slip into the body of her scared and alone nine-year-old self in the woods. "It was easy to blame Valgard, the kingdom we're all taught to fear. But what it if it was Marvellas? What if she was the one my mother tried desperately to run from? Her life in Rhyenelle was secure, comfortable…but completely public and therefore vulnerable, and fleeing was her desperate attempt to hide us from her reach. But what if Marvellas finally found her? Alone in High Farrow, it would have been the perfect opportunity to take her." Faythe didn't know how to go on. There were so many unanswered questions surrounding her mother and her death that threatened to be her undoing. Questions that crushed her to think she would never receive answers to.

Reylan's face creased in sadness, but she couldn't be sure if it was for her or himself. "I'm sorry you shouldered that burden alone," he said with all sincerity. "But you're not alone anymore—never again. I vow to do whatever it takes to avenge Lilianna and find the truth you've longed for."

Faythe's eyebrows knitted together as she fought back the burning in her eyes at his declaration. She didn't deserve it, but she was grateful for him. "I was so young I didn't get to know her in adulthood, didn't get to understand who she really was," she admitted with a stabbing pain in her heart.

"She was…a lot like you, actually." His lips curved, eyes holding something that fluttered in her stomach. "Headstrong, fierce, but with a tender heart. As golden as her eyes—*your* eyes."

A warm, genuine smile found her lips. Faythe nestled into the armchair, curling her legs up and fixing the blanket. She lay her head against the tall side of the chair. "Can you tell me more about her?"

Reylan's mouth curled, and her heart skipped a beat at the sight. He too leaned back, getting comfortable to begin a short string of stories about her mother in Rhyenelle. Stories she'd only ever dreamed of being able to hear.

All the heavy conversation and sadness became distant while Faythe tuned in to the gentle roughness of Reylan's voice telling those tales. Of peace, of antics, of bravery. Soon, she couldn't fight the weight of her eyelids. Words blurred, leaving behind a soothing, deep hum whose serene waves softly pulled her under, into a blissful sleep.

Reylan's voice… It felt like *home.*

CHAPTER 13

Reylan

REYLAN WATCHED FAYTHE'S peaceful face for a few minutes once her breathing had slowed and deepened. She was soundlessly asleep. He was glad for it, knowing she'd had little proper rest since leaving everything she knew behind. He too had been plagued with horrific nightmares and found himself often waking up with her since his temporary move to the room across the hall—his attempt to keep some of the familiarity of High Farrow. Every time he knew she lay awake, he wanted to go to her. Yet he kept his distance to give her the space he thought she needed to adjust.

Tonight, after riding for days without rest to return as quickly as possible, he couldn't retire for the night without checking in on her. It was far too late for him to simply knock on her door, so he'd wandered by Izaiah's room, taking only enough of his ability to transform and glance at Faythe from a distance to curb his rattling mind. It hadn't surprised him to find her pulled from sleep but seeing her seated so beautifully before the pianoforte was a sight that struck him. He'd long since hardened himself to the memories she brought forth—of Farrah, who had been a keen player of many wonderful instruments, and he'd silently picked up on her favorite of all from watching her so often by the piano.

He couldn't be sure if his pain upon seeing Faythe there was from the reminder of a dark past or his guilt for the present—that he couldn't help her with her night terrors and had been party to convincing her to cross the kingdoms to Rhyenelle. Perhaps being with her friends would have helped her to overcome them by now.

Right now, she looked peaceful. He couldn't imagine what she'd endured in High Farrow when she was dragged out of that tower cell away from his watch. He couldn't...because even though the captain was dead, the thought of what he did to her made him want to rage and kill to no end.

Reylan stood carefully, deliberating. He couldn't leave her in that armchair. If she did, by some mercy, manage to stay in undisturbed sleep for the rest of the night, she would wake with horrible aches from the crooked position by morning. He sighed, taking the few strides over and pausing in front of her. Knowing everything he did about the impossible woman who had defied the odds to exist, shouldered so much burden, and loved and lost more than anyone should in such a short life-time...he felt momentarily struck by her quiet, sleeping form, stripped back to the innocent, fragile human she was. Not the Heir of Marvellas; not the daughter of a great king; not a keeper of powerful magick; just...*Faythe.* And that was enough. She didn't deserve to carry the weight of the world.

His hand came up before he knew what he was doing, and he gently brushed the hair that fell limp over her face in her unconscious state. Then he stealthily, carefully, lifted and cradled her body to him along with the bundled blanket. He carried her over to the bed, having to focus on calming his mind as it flashed between now and the last time he'd held her in such a way, when she was within death's reach in the throne room of High Farrow. The uncertainty of those few days that followed—Reylan hadn't felt such a deep-seated fear and dread since… since that dark day in Fenher.

He laid her down gently and moved to step away completely and leave her rooms. A soft hand encased his wrist.

"Stay," Faythe said in a sleepy whisper.

Reylan froze, positive she must be dreaming as her eyes remained closed, her fingers limp against his hand. Just as he was about to try straightening again, her tired lids fluttered open.

"Please."

Reylan didn't think his heart was still beating. Faythe lazily shuffled over, barely able to remain awake, then patted the bed next to her. He confirmed his heart was still beating—more than that, as it picked up a frantic sprint. Her request was achingly innocent, a silent desperation not to be alone if she were to face the fears in her mind. Yet he couldn't shake the guilt of his past; the *fear* that he was selfish for letting her get close to him.

Reylan pushed aside those wicked, tormenting thoughts. Tentatively, as if one wrong move could spook her, he dipped onto the bed beside Faythe, remaining above the covers. He kept his distance despite the faint itch to shuffle closer and feel her warmth. He could fight against his own need for rest and stay until she was in a deep sleep once more. Faythe already had her eyes blissfully closed and looked delicate, peaceful. He watched her breathing, transfixed by the rise and fall of her chest. As though it might still. As though the beat of her heart were tied to his own.

Yet he didn't fear it. Not in the slightest.

CHAPTER 14

Nikalias

THE KING OF High Farrow sat in the grand chair of his private
council room, fingers pressed into his temples as if it would
soothe the throbbing in his head. It didn't, and he was close to shouting
in frustration at the pain that seemed constant with the pile of woes and
matters that never slowed, never gave him a break. How had his father
kept his sanity—before his mind was twisted by Marvellas? Nik was
beginning to sympathize with him for the scale of what it took to run a
kingdom.

He'd convinced himself his internal doubts and overwhelm would
pass, that this was only a phase. Now, over three months since he
became king, Nik was dealing with a sinking feeling in his stomach that
perhaps everyone was wrong and he wasn't ready. And maybe he never
would be. Fearing he would go out of his mind if he was left to his own
destructive thoughts any longer, Nik bounded to his feet, ignoring the
stabbing in his head with the sudden movement.

He walked the halls in silence. Usually, he would plaster on a mask of pleasantry to give the guards and those he passed a warm reception. But he was far too exhausted to even try anymore. He had one destination in mind, one person he longed to see—someone he always confided in and who always seemed to know how to lift his spirits and soothe his emotions. He had no right to go to her, but he planned to offer her the apology she deserved and assure her she would never owe High Farrow anything in exchange for her safety here. Whatever it took to bide the nobles, he would promise her that.

Standing outside Tauria's rooms, Nik knocked in his usual pattern and waited a short while, giving her the chance to call out if she was indisposed. When all was silent, Nik twisted the handle and welcomed himself inside as she had long granted him permission to do so.

Quickly scanning the bedroom, he knew it was empty without having to check any of the adjoining rooms. His disappointment settled horribly, only adding to his growing despair.

He left, and just as he was closing the door he spied a familiar blonde head down the hall, fully engrossed in the book splayed over both her palms. Marlowe's eyes flashed up briefly, and she smiled warmly, closing her book as they both halted where their paths crossed.

"Have you seen Tauria?" he asked, feeling shameful that he'd skipped a greeting.

Marlowe's face fell solemn, and Nik was hit with panic. "You don't remember?"

"Remember what?"

"What day it is."

It didn't take him long, and when he caught on, Nik's eyes widened and heart cracked at the same time, riddled with the most gods-awful guilt that twisted his gut painfully. He'd never forgotten before, not in over one hundred years. He'd never forgotten the anniversary of her parents' deaths—the day everything was taken from her. He'd been so damned distracted by his new mountain of duties that he didn't realize what day it was. And the thought that struck deepest...was that Tauria, selflessly, hadn't thought to remind him.

His guilt was overshadowed by anger at himself. He was becoming the kind of ruler he tried desperately not to be: one too consumed by duty to balance it with caring for his friends and family.

"You know where she is, don't you?" Marlowe asked quietly, looking at him with a touch of sympathy he hated. Though he didn't blame her for it.

"I do." Nik mustered a weak smile, resting his hand on her arm in thanks for a quick second. He knew exactly where she would be when she was still confined to High Farrow. Tauria always headed to the one place in his kingdom that remotely resembled her home: a spot on the outskirts called Springhill.

Nik was at the stables and had a horse ready right away, barely even registering his own movements.

"Should I alert some guards to accompany you out of the city, Your Majesty?" A timid voice came up behind him.

Nik turned to the stable boy. "That won't be necessary," he answered quickly, mounting the horse in one swift motion. "Did any of them leave with the Fenstead queen?"

The boy paled, and Nik flared in anger that she had been able to leave the city without an escort or his being notified. Even though he knew Tauria would have bribed and silenced whoever necessary to slip out alone, he still made a note to unleash some of his pent-up frustration on his royal guard.

With a new flare of urgency, Nik took off in a fast gallop out of the castle grounds.

King Nikalias slowed his horse after three hours of exerting himself and the beast. He patted the mare's neck in silent thanks for keeping the pace while his mind raced in panic at the thought of Tauria being all the way out here, alone in the hillside. There could be any number of bandits, fae or human, who would target her for her obvious wealth even if they didn't realize who she was.

His frantic heartbeat finally had a chance to calm when he spotted her sitting by the giant lakeside. Nik dismounted, tying his brown mare to a nearby tree at one of the adjoining streams. He started the walk to her slowly now it was confirmed she was safe.

Springhill was beautiful and one of High Farrow's most treasured locations. It reminded Nik a lot of the Eternal Woods in Farrowhold, but on a far larger scale. He'd only visited Fenstead once before when he was a few years past his first century. Here, the open green hills were scattered with colorful blooms, the lake broke off into a small maze of streams, and the verdant forest sprawled on for miles. Springhill was as close to Tauria's homeland as she could get from so far away.

As he approached, Tauria was making flowers bloom in the grass around her with her ability. Spindlelillies. They were white-petaled with a brilliant red center of fine veins, a flower that first bloomed naturally in Fenstead many millennia ago, on a battlefield that saw much tragedy, and had since became a tribute to their fallen. Tauria delicately arranged those she had mimicked into a small, beautiful garland. She would no doubt have detected Nik's presence by now, but she didn't pause her sorting of the arrangement.

"Tauria, I am so sorry," he began quietly when he was close enough.

Her brown eyes glittered a beautiful hazel in the sunlight when they slid up to him, and her small accompanying smile took his breath away but further clenched the guilt in his chest. Tauria motioned for him to join her. Nik swallowed the raw emotion in his throat and obliged, lowering down to sit beside her while he watched her pick at the leaves and stems, head tilting as she observed her work. Her peaceful composure made him feel lower, thinking perhaps she was holding back her grief for his sake.

"Why didn't you come to me?" Beneath the guilt, Nik was silently heartbroken, fearing Tauria had begun to distance herself from him over the past few months since he'd inherited his new status.

Tauria stopped arranging the flowers, her hands lowering as she turned her attention to him. "I understand the commitment of the position you are in, Nik. We are both changing; both growing into the crowns we were born with. Duty comes first, and I understand that."

Nik's brow furrowed in protest. "I will always have time for you," he insisted as it felt as if she were pushing him away. "What I said to the council, I didn't mean it. Not for a second. You are safe here by no obligation. Always."

A pain filled her eyes, creasing the smooth golden skin around them. Nik's panic hitched at the sight. It had nothing to do with the tragic day, nor the reminder of her dark past. Tauria looked away from him, which only added to his growing anxiety. She raised her chin as she stared at the shimmering ripples of water.

"One hundred and seven years to this day since they killed my parents and slaughtered so many innocents," she said, eyes darkening as if she were traveling to that fateful day. Nik shuddered at the thought of what she had endured. It always stabbed his chest with the pain of grief and destruction, a desire to rage for revenge on her behalf. "I plan for this to be the last year I mourn them away from the kingdom they died for. Away from my home. I may not have their bodies to bury, but my parents deserve to be memorialized in the tombs where they belong, my people commemorated for their sacrifice. It's been too long, and I won't hide anymore."

"I don't know where you're going with this," Nik said carefully, but his chest rattled.

Tauria placed down her flower arrangement. Reaching to her other side, she produced a small stack of letters and extended them to him. Nik took them warily, and as he glanced down, his blood ran cold. His wide eyes snapped to hers, but her expression was determined. He looked back at the letters in his palms, each featuring a broken purple seal… The sigil of Olmstone.

"I've been exchanging letters with Varlas, and some with Tarly," she explained, her tone yielding nothing but fact.

Nik opened one of the letters incredulously while trying not to crumple them to nothing at hearing the Olmstone prince's name. He couldn't speak as he skimmed over the words. His pulse was in his ears as certain words flared his anger, his sorrow, his defeat.

"They are open to negotiating an alliance," she went on, but not with an ounce of joy or hope. Nik skimmed over the next letter, then the next, unable to stop despite the torture it inflicted on his heart. "Between Fenstead and Olmstone."

The news hit him like a punch to the gut. The letters crumpled as he couldn't prevent the curl of his fist. Because she had confirmed what he'd already concluded: Tauria meant to secure allegiance with Olmstone as Fenstead's queen alone, not as High Farrow's ward.

His fury forced him to his feet. He couldn't subdue the stab of betrayal as he looked down at her. "How could you do that? How could you trust them with all we know?"

"If you would let me explain—"

"They will use you and then diminish all that you are as soon as they take your throne back." He couldn't stop the words that poured from him.

Tauria was calm as she stood. "Nik, just—"

"After all we've been through, how could you—?"

"Nikalias!" Her voice snapped and took him by surprise. "Gods, if you could stop enjoying the rant of your own voice for two minutes to let me explain!"

Nik's mouth pressed into a firm line. He focused on his breathing, defusing his wrath enough to realize he owed her that.

"You said we needed a way to get eyes in Olmstone. Well, there you have it." She cast her hand to the letters he gripped tight in anger.

The plan fell into place, and every ounce of rage spread into cold, desperate dread. He shook his head. "Not a chance in rutting damn," he snarled.

What she implied he couldn't bear to think of. Not only imagining her in the arms of the enemy, but if she were to go to them as a spy… He didn't believe her name and crown would be enough to save her from Varlas's fury.

"I wasn't asking for permission," she shot back.

His nostrils flared as he took a step toward her. "You are *not* dangling your life at their mercy. If they found out about your intentions, not even I would be quick enough to intervene and save you. He would have cause to execute you on the spot."

"I meant what I said." She spoke firmly. "I'm done being idle. I'm done waiting for *nothing* while I cannot be sure how many of my people survived, nor my court, only to watch me sit comfortably in High Farrow with no plans to *fight back.*"

Her passion stunned him to silence. She was coming into the fierce queen he knew her to be.

"I will do this for High Farrow; for everything this kingdom offered me when I had nowhere else to turn. But most of all, I will do this for Fenstead. If there is a chance Varlas could be siding with Valgard, I can't let that happen. They took everything from me, and I plan to take it back."

The prospect struck him with a fear so great it was an effort not to break down and protest that she change her mind. As her friend—as more than just her friend—he would do anything to get her to stay. Yet as a king, from one monarch to another, he knew why she had to do this.

"I can't protect you there," he said in defeat.

Tauria's face finally softened. "It's time for me to protect myself. I will forever be grateful for everything you have done for me, Nik. But it's time for me to move on and start thinking of my kingdom. There's nothing left for me here."

That final statement felt like a blow to his gut, winding him entirely. It repeated in an echo of torment, and he knew it would continue long past her days in High Farrow. He would never stop hearing those soul-crushing words.

There's nothing left for me here.

"You're not protecting yourself; you're offering yourself up for execution should they have the slightest suspicion about your intentions."

"My intentions are true." Her calm, cold voice stiffened his spine. "I will be accepting their invitation to Olmstone to entertain the prospect of a marriage alliance with Tarly."

Nik flared. "How could you? After all they've done and could be plotting!"

"We don't know what their movements are yet. If your information turns out to be false, I cannot deny a secure alliance with Olmstone would benefit Fenstead. And if they are colluding with Valgard, that is my revenge to be had more than anyone's. I will tear them apart from the inside if I have to—I don't care what it will cost me."

"I care," Nik snapped, his anger rising, fear rattling at the mere thought. "You can't walk into the lion's den dressed as a lamb. They'll snuff you out quicker than you can get a single piece of information, and even if you did, what will you do with it?"

"They won't suspect me, and if they do, I'm more use to them alive than dead. You said you needed eyes on the inside and that you couldn't risk Nightwalking in case your spies were killed. They won't kill me, Nik —not straight away. They'll only risk making me a martyr for Fenstead and causing an uprising."

What she said made sense. Brilliant but damning sense. Nik couldn't see the merits; didn't believe anything was worth risking her life for.

"If they suspect me, I'll have time to warn you before…" Tauria cut herself off.

There was something haunting in her hazel gaze that made every cell in his body tremble and wrapped him in ice. He couldn't stand the lingering tension as he pressed, "Before what?"

For the first time, Tauria's determined gaze fell to sadness, and she looked away from him, over the glittering lake. "Fenstead fell, and I ran. My people gave their lives for me, and I've sat idle for over a century. I owe them that devotion. If Olmstone detains me in thinking I'm a spy for you, they'll want to use me as much as they can before executing me. If it ever comes to that, I won't risk them using me to lure in what could be left of Fenstead's court. I won't let them use me…to get to you."

Nik's heart stopped cold, dead. He didn't care if it never beat again when the meaning behind her words shattered his soul. He shook his head, something dark and primal overcoming him. "No."

"I'm not asking for your—"

"Permission. I know." His tone was shadowy, and Tauria's brave face wavered. "But I will not stand by and watch you recklessly, *foolishly*, end your life for this cause. There will be another way—"

"This is the best solution, and you know it."

"Not at the cost of your *life!*" His chest heaved; he couldn't stop his anger. Toward Olmstone—toward the *world*. For dealing them such a screwed-up hand that knew no happiness. Not when war and devastation found them at every turn; not when they were forced to be leaders through such hardship. "What you propose is suicide, Tauria. It is not a plan. It's a tragedy."

"I've made up my mind, Nik." Tauria tried to regain her composure, but he could see the fear in her eyes. "It is done. Varlas expects me in two weeks and will be sending his warriors and the prince to escort me."

Nik's nails bit into his palms as they shook at his sides. He wanted to rage, to kill, to storm to Olmstone and execute Varlas himself before he would allow her to walk into his domain and be at his mercy.

"Nik, listen to me." Her voice dropped to a calm, serene tone she had used before, but so long ago. The same tone as when he was consumed by endless anger over the death of his mother and her gentle coaxing was the only thing that brought him back from a path of reckless destruction. With the notes of her voice, she closed the distance with slow, careful steps. "I'm going to be okay. This is for me, but this is also for you."

Nik couldn't bear to look at her, but he couldn't fight her when he felt her soft fingers under his jaw, forcing him to lock onto her hazel gaze.

"Let your nobles think this is your idea. That you are sending me as High Farrow's ward with the hope of negotiating ties in Olmstone and Fenstead. They will never need to know any different as we will always be allies. We will always be friends."

The last word clenched in his chest to the point of pain. His hand met with hers at his face while his brow pinched with so many declarations drumming his heart to be spoken. As he held her glittering eyes, he saw it. She needed this. For herself and her kingdom, Tauria needed to take back control of her life, and this was her chance. As much as every internal fiber begged him to make her stay, for her to be safe…he couldn't take that from her.

"If anything happened to you…" Nik trailed off, unable to finish without the air that had left him completely.

Tauria smiled sadly. "I know," she said quietly. "I know."

CHAPTER 15

Zaiana

"AGAIN," ZAIANA COMMANDED the young dark fae with no sympathy for her fatigue. Amaya looked at her incredulously, and Zaiana answered with a firm look of her own that dared her to protest. With a suppressed sigh of reluctance, she splayed her wings and took off into the air she hadn't long dropped from. Zaiana tracked her from the stone fringe viewing platform of the pit, assessing her every maneuver and weakness while she completed the basic flying drill.

"She's slow," Tynan remarked from beside her. His distaste for her choice wasn't subtle. She knew none in her inner circle were particularly thrilled with the new addition.

Zaiana spared a look in his direction and noticed the nods of agreement from the rest of the group. Her irritation grew.

"I hate to agree, but Kellias and I have been overseeing her training, and she's among the weakest in the grade," Acelin added.

"It's not about speed or strength," Zaiana snapped. "I didn't choose any of you for those particular traits." She didn't need to defend her decision, but she did want to assure her group that nothing would get in the way of them winning the trial for the quest. She tore her eyes from Amaya's training drill to turn to the five who stood behind her. "I know we could beat Maverick and his rogues just as the six of us, but those aren't the rules. We need another player, and Amaya is simply a body to fill that space. On that field, no one concerns themselves with anyone's role but their own. If she can't handle herself, if she can't keep up, she'll face the ultimate punishment. But she will not hold any of you back from victory."

Her companions all nodded simultaneously in fierce understanding and respect. They weren't friends, as to be friends required feelings none of the dark fae were capable of. Care and love. A beating heart. They shared a bond of respect and obedience only, and out of duty, any of those in front of her would lay down their life for her.

With their concerns addressed, Zaiana turned back just in time to catch Amaya clip the tip of her wing on the edge of the protruding stone wall. It sent her into an embarrassing tumble before she floundered to regain composure, still in flight. Zaiana momentarily pinched her eyes closed, grinding her teeth in frustration. She knew it would be a challenge to address Amaya's physical weaknesses. Her crooked wings and sloppy flying could end her in a heartbeat in battle. Zaiana didn't look to Tynan again, knowing he would be suppressing his "I told you so" look and she'd have to hold back the urge to unleash her anger on him.

"That's enough," Zaiana bellowed into the empty space.

Amaya paused, her face falling in defeat. As it should. When the young fae dropped to the pit floor, Zaiana took a step off the balcony, wings splayed, to swoop down in one graceful movement. She tucked them in tight when her feet landed weightlessly. Amaya shifted nervously under her irritable gaze.

"Do you have any strengths?" Zaiana's words weren't slander; rather, she asked this to gauge how well the young fae knew herself and if she possessed any confidence in her capabilities at all. At Amaya's silence, Zaiana was one short fuse away from casting her out of sight. It wasn't too late for her to find a replacement. They still had over a week.

"I—I can use a bow."

Archery was a skill most of them had perfected. It wasn't exactly impressive. But Zaiana's interest was piqued. While those in her inner circle could use a bow well, none of them were specifically honed for the weapon. She cantered her head.

"Can you glamour?" It wasn't a common ability. The only two who couldn't in her group were Drya and Selain. It wasn't a weakness for them as they had a natural skill to become like living shadows, making them invaluable as spies.

Zaiana didn't expect it, but Amaya's small nod lit a flare of triumph within her. She knew what to do with her then. She was small, so stealth would be her best attribute. Her position wasn't to be in the skies; she would be invaluable on the ground.

"Why wasn't I told this?" She directed the question to Acelin and Kellias specifically.

They looked between each other before Kellias spoke up. "Archery isn't something we've been actively practicing yet."

Zaiana glanced back at Amaya in curiosity. "Then how is it you're so confident in your skills as an archer?"

Amaya shifted her weight, sparing a guilty look at her training over-seers. "I know I shouldn't have…but sometimes, when the pit is quiet, I come here to borrow a bow and some arrows. And I know we're not allowed, but I take them to the range above the mountain and practice. I don't mean to disobey, but it's the only thing I've found I'm good at." Amaya was quick to ramble her confession.

Zaiana should have been outraged. It was a grave insult to go against basic orders and venture unpermitted and unsupervised to the range outside. Yet her eyes flashed with something else: admiration for the young fae. Not for her disobedience—that she would find suitable punishment for, as was to be expected—but she had to credit Amaya for playing into her strengths and not submitting to being useless in the training drills she was forced to participate in.

Zaiana's mouth curled in wicked delight. "Let's see if your words have merit." She turned to her five. "Someone retrieve a bow, and let's take this out to the range, shall we?" Her voice sang. She felt a glimmer of victory that she wasn't wrong. Amaya could prove to be an asset instead of dead weight in their ensemble.

Her companions looked hesitant, but reluctantly, Acelin and Kellias went to fetch the weapon.

She turned back to Amaya, voice turning deadly low. "If you make me look a fool for trusting you, death will be the least of your fears."

Out in the training range, Zaiana didn't register the bitter nip of the whistling wind in her rare high of excitement. Along the narrow gap between mountain peaks the archery range stretched, consisting of fifteen targets. The target heights were staggered, the distances progressively farther and all in varying sizes, the smallest being no bigger than an acorn.

Amaya stood timidly behind the line where most would stay to practice stationary archery. As creatures with the ability of flight, archery wasn't a skill a lot of dark fae felt necessary. They would rather practice dodging fatal darts from the enemy in the skies. But Zaiana had a giddy thrill that she could perhaps add someone to her ranks who would further strengthen her group—another lethal, unique skill.

Acelin came over to hand Amaya the bow and a quiver of arrows, and in the way she took the items with hesitance, Zaiana's confidence in her faltered dramatically. If she'd misled her on how well she could use the weapon, it would be to Zaiana's embarrassment for trusting in her word. And to display her poor judgment in front of her companions weakened her as a leader. Her fingers curled in anger at the thought.

"Stationary first. Hit all fifteen targets from where you stand." Zaiana's voice was hard, almost threatening. Amaya's answer was a shot nod, and then she equipped the quiver to her back, pulling one arrow out.

No one spoke, no one moved. Zaiana observed Amaya's every flicker of movement and assessed her methods. Amaya paused and took slow, concise breaths while her eyes scanned every target with focus. Zaiana tilted her head in curiosity as she studied the young fae. Tynan opened his mouth to speak—likely to voice his impatience for her to hurry up as Zaiana herself had the same thought. She held her hand up to silence him before he could, not taking her eyes off Amaya. Her feet moved into a steady stance to brace, her chest rose and fell in perfectly timed breaths, and she fixed her arrow into the string, but she didn't raise her arms to aim. The wind whistled more, and Zaiana knew it would take extra precision with the effect the air could have on the projection. Amaya would have to purposely offset her aim to compensate and adjust each fire since the force and direction of the wind could change at any moment.

Just when Zaiana was beginning to doubt that her pause was for calculation and not out of fear, Amaya raised her bow and let loose in the space of a breath.

It hit dead center, but Zaiana expected nothing less for the first five targets in the range at least. That wasn't what was impressive; it was that the darkling didn't stop for a second. She swiped an arrow from her back, aimed, and let loose. Again and again and again. Unfaltering, unflinching. When it got to the final and farthest target, Amaya did halt, just for a split second, as the wind blasted a quick gust. Then she let her last arrow fly, and it hit with perfect precision.

There were very few times in Zaiana's life that she had ever been stunned. When Amaya lowered her bow, she turned around to her with a sheepish look, back to appearing as the weak coward she allowed herself to be. Zaiana couldn't be sure if the young fae was brilliant for hiding her skills behind a mask or simply lacking in confidence. Nevertheless, her lips curled in satisfaction. She glanced at Tynan, who was staring at her wide-eyed like the rest of them. Zaiana smirked at their reaction, eyes twinkling with delight when they turned back to Amaya.

"Very good." She stalked up to her, dropping her grin. "Why would you keep such talents hidden?"

Amaya straightened, relaxing with the knowledge she wasn't to be reprimanded. At least not yet. "I didn't think it was something that would be useful," she admitted.

She wasn't wrong. To anyone else, the skill of archery would seem insignificant considering the many alternatives. Swordsmanship, agility in the skies, and abilities were all ranked far above a bow and arrow to a dark fae. But Amaya wasn't just a fine archer; she had honed the skill, become the weapon, and it was something no one could expect. Zaiana's instincts had once again proven to be right, and the darkling in front of her could make a spectacular ally.

"Your skills are impressive. Don't discredit what you're good at." Though she admired the talent and Amaya's intuition to train herself, she had still broken a rule when she took it upon herself to venture outside unpermitted. Zaiana couldn't be seen as weak for letting that go unpunished. "Since you thought it appropriate to disregard basic rules and venture out here, this is where you will stay. Practice, rest, and don't come back into the mountain for three days."

Amaya's eyes widened in a plea, but Zaiana's look warned against it. Her face fell, and she nodded in acceptance of her punishment. While Zaiana knew it wasn't as brutal as expected, she couldn't inflict any serious harm on the young dark fae, if only because she was to participate in the challenge by her side and would need to be at full strength. After suffering three long, freezing days and nights without a proper meal, she would have at least a week to regain her strength for the match ahead.

Zaiana turned to her companions with a cunning smile. "Her skills in stationary archery are impressive, but what about moving targets?"

Tynan caught on immediately, his face falling in a scowl.

"Oh, Tynan, when was the last time you exerted yourself outside the comforts of your bed...or another's?" His deviant grin made her smirk. She turned to the rest of them. "All of you pick up a target. Or don't. If you still doubt her ability not to spear an arrow through your chest."

Their hearts may not beat, but they weren't immune to a fatal wound. A timid smile of amusement curled Amaya's lips, but it was gone when she caught Zaiana's eye. It shouldn't have bothered her. After all, she was supposed to be feared, respected, and obeyed. Though, she wasn't a complete monster; she could enjoy a little fun now and then. What constituted as "fun" varied, but she felt a stab of sourness that she seemed to kill the mood wherever she went.

Zaiana often wondered how different she would be if she hadn't become the delegate. If she hadn't been pushed and trained ruthlessly to win the position since birth. If she never had...Finnian would still be alive.

And she would still be weak.

With grumbles of reluctance, her five stemmed off to equip and position themselves as targets around the gap. Zaiana approached Amaya, whose confidence looked truly shaken at the prospect.

"Have you ever tried hitting something that isn't still?"

Amaya, to her surprise, nodded. "Birds fly over these mountains sometimes," she said, head tilting up as if she'd see them.

There were none when Zaiana followed her line of sight over the clouded, misty skies, and she didn't think it was very often birds flew over these mountains. Still, she continued to be pleasantly awed by the darkling's intuition.

"They're going to be far faster than birds, and they won't hold back.

This isn't child's play. Imagine each of them as your death approaching, and make it known it won't claim you today."

Amaya's green orbs met hers, and she felt the silent gratitude in them. With a nod of new confidence, she straightened her posture. Zaiana felt a pang of something she wasn't used to—something faint and oddly warming to her cold chest. Pride.

She walked a few paces ahead, raising her voice so the others could hear. "On a battleground, there are very few moments in which you can pause to fix your aim. There are no rules, and an enemy could approach from any angle." Her companions would know what she required of them. She twisted back to address Amaya alone. "Your task is simple: make it to the end of the gap. Striking the last target will signal your victory. Be aware of those who try to stop you…to end you."

Amaya didn't speak or move, but the hard determination in her look was far louder than words.

"Glamour your wings—they will only slow you down." With that, Zaiana splayed her own and shot to the sky with a few powerful motions. She flew to the end of the gap. She had no intention of sitting on the sidelines and would be Amaya's final obstacle in the way of the small target now positioned behind her. She straightened, hands clasped behind her back, to enjoy and observe if Amaya even made it far enough for her to be needed.

"On your mark, Amaya," Zaiana called. Her fae ears would pick up on it from across the stretch of stone with the added lift of the wind.

The young dark fae was a slender, dark silhouette in the distance—more so now she'd taken Zaiana's advice and glamoured her wings away. Some might see it as an insult, disregarding their heritage, but Zaiana played to everyone's strengths no matter what it took. Amaya would have far more agility in a sprint to maneuver the obstacles around her, and far better balance to use her bow on the move without the added weight of wings to account for. That, and if she wasn't to use them, they would only be vulnerable to an enemy strike. Amaya's greatest strength was her size. The smaller she could make herself, the more lethal she would become with her dead shot.

Zaiana scanned the angry, jagged rocks of the surrounding mountain peaks. She couldn't see any of her companions, but she didn't need to. She knew exactly where each of them was lying in wait for their turn to catch Amaya off-guard. Over the centuries, it was as if she'd developed a sixth sense for each of them. With their distaste for the darkling, they would be even more determined to see her fail.

Good. She wanted to see Amaya challenged to her full extent.

Zaiana shouldn't care if Amaya succeeded or not; she could find another stand-in for the trial. Yet a small part of her was rooting for the darkling. Not so she would be proven right in her decision, but for Amaya to prove to herself she could rise against odds and expectations.

Only the wind whistled its presence, billowing her cloak sideward. Zaiana was still, watching, waiting, silent.

Amaya fixed the bow and arrow in her own expert way, inhaled a long breath, and then took off running. She didn't raise her bow immediately nor clumsily scan the area for the impending attacks. Amaya ran straight ahead, focused, using her hearing to detect the threats instead. Smart.

Kellias was first—he came at her from the side, floating downward from the skies. Amaya was quick. She didn't pause her running as Kellias swooped in. She had an arrow nocked and fired, but it missed as he spun around the dart. Landing, he sprinted for her. Amaya paused, turned back, aimed, and let loose. She hit the target he held.

Zaiana's eyes flashed in delight at her swiftness as Kellias stopped advancing.

Amaya didn't pause to bask in her triumph. Clever young dark fae. She didn't reach for another arrow, choosing to gain some distance in a long sprint without a poised weapon instead. Drya and Selain were next. Together they came from each side—only, one was in flight, and the other on foot. Amaya drew an arrow, nocked it, and released it at

Drya who advanced at her level first. Her arrow met its mark. In the same breath, Amaya abruptly halted. The arrow in her bow met with her line of sight, tracking Selain who darted for her, zigzagging her flight path to throw off her aim. The young dark fae didn't immediately try the shot. She kept still, arms poised. When she was close enough, Selain swooped down in one clean glide. Zaiana thought it would be over, but then Amaya loosed her arrow. It hit the target seconds before Selain would have landed and took her out.

A smile twitched Zaiana's lips.

When Amaya turned, Acelin was already in her path, racing for her on foot. It caught the young fae by surprise, and she left her beeline path to dart to the side. Pulling an arrow free, she nocked and let loose, but in her flustered lack of awareness it was completely off the mark. She tried again and missed again. Zaiana's smile faltered. Acelin was closing in fast, and Zaiana's hands tightened together, believing she would be the one to end the game.

Acelin shot to the sky, meaning to swoop down and knock her out in one clean motion. Amaya, to her credit, didn't succumb to the low odds. Instead, the darkling inhaled deeply. Then, so fast she would have missed it if she blinked, Amaya retrieved an arrow from her back, aimed, and let loose. It hit. Zaiana's eyes widened a fraction in surprise, and Acelin also halted her fast descent, looking down at the arrow protruding from her small target in bewilderment.

Amaya didn't pause for celebration. She took off, and it was now Zaiana's turn to have her fun. A wicked smile curled her mouth as she unclasped her hands, reaching to unfasten her cloak as she tracked Amaya's run. She allowed the vibration of her lightning to hum through the veins in her arms and form delightful pricks of vibrant amethyst bolts through her two iron-clad fingertips. Zaiana glamoured her wings and took off running toward the young fae.

It clearly wasn't what Amaya expected as her eyed widened and her pace slowed. Zaiana didn't hesitate. Casting out a hand, she shot a jagged bolt of lightning at Amaya, who shrieked, narrowly twisting around it. Zaiana was already sending a second flash of moderately charged lightning her way. She ducked in time to avoid its blast. Bolts formed at her fingertips without much effort, and she fired them again and again. Amaya danced around them, her small build meaning she was light on her feet, quick to move, and hard to lock onto for a precision aim.

Zaiana's early advancement was purposeful. She anticipated it would distract the young dark fae enough that she would fail to remember there was still one other player in the game. Zaiana caught a glimpse of Tynan's dark splayed wings swooping down behind Amaya while she held her focus dodging Zaiana's attacks. She had yet to notice the threat as he closed in fast and without an equipped target for her to strike. Tynan was an arrogant, stubborn bastard and would rather accept the pain of defeat if he overjudged a situation in his confidence. It was something Zaiana greatly appreciated about her second-in-command.

It was about to be over though as Tynan was a few seconds from crashing down on Amaya. But as she held her eyes on Zaiana, whatever she read in her expression translated to alert and sudden awareness. Zaiana halted and watched in surprise as Amaya's arm reached back for an arrow and she twisted a split second from colliding with the dark fae. She released her arrow, striking just as Tynan crashed into her. They both skidded across the jagged ground.

Zaiana winced at the sound of the impact that sent Amaya rolling and the rest of her arrows flying from the quiver on her back. Tynan groaned as he regained his composure and peeled himself off the ground. He blazed at the arrow protruding from his shoulder, clenching his teeth as he pulled it out with a hiss of pain. It momentarily poured shining silver blood.

But the game wasn't finished, and Zaiana had no plans to go easy after that brutal display. She began her onslaught of lightning attacks once more. Amaya cried out, rolling to dodge a couple before scrambling to her feet. She had her bow but no arrows. Her eyes flashed to the ground where a single dart lay a few meters away. Zaiana struck over and over as she made a run for it, hopping between the wicked bolts of purple, on her toes like a gracefully mastered dance. Zaiana felt frustrated she had yet to make her falter, mesmerized by the way she moved as if she were a feather in the wind.

Amaya swiped the arrow, nocked it into place, and aimed. Not at the target; she aimed for Zaiana as the target was offset to her left.

Zaiana blazed at the threat. She opened her arms, summoning the strength of her bolts through both hands. Amaya didn't balk. She held Zaiana's eye, unflinching. Zaiana couldn't decide if she admired or despised Amaya for her bravery and defiance. The challenge canceled out all thoughts of mercy, and she didn't hold back the strength in her currents. Just as she did with Maverick, she joined her currents and sent the forceful blast shooting from the iron tips of both hands.

Amaya didn't move out of the way like Zaiana expected her to. For a moment, she felt a stroke of fear, perhaps even regret, as she realized the strength of her joined currents could very well be enough to kill such a small form. Amaya's life shouldn't concern her. It didn't. But what a waste it would be.

Then the most unexpected, cunning, brilliant thing happened.

Amaya shifted her legs, bracing to absorb the impact of the lightning strike. And she did. The tip of her arrow connected with the bolts first, and Amaya clenched her teeth, not spared from the shockwaves completely through the conduction of the iron tip. She shifted her aim, letting her final arrow fly. It soared beautifully through the length of the space, right by Zaiana's face, charged with a mesmerizing vibrant purple. The arrow hit—no, *exploded*—the farthest target.

Zaiana stared at the broken fragments on the ground, bewildered and in awe over what she'd just seen. When she turned back, Amaya was on her knees, breathing heavily as she attempted to recover from the aftershock of Zaiana's blast. For a moment, she thought she felt guilt or something akin to sympathy. It was an odd pang in her otherwise emotionless mind and still chest.

She approached the darkling, looking down on her. Amaya raised her eyes to lock onto her stare. They were clouded with fatigue, but she held fierce.

"You did well," Zaiana said, and the young fae managed a small smile of relief. Zaiana lost the fight against her own lips as they curled up. "Keep it up. You have the potential to do great things, Amaya. Believe it."

With that, Zaiana passed the darkling. As she left her on the mountainside to live out her punishment, she tried to ignore the new, damning flare of something she wasn't used to. Something like *hope*.

CHAPTER 16

Faythe

FAYTHE AWOKE FEELING colder than she remembered when she fell asleep. Her arm stretched out as if she expected to find someone there. When she was met only with a soft sheet, it came flooding back to her exactly *who* she thought would be there, and her eyes snapped open with the skipped beat of her heart.

She was alone.

Faythe pushed herself upright, feeling her body flush as she recalled the previous night. In her state of exhaustion, she'd asked Reylan to stay after their late-night conversation. And he did. The slight impression of his form left behind in the space beside her confirmed she didn't imagine her shameless request. She couldn't decide if she felt relief or disappointment that he'd left at some point in the night or early morning. Her heart thundered. Had he thought it inappropriate and left the moment she was asleep again? The thought dropped her stomach, and she pulled the covers back to cool her heated skin. Taking a long breath, with a look out over the sunny sky, Faythe felt…refreshed.

Then it dawned on her. She didn't dream of anything. Not after she fell asleep for the second time last night. A triumphant smile tugged at her lips. *Finally.* Though it was short-lived when she realized it wasn't enough to give her the strength to attempt to Nightwalk to Nik in High Farrow. She needed more nights of blissful, dark rest and was suddenly overcome with dread that her nightmares could return any night to ruin the small bit of strength she'd regained.

Faythe heaved a long sigh and pushed herself out of bed. Walking over to the balcony doors, she stared out at the magnificent surrounding city, vibrant with the sun that kissed the array of impeccable dwellings beyond the castle's fortification. Faythe was high enough that she could view both the inner and outer rings' circumferences far into the distance.

Aside from the man-made fortifications, Ellium was surrounded and protected by beautiful crimson-peaked mountains that glittered like rubies in the sunlight and added a perimeter of sparkling stars at night-fall. The magnificent sight from her vantage point was breathtaking, humbling...empowering. A city of fire and ash.

Her wandering thoughts were disrupted by a polite knock on her door. Faythe whirled, heart leaping. Subconsciously, she pulled at the hem of the robe she'd fallen asleep in, stupidly nervous imagining the head of silver hair she expected to see as the door handle twisted. However, her shoulders immediately slumped with a small exhale at the sight of her handmaiden, Gresla. She was an older woman, her apron a little too small to wrap around her plump form. She cast a bright smile, and Faythe retuned it in a bid to hide her disappointment. Gresla was human and had been a great comfort in easing Faythe's doubts and stresses during her months in the castle. Faythe felt able to confess every-thing to the humble woman as if she were her own grandmother, a matronly figure she never thought she would have the pleasure of knowing in her life.

"Good morning, Lady Faythe," she chirped. It was the same

greeting every morning, yet Faythe cringed each time she heard the formality. No number of protests worked in getting Gresla to drop the title.

"Good morning, Gresla." Faythe bit her lip, trying hard to choke back the question that burned to follow. Unsuccessfully. "Did you happen to see—?"

"The general left your rooms early this morning," Gresla answered before she could finish. It amazed Faythe sometimes how often she seemed to know exactly what she was pondering. "He told me to allow you to rest in and come back when you awoke." Gresla's slight smile was almost teasing as she went about fixing the bed.

Faythe didn't have a second to feel embarrassment as she frowned. "What time is it?"

"Midday, my dear."

Her mouth popped open. She'd slept in that long? A warmth filled her chest at the small detail she'd gained from her handmaiden. Reylan had left this morning, not as soon as she fell asleep again last night. Giddy nerves trembled through her. Though perhaps he'd simply fallen asleep himself and found it inappropriate when he awoke, leaving swiftly. That thought put a cold dampener on her bright mood.

Faythe straightened, not allowing her moment of triumph over a full night's rest to be ruined by irrational, petty thoughts. It had taken last night for her to realize how close she was to being crushed by the weight of her own confrontations and how desperately she needed the release of sharing her burdens, coupled with a full night of undisturbed rest. She had Reylan to thank for it, whether he knew it or not. She wanted to seek him out, to be certain his staying last night hadn't tainted the air between them, and to express her gratitude that he'd listened to her heavy confessions and uplifted her spirit with tales of her mother until she fell into a deep sleep. Faythe almost skipped to the wardrobe, the soft chuckle of Gresla following her.

"Eager this morning, Lady Faythe," she commented at her back. "Nothing to do with the handsome general now, is it?"

As she rustled through the various garments, Faythe replied, "Not at all." Though it was hardly a convincing statement. Gresla appeared in the doorway, and Faythe paused her searching to return her pointed look. "I wish I had more scandalous news for you, Gresla, but we simply talked last night and the hour got away from us. Nothing happened."

"I would never assume it did. Though I'm glad it has seemed to lift your spirits." Gresla passed her, reaching for a gown without a pause for deliberation.

Faythe smiled sheepishly at the crimson-embroidered asymmetrical gown as Gresla also snatched up a pair of fine black pants. Faythe wasn't exactly the most stylish, and she admittedly would be lost in the sea of vibrant fabrics and accessories were it not for her wonderful handmaiden.

Once dressed, Gresla was finishing her work on Faythe's hair when Faythe interrupted the silence. "Do you know where he went this morning?" Something about saying Reylan's name to Gresla felt confessional. Faythe avoided it as if it would deny the fact she'd had the stunning fae general in her rooms at all last night.

Gresla cast her a knowing look in the mirror, taking the pin she'd pinched between her lips and sliding it into the lattice of braids that bound her hair half-back. Faythe's cheeks flushed pink, and she had to avert her gaze.

"I think he said something about the drawing room. A meeting with another commander, I believe. He said to tell you he'd come for you after."

Though he usually appeared at her rooms to escort her for the day, something about this made Faythe giddy with a thrill. She had acquired another piece of knowledge that soothed her anxious worries: Reylan must have left out of duty, not regret for staying the night. She tried to force down the wide smile that bloomed, if only to prevent it from adding to Gresla's growing assumptions over what was going on between them. She said nothing further.

Faythe got to her feet when Gresla went to retrieve another pin. "I think I know the castle well enough by now. I'll find my own way."

Gresla didn't protest. A warm smile split her round cheeks instead, and her eyes looked over Faythe with a hint of humble pride. Then her hand lightly touched Faythe's back, steering her sideward before she could make a break for the door. "First, breakfast," she said in a firm way that showed she'd already anticipated Faythe's plans to skip eating.

Faythe grumbled reluctantly and headed to the adjoining dining area where a cold spread had been laid out. Her appetite was completely diminished by her need to confront her antsy feelings. As she sat down, a knock sounded at her door, and her heart battered against her chest as she whipped her head toward the sound. Gresla cast her a teasing look at her response, but Faythe tried hopelessly to appear unfazed while she moved to answer it. Her anticipation once again diffused completely when a familiar blond set of curls caught her eye. The slight pang of disappointment was quickly swept away as she grinned at Reuben.

"I'll leave you two alone. You know how to find me if you need anything, Lady Faythe."

Faythe found herself sliding a look at Reuben to catch his reaction to the formal address. His brow quirked, but his expression gave nothing away. She cast a grateful nod and smile to her handmaiden, who swiftly left.

"Lady, huh?" Reuben commented with a suppressed smirk. "I'm surprised it's not *Princess.*"

Faythe scowled at him, turning to take her place at the table before digging into the delicious pastries. Reuben took the seat opposite and began to help himself, eager with bright eyes. The sight pained her as she wondered what kind of treatment he'd received over the sea even though he'd relayed that he was well cared for after taking up refuge with a human family in Lakelaria.

"How have you been settling in?" Faythe asked after a silent pause.

"Good," he said with his mouth half-full. Faythe chuckled as the sight brought forth warm memories from her childhood. Carefree days she pined after now she was reunited with her lifelong friend. "They've been very welcoming here. Thank you, by the way. I don't know what the alternative would have been were it not for you." His body gave off a slight tremor.

Faythe shook her head. "You don't have to thank me. I'm glad you're here, Reuben. I'm glad you're safe." After a short pause, she had to ask the question she'd been holding onto, wanting as many precious moments with him as possible. "When will you go back to High Farrow?" Although she wanted to spend more time with him, she needed him to go back to their home kingdom, where he would be safe and with their other friends. Faythe's days in Rhyenelle were numbered with the perilous journey she would have to take in a month's time. The solstice was too near for her to delay it any longer, and she didn't want to leave Reuben in a foreign kingdom without a friendly face once again.

"Actually, I'd like to stay."

It was not what she expected. It was both a happy and painful notion that this was what he would choose. But she couldn't give him that choice. "You can't. You need to go back. Nik is king now; no harm will come to you. I promise."

"No harm will come to me here. You're the princess, are you not?"

Faythe was conflicted in her answer. She had decided to embrace her heritage and put herself forth for the position of Agalhor's heir, but it was not guaranteed. Not with Malin standing in her way. She decided to divert from the lingering question.

"I'm leaving Rhyenelle. You'll only be a stranger in a foreign kingdom once more."

"I want to come with you to the Isles."

Faythe recoiled, straightening in her seat. An unsettling feeling rose in her stomach as she stared at him for a few long seconds. Her brow pinched as her mind reeled at his words.

Reuben's face was innocent, but Faythe's heart quickened.

"I never told you where I was going," she muttered, alarmed as she continued to wrack her brain for the missing conversation.

He only cocked his head in confusion. "Yes, you did. The day I arrived, remember?"

Faythe tried to recall everything they had spoken of. It was a lot, but she had no recollection of mentioning the Niltain Isles at all, feeling certain the first she spoke of it was to Reylan last night. She and Reuben had caught up on so much that perhaps it had been thrown into conversation. Still, her edge of wariness remained. She had no reason to distrust her old friend who had been through so much, and he had no reason to lie to her. Faythe shook her head to dismiss her suspicious thoughts.

"You can't come with me."

"There's nothing for me in High Farrow anymore. I don't want to go back to that mill." His face turned desolate and pleading.

Faythe was torn with sympathy, but she couldn't risk taking him with her. There was no guarantee she would make it back. "You'll only be in the way. Where I'm going, I can't afford to look out for you," she said firmly, though it pained her to be so harsh to him.

Reuben didn't balk at her dismissal. Instead, his expression turned dark, hard, and it struck her enough to listen. Reuben was no longer the boy she'd always felt the need to protect.

"I faced things you couldn't imagine in Lakelaria. I stood up for myself, and I fought for myself. I'm not the same person you parted with on Farrow Harbor. I don't need you to look out for me." His firm look of determination gave his words merit. He *wasn't* the same boy she'd left close to a year ago. He'd aged in spirit, even appearance, far more than she could have imagined. His features were more prominent, as though hardship had weathered his face. He was definably handsome now, rather than boyishly good-looking.

"We might not come back," she said in barely more than a whisper, a quiet plea for him to change his mind.

Reuben smiled, lifting his glass to her. "Then let's not come back together."

It didn't frighten him. Not in the slightest. And it filled her with far more dread then joy. Not for his life, but the small seed of apprehension as she held his eye. Those eyes, for a split second, she thought were a shade darker than she remembered, and his thrill for the dangerous quest belonged to a stranger.

Then it was gone. His attention was back to the breakfast in front of them as he took her silence as acceptance.

Faythe cast out her reservations, but the drop of guilt that there was yet another life on the line against her will remained.

Faythe walked the halls poised and confident. The drawing room was one of the few places she knew how to easily navigate to as it was somewhere Reylan frequented. He dragged her there often to retrieve battle plans and other items related to the royal armies and defenses, often trying to explain things to Faythe when she pestered him about it. Reylan could talk for hours about his passion and admiration for the kingdom, and it was wonderful to be swept away by his voice for a while.

Rounding the last corner, Faythe slowed her brisk pace, finding the doors to the room already ajar. She approached cautiously, hearing the soft murmur of voices carrying down the hall. Two voices, one of them soft and feminine. When she got to the door, she stopped to glance inside first, not wanting to interrupt if the meeting was still underway. What she saw, however, instantly made her stomach drop.

Reylan was leaning back casually against the long center table while a breathtakingly beautiful female fae loomed close enough to touch. Her auburn hair was reminiscent of autumn in full bloom, tied in a long braid. She wore the same form-fitting combat suit Faythe now possessed, exposing every enviable full curve of her strong body. This fae was a warrior. Her features were soft yet delicately stunning with gold accents decorating her pointed ears.

The pair looked engaged in bright conversation along with one other, a male warrior fae, whose rich brown skin and cut features parted Faythe's mouth. He was stunning. Yet her attention was fixed solely on Reylan. His eager smile was rare, and it warmed her as much as it pained her to see it brought on by another while he looked at her with adoration. The female fae laughed, the sound a wondrous melody, and her hand went to Reylan's arm as she leaned in closer, chuckling over something he said.

Faythe sucked in a sharp breath just as Reylan turned his head to catch her intrusion. She spun on her heel, taking off in a fast, light walk away from the drawing room, knowing heavy footsteps would certainly draw his attention. She eyed the corner, willing it to meet her so she could disappear around it and save the embarrassment of a confrontation.

"Faythe." His voice called at her back and halted her movement. She swore inwardly, wishing more than anything to turn to a pile of ash where she stood. Instead, Faythe schooled her face and twisted to him in one fluid motion.

He was walking toward her, his companions in tow. Their smiles were warm, welcoming, and Faythe tried her best to reciprocate them despite the horrible sting of...*jealousy*. She was wrong to assume anything from her brief observations, but their closeness had her mind already sprinting to judgment.

"I, uh...I was looking for Kyleer," Faythe lied awfully when they caught up to her. It was the first thing that came to mind to explain her aimless wandering without admitting she was looking for Reylan.

"What for?" He knew she was lying, and she wondered why he didn't call her out on it.

"Training," she blurted.

His eyes roved over her in accusation, and his brow arched at her attire. Faythe looked down at herself, not dressed for combat of any sort. Trying to salvage her awkward situation with the thickening tension, she inhaled a long breath.

"I'm just heading off to change," she added, jerking a thumb behind her and hoping he'd allow her to leave.

He didn't, but just as he opened his mouth, a melodic voice sounded instead.

"I've heard your skills are quite impressive in the training room. I hope we get the chance to spar sometime," Reylan's companion said eagerly.

Faythe was oddly nervous at her attention, shifting at the mention of her *skills*. How often was she talked about when she wasn't there to defend or counter for herself?

"Since General Killjoy over here isn't going to introduce us, allow me. I'm—"

"Commander Livia Arrowood," a voice filled in from behind Faythe.

Livia beamed brightly when her eyes fell upon the fae. "Five months apart and you address me formally, Izaiah?"

Faythe twisted to spot the youngest brother strolling leisurely toward them, his hands stuffed into his pockets and a devious smile at the edge of his lips. Livia passed Faythe to meet him, and the pair exchanged a tight embrace. It lasted long enough that Faythe felt the need to avert her gaze from their moment of reunion. She shifted back around, immediately meeting the hard gaze of Reylan. Her cheeks heated, and it felt odd that she didn't know how to act around him. Not when they'd shared a bed last night, as innocent as it was, and she had yet to find out if he held any feelings of regret or awkwardness. His expression gave away nothing.

Then Faythe's gaze caught on the stunning fae beside him, whom Reylan introduced. "This is General Lycus Warner. And may I introduce Her High—"

"Faythe," she cut in. "Just Faythe."

The general smiled, flashing a perfect set of white teeth and creating a dimple on his smooth brown skin. His eyes were an inviting deep chocolate hue that sparked with wonder as he fixed his gaze on her. "I believe you are far more than just Faythe, Your Highness." He gave a short bow, and Faythe didn't know how to react.

When his tall, built form straightened, she took a second to glance over him, dipping her head in acceptance of his respect, however odd it seemed. The first thing she noticed was that he wore all-black, unlike Reylan, who usually sported crimson accents on his attire. Then her eyes caught on the intricately carved emblem pinned to his shoulder. Her eyes widened.

"You're from Fenstead?" It wasn't really a question when the side-profiled stag symbolizing the great conquered kingdom was confirmation enough.

He nodded, his smile pained. "Indeed."

It was then she believed the lack of color in his attire, the emerald of his kingdom, was perhaps absent in respect of the kingdom they sought refuge in. Or in mourning, saving the added vibrancy for when Fenstead was reclaimed. The thoughts that swirled in her mind were dizzying, but she got out, "She's alive." Tearing her eyes from the clasp at his shoulder, Faythe met his gaze with hope. "Tauria Stagknight—she's in High Farrow."

General Lycus's face was full of understanding. "I am well aware my queen lives."

She shook her head. "Then why haven't you gone to her? She needs you. Her commanders, her people—she doesn't know how many of you survived." Faythe couldn't help the accusation that slipped into her tone, but in picturing her wonderful friend and how she longed to take back her home someday, it didn't make sense that those who could aid her— her own people—hadn't made themselves known.

"Queen Tauria Stagknight is exactly where she needs to be, safe and protected," he answered calmly.

"You're wrong."

"Faythe—" Reylan cut in, but she couldn't stop, feeling she owed it to her friend to voice what she'd heard Tauria lament over. The sorrow and guilt that was a permanent shadow across her gracious face.

"I think you'll find in the time you've spent away from her that Tauria isn't some frail princess. Not anymore. She doesn't need to be shielded. She is a queen who needs the strength and belief of her people."

"You were close with her?" Lycus observed.

"She helped me see a lot of things in myself. Her resilience is admirable. She also helped me feel welcome where I wasn't. If you're waiting for her to be ready, let me tell you, she has been for some time, and if you don't go to her, she may already be making plans to take matters into her own hands, General Lycus."

His expression firmed. Not in anger or irritation over what Faythe had brazenly said. He was calculating her every word as he stood with hands clasped behind his back. With her words spoken and passion dwindling, Faythe's nerves returned at his assessment. He was intimidatingly stern and beautiful, his hair dark, so short, and upon closer attention, textured with tight curls. When she tore her eyes from him to remember the fae behind her, something clicked.

Arrowood.

"My cousin." Reylan answered her curiosity.

Livia tilted her head at the mention. "Tragic, really. To be blood-related to someone so stern and boring. First day back, and all he can talk about is war camps, strategies, blah, blah, blah…"

Reylan scowled at her, but she responded with a teasing smirk. Faythe found herself smiling, amused by Livia's boldness. Her chest opened in relief that she was a relative of his. Faythe looked away, guilty at the thoughts that had swirled in her mind when she saw the pair so close.

Livia leaned a forearm on Izaiah's shoulder, and together with matching devious looks, Faythe imagined them running rings around Reylan.

"It is your job to report back," Reylan grumbled in defense.

"Allow our little Liv a moment to breathe," a new voice called from down the hall.

"*Little?*" Livia challenged, turning her head to track Kyleer as he approached with a wild grin. She dropped the threat when he got close enough for her to throw her arms around his neck. He embraced her tightly back.

"I thought I smelled trouble in the air when I woke up this morning," Kyleer mused when they released each other. He lifted a hand as if to tousle her perfectly formed braid, but she caught his wrist before he could, shoving it down while he rumbled a chuckle.

The sight stabbed Faythe's chest, causing a flashback of memories of her own best friend back in High Farrow. The solemn mood clouded her mind in an instant. She had exchanged a couple of letters with Jakon since she left, but they were vague in her guilt and shame that she had yet to Nightwalk and confirm she was physically well through Nik. What would he think of her?

A light hand on her back made her jolt, bringing Faythe back to the hallway where the brothers and Livia were in quiet chatter with the Fenstead general. Her head twisted to meet Reylan's concerned look.

"*Do you want to talk in private?*"

Faythe's heart skipped a beat at the question. Strangely, she couldn't bear to hold his gaze, flushing every time. She shook her head. "I have to go check on Reuben." Another lie that settled horribly in her stomach.

Faythe had hoped she would find the general alone, but with the eyes of four others on them her stage fright got the better of her, and the churning-up of old memories of her friends in High Farrow pushed her into a pit of despair. Everyone looked to her, and Reylan strained as if he were about to protest, but with a sweet smile, Faythe passed them all and took off back the way she came. Mercifully, no one followed, though she swore she felt Reylan begin to. The faint ripples of his want to go after her shivered at her back until something halted him.

Faythe was down her second corridor, about to turn the next sharp corner, when she sucked in a breath of horror, stopping abruptly as if she'd connected with a wall, mere inches from colliding with a tall, solid form instead. When her eyes traveled up from his chest, she was doused in ice. She stared wide-eyed in shock into the bright hazel eyes of the King of Rhyenelle. He stared back in mild surprise. Faythe didn't think she was still breathing. Immediately, she stepped aside, head bowed in submission on instinct.

"Forgive me, Your Majesty," she choked through a short breath from her racing heart. She had to clasp her hands at her back, tightly balling them to suppress the trembling. Faythe silently prayed he would continue on without further acknowledging her.

"There is no need for the formality, Faythe." If she didn't know any better, she might have believed the note of pain in his deep voice.

Faythe forced her gaze up and connected with solemn eyes that held hidden longing. In her gold irises he would see her mother, his lost love. Perhaps Faythe's being here was a mistake after all; she only served to remind him of the life he lost and the child he didn't know…possibly didn't even *want*. The thought twisted her gut with shameful guilt.

Agalhor inhaled visibly, his broad shoulders lifting with grace. His mouth opened without words as if he were deliberating. It seemed ridiculous, but Faythe thought she caught a hint of nervousness in his poise as he addressed her.

After some hesitation, he finally said, "Would you care to join me? I was just heading to the Glass Garden. I would very much like to show it to you."

Faythe was stunned. Though he'd invited her there many times since she arrived in Rhyenelle, sending a messenger and keeping his distance while she adjusted to her new surroundings, the offer coming direct from the great king struck her with the reality of her situation. Before her was not the King of Rhyenelle, but her *father*. Her hands fell to her sides, mouth opening to form a response. He was patient, but his eyes were laced with a twinge of sadness as if he anticipated her refusal.

"It's a kind offer, but my friend—"

"Is being taken care of as we speak," he assured her.

Faythe shifted her weight between her feet, having no excuse to spare her from the alone time with him. She couldn't avoid it forever—she knew this. Then Reylan's words of encouragement from last night echoed through her, along with the flare of hope that Agalhor might hold the answers she needed to cure her night terrors. At that thought, at what it could mean—granting her the opportunity to see her friends again if she could Nightwalk—Faythe took a deep breath and let some of her pent-up anxiety release in her exhale.

"Then I would love to accompany you, Your Majesty."

Agalhor's brow arched faintly in surprise, but then he matched her smile with a bright one of his own. "Please, you need not address me by my title. My home is yours. I hope in time you will find yourself at ease here." He motioned for her to walk, and she took the lead while he strolled beside her.

Faythe tried to maintain her outward composure, but internally, she was in nauseating turmoil. Her history with kings in the past was far from pleasant, but Agalhor was…*different*. She stole a sideward glance and wondered if anyone saw the resemblance they bore. Her hair perfectly matched the shade of the king's beside her: fair brown with hints of gold throughout. Her jaw was angled like his, only with a soft feminine touch.

When he looked down and caught her eye, she immediately averted her gaze with a hot flush.

Faythe didn't know what it was to have a father. She didn't know how to *act* now she was within reach of the one figure in her life she'd silently, sometimes painfully, longed for. Part of her wanted to resent her mother for depriving her of the bond they could have had, the lessons she could have learned, and the love that couldn't be matched by any other. Yet she couldn't. Couldn't bring herself to think one ill thought about her mother, who had given up so much to keep her safe, and who had ultimately sacrificed her life for it. All she could do was start building the life she could have had now she'd found the missing piece to fill the puzzle of *where* she came from.

They walked for some time in silence. Faythe flexed her fists to distract herself from the awkwardness. She didn't know what to say and couldn't be sure if Agalhor felt the same or was simply enjoying the peaceful walk in her company. He relieved some of her tension when he finally spoke.

"How are you finding Rhyenelle?" It was a boringly vague question, and she supposed he may as well have asked her about the weather. Nevertheless, she had to clear her throat, which felt uncomfortably tight, perhaps constricting to prevent her from saying something stupid.

"It's different," she said meekly. "In High Farrow, I didn't know any sort of luxury until…" She halted as dark memories flashed to the forefront of her mind. All her happy memories in the castle with Nik and Tauria, despite everything, were cruelly overshadowed by the torture and horrors she'd endured there. Faythe looked to the ground in shame.

"You don't have to explain your past to me today. Or ever, should you choose not to," he said softly.

She cast him a weak but grateful look, but she didn't miss the hint of sadness in his voice. He wanted to know her, and she wasn't scared to admit there was a large part of her that wanted to know him too and try to make up for lost time. She damned her own cowardice.

Faythe knew straight away that they were approaching their destination by the grand glass double doors that gave away the interior. Her breath was stolen from her at the beautiful sight: a room of endless white roses. The guard posted outside didn't hesitate to open one of those doors upon their approach, but Faythe halted anyway, looking to Agalhor—perhaps foolishly—for permission to enter the space that radiated purity and beauty. His face was eager, and he nodded for her to go in first.

It was a room made entirely of glass. Green stalks climbed the panes, perfectly tamed, with the most innocently blooming bright white roses in varying sizes. Faythe walked around the room in awe. The center held a circular bed of equally untarnished roses on a raised platform. She approached them, compelled to reach out and hold one. It hovered delicately in her palm. The stalks still had their thorns, reminding her of the hidden danger under their guise of beauty.

"You look just like her." Agalhor's voice was hushed as he remained by the door, silently observing.

Faythe felt a pang of guilt at the sad look on his face, his hard features softening, and knew she was stirring up old memories. She couldn't begin to comprehend the relationship he had with her mother —how deeply their love might have settled. The brokenness that flashed in his hazel eyes pained her heart, making her think of the loss he had suffered. The loss they *both* had suffered. It was clear in the look they exchanged that they were connected through that mutual devastation; they understood each other. Faythe had to look away to breathe for a second, forcing down the lump in her throat.

"This place is beautiful," she admired.

He gave a quick look around with a saddening smile. "Your mother loved to come here," he began, finally taking his own steps around the room. His fingers caressed the petals of a nearby rose, and she wondered if he was imagining their softness as her mother's face. "She would spend endless hours tending to them. I never understood her fascination. Not until she left and I began to come here myself."

Faythe stayed silent, but her heart began a hard beat, at risk of fracture, while he spoke of her.

"It's peaceful. I have spent many evenings here since. It opens the mind to quiet thought and calm emotion, though I am hopeless at gardening. I cannot take credit for its maintenance." He gave a soft chuckle, and Faythe's heavy mood lifted with the sound, a smile tugging at her lips.

She knew she could ease the king's burdens with what she knew was the real reason for her mother's leaving. Nerves gripped the words as in turn they would reveal everything about *her*. What would he think about his only child being a descendant of such a wicked evil? An Heir of Marvellas. The power she held, the weapon she could be become... It filled her with nauseating fear of his rejection. She couldn't stand to lose someone she had only just found.

"Something weighs on your mind," he observed, casting an encouraging look in her direction. "You can speak freely. I know this must all seem overwhelming, but you are free here, Faythe."

You may have been born in High Farrow, but you will always fly with the Phoenix. Her mother's words. She had wanted this, for them to find each other, and Faythe trusted her mother's encouragement.

"She didn't leave out of want." Faythe let the words fall from her mouth before she could allow her cowardice to stop her.

Agalhor looked taken aback. He straightened with piqued attention but remained quietly patient, as though he wouldn't protest if she didn't explain further. But Reylan was right. He deserved to know. Despite what he thought about Faythe when all was said and done; when he knew she was the reason his love was torn from him. If he resented her for it, Faythe would be able to live with it knowing she'd answered his decades-long question.

"She left to protect me," she admitted. "And I fear…I fear it was in vain. I'm sorry—"

"Faythe," he interjected, brow furrowed in distress. "I do not accept your apology as it is not needed. Not for anything."

Faythe shook her head. "I am to blame. You don't know everything—"

"I do not need to. You were but a child, unborn when she made her choice to leave."

"She thought she was protecting me from a fate that caught up to me all the same." Faythe's tone was harsh—she couldn't hold it back. She didn't deserve his defense. "She left you for nothing. She gave up the life she had here, people who loved her, for nothing. She died for *nothing!*" Her voice rose a note, feeling the need to argue *for* her guilt as it had been slowly eating away at her for over ten years. "Before you decide what to do with me, what you *want* from me…you need to hear the truth. Everything I am, everything I've done, and everything I'm set to do. I need you to hear it all before you waste your time on me." Her heart thundered to talk assertively to the king in front of her. Her *father.*

He rolled his powerful shoulders, hands clasped behind his back, as if to give her his full, undivided attention. It rattled her nerves awfully. "I am all ears, Faythe. But you should know, not a minute of time is wasted with you. Not when we have so many years to make up for."

Faythe's eyes burned, her forehead crumpling to suppress her tears at the genuine passion in his tone. It was exactly what she needed to hear, but she couldn't let herself relax. Not yet.

"Tell me that again once you've heard everything."

CHAPTER 17

Faythe

THE KING KEPT respectfully silent while Faythe paced around the Glass Garden. She spoke her story to the brilliant white blooms, terrified to meet the hazel gaze of her father and gauge his reactions. Faythe's past was woven with tales of dangerous antics, fictitious-sounding truths, and a lingering sense of unfulfillment. She told him of all she could remember about her mother in her early years, then her impoverished but loving years with Jakon. She spoke of her fighting days and the impossible ability she never knew she harbored. How her savior came in the form of Nik, and how she landed in his father's service and suffered at the hands of Captain Varis. Faythe didn't hide anything, admitting her role in his death.

She had come to terms with what she was and what she was capable of. Every action she'd taken she owned, and if anyone else might judge her for it, she would accept that judgment. Even from her own father.

"So, now you know," Faythe concluded. Her breaths were labored as if she'd exerted herself through exercise, emotions fluctuating from telling the tales as quickly as possible before they were swallowed by her cowardice and shame. "Her leaving was never because she fell out of love or changed her mind about the life she wanted for herself. It was because of me. She thought she could avoid a fate that was already in motion."

Faythe finally mustered the courage to face him, but his expression gave little away. He was contemplating, likely trying to absorb everything, a decade's worth of knowledge crammed into the space of a few hours. It was her turn to be patient as she counted the hard beat of her heart while he deliberated his verdict on her mess of a life. What made her thoughts wild was that she couldn't be sure which part he was stuck on.

After a few painful minutes, he saved her from being crushed under the weight of her own anticipation. "Then she did not die in vain," he said, heartbreak singing in his tone.

Faythe frowned, about to argue against his statement, bewildered he hadn't been paying attention after all, but he went on.

"Make no mistake, Faythe, there is *nothing* I would not have risked to keep you both safe. Though I do not fault her for leaving now I know the truth." He paused, and the hard shift of his expression was akin to how Reylan responded to the revelation of her ties to Marvellas. She couldn't be sure what he was calculating.

"She bought you time," Agalhor pondered, not meeting her eye. "Had she stayed, had you been born here in the public eye...perhaps Marvellas would have found you sooner. By the *Gods*, Faythe, it is inconceivable to believe, this prophesy you speak of, but I will choose to believe you. And to believe in your mother, who left out of love for you."

Faythe's eyes stung as a sorrowful marble formed in her throat. She didn't know how to reply, and as they stared at each other...something changed. She felt the connection to him in that look; saw what she knew her mother saw. The male without a crown. Agalhor was a fierce warrior and protector, loved by his people, feared by his enemies. And

Faythe... She was half of him. Or at least, she believed she had the potential to be, strengthened by the pride in his eyes, which she allowed herself to accept, but which left her at a complete loss for words.

"There were a lot of people who didn't understand our relationship." He moved around the center bed of flowers between them. "How could a fae love a human and expect anything lasting to come from it? There were a lot of people who were against us, claiming I was weak, that perhaps I'd let your mother cloud my judgment. Or wicked, and that she was by my side against her will." Faythe noticed the twitch of anger on his face at this assumption. "We didn't listen to any of it. I knew what we had between us was more than infatuation. Something far, far more." He stopped a few feet away, and Faythe opened herself up to feel the echo of his heartbreak. "No one understood, and I'll admit, even I couldn't comprehend it at first. What I felt for her...I could only describe it as if we were mates. Impossible? Perhaps not. Perhaps we've allowed ourselves to become too ignorant in our beliefs to ever conceive of something that defies what we think we know."

Faythe was stunned by his passion and moved by his wisdom. His thoughtful face turned upward in a warm smile that eased the sadness.

"Come—I would like to show you more."

She matched his eager look, wanting to see and hear more from the king who could tell her so much about her mother and everything she loved about the Kingdom of the Phoenix. Slowly, she felt her confidence rising, her walls crumbling—but Agalhor didn't once look at her with doubt or dismay, and Faythe allowed herself to believe she could finally set aside the heavy fear of being cast out or rejected. For now.

Together, they left the Glass Garden and walked the halls lined with crimson tapestries. Faythe was mostly silent, tuning in to the serene sound of his rough voice as he told small tales of Rhyenelle's history. She was fully engrossed and didn't think she could ever get enough knowledge, nor would there be enough years in her mortal lifespan to learn every intricate wonder of the Kingdom of the

Phoenix, mighty, powerful, and so highly regarded as it was. It was no surprise to her that Rhyenelle had never been conquered in all its existence.

Faythe followed without question, too hypnotized by his words to care where he led her as she spied massive glass doors at the end of their next corridor. Like every other door, they were opened before they reached them, and the two walked out onto a large stone-walled balcony. She continued walking all the way until she braced her palms on the cold rail, breath catching at the view.

They were looking out over the entire courtyard, and from this height, the first thing to grab Faythe's attention was the intricately painted giant symbol adorning the center. She'd known it was there from having walked over it, but taking in the full image—the sigil of Rhyenelle, a Phoenix with wings splayed—was humbling and strength-invoking.

"Did you know our ancestors were among the first of the Phoenix Riders?" Agalhor questioned, though he knew it was likely she didn't.

Her stunned look made him smile wider, and a gleam of excitement caught his eye as if he found great delight in her eagerness to know more.

"King Matheus was the first King of Rhyenelle. Your direct ancestor, Faythe. He led a legion of warriors through the Fire Mountains in an expedition to the Niltain Isles almost ten thousand years ago, and it was there they discovered the first nests of the Phoenix."

Faythe's eyes alone begged for him to continue. He huffed a short laugh at her enthusiasm.

"Magnificent creatures they were. But they were wild, rogue, and attacked at first sight as I would imagine it was the first time either species had encountered the other. The Red Years is what they were named in history, an age of blood and fire."

"Did they kill them all—the Phoenix birds?" Faythe's chest tightened at the thought, but she felt she already knew the answer as she, like everyone else, believed the creature was a myth. No one had seen a Fire-bird in thousands of years.

"Not at first," he answered. "No. Something unexpected happened." He looked over the grounds, straight and poised, and Faythe had to swallow hard, intimidated by the great ruler. How would she ever be able to hold herself to that standard? How would she ever convince an entire kingdom she could walk in the footsteps of someone naturally born for the role like Agalhor? The sinking thoughts didn't get a change to make her spiral as the king spoke again without taking his eyes off the grounds below.

"This castle was rebuilt and expanded on to accommodate the Phoenix Riders. They would land in this very courtyard. Once they succeeded at making peace with them, that is. Those with the gift to tame the creatures, connect with them, were of the highest ranking and regarded as warriors in Rhyenelle, respected across all seven kingdoms of Ungardia and even beyond."

"What happened to them?" Faythe asked in awe. She couldn't imagine what could have made them extinct if what the king said was true.

He left the story hanging, and Faythe almost bit out a protest as he turned from the stone rail, giving a nod for her to follow before retreating inside. She swallowed her protest, knowing better than to demand answers from a *king*, estranged father or not.

They walked together through another series of passages, some she had not ventured through before. He kept the conversation flowing but to her slight annoyance diverted it from the tale of the Firebirds she held onto at the edge of her mind. Still, she immersed herself in his recount of smaller historic events and antics from his days with her mother that brightened Faythe's mood immensely.

Down a long stretch of passage, Faythe's attention was stolen, the breath taken from her when she glimpsed the sea of color adorning the walls. Intricate paintings, mesmerizingly beautiful, and when she got close enough to make out the details, every picture held a story. The main attraction that caught her attention were the many depictions of the Phoenix in battle. She concluded these must be the visual representation of the "Red Years," as Agalhor had called the period of carnage. While there was blood and war and creatures fought out of fear...the paintings almost made it seem poetic.

Agalhor picked up on his storytelling exactly where she'd hoped, and she tuned in to his words while the colors in front of her added a whole new depth. "When they came across the creatures in their nest, the fae and humans were in the wrong. They had unwittingly ventured onto occupied territory. Matheus knew this and had every intention of retreating his forces and leaving the beasts in peace."

She realized why he'd held onto the rest of the story until now. It was easier to see, to *feel*, the emotions and be able to understand while he spoke his tales into the paintings, filling the gaps the visual depictions couldn't communicate.

"Though the Fire Mountains are under Rhyenelle jurisdiction, Matheus wanted no conflict between any species in his kingdom. He planned to let them be, perhaps figure out a route through the mountains that wouldn't disrupt them. They returned to Ellium straight away, but King Matheus couldn't get the creatures off his mind and felt a silent call to go back...alone."

Faythe raised an eyebrow, meeting Agalhor's eye. He gave a small nod and a smile.

"He went back without a single guard, knowing the dangers. I believe there are some things in this world that we can't explain. Feelings, energies, *fate*, as one might call it."

The next painting brought the scene Agalhor spoke of to life. Faythe couldn't help her small gasp at the artwork. A lone figure stood on the mountain's edge, barely more than a speck of shadow between the tall, jagged peaks. The fae stared off against the most beautiful creature Faythe had ever seen. It was huge, reducing the fae to less than the size of one of its powerful taloned feet. The bird's splayed wings were vibrant against the dull stone of the mountain. Hues of red and amber infused with faint flecks of yellow, torched at the tips with blazing fire. Faythe was captivated and couldn't stop the hand that reached out to trace the flames that licked along its feathers.

"When Matheus arrived at the same place in the Fire Mountains, he was greeted by the Great Phoenix who would come to be named as Atherius in legend. She was their leader, their protector, and Matheus faced her with no fear. Not because he was exceptionally brave, but because he understood her, one monarch to another. But Atherius was not so quick trust." He took a step closer in a silent push toward the next painting.

Faythe reluctantly forced her eyes from the beauty with splayed wings. The next depiction quickened her pulse, as if she could feel herself in the scene as fire blasted over a rock the small figure of the king crouched behind. She felt her body flush, imagining the blaring heat that would have encased him around that stone shield.

"Was he killed?" she asked breathlessly.

Agalhor huffed a laugh. "I would not waste my breath on a tale with such a disappointing ending." He shot her a teasing look. "No—quite the opposite happened. You see, the Phoenix is a fiercely protective bird, but also incredibly loyal and intelligent. Some believe the king reached a point of insanity with how he sought to gain Atherius's trust. He didn't fight back and allowed her to blast her fire over and over while he merely focused on hiding to stay alive. Soon, she stopped. Matheus faced off with her once again and heard her name through her eyes. He believed they were bonded somehow, and to prove it, he turned and ran until he leaped off the mountainside."

Faythe snapped her head to him with an incredulous look. He only nodded to the next painting. When Faythe's eyes landed on it, she was stunned.

"Madness or brilliance, no one will ever truly know. But Atherius caught him, and from then on, an unbreakable bond was forged. Soon after, he took more of his warriors to the mountains, and more alliances were made, but not all were able to capture the mind and soul of a Phoenix. It is still unclear what it was about these particular fae that made them *worthy* of a pairing with the Firebirds. I believe it had something to do with a pure soul, those with the right intentions and goodness in their hearts. The Phoenixes were a highly intelligent species. Some believed they could see right through to the very essence of a person."

"I don't understand… What happened to them?" If his story was real history—and perhaps naively she was falling for it as he spoke with such passion—it didn't make sense that they would cease to exist.

"They lived in perfect peace for many centuries. They were invaluable allies and strengthened the kingdom immeasurably. That is, until Matheus was betrayed by his brother, Balemorus. His younger sibling didn't succeed in forging a bond with a Phoenix, and it drove him wild with jealousy and resentment. Matheus had everything—the crown, the people's love, the most powerful of companions in Atherius." Agalhor's voice dropped darkly, and Faythe gleaned the grim look in the deep creases of his face, anticipating the story was about to take the most sinister of turns. "The birds had long settled into peace with the fae and humans. They still lived in the Fire Mountains and were called upon by their bonded through an internal channel. Balemorus killed her—Atherius—when Matheus was not there to protect her. He assembled his own legions loyal to him, and in the dead of night, he attacked. Atherius was the one to let them pass, so they killed her first."

Faythe had to blink hard at the pools forming in her eyes as she landed on the final painting. Her heart fractured, the cut so deep and painful. She couldn't understand why she felt so moved to see the slain Phoenix birds. The carnage of wings and blood that painted the scene.

"I am sorry, Faythe. It was not my intention to upset you with this—"

"No, please. I want to hear the rest."

Agalhor looked reluctant, but she took a deep breath to collect herself and gave him a nod of reassurance. "No one really knows what happened next, but they were all gone by the time Matheus felt Atherius's pain and raced to the Fire Mountains, only to arrive to complete devastation. A lot of them were dead, both bird and fae, but there are some who believe perhaps Balemorus did not succeed in annihilating the Firebirds completely. That maybe some managed to flee and now reside in another part of the world."

"The Phoenix regenerates, does it not?" Faythe perked up slightly, hoping perhaps the story could take another turn and would finish with a somewhat happy ending.

Agalhor's sad look killed her hope in an instant, and her face fell again.

The end of the corridor of art opened up into a grand library. The hall was triumphant. Faythe cast her eyes up to the dauntingly high domed roof, in utter awe of the model Firebird that flew over their heads, taking up the whole space. She wondered if its size was an accurate representation and felt her throat turn bone-dry at the prospect, but she remained giddy with wondrous thrill.

They kept walking inside, and straight ahead she spied a long glass case on a podium. Even from this distance, Faythe knew exactly what it was and subconsciously quickened her steps, in complete shock until she was right in front of the artifact.

A single feather was displayed as if it were floating within. A pure crimson red with tendrils of amber and the faintest flecks of yellow. It spanned at least the length of her arm. Her mouth was wide as she gawked at it. All reservations about whether the tales were fact or fiction were made indisputable by the evidence in front of her. How many knew of its existence?

"Every thousand years, the Phoenix dies naturally and incinerates itself. You are right: from their own ashes, they regenerate and start their life cycle once again. Unless…"

"Unless they're killed," she concluded on her own, not taking her eyes off the feather, transfixed by its silent beckoning.

"Yes, I'm afraid so. But killing a Phoenix is not without consequence. As a result, Balemorus and all those who committed the heinous crime were cursed. Many of them never left that mountain, damned to some disease that turned them into hideous, disfigured beings people say roam there still and have multiplied in numbers to make the mountains dangerously impassible. Others who managed to make it out found they could not produce heirs, could not attract an ounce of love or kindness, and were stripped of any abilities they had, leaving them alone and bitter. Many took their own lives, but Matheus wouldn't allow Balemorus that mercy. He kept him alive and locked up for well over a millennium, until they both faded on the same day. Matheus would have left this world for the Afterlife, but Balemorus was damned for the Netherworld, where his soul will be suffering the consequences of his actions still."

Faythe involuntarily shuddered at his dire fate in both life and death. It was what he deserved, but it was horrific to conceive of. Fixing her eyes on the feather once more, she strangely felt its pull as if it were a life force within the glass case. The more she stared, the more entrancing and vivid it became. It was no longer just an artifact; not a decorative monument. She thought she could see sparks of flame, tendrils of live, lapping fire, woven between each strand of fine hair.

"You feel it too, don't you?" Agalhor's voice stole her attention, and she pulled her head back, unaware she had been inching it slowly closer to glimpse every detail of the magnificent feather.

"What is it?" she asked, stunned by its silent enchantment.

Agalhor cantered his head as he observed it. "I used to believe it might belong to Atherius herself and that Matheus had kept it to commemorate her long past his days. But then I came to discover the feathers of a Phoenix don't hold their vibrancy in death if slain. They dull and lose all the effects of enchantment and fire so no one may use them. They are powerful, believed to hold great healing properties, and can be made into elixirs for all kinds of strength-heightening potions. So, you see, it cannot belong to Atherius." His deep frown told her he too was puzzled by its origin. "I've never known anyone else to feel its pull like I do, but perhaps it has something to do with our bloodline."

Agalhor used the term so casually. "Our bloodline." It meant more to her than she thought it would, and she glanced at him at the subtle declaration. She was part of him. And that thought brought forth another line that connected them both: Nightwalking.

"Have you ever been afraid? So terrorized by your own past that it haunts you in sleep?"

His features creased, and she couldn't be sure if it was because she'd disturbed his memories with the question or because it pained him to know Faythe spoke of her own experience. "Many times," he said, and she was grateful he was willing to share his vulnerable side. "Why do you ask?" His question felt loaded, but out of respect, it seemed he wouldn't assume anything without her willingness to open up unprompted. Perhaps Reylan had already informed him of her night terrors and he was waiting for her to finally come to him.

"Nik—King Nikalias," she corrected, thinking it more appropriate to address him by title, as odd as the formality sounded. "He once told me Nightwalkers don't have their own dreams and nightmares. Yet... I've suffered with them nearly every night."

Agalhor gave her a knowing look, confirming he anticipated exactly what was troubling her. "What you're experiencing, Faythe, is your own tormenting guilt," he explained. "The mind is a complicated thing. It is our biggest asset, yet it can be our worst enemy. Whatever horrors befell you or others, you've taken them all on your own shoulders, and until you let go and find acceptance you will keep reliving those nightmares as your mind's way of punishing you."

Faythe's shoulders fell. She felt as if she had already tried to let go—had spent all these months since leaving High Farrow trying to set aside her fears and convince herself she was safe. "How do I make it stop?"

He offered a pitiful smile. "For me, your mother helped," he said, and Faythe perked up at the mention. "After the Great Battles, I was riddled with those night terrors for decades. Until I came across a wondrous young woman in the outer ring of Ellium. She sold baked goods at a market stall, but I knew straight away there was far more to her than her delicate nature."

"So they went away…because you fell in love?" Faythe interjected, her hope deflating a little.

Agalhor chuckled softly. "No, not at all. The nightmares have nothing to do with how others perceive you. They key is in your own self-acceptance. Your mother helped me to see the strength I'd buried under mountains of grief and guilt. She helped me to see I was worth something and that my time here wasn't finished. I couldn't submit to those terrors that would have ultimately driven me mad beyond salvation. She helped me believe I was worth the life I still held when so many others had lost theirs at my hand—literally or collaterally."

Faythe's chest filled with warmth at the way he spoke of her. She would never get to see her parents together, but she *felt* the love he harbored for her even to this day, and she knew he would for the rest of his days. It gave her the small hope that perhaps such an unbreakable love existed in the world for her: a love that defied death to keep on existing past their time in this world. Perhaps she had already found it, as she held Agalhor's eye and thought she saw it there. A father's love. Her eyes burned, and she had to furrow her brow to force back the wave of emotion as she looked at him from a new perspective. Not as a daunting king, nor one who held so much influence and power. In that moment, all she saw was her father.

"I never thought I would have this chance in my life—to feel happiness again. After your mother, I vowed never to seek another. Rhyenelle still had an heir thanks to my brother." Agalhor paused as if he too was fighting his emotions. He saw beneath all that was impossible and dark about Faythe to find some tiny beacon of light that he believed was worth a chance. "Then there you were, with her eyes, the most precious gift of all. A daughter I didn't think I deserved."

Faythe felt a wetness trail down one cheek, but she made no sound.

"When you spoke among the chaos of the High Farrow throne room and everyone listened, I saw her spirit in you then, and I saw myself too. Dear Faythe,"—he took a step toward her, and she didn't flinch as his hand brushed her face—"I am so proud of the woman you have become despite all that was kept from you, and I know your mother is smiling at us now. We may not have the past to reflect on, but the present is all the brighter, the future all the more hopeful."

Faythe couldn't stop herself and fell into him, needing to convey how grateful she was. She had no words as he'd stolen them all. All she could do was show him she agreed; she was happy to have found him.

Agalhor tensed for just a second, but then he relaxed and encased her in his arms.

For a suspended moment in time…she was nothing. Nothing but her innocent child-self. She closed her eyes, needing to savor this moment for that little girl who'd spent years longing for this feeling of safely, protection, completeness…

For her father.

CHAPTER 18

Nikalias

"I DON'T NEED to advise you of how dangerous this plan is, do I?"

Nik paced the length of his council chamber as he relayed everything to Jakon. It seemed ridiculous that the only person he'd thought to confide in was the human. Though, to his surprise, Jakon had been the one to come to him. Nik couldn't hold back the outpouring of his building rage, frustration, and helplessness against Tauria's reckless plan. And he couldn't deny it was a relief to know he wasn't alone in thinking it was too much of a risk.

"She won't be dissuaded," Nik grumbled. He stopped pacing at his desk, bracing his hands on it while he clenched his teeth and shook his head. "Damn it, she's too headstrong and stubborn for her own good."

Jakon's chuckle stole his attention, and Nik whipped his head up, incredulous. "Sounds a lot like someone else we both know."

Just for a second, Nik's rigid shoulders loosened, and he even smiled at the face that was brought to the forefront of his mind. The brightness they exchanged was short-lived, however, as even in reflection of Faythe,

the sadness of her not being nearby overshadowed everything. "I'm sure she'll contact us soon," Nik said quietly. It was a weak assurance when he couldn't be certain Faythe was even capable of Nightwalking so far. He figured if she were, she would have tried at least once by now.

Jakon only nodded, averting his gaze to conceal the void left in her wake. While Nik felt her absence strongly, he couldn't imagine what it was like for Jakon, who had never been parted from her for so long and from such a distance. With that thought came a sharp pain in his chest —because how Jakon felt about Faythe was exactly how Nik would feel about Tauria when they were torn apart.

"Marlowe has a couple of clients who need work finished. I think we're planning to leave for Rhyenelle by month's end."

This news only made Nik's sinking gut heavier. Never in his lifetime did he think he would be pining after the company of two ordinary *humans*, yet aside from Tauria, their company was effortless and freeing. There was no one else in his court who didn't see him simply for the crown he wore, either as a means to gain or a pawn to manipulate. It was a desolate thought to imagine his days without a friend he could confide in without question.

Nik's answering nod was vacant while his mind started to darken with ghostly thoughts. Like loneliness circling, tormenting, before it finally settled in permanent residence when they were all gone. He was a king, a figure who should place duty before all else, and only with a steel mind would he find the will to go on for his kingdom no matter what.

Jakon's deep breath as he rose from the chair snapped him from his dark spiral. "What Tauria poses is a risk—a huge risk. But I can't deny it is also brilliant. She may be our best shot at getting reliable eyes in Olmstone."

"It's not worth the cost of her life."

"Of course not. But personal feelings aside, she's not doing this for you or for High Farrow. She needs this for herself and for Fenstead—to regain what was stolen from her, and I don't mean her land or title.

188

You've protected her, and I know you want to shield her from it, but you may need to be willing to let her go so she can rise to be the queen she is supposed to be."

Nik was stunned for a second. The counsel Jakon offered was unexpected, but every word he uttered came from his heart. He had underestimated just how observant and attentive the human was, and in that moment, he saw every admirable trait Faythe had spoken of many times.

"I distrusted you for a long time, Nik. I resented you, thinking you had used Faythe, led her on with a false identity, and claimed her heart with no intention of holding it."

Nik refrained from dropping his head in shame.

"But I realize now…that you have held it. Protected it—just not in the way you both might have felt a pull toward, to see if there could be more between you. There's no fault in that."

The look they shared was one of understanding. It was the first Nik remembered from his observations of Jakon before they met—before he met Marlowe. While it felt liberating to hear Jakon voice what he tried to convince himself of to soothe his guilt, the fact remained he *was* wrong to pursue Faythe as more than a friend to help train her in her abilities.

His chest hollowed out at the thought of Tauria and how badly he had wronged her too. If there was a chance she could find happiness with another, find the dedication she deserved, perhaps letting her go was the best way—the *only* way—he could truly show his love for her.

"Are you going to be all right without her?" Jakon's question was filled with a knowing sadness. "Without all of us?" he added.

Nik appreciated the subtle meaning. Against all odds and obscurities, they had become friends, and while Tauria's absence was near unbearable to imagine, he couldn't deny a void would be left with the humans gone too. Mustering a nod, he added a forced smile. For his duty and his kingdom, he had to be.

CHAPTER 19

Zaiana

ZAIANA FELT NOTHING. Heard nothing. She was weightless, sinking slowly, suspended in time. She imagined she was falling as she submerged herself in the body of black water, letting herself drift into a depthless void in her mind where she was simply…nothing.

When her body defied her desire to sink deeper, she reluctantly forced herself to swim up. Zaiana inhaled deeply as she broke through the surface water, smoothing her long hair back from her face as it clung to her skin. When she opened her eyes, she didn't hide her deadly glare from who she spied across the baths.

Maverick's smile was devious where he leaned against a bulge in the cavernous stone wall, hands in his pockets as he watched her. The black waters concealed her naked body as she was submerged to her shoulders, but she specifically chose this hour, in the dead of night, so she would have the place to herself. As she always did. The dark demon's presence riled her annoyance as he likely knew this and had decided to impose on her private time anyway.

"Get out," she demanded in a cold, dead tone.

It only made his smile grow, and she flexed in irritation. "This is a public space," he answered casually, in a way he knew tested her patience.

It wasn't out of modesty Zaiana kept her body hidden in the water up to her collarbone. She never let anyone see her marred flesh from the many punishments she'd earned. It was the main reason she bathed when she knew she'd have the baths to herself.

"What do you want?" she asked, trying to keep her tone disinterested. Any reaction was entertainment for Maverick. She often found no emotion was the quickest way to lose his interest and get him to leave.

He didn't respond with words. Instead, he peeled himself from the wall, not taking his eyes off hers. His mouth curled in feline delight as he reached for the buttons of his tailored jacket. Zaiana ground her teeth, realizing what he intended. She wanted to turn away from him, damn what he would make of her naked body, and leave him to bathe alone before she would share the water with him. But a part of her flared in defiance. To leave now would be an act of defeat. They held each other's stares in silent challenge to see who would balk first as he began to undress. She'd be damned if she lost to him.

Maverick removed his jacket then his shirt. Zaiana didn't blink or look away. He was a glorious being, and she would be a fool to deny he was beautiful. He flexed his impressive wings as he undid his pants next and let them fall. She refused to avert her gaze from his black orbs. He smirked, and she cursed colorfully internally, thinking perhaps he'd caught the flinch of her eyes that gave away her curiosity. He took the stone steps into the black waters deliberately slowly until he was submerged past distraction.

His hair caught the moonlight that flooded in from the open cave roof, and the strands of silver across the midnight hue were stunning. They further defined the contours of his impeccable face, but she didn't give him the satisfaction of a reaction as he inched closer. She kept her eyes hard, her expression cold.

"A little chilly in here, don't you think?" he remarked with a smug look. "Allow me." He raised his hands to float just below the surface, and Zaiana watched bubbles form from the heat emanating under his palms. It was impressive, she had to admit, that he could conjure the heat of fire without flame. Water should be his natural enemy, but his ability was adaptable. Zaiana, on the other hand, always held an edge of caution around water. If she wasn't careful, her bolts could strike whoever was in contact with the water. She wasn't immune to a blast of her own current if it was conducted back to her.

Heat encased her, and she shivered as she'd grown accustomed to the cold. She wouldn't thank him for it, but she enjoyed the warmth that relaxed her tense muscles.

Once he was satisfied with the temperature that misted around them, Maverick splayed his wings and leaned against the bath edge with an overexaggerated sigh of relaxation.

"Why are you here?" she asked in a flat tone, wishing nothing more than to be alone.

He remained unfazed by her obvious hatred for his unwanted company. He lazily swirled his fingers over the water, creating ripples to disturb its stillness. "You should be thanking me, you know," he said casually, ignoring her question. As if he felt her simmering anger, a curl of amusement appeared on his mouth without looking at her. "The High Lord got to witness you at the height of your power. How easy it was to get you to unleash a glimpse of what you're truly capable of."

Her fists clenched under the water even though the way he spoke, she dared to believe, held mild admiration. "You would be dead if that were the height of my power."

Maverick didn't bother to counter.

Zaiana went on. "You knew Mordecai was here, and you knew it could have gotten me executed." She'd broken the law against attacking

A THRONE FROM THE ASHES

Maverick before. It was perhaps the hardest law for her to uphold, and by far the most foolish law to exist. It always resulted in some brutal physical punishment, but they wouldn't kill her. She held slight satisfaction in the knowledge she was too useful to them to be killed. But in the presence of the High Lord, they wouldn't have second-guessed the command for her to be put down if he gave it.

"I *knew* that if you attacked first, you would be far less likely to be given a death sentence than I."

Zaiana couldn't suppress her frown. "What are you implying?" she demanded even though she already suspected what he meant.

He slid her a knowing look. "I don't know what he told you, but you and I weren't the only candidates for the quest Mordecai posed. I overheard them mulling over some others. Even the masters were eager to put themselves forward for the esteemed role. Whatever it is, it's important. I simply made sure out of all the names he heard, you and I were the only ones who stuck."

Zaiana's eyes narrowed on him. He had no reason to lie, and his plan was just as self-serving as it was almost a favor to her. It remained a matter of mercy and luck she hadn't been fatally reprimanded for the fight. But perhaps he was right. After remembering the leniency the High Lord had with her, she had to wonder *why* he'd spared her from punishment. She could admit she thought Maverick brilliant for the dangerous scheme, but she would rather be killed by Mordecai's hand than give him the satisfaction.

"I'm looking forward to our little battle," he said casually as he closed his eyes and tipped his head back, basking in the moonlight.

Zaiana scoffed. "Calling it that would imply significant time and worthy opposition. I plan to make it quick."

He straightened his head, black eyes twinkling with a thrill at the challenge. "Have I ever told you your confidence is wickedly attractive? Even if misplaced."

Zaiana rolled her eyes, grinding her teeth to prevent herself from reacting in the way she knew he was trying to provoke. He delighted in anything he could get out of her, good or bad, though the former was almost nonexistent. She would have despised him, but even that inspired great satisfaction in the sadistic demon. So she tried not to feel anything toward him at all.

Maverick braced his elbows on the uneven stone edge of the bath. Her traitorous eyes flashed to admire the flexed muscles of his torso as he did, but she didn't allow them to linger. If he noticed her looking he said nothing. Not even a smirk to gloat as he held her gaze once more. She broke first, twisting to also lean back, wings splayed, drifting at arm's length so she could keep a close eye on him.

"I only got us the game. I still have every intention of winning," he went on.

Zaiana smiled to herself with the excitement that pulsed through her at his opposition. Like her, Maverick relished in competition. It was *fun* for them, even when it involved pain and brutality regardless of whether they won or lost. It was one guilty pleasure they shared. As creatures born to feel nothing, they indulged in the opportunity to feel *something*.

"You're lucky no one's here. It would only add to your humiliation when you can't put skill to your arrogance."

Maverick chuckled—a low, deep rumble that vibrated over the ripples of water. She even felt a faint flicker of desire at the sound. Out of the corner of her eye, she caught the movement of his arm reaching over to her.

"Touch me with that hand, Maverick," she warned without turning her head to him, "and you'd best be prepared to lose it."

His fingers lingered over the curve of her wing. The pulse from the near touch was enough to make her shiver. It was a bold move even for Maverick, and she could tell he relished in her threat. Wisely, he retreated his arm, but his gleaming reaction told her he'd gotten what he wanted from her even without the connection.

Maverick glided through the water to reach the other side, twisting so he could face her instead. She kept her face emotionless as she was forced to look at him. Tresses of his thick midnight hair curled over his forehead, and a small dimple indented his cheek on one side. As it always did when he wore the taunting smirk she hated. Hated because it was a sign of the unique amusement he got from her alone. And for her own thoughts that scattered for a split second when she saw it.

"I heard about your new little recruit," he drawled, once again settling against the stone edge. "Are you turning soft, Zaiana? Or perhaps you're looking for someone to blame when you lose."

Zaiana smiled deviously but didn't let it reach her eyes. "I don't need to explain my reasons." She played it off to avoid giving away her confidence in the young dark fae, who she had high hopes would be the complete opposite to a simple filled space. "And you need not concern yourself with my choices."

Maverick's brow arched, his smirk remaining. "Your choices are highly predictable, which makes it all the easier for me to prepare to take you and your little team down."

She itched to lash out in defense, but she saw the gleam in this eye that expected it from her. *Wanted* her anger to expose her weaknesses. Instead, she raised her chin after taking a few seconds to calm down. "You might think you hold a hand of surprise, but the truth is, it doesn't matter who you force to side with you in this fight. We may require a team in rule, but when it comes down to it, only two on the field really matter. You against me. We've battled many times, Maverick." She cantered her head as his gloating faded. "We both know the odds don't hold in your favor."

"Odds," he scoffed. "People listen to the odds when they're afraid. In favor, odds are a reckless confidence. Against, they hold one back from believing in their strength to win. I can tell how much this quest means to you—the chance to get away from the mountain for however long they relax the leash. If you beg, perhaps I'll go easy on you."

Zaiana flared. It was a lie as there was nothing that would make Maverick concede. He was arguably even more stubborn and proud than she was. Even still, the suggestion that she would ever resort to such measures itched her temper.

"Did you only come here to insult me?" The hum of lightning in her veins stung the surface of her skin as she held the bolts back, realizing now that perhaps the most lethal combination was her, Maverick, and a body of water. Part of her thought it might be worth suffering the pain of her own currents if it was inflicted on him all the same.

"I came," he drawled, hand swirling lazily around the surface water, "to enjoy a peaceful bath."

Zaiana bit back her scoff, having had enough of the jesting for one night. She swam for the edge, but when she got to the shallow end, which ascended into natural, uneven stone steps, she halted. It flared her anger that she wouldn't get to storm away without further acknowledgment of his presence, but reluctantly, she turned her head back to check if he was staring before exposing herself. Her scars were a hidden armor she didn't reveal to anyone.

Maverick *was* staring, as she expected, and at his smirk of amusement she was about to screw what he saw to make a point. But then he turned his head away, fingertips tracing the jagged ledge as if to occupy himself.

Zaiana didn't hesitate and took the opportunity, not knowing how many seconds his subdued deviance would hold out for. She quickly slipped into a robe that hid the lattice of her back and chest at least then snatched up her clothes, making to leave as his voice traveled to her with a darkness that swept a shudder over her body.

"Which of them hurt you?"

She dared a glance back. Maverick's expression was hard to decipher. There was a coldness that was always present, but now it seemed woven with a chilling wrath. He meant which of the masters had inflicted her *punishments*. Why he cared to ask she couldn't be sure.

Zaiana raised her chin, casting her eyes to the exit as her feet pressed for it.

She didn't look at him again as she muttered coldly, "All of them."

The wind howled, and bitter air whipped at her damp hair in the dead of night. Zaiana sat perched on the high peak of the mountain's edge, observing the young dark fae who had found a dipped alcove of stone to curl into that would shield her from the harsh blasts. She'd somehow managed to gather provisions for a small fire. It was impressive as this wasn't a skill they were commonly taught. Once again, Amaya had proven herself to be smart and resourceful.

Zaiana didn't know why she'd bothered to come out here after her disrupted moment of quiet in the baths. Perhaps to see if the cold had claimed Amaya's life on the first night, or to gauge if she would make it through the whole three. Even though Zaiana had fully exposed herself to the elements in her position, paired with her wet hair she could hardly stand the icy temperature and wanted to test how long she could last before she broke. She thought an hour would be commendable.

She couldn't revoke her punishment. She had made it in front of her inner circle, and to go back on it would discredit her as a leader. They would be well within their rights to demand she was removed from her position by the masters. She highly doubted they would, as she liked to believe their loyalty to her trumped their loyalty to the masters. Though, they would never of speak it, as to do so would seal their end.

Zaiana debated retreating to shelter under the mountain or swooping down to confront the young dark fae. She had no reason to— nothing in the way of conversation or lecture to impose on her—but oddly, it was as if she wanted the company. Deciding she'd had enough of seeing if she'd freeze to death, Zaiana stood, splayed her wings, and stepped off the high peak. She cut through the air like the edge of a blade, gliding down in a single swift motion. Near to the ground, she worked her wings a few times until she was able to land directly in front of Amaya and her fire.

As she did, Zaiana's quick senses had her detecting Amaya's fast movement, followed by the whizz of an arrow flying straight for her. She pivoted on the spot, hand coming up to catch the arrow that was a mere second from piercing her chest. Zaiana stared at the arrow within her grasp, dumbfounded. When she turned her head with raised eyebrows, Amaya's face was pale with horror.

"*Oh Gods.* Forgive me, Zaiana." Amaya dropped the bow she held, forcing her body forward in submission.

Zaiana was still too stunned to accept or decline her groveling. She spun the arrow between her fingers with a curious hum. "Impressive," she said at last.

Amaya seemed to relax, thinking she had been spared from wrath at the error. Zaiana should punish her. She should be far more outraged over the attack that could have lethally wounded her. But in hindsight, she was in awe.

"How did you learn to start a fire?" she questioned, using the iron tip as a pointer.

Amaya hesitated, but Zaiana gave her a small nod to confirm she could speak freely. There was no one here to assess or question her judgments. If she chose to be lenient, Amaya could easily be silenced if she ever thought to speak a word of it. And if she dared, her silence would be permanent.

"I read books," she confessed.

Zaiana's eyes narrowed. "From where?"

Amaya shifted uncomfortably. Zaiana already knew there were only two places literature could be found, and those were in the council chamber and her private section. Perhaps Maverick also kept such luxuries in his side of the mountain, but she didn't picture him as one who would find any sort of joy or entertainment in useless stories. Zaiana wouldn't admit to anyone she did, but the collection of books they had accumulated over the centuries was not of her own doing, and she had not touched one since their collector passed. At Amaya's reaction, she knew exactly which of the forbidden sections of the mountain she'd obtained her information from.

"You welcomed yourself into *my* private space?" Zaiana's voice dropped low. Her domain was strictly off-limits to all but her inner circle.

Amaya quickly shook her head, which eased her temper just a little. "Then where?"

The young dark fae shifted, tucking her knees under her arms, and inched closer to the flames. "You told us never to speak his name," she said quietly, but she didn't balk at the stare Zaiana pinned her with.

Zaiana clenched her teeth, knowing exactly who she meant. Finnian had been many things—many weak and spineless things. She knew that now, though her naïve younger self did not. She had allowed herself to believe kindness could exist among their wicked species, but he'd proven to be a master of deception.

"Why would he help you?" She kept her tone emotionless, but a dark part of her memory awoke like a long dormant demon with the want to torment her with the stirring-up of the past. Zaiana crouched low, eager to feel the heat of the flames to take away the chill that coated her skin.

"He was kind to me… I don't know why, but he used to bring me books when I was a child. I'd never felt accepted by anything until I found out what it was like to lose oneself in the wonders of a story. Lose, only to emerge from the pages so much clearer about who I was."

Zaiana had to glance away; she couldn't bear to look at Amaya. When she did, with those dark tresses and innocent speech, her fists curled at the overwhelming sense of being dragged into the past. Looking at Amaya now…felt like looking straight into the eyes of her own foolish child-self, even though Amaya was near full-grown. "You'd best keep that kind of romantic poetry to yourself. Ridicule will be the least of your worries should you speak of it to anyone else."

"I wouldn't dare. I've kept it to myself for this long, but I do not mind it."

Zaiana stayed silent, staring off into the dark void of the mountain pass, trying to drown the thoughts and memories that flared to life from the pits of darkness in her mind. It was a mistake to come out here.

"Why do you no longer speak of him?"

Zaiana snapped her head to the young dark fae, unsure whether she admired her or wanted to reprimand her boldness. No one ever questioned her about personal subjects as she had succeeded in making it known pain would befall those who dared. Yet she didn't feel the urge to punish Amaya.

"How old are you?" Zaiana asked instead.

Amaya's shoulders relaxed as if she had expected a lashing for her curiosity. "Halfway into my second century," she answered cautiously.

"Then you would have been old enough to witness and understand the Blood Trials."

Amaya nodded, but her eyes still held the lingering question. To most, it would be obvious why the name triggered her. A demon of weakness she had slain.

"I killed him. He was a coward and does not deserve for his name to be remembered in this world." Even though not a day went by that he didn't cross her mind. Like a vicious eternal plague; a punishment for her own foolishness.

"You loved him."

Zaiana flared, barely able to contain the sparks of lightning that pricked her body at the words. She had to take a second to breathe consciously and not give in to the impulse to strike. She was a master of control, had been trained in how to keep her anger and emotions in check since birth and harness them as a weapon when the situation called for it. This was not one of those moments. Harming Amaya would only damage her with the need to find a replacement for the battle against Maverick.

Her voice dropped deadly low when she spoke again. "We are creatures of darkness. Soulless, heartless. Put a hand to your chest, Amaya—you can't deny that truth no matter how many romantic tales you fill your head with." She stood, her chest heavy with the rage that built, lightning collecting like a storm. "You ever speak of such a thing again, it will be the last thing you speak of at all."

CHAPTER 20

Faythe

FAYTHE WATCHED THE descending sun, feeling a new sense of completeness. A void within her she believed would always remain hollow now began to fill with strength and pride after her time with Agalhor. Her only regret was that it had taken her so long to overcome her fear of rejection and face him, but now she had, she could only picture the bright future they would have together to make up for lost time.

She smiled, genuine and weightless, as the glowing star diffused vibrant amber and yellow notes across the sky. She'd come to the balcony overlooking the courtyard to bask in her favorite time of day as the colors invoked a sense of serenity for her to think with a clear mind. Or to reflect, as she did now, relaying everything she had learned today. Tales that filled her head with wonder, love that filled her heart with pride, and prospects that filled her future with bright opportunity.

"Mind if I join you?"

Faythe twisted in fright as the cheerful voice sounded behind her.

Her eyebrows raised to find Livia walking out to greet her. Her words were choked with foolish nerves, so Faythe offered a small nod even though it was clear Livia wasn't about to take no for an answer when she came up beside Faythe, casting her eyes over the horizon.

"You are some woman, Faythe. First day back, and all I've heard since I've been here are stories about the impossible human with fine sword skills and a surprising mind ability," Livia said, sliding her eyes to Faythe with a small smirk. "An Heir of Agalhor's who was never known to exist. The news has already traveled throughout Rhyenelle and likely beyond. You're quite the miracle."

"Sorry," Faythe answered sheepishly, cheeks aflame that the commander had been forced to listen to boring tales of her life. It was embarrassing she'd become the topic of conversation at all.

"No need to apologize—it's quite fascinating. Though Reylan does tend to go off on tangents sometimes… You're someone I think he could talk about for centuries if nobody stopped him," Livia teased, and Faythe's face grew hotter. The fae chuckled at her reaction.

Faythe looked over at Livia, really taking in her appearance for the first time. What she'd failed to notice before was the long, slightly raised scar that began at her left temple and trailed past her eye before breaking off into two lines like jagged lightning down the side of her face. Faythe found the imperfection…beautiful. Livia wore her scar as if she were born with it, as if she wasn't afraid of the story attached to it. Faythe's eyes must have lingered for too long because Livia smiled knowingly.

"What happened?" Faythe couldn't help but ask.

Livia looked away from her, flinching for a second as if she were reflecting on a dark and distant memory. "I wasn't always a commander; I wasn't always able to stick up for myself." Livia locked her gaze, and her eyes were fierce. "Reylan, Kyleer, and Izaiah saved me from the circumstances that ended in that scar. Then I vowed never to be weak again."

Faythe didn't know Livia, but her chest panged to know the permanent marking was not an outcome of battle, but that someone, or maybe several people, had personally harmed her. Seeing how strongly and confidently she carried herself, Faythe found herself in awe of her resilience and strength.

"I'm sorry."

Livia smiled a little. "I'm not. I've long had my revenge and built myself up from what happened to me. But while my story may be visible, the scars that cut deepest are often those we harbor within." They held each other's eye, and as much as she felt utterly exposed by the way Livia studied her, Faythe couldn't look away. "Don't be afraid of the past that has made you stronger."

The words struck her, pained her, as she realized the fae in front of her knew everything. Faythe couldn't find the emotion to be angry or embarrassed that Reylan might have told her everything she suffered back in High Farrow...because her words were exactly what Faythe needed to hear.

She didn't know how to respond as her eyes pricked and she forced back the desire to break down in front of a stranger. Livia gave a small nod of her head as if she were silently accepting Faythe's gratitude and understanding without having to voice any of it.

Livia took a deep breath, and at her hard look, Faythe braced herself. "Reylan told me of your intention to cross to the Niltain Isles," she began. Whatever she gauged from Faythe's reaction, Livia's face twisted in understanding. "He asked if I'd be willing to accompany you. He only means to gather those he can trust. I thought he was joking at first. The journey you plan for, Faythe...it is almost as good as suicide."

Faythe flared in defense, feeling as if she were being scolded by the commander. "You don't understand what's at stake—"

"He told me everything."

"He told you facts. Let me guess—foolish, naïve human thinks she can cross unventured territory and save the world, right?" She laughed without humor. "I'll admit it must sound ridiculous. But no one else need risk their life for it."

"You're wrong," Livia answered coolly. At the flash in Faythe's eye, she gave a look of her own that made Faythe swallow her desire to object. "Accepting help is not a weakness, Faythe, and Reylan warned me you may fight against it. But a legion is far mightier than a lone soldier. Strength is in those who know when help is needed and are not afraid to ask for it. And in those who listen, even when the truth is hard to hear."

"Why are you telling me this?"

Livia turned to her fully. "I'm telling you because when Reylan told me everything, every detail about who you are and what you plan to do, I didn't question it for one second. I told him I would go with you, but while he believes in you more than he believes in anything he's ever committed to, he won't tell you the harrowing truths of the mission you propose. No soul who attempted the journey to the Niltain Isles has made it back alive in centuries. The odds of survival don't exist as far as any of us are aware. So, as with any battle, we all stand together, but be sure you come to terms with the high chance a walk onto the Isles could be a one-way trip."

Faythe's heart was a hard beat, twisting at the notion of the lives at risk on the quest she must take. But Livia was right, and Faythe was immensely grateful for her honesty. What she didn't know was that Faythe had long come to terms with the possibility of her life ending, and she still planned to set out on this journey as long as it meant she would take the evil in Ungardia with her. What turned a new dagger in her gut was that she would have to accept Reylan and Livia's lives could also be taken on the dire quest.

She looked into Livia's blue eyes, and they were hard with determination, waiting for Faythe to confirm she accepted the fate she was condemning them all to. But she had no choice. Dakodas's ascension had to be stopped before she joined Marvellas in their world and all would be lost. A few lives to save many, many more was perhaps the cruel trade Faythe had to accept. So, she nodded, and in accepting Livia's help, Faythe hardened her heart to what she was imposing on them all.

"Thank you," Faythe said, but it didn't feel like enough for her loyalty and courage.

Livia gave a short nod and a light smile. "Good. Now that the heaviness is out of the way, you seem to have my dear cousin quite wound up in other ways." Her grin turned devious as Faythe's mouth popped open at the suggestive tone.

"Me? I—no, Reylan is just…he's just…" Faythe's body flushed as she floundered for a response to counter the commander's observations.

Livia laughed, making Faythe want to hurl herself over the balcony to save herself from the rising embarrassment. Her chuckles ceased, and then her face turned soft. "He's had a hard time this past century. I'm sure you know the vague details, but after those Great Battles, after losing so many and blaming himself so deeply for it, we all worried we'd never get him back."

Faythe's chest tightened at the mention. She wondered why Livia chose to share it with her. She knew what happened all those years ago, who he'd lost, but she so far believed Reylan had hardened himself to continue in his role and carry on living.

"Farrah was a sweet fae. Truly, I have no bad words about her. But she was never right for him. Too gentle, too delicate, but he cared for her deeply. After he lost her in Fenher, he left. We didn't see him after those battles for decades. Kyleer, Izaiah, and I searched endlessly, but Reylan didn't want to be found, and he was good at remaining hidden."

Faythe tuned in to the tale with utter heartbreak, part of her wanting to stop Livia's words because they pained her to imagine, but the larger part of her needing to hear. To understand Reylan from another perspective. "How did you find him?" she choked out with quiet emotion.

"We didn't. He came back on his own, no explanation of why or where he'd been…" Livia looked to her then, and there was something in her eye like disbelief. "It was around the same time Agalhor met your mother. She and Reylan, they became pretty close, and it was exactly what he needed to fill the void of not having his own parents. When she left, Reylan closed himself off completely once more."

She knew Reylan had some kind of relationship with her mother. It was always clear in the bright way he spoke of her. Knowing she had also cared for him deeply, the warmth in Faythe's chest made a smile bloom on her face.

"I've been looking for you."

Both their heads snapped to the silver-haired warrior they spoke of, and her heart skipped a beat to see him in the doorway.

"Ah, yes, I guess I forgot to mention that," Livia said, shooting Faythe a devious side-smile. Faythe chuckled a little at Reylan's scowl in response. "I'll take that as my cue to leave." She walked to the glass doors, pausing before spinning back to add, "I'll make sure we get some time in the training room before we leave."

Faythe gave a nod in promise, giddy at the prospect of getting to train with the commander. Then she was gone, leaving Faythe and Reylan to tune in to the peaceful stillness of evening for a few seconds.

"You spoke with Agalhor." He broke the silence with careful words.

She smiled, and he seemed to relax his shoulders as she did. As if he had come fully prepared to help her through the emotions if it hadn't gone well. The sun illuminated where he stood before her, and she couldn't be sure what she had ever done to deserve him by her side, where he'd always been since the day they met. She wished she could capture the picture of him right there, burning against the sun's colors, Rhyenelle's protector.

He waited patiently for her to speak, and she took a final deep breath of cooling air.

"I want to tell you everything."

Faythe lost herself in relaying the stories her father had filled her with while she sat across from Reylan at the dining table in her rooms. She barely touched the delicious food that was laid in front of her, fully immersed in adding her own thoughts and feelings about the Phoenix birds that had stolen all her headspace for the day.

Reylan also sat with a near full plate, adding his own take on some of the tales, but mostly, he gave her his undivided attention while sitting back in his chair and watching her with a rare warm smile, letting her rant. She didn't know how much time passed, but she was glad her meal was a cold selection of meats and cheese as she was sure nothing would hold any warmth by now otherwise.

"Eat," Reylan instructed as he straightened, interjecting with the command just as she finished one thought ready to skip straight ahead to the next. He looked at her expectantly when she didn't immediately react.

Faythe rolled her eyes. Grabbing her fork, she speared a cube of cheese and shoved it into her mouth. He huffed a laugh at her childish display, going for his own silverware.

When the distraction of her excitement had subsided, Faythe began to feel the horrible creeping of nerves instead. Something was playing on her mind to make her cower out of confronting the subject with him that morning. Her appetite left her.

"You stayed last night," she blurted when she couldn't stand it any longer. She needed to know he didn't regret it.

"You asked me to," he replied with an edge of defensiveness.

She dropped her gaze, realizing it was not the reaction she hoped for. Just before her disappointment could settle, Reylan sighed, setting down his fork.

"I'm sorry. I didn't intend to fall asleep," he admitted.

Faythe glanced up to catch the apology in his wary eyes. "Why are you sorry?"

"Because it's not proper for—" He stopped himself, taking a pause as he deliberated.

Faythe leaned back in her chair, crossing her arms. "You're worried about what people will think?"

"People don't just think; they talk."

"Then let them. Those who are petty enough to spread gossip never care for the truth anyway."

Reylan's look softened as if he were trying to let her down gently, and she hated it. "They might say I'm taking advantage of you."

Faythe arched a brow in humor. "How shocking."

"They might assume we do far more than sleep," he went on, his lips fighting the amusement.

Faythe had to press her thighs together at the unexpected heat that rushed down her body. She leaned forward, popping her chin over her clasped hands on the table. "How scandalous."

"They might decide I'm a bad influence on such a delicate human." His voice changed, dropping in tone, as he mimicked her across the table.

Faythe's head tilted, but she couldn't ignore the skip of her pulse. "What kind of *influence* might they think you've spun on me?"

A smirk formed on his mouth. "I'm more curious to hear what your imagination is conjuring right now."

"I'll bet you are."

"Not willing to share then?"

Faythe damned the Spirits to burn, having to avert her gaze with a deep breath to regain her composure. When she cast her eyes back to lock on his, something had changed between them. It was there in the current of their stare.

"What if I asked you to stay again?"

Reylan didn't answer straight away, but his look gave away his deliberation, and it lifted her spirits that he didn't immediately reject her. His consideration was for the benefit of her reputation.

"I don't know if my night terrors are cured yet, and I…I don't want to be alone."

Reylan's face fell in understanding. "Are you sure?" he asked carefully, giving her another chance to fully realize what she was asking.

Her stomach knotted with nervous thrill as she took this as his acceptance. It was an innocent ask, and she knew he had no further expectations of her, nor she of him. But he was right: in a castle full of high fae and human servants who had it in their nature to gossip, there would be no small amount of speculation when he was undoubtedly caught leaving her rooms by morning. Faythe didn't care—not in the slightest—as her desire for his company, not to be alone with her fears anymore, drowned out all worry of mindless people's observations.

"Let them whisper."

Reylan's smile of agreement held something more. Something like *relief.* Before she could ponder it further, he resumed eating then swayed the topic of conversation, "Did you tell Agalhor of our perilous journey?"

Faythe shifted in her seat, grabbing her own fork again to distract herself with the items on her plate. "The right moment never came up."

At his short silence, Faythe peered up and found him pinning her with a small frown of disapproval that called out her lie. She sighed, setting down her silverware.

"You should have seen how happy he was," she said quietly, face wrinkling. "He spoke of the future, of making up for lost time, thrilled by the prospect, as was I. How could I take that from him?"

"Why do you sound as if you're not planning to make it back?"

"I know the odds."

"Screw the damned odds."

Faythe was taken aback by the bite in his tone, but it was not directed toward her lack of hope for survival. Because his hard eyes were split with a hint of terror that gave away he also knew of the dangers that made it a real fear they may not return.

"Livia told me to prepare for a one-way trip, but I always knew the risk I was taking." Her life—her single human existence—would be a small price to pay for the millions that could be saved. It was a sacrifice she was willing to take, until...

Staring at the silver-haired warrior across from her stabbed her painfully with her first dose of selfish guilt. Both for the pain she wanted desperately to erase from his face, and for the time with him she would be robbed of. Whatever would become of them, however short or long, she wanted all the time that had now been put on a cruel, unstoppable countdown.

"You defied the odds to exist. You'll defy them again to survive." The way he spoke those words, sapphire forging with gold, struck her with a new will—a *reason*—to take a stand against fate. To *live* and see the world reemerge from the clouds of war and evil. And she wanted to see it all, feel it all, with him by her side.

"Is that an order, General?" Faythe said, a little breathless from the gaze they shared.

Reylan's firm look was cut by the flash in his eye and slight upturning of his mouth, telling her she'd roused something in him with the use of his title. "Yes. Now, *eat.*"

CHAPTER 21

Reylan

FTER DINNER, REYLAN stood with arms crossed against the closed balcony doors, failing to distract his mind from the fact Faythe was changing for bed in the closet a few meters away. He shouldn't be here—shouldn't have agreed to stay. Yet it was his own selfishness that faltered his protests against the proposition. He'd rested better than he had in months last night and couldn't deny her plea for company if there was still a chance she might relive those nightmares. Even though she'd succeeded in evading them for the first time. If his presence could help her, it made the decision easy.

He heard her reemerge into the bedroom, and as he turned his head, he peeled himself from the casual position instantly.

Faythe was pulling subconsciously at the hem of the shirt she wore. The *male's* shirt, which was all that covered her, reaching to mid-thigh on her bare legs. There was a raging conflict in his mind at the sight, an irrational flare of something dark and ugly as he wondered who the garment belonged to, but even more dominating was the sensation that tensed his body when he lost the fight with his own traitorous eyes and let them trail the length of her glorious exposed skin.

Gods above.

She was trying to kill him. Truly.

"It's Jakon's shirt," she muttered quietly, and perhaps she read the question in his hard expression.

The quick flash of primal anger dissipated completely. His poise loosened. Faythe couldn't hide the flicker of sorrow at the mention of her best friend, and Reylan's gut twisted with a bout of guilt. All he gave was a nod in understanding.

Faythe wandered over to the bed. Pulling back the covers, she propped herself up but neglected to fold herself under them. The shirt rode up further, and Reylan choked on a groan as he slowly edged toward the bed and refrained from drinking in the length and poise of those smooth, enticing legs. He had a hard enough time staying focused while she trained. Pushing them, strengthening them, beyond what a human should be capable of.

Faythe's amber eyes slid to hold his. Seconds of silence passed.

"You're staring, General," she said casually, but his throat bobbed at the caress in those words.

"Are you really going to sleep in just that?" he countered thickly.

There was a twinkle of deviance in her eyes. "Would you prefer for me to change into one of the dainty pieces of silk instead?"

Reylan had to breathe consciously at the memory of *exactly* the walking temptation she was in the nightgown she wore the night he intruded on her after returning from Fenher. Not even her robe had been enough to cover all that was exposed beneath.

Faythe shuffled down until she lay on her side. She folded her hands under her head and bent her leg a fraction, torturously slowly, for comfort. The movement exposed her to the top of her thigh. All without taking her eyes off him. He gauged the hint of challenge that sparked in her irises as he fought to keep his own gaze locked on hers.

Reylan conceded, but he didn't glance down at the maddening sight of her. He looked anywhere *but* at Faythe in an attempt to calm every damning, raging thought that swirled within. He should leave. Before he ventured down a dangerous path there would be no backtracking from.

He heard the faint rustle of material and knew the distraction of her body had been stolen by the covers as she folded herself under them. Relieved, he dropped his eyes back to her. While he remained utterly still, the teasing in her face smoothed out into a small smile, and she might have mistaken his stillness for discomfort. But that was so gods-damned far from what coursed through him as he watched every flicker of movement, every flex of exposed skin that had him fighting against restraint.

Faythe casually patted the empty space next to her in a silent invitation, no expectations.

"Are you sure you want me to stay?" he asked once more, to be certain there would be no regrets on her part should any hollow rumors spread. There would certainly be none on his.

"I'm not trying to seduce you."

She didn't have to *try*.

Fatigue started to cloud the gold of her irises. Reylan took a breath to calm the raging thoughts he couldn't subdue. He unbuttoned his jacket and removed his boots. Then he sat on the edge of the bed, taking a contemplative pause with his back to her. Before he could listen to the dark chants of his mind, Reylan reached back and pulled his shirt off.

He heard Faythe's shallow inhale, which she tried to disguise, and he stilled, going utterly rigid. This was a mistake. He didn't move to gauge her reaction, afraid of repulsion or worse: sympathy. He couldn't bear it —not from her. He could have been holding his breath from the tense-ness that coated his body.

Faythe wordlessly shifted on the bed behind him. Slowly, she inched over to him, the faint embrace of her presence closing in. Her hand raised, and he felt the warmth as her touch hovered over the skin of his back as if waiting for his permission before she laid her hand on him. Despite his fear that she would shrink away from him if she did, he turned his head just enough to let her know he understood what she was about to do.

When those delicate fingers grazed his marred skin, Reylan clenched his fists tightly in his lap. Not out of fear or discomfort. As her touch traced over the lattice of raised scars, he felt his muscles loosen, his insecurities dissolve, and his mind calm.

"Are these from war…?" Her voice held an edge of sharp anger quietly infused with pain. "Or from *him?*"

Reylan couldn't stand her ache. It was even more heart-wrenching that Faythe's pain was for him, and the realization of that twisted something deep inside. He turned around to her fully. Their eyes locked, her amber pools glistening against the moonlight, and he saw something in them he never thought he would. Didn't think he deserved.

Acceptance.

Faythe's gaze fell, and she scanned the markings on his chest too. Her hands raised, hesitating once again. He didn't move or speak, and she read this as permission. While they sat there knee-to-knee, Faythe rose to run her soothing touch along each scar carefully, purposefully, as if she were memorizing a map. As if she longed to trace and discover the story inside each one.

"Both," he answered in barely more than a rasp of air as he watched her thoughtful face. Beautiful.

He thought he would risk hurting her, based on his response to anyone who had tried to touch him before. But all he could do was watch her face as her golden eyes searched his past. Every dark and unforgivable thing branded onto his skin. She didn't look at any of them with a hint of disgust; rather, her eyes glistened with silver, her brow pinched with pain, and her features sharpened with the steel edge of anger.

His hands wrapped around her wrists, and she seemed to snap out of whatever tunneling thoughts she'd spiraled into. Her gaze met his, and it took everything in him not to give in to the need that burned. A need to take her pain and share it. He wanted to share every piece of himself with her, and it terrified him.

Her eyes flashed to her wrists he had yet to let go of. He uncurled his fingers, releasing her despite his want to draw her close.

"You should get some sleep."

Faythe held his gaze for a moment longer, and for once, he wanted to ask what she was thinking. He had no idea what she pondered, what she saw, as she looked at him now she knew everything—*saw* everything. Maybe he would never get to know, as she nodded before backing away from him. Faythe shuffled over the bed before folding herself under the covers once again. He hated that even the short distance across the absurdly large bed felt too far. There was a pitiful passing thought that she *wanted* distance after seeing his tarnished skin.

He tentatively lay back. In the dark, he felt both calm with relief and rigid with fear that she might change her mind now they lay together.

After a still minute, her small voice cut the silence. "Are Kyleer and Izaiah joining us too?"

He shifted his head on the pillow to look at her where she lay on her side facing him. A part of him—a large part—flared irrationally for a second at the mere thought of another male in her bed. She eyed the large space he'd left between them.

"You're almost hanging off the bed, Reylan. I don't bite." Her eyes fell closed, but a small, devious smile tugged at her lips.

Every tense and horrible thought dissolved completely at those words because he knew it was her acceptance. Of him—of his presence. It settled his mind into contentment but rushed his body with such heat he had to stifle a groan. He paused to take a few long, deep breaths to calm his raging thoughts.

Reylan shuffled closer until he felt the faint, radiating warmth of her body and relaxed in the comfort of it. At knowing she was close, and safe.

CHAPTER 22

Zaiana

"THE FATE OF the quest is being decided on a game of Flag Runner?"

Tynan's bored voice sounded at her back as Zaiana stood facing the firepit while the rest of them sat splayed over the couches in their lounge area. She folded an arm across her chest to prop up the elbow that supported her chin, contemplating their thoughts on the challenge against Maverick in five days. She had to agree the chosen game was almost laughable, yet most of their strategic suggestions so far were too obvious, and frankly, she was growing irritable at their lack of useful ideas. She pressed her hand to her forehead instead, massaging the tension that grew.

Kellias chimed in. "Unlike us, there is no sure way of knowing who he'll pick for his side. It would be too much of a risk to assign one-on-one at the last minute."

Tynan answered with a grumble. None of them liked to be contradicted, and it was making her head spin to listen to their petty bickering that held no resolutions.

"And even if we did, it would all go to shit if they have a group target approach." Acelin weighed her opinion with Kellias.

"You two have found nothing on Maverick? So much for spies," Tynan scoffed.

Drya and Selain had been all but mute in the discussion. Zaiana refrained from unleashing her disappointment on all of them. She couldn't be sure what it was that had set her in a sour mood for over a week, but her last discussion with the dark bastard when he intruded on her time in the baths still reeled in her mind. Along with the secondary encounter with Amaya that was of her own doing. Both of which had grated on her nerves more than she cared to admit.

Exasperated, she whirled to her companions. All eyes pinned her, and at their slight recoil, she was sure her face was far from pleasant. Or even content. "Half a damned hour, and all you can come up with are novice tricks and sloppy field stations," she blazed. They were unfortunate bystanders of her wrath that wasn't really of their making. "None of you have even remotely considered the new weapon in our arsenal." While she'd let them battle it out for how best to approach the tournament on the trial ground, Zaiana had been churning over her own plan. She'd hoped at least one of them would come up with what had lit like a beacon in her mind. She'd left them this long as a test, to see if they really were too stuck in their own resentment and defiance to include the young dark fae, Amaya.

When Zaiana's eyes slid to her, the darkling stiffened in her position in the far corner, keeping a good distance from the others who were sprawled out lazily.

"No offense," Tynan began, speaking to Zaiana, not the young dark fae he was indeed about to offend, "but we don't exactly consider her an advantageous weapon."

Amaya showed no emotion, but she didn't break Zaiana's stare.

Zaiana tilted her head as she asked the darkling, "Do you agree with him?"

Amaya's gaze drifted across the others, who pinned her with intimidating stares in challenge. She shifted in her seat but raised her chin a fraction.

"I believe I could help," she answered timidly. The poor response of a child.

Zaiana's chest heaved with a breath of growing impatience. She hated that she had to press and usually wouldn't give any of the others another chance. "Never assert your worth without backing it up with merit," Zaiana warned.

Amaya's throat bobbed, but to Zaiana's surprise she stood, going around the center table to mirror her position to address the room. It was bold, and Zaiana's temper cooled slightly, hoping perhaps Amaya was thinking the same thing while the others refused to acknowledge her. Perhaps her silence was her way of biding her time so she wouldn't speak out against any of the others who were still wary of the new presence in their close circle.

She locked eyes with Zaiana as if asking for silent permission to speak. Zaiana gave a slight dip of her head to signal she had their attention.

Amaya cleared her throat before saying, "It's obvious in appearance I'm the weakest one here—"

Kellias snickered, and Zaiana's warning glare was nothing short of deadly. He straightened in his seat at the look, fixing his attention back on the young dark fae without so much as a twitch of amusement.

Amaya, to her credit, didn't lose her small dose of confidence at the sneer. "Maverick and the others won't consider me a threat. They won't expect what I can do with a bow. I'll be their first target. I think it's quite obvious, really."

Zaiana allowed the slight curl of her lip as the direction of Amaya's plan was beginning to sound a lot like her own. Her group were far from impressed at the subtle gibe that their half hour had been squandered when they'd failed to see it in their arrogance.

"I have to be the runner," she said as though it were a game. "They won't pass up the opportunity to strike meek prey. If I can attract their attention one by one, they might take the bait and be distracted for long enough that one of you can take them out—or for them to find out too late how accurately my arrows can hit."

Zaiana was grinning now. And at the perplexed looks of the others, she knew they too thought it a brilliant plan. Dampening her approval, she said, "Good. At least someone is accounting for the team and not just themselves."

Everyone snapped their heads to her, incredulous. Zaiana ignored them.

"Maverick knows Amaya is within our ranks now, but he's no fool. He'll likely enlist Berrik and Jesper out of brute structure alone. They'll want to team up and target Tynan, perhaps even Kellias too."

"I can take them—"

"This isn't the time for arrogance. I don't doubt you, Tynan. In one-to-one combat your skills could certainly outsmart them. But I won't take chances on the field. You'll cover Amaya at all times. No one goes off alone, no one allows themselves to be in a position where they are outmatched or outnumbered." She cast a subtle, deliberate glance toward Amaya, and the young dark fae winced. "One you've got the flags and I'm free, it's just me against Maverick. He is mine. I am his. It's how it has always been, and he'll expect it too. That fight I'm more than willing to walk into."

"How is the game won?" Amaya asked. She didn't balk at the attention that fell to her. "If we're not allowed to kill, that is."

"I have to locate the final flag before Maverick does. It will be black and hidden within the mountain range. Your job is to gain me as much time advantage as possible for that final task." Seeing faint fear cross Amaya's eyes, Zaiana did something she never thought she would do.

"You cannot kill out of malice. They have the right to demand your life if you do." She took a step closer to the darkling. "But if you feel it is a choice between your life or theirs, you have my protection."

"Zaiana." Tynan straightened in his chair. "You can't be serious."

She cast him a bored look. "Am I ever not?"

"You would really put your life on the line in her place?" He cast a dismissive hand toward Amaya, who had gone chalk-white.

What Zaiana proposed meant should Amaya be forced to take a life during the battle, it would be Zaiana who took the blame, not the darkling.

"Yes," she answered simply.

"That's absurd!" Tynan shot to his feet, and Zaiana instinctively flared at the challenge. She pushed her damned dominant nature aside, in no mood to bicker with any of them. She knew it was his own inherent drive to protect her that fueled his anger, and perhaps he was right. Zaiana couldn't be sure what made her extend the offer of protection. She wanted to believe it was in aid of nothing more than avoiding wasted potential, lost talent, should she be forced into a situation that would make her fatally harm a Blackfair. Zaiana was confident she could avoid a death sentence as compensation, but the masters wouldn't give a second thought to letting Maverick take a lowly young fae's life if it kept him happy. She couldn't let that happen.

"I think we are done here," Zaiana dismissed. It was close to midnight.

Her companions rose, albeit disgruntled and far from satisfied with the night's affairs. She couldn't take on the weight of their emotions right now, so she tried to ignore them completely. They gave her a nod in parting, but their eyes were wary. They were concerned for her; their whole existence revolved around keeping her alive. Zaiana often wondered if they too were wasted potential, living to protect something so hienious and evil.

Tynan was the last to leave, coming up close with his back to Amaya as though she wouldn't hear what he had to say. "Why are you doing this?"

Zaiana slid her eyes to his, mere inches away. "To win."

He held her gaze for many ticks of the clock perched on the mantel to the side of the room. She didn't balk at his intensity, but she could see the word he wanted to voice but would never dare.

Liar.

As expected, Tynan broke the stare first. With a sigh and a shake of his head, he turned and strolled for the exit in the wall after the others. He didn't refrain from shooting a look of distaste at Amaya, who didn't falter from it. Slowly, her instinct to shrivel and cower at the slightest confrontation was lessening. She took her first step to leave.

"Not you," Zaiana said to halt her.

Her whole posture stiffened as she twisted to face her delegate respectfully. Amaya copied her stance. Standing straight, shoulders squared, hands folded behind her back. For a second, it was like looking in a mirror. For a second, Zaiana felt a pang of something she wasn't used to. Something like sadness.

She banished the emotion as quickly as the flash came and studied the young dark fae from head to toe. She'd yet to shift or speak. Commendable. Then she felt a sudden sense of responsibility as Amaya matched her stance. How much had the young darkling studied her to have become so in tune with her in such a short time? Zaiana dropped the hold on her own wrists, arms falling to her sides. Amaya did the same. The flare of ice that shot through her had nothing to do with anger. In fact, she even dared to admit it was a flicker of dread. Watching Amaya take her lead, as if she were someone to be admired, someone to be made the image of, was a damning notion to any poor soul who believed she was anything of a role model.

Zaiana was the leader, the delegate, for a reason. But that reason was down to her ruthlessness alone. Not any admirable traits. No—

beneath the title, she was nothing. Nothing but all that was cold and wrong.

"You need to learn who you are," she said, voice distant as though she were speaking to herself. "You need to figure out who you want to be in this world and what impression you want to leave behind. You can follow orders, soldier in an army, but no one can make you who you are —not if you don't let them."

Amaya's faltering confidence returned in the way she shifted on her feet. The young dark fae didn't respond. Zaiana didn't need her to.

"Where do you sleep?"

Her green eyes lifted to Zaiana's once again. "In the dorms."

Zaiana suppressed a wince at the memory. She'd begun in there too —in the cold, wretched halls that housed the new darklings who were yet to prove their worth. Or those too low on the chain to ever rise from the pits of the darkest level. "Dorms" was a civilized name for the open cave lined with sunken alcoves, three high, barely big enough to accommodate wings. Down there, the ability to glamour was the most envious possession.

The next step up from the dorms was the common level, which was far more comfortable, with single cots and usually only six dark fae per room. Zaiana thought Amaya would at least be there by now given her age, though it was clear her lack of progress in the training grade and her crooked wings made her constantly tumble to the bottom of the social ladder. Her fists curled of their own accord at the dark memories that flashed from those early years she'd suffered like any other.

"Not anymore," Zaiana said, voice hard.

Amaya opened her mouth.

"You have ten minutes to gather any things you might have and be back here. Go."

Amaya stood stunned for a second. A second long enough for Zaiana to need to bite back a snapping remark. Then she nodded, stumbling over her feet as she hurried from the common room.

Alone, Zaiana swore.

What was she thinking? The darkling was not her problem. Her well-being should not be her concern. But she had made it hers the moment she allowed Amaya to join her ranks. Even if she only intended for her to be in the battle and nothing further, she was opening herself up to another responsibility she didn't want. Didn't need.

And yet she couldn't turn her back.

"Where are we going?"

Zaiana didn't respond to Amaya. Not this time, nor the first time she'd asked with different words since leaving the common room. She simply charged ahead, letting the darkling trail after her while she went over the many reasons why she shouldn't be extending this special treatment in her mind. She tried to soothe her anger over what others may think if they caught wind of her mercy; over the thought of appearing *weak*. Amaya, in her judgment, had earned at least the decency of more comfortable accommodation, especially if she were to become known as one of her inner circle. Each one of them was tied to her reputation; everything they did was a reflection of Zaiana. Their failures were her punishment, and their triumphs were her merit.

She should have simply found her a cot in the common halls. It would have been a generous comfort in comparison to the dorms. Yet Zaiana couldn't stand the thought of her being exposed to other wicked darklings, both Silverfair and Blackfair. With her outward appearance small and feeble, she would be easy prey to their taunting and malice. Amaya had a long way to go before her confidence was to Zaiana's standards, and she wouldn't have anything getting in the way of her progress. She was her weapon to hone now.

Only the highest-ranking were given the luxury of the few private living spaces. Under the mountain was a labyrinth of spaces that had been carefully crafted over millennia to accommodate the rise of their species once again. They had succeeded in saving the dark fae with the help of the Blackfair transition rituals, and space was beginning to fill.

Zaiana felt this more than anyone. Living under obsidian rock for over three centuries never got easier. She'd always felt trapped, suffocated, and the numbers that crowded the cavernous halls were becoming too much for her to withstand. She spent as little time as she needed to here. If she hadn't become the delegate and didn't have the freedom to roam the towns, glamoured, at her leisure...she often wondered if she would still be alive. Physically, perhaps, though not out of choice. But she believed her mind would be the first to lose its tether on sanity.

She'd seen it before. There were many in the Blackfair line, and some within her own, who seemed to have completely given over to the madness that lived within them all. No shred of humanity remained; they had turned into the most lethal and savage of them all. Zaiana knew she harbored the same demons, but she wouldn't surrender to the beast within completely.

Zaiana halted outside a door. One of the very few dwellings with such privacy. Beyond it was her only slice of absolution. She didn't know why she'd brought Amaya here; it wasn't often she allowed any of the others into her rooms. Except one, a long time ago.

She didn't give herself time to change her mind, pulling down on the handle and storming inside. She didn't invite Amaya to follow her in either, as if doing so would acknowledge the invading presence and snap her into changing her mind. But she felt the darkling enter after a small hesitation. Zaiana didn't turn. Instead, she eyed her large room. She supposed the space was as close to what a mortal would call home. She wasn't one for sentiment, but her whole body relaxed the moment she entered every time.

No eyes, no pressure, no expectations. Just...quiet.

The large quilted bed was a luxury very few had ever come to glimpse under the mountain. She had her own desk, sitting area, and firepit. A part of her used to feel guilty for the riches, but Zaiana had earned her place. Through blood; through sacrifice. She'd worked from the bottom just like any of them.

Zaiana didn't plan to bring Amaya here. There was one smaller private living space she knew had been vacant for over a century. But in a flash of cowardice, she couldn't bring herself to go there. Not when memories of its previous occupant and what she'd done with him there throbbed in her head. It was a last-minute decision to bring Amaya to her own rooms. Though even as she felt the young dark fae timidly at her back, she was relieved to feel no regret.

Zaiana finally twisted to her, finding Amaya barely over the threshold, scanning the room while she clutched a small bundled cloth. "Close the door."

Amaya quickly did as she asked then took a few tentative steps inside. Zaiana let her observe it all, not really caring what she made of her private space. Going over to the firepit, she summoned the sparks of her lightning to her two fingertips, enjoying the vibrations along her skin. She played with the purple bolts that weaved between her fingers. Then she cast her iron-clad fingers down, sending the collective bolt to strike the wood. The logs popped and crackled, slowly catching in a flame that merged until an inferno filled the darkness. Zaiana breathed in the wholesome smell of burning wood and eased her muscles against the glorious heat.

She forgot about Amaya for a few seconds, silent as a ghost. Turning her head, she found her observing the bookcase with curiosity. Zaiana's personal collection. None of the scriptures she'd touched in over one hundred years.

Zaiana expected her to say something of her rooms or at least ask why she'd been brought here. Amaya didn't tear her eyes from the books as she said, "They're all stories." Her observation held a question Zaiana didn't answer. "I didn't imagine you as one to read fantasies."

"I don't," Zaiana said foolishly, with a bite of defense. She turned to the darkling fully, hands folding behind her back as she enjoyed the warmth behind her. "Not anymore," she amended.

Amaya raised her hand to caress the spines. They were all covered in dust from neglect, not that Amaya showed any care for it. She halted on one, twisting to catch Zaiana's eye. "May I?"

Zaiana's head cantered out of curiosity, but then she gave a small nod in affirmation. She watched Amaya drop her small bundle of belongings onto the long lounge chair before peeling the chosen book from the case. Strangely, Zaiana was fascinated. She couldn't be sure what it was about the young dark fae that made her want to know more, as if the depth of her person was endless yet no one stopped for long enough to figure her out.

The book opened, and she splayed it across her hands. Then a small smile spread over her cheeks, suppressed as though it longed to be a grin. Zaiana frowned, but her question was answered when their gazes met.

"I definitely didn't take you as one to read romance," Amaya commented. There was a hint of teasing in the darkling's voice that took Zaiana aback. Very rarely did anyone use such a casual tone with her. Her inner circle was not always so formal, but it wasn't often Zaiana felt her face twitch in genuine lighthearted *amusement.*

"If you value your innocence, I'd be selective about which books you dive into from that particular row," Zaiana said, only now realizing which set had caught her attention.

Amaya's cheeks flushed, and Zaiana's eyes danced. She found her reaction oddly endearing.

"Sorry," she muttered in slight embarrassment.

Amaya closed the book, but Zaiana said, "You should read it. You're old enough to find enjoyment in such…descriptive texts. Though I would wait until you move to your own room," she said as casually as she could at Amaya's amusing flustered look. Zaiana schooled her face.

"There's no shame in finding out what brings you pleasure. Just as there's no shame if you find those books aren't to your particular taste."

The darkling's stiff posture relaxed, and she offered a timid smile, laying the book down next to her things. "I'm getting my own room?" she asked in disbelief, doubling back to the detail.

Zaiana nodded. "If you're to be one of us, I can't have you undermined in a hall of rogues and imbeciles." She eyed Amaya then her pitiful bundle of belongings. "You'll stay here tonight. Tomorrow, you'll have your own room."

She had to face it. Finnias's old room. She refused to bow down to cowardice over foolish memories. Mercifully, Amaya didn't deign to ask why. Perhaps she was becoming in tune with Zaiana's signs and knew when not to question further. The darkling was a quick learner—Zaiana had to admire it.

Fatigue started to weigh on Zaiana's eyes. She unbuckled her sword belt, discarding it by her bed as usual. She said nothing as she went to the trunk at the foot of the bed and found her nightclothes, giving no warning as she began to change. Sliding a glance at Amaya, she found her rustling through her own pile, but she didn't seem to have anything even mildly comfortable to sleep in. Zaiana realized she likely slept in what she wore and had only one alternative outfit. A lack of basic essentials Zaiana once knew.

When she was in her sleep leggings and had pulled the thick jumper over her head, Zaiana sighed. She opened her trunk once more, finding a spare set of pajamas that would likely be too big for the small dark fae. But at least they would be comfortable.

"Here," she said, and as Amaya caught her eye she tossed the items to her.

Amaya's eyes widened as she looked between Zaiana and the articles of clothing. She seemed inclined to thank her, but Zaiana's look warned against it, so she offered a small smile instead. An act of simple decency didn't need to be commended.

Zaiana busied herself with preparing her bed for sleep to give Amaya some privacy to change. She sat on the edge and pulled at the piece of cloth that bound her long braid, unraveling her waves of ink-black hair. Figuring Amaya had finished slipping into the nightclothes, Zaiana stood and grabbed the blanket folded over the foot of her bed. She walked the few strides and held it out to the darkling. Timidly, Amaya reached for it. Zaiana turned to leave her to get comfortable, but Amaya's small voice halted her.

"Why are you being so kind to me?"

Zaiana stiffened with her back to Amaya. The question inspired a need to take it all back, to cast her back to the dorms and rescind her offer of sanctuary. Kindness was a weakness—it was what she had always been taught. She didn't turn to her as she said, "You're to be a weapon in my arsenal, Amaya. Don't mistake this as anything more than my doing what is necessary to keep you out of the hands of those who will attempt to dull the edge of your blade while I sharpen it."

As she made it to her bed and pulled back the covers, she dared a look at the silent darkling. Amaya was fixing herself under the blanket so her wings dangled off the long cushioned seat. She didn't speak again or even respond with one of those insufferable innocent looks—eyes that pinned Zaiana as if she were someone not to simply follow and obey, but trust and admire.

Zaiana knew it was for the best she set the rules down hard on the darkling. She trained warriors, not puppy dogs. Yet as she climbed into bed, she couldn't shake the feeling her last words weren't entirely the truth.

CHAPTER 23

Faythe

"**B**ETTER, BUT STILL LACKING."

Faythe panted, spinning around to stare down at Livia in incredulity as she finished the assault course for the third time that afternoon.

"She's doing great," Reylan defended from the sidelines. He stood with arms crossed and frowned in irritation at his cousin. Faythe didn't need him to stick up for her, but she didn't have it in her to scold him for interjecting on her behalf.

Livia cast him a flat look. "This is why you weren't invited to this session." She paced over to Faythe, poised, and looked her over with a commander's assessing gaze. "Am I being too harsh on your sensitive feelings, Faythe?"

She ground her teeth at the mockery. Then she directed a subtle glare at Reylan as a warning to stay out of it. Livia smirked at the exchange, and Faythe couldn't be sure if her taunting was purposeful, intended to rouse a reaction and expose her reckless, unhinged side.

"You're fast, agile, but this is a game, and it shows that's all it is to you. On the battlefield, you'd be wiped out within minutes." She glanced over at Reylan and Kyleer who stood on the sidelines. Neither said anything, and Faythe was quietly taken aback, caught between anger that they had kept such insight from her out of concern she would be offended and embarrassment that they thought it necessary. "It seems I may have to be the one to state the obvious here, but you're human, Faythe, and you need to stop trying to rise to the expectations of a fae you'll never be able to compete with in strength and stealth. But you're smart, and you have the advantage of your ability. You shouldn't be wasting your time running a course that does nothing to train your biggest weapon: your mind."

"She has a point," Kyleer chimed in casually. He stood mimicking Reylan's position, and the general slid him a warning glance for siding with his cousin. It was oddly amusing.

Clashing steel preceded a loud *thump*, and an audible groan had them all snapping their attention to across the hall. Reuben lay on his back in the training ring, clutching his shoulder while Izaiah propped himself up with his sword. He looked thoroughly unimpressed.

"Don't even get me started on him. He could get us killed, and I hope seeing this might get you to change your mind about allowing him to come," Livia commented with a disapproving shake of the head as she stared at Reuben now fumbling to his feet.

Faythe winced but flared in defense. "It's not for me to *allow* him to do anything."

"He could get us all killed out there."

"You don't have to concern yourself with him."

Livia backed up a few paces, going over to the weapons rack and retrieving two swords. As she returned, Izaiah and Reuben also ended their session to come over to the training ring Livia and Faythe occupied. The commander extended Lumarias expectantly, but her expression was hard. Faythe took her sword with apprehension.

"When we stand on the lines of battle waiting for it to begin, do you think I don't care for each and every soldier regardless of their station?" Livia angled her blade in a silent command for Faythe to take her stance.

Faythe swallowed hard but braced her legs in a firm defensive position. Livia moved, and she was fast. Faythe honed in on her mind to keep up as they began a loose parry around the ring. "Of course not," she breathed, trying to stay focused.

Livia twisted around her, switching sides. She was incredibly swift on her feet, and Faythe found herself challenged more than she had been in some time. She was so used to sparring against tall, broad warriors like Reylan that she'd allowed herself to get complacent against opposition who almost matched her in height and build. Fighting Reylan required strength and speed; against Livia she needed focus and attention as she too was a master dancer with a blade.

It wasn't long before Faythe was caught in a killing strike when Livia's blade hovered at her throat. "Of course not," Livia repeated, lowering her sword to give Faythe a chance to collect her breath. "Regardless of what I think, out there, we're all equal. The strike of a weapon knows no rank. Everyone watches each other's back." Livia cast another look over to Reuben, who shifted under her gaze.

None of her companions had been particularly pleased when Faythe informed them of their last-minute addition over a week ago. None of them had been subtle about it either. Still, there was no dissuading her friend. They were set to begin their journey by week's end and had spent every day since either in training or in the drawing room going over logistics. There were so many conflicting opinions on every decision Faythe had to make that she had been forced to have no input at all, letting the fae—who were at least acquainted with the lands beyond Ellium—battle it out for who would lead in terms of direction.

"You want to be the commander of this mission, Faythe. Everyone you bring along with you is on your neck." Livia backed up a few strides then twisted to angle her sword again. It was a silent taunt for Faythe to advance first.

"I didn't ask any of you to come." Faythe lunged but cleaved nothing except air as she struck out a round of offense attacks. Livia moved like the wind out of the path of her blade.

"Because you're weak and afraid," Livia remarked, clashing swords with her.

Faythe spun low, but Livia caught her blade while simultaneously spinning around and kicking the backs of her knees. Faythe fell but didn't allow herself to stay down for Livia to end it again so fast. She rolled, pushing herself to her feet just in time to lock blades with her before Livia could claim victory.

"You don't know anything about me," Faythe hissed in defense, feeling her fury rise at the taunting insults.

"I know enough," Livia dismissed casually.

Steel sang, and Faythe forgot about their companions who stood as onlookers as she honed in on her moving target. The more Livia riled her, the more her determination rose to prove her wrong. The commander's smile was goading, and Faythe didn't hesitate to clash swords with her once more. The room became a blur, and the steel sang to her senses. She canceled out friend from foe, desperate to wipe the victorious look off her face.

"Slow," Livia chanted. "Weak." She folded one arm behind her back as she continued to deflect against Faythe's blows as if to mock her further. Her anger built, almost overflowing into recklessness. "A *coward.*"

The final insult flashed across her gaze in a white rage, and Faythe delved deeper into Livia's mind—farther than she should. The commander gasped, dropping her sword when Faythe commanded her to through her ability. Then she forced Livia to her knees, taking a step forward to meet her, and braced her arms to plunge Lumarias into her chest.

Faythe panted heavily in her anger, but when it subsided and she realized what she'd done, she backed up a few strides in cold horror, severing her connection to Livia's mind all at once.

"I'm sorry," she said quickly.

She watched in wide-eyed guilt as the commander rose to her feet again, looking oddly awed. Faythe glanced at the others at the side of the ring who also looked quietly stunned. Reylan had one foot braced in the training platform as if he were about to step in and intervene before Faythe's final maneuver.

Livia grinned then huffed a laugh along with a shake of her head. Faythe was quietly taken aback by the reaction considering the invasive cheat she'd used.

"You've been holding back, Faythe. I knew you had more in you than just being able to glance surface thoughts during combat."

Faythe blinked, realizing now that Livia had purposely roused her past breaking point with her words.

"Don't limit yourself. The battlefield is never a place to think of fairness when your life is on the line. You have a great advantage. Use it."

Faythe's heart calmed, and her guilt eased that there was no resentment from Livia for her invasion of her mind.

"Your anger, however, could get you killed no matter how skilled you are. I've seen the way it consumes you, and if you don't learn to tame your storm you're as good as useless," Livia went on, pacing toward Faythe. When she got close enough, her face held understanding as her voice dropped low, personal. "You're right—I don't yet know much about you. Those were just hollow words, Faythe, but they strike you because you believe them to be true. Only you can be the one to prove otherwise within yourself."

Faythe dipped her head in appreciation of Livia's guidance, even if it were more obscure and brutal than her cousin's. She cast a look over to the silver-haired warrior who was frowning at them intently, offering a weak smile as she strolled over to her friends, finished with combat for the day.

It pained her as she looked at their faces. Reylan, Kyleer, Izaiah, Livia, and Reuben—they were all ready and willing to follow her in an uncertain quest across perilous territory. But she no longer felt the stabbing guilt. They had all made their choice, and she was filled with more strength and pride than she'd ever felt before at having them by her side.

"I can't thank you enough for all you're risking for this," Faythe said quietly.

The quest loomed closer by the hour. Soon, they would leave their comforts behind and not be sure when they would return.

"Why is everyone so gloomy about this? See the adventure! You all just need to have a little..." Izaiah paused as his gaze fell to her, a cunning grin splitting his cheeks. "Have a little *Faythe.*" He shot her a wink, reveling in the play on her name.

Faythe rolled her eyes as she stepped down from the training platform, and they all turned to leave the hall. "I don't think faith and belief are going to help us out there," she commented.

Izaiah smirked. "Oh, I don't mean in the literal sense." Faythe's brow curved in question, and he grinned wickedly. "To have Faythe: to live like death is a game, love is a prize, and danger is desire."

Livia giggled, and even Reylan's stern face upturned in amusement.

"Who knew you could be so poetic, Izaiah?" Livia remarked. "It's quite fitting."

Faythe's cheeks heated while they all teased, but her embarrassment was cast aside by the smiles upon their faces that brought her great joy to see. Reylan caught her eye, sapphires bright with the warmth on his face. The others were ahead, chatting between themselves.

"To having Faythe," he declared quietly.

CHAPTER 24

Faythe

FAYTHE STOOD IN the familiar comfort of her gold-and-white mists, anxiously working herself up for what she was about to attempt. It had been over a week since her first full night's rest followed by her talk with Agalhor and his helpful advice about how to cure her night terrors. So far, she'd only succumbed to them twice and was slowly managing to rest her mind and find her subconscious before the nightmares gripped her first.

Reylan offered invaluable support, and every time she awoke unable to reel in her terror-filled mind and grasp where she was, he was right there to ground her instantly. He would stay awake with her for hours after those nightmares, and they'd simply talk until her mind found peace once more.

Faythe observed the colors of her mind as if they would turn to the black-and-gray smoke she so desperately longed to see. Every night she made it here she tried to project herself across the kingdoms, but she was never strong enough. Maybe it was the intermittent nightmares that still dampened her strength and ability, but she was starting to fear more than anything that perhaps she had never been strong enough even without the strain on her magick.

With a deep breath, Faythe reached up to hold Nik's star pendant in her palm. She closed her eyes and prayed with everything she had that she would be able to make it there this time. She focused all her mental energy, pictured the prince, imagined High Farrow, and visualized the clouds of his subconscious. She pulled on all her memories of him and forced her will to see him.

She felt herself projecting, casting far out into an endless oblivion where she floated through a void without time; a space with infinite destinations. But it wasn't long before her collected hope shattered as she felt the familiar damning force wrap around her, eager to pull her back to confinement. Her mind had reached the end of its elasticity. She tried to push past that hold and defy magick's dark chant that it would take far more of her if she dared. Faythe kept pushing, even past her throbbing headache that rang with alarm. She knew the consequences could be fatal if she kept trying as Reylan's warning about her limits rang through her desperation to just. Keep. Pushing.

With a sob of defeat, Faythe let go.

She was thrown back into the confines of her subconscious, landing painfully with force. She didn't bother trying to stand up as she curled into herself and cried. *Gods*, she missed her friends so hard it cut deep and physical. All she needed was to see Nik and hear the others were safe. Even if just for a minute. Faythe trembled as she thought of them and what they might think of her as she'd failed to check in even once in months.

As she lay there, she felt something trying to pull her from her subconscious. She wanted to fight it and stay, to wallow in her own self-pity and failure, but it became far too strong for her to resist, and reluctantly, she gave in to that pull.

Her eyes fluttered open—not to meet darkness as she expected. Instead, familiar sapphire eyes looked down on her. Then she felt his hand at her face, his warm palm at her cheek momentarily soothing the pain in her heart. He pulled it away once she was awake, the cold breezed across the damp trails giving away that she'd been crying.

Reylan's face was deeply disturbed and etched with concern. "Another nightmare?" he asked softly.

Faythe bit her lip, shaking her head, and had to cover her face out of shame and defeat. "I can't do it," she croaked.

She felt the bed dip as Reylan inched closer. Then his hands went over hers to guide them down from her face. "You don't have to hide from me, Faythe." His words were enough to soothe some of her grief, and she composed herself. She shuffled up to sit against the headboard as she took deep breaths to calm down.

"I can't Nightwalk to Nik. I'm not strong enough. We leave in a couple days, and the journey will take me farther from High Farrow. I won't get to see him or hear about Jakon and Marlowe and Tauria before we go, and…and perhaps I never will. And they'll never know why I had to do it." The truth crushed her spirit all over again. That should she not return, she would never get the chance to explain to him, nor to see him one last time.

Reylan sat up abruptly before getting out of bed. Faythe's panic surged.

"Where are you going?" she asked as she watched him reach for his shirt, thinking perhaps he'd had enough of having to console her with no result. Her fear was momentarily overshadowed as she couldn't tear her eyes from his toned torso in the moonlight that highlighted his every impressive contour. When he pulled his shirt over his head, she was glad for the darkness to disguise the heat that flooded her cheeks—and her whole body.

Reylan hastily pulled on his boots and must have read the worry on her face as his features softened from hard determination. "I'll be back in a few minutes," he assured her as he stood and made for the door.

Faythe relaxed at the promise even though her heart still sank the moment she was left alone in the dark solitude of her rooms. She tucked her knees to her chest as she waited, unable to peel her eyes from the door as if she didn't believe he would return. She wouldn't blame him if he decided she was a lost cause and didn't want to suffer sleepless nights with her any longer. But her heart selfishly ached at the thought.

Faythe counted the minutes, the stillness chanting cruelly that she deserved to be alone. Then the door creaked open, and she jerked up, overjoyed at the silver hair that wandered through it. She loosened off as he once again settled in beside her. Faythe stayed silent, waiting for him to explain.

"I don't know if it'll work," he said apprehensively. "I borrowed power from another Nightwalker."

Faythe's eyebrows rose. "Have you ever Nightwalked before?"

Reylan nodded. "Only to see what it was like. I've never had a personal use for it—I tend to prefer more physical abilities." He paused, and she could see he was deliberating. "I've never been able to pass power that I've taken to anyone else, but in High Farrow with the temple ruin, when we touched…it was like I could feel you, but you could also feel me." He scratched the back of his neck, and she almost believed it was out of nervousness or embarrassment for what he was going to propose. Faythe bit her lip, finding his flustered look highly amusing. "It seemed worth a try to see if I could somehow strengthen your Nightwalking with what I have within. Just like with the power of the ruin."

Faythe blinked, astonished they hadn't thought to try it sooner. It made sense, but at the same time, it seemed like a shot in the dark. "How do we try?"

Reylan shifted down the bed until he was lying flat. Faythe did the same and waited expectantly. Hesitant, Reylan held out his palm to her, and her heart skipped a beat. Slowly, she reached over, sliding her fingers over his, holding her breath at the warm trail that shivered up her arm and through her chest, until their fingers were entwined and palms joined. Reylan looked at their joined hands, but she couldn't read what passed his thoughtful face in the few seconds of silence.

"Once you fall asleep, wait for me in your subconscious."

Faythe didn't have words to respond with when his voice seemed to thicken as if he were holding back a desire to pull her closer. The gap between their bodies held a noticeable coolness. When her quickening pulse prevented her from speaking, Faythe nodded in understanding then let her eyes flutter closed. She willed her heart to settle and tried to ease her racing mind, but her thoughts were tense. Then she felt the gentle caress of Reylan's thumb over her own. The movement was soothing and a comforting sign of his patience as he waited for her to fall asleep. It tamed her restlessness and slowed her thumping pulse. Soon, sleep beckoned her, and she let the shallow vibrations of Reylan's touch send her into the blissful arms of darkness.

Faythe waited patiently in the confines of her gold-and-white mist. Irrationally, she felt *nervous* at the thought of Reylan's presence in her mind. Although she'd allowed Nik in many times, it felt different with the general, perhaps more *intimate* as she welcomed him into the deepest, most personal part of herself. Faythe foolishly observed her colors as if this were her home and she was inspecting it for disarray before hosting guests. But she didn't get the chance to work herself up further when she felt a familiar impression in her mind. She released her barriers to him completely, feeling no need to hide anything.

Reylan materialized before her, and a smile bloomed across her face of its own making. Reylan didn't return it. He had yet to glance her at all while his eyes roamed over their surroundings instead.

Faythe watched him carefully. He was slow to walk to her, his reaction not what she was expecting. He looked around her mists as if he were *searching*. No lines creased his face, but in his wandering gaze it was as though he traveled elsewhere while observing her colors. Then his eyes met hers, and Faythe was claimed by his look. Just for a split second with their air of wonder. A tremor swept through her as he neared, stopping close enough to touch.

She wanted to ask what he was thinking, noting he'd closed off all his own emotions in here. Never would she think to break past those boundaries though it was within her power to do so. Before she could, Reylan cast a look around once more, the tension shifting as he made a casual, curious sound.

Faythe folded her arms. "You don't seem impressed."

Reylan chuckled at her reaction. "I guess I'm just not surprised." He stuck a hand out, and in his palm a small tornado swirled beautifully, slowly separating the white until it was a flurry of pure, glittering gold.

Faythe was momentarily awestruck. Nik had never been able to manipulate her mists. Or at least he'd never tried to. But even in Nik's mind, she couldn't recall having an influence on its appearance or otherwise.

"What color is yours?" she asked when he let his display dissipate.

"I don't have one."

She heard the lie. "Tell me!"

When he stayed silent in amusement, Faythe huffed. "You know I could just find out for myself."

He huffed a laugh. "I may not be a Nightwalker, but I would know if you tried to enter my mind."

Faythe grinned in challenge. "We'll see." Then, dropping the subject, she asked, "So, how do we do this?"

"I don't know if it will work," he began as if in apology before even trying. He looked afraid to give her false hope.

Faythe offered a warm smile. "It's worth a try no matter whether it works or not," she assured him, making sure he knew her disappointment would never be directed at him.

His nod was wary but accepting. "When you Nightwalk, I'll be forced back into my own mind while your mental being channels to Nik's. I'm hoping if I remain in my own subconscious until you return, through our mental and physical connection I may be able to pass some of my power to you and strengthen your reach."

As he explained his plan, Faythe stared with raised brows. Reylan was brilliant. Utterly, mesmerizingly brilliant. Her smile stretched out into an eager grin, giddy and hopeful it could work. His own reservations seemed to loosen off at her reaction. Then, wordlessly, he once again held out his hand to her with an encouraging smile.

Faythe's heart fluttered at the sight, and she took one step forward to close the distance. She slid her palm into his with a quick burst of warmth at the thought nothing would ever feel so safe and *right*.

"Thank you," she muttered quietly, not feeling words were enough to express her gratitude for everything he'd done for her.

He didn't respond. She didn't need him to as his soft eyes spoke everything.

For a moment while they stood, she felt nothing. But she continued to stare into the depths of his irises as if she could make the connection through them alone. Then she felt it, starting as a tingling through their joined hands and crawling slowly up her arm. Waves of power—*his* power—humming through her veins and adding new heights to her own. It encased her body, and Faythe felt a strength like never before. It were as if her mind lay dormant until it was sparked to life once more with the joining of their essence, and it filled her with new confidence she would be able to make the leap to High Farrow.

She breathed consciously, adjusting to the surge of energy that awoke all her senses. Reylan's face said it all: he knew it had worked. At least the transfer of his power. She had still to test if it was enough to add to her Nightwalking ability and help her reach Nik. Reylan gave a single nod of encouragement, a silent push for her to try.

So she closed her eyes and thought of Nik, praying with everything she had that it was enough and she would finally see him again.

CHAPTER 25

Nikalias

N<small>IK WAS LOST</small>, hopeless, and alone. With the friction between himself and Tauria, he had no one else to turn to for relief from the emotions that wrecked him from the inside out. He was almost desperate enough to go to Jakon, but while he considered the human a friend, they weren't nearly close enough that he felt comfortable taking his woes to him—not if they would likely flow out of him in insufferable whining.

His mind was a storm with the weight of the duties required to run the kingdom along with the crushing feeling in his chest at the possibility of parting with Tauria. With a long sigh of defeat, Nik walked to his bed, hoping to soothe the pounding in his head by morning with a deep, restful sleep.

Sitting on the edge of his bed, Nik eyed the sleep tonic on the night-stand. He'd become dependent on it to get his turbulent mind to settle, or he'd never manage even a couple hours if he relied on falling asleep naturally. With a huff of anger, he swiped the bottle, dropping the required dose of the foul-tasting liquid onto his tongue before settling into bed.

As his lids grew heavier, he let his pain and sadness drift off, giving in to the clutches of darkness.

Nik waited in his subconscious, as he always did, for a while. Perhaps foolishly, as he was waiting to see if tonight would be the night Faythe finally made it through. As the weeks passed, he understood perhaps she needed time to adjust. As the months passed, he began to dread gifting her the necklace was a futile effort at keeping her close. It was hopeless to believe she could make the subconscious leap so far.

The black-and-gray smoke around him swirled angrier than usual. He couldn't tame it. He didn't want to. With every day that passed, he felt himself slipping into a dark pit of despair he feared could permanently grip his soul.

Nik stood with his hands in his pockets, simply staring into the depthless void ahead as if it were a door that he expected the familiar sight of gold eyes and fair brown hair to walk through. She never did, and he was losing out on much-needed hours of rest by waiting. He knew it would be easier for her to channel into his subconscious if he were present. In his deep rest, she might not be strong enough to wake him and enter.

His shoulders fell as he turned and closed his eyes, about to will himself into the arms of the darkness that would offer temporary numbness...

Then he halted. A faint impression, barely there, made him glance back.

Nik stilled completely, extending his senses and releasing every single barrier in disbelief. Nothing happened, and he began to believe he had imagined the familiar essence imprinting on the edge of his mind. His heart thundered as he waited.

Then color flickered through the dark folds, so faint he had to blink long and hard to be sure this too wasn't of his own imagination.

It was more a ghost forming from his shadows. Until a gold flicker broke the darkness. Then she looked at him, her ghostly form becoming full.

It was Faythe. Unmistakably.

Nik didn't move, in complete terror that he might be conjuring her image on his own, a cruel trick of his desperate mind. But Faythe's brow pinched together, and a shallow cry left her that felt like a tear within himself. It was enough for him to know Faythe was *real*. She was here.

She ran to him, and his arms opened to catch her as they collided. Hers clamped tightly around his neck, and he closed his eyes, breathing deeply into her hair. It relaxed his tormented mind after being so painfully on edge to see and feel her again. Faythe shook in quiet sobs into his shoulder. He didn't know how long they held each other before he released her, letting her toes meet the ground to study her face.

"It's about time you paid a visit," he teased lightheartedly.

Her face fell, a sight that tugged his chest as she buried her face into him again. He held her for as long as it took for her to calm, but his mind reeled. Perhaps she hadn't been well all this time in Rhyenelle. And he'd left her there.

In a flash of panic and rage, he took her shoulders to peel her away from him and scanned her for any possible sign of injury or distress. "Did something happen?" he asked calmly, but he was one short fuse away from erupting if she had been mistreated in any way, by anyone.

Faythe shook her head and wiped her face with the backs of her hands. It was a small relief and relaxed his rigid posture, but something was still wrong.

"I'm sorry I didn't come sooner. I—" Faythe paused, choking up again. Nik tried to be patient, his hands curling into fists as he waited for her to explain. "I haven't been strong enough."

His whole body loosened, and he released his anticipation in an exhale. "You're here now."

Her small smile wrenched his heart. "I don't know how long I have. Reylan is helping me, filling in the strength I can't gather on my own to channel here. At least not while...not while I'm still having nightmares."

Nik pulled back, running a hand through his hair. "Shit," he swore in a wave of immense guilt. How could he not have thought her trauma might affect her Nightwalking? He'd been plagued with nightmares before and could have warned her if he hadn't been too overwhelmed to ignore everything she went through in High Farrow. "I should have thought... I should have warned you."

Faythe shook her head to halt him, but it didn't ease his self-loathing that he had failed her by letting her traverse across kingdoms to suffer in silence for months while he was wrapped up in his own problems. The only consolation was that she was here now, and from the look on her face, it was exactly what both of them needed.

When they released each other at last, Faythe shivered, and as she did, Nik took in the sight of her in the short nightgown. Clearly, she didn't anticipate making it here tonight. Her whole face flushed as she too looked down at herself and tugged at the hem. Nik smirked, and his hand came around her shoulders once more. In his subconscious mind, he materialized a cloak and fastened it around her. Faythe's gratitude flowed through him while she left her mind open and vulnerable.

"We have a lot to catch up on, and not a lot of time," she muttered quietly.

He didn't hide his sadness. He didn't hide anything and knew she would be able to feel everything while she was in his subconscious anyway. He didn't care. He wouldn't risk putting a strain on her link here by trying to shield anything. He wasn't afraid. Faythe would never judge him for his vulnerability.

Nik conjured a bench, and they sat, neither knowing where to begin but also acutely aware of their precious time counting down rapidly.

"How are Jakon and Marlowe?" Faythe asked, trying to muster a brave face that was discredited by the creases of longing in her expression.

"They're well. Jakon makes a fine emissary, and the gates to the Caius City have been opened indefinitely for both fae and humans. Marlowe insists on keeping up with work at the blacksmiths, but her home is at the castle." Nik felt Faythe's joy, and it thawed a small piece of the ice that had started to freeze his chest.

"I knew you would make a fine king," she said quietly, choked with emotion.

He was humbled by the comment, but he didn't feel deserving of it.

"And Tauria?"

He had to look away, but his pain at the mention must have alarmed Faythe as she shifted closer, body angled to face him.

Nik took a long breath. "She plans to leave for Olmstone."

Faythe's inhale was audible enough that he turned to see the shock on her face. Her wide-eyed look fell quickly into a firm, lecturing frown. "What happened?" Her voice didn't hide her accusation, and Nik's gut twisted.

He took a deep breath, knowing this was his first chance to get word to Rhyenelle about what he suspected of Olmstone. "I think Varlas might be looking to Valgard for aid. I don't believe he has given up on his path of vengeance."

As Nik relayed the rest—everything he knew, and Tauria's brilliant but dangerous proposition—Faythe fluctuated between shock, anger, and disbelief. "She can't," she said firmly. "How can you let her walk right into the arms of the enemy?"

Nik flared. "It's not *my* decision. She is a queen, Faythe—her actions are for the good of her people and the prospects of her kingdom. It's not an easy responsibility."

Faythe winced, and Nik immediately realized his error as his harsh tone came out in a bitter gibe. He didn't know what she was going through in Rhyenelle, and if she too was beginning to experience the weight of the monarchy…

"She's not safe there alone," Faythe said quietly, but she knew as much as he did that there was no dissuading Tauria once she'd set her mind on something.

"She won't be alone. At least, not in her mind. I'll be Nightwalking to her to gather information. I won't be able to interact with her in her subconscious like we can, but I'll be able to plant thoughts and feelings. I won't allow her to feel alone."

Faythe smiled warmly, reaching to take his hand. "You are good, Nik."

He shook his head. "No, I'm not. I should find another way that won't risk her being in their grasp should things take a turn for the worse. But I have nothing else—not to offer her—and no other plans to get us what we need."

"She'll be okay. Tauria is one of the smartest, most resilient people I know. She'll know what to do in any situation. Once she's achieved what she needs, she'll come home."

Nik wasn't going to tell her about Tauria's very real, aching plan should Olmstone not turn out to be a threat, but he felt Faythe's grip tighten and imagined his desolation was suffocating the air. "I don't think High Farrow is her home anymore," he admitted quietly. "She may be going to find out if Olmstone has malicious intent, but should there turn out to be nothing, her true intention is to entertain a marriage alliance with Tarly."

Faythe's shock rippled through him. "She can't be serious."

"I can assure you she is."

"She doesn't have feelings for Tarly."

Nik couldn't deny the satisfaction she stoked with those words, but he wasn't an arrogant fool to believe Faythe knew how Tauria truly felt despite what she may have confided in her. "Feelings are often a luxury we cannot afford," Nik answered quietly. He felt Faythe's understanding —perhaps even her fear should the same fate befall her if she decided to embrace her heritage.

"I know you, Nik… Are you really willing to let her go?"

Nik stood, sliding his hands into his pockets as he stared into the darkness. "If it is what will keep her safe, then yes, I am."

"I don't understand…"

Nik's heart pounded, and he took a few long seconds to collect his thoughts, feeling the overwhelming need to explain, to have someone other than his demons know the truth. He glanced over the black-and-gray whorls of his grim subconscious mind. "It used to be green," he said vacantly, pausing to swallow the hard lump that choked his airway. "My mist…it has always been a darker tone than yours, but the gray—it used to be green. It's been over a century now, and I often forget about it." He turned back to her, and Faythe stood, glancing around with a note of sorrow.

"What happened?"

Despite what she might think about him after he voiced his eternal torment, a small weight lifted at what he was about to confess—a story he had never told a soul before. But he had to tell her; had to make her understand.

"After my mother was killed, I was so consumed by my need to discover the culprit. My father tried, but I always believed he could have done so much more considering she was the queen—his *mate.*" Nik's fists curled, but Faythe's comforting warmth embraced him through the tether of their minds. "I spent days on end tracking and seeking out those who claimed to be experts in the field. Tauria was the only one that kept me grounded, or I might have gone insane in my *need* to find them. She talked me down from many reckless, harrowing ideas. I would be a completely different person now if it weren't for her becoming my conscience. Tauria…I owe her everything. And I have treated her so awfully, but only because I thought it would be better for her *not* to want me. Because I thought I was protecting her…from me."

He had to pause to ease the tightening in his throat, his chest. Faythe stayed silent, letting him relay his story.

"I found someone who led me to a woman who claimed to be a seer. Someone who could glimpse pasts and futures. I was too desperate to even question the absurdity of a human having such talents. She wasn't like Marlowe, and technically, she was nothing beyond mortal. What she had gained a name for was the item she possessed: a Mage Mirror." He heard Faythe's heart quickening and stole a glance at her reaction as he paced. She'd dropped a shade paler. "She lived in a rundown trailer and traveled through kingdoms luring people in to glimpse knowledge they thought they wanted. I was warned by those who knew of her that people who went to her didn't gain hopeful insight. Many of them fell to insanity, some ending their own lives over what they discovered through the Mage Mirror. I didn't care—I *had* to try. Yet what I learned that day haunts me still and will for the rest of my days. It is not the mirror itself that should be feared, but what lives within it."

Faythe's breath caught, and he halted his steps, thinking he'd shared too much and frightened her.

"Did it have a name?"

Nik's brow furrowed at the odd question, and he thought back. "Not exactly. Though I believe it was a creature called—"

"A Dresair."

Nik's pinched brow lifted then. "How do you know?"

"Because I have encountered one before. Below the castle in High Farrow." A second passed. Then realization dawned on him all at once, striking him cold and still. "I saw it when I went to retrieve the ruin, and the only way to leave with it was to accept the knowledge." Her voice cracked; her eyes glittered. "I knew he was going to die," she whispered.

Nik was stunned, having already concluded what she meant. *Who* she meant.

Caius.

Faythe dropped her eyes to the ground as if they were weighted with guilt. "Or at least, I knew one of you would die while we tried to stop your father. If I had known it would be Caius, if I had considered him more, perhaps he would still—"

Nik took the few steps to her. His hand grasped her chin, and his eyes were fierce as he said, "His death is not on your conscience, Faythe. Not even for a second."

Faythe's lip wobbled, but she gave a small nod. When he released her, she took a calming breath, throat bobbing to swallow the immeasurable grief. "What did you find out when you faced the Dresair?" Her question was careful, and Nik's gut twisted with the knowledge he had harbored all this time.

"It told me it would give me what I needed, but in return, I would shoulder the burden of a dark glimpse of the future."

Faythe nodded, painful understanding clear in her wince.

"I didn't get the information about my mother's murderer. That was the first trick I fell into. Apparently, that was not what I *needed*. Instead," —Nik raised an open palm and materialized a version of the item he received that day—"it gave me this."

Faythe gasped, eyes widening as she raised delicate fingers but made no move to take it. He almost wished she would as even the sight of the thing—a single small red feather—had mocked him for nearly a century, having no purpose in exchange for the burden of knowledge he was left with. He was a fool to trust the Dresair.

"Do you know what this is?" Faythe asked through a breath of disbelief.

Nik furrowed his brow, dropping his hand. Faythe squinted to catch the odd-colored feather, but it remained suspended in the air at his command. He slid his hands into his pockets as he examined it.

"A waste of my time is what it is."

"You're wrong."

Nik curved an eyebrow, but she didn't meet his eye.

"You have a Phoenix feather. Albeit a very small one, perhaps from a young Firebird."

Nik almost scoffed, but watching her tenderly trace her fingers over the feather in complete admiration, it seemed it would be an insult to her childish fantasy. "It is nothing but a pheasant feather dyed red. I was tricked. The creature I faced was simply a masterful jester."

Faythe's expression of wonder fell as she angled and dipped her head, glimpsing every possible angle of it as though it would reveal his words to be true. "I can't be sure without seeing it next to the real thing, but if it is real...do you know what it can do?"

Nik wracked his brain for loose teachings. While he found the myth of the Phoenix mighty and awe-inspiring, there were very few who believed it to be true. "The Firebird feathers were said to have healing properties," he recalled from a spark of memory. "If they roamed the land and skies in our history, they were highly protected so they wouldn't be hunted and used for their feathers, which could not only heal, but amplify powers unimaginably."

"Yes," Faythe confirmed, and he wondered what tales they had been filling her head with in Rhyenelle for her to be so entranced. "It's real, Nik. All of it. I've seen it. Agalhor guards a full-grown Phoenix feather in his castle. It's...*alive.*"

Nik shook his head, trying to find the words to gently diffuse her naïve hope. "Even if it were real, it makes no difference. I have no use for it."

"Perhaps you will." Faythe's sparkling amber eyes finally looked up to lock with his. "Retain your ignorance and defiance if you want, but there must be a reason you were given this. Always keep it close to you."

By his command, the feather dispersed into glittering embers until it was engulfed by his darkness.

"What knowledge did the Dresair burden you with in return?"

Nik was embraced by ice at the mention, riddled with the same damning feeling at the mere recollection of that day he was forced to hear the unthinkable. Instead of replying, he wordlessly unfolded the scene around them. Much as it stiffened every muscle in his body to be back, he had to show her, unable to voice the words himself.

From the black-and-gray whorls, faint color filtered through—mostly hues of a saddened brown—as he stepped back into the place that haunted him still. Where everything changed and any prospect of happiness died. They stood inside a sad, rundown trailer that belonged to the one he believed to be a seer. The plump old woman looked as neglected as the home she occupied. Nik might have felt sorry for her had she not been so wicked and cold.

"Look into the mirror and you shall see," the woman's voice croaked. Spindly fingers encased his arm and guided him over to the distorted shape of a tall mirror against a wall.

Nik was staring at his reflection, his face, yet he could no longer associate it with that fae.

"A past, a present, a future to be free."

Nik breathed hard, eyes transfixed on the memory. Warm hands encased his tightly clenched fist, and it was enough to ease his tenseness and stop him from casting the memory away before she could see it. He opened his hand to allow Faythe's palm against his. It was the only thing that kept him grounded. Kept him from wanting to collapse in defeat as though he were hearing the damning knowledge for the first time.

His reflected self smiled: the Dresair wearing his face, so wicked and goading, challenging him without a single word, knowing how tormenting its knowledge would be. "Are you sure you wish to accept what I am about to tell you? It cannot be unheard, prince."

Nik didn't recognize himself in the vision—so detached and cold. He had been so Nether-bent on finding his mother's assassin he had parted with any decent traits he harbored. This version of him was one he wanted to bury and never allow to surface again. It sank his heart to think he had been so emotionless back then…and Tauria still didn't abandon him. She stayed. He pushed and pushed, and she still came back.

When the vision of him nodded in confirmation, the Dresair straightened. "Very well," it sang. "In your quest to stop great evil, the one you are soul-bonded to shall lose their life by *your* hand, and yours alone, prince." The words echoed and taunted. Chilled and swirled in his mind, his gut, his *soul.* They had not stopped replaying since he first heard them.

His hand clenched. No—it was Faythe's grip on him that forced him to glance sideward for her reaction. She stared with a puzzled vacancy at the vision of him.

Nik stilled the memory, not wanting her to see the outpour of rage that followed that confrontation. In truth, he was ashamed of how he reacted, destroying so much in his path he couldn't fully recall the details after his anger had consumed him so wholly. He'd refused to believe the knowledge at first, but if there was a chance it were true...

"I still don't understand," Faythe muttered. She shook her head as the vision dissipated around them, returning to the gloom of his subconscious mist. With nothing to fix her gaze upon, she finally settled her eyes on him. "Soul-bonded? As in—"

"My mate."

Faythe's face was unflinching, but she was clever. Nik watched her fitting the conclusion together on her own. His heart was a hard rapid beat in anticipation. Never before had he been so fearful of judgment, so concerned over the opinion another may have of him. Time crawled as he studied Faythe's every flicker of expression until he saw the exact moment she figured it out. Her face paled; her eyes widened.

Faythe's mouth parted with a pause before out tumbled, "Tauria?"

Nik didn't move. He didn't need to confirm it. This was it: the moment all was revealed to Faythe. His confession that he had used Faythe all that time ago, and that he had pushed away and hurt Tauria more times than he'd ever be able to atone for. The truth about who the

Fenstead princess was to him that he'd buried so deep and never told to a soul.

"Oh Gods." Faythe turned away from him, and each step she took clenched his heart. He couldn't be sure what she was thinking, but the waves of her disbelief were mixed with…anger.

He expected it and was wholly deserving of it. Nik waited for her outpouring of betrayal and rage. But she was silent for far too long, as if calculating where she hurt the most.

"How could you?" she whispered with her back to him.

He opened his mouth to form some kind of pitiful explanation that would never justify his actions, but Faythe turned to him before he could, and something far worse than anger was etched in her expression.

Disappointment.

"How could you do that to her?"

Nik blinked, taken aback. He didn't expect Faythe's concern to be for Tauria before herself. Though it seemed she was already long past what was once between them.

"I didn't want to, and I tried…I tried to resist what I thought I felt for you."

Her brow flinched. Nik's self-resentment swirled like shadows in his gut.

"I wanted to protect you. I wanted you to need me, and I…I led you into something when you were the most vulnerable, if only to keep you close. I'm so sorry, Faythe. You did not deserve that. But you should know what I felt for you then was real. I fell in love with you, just not in the way either of us believed." For a second, he thought he felt her agreement, yet her eyes were pained as she kept her distance from him. "Can you ever forgive me?"

Faythe shook her head, and he wanted to go to his knees if that was what it would take. But she asked, "You haven't told her?"

The diversion from herself, from *them,* took him by surprise. "I knew who she was to me that first night we spent together. I think she might have had her suspicions too. But then my mother died, and I was overcome with grief. I pushed her away in my madness to find her killer. Then I learned the knowledge from the Dresair, and suddenly nothing else mattered. Nothing but keeping her safe. I knew the only way to do so was to make her believe we weren't mates. That what we shared was nothing but a one-night infatuation."

"Nik…" Faythe's voice fell to a sympathetic plea. He hated it. "She deserves to know."

"She wouldn't understand."

"You would never hurt her."

"I don't believe for one second I could ever harm her. I would kill myself before laying a hand on her. But you have only confirmed the worst of my fears, Faythe…" He had to pause. The air left him completely at the thought. "What you learned from the Dresair came to pass. I cannot take that chance. Maybe it's a stab in the dark, but the only way I could think of to *try* to prevent it is to never truly mate with Tauria. There will always be a lingering bond between us—the tragic reason she doesn't know is likely why she hasn't given up on me yet—but without the mating, we are not truly *soul-bonded.*"

Faythe's silence was excruciating, her judgment impossible to decipher. So many emotions filtered between them he couldn't be sure what was his or hers. Finally, she released a long sigh and ran a hand over her face, her fingers pressed to her temple a little longer, but then she strolled over to him. Nik's stiff shoulders relaxed when she was close enough to touch, all tight lines of anger smoothed into sympathy.

"I know how it feels to harbor a secret under the belief it will keep others safe. Sometimes, it's not always what is best." She reached for his hand, and he didn't stop her despite being undeserving of her forgiveness, if that was what this was. "What I felt for you was as real then as it is now, Nik. There is nothing to forgive because I think a part of me has always known that I was right to want you—to need you.

You are right: it was just in the way we both thought. But I regret nothing."

He nodded his understanding, having no words to convey his relief.

"I can't tell you what to do, but you are *good*, Nik. You deserve to be happy."

A deep pain shot through him and stiffened his spine with dread. It was Faythe's pain. And on her face, it was as though she were holding something back.

"What's wrong?"

Faythe dropped her gaze—and his hand. After a short moment, she lifted her eyes to stare ahead in silent contemplation. "You will need each other when I'm gone."

"Gone where?" he dared to ask, on edge while he watched the slow pooling of tears form in the eyes she kept off him. He couldn't bear it, and his hand went to her chin to force her to look at him again as he urgently scanned her face in aid of understanding her sadness. She was putting effort into calming her features as her fingers took his hand. Her eyes turned hard, fierce, and he braced himself.

"We knew it wasn't over, that the conflict with Olmstone was merely a diversion. A distraction." Faythe rubbed her temple again, and his panic surged at the indication she couldn't hold the link much longer.

"Faythe, whatever you're planning, let me help," he begged.

She shook her head. "Marlowe knows. Tell her you saw me tonight and let her tell you everything. Everything I'm sorry I never got the chance to tell you myself. Nik—" She paused, choking on whatever her next sentence was meant to be.

"Don't do anything foolish. I'm coming with you. I'll come to Rhyenelle—"

"No." Faythe blinked slowly, leaning more of her weight onto him as he braced an arm around her. If she didn't go back to her own mind soon, she was risking her life trying to exhaust her ability past its limits. "I have all the help I need. Reylan is coming with me."

259

Nik's pained wince almost broke through at the mention of the general. A lingering guilt twinged every time he pictured the two together. But above all else, Nik was relieved.

"Then you are with the best of us all." At least, the best for *her*.

Faythe's smile was sad but grateful. "Speak with Marlowe—she will help you to understand why I had to do this. Marvellas has to be stopped, and it can only be me." Her warm hand raised to his cheek, but he was too rigid in dread and panic over something that didn't even make full sense to take comfort in her touch.

"Nik—"

"No, Faythe," he said quickly, knowing he only had precious minutes left. "No goodbyes. I will see you again. We all will."

She released a sob and fell into him. He held her as if the moment could last forever. "I hope so," she whispered.

He felt her presence fading even though she grappled to stay a little longer. "You can let go now, Faythe. I'll see you soon," he promised.

Her arms tightened, but their grip was weak as her strength rapidly faded. "Tell Jakon and Marlowe I'm safe and that I miss them."

"You'll get to tell them yourself," he said quietly.

A guilty pain stabbed his chest knowing he wouldn't get the chance to apologize for breaking his promise by sending her friends across the sea to Rhyenelle. All he could do was pray they made it safe to explain it all to her themselves.

"Tell Tauria…tell her I know she can do it. And that her people live. Many of them are in Rhyenelle waiting for her." Faythe pulled back to look at him. "And Nik, thank you. For everything." A single tear fell down her cheek, but as his hand lifted to wipe it away, Faythe faded in his arms, her image becoming transparent. She faded and faded until she was gone and he embraced nothing but darkness. The ghost of her presence lingered to spear a dagger in his gut.

Then he was completely alone again.

Nik couldn't settle the anxious feeling that grew in the pit of his stomach at the knowledge he had to speak to Marlowe straight away to make sense of what Faythe said. He feared for her. But in seeing her, in getting to voice his truth and absorb some of her effortless comfort, a weight had been lifted—one that was close to crushing him completely.

With a heavy heart, Nik turned to take the door to dark oblivion before his demons resurfaced to steal the precious dose of peace Faythe had left behind.

CHAPTER 26

Zaiana

I T WAS A horrible day to stand exposed to the elements on open ground. Wind cut through the passage between the mountaintops surrounding the trial arena, howling like a jeering crowd of onlookers. The mass of bodies and wings actually watching them was utterly silent.

Everyone had gathered outside the mountain to witness the showdown between Zaiana and Maverick. She couldn't blame them. This was likely the highest glimpse of entertainment any of them would get to experience in their lifetimes. Though she certainly had no plans to be ridiculed in the spectacle that was about to unfold.

A dreary, overcast sky dulled the daylight and restricted visibility. Zaiana didn't fret in the slightest that the weather was unfavorable—she liked a challenge. She even hoped it might string out the otherwise easy defeat. The dark fae spectators weren't the only ones giddy with excitement for the battle after all; she was high with adrenaline, every dormant sense rattled awake to her dark pleasure in the face of a fight.

Zaiana unclasped her silver-lined cloak, and it was swiftly taken from her by one in her ranks whose name she didn't know nor care to glean from their face. Her focus was solely on the opposition, who were no more than specks of darkness across the long arena where they huddled before the battle began. Even still, she could make out Maverick's frequent and equally arrogant glances at her. Good. She enjoyed his confidence. It would bring her far greater joy and satisfaction to see him at her mercy once this was over.

She scanned the onlookers, a wave of darkness over every mountain edge and peak. Thousands had crowded to observe, but they were only a fraction of the current line of dark fae. Over a millennium of rebuilding their race and biding their time to raise armies, and the dark fae had amassed in the tens of thousands, many of whom were to be spread out between the conquered kingdom of Dalrune and their High Lord's domain of Valgard.

The observing crowd gave Zaiana conflicting emotions. Pride for those of her blood who were not savage beasts; for the rise of the Silverfairs she had watched unfold. But there was also a small coil of damning darkness at the knowledge she was also akin to those who were beyond humanity.

With a deep inhale, Zaiana tore her eyes from Maverick to turn to her companions. She looked over them all, a smile of pride curling her lips at the lethal ensemble. Dressed in all-black leather fighting attire of the highest caliber, equipped with just enough steel and iron to suit each of their fighting styles. As individuals, they were dangerous. As a team, they were untouchable.

They all stood poised, attentive, and focused, with their undivided attention on her. She was pleased to see even Amaya blended in well as their unexpected seventh member. She'd had small bouts of creeping doubt about the darkling over the past few weeks, but each time she was pleasantly surprised by her, and seeing her now, Zaiana didn't have one single regret about her choice.

"We all know how this ends." Zaiana addressed her inner circle, the closest to what she would ever call real joy or excitement reflecting on her face. "But let's at least have fun with it, shall we?" The same wicked amusement was mirrored on the faces of those in front of her, which added some warmth to her cold chest.

They all gave one short nod of agreement in unison.

"Good. Let's go."

Twisting on her heel, Zaiana led the way out of the alcove where they lingered in wait. They didn't need pep talks; didn't need time to strategize. Zaiana and her six were always one step ahead, solving problems before they were posed. Of course, nothing in battle was ever certain. Planning always came second to mastering adaptability. To expect the unexpected and be able to use mind over body was key to not getting caught out. Zaiana had every faith in herself—not out of arrogance, but from spending every year of her existence learning not only how to stay alive, but how to rise against the odds.

Out in the open, the bitter wind hit hard and cold. Zaiana didn't feel it; with each step she tunneled down into a dark, focused state. The whistling air was silenced, and the thousands of eyes that tracked her disappeared. Down and down she went into the well that canceled out her mercy, straightened her poise, and drowned out every objective in her mind but one. To win.

Maverick locked eyes with her as he led his own band of rogues onto the stone field. Her eyes drifted briefly over to glance at his chosen ensemble, and she didn't refrain from matching his gleeful smile. He may like to poke fun at her obvious choice of soldiers, but Maverick was equally as predictable. What made his choices even more humorous was that he tried not to be. Those behind him were almost carbon copies of the savage brute force. Unlike Maverick, who held a shred of humanity —albeit questionable and lacking a lot of the time—those behind him had cruel, cold expressions and nothing but one goal in life: to kill and not think twice about it.

Momentarily, she wondered what tactics he might have imposed on such heartless beasts. They were prohibited from killing unless in defense of their own lives, but Maverick was cunning and smart. In the gleam of his eye, just for a second…she felt a pinch of what she dared to call fear. Zaiana's identical goading smile faltered, her face falling to a hard promise of death for any of them who thought to cause real harm to her companions. Not even the might of Dakodas herself could save them from Zaiana's wrath if they dared.

Drya and Selain occupied the back-left quarter while Acelin and Kellias took the right. In the center two zones, Amaya was behind her on her right, and Tynan on her left. Zaiana kept walking, out of their zones and into the center half-circle, where she came to a halt at the same time as Maverick.

While she tracked him with a look of violence, his crooked smile remained as if they weren't standing in a battle arena about to face off against one another. His expression was as unfazed and arrogant as ever —a look that would get him killed one day, when she finally took a blade to his pretty smirk.

"You look simply exquisite, Zaiana." Maverick's voice was carried on the wind with a seductive caress.

"We're here to fight, not… What *do* you call your poor performance in the bedroom?" Her tone was shallow enough it wouldn't be caught by anyone but him.

His grin turned feline. "You sound curious to find out. Perhaps after your defeat I can offer you consolation with my *performance.*"

Zaiana gave her best sultry smile, one she knew inspired a lustful shift in him. If it wavered his focus and cracked his guard, she didn't see the harm in playing. "This little battle is likely to be short. I think I'll pass on following one disappointment with another."

Maverick chucked, delight twinkling in his black eyes. She looked him over from head to toe, never one to deny something impeccable to look at. Slender, tall, lethal. The clawed tips of his wings hovered impressively high, splayed slightly apart, and she couldn't be sure if it was to appear all the more intimidating or to shield him from the cold. Zaiana guessed the former as he stood so casually, idly adjusting his cuff as though warm tendrils of sun, not freezing clouds of mist, kissed his skin. The droplets glistened in his hair. They may as well have been enjoying a leisurely bask on a field in spring rather than preparing to face off in battle for all the reaction he gave to his surroundings.

Zaiana turned her gaze to the main viewing platform where the four masters and Mordecai observed from under the cover of a tent that hosted four chairs and a central, more prominent seat of importance. Even from such a height and distance, she could make out the High Lord's feral grin as his eyes pinned her. She didn't balk at the attention even as he rose from his throne and came to stand at the stone edge overlooking the arena. In every visual aspect of the word he appeared a king, broad shoulders clad in the thickest furs over the finest tailored garments, his poise radiating dominance and authority.

"Welcome all to the trial ground," Mordecai's voice bellowed, and it would have been swallowed completely by the whip of the wind were it not for the magick he used to amplify it. "Today, we observe a challenge of strength—and leadership. One will emerge victorious and claim the honorable prize of my utmost commendation." His pause was accompanied by a lingering look directed at her. "To be recognized as the fifth master."

A buzz carried over the cries of the weather—the murmurs of the onlookers. Zaiana's gaze was hard. She didn't want or need his *commendation*, though she supposed whatever his quest was—the real prize to be won—it was to remain a secret. But to become the fifth master... Zaiana couldn't be sure if it was thrill or dread that straightened her spine.

His declaration, and what it meant to every soul watching the delegates, sharpened her desire to win to a dangerous extent. Victory would not only secure her the fate away from the mountain; it would officially rank her above Maverick and place her as equal to those she promised to get vengeance on someday. She couldn't decide what would bring her greater pleasure: Maverick's humiliation to lose and bow to her or the masters' rage that she would match them in station.

Giddiness fluttered her stomach like the lick of a delightful burning flame that blazed higher as she pictured them submitting to her status.

"On the mark of the drum, the trial will begin," Mordecai announced. The crowd grew silent. "Runners and first player, take your positions."

Zaiana didn't glance back at Amaya and Tynan who would be taking stance behind her as they had rehearsed many times. It was a waiting game for the two delegates once the match began. Time to rile the dark bastard and imagine his fealty to her.

"In darkness may you triumph." With the saying of their people, Mordecai flashed her one last gleaming look of satisfaction before he lazily occupied his throne to observe the show.

Zaiana diverted her bored attention from him, switching from one cruel gaze to another when she found Maverick already staring with a sly smile. She held his depthless stare and let the breeze of the chilly air circle her head, her mind, calming it in a serene tornado with cooling notes from the shimmering mist. Neither of them moved. Though she faced the opposition, her attention was masterfully divided to note every flicker and intention of her team behind her. Perhaps the biggest advantage she had was how in tune she was to her companions. She knew Maverick held no bond or relation to those behind him who seemed to have been chosen for nothing but brutality and muscle.

"I'm looking forward to watching you do what you do best," Maverick said.

She wouldn't have reacted to it as she was stilling her mind to a lethal calm for combat, but curiosity got the better of her when she swore among the taunting and arrogance that the twinkle in his eye was genuine admiration. "And what might that be?"

The curl of Maverick's mouth was devastating. "Making it storm."

In her moment of distraction, the loud pound of the drum made her flinch. Before the vibrations ended across the length of the arena, Amaya and Tynan had already taken off.

Zaiana and Maverick would remain with the inner circle until all three of the opposition flags were in the hands of the runner. But they weren't prohibited from fighting to wear down their opponent in the meantime before they raced to locate the final black flag.

Neither delegate moved. Challenge was thick in the glaze of their eyes, and she knew he'd fallen equally into the laser-focused mindset she knew all too well. This combatant was one she had fought and beaten, but she was not immune to defeat with his ruthless determination. He was the single person under the mountain—she admitted with great internal reluctance—who was a worthy opponent.

Maverick's eyes flashed behind her to where she knew her little darkling was displaying her weaknesses in the sky with Tynan covering her. Zaiana refrained from smiling in delight at his scoff.

"This shouldn't take long."

She couldn't fight the upturning of her mouth. "No, I don't think it will."

His eyes narrowed with a canter of his head. "Steel or storm, Zaiana?"

In answer, she drew her sword. Slowly, deliberately, not dropping his stare, which was lined with a dark hunger. With a twist of her wrist, sparks hummed through her veins, prickling her skin, and shot down the length of her blade to turn it into a lethally blazing amethyst. "Both."

He matched her predatory gleam. "I was rather hoping you would say that." Maverick drew his own blade, casting a blue flame to engulf the silver glint in his own signature flare. She expected nothing less. Fire on fire was how they always played. It was beautiful, dangerous, and entirely exhilarating when their energies collided in combat.

"I'm looking forward to seeing you kneel before me."

"I'll get on my knees for you anytime, Zaiana. You know you need only ask." Maverick used his flaming sword to prop himself up in front of her.

"I want your fealty, not your disappointing bedroom favors."

"In the bedroom, I might just yield both."

"If you were the last male on the continent, our species would cease to exist with us."

His deviant grin stretched to his eyes as he took a few slow steps forward, right until he toed the line between their halves. Zaiana didn't display her satisfaction. "We both know I don't need to be the last male for you to finally submit to what you truly desire."

"What I *desire* is to rip the dead heart out of your chest." Zaiana raised her chin. "And I will."

Maverick held a hand to the cold, still organ. "You wound me, my dear."

The sudden roar that broke in a wave over the open space snatched their attention, followed by the single beat of the drum that signaled a captured flag. It didn't come as a surprise to Zaiana, who had been tracking the darkling with every sense she could spare while distracting Maverick. She knew Amaya held the first flag of the game with the aid of Tynan without looking.

Taking the second she gained from Maverick's bewilderment as he twisted his head to glance back, Zaiana struck. Casting her sword arm out, the impact of her lightning blast hit him harder from his foolish proximity. It sent him shooting backward, and he splayed his wings to catch the air and avoid an embarrassing tumble to the ground. As he landed on his feet, boots scraping over the stone, he curled into himself with gritted teeth while the aftershocks subsided. Zaiana beamed in triumph.

Her strike had been enough to send him marginally outside his inner circle. Every time they were forced out of their zone before their turn in the game, it added a penalty time of sixty seconds. Even if his team managed to capture all their flags and release Maverick first, he would be stuck here for however many precious added seconds she could pull from him.

When he straightened, his look was nothing short of shadow-kissed rage. A pissed-off Maverick was perhaps the most pleasing sight to exist. Zaiana kept her sly composure as he stalked back to her.

"You make it too easy, Maverick," she goaded. The more she could rile his anger, the more reckless he would become when it remained the two of them.

"Cheap tricks, Zaiana. I expected better."

"It seems we were both disappointed."

The shift in his arm alerted her to his next move. Just as she caught the flicker of light appearing at his fingertips, Zaiana cast her free hand out, iron claws pointed to strike lightning to flame. When their powers met, they shook the ground beneath them. Zaiana shifted her stance to absorb the impact while amethyst and cobalt fused to create a flare of blinding light. He was strong, but it wasn't the first time she'd tested her ability against his. In a challenge of raw power against power, they would kill each other. The only way to triumph against him was in cunning tricks and agility.

Zaiana took the liberty of casting their beam of merged power skyward, and the echoing beat of two drums was quickly swallowed by the resonating boom of thunder that exploded ferociously over the bleak clouds. The sudden sever of energy had them both panting, and Zaiana took the moment of recovery to spy Amaya just as she sent an arrow into the leg of one of the opposition. What was more satisfying were the two blue flags tied around her belt. The other drumbeat was to signal Maverick had acquired one of theirs, but at least she held the lead. All her players now swarmed the board, and Zaiana inwardly beamed with pride.

Straightening, she dropped her eyes back to Maverick, but his black orbs turned to twin white spheres of fire that hurtled for her, turning a bright blue as they expanded. She twisted around one of them, but her moment of distraction scrambled her mind, preventing her from avoiding the second, which hit her chest like a searing brand. It sent her sprawling back, but she allowed herself to fall to the ground instead of splaying her wings for the air to catch her. The wind would have carried her too far, whereas the harsh scrape of loose stone that cut her palms and wings slowed her.

When she stopped moving, she immediately pushed herself to her knees, glancing to her side. The injury was worth it to see herself still within her circle, a mere inch from being outside of it. Zaiana chuckled then tipped her head back, laughing harder with a haughtiness she knew would entice those shadows of rage that circled Maverick's eyes whenever she bested him.

She stood slowly, dusting herself off with nonchalance. "You can do better than that," she called to him.

In response, another ball of flame was sent for her. Zaiana lifted her sword and braced, allowing the steel to cut through his pathetic shot. Good. She wanted to wear him down. He seemed to realize it, and his fists curled tightly to refrain from brazenly attempting to strike her and deplete his strength. She figured she held the advantage already. She'd succeeded in riling him.

Another sound of the drum, but it was not her final flag that was captured. Maverick's rogues had caught up. Zaiana would have ground her teeth in irritation, except a glance at her team made her wish she didn't have Maverick to be wary of so she could enjoy the entertaining show of Amaya acting exactly as they'd planned. Feeble and weak, scurrying around with glamoured wings that made the brute vultures circle her, so tempted by an easy takedown that they focused on gaining her flags rather than securing their final one to release Maverick.

"We both know they are just for show. The real battle is between you and me."

Zaiana looked to Maverick, who had regained his cool, masterful composure. The insufferable amusement had returned to his cunning little face.

"Just like old times," she responded.

His grin was enticing. "I have missed this."

"Getting your ass handed to you?"

"Watching you"—his eyes trailed her from head to toe—"become beautifully untamed."

Before she could respond, one beat, followed closely by another, sounded over the ground. This was it, as Amaya raced for her with all flags in tow—but to her horror, three of Maverick's rogues where hot on her tail, and none of the others were covering her. Instead, Drya and Kellias were fighting two others, Saline lay unmoving on the ground, and Tynan and Acelin were advancing on Maverick's runner to delay him from reaching the inner circle. It was distorted chaos and not their plan.

Zaiana couldn't concern herself with any of the others; all she could do was watch in rigid anticipation while Amaya ran, occasionally twisting to shoot arrows that missed their marks since she had so many to consider. She was a fine archer but required far more fine-tuning on a battleground to be able and aware to dodge and strike multiple threats.

Zaiana caught the glint of a blade seconds before the dagger went hurtling from the sky directly toward the darkling. A drop hollowed Zaiana's stomach, and her eyes widened. She opened her mouth to warn Amaya, but she was too late. Just as Amaya turned to release another arrow, the dagger lodged into her side. She cried out, and Zaiana lost complete focus on Maverick as she ran to the edge of the circle and watched helplessly as the darkling fell.

"Get up!" Zaiana shouted. She was close—so damn close.

Amaya's eyes snapped to hers, ghostly with a fear that stilled her cold.

"*Now, Amaya!*" Zaiana coated the words with as much will-bending authority as she could, flashing her eyes to the three dark fae who were closing in like wraiths. They would kill her as a punishment for Zaiana no matter the repercussions.

She saw the moment in Amaya's eyes that fear turned into hard determination. To survive. She pulled the dagger from her side with a cry of agony. Zaiana winced and only hoped she could heal just enough for the blood loss not to be fatal. Pushing to her feet, Zaiana could only watch in sickening *fear*—something she wasn't used to. Even in the face of the most perilous battle she never felt fear. But it quickly turned to awe as Amaya retrieved her bow, reached for an arrow, took her stance, and released. Then again, and then again. The fierce cry that came from her with each agonizing movement was utterly inspiring.

Seconds away from being pommeled into by the final male, she released her final arrow. It met its mark, plunging through his throat and killing him instantly so he wouldn't feel the cracking of his bones as he plummeted down.

Amaya didn't waste a second despite her wound, which poured silver blood over the hand clutched to it. With gritted teeth, she started running again, and when she reached the circle, Zaiana would be free.

Maverick hadn't struck her although she'd been fully vulnerable for him to have gotten his own back several times over. She didn't look at him to gauge what could be occupying his attention while her eyes were on Amaya. *Just a little farther.* She was stumbling now. *Come on—just a few more steps.* Her labored breathing was audible, her pace slowing. Zaiana's arms opened of their own accord, and Amaya fell straight into her. She lowered the darkling until they were both on their knees. The shrill of a siren signaled her release.

"Go," Amaya breathed.

Zaiana's hand went over Amaya's on her wound. It was still gushing, and the panic that clouded her head was so rare she didn't know what to do with it. So much silver blood when it should have stopped by now.

"I think..." Amaya panted—and not from physical exertion. "I think it was Niltain steel."

An all-consuming hot rage flashed across Zaiana's widened eyes, and she snapped her neck toward Maverick with a promised mark of death. He was masterful in maintaining a look of innocence, his expert acting even portraying shock as if she would believe he knew nothing of the illegal weapon his rogue had smuggled onto the field. A metal that could be fatal to their kind.

"You need to *go*," Amaya said weakly, bringing Zaiana's attention back to her. Her face was paler than usual, and she couldn't be sure if it was sweat or the mist that slicked her skin. Her eyelids dropped a couple of times, and though her words rang in her ears with the urgency that she needed to leave her if she stood a chance of retrieving the last flag before Maverick...

Zaiana couldn't move.

A second siren sounded, and she knew Maverick's runner had made it back to him too. But she still had sixty seconds' advance on him.

Zaiana fought internally, not knowing if the young dark fae would make it if she left. She needed a healer, fast. In her hesitation, she was sacrificing the opportunity to have everything she'd ever wanted. She was being weak. Zaiana ground her teeth at the tornado of chanting conflicts that beat hard with each passing second.

She was about to settle on her choice and damn to the Nether what that made her. But she didn't have to. Tynan swooped down, landing and crouching next to Amaya, taking the darkling from her arms.

"Go, Zaiana!" he barked.

It was enough for her to see sense, and she met his hard gaze as she straightened. Tynan took her place, bracing a hand on Amaya to keep pressure on her wound as her strength faded.

With a nod, Zaiana splayed her wings. Just before taking flight, she said, "You stay alive, Amaya. That's an order."

CHAPTER 27

Zaiana

WITH A STRONG pulse of her wings, Zaiana shot to the sky, catching the faint breathy chuckle of the young dark fae before the mist engulfed her. It was enough to calm her panic and reel her back into that laser focus.

She'd wasted too much time, foolishly, weakly, and it had almost cost her everything. Zaiana collected her anger, embraced and harnessed it, ready to unleash in a raging storm on Maverick. She cut through the misty clouds, hair dampening the higher she went, until visibility was near impossible. But these mountain passes were ingrained peak for peak in her memory. She completely blocked the flashbacks from the last time she'd battled through these passes on that ground. Her mind only honed in on two goals that made it easy to forget everything else: find the flag and release her retribution on Maverick.

She knew her time of advantage was up, and she extended every one of her senses to detect him if he chose to come after her. Zaiana dipped and weaved over the jagged stone of the mountains, eyes scanning fervently for the flicker of the black flag that was deliberately near impossible to detect against the obsidian terrain. If she wasn't careful, she could pass it by embarrassingly without realizing.

Slicing through the fallen clouds, her hair turned wet and heavy. She was about to fold into a dive to get a closer look, but she felt the invasion in time to twist and bring her blade up before the strike of the blue-flamed steel hit her. In the air, Maverick was hard and determined as they locked gazes through crossed blades. Cobalt and amethyst met in a beautiful blazing tango. Zaiana could see nothing but white rage. She pushed off his blade and swung again, and he deflected with his own.

The gray gloom of their surroundings exploded in sparks and embers of electricity and fire every time their blades met. Zaiana didn't relent in her offense attacks, striking over and over in a perfectly controlled and channeled anger that made Maverick falter. He seemed to know it, and before she could bring down the next swipe of her sword, he tucked his wings in tight and dove headfirst out of the path of her lightning blade. He was swallowed whole by a cloud of angry darkness, and she brazenly cast a bolt through her fingertips after him in her frustration at his retreat.

She didn't let it curb her focus. All she had to do was find that damned flag. Maverick had yet to feel a fraction of her full, undiluted fury over his cheat that could cost Amaya her life. She cast out the thought of the darkling and began a steady sweep over the mountains once more.

After a few minutes, Zaiana's irritation grew to the point of recklessness. It was as good as searching blindfolded. An idea came to her, and she aimed high, flying and flying, her wings pounding furiously against gravity to triumph the skies.

Feeling high enough, Zaiana closed her eyes and focused on her breathing. She calmed her mind and dove for the stormy well of power that lay within her. She felt its pulse like an orb of living light, in stark contrast to the darkness that lived in her mind and heart. Zaiana sheathed her sword and held her palms as if that ball of power were within her grasp. She yielded and harnessed, and it became a tangible force. The currents filled her veins, taking away the chill of her damp hair that hung limp around her face. All she felt was power—electric, magnificent power. It sparked to life at her fingertips, and when Zaiana opened her eyes, the space between her palms grew a lethal ball of charged lightning. She let it build, patiently and meticulously, knowing any wrong conduction could backfire horribly. Beautifully jagged strokes sparked and danced over her hands and into the orb that grew. It was truly mesmerizing.

Then, when she felt the well straining, warning her she was testing the limits, Zaiana let go.

As she cast her hands out, the orb flattened and expanded, and she watched in awe of her own ability as it conquered the mist and darkness across the entire training arena, chasing away the overcast gloom for her to see every dark fae that now looked up at her. The gleam of the High Lord caught her eye, but she paid none of them an ounce of attention.

She didn't waste a second of the time she'd bought for herself before the mist crept back to shadow everything once again. Zaiana flew away from the open ground below, knowing they would never make it so easy. The flag would be somewhere within the mountains.

If she'd blinked, she would have missed it. A slight flicker in the distance. These mountains held nothing that moved naturally. And knowing her blast would have chased away any other creature in flight, Zaiana smiled in victory. She darted for the flag.

Landing on the narrow, flat plane, Zaiana tucked in her wings as she stalked for the billowing black fabric that sang with her success. She got all of a few steps before she had to twist in time to cast out her lightning in defense as Maverick's fire shot for her.

She growled in annoyance.

Maverick closed in the distance without attack. Zaiana didn't feel so restrained. Bracing, she strung out a precise dance of movements that correlated with her lightning strikes. He deflected some of them and narrowly avoided others. But she was only warming up. With the next charge of her bolts, she pointed her iron-clad fingers and brought them together in front of her, sending a bright flare after him. It stuck—hard enough that there was nothing graceful about his hurl backward until he slammed against the stone.

Zaiana should have turned and raced to capture the flag once and for all, but in her fury, she advanced for him again. Maverick was on his hands and knees, spitting black blood onto the ground. Straightening, Zaiana drew her sword and held the point to his dead heart. Her chest rose and fell deeply, the dark chant to drive her blade through him near maddening.

"I always knew you were a spineless coward," she hissed through clenched teeth.

Maverick didn't show any anger, nor any sign that he intended to fight back. Her nostrils flared, hating his submission. This wasn't him; he didn't concede.

She pressed her blade harder, and his jaw flexed. "I promise you, Zaiana, I had no knowledge of Berrik's intention."

She didn't want to hear his name, and the sound of it added more pressure to her arm until she felt the tip of her blade pierce his skin. He winced but made no sound.

"You expect me to believe that?" she said, keeping her voice steady. "Do you think I'm a damn fool?" *Gods,* she hated him. She despised him so much it was almost a physical burn scorching her chest. Or perhaps it was the wild awakening of her lightning that demanded she end him here.

"You are no fool. Which is why you will not kill me."

Zaiana flared in challenge, gripping the hilt with both hands and angling her arms in the perfect position to drive her sword clean through his chest. It wasn't just a want; a petty chance at revenge. As she looked down at Maverick, all she could see was every wicked, horrid, and abominable thing in the world. All she could see…was herself.

She clenched her teeth. Staring into those depthless black eyes, she saw a flicker of something damning. Understanding. His wet midnight hair clung to his face at all angles, and for a moment she saw him as his younger self. Maverick wasn't always like this. He wasn't always a dark fae. But she was. She was *born* this way.

"I will kill you, Maverick. Maybe not today, nor in a hundred years, but I will. I hope you spend the rest of your life watching your back for me, because I will always be there. Waiting. A shadow that lingers even in the dark." With a long stride backward, her blade left his chest.

Maverick hissed, hand going to the wound that leaked black blood. Zaiana turned from him and stalked for the flag once more.

It was a foolish move made in the glimmer of defeat she thought she saw in the demon's eye. Zaiana should have known better, only realizing her mistake when the sear of hot flame struck her back. She cried out in surprise, crashing to her knees to cool the burning with the breeze and wet mist. But it was too late, and as she straightened, Maverick passed her in haste, coming to stand in front of the flag. Her eyes went wide in disbelief, unaccepting of the failure that ridiculed her as he reached out a hand to claim victory. *Her* victory.

Zaiana snapped, all pain diminished in an instant as she rose, and threw out her ability in the form of a lasso that whipped around the wrist mere inches from the flag's material. Maverick shouted as the rope of electricity held him and pulsed through his body, heightened all the more by the wetness that coated him. Zaiana pulled with all her might, yanking Maverick back, and he went sprawling before her. In the same breath, she lunged and ran. Just before he got to his feet, she gripped the damned flag and ripped it from its pole with a roaring cry of victory.

Her breathing was hard as she turned to face Maverick. Holding the flag, she glared at him. The siren that sang over the mountains was a wondrous melody. Zaiana breathed, she blazed, she raged within.

She had won.

CHAPTER 28

Faythe

FAYTHE STIRRED, WRAPPED in something firm and warm that filled her with a sense of contentment and safety. She fluttered her eyes open, only to be met with the steady rise and fall of a muscular torso. At some point in the night, she must have shuffled closer to Reylan, likely for comfort as his fingers were still entwined with hers and their joined hands lay over his chest while she curled into him on her side.

She held still, registering their position and closeness, but not out of embarrassment or fear. As she carefully tilted her head back, she looked upon Reylan's peaceful sleeping face. Soft silver curls had fallen over his forehead, and every stern line of his face was smooth and unburdened. She didn't want to disturb him, savoring the sight.

After reluctantly parting with Nik and returning to her own subconscious, Faythe had collapsed from the exertion of her ability. She knew she was dangerously close to harming herself—or worse—but she couldn't help but grapple onto every precious second she could get with her dear friend. Faythe didn't have the strength to check in on Reylan and confirm she had made it across. She'd succumbed to the dark pull of sleep instantly.

They must have slept in, as Faythe felt rested and refreshed. It seemed Reylan had needed the extra hours too, and her chest twinged with guilt that he had exerted himself by gifting her his power. She didn't know how to express her gratitude that he'd stayed awake for as long as it took for her to see Nik, draining his own energy in the process. Words were never enough, and she couldn't help but feel she had nothing of value to offer the selfless warrior. Her sadness tore her heart.

With caution, she slid her hand free from his. He was soundless, and his chest remained in a steady, even rhythm. Faythe shuffled a short distance away before peeling herself upright, tucking her knees to her chest as she glanced sideward to catch a glimpse of the cloudless daytime sky beyond the balcony. She managed all of a few quiet seconds before Reylan's deep inhale signaled he was awake. Faythe glanced down at him as he propped himself up on his elbows. He looked at her expectantly with a frown knitted in concern, and she realized he must not know she'd made it last night.

"Did it work?" he asked carefully.

A smile bloomed on Faythe's cheeks, and it relaxed Reylan's tense shoulders. She nodded. "It worked."

Reylan fell back down with a breath of relief. "What does High Farrow's king have to report then?"

Though he said it in humor, Faythe had to turn away from him at the question, not wanting to dampen his obvious elation that she had managed to speak with Nik when the happiness was cruelly overshadowed by sorrow in their difficult conversation. But she could never hide anything from Reylan, and he sat up next to her without hesitation.

"You told him about the journey to the Isles, didn't you?"

Not directly. But it was only a matter of time before Marlowe did. He read the answer in her pinched brow.

"It made it real," she said quietly. "As if all this time I didn't really believe I might not see him again. Jakon, Marlowe, Tauria..." Faythe closed her eyes, needing to calm her racing heart as it tightened her throat.

"You will," Reylan said firmly. "On my life, Faythe, you will see them again."

Gods, the mere thought of his life being in the balance to save her own made her chest twist awfully. Though he said the words to comfort her, the promise that he would protect her life with his own if need be pained her far more than comforted her. So much so, she felt a wave of dread that made her want to find some way—*any way*—to get him to stay behind. If only so he would be safe. It would be a futile effort because she knew Reylan would never abandon her. And she would never abandon him.

They would start the journey by week's end, and the hourglass counting down their peaceful time was draining faster than she anticipated.

Reylan's hand fell on her back, and the spark of it made her tense in surprise. He must have gauged it as unwanted contact, quickly letting his arm drop, but the touch tingled through her as the opposite, and she turned her head to meet his sapphires again. The look they shared held something...*igniting*.

Before the intensity could grow, Reylan pulled back the covers and twisted out of bed. She watched him slip into his jacket and boots. He'd freshen and change in his own rooms, as he always did. She didn't let her disappointment settle that their alone time was over once more.

"I have to brief the guard on their new measures for while I'm gone," he said, buttoning his jacket to look semi-presentable and not like he'd just tumbled out of her bed. It was sure to fan the flames of gossip.

Faythe gave a short nod. "Agalhor invited me for another tour of the castle," she told him.

Though it still swept her with a nervous unease, it no longer frightened her to see her father. In fact, every time he suggested some time alone, she felt giddy with thrill like a child, both to learn more about the history of her heritage and the kingdom and to recollect on the memories she secretly stored in a precious part of her mind, not sure how many she would have the privilege of experiencing with her father should the worst happen on their journey.

Reylan grinned wide at the mention, a rare bright smile that fluttered her heart to see. "I'm glad," was all he said, but his tone perked up in joy.

It was clear from the moment she saw them together that Reylan and Agalhor held a bond that ran far deeper than a king and his general. Faythe thought she would be jealous of the connection they shared, which she had been robbed of establishing with Agalhor, but it filled her heart to see.

Reylan strode for the door, pausing at it. "I'll find you later." It was the promise he always made, right before he left to fulfill his duties for the day. Sometimes more reluctantly than others. She didn't envy him for the weight of responsibility and the stack of tasks that required his attention. He suited the role and dealt with everything no matter how grueling and tedious it seemed. Faythe admired him greatly for it and was learning so much from him about what it took to be a figure who stood to be respected. What it took to *lead*.

Faythe wasn't alone in her rooms for long before a delicate knock, followed by the opening of her door, signaled her day beginning. Gresla strolled in as usual, casting the same knowing look she always did when she timed her arrival just as Reylan left. She never said anything, but she didn't have to, and Faythe couldn't prevent the color that seeped into her cheeks no matter how many weeks had passed.

Faythe was fully enraptured by Agalhor's rumbling voice as she tuned in to a tale about the Ashfyres' royal line. She was completely in awe—and admittedly daunted—at being a relation of such an ancient and powerful bloodline. The Ashfyres were fabled, dating right back to the first ever King of Rhyenelle and the first Phoenix Rider, Matheus Ashfyre.

"My brother was like Balemorus in a lot of ways, and it was his own need to *prove* he was something more that got him recklessly killed during a horrible battle many centuries ago, near to when the conflicts with Valgard began," Agalhor explained while they observed a new set of paintings along a separate hallway leading into the library.

Faythe's brow knitted, and she stopped in front of a family portrait. She identified Agalhor straight away even though he looked no older than Reylan in the image. Next to him, she could only assume, was the brother he spoke of and the only other person besides their parents who stood behind them. Strangely, Faythe felt an odd, nervous chill curve her spine, as though there were an essence left behind in the still gaze of the fae in the painting. Her grandparents and uncle, it struck her to realize. Never in her orphaned life did she believe she would ever get to know any of her lineage on either of her parents' sides. Being confronted with it now brought about a wave of emotions she couldn't separate. Sadness, joy, fear, unworthiness—they all swirled nauseatingly in her stomach.

Faythe's eyes lingered on her uncle a little longer. Unlike Agalhor, his expression was colder, firmer, and a sharp tremor shook her body as she felt as if she were staring into the detached eyes of Malin. "He wanted the throne?" Faythe asked, though she already knew the answer.

Agalhor nodded, and she followed him away from the painting until they entered the magnificent library. Faythe's eyes were instantly drawn to the Phoenix feather once again, but she didn't advance to it this time as the king diverted over to a reading area.

"We all harbor demons, but his chanted louder than most. I was the oldest, and my father always favored me. As much as I tried to include my brother, we were always separated. I was brought up to rule, and I suppose he felt the lack of attention as a lack of worth. We quickly grew apart when we became old enough to learn our duty." Agalhor spoke of his brother sadly, like one who knew how it felt to grieve for someone who was still alive, and she pitied him.

"And now...Malin is next in line for the throne?" Faythe asked. She needed to know from him and watched every flicker of expression that could betray his next words. She already knew the answer, but she'd rather ask the question to detect if Agalhor had revised the prospects; if he considered her a real candidate at all. As the king or as her father, she couldn't be sure which opinion she found more important.

Faythe wouldn't blame him if Malin was the favored option. He had grown up here for centuries and knew the way of life, the structures of the court, and had the backing of the high fae nobles as far as she had observed. Faythe had...nothing. Nothing to show for herself. The only thing that kept her chin high in determination was that she had everything to *learn* and had never felt more eager and willing no matter what became of her residence in Rhyenelle.

Agalhor stopped walking and turned to her. His poise was dominating as he stood with hands clasped behind his back, but it was not in intimidation or scrutiny; it was simply a natural stance for the king. He didn't respond immediately, and Faythe stood rigid as he looked at her, *studied* her. In the space of a few excruciatingly long seconds, Faythe felt as if he reached into the depths of her soul with that look, gauging if she could handle his honest judgment, or perhaps to prove himself wrong or right in whatever he saw in her. He spoke when Faythe was close to turning to stone in anticipation.

"From the moment I laid eyes on you, I knew that you were destined for something great, Faythe. For when I looked at you, I saw exactly what I saw in your mother. A fierceness, a rare determination. To live, to fight, to stand up for what is right."

Faythe's heart beat hard, moved by his words and the mention of her mother.

"Then you spoke—like a leader and a protector. A peacemaker. I saw a ruler worthy of being my successor." Agalhor bowed his head to her. *Bowed.*

Faythe was stunned, unable to comprehend what she was hearing and seeing. A great king stood before her, offering his respect as though she were another monarch. When he straightened and locked eyes with her, Faythe instinctively dipped her own head back to him. In the movement was a silent acceptance. Of his belief in her; his *want* for her to follow in his footsteps. It daunted her, thrilled her, but most of all…it strengthened her. Having Agalhor's blessing dispersed the shadows of uncertainty, and Faythe claimed every ounce of that newfound strength. She would rise and fight and *hope* the people would see her as they saw her father, and as they once saw her mother. As Rhyenelle's queen.

"Thank you," Faythe said, straightening with confidence.

Agalhor's smile was warm, eyes twinkling with a pride that brightened her soul. Then the determination of a king fell to the worry of father. "General Reylan has informed me of the journey you are to take," he said. Faythe prepared herself for yet another lecture on the ridiculous expedition to the Isles. "I understand the need to put duty and destiny before your own wants and safety, but is this truly an unavoidable cause?"

Faythe's face fell with guilt as she glimpsed the concern that aged his face. "It has to be me."

"And it is not for me to stop you. Though might I at least send the aid of soldiers—?"

"If Marvellas finds out, she will move to stop me."

"We only just found each other." Agalhor's voice grew quiet as though it were a traitorous slip of thought, along with the near undetectable deflation of his shoulders. He was quick to compose himself. "I apologize. I do not wish to incite guilt."

Faythe swallowed, but it did nothing to relieve her tightening airway. Because he was right, and the thought of venturing away from him so soon after being united with him was the one heartache that clenched her chest with heavy, selfish longing to stay and damn the consequences. She was selfish for allowing Agalhor to bond with her, to have given him hope and a reminder of his lost love. If Faythe didn't return…she hated the thought of becoming another immeasurable loss for him to bear.

"I'm sorry." She didn't know what she meant by it.

Agalhor reached out a hand but hesitated, only for a second, before his warm palm met her shoulder. It was a small comfort, an acceptance, that burst in her chest. They shared a sad but grateful look, seeming to communicate their mutual alignment of thought. They were blessed to have even their short amount of time together no matter what became of the future.

"All I ask is that you be careful and remember your destiny is far greater than *what* you are. It is *who* you are that carries the hope for this kingdom. I know you will return to us."

Faythe blinked back the wave of pride that pricked her eyes. She had no words to utter in her gratitude, and no words to console him. She couldn't promise what wasn't within her power to ensure, but knowing what she had to return to gave her a fierce will to *live*.

Agalhor dropped his hand. In his small smile, it was as if he'd read her thoughts without her need to voice them. He turned and strode for a table stacked with open books and parchments. "I should like for you to dine with me before you leave. All of you who are to take this journey."

Faythe followed. "I would like that," she answered with genuine sincerity.

They stopped before the disorganized table. It was very out of place in the impeccable library, and she noticed all the books and parchments held a coating of dust. No one had touched anything on this table in a very long time.

In answer to her observations, Agalhor said, "Your mother loved to read." He reached out a hand, disturbing the neglected books as he aimlessly flicked through a couple of pages of one that lay open. She understood then that the discarded array of books lay exactly as her mother had left them. Never touched, never returned to the shelves, as if it might erase the image of her standing here studying the texts. It was a tragic thought that settled in her stomach. Even after all this time, Agalhor's loss clung to him as if it were still fresh. But he was resilient and hid his sorrow masterfully so he would not come apart in front of a kingdom that needed him. He was one of the most selfless and strong people she'd ever had the privilege of getting to know.

"For weeks before she left, I would always find her here. Sometimes it took great persuasion to peel her away from her ancient wonders and scripts." A warm smile graced his cheeks as he looked over the pages, reminiscing on the memories. Then his head turned up, and he gave a quick glance around.

Faythe followed his gaze, but they were completely alone in the library as far as she could tell.

"What I am about to share with you has remained a secret from all, and I thought it would remain so forever. But you need to know, Faythe. Now you are here, now you are known to be my blood, it changes everything."

Faythe braced herself, but it didn't prevent his words from striking her with clashing emotions.

"I must start with the fact your mother believed in the Spirits you speak of and spent endless days reading any scripture she could get her hands on, all in aid of one purpose. The fae were made of human origin by the power of the Spirits, and Lilianna believed there may have been some way to make contact with the Spirit of Life. If not to have her turned fae, then to have me turned human." Agalhor paused, gauging her reaction.

Faythe was stunned and pictured her wide-eyed disbelief at the impossible notion. A faint smile twitched the king's lips as he looked away and turned.

"There's something I would like to show you." He began to walk off.

Faythe didn't immediately follow him as a flash of memory—a question —was answered unwittingly by Agalhor's information. Her heart pounded, picking up a rapid, uneven tempo as the puzzle pieces slid together on their own. Her pocket watch—or more specifically, the note she'd found within... Did Agalhor know her mother had found out how to contact Aurialis? That she had discovered the locations of all three Spirit temples.

Faythe looked down at the scattered books and loose papers. Her mother had made it to Aurialis's temple—which finally answered Faythe's question of why she had chosen to go to High Farrow. Yet she couldn't figure out what the Spirit could have told her for her mother to decide not to return to Rhyenelle. Perhaps she was wrong to assume it was simply an attempt to stay out of sight of Marvellas wherever the Great Spirit lay in wait. It didn't make sense that she had chosen not to tell Faythe of her ability when she was old enough to at least begin to understand it. She couldn't wrap her head around why she had also been deprived of knowing a single thing about her father.

Her mind reeled, and the room tilted. Faythe shook her head. She couldn't overwhelm herself just now—not with Agalhor present to question it. Turning to him, she found the king waiting patient and poised by the far door. She took a long breath to calm herself and moved to follow.

They came to stand in front of two massive, intricately carved oak doors. No guards stood outside, but the longer she stared at the glittering wood, she began to see the faint shimmer that radiated from them.

"This room is warded against anyone without my blood." Agalhor answered her curiosity. Reaching out a hand, the king pressed his palm lightly to the veil, and at his touch it rippled and dispersed like the parting of shallow water. Faythe was mesmerized.

As Agalhor entered, Faythe was giddy on his heel, excited to find out what lay beyond to warrant such magickal protection. Inside, her eyes went wide at first glance as some other kind of magick illuminated the space in response to their presence. The room glittered like a sea of crystal. Jewels, artifacts, scriptures. But what caught Faythe's attention was the prominent centerpiece. Upon a velvet-covered mannequin sat the single most magnificent gown Faythe had ever laid eyes on—one she knew nothing would ever compare to. A crown adorned the head of the figure, but not in the traditional sense she would expect. This one was a halo of wavy peaks like a blazing sunrise floating behind the mannequin's head. Faythe circled around, needing to see every angle. She almost gasped at the image of power crafted masterfully on the back of the garment. While the front was all crimson and embellished with red crystals, sewn onto the back was a sheer material, which attached to the wrists in hues of crimson and gold. Faythe reached for the sleeve, extending it and watching as the illusion of a Phoenix's wing came to life before her.

"I have to tell you something, Faythe. Knowledge I have confided in no other who didn't absolutely need to know before. But you have every right to know, and so will the world if you choose." Agalhor's voice was quiet, uncertain. When her wide eyes met his, she dropped her hold on the garment, glancing his pride laced with reservation as he observed her. Faythe was riddled with nervous anticipation over what he wanted to confess, feeling her palms slick with sweat.

"There are many who will object to me instating you as my heir, Faythe. Because they believe you to be illegitimate."

Faythe's stomach sank, the ugly sense of her twisted, unwanted existence returning. But Agalhor showed no concern, and his next words struck her still.

"They are wrong, because Lilianna and I *were* wed, in private, but it was legal and binding all the same, and I have the documents and witnesses to prove it."

Faythe was stunned. She couldn't be sure of what she felt at the knowledge. Relief, joy, triumph—all for her parents who had defied harsh prejudice to be together. Then there was a daunting sense of responsibility. Having legitimacy sealed her rightful claim, but she would be a fool to think that was all it would take. Faythe still had a fight ahead of her to prove herself worthy to the court and citizens. She still had a fight against Malin.

Agalhor took a few thoughtful steps toward the masterpiece of a dress, staring at it but seeing far more than material and jewels. "This was to be her wedding and coronation gown. We were biding our time on making it public, anticipating the outcry over our mortal differences. I didn't care, but Lilianna insisted on more time, convinced she would find a resolution to ease the minds of the people and nobles who would undoubtedly object and perhaps put all effort into abdicating me and removing us both from power."

Faythe circled the dress, feeling an odd sense of strength and power. Coming to stand before it, she was transfixed. The longer she stared, the more the image in her mind became vivid. She pictured her mother instead of the velvet mannequin, and she was breathtaking. Then, just for a second, she saw herself. Blazing and triumphant in the Phoenix's colors.

CHAPTER 29

Nikalias

TWO WEEKS FELT like mere days. Nik clutched onto every precious minute he ultimately wasted. Now his hourglass had nearly run out, and in his torment and sorrow, he had never hated himself more for not spending what little time he had left with Tauria.

She was set to leave by the afternoon, when Olmstone's cavalry would arrive to steal her. He had to remember she wasn't his—or anyone's. This was *her* choice. And Queen Tauria Stagknight of Fenstead was to become the ultimate weapon in disguise.

Nik had called her to his council chamber, but not for a final private goodbye, as Jakon and Marlowe lounged on the seats behind him while he stood staring out the window in solemn silence. The humans didn't speak either, and he might have felt bad for his bitter mood that weighted the air, but he had to set his turmoil about Tauria aside for this. To inform them he had finally seen Faythe.

He felt Tauria's approach from down the hall, and his shoulders locked as he tuned in to her gentle footsteps that he would miss. So many small, simple things had become so much more treasured and painful to imagine parting with. It seemed foolish, but he didn't care.

She entered through the door after a short knock, not waiting for a call of invitation. Nik felt her at his back and turned. A pang emitted from his chest at the sight of her. She wore a cloak for the outdoors, and a pair of gloves dangled in her grasp. Their time would be up as soon this meeting was over with. For a moment, they stared at each other, and he thought he saw the suppressed pain in her brown eyes before they dropped to fiddle with her gloves. Then Tauria spared a glance at Jakon and Marlowe, and they offered warm smiles of reception. Nik couldn't bear to look at them for the most selfish, ridiculous reason as their hands entwined affectionately where they sat in their effortless closeness.

Gods, had he really fallen to such pitiful levels that he was *jealous* of the humans? He was a king, a powerful Nightwalker...but even reminding himself of those things did nothing to cure the ugly seed that grew, watered by his loneliness.

"Why are we all here?" Tauria asked when Nik didn't immediately say anything.

He settled his eyes on Jakon. "Faythe came to me."

"How is she?" Jakon asked quickly, straightening with full attention while Marlowe's eyes widened with hope.

Nik mustered a hollow smile. "She is well. Thriving in Rhyenelle, it seems, but she still has a lot to overcome with her father."

Jakon's stiff shoulders relaxed a little. "Did she say anything about coming back? Or...about us going to her?"

Nik had to look away from him. He wanted to soothe his worries, assure him Faythe thought of and missed him dearly, but something else needed to be voiced far more urgently. Faythe wasn't coming back. Not anytime soon.

"She misses us all, truly, but—" Nik slid his hands into his pockets, pacing over to the empty fireplace. "We all knew the war against Marvellas wasn't over."

He heard Jakon rising to his feet. "If she's planning something, she'll need our help."

Nik shook his head. "We can't."

"Of course we can!"

Nik turned to him, gaze hardening at the flare of challenge. "Even if we wanted to, she'd be well on her way there before we could reach Rhyenelle's borders."

"Where?" Jakon snarled, fanning Nik's anger even further. It was irrational, but he couldn't help it. Especially when the human pinned him with an accusatory look that suggested Nik was content in letting Faythe face the quest on her own. It was so far from the truth, and he'd raged and wrecked several rooms in turmoil because he wanted to aid her. Faythe had made it clear she had to go now, and that Reylan would be going with her. She was already with the one who would protect her like no other.

"She's going to seek out Dakodas's temple on the Niltain Isles," Marlowe's calming voice answered for him.

They all snapped their gaze to the blacksmith. The *oracle*. She wore a sad smile.

Nik had to walk over and perch on the edge of his desk, feeling his stability falter as he thought things through. He folded his arms, pinching his brow between his fingers. "Dear Gods," he muttered with a shake of the head, mulling it over. "She's been planning this for a while." Even though he wasn't looking in her direction, he pictured the blacksmith nodding her head in confirmation as silence answered him.

"We should go to her," Tauria said in disbelief.

Nik looked up, and her face was creased in deep concern. Would she really give up her chance in Olmstone to go to Faythe's aid? He felt guilty for questioning it. Faythe had been invaluable as a friend to Tauria during her time in the castle—of course the princess would care deeply.

Nik switched his gaze to Marlowe. "Faythe said you would be able to explain."

The blacksmith stood but didn't go to Jakon's side. She moved to a space where all their attention was centered on her, and she was calm and composed. "In the past few months, I've seen far more than I have in my whole life. Sometimes it's very cryptic; other times it's so clear. Though one thing remains the same: the war will not come because it has surrounded us for centuries. Not a war of man against fae, or fae against fae. This was never a war against Valgard, but a war against the Spirits."

"We know this," Nik said as gently as he could. He was desperate to hear more of what this meant for Faythe.

"Yes. But what you do not know is that Faythe is not just human, not just half-fae. She is an Heir of Marvellas, born of a line of direct ancestors that can be traced over the centuries, right back to the Spirit herself in fae form."

Nik had never been so struck still by shock that he had to brace both hands on the desk to keep from swaying. It was mirrored on Tauria and Jakon's expressions as they looked to Marlowe as if she were out of control.

"There is something else. Faythe is born of a bloodline-blessed—Agalhor—and a direct descendant, Lilianna. It is why she has manipulation of the mind, both conscious and unconscious. Whatever that means, it is important to Marvellas."

Nik began to feel nauseous. It didn't make sense—not in the history of the world he knew, not in all he believed to be *real*, just as he knew it wouldn't make sense to anyone else. Impossible didn't even seem appropriate. He vacantly shook his head while letting the information settle. "So why does she seek out Dakodas's temple?"

Marlowe's face paled. "Marvellas broke many fundamental laws when she transitioned to our world nearly a millennium ago. It required the sacrifice of those blessed with pure spiritual ability. Those like me, though I can't be certain how many. It also required a specific moment in time: a solar eclipse, during which the veil between this world and the spiritual world was thin enough to be broken. A time that only occurs once in a millennium." She paused, glancing around the circle as though one might be able to race to the conclusion before she explained it. Everyone remained still with horror-struck faces. "It seems history plans to repeat. Dakodas, Spirit of Death and Goddess of the Moon, intends to follow her sister and be bound in a form that can walk our world. If she succeeds…may the Gods have mercy on us all."

Silence settled around the room—one so cold it seeped into Nik's very bones and rattled a chill. Everyone mulled over the revelation. The damning, the inconceivable. And the knowledge that their mutual friend was not only at the forefront of stopping it, but she was also *connected* to it.

It can only be me.

Nik's panic surged at the thought of her facing the grave danger alone, but he quickly remembered that was far from the truth. She had Reylan, whom Nik had observed over his time in High Farrow more closely than he should have, always out of concern for Faythe. He had been wary of the general's intentions, but the way he was with her, his defensiveness and protectiveness…

Nothing was impossible—not anymore.

It was enough to soothe his worries and discourage him from doing something reckless and impractical. Marching to Rhyenelle wouldn't help her, and he could only pray she made it back safe. He wouldn't accept an alternative.

No one else spoke, so Marlowe continued. "She faces a great trial, and she will need us. Not to aid her in this quest, but to accept her when she returns."

Nik's brow furrowed at the cryptic message. "Of course we will," he all but snapped, knowing there was nothing that could make him turn his back on her.

Marlowe's smile was knowing but solemn. "She might not be the same as you once knew."

What that meant Nik couldn't be sure. But his view remained the same.

Jakon moved, an arm going around Marlowe's waist. "The plan remains the same. Marlowe and I will still go to Rhyenelle to aid communications between you and Agalhor. Faythe will appreciate our being there when she returns."

Nik wanted to protest, suddenly overwhelmed by the notion of them setting off on the uncertain journey across the sea. It was a helpless feeling of confinement, as though his throne were a cage and his crown the shackles that held him back while everyone close to him set off on their own perilous quest and he could do nothing but watch.

Tauria's voice cut through his desolate thoughts. "Olmstone will be arriving shortly."

The declaration sank him further, and he wondered if there was no end to the well of torment he had been slipping into all this time. There were short moments in his life that had kept him from succumbing to the wildness of such a dark and bleak existence, but they could all be traced back to one person. Nik feared that without Tauria, he might just be willing to fall completely.

Tauria closed the short distance between her and Marlowe. "Thank you. For being a friend, and for telling us all you know about Faythe— all you *can* tell us. I do not envy your gift and the curse of knowledge you bear. You are the bravest of us all."

The two embraced for a tender moment.

"Good luck to you, Your Majesty," Marlowe said, pride coating the title.

Tauria's eyes lit up with fierce determination, and it was inspiring to see, but it also twisted his self-guilt. He should have done more for her. *He* should be the one to strengthen her belief in herself. As a mate and as a friend, he had failed her. Tauria deserved far more.

The Fenstead princess stepped out of Marlowe's embrace, and even though they weren't as close, Tauria didn't hesitate to walk into Jakon's open arms. Watching their goodbyes, Nik had to focus on his steady breathing to distract from the crushing sadness that swept him at knowing this was real. Their time was up.

The humans left, their final farewells heartfelt but sad. Nik and Tauria stood in a thick, palpable silence. Nik remained leaning on the desk, unable to shift his eyes from the ground while his heart was shattering piece by piece with each tick of the phantom clock. Finally, after a long, shaky breath, Tauria spoke.

"I guess I should give you something of mine, for the Nightwalking—"

"Do you remember the day we first met?" He met her hazel gaze, and the question seemed to stump her.

"When I arrived in High Farrow?"

"Before then."

Creases formed around her eyes, but she nodded.

"My parents dragged me to Fenstead against my many protests for your Winter Solstice Carnival. I found it over the top, pretentious, and wanted nothing more than to be back in High Farrow the moment I arrived."

"Yes. I'll never forget your sulking face as you sat glaring at everyone," Tauria mused. For a moment, the brightness of her smile eased the melancholy of his heart.

He mirrored her expression. "And I'll never forget how every single protest and irritation dissolved the moment I saw you. Your gown was ridiculous, but the emerald color was so striking on you."

"You made fun of me the whole time," she grumbled. "Young Nikalias was a menace."

A light chuckle left him. "Would you believe me if I said it was because I found you the most magnificent thing in that ballroom?"

"Not for a second."

"Good. Because you were the most magnificent thing I'd ever seen at all." Nik reached into his pocket, and Tauria's eyes widened at the item. He held it up, observing the light that bounced from every angle of the emerald-jeweled comb. "I plucked this from your hair, claiming you had far too many and that they were wearing you instead of you them. And as I handed it back to you, you said—"

"Keep it. It would match your eyes if you dared to let a sparkle of joy into them."

Nik's mouth twitched in bittersweet reflection.

"Why do you still have that?" Tauria asked quietly.

Nik's face pinched as he fiddled with the comb between his fingers. "I kept it with the intention of giving it back to you one day. Over a century passed, and I always thought about going back to Fenstead, if only to tell you it worked. That every time I looked at the damn thing it brought me joy to remember that moment. But we were preparing for the greatest battles Ungardia was to face. Training became the only thing that mattered, but I never forgot about you. Never forgot that I would one day follow through and return this to you. I thought about that every time I went onto those battlefields. It was my determination to walk off them." He shook his head, eyes finally glancing up to catch hers. He didn't expect the glitter that danced across the hazel. "Then there you were. On my doorstep, so haunted and broken. Above everything, I was relieved. So gods-damned relieved you had come to High Farrow. To me."

Tauria moved toward him slowly. Nik remained reclining against the desk, his heart beating harder with each step she took to close the distance.

"I could have gone to Rhyenelle. I could have gone to Olmstone." She stopped closer than he expected, looking down at him and searching his eyes with a hint of hesitation. He stayed silent. "Both kingdoms were far closer, both with kings who were close to my father. They would have easily taken me in. Yet I kept going, kept riding, because…"

—her gentle hand trailed over his jaw, igniting his skin—"I remembered the sulking prince who stole that comb from my hair. Who jested and teased the whole damn time. I remembered that there was no one else at that ridiculous, over-the-top ball I wanted the company of more that night despite how much of a pain in my ass you were."

Warmth filled his dying chest, and it took every single piece of restraint not to reach out and feel her, to pull her to him. Nik had never been so stunted by such raw, desperate emotion with no way of release.

"Can I ask for something?" Her voice was hushed, uncertain.

His chest rose and fell deeply, not breaking her hypnotizing stare as he got out, "Anything."

Tauria's throat shifted as she swallowed, and he couldn't help but tune in to her heartbeat as it picked up tempo. The few seconds she deliberated continuing with her request were maddening.

"Kiss me."

His heart might have stopped completely. "Tauria—"

She interpreted his response as a rejection before he could continue. She dropped her eyes, about to take a step back, but Nik moved on instinct laced with desperation and desire. His arm hooked around her waist as he lifted her and twisted with her. She let out a breath of surprise when they stilled, and then she sat on the desk he had been perching on a second ago. He stood between her legs and leaned into her. Tauria's hands gripped the folds of his jacket as though she thought she would fall, but Nik's arm didn't release her. Their faces came so dangerously close he felt the warmth of her breath against his lips.

"If I kiss you, Tauria…I won't be able to stop."

They shared a breath, and he swore he felt the tightening of her legs around him that made him force back a groan.

"I don't want you to."

He did groan then, his forehead falling to rest on hers while he fought with restraint. One hand traveled from her waist to hook under her thigh, clad in such form-fitting riding leathers the sight was enrapturing, but the feel was nearly his undoing. The position he'd put them in strained the last tether on his control.

"You don't want this this. Not when you're about to leave with prospects for another." He pleaded with her as though she might have the will to pull away when he lost his.

Instead, her palms flattened against his chest. Slowly, torturously, they trailed up to his neck. Her soft fingers over his skin made his whole body shiver until her fingers weaved into his hair. "I have promised nothing yet. Can't I have this one moment for myself?"

Nik's hand clenched lightly on her thigh. "This won't be just a moment."

"Please."

He pulled his head back, locking onto her hazel gaze. Beyond the haze of lust lay the vulnerable longing he couldn't deny. A desperation sent to pull them from the paths that would force them apart.

"If we do this, there's no taking it back."

"It's not as if it'll be the first time."

No, it wouldn't. The memory of their first night together was one he often thought of. Alone. When nothing else could sate the pent-up need for release in the darkest hours of the night. Or after having spent a day with her. Or when his mind didn't care what time of the gods-damned day it was, Nether-bent on sparking his desire for her.

"Why now?"

Tauria's fingers uncurled from his hair, and Nik's breath sharpened as she went to unfasten his jacket. "I want this for me," she said, voice turning to an alluring whisper. "I want this to remember I had a time of freedom to do as I desired before my duty."

He didn't stop her when she pushed his jacket from his shoulders. He could do nothing but hold her, letting her take every ounce of control. A part of him hated the satisfaction that caressed him from within, but the twist of pain, the seed of guilt that he should stop this for her sake, was drowned by such a strong force, heightened even more so now he might not get another chance to show her how much she meant to him.

"And after?" Nik ground out as she unclasped her cloak and let it fall.

Her hand encased his cheek. "After…" He almost missed the faint wince that flashed across her expression. "I go to Olmstone. We go back to how things were. No expectations."

His heart squeezed so tight his teeth clamped together. But against his will to protest, he nodded slowly.

"Nik," she breathed, and her need filled the room with the sweetest, most desirable scent. His name—on her lips, and in the sensual way she spoke it—was his undoing.

Nik crashed his mouth over hers. A soft moan left her, and he pressed into her tighter. Tauria ground her hips against him as he did, and he lost all tethers to his reserves, control, and sanity. He lost himself in her, and he knew he didn't care if he ever came back. Every feel of her was glorious, every taste like an insatiable craving. The way she moved for him, it was as if her body harmonized with his. The material of his pants felt torturous, and he became unhinged, unable to stop the jerk of his hips that answered to the way her legs around him pulled tighter, impossibly close. Tauria's noises were of the sweetest notes.

His lips found her neck, and Nik panted with restraint—against every primal instinct that roared to claim what was his. It was dangerous for him to be this close to her, but he wouldn't mark her. He would never take that choice from her, and the risk to her life if he gave in was enough for him to resist the drag of his teeth over her long neck, which she exposed to him so eagerly. Her fingers in his hair curled tightly, almost to the point of pain, and he relished in her abandon.

A knock on the door made him emit a low growl from his chest. He couldn't stop; the need to be buried so deep in her there would be no disentangling them was like fire coursing through every inch of him. It was utterly claiming and changing, and his fury at being interrupted when the intruder knocked again shot all kinds of murderous thoughts through his mind. He heard the guard nervously clear his throat before his muffled voice sounded through the wood.

"The Prince of Olmstone has arrived, Your Majesty."

If his rage weren't a dangerous force before, it near shattered at hearing that name. It took great will to pull back, but not completely, as he rested his forehead on Tauria's while they caught their breath.

Knowing this was it, their time was up, his heart clenched and clenched so painfully he couldn't stop himself as he blurted, "I want you to come back."

Tauria pulled away, surprise defusing her lust. "Nik—"

"I don't know what they'll offer you. I don't know if I can compete. But what I promise you is that you will never need to commit yourself to marriage or surrender anything in return for High Farrow's protection and allegiance. I will respect your choice and what you need to do for the good of your kingdom. But know, should you ever change your mind, you can always come home."

Her hand caressed his jaw, and she brought her lips to his in a single soft kiss. Nik groaned as his lips found the soft spot below her ear. "Until you do, I'm going to be thinking of all the shameful things I never got the chance to do to you right here." He leaned into her further, and a breath left her as she clutched onto him tighter. "I'll always be thinking of this. Of that look on your face. Of how I would have scattered everything on this desk to worship every inch of you over it. Of how beautifully you would have screamed for me." He memorized the staccato of her desirous breaths and how her thighs squeezed around him.

Another knock turned him rigid, and he had to breathe consciously not to snap.

"Your Majesty, Prince Tarly Wolverlon awaits in the reception hall. He's…impatient."

Nik smiled against Tauria's throat. It was a wicked joy to imagine his irritation at being kept waiting. Nik didn't care, and there was a large part of him fighting internally not to make him wait *far* longer so he could fill his words to Tauria with memory rather than promise.

Tauria forced him to straighten, pushing his chest. "Menace."

He gave her space after setting her back down, and Tauria righted herself, adjusting her askew clothing before fixing herself back into her cloak. Nik's desire for her still pulsed so strong he had to avert his gaze and think of something, *anything*, to subdue his raging thoughts.

"I trust you won't go poking around for things you shouldn't when you Nightwalk to me," Tauria said, her breathing still delightfully uneven.

Nik gave a devious smile. "What dirty secrets might you have to hide from me, Tauria?"

She scowled, and Nik chuckled, grateful for the distraction—for the small dose of lightheartedness he would cling to, not knowing when he would see her again.

"You have my word. I will only be looking for information regarding Olmstone. But Tauria..." Nik paused, face falling serious. "You give me one word, one sign, if they ever give you a reason to think for a second you are not safe there, and I'll come for you. I don't care what it takes."

Tauria smiled sadly. "Thank you, Nik. I won't forget all you've done for me."

The crushing pain in his chest returned. "This is not goodbye."

She closed the distance to him, and he didn't stop her when she fell into his embrace. They held each other for a short, tender moment. Her voice was barely a whisper as she said, "I hope not."

CHAPTER 30

Nikalias

TARLY WOLVERLON WORE a divided expression as they met on the portico outdoors. There was the gleam of excitement of someone eyeing a prized jewel as his eyes landed on Tauria, but something about it was triumphant rather than endearing. His look of suppressed ire, however—that only surfaced when his gaze shifted to Nik. The challenge that radiated between them was a familiar energy that grated on his nerves. Perhaps it was a fool's move, but as they approached, Nik couldn't help the hand he lay on Tauria's back to guide her out. His touch didn't go unnoticed by the prince. He didn't want it to.

"I have been here some time," Tarly spoke with a hard edge.

Nik fought the curl of his mouth. "I must accept fault and offer my apologies. I kept the princess back for final preparations for her long trip. Tauria is still High Farrow's ward after all."

Tauria's spine stiffened as she caught onto the subtle emphasis he put on their *preparations*.

Another wicked voice cut through the tension. "I wish to bid you farewell, Tauria Stagknight." Zarrius wore a triumphant gleam as he stepped outside to join them. "I look forward to watching our kingdoms strengthen at the prospect of this wonderful union."

Nik tried not to lash out, knowing the anger that flexed his fist was not the best approach to dealing with the lord. Instead, he schooled his face to a cool calm. His fingers trailed Tauria's spine deliberately as he let his hands fall then clasped them behind him to straighten his posture. Her lips parted, but she otherwise kept her composure.

"Indeed," Nik said, matching Zarrius's cheerful tone. He had to play smart. "High Farrow, Olmstone, and Fenstead could thrive greatly with this binding alliance. I look forward to corresponding with your father on the matters once you return and the princess has had a chance to settle." Nik was purposeful in pointing out Tarly was not a voice of authority in the negotiations. It was a move of arrogance and perhaps spite, but it was also the truth: Nik outranked the Olmstone prince now.

To his surprise, Tarly didn't balk. "I'm afraid my father is preoccupied with other matters at present. Most of the negotiations will be made with me."

While the thought riled him and the smug look on Tarly's face flared his violence, the prince had unknowingly provided Nik with his first insight into the Olmstone king's suspicious activity. He couldn't imagine what would be more important to Varlas than securing the Fenstead princess for his kingdom. The wave of urgency to protect Tauria was so strong he almost damned the guise to demand she wasn't to leave his side. He couldn't shake the settling anxiety that he was sending her straight into the arms of the enemy—to the ones who had killed her parents and conquered her kingdom.

Tauria's eloquent voice interjected. "I will of course be included in all correspondence and negotiations, as I not only stand as High Farrow's ward, but as Fenstead's queen."

"Of course," Nik agreed, pride chasing away the uncertainty.

Tauria was strong and resilient and smart. He had to believe she could take care of herself, and if her position became compromised, he would storm Olmstone with everything he had. It was a harrowing thought, but if they threatened to harm her, he would incite a war.

"We shall see," Tarly said, eyes flashing between him and Tauria. Nik's rage didn't get the chance to surface recklessly when the prince extended a palm to her. Everything else dissolved to twist his stomach with jealously and sorrow. "Come, Princess."

Tauria gracefully accepted his offer, but her smile was hollow. Nik fixed his eyes on her palm as it slid into his, his tormenting demons mocking and laughing at the contact, flaring his every instinct to remove the touch of another from his mate. Tauria didn't deserve to be fated to one so spineless and pitiful.

Neither of them looked back as they descended the stairs to where a carriage lay in wait. His rage at imagining them in such a confined space together was drowned by the wave of his grief as Tauria took steps away from him.

"I'm glad you came to accept my counsel, Your Majesty." Zarrius came up to stand by his shoulder. Nik couldn't take his eyes off Tauria despite the irritation that clenched his fists. "Using our best pawn to secure a stronghold."

It was an effort not to take his trembling fist to the lord's face at the way he spoke of her. Zarrius was brazen, as though he were goading Nik to break, to expose whatever suspicions the lord might have about his feelings for the princess. Nik yielded nothing. He tunneled so far down into a coldness he knew all too well, detaching himself from the world. A place built of his own self-loathing.

"You were right." Nik forced the words from his mouth. "Tauria as an asset could be very advantageous if we negotiate well." He had thought about how to handle Zarrius for some time and knew the only way to tide him over while he worked on his own silent plans was to give him everything. At least make him *think* he had everything. "You were close to my father, Zarrius; I trust you by my side. As I trust you will be invaluable in these upcoming negotiations." It was like spilling acid from his mouth, and the ripple effect of the lord's inflating ego was suffocating.

"I serve no greater honor than aiding in the rise of High Farrow. I am glad we see eye to eye, just as I did with your father." Zarrius spoke with cruel confidence.

Nik would allow the lord to bask in his triumph. He would allow him to build himself up in such high regard so it would be all the more satisfying to watch him fall. All Nik had was time, and he had to bide it well. For Tauria and for his kingdom, he had to be smart, but most of all…he had to be patient.

There were no words to describe the way he felt watching her travel away from him. Nik stood on the portico, hands clasped formally to straighten his posture while he and the other members of the court bid farewell to the princess as she rode off with the Olmstone escort. The carriage had almost reached the gates, and his heart was such an uneven mess of shards he didn't care if it stopped there and then.

Please look back.

Perhaps it was a foolish thought. Childish even. But he found himself needing it, the knowledge she had thought of him in her last moment leaving the castle grounds. The knowledge it was hard for her to leave, even if it were just a fraction of what he felt.

The horses trotted to the gate, a steady pace that quickened in his frantic mind. Too fast.

Look back. Look back. Look back.

He flexed his fingers but refrained from moving otherwise. From running after her in an epic, disgraceful display as his mind taunted, *She's my mate, and I'm letting her go.*

At the gate, his eyes bore holes into that damn carriage.

Then, at the last second, Tauria looked back. Her beauty was radiant even from this distance as her head twisted out the window. He was mesmerized by the flowing waves of her brown hair, the gold accents that adorned her ears glinting in the sunlight. It was an image he held still in his mind, savoring it then storing it.

That second of suspended time was far too short. Tauria dipped back inside just as the ornate carriage disappeared out of sight completely.

"This could be a great merger between courts," Zarrius muttered. Nik didn't want to pay him any mind, but he was completely vulnerable with his guard down in the moment as he fought against every instinct to abandon the plan; to declare what was his and should have been all along. "Don't let it become a clash between courts. A word of counsel, Your Majesty. One heart can tear down an empire faster than any army."

Perhaps he was already a losing player if he couldn't find it in himself to convince his council, the world, that what he likely wore on his sleeve wasn't true. His love for Queen Tauria Stagknight.

It was sheer will that kept him from buckling where he stood, unmoving.

He didn't know how much time passed, but he found himself completely alone. The sky fell a few shades darker, and bodies occasionally filtered across his inattentive vision. Then finally, as the sun made its final descent, Nik looked away from where she had vanished. He turned back to his castle knowing Tauria Stagknight had been willingly sacrificed as the opening gambit in their deadly game.

CHAPTER 31

Faythe

IN THE GREAT dining hall, Faythe could barely touch her food from the knots in her stomach. There was a lingering sadness that clouded the air at dinner with her companions and the king—their last supper before they left tomorrow. The dinner Agalhor had insisted they all spend together. She pushed around the selection she'd forced onto her plate from the glorious spread. All this effort, yet she felt guilty for her lack of appetite.

"We plan to take the known passes through the Fire Mountains. Diverting through Balmore would be far too much of a risk lest we run into Valgard armadas in the Southern Gulf." Reylan sat opposite her, explaining their route while casting her several looks laced with worry.

Agalhor leaned back in his chair as he pondered the information. "I suppose you are right. Though you will be unable to go on horseback and will need to make sure you are well-stocked with provisions. I do not believe there is anything left of civilian life on the Isles. Beasts and creatures are all that are said to remain. You will be cautious."

Faythe shifted her gaze to the king. It was the first time she'd ever heard him speak to Reylan so informally and on such a personal level. His concern was clear in his tone as well as in the slight crease of his brow. At his quick flash of a look in her direction, she saw the hidden plea in his words. To protect her. Faythe dropped her eyes to her plate in guilt.

Reylan gave a nod. "Of course. We have devised a plan for every stop and considered all threats that could greet us. We are well-prepared."

While Faythe and Reylan sat on either side of the king, Reuben sat next to her, along with Livia, and across from her Kyleer and Izaiah were enjoying their final dinner in comfort, for none of them knew how long it would be before they returned. If they returned at all.

"And you are sure it cannot be delayed any longer?" She felt Agalhor's words directed at her.

Faythe took a deep breath as she raised her head, slipping on a firm mask of confidence while also trying her best to ease his concerns. She knew exactly why he agonized over the sudden announcement of their journey. While she'd been in Rhyenelle for over four months now, like a coward she had avoided any kind of bonding with her father until only a few weeks ago, and she cursed herself relentlessly for the time she'd lost that may never be regained in their uncertain future.

"The Summer Solstice is a mere month away. If we do not go now, we risk not making it to the Isles in time to stop Dakodas." Faythe felt strange to speak of the Great Spirit out loud as it felt like a fable in her mind. She forced a smile to conceal her unease. "The sooner we leave, the sooner we can return." The words burned in her throat as she felt the guilty drop in her stomach that they could be a lie. That a promise of return was not her gift to give. It seemed to ease his tension, and he returned her warm look.

No one was really enjoying the food with the heavy conversation except for Reuben, who was fully engrossed in inhaling the pile on his plate. Faythe didn't fail to notice the wary looks of her companions, who were still holding back from outright banning him from coming. Faythe didn't admit it, but she was silently glad he was accompanying them—as another human and lifelong friend she'd missed dearly. It was at least a familiar reminder of her life back in High Farrow even if she didn't hold out any hope of Reuben being of use in the expedition.

Faythe was eager for the feast to be over so she could crawl back to solitude. Well, as solitary as she could be when Reylan refused to let her sulk on her own. But he never pressed or forced her to talk, and even in silence it was comforting to have him nearby.

As if reading her thoughts, Reylan cleared his throat. "I suppose we should see to it that the last-minute preparations are in order. We should like to leave by first light in the morning." He cast her a look, and she read the meaning in his eyes. He was giving her and Agalhor the final hours of the night to be alone together, and she could have embraced him for it. Faythe wasn't ready to say goodbye to her father when they had not been blessed with nearly enough time together.

Livia, Kyleer, and Izaiah understood immediately, and they all began to rise, each giving a short bow to their king before strolling from the hall. Reuben caught on a delayed minute later as Reylan stood behind his chair expectantly to lead him from the hall. His pale cheeks flushed, and Faythe suppressed a genuine smile at the sight of the young boy he looked in that moment—the one she knew from happier memories.

Reuben quickly wiped his mouth and fumbled to his feet, but he hesitated before swiping one last slice of bread. "Thank you. The food was delicious," he mumbled ungracefully to the king, mouth half-full. Then he strolled out of the hall after the others.

Faythe bit her lip to hold in her chuckle at his completely innocent lack of manners. Reuben had never been in the company of the high fae before, let alone a *king*. She caught Reylan's eye one last time.

"I'll meet you at your rooms later," he said to her privately, and she gave a subtle nod of acknowledgment.

She watched his back as the final member of their ensemble left. Then, alone with Agalhor, silence settled. Faythe didn't know what she wanted to say to him as she didn't think she could acknowledge this as their last moment alone together for however long life ripped them apart this time.

"There's something I've been waiting to give to you," Agalhor said thoughtfully.

When Faythe turned to him, he waved over a nearby guard who held something wrapped in a crimson velvet cloth. The king stood as he got close enough to take the item into his own hands. As he came around to her side, Faythe also felt compelled to get to her feet. When they stood facing each other, Agalhor unwrapped the item that stole Faythe's breath the moment she laid eyes upon it.

"They call it the Eye of the Phoenix," Agalhor said as he admired the amulet he held. It was a fitting name. The intricate ornate silver band held a single brilliant amber stone in its center, but it moved ever so faintly with tendrils of red like a live flame. "It has been in the Ashfyre line since the age of the Phoenix Riders. It is said to have been forged in Phoenixfyre, a deadly weapon, but also great protection. It may all be superstition, but it has always been passed to the first-born child in each generation." Agalhor held out a hand, but Faythe was too stunned.

"I—I can't accept that." She stumbled over her words, feeling wholly unworthy of the ancient heirloom he wanted to bestow upon her.

"You are my daughter, are you not?" he asked carefully, in such a way that it was left open for Faythe to deny without judgment. But this held more meaning than a simple declaration. With the acceptance of the gift, he was all but crowning her head.

Faythe slowly reached out her hand in answer, and his calloused fingers grazed her skin as he went to adorn her wrist with the Eye of the Phoenix. She couldn't hold in her gasp as the cold metal touched her skin. The faint prickling of unexplainable energy tingled over her hand, up her arm, and ignited in a small burst of flame in her chest, snuffing out the darkness that clouded her mind, like a shockwave of strength.

She looked to Agalhor with wide eyes. He looked back with a pride she had never seen before. Pride reserved for a father to his child. With the acceptance of the amulet, Faythe felt something far more powerful and heavy bearing down: the weight of the phantom crown that had her straightening in turn to bear the acceptance of that too.

"Thank you," she said quietly through the emotion that choked her.

Agalhor was slow to release her wrist. "I shouldn't say this, as it is not certain with the challenges that lie ahead when you return from your duty. We may not have had the privilege of filling these halls with your laughter as you grew, of collecting the memories of your child-hood, or of watching you bond with the people as their princess, Faythe, but I still see it all the same, and I know I am not alone." His hand raised to her cheek, and her vision blurred around the edges at the wave of his pride that pierced her chest. "My daughter, Rhyenelle's lost flame returned. Just like your mother…you would make a gracious queen, Faythe Ashfyre."

CHAPTER 32

Zaiana

ZAIANA WAS JERKED awake by a faint knocking against wood. When her eyes snapped open, it took all of a second for her to remember she was in her rooms. When she moved, she winced, straightening from the awkward upright position she'd fallen asleep in in the armchair she'd pulled to her bedside.

She hadn't meant to fall asleep, and in a surge of panic she studied the chest of the darkling who occupied her bed. Amaya's chest rose and fell, but her breathing was still shallow and labored. As Zaiana shuffled to stretch her aching muscles, a blanket she didn't remember covering herself with fell to bundle in her lap. She frowned at the material, but the gentle knocking sounded once again, reminding her of the presence that lingered.

Zaiana rose, rolling her neck and arms to ease the stiffness. She cracked open the door. Upon seeing Tynan's concerned face, she wordlessly widened the gap for him to slip inside.

"You didn't bother to knock the last time," she commented quietly, not wanting to disturb the darkling who needed all the rest she could get to heal.

Tynan looked to where she lay with a hint of pain disturbing his hard face. He had failed in his role to cover her when the attack happened, and she expected he would feel some responsibility for her condition. They had yet to discuss anything of the battle from two days ago, and Zaiana had yet to face Mordecai to be commended for her victory.

"None of us have seen you since the battle. You told us to stay away."

Confusion twisted Zaiana's expression, and she glanced at the blanket on the chair. She said nothing about it.

Tynan passed her to get a better look at Amaya, whose face could almost be mistaken for dead with its hollowness and dry lips. "I knew Niltain Steel was lethal to our kind, but—" He stopped himself, and they shared a grim look.

Neither had predicted just how deadly it could be.

"She's small in form and not as well-fed or trained as she should be." Zaiana's fingers curled. "I imagine it's attacking her system faster than if it were inside you or me. Her body can't heal fast enough to counteract the metal poison."

Niltain Steel could incapacitate and torture against the skin, but if it entered the bloodstream, it could be fatal, like a spreading poison. Zaiana didn't have an ounce of pity for Tynan, who didn't even try to hide his guilt. She wondered if it was simply for her being hurt when he should have been covering her, or if he was regretful of how badly he'd underestimated her before. Amaya had proven herself without a doubt on that field, and if any of them tried to devalue her worth now, it would be on Zaiana's wrath.

The only thing that churned her stomach to a feeling she was not wholly accustomed to was the prospect of Amaya not waking up.

There were no healers under the mountain. Such a talent as magick healing was only known to exist in fae, and Zaiana was forbidden to bring one here unless she was prepared to kill the captive afterward. She was ruthless, born heartless, but even if she were to find one with the rare skill, she was conflicted about wasting such a life. But Amaya was coming to end of her luxury of time, and she was deteriorating. If it came to a choice between one of her own and a stranger, the answer was obvious. She had already wasted enough days.

"Tomorrow, I'm going to find a healer," she announced.

Tynan whirled to her. "What about the quest?"

Zaiana had won it, and if she left, she couldn't be sure it would still be on offer by the time she returned. She would be all but submitting her reward to the insufferable Maverick. Perhaps this had been his plan all along. If he couldn't best her in battle, he would still find a way to steal the prize.

Lying, cheating, arrogant bastard! Zaiana's anger was razor-sharp at the mere thought of him. "I'll speak with Mordecai," was all she said.

Tynan's look of understanding laced with disappointment ground her nerves further. It wasn't directed at him, but they both knew the High Lord would not have the patience to hold off the quest for her. Even more, she risked losing the promised status of master and being seen as weak. For caring for a life beneath her own so much she would risk everything. Zaiana was a fool, and it had been tormenting her to distraction the past couple of days. She should let Amaya die if that was to be her fate. It was expected of her. She was just another darkling. Replaceable.

Yet every time Zaiana imagined the chest she studied stilling for good, she couldn't explain it. It was as if in failing Amaya, she would be failing a piece of herself. One that couldn't be forgiven with time.

"Watch her." Zaiana didn't wait for his response. Spinning on her heel, she marched out of her rooms, high on rage and resentment. If she had to leave to find the healer tomorrow, she wanted to get the humiliation over with by explaining her absence to Mordecai.

She was seething as she stormed the halls. The few dark fae who littered the cavernous space averted their gazes, shrinking out of her way quicker than usual. She was at risk of recklessly harming anyone who got in her way in her current mindset.

Zaiana focused on reeling in some form of composure to face the High Lord. It would not win her any favors to arrive unhinged, or she risked far more than verbal disgrace for what she was about to propose.

Then, just as she was calming into some form of sedation, around the next corner her vision flashed white at the person who stalked her way. In the space of a breath, Zaiana drew the dagger at her thigh, crossed the space, and slammed Maverick to the wall, settling her blade across his throat. She bared her teeth while he took a second in his bewilderment to register the threat.

"I should have known," she snarled. "You never have been anything more than a spineless, cheating *coward!*"

Two dark fae rounded the corner, taking in the sight of their delegates. She didn't even have to turn to them before they hastily shuffled back out of sight.

Maverick said nothing. His face was calm and cool, devoid of all emotion. Zaiana clenched her teeth, pressing her dagger harder until it made a shallow cut, slicing the edge with a trail of black blood.

"Say something," she demanded.

He stayed silent. Zaiana gripped the folds of his jacket and slammed him against the wall again. He yielded no reaction but a faint grunt at the force.

Stepping back, she held the point of her knife to his neck, her breathing heavy. "I could kill you right now."

"Then do it," he said at last, tone soothing as though he were trying to encourage her.

Zaiana's nostrils flared. Everything was a game, a trick, with Maverick. Yet there was nothing taunting or teasing on his face. No victory. Nothing. It was unlike him to be so detached.

"You are pathetic," she spat.

Both of them stood in thick rising tension for a few deep breaths of cool loathing. She had half a mind to rip his head from his shoulders for what he had done. But Maverick simply watched her, black eyes fixed until her breathing slowed and came easier. Until sense weaved through the all-consuming hate. All he did was watch her steadily.

"Berrik and Rex are dead," he said quietly, cautiously, knowing she was teetering on a razor's edge with the little humanity she held.

Saying those names was certainly a risk to her murderous ideals. Hearing they were dead by Amaya's hand rallied two prominent thoughts. The first was that in extending her protection to Amaya, their deaths were her punishment to face. The second was dark and gleeful satisfaction that the darkling had gotten her own back. Twice.

"I told Mordecai I don't stand to challenge their deaths. The end they met was fair game," he went on with equal calm.

Zaiana's eyes narrowed a fraction, but she did not lower the blade she threatened him with. Whatever he read on her face gave him the confidence to slip his hands into his pockets, and the bastard had the audacity to shift into a leisurely lean against the wall. She tried to ignore the flare of anger. It was as though he didn't believe she would follow through and plunge her dagger through his throat. Or he simply didn't fear it.

"Why?" she ground out.

"It *was* fair game." He gave a one-shouldered shrug. "They brought illegal weapons onto the field—"

Zaiana stepped forward, leaning into him once again to press the length of the blade against her last cut. "*You* brought illegal weapons onto that damned field! And if Amaya dies because of your cowardice, so help me, Maverick, I'll be coming for you."

Their closeness was deadly and intimate, faces almost level from his slant against the wall. She straddled his extended crossed legs. For a split second, she almost retreated at the dark flash of desire in his depthless onyx eyes, there and gone so fast she would have missed it if she blinked. She recoiled internally. Not at that look, but because her body betrayed her mind with a flush of heat in response to it.

"Are you quite done threatening my life?" he said with a low gravel tone he didn't try to disguise.

Zaiana didn't respond, but she supposed the edge of her unmoving blade was answer enough.

Maverick's insufferable smirk returned, sadistically delighted by her threat. "I thought you might like to know I have a healer for your little darkling."

Her breath stilled. "What?"

"I said—"

"I know what you said," she flared. "Where did you get a healer?"

"I have my ways."

Zaiana stared into his eyes, searching them for any indication he was playing her for a fool. "Why?"

Maverick seemed to calculate his next words carefully. "She was impressive out there. It would be a shame to see such talent go to waste."

Lies. He was lying, but it didn't seem as if he cared whether she believed him or not.

"One of my *rogues* should have escorted her there by now while we've been…chatting." He slipped back into his insufferable arrogance, but she didn't care. About him, about his pitiful life, nor about his reasons. Tension vibrated an exhilarating current between them, and their faces came so close they shared breath.

Zaiana's voice dropped to an icy warning. "Mark my words, Maverick,"—she locked eyes with him to deliver her promise—"if she doesn't wake up, neither will you."

They stared off in thickening silence. Neither flinched from the compromised position. He wanted to rise to her threat but debated it if it was worth her anger.

"Ah, there you are."

At the voice that carried down the hall, Zaiana instantly pulled away from Maverick with a forceful shove. He straightened, and both of them bowed at the waist to Mordecai as he strolled toward them.

"Interrupting something, am I?" he asked, voice dancing in amusement.

Zaiana straightened, clenching her wrist painfully tightly behind her back. "No, High Lord," she answered before Maverick could.

Mordecai looked between them both, a brow curving at the obvious conflict that was palpable between the delegates. "I imagine the emotions of the battle are still running high," he observed. It was a light way of putting it, but Zaiana remained silent. "What an impressive show you two put on."

Zaiana hated the comment. As if they were no more than pretty weapons for his entertainment. She wouldn't out Maverick for his use of Niltain Steel. It would only serve to make her look weak, and she wouldn't have them punish him. No—she would exact her revenge on him in her own way.

"Come," he said simply, turning on his heel to stalk back the way he came.

Zaiana moved while Maverick stayed put, figuring Mordecai's summons was regarding the task he was about to finally disclose. But Mordecai paused after a few steps.

"Both of you," he added with a quick glance behind him.

Zaiana flexed her fingers but said nothing as she continued to follow the High Lord through the maze of passageways. She did, however, cast a glower of hate toward Maverick. Childish perhaps, but the petty side of her always came out around the dark demon.

Maverick fell into step beside her, much to her irritation. She was supposed to be his superior now, though this was still to be formally imposed. She had beat him and hated that it felt as if she had gained nothing in return.

Upon their arrival at the council room, they found the masters already seated, and Mordecai went around the table to take his own grand place. He didn't sit. Instead, he stood proud and silently assessed the two delegates in front of him. They stayed silent and obedient. *Speak when spoken to.* His eyes darted between them, but Zaiana couldn't be sure what he was pondering. He looked at them as though he couldn't tell them apart. And that unnerved her more than she cared to admit.

"It has been two days, and you have not come to seek your reward."

Zaiana's spine stiffened. "One of mine was wounded in battle," she explained.

His emotionless face seemed to have already rejected that as ample reason. "Maverick lost two in that battle, yet he came to me straight away."

Zaiana had to fight against snapping her head to him in accusation. Instead, her claws cut into her wrist behind her back, enough to be painful.

Mordecai went on. "He came to tell me he seeks no justice for those deaths at the hand of your darkling. I must admit she has impressive potential."

"Which is why I have been absent, High Lord. I plan to finish crafting the weapon I will make of her. I won't let her die and lose that hard work."

"Is she recovering then?"

Zaiana couldn't help the look she slid to Maverick. "Yes," she answered. "She just needed firm encouragement dying wasn't an option." She hoped her words were convincing. That he wouldn't find out Zaiana had sat like a shriveling coward at Amaya's bedside instead, muttering pitiful prayers to whatever creature would listen that she would wake up again.

Mordecai answered with a bored hum, seeming to accept her absence but not pleased by it. "The quest I propose looms closer. Two weeks, to be exact, until you shall embark."

Zaiana straightened. A thrill tingled her chest and brought a flare of momentary joy. This was it. Her quest to freedom. One she had proven herself worthy of. All her negative sentiments were swallowed by giddy anticipation.

"The time we have been waiting a millennium for is finally upon us," he said. "It is a little over a month until the one who guides us shall join us." He had Zaiana's full, undivided attention. Her breaths were steady, and she knew what Mordecai referred to. *Who* he referred to.

"Dakodas's ascension," Zaiana let out. She couldn't believe it. Couldn't believe it was real and that she was to be a part of such a brilliant event that would go down in history for all eternity. The Spirit of Death, the Goddess of the Moon, the one they owed their survival to, would come to walk on their land. It was an exhilarating concept.

A triumphant smile appeared in the corner of Mordecai's mouth. "Yes, Zaiana. When you leave this mountain, you will come back having made history. And she will reward you with something far greater than anything you could have wished for."

A surge of pride and determination raised her chin and allowed a smile of her own to disturb her calm face. Only, it was quickly dulled by a cruel tug of the phantom leash that had been tied around her neck since birth.

You will come back.

Suddenly, the prospect of leaving, of going on the quest, didn't seem as freeing and exciting with the knowledge she would always be called back here; always be at someone's mercy. It was a darkly damning feeling, but she had never been taught anything different. She had been taught to always belong. To obey and to lead. Zaiana's life had never truly been her own.

"You shall not go alone." Mordecai's voice snapped her from her clouded thoughts of resentment. "Choose whomever you wish, those who can glamour, to aid you in your quest. The existence of our kind should remain secret until the time is right. Fly to where you can and where there is cloud cover, but otherwise, this journey should be taken by foot."

Zaiana wanted to groan out loud. She knew where Dakodas's temple lay: on the Niltain Isles of Rhyenelle. They would miss the day of the solstice completely if they didn't plan their journey wisely, and indeed, some flight would be necessary to make it there at all.

"Should I not have left far sooner, High Lord?" She felt the need to state the obvious.

He smirked, seemingly anticipating the question. "If we had the luxury of deciding, you would be right in your observation." Mordecai tapped aimlessly against the wood of the table. The rest of the masters were silent and expressionless. Zaiana wondered why they were here at all. "We do not hold the key to the temple, and the one who does also happens to be exactly what we need for the ascension."

Mordecai finally occupied his throne, and Zaiana gauged they were about to dive into a long string of details. She was a fool to believe ensuring Dakodas's ascension would be without challenge; that she could face the task with ease and perhaps even excitement.

The High Lord's hard look braced her for grim details. "Does the *Heir of Marvellas* mean anything to you?"

Zaiana's brow furrowed. "The ones descended from Marvellas as fae, yes. But her descendant lines were all hunted and slaughtered. The Heirs of Marvellas are a fable now."

Mordecai gave a brief chuckle. "It seems her kin are far more cunning at elusion than even the great Spirits could have prepared for." He leaned back casually, clearly reveling in the tale.

Zaiana stared back with a frown, growing irritable at his dance around the point.

"One lives. Not just any heir, but one conceived of both her direct bloodline and one blessed with her magick. The divination is in motion."

Zaiana fit the pieces together. "He seeks out the temple to stop

Dakodas, knowing she will band with Marvellas?"

He gave a nod of approval. "*She* is set to take the same quest as you. *She* is the one who holds the key we need. Both to open the temple and to open the veil." A dark chuckle rumbled through him. Humorous disbelief. Zaiana couldn't see what was of amusement; she was more than capable of taking down one person who stood in their way. "As it would seem, fate has a wicked sense of humor," he went on. At her pointed look of question, his grin widened. "*She* is Faythe Ashfyre of Rhyenelle."

Ashfyre. Zaiana knew the royal house of Rhyenelle. Only, in all her teachings of the ally kingdoms' lineage, particularly those they were still to conquer, she had never heard the name "Faythe."

"Agalhor has a daughter? How did he keep that a secret?" Maverick asked with pressing disbelief. Zaiana had forgotten about his presence in his silence, and she twisted her head to him to match his look of confusion.

"He did not know himself until months ago when conflicts stirred between the allied kingdoms. It seems her mother fled with the unborn child without his knowledge. We can all assume her foolish reasons were in vain."

It started to make sense. If Faythe's mother was a descendant of Marvellas, she would have found out what a child conceived with a Nightwalker was destined for. She faintly pitied the tragic soul—born without any idea of the fate that would befall her. And her mother, who seemed to have failed in her attempt to keep her from it.

"So, am I to kill her?" Zaiana asked, not particularly enjoying the fact, but hardening herself to accept it.

To her surprise, Mordecai shook his head. "She doesn't just hold the key to the temple…she *is* the key."

Zaiana would never admit it, but Faythe's death not falling to her hands was a relief. Then a spark of remembrance had her locking eyes with her High Lord. "The Heirs of Marvellas…they were human."

"As is she."

Zaiana couldn't be sure why that fact made a difference. As though the girl never stood a chance in this world from the moment she was conceived. Weakly human, but different from her kind. She would have power at least, though Zaiana didn't believe it could be substantial enough to stand against the dark fae who were about to be set on her.

"You should not be so quick to underestimate her. She is powerful and is said to have harnessed the Light Temple ruin. You would be wise to take caution."

She didn't like that it felt like a challenge.

"You will need this." Mordecai gestured to his side, where a Black-fair stood cradling an object wrapped in a cloth. Upon removing it, Zaiana's blood stilled. She didn't let it show but snapped her eyes back to meet Mordecai's.

"I said you may take whomever you choose, but I have decided to add one to escort you of my own choosing," he went on without acknowledging her wide-eyed look. Zaiana's jaw flexed, and her clawed fingers broke her skin. His eyes flashed to beside her, and she heard his declaration before it was spoken. "Maverick shall accompany you. Under your authority, Zaiana, you have proven yourself worthy of the strength and leadership."

She heard nothing after Maverick's name. Not when rage clouded her senses and set her thoughts aflame. Zaiana said nothing, focused on her breathing to calm the storm of her mind, which translated to the awakening of her lightning that prickled her whole body. *I was played for a fool.* Zaiana stilled her mind, reeling her emotions in as she'd been disciplined to her whole life. *I never should have believed winning would grant its merits.* Her breaths cooled her hot wrath and smoothed her skin. *Liars. They're all liars.*

Finally, she rallied enough composure to reply. Her tone was hard and ice-cold. "I do not need him."

"It is not up for debate," Mordecai dismissed, triggering her gruesomely violent thoughts. "Faythe is powerful, and she will not be without the company of others with abilities. You will need both of your powers if you are to succeed."

Zaiana wanted to shout and rage and kill, wondering why they'd suffered the damned battle at all. It was all for nothing as she should have been chosen to lead without it. She'd spent three centuries of existence proving she was worthy, proving she was the best, and he had belittled everything she had worked for by demanding a pageant of talent that ultimately reaped no real reward except a damn High Lord's favor.

She stared at him with cold, simmering fury that she masterfully kept off her face. But in that stare, she marked him.

Zaiana stormed the halls to her rooms, aware of but too enraged to pay notice to Maverick who followed her. Arriving at her door, she barged through it, halting in the doorway. At the sight of Amaya sitting up in her bed grasping a steaming cup, every other emotion that boiled in her blood cooled with a wave of relief. The darkling wore a smile as she chatted to a female fae sitting on the edge of the bed, and her smile widened when her eyes met Zaiana's.

She was too dumbstruck to return it, seeing the healthy glow had returned to her skin although she'd left her only a couple of hours ago looking close to death's claim. Then Zaiana took in the presence of Tynan, who stood with arms crossed and a hard look of threat, pinning the Blackfair from across the room. Maverick's rogue equally stared off in challenge, neither acknowledging the delegates who entered.

Zaiana didn't care that Maverick was at her back; didn't even care for every other invading presence in her safe and private space as she walked right up to the bed and stopped at the foot.

The fae met Zaiana's cold look with a warm reception. Despite where she was, despite the dangerous, foreign, winged species that surrounded her, she wasn't afraid. At least, if she was, she kept it masterfully suppressed.

"How?" Zaiana demanded. She'd been hopeful a healer could give the darkling the boost she needed to heal herself, but Amaya looked as though she had never been wounded.

The fae stood, casting one last smile to Amaya. "She's strong, this one. As soon as she felt my magick, it was as if she was determined to work with it. It will take a couple more days to fully burn out the remains of the Niltain poison, but she'll make a full recovery."

Zaiana stared at the fae, so soft-spoken with an accent that was faintly familiar. Kindhearted when she had no reason to be. It didn't make sense. She couldn't decide if her lack of fear was foolish, for being so trusting that she couldn't see her life was all but sacrificed in being here, or if she admired her selflessness in aiding without resistance despite her grim fate. The fae was strikingly beautiful. Loose white tresses curled around her face, overspilling from her long braid. The paleness of her hair was in marvelous contrast to her glowing bronzed skin. Her eyes were a wondrous bright hazel.

"I should like to stay a couple of days if that's all right. To be sure there's no setback with the poison."

Zaiana stiffened, feeling a wave of something that churned her gut, akin to regret. No—deeper. Remorse? For the kindness she didn't know how to receive and didn't deserve when she would be forced to end the fae's life for her exposure to their existence. She shouldn't have accepted, but Zaiana's head nodded of its own accord. Because Amaya *did* deserve her kindness.

"Thank you," she said to the fae. The words were so unused they felt foreign on her tongue. Her cruel mind sang weakness, but her gratitude was too strong to listen to its taunts.

She looked back, catching Maverick's eye first. He stood by the door with his hands in his pockets, observing her with a frown.

"I was of the impression I would be escorting our guest...out," he said carefully.

Maverick had planned to take her. Did he plan to take the task of her execution too? Zaiana figured it was the least he could do when he was the reason they were in this mess. Yet he didn't need to. He could have left her and not bothered himself at all with Amaya's fate. After all, he wouldn't receive punishment. She couldn't figure him out. Why would he help? He owed her nothing.

Zaiana knew she should let him take her, to get it over with instead of stringing out the inevitable for a couple of days, allowing the fae to think her goodness would be rewarded with freedom, unaware that these mountains had claws, and once within their grasp, it was stay or die. If anyone else found out she was here, the fae's fate would be far worse than death.

Zaiana didn't waver her firm expression. "You heard her. Amaya could decline again; she needs a few more days." She switched her gaze to Tynan. "Leave us. And I don't want to be disturbed. I will come to you when it's time to discuss and prepare for the quest we will take in two weeks."

Tynan gave her a single nod then fixed his stare on the Blackfair across the room expectantly. He, in turn, glanced to Maverick for instruction. A dip of the head was all he gave to his rogue. With a grunt, the Blackfair left, and Tynan followed after him.

Maverick lingered. "A word, Zaiana?"

"Later," she dismissed.

His jaw flexed in protest.

She walked over to the door, and Maverick twisted smoothly to walk out of it. A few steps past the threshold, he sang behind him, "Seems like the perfect night for a late-hour bath."

CHAPTER 33

Zaiana

ZAIANA STOOD BY the firepit staring into flames that soothed her senses so she could think peacefully. Amaya was once again in a deep slumber behind her, and Zaiana couldn't relax in the presence of the fae, who sat by the bookcase on a lounge chair casually flipping through pages. Zaiana didn't know what she read, nor did she really care. They had barely spoken a word since everyone left and the fae purposely sedated Amaya for better healing. Zaiana felt…foolish. For not knowing how to approach a topic of conversation with the fae. Any she had encountered in her lifetime she had usually killed, or she'd watched their death during Transition.

With the awkward silence grating on her nerves, Zaiana swiveled to the fae. "What is your name?"

Peering up from her book, her cheeks flushed rose as she blinked to refocus her vision after reading for so long. Flicking her eyes down to the pages, Zaiana realized exactly why the hint of embarrassment flashed across her expression as she recognized the title. Amaya had given off the same shyness, and she had to wonder if it really was so scandalous to own such books.

The fae straightened from her curled-up position on the chair. "Nerida," she answered. "And yours?"

Zaiana shifted on her feet, oddly nervous at the question she passed back to her. It wasn't often she was asked anything about herself. Outside her close circle, her social skills were severely out of practice.

She shouldn't bother to engage with her, knowing Nerida's days were severely limited, but curiosity got the better of her. "Zaiana," she answered.

Nerida closed her book, shifting in attention. Zaiana stiffened with *anxiety* under her awe-filled gaze. She was an odd creature. A happy lamb in a lion's den. She couldn't be sure whether the fae was simply naïve or incredibly brave.

"Why are you not afraid?"

Wisely, there was a wary shift on Nerida's face. "Why should I be?"

Usually, such idiotic questions would irritate Zaiana into snapping back with disciplinary sense, yet she could only stare pointedly like a gawking fool. Nerida huffed a short laugh at Zaiana's expression, which twitched her face into a firm scowl. With hesitation, Nerida stood and walked over to where Zaiana was posted by the fire. Zaiana tracked her every flicker of movement. It was ridiculous to think of her as a foreign species. Aside from wings and the color of their blood, they were almost kin.

"I've read a lot about your kind, you know," she said casually as she took up the armchair by the flames instead. Zaiana couldn't help but be bewildered by the prey getting comfortable in front of the predator. "It's fascinating to find out so many of you lived—and have been living—in secret, building your species once again. It's remarkable."

The knowledge should have frightened her, but Zaiana was baffled by her intrigue and awe. "I wouldn't believe what you might have picked up in scripture." Zaiana turned her eyes from the fae, perhaps acknowledging her own shame. "We are made of nightmares, not dreams, and you'd be wise to be fearful of that. Your kindness is what will get you killed."

As it already has.

"Nightmares are made of monsters, are they not?"

Zaiana followed the fae's line of sight to the peacefully sleeping darkling in her bed.

"That is not all that I see here."

Zaiana paused. Within, she fought with…agreement. Nerida was strange. Foolishly, naively strange in her perceptions. "Where do you come from?" She couldn't figure the fae out. Her calm optimism—it was a trait Zaiana didn't think she had come across before.

Finally, Nerida seemed to guard herself sensibly from the question. Good. At least she wasn't a compete fool and held some reservations about what she could share. "Nowhere." When Zaiana arched a brow, she added, "I travel."

It wasn't an answer Zaiana was willing accept. "Where were you born?" A hint of a warning seeped into her tone. She couldn't help it, hating for her question to be evaded. It was so rare for someone to challenge her or try to withhold information from her.

Nerida studied her for a few seconds. *Studied,* and Zaiana's hideous defensive side took it as an insult; a question of her authority. Lightning rippled across her fingertips as an instinctive reaction. The fae's eyes shot to her hands at her sides, widening as she caught a glimpse of her ability. But to her displeasure, it was not in fear.

"Remarkable," Nerida breathed. "I should have realized sooner by the vibrant core of purple in your eyes."

Zaiana's lightning winked out. This fae was impossible. It was a miracle she had survived this long with her stupidity.

"You're a Stormcaster."

Zaiana blinked. "A what?"

Nerida's eyes met hers with a frown of confusion. "You've never known what you are?"

"I know exactly who I am," she snapped. *Liar,* her cruel mind hissed.

"No one's seen a Stormcaster since the Old Age of the fae, and even then, they were extremely rare—an unexpected development of the Firewielder ability, but far more lethal."

Zaiana's mind raced, *pulsed,* with a wave of knowledge she didn't want to hear. Or believe, as it made her question everything she thought she knew about herself. She knew her ability was rare, but to be spoken of as if she had no clue about herself... She hated that it felt like another lack of control on her life.

Zaiana's voice dropped, becoming cold and threatening. "First lesson, Nerida: I don't often give second chances. You've earned one pass for helping Amaya, so I'll ask again." She focused her breathing to calm her anger. "Where do you come from?"

Finally, the naïve fae had the good sense to look afraid. Her throat bobbed. "I was born in Lakelaria," she confessed.

Zaiana straightened, finally realizing why her accent sounded familiar. Nerida must have read the recognition on her face.

"You have been before." It was an observation rather than a question, but Zaiana turned from her, not deigning to give her confirmation. She had only been to the great western isle a handful of times. Every time she did, she felt her presence alone was a dark stain on the beauty of the kingdom of ice and water.

Zaiana diverted. "Did Maverick retrieve you from Lakelaria?" Though even as she asked, her mind calculated the round trip would be impossible in the length of time he'd had.

Nerida shook her head. "I left there a long time ago. I lived in Fenstead for some time, until..." Her face fell in sorrow. "Well, after it was conquered, I fled to Fenher in Rhyenelle as one of the closest towns. The Great Lake there is marvelous—it almost rivals the pristine crystal waters of Lakelaria." Nerida's eyes wandered, looking to nothing in particular while she seemed to travel to her homeland in her mind. Zaiana envied her for having such bright joy to reflect on. She found bliss in the stars—the one thing of beauty that would remain the same no matter where she went. It could not be taken from her.

"How did he know you were there?"

"There aren't many Waterwielders on the mainland, and I was certainly the only one in Fenher. I guess it wouldn't haven't taken much if he asked around, as discreet as I try to be. But not all of us have healing abilities."

Zaiana processed this information, matching it to what she already knew from centuries of schooling. Water and healing: a rare and invaluable combination. It only twisted her gut with regret even more to have to waste such a talent for saving one life of the wrong kind.

"He was surprisingly kind, you know," Nerida went on, perking up.

Peering down at the fae, Zaiana saw she'd settled against the back of the chair, perfectly comfortable with her surroundings, her company, and her situation. It was unbelievable.

"Dark and mysterious turns out to have a soft side. He was calm in explaining what he was and what he needed of me. You can imagine my shock. I might not have believed him until he showed me his wings. It's truly astounding." Nerida's eyes fell on Zaiana's wings. She tucked them in tighter in subconscious defense. "I couldn't leave a young fae to die— dark, believed-to-be-extinct species aside." Nerida's smile curled in teasing amusement.

What Maverick had failed to include in the terms of her duty was that her life would be the price for Amaya's. But something about her made Zaiana wonder if she might have still agreed even if she knew. Her frustration grew at the horrible rise of...*guilt*. She shouldn't care, and it was becoming a constant drain to fight the fact she did.

Without warning, Zaiana stormed for the door.

"Where are you going?" Nerida called, twisting over the chair to track her.

"There's something I need to do." She yanked the door open but paused, turning her head back. "If you're smart, you'll stay silent, sit still, and won't leave this room."

Zaiana traveled the maze of the underground with one specific vicinity in mind. Even as her feet pressed forward, her mind screamed at her to turn back. Getting answers wasn't worth suffering Maverick's presence. But it seemed he too had things on his mind that needed to be said.

Seems like a perfect night for a late-hour bath.

Sure enough, she detected his insufferable scent down the hall leading into the baths and focused on taming her irritation that stirred at being near him. Rounding the final corner, she found the bastard in the black waters. Zaiana felt the heat he added to the chilled pool, giving off a light steam in the air. Maverick's head was tipped back with eyes closed as he basked in the moonlight pooling in from above, highlighting every impressive contour of his glistening bare chest and arms that he splayed over the edge as he'd glamoured his wings, as though he were in a hot spring in summer.

"Care to join me, Zaiana?" he asked without opening his eyes. A curl formed on his mouth. "You'll find the temperature to be quite pleasing."

If she didn't despise him, she might have admitted the offer was tempting. It wasn't often she bathed in warm water—only in the prime of summer when the rays of the sun penetrated the overcast mountain with their shine for long enough to add a faint warmth.

"Why did you bring her here?" Zaiana ignored his invitation.

He lifted his head, black eyes sparkling as he looked over at her. She held his gaze, willing her traitorous eyes not to travel as he twisted in the water to face her.

"Join me."

"Tell me."

"I will if you join me."

Zaiana ground her teeth. She was of the right mind to storm away, but she had a feeling it would only be a matter of time before their unspoken conversation brought them right back here. Both about Nerida and the quest ahead.

Maverick rolled his eyes at her stance of defiance. "Don't make this glorious hot water go to waste." Shifting back to his previous position, he turned his head from her.

Zaiana muttered a colorful string of curses, both internally and out loud, as she began to undo the fasteners on her jacket. She was still mumbling her dismay when she stood bare and slowly eased into the pool. Her words ceased the moment her legs felt the blissful heat, and she bit back her sigh of contentment instead. How could something so simple feel so good? Her skin loosened, muscles easing, and she took a moment to close her eyes and breathe in relaxation when she was fully submerged.

Remembering she had company, her eyes snapped open. Maverick still looked away from her, but the knowing curl of his mouth itched her skin.

"Lose the gloating," she grumbled.

Finally, he looked to her, focusing on nowhere but her eyes. Zaiana drifted through the water, glamouring her wings to settle against the edge opposite him.

"I suppose I should congratulate you," he said loosely, fingers tracing the surface water.

Zaiana scoffed. "No need. It's not as if either of us expected any different outcome."

Maverick's grin turned feline, relishing in her confidence, which seemed to overcome any bruise to his ego from the loss.

She added, "Though it seems I reap no reward regardless of my victory."

"We're nothing more than pretty show dogs to them," he said, stretching back. She didn't glance at the flexing muscles of his chest, but the awareness surrounded her. "We both knew it was nothing more than a game laid out for their own amusement. Though I would be lying if I said I didn't also enjoy it." He cast her a wicked smile.

Zaiana rolled her eyes. "It worked out perfectly for you regardless."

"I was just as surprised as you were to find out he would be sending me with you."

She met his depthless gaze and narrowed in on him to detect if he spoke the truth. Nothing about his expression was gloating.

"You think I want to spend weeks among you and yours?" He huffed. "You'd better keep that insufferable dog of yours on a leash."

Zaiana flared at the insult, knowing it was Tynan in particular he referred to, though he held no fondness for any of them. Over the past century, Tynan and the Blackfair delegate had gotten into many violent altercations. It always started in defense of her and ended in Tynan's punishment no matter who was at fault. What was worse was that as his leader, Tynan's brutal and public punishments were always hers to carry out. Such gut-twisting memories she stored behind a solid block in her mind that only broke each time she was forced to add another.

"Don't be a bastard and he won't have cause to bite."

"Out there, the laws of the mountain don't exist."

"Out there," she warned, "you answer to me. Just like the rest of them."

His eyes flexed at the tone. The dominance in him rippled like the waves of the water. He unhooked his elbows from the bath's edge and floated closer to her. She didn't balk, nor did she allow her eyes to leave his. He stopped just shy of arm's reach.

"You've let the win go to your head if you think I'll submit to the same obedience as your dogs," he rumbled, voice quiet but firm. "I will honor your victory, and by that I mean I will yield to you. But try to mock me, belittle me, in front of your *underlings*, and I think you'll find yourself on a field where there are no rules and you might not emerge so triumphant."

She held his black stare like fire on fire. Felt it in the heat of the water as the tension grew thick. Zaiana couldn't decide how she wanted to respond: in violence at the threat he laid down in his words or indifference because she understood. She despised him for so many wicked reasons, some not even his own fault. But she respected him as sometimes…she couldn't deny they were one and the same.

Zaiana decided not to respond, but her silence was enough to assure him as he gave her a short nod. Cutting through the water, he came to lazily prop himself against the edge next to her.

"It will be refreshing to taste air not so tainted by pent-up malice and aggression," he diverted casually.

Zaiana snickered, glad for the dissolved tension she didn't have the energy to battle with. "Don't pretend like you don't thrive on such things."

"Oh, we both do. But it's only fun when it's our own, not that of untrained darklings unable to turn it into pleasure. Just pure, irritatingly unfocused wrath."

Zaiana couldn't fight it: she smiled. Not out of slyness or cunning; it was a flutter of unusual warmth to acknowledge her genuine light-hearted amusement. What was even more jarring was the one who inflicted it.

"How is our little darkling?" he drawled, trying to sound as if he didn't really care.

Zaiana shifted to look at him. "Why did you help her?" It had been tormenting her all day. Maverick had no reason to offer such mercy and nothing to gain. Or so she thought. It set every nerve of irritation on edge that perhaps there was a personal goal behind his actions. There always was. And Zaiana hated nothing more than to feel as if she owed a debt.

"I have my reasons," was all he said, and she wouldn't grovel for an explanation no matter how much it clenched her fists to wonder. "You do know we will have to kill the healer," he drawled coldly. "I hope you're not growing attached as quickly as you did with your little darkling."

The mocking tone itched at her violent thoughts. She couldn't understand why her emotions had decided to turn on her now, when she was so close to getting everything she wanted. Before she could remind herself who she was in the company of, she blurted, "What if we take her with us?" They couldn't let her go. Zaiana wasn't completely blind-sided by foolish emotions to trust Nerida wouldn't talk. It wasn't yet the time for their exposure, and it could ruin everything. Yet even barely knowing the fae, Zaiana couldn't stand the thought of such a waste of talent.

She felt Maverick's pressing judgment lock on her and swallowed the grating sensation that she had exposed a weakness to him. Mercy. He was silent for a long moment, and she almost slid her eyes across to gauge his reaction.

"I'm deciding if I should forget you just suggested that," he said carefully. "As I assume you're going to take it back."

"I wouldn't say something I plan to take back," she snapped. Perhaps she'd lost control and finally cracked. She'd spent centuries under this mountain and killed countless fae, humans, and dark fae. Her hands were coated with the blood of all species, and she didn't think it would ever wash off. Yet in the span of less than a month she'd shown more weakness and, dare she believe it, *compassion* than she had in her entire life. They weren't feelings she should harbor—no dark fae did. She didn't want them, yet they stirred in her mind so irritatingly it was impossible to ignore. And exhausting to hide.

"By the Dark Spirit," he drawled, not meeting her eye as he tipped his head to gaze at the moon through the open mouth of the cave. "Our esteemed delegate, the notoriously ruthless, highly powerful and feared Zaiana Silverfair…has grown soft."

"Not at all," she hissed, hating that the comment reduced her to nothing, discrediting all she had built herself to be. "The fae is useful. She's a Waterwielder and a healer. You heard Mordecai—this human girl is powerful and will likely have companions who are too. Nerida provides another weapon in our arsenal."

"Oh, she has a name. How lovely of you to care to find that out."

She ground her teeth. "Unlike you, I don't fail to see past a single task someone can perform."

A deviant smirk curved his lips. "I bet not." He glided through the water until he was right in front of her. "I bet you're good at discovering *many* tasks that can be performed by a person."

It was incredible to witness where the bastard's mind could jump to so quickly. Incredibly infuriating. She blamed the heat of the water for the flush of her body at the gaze that accompanied his statement—the twinkle of mischief in his depthless eyes that made her want to gouge them out of his hollow skull.

"You're insufferable."

His smile only widened to a grin that showed his elongated canines. Unlike her, the Blackfairs could not retract the teeth they needed to feed. Silverfairs didn't need mortal blood to survive like them. It was a curse of the ritual performed to change their species.

"I think you like it."

"I think the heat is getting to your head."

He inched a little closer, and Zaiana's eyes flared in a deadly warning, all too aware of every inch of her skin that was exposed under the black water, only a slight shift of movement away from touching his.

"The heat is getting to a lot of things, I can assure you."

It took a conscious amount of will not to look down despite knowing she would see nothing. But it were as if he could see past the cracks of the hard expression she tried to maintain while they stared off against each other. His grin turned roguish as if he knew exactly what she was thinking.

He tutted, floating back to rest side by side with her. "What scandalous thoughts you have, Zaiana."

"You know nothing of what I'm thinking." She passed it off as nonchalantly as she could. She didn't have to look; his sly amusement was palpable, and she wanted nothing more than to carve it from his face.

"I sometimes think I know you better than you know yourself."

"Then you'll know my only thoughts of you are about how painful I can make your death."

The bastard chuckled. "I think anyone can sense that," he said. "But not the other things you wish to do with me before that gruesome end."

Zaiana's mouth fell open. It wasn't often that she was so at a loss for words. Maverick's brazenness and over-inflated ego had taken on new highs of stupidity. It only added to her loathing and stirred her violent creative thinking.

To wipe the smug look off his face, Zaiana decided to act rather than speak. She moved through the water, aware of his eyes that tracked her. Then she did something she never thought she would. She continued to the shallow end, inches of her skin slowly becoming more exposed. Her shoulders, her chest. Zaiana held her breath, stepping out past her breasts even though her back was to him. Her marred, torn back from many, *many* lashings between and around where her wings expanded. She didn't even release her glamour so her wings would cover her. She felt Maverick's stare like a branding, surprised to feel nothing but blazing triumph that she'd silenced him; that she could no longer feel his arrogance and teasing in the hushed air. The water lapped around her navel, and she didn't falter a step as she continued out of the bath. The cold air kissed her behind, tingling over every inch of her once she was fully out the water. It cooled her heated skin, made her body shiver. Zaiana didn't look at him as she began to dress, the material clinging to her wet skin.

"You will keep silent about this," she said casually, knowing he watched every movement, devouring every piece of her. "Nerida will stay in my rooms until it is time to leave. She will accompany us, and you will say nothing. I don't need your opinion, and I don't care for it." She was buttoning her pants, having already flung on her light shirt that likely exposed as much as if she were still naked in its dampness. She turned to him regardless.

Maverick was unmoving. Not a single ripple disturbed the water as he fixed his eyes on her. A spark of hunger hardened his black stare, but there was no smile on his cut features. A conflict of rage and desire danced in his onyx orbs.

"Out there, you are under my leadership. You all are. You say you think you know me, Maverick—then you should know I don't act without reason. I'm not afraid to challenge you. Not in here, nor out there." Fully dressed, Zaiana stalked for the exit without looking back. "Don't give me cause to."

CHAPTER 34

Faythe

FAYTHE STARED AT her reflection in the mirror, feeling…vacant. Over the week, she had succumbed to the stresses that drove her from sleep. She embraced every fierce word of her friends and father that filled her with determination. She mulled over every happy and perilous outcome of the path she was set to take. Now the day had dawned, all she could do was adopt a cool indifference to force her to take her first steps onto that road of uncertainty.

Gresla was finishing off the elaborate braid she'd spent more time than usual styling half-back for her journey ahead, making sure it would remain out of her face and not bother her. Faythe caught her occasional sad gaze as she secured endless pins behind her head. She had no way of knowing how many days or months counted down until her end, and no sure confidence she would succeed in her end game to rid the world of Marvellas once and for all. But what she was sure of was that while she lived, she had people who were counting on her, and those she was counting on all the same. For them, she would be brave. For them, she would *fight*.

Reylan had left earlier that morning before the sun began to rise—as it was now—to prepare himself for the journey. She knew the others would be doing the same. It was time. Faythe was no longer afraid and had learned to let go of the weight of emotions over everything she could not prevent or change.

When Gresla finished, Faythe stood and turned to her. She had nothing to offer the kindhearted woman who had done so much for her during her time in the castle. Nothing but endless words of gratitude.

Her small, plump fingers reached to Faythe's cheek with a smile that reflected in her eyes. "You look just like your mother the day she left."

Faythe's eyes widened. "You knew her?"

Gresla winced. "I was her handmaiden too," she confessed, striking Faythe with a sudden twist of emotion that pricked her eyes. "I was the only one who knew of your conception. But she swore me to secrecy, and I couldn't betray that. I always had"—she gave a loose chuckle, silver lapping her gray eyes—"*faith* that she left for good reason, that it was somehow tied to you, and whatever it was, I knew you would be safe with her."

"Why didn't you tell me before?"

"Because while I see the spirit of your mother and the will of your father…you are someone else entirely, Faythe. It gives me hope for us all."

Faythe didn't feel deserving of her powerful belief, but she didn't shy away from it. Her palm encased Gresla's at her face. They exchanged a pained smile, neither letting their tears of farewell and gratitude shed.

"Are you sure I can't stay to help you dress, dear?"

Faythe gently shook her head. "You've done more for me than I can ever thank you for, Gresla." She didn't mean for it to sound like a permanent goodbye, but Gresla's face fell further as if she felt it as such.

"You will come back, Lady Faythe. I will be waiting with your favorite meal and a warm bath for your return."

They embraced each other. Faythe savored every second of her comforting warmth.

With a final squeeze, Gresla said quietly, "Be safe, my dear."

All Faythe could muster was a nod in hollow promise when they parted. Then the handmaiden turned for the door and didn't look back as she left silently.

Faythe took a deep breath to calm down, letting the first rays of the sunrise caress her face and offer solace. Then she approached the ensemble laid out by Gresla on the bed. Her fingers grazed the black-and-crimson leathers and various weapon holsters. It was an exquisite combination. Everything had been specifically and carefully made for her, with requests from Livia for the clothing to be added to and rein-forced for their journey.

Faythe took her time stripping out of her nightclothes and into her Rhyenelle leathers that were gloriously form-fitting for the best freedom of movement. They were textured with scales dipped in crimson, reminding her of fire and ash—a powerful masterpiece. She equipped herself with every item like armor in preparation for battle, for the journey they would take was just as variable, uncertain, and perhaps equally as deadly.

She was fiddling with the buckle on her upper-thigh sheath when two knocks sounded at her door. Reylan entered through it when she didn't call out to him, and the sight made her straighten in awe. He looked...

Gods.

Words left her completely, no way to describe what she thought of the great general dressed like death incarnate. Though he wore no steel, as they would all stop by the royal armory to equip themselves before they left, Reylan looked even more lethal in his battle leathers. Her throat turned dry as he approached her slowly. Neither of them spoke, but a dark look of appreciation glazed his eyes as he glanced at her from head to toe with each step closer he got. She felt his gaze like an impression over every inch of her skin. Her heart picked up a quick tempo.

Reylan said nothing as he stopped a mere foot away. Faythe's head tilted to hold his stare that fluttered a giddy tension in her lower stomach. Then her eyes widened, following him as he dropped to one knee before her. Faythe's breath hitched when his fingers grazed her upper thigh, working on the dagger sheath she'd been in the midst of securing. When he pulled to tighten the buckle, she jerked, her hand instinctively raising to his shoulder for balance. As it did, Reylan's sparkling sapphire eyes flashed up to her through long lashes, and Spirits be *damned,* she hoped he didn't detect the desire that flushed her body at his gaze.

When he finished, Reylan rose deliberately slowly. Faythe began to feel mildly dizzy from her uneven breaths with each of his movements. The trace of his stare that was claiming. He didn't stop there. His hands came up to her shoulder next, adjusting another strap. Then, as his fingers grazed across her chest, she thought he was going for the other side to fix the buckles there too.

But his hand halted at her chin.

Faythe held utterly still, and when Reylan's fingertips grazed her bare neck, her lips parted at the sensations that crawled delightfully over her skin. He paused for a few tense seconds as if to read her reaction. Faythe didn't move, didn't speak, out of fear that if she did, he might retreat from her.

Whatever he deciphered in her expression made his eyes flash to her mouth then back to her stare. Faythe couldn't even be sure her heart was still beating. His hand curled slowly along her neck until his fingers trailed over the tip of her spine, and the touch angled her head back on instinct.

Finally, Reylan spoke when she was close to coming apart completely. "There's something I've been waiting to do," he said in barely more than a husky whisper that weakened her knees. "Something I never got the chance to do back in High Farrow."

Faythe's heart reached a tempo she feared could break through her rib cage. She wanted him, but one thought sang cruelly above her need to give in to desire. "This can't end well for either of us." She choked the gut-wrenching truth.

She was human. And she'd ignored the curse of time once with Nik. Yet to deny Reylan twisted her heart like nothing she'd felt before. Faythe wanted to bow her head in disappointment, but Reylan didn't release her. Instead, his eyes searched hers, looking for any sign her reservations were her own and not simply for her mortality. He seemed to find his answer when his gaze turned soft but fierce.

"Why think of the ending of something that has not been given the chance to begin? Why deny yourself the chance to be happy and damn whatever the ending may be?"

Faythe's brow pinched together as she fought the lapping pools in her eyes. Reylan never once shied anyway from everything she was. Everything she *wasn't*.

His face inched closer, so tensely slow, as if he left each second as a chance for her to object. She didn't. She couldn't. Every impulse and instinct within her longed to close that distance. When she couldn't stand the growing need any longer, Faythe closed her eyes and made the last move to push up on her toes and meet him.

Then the sun and moon collided. A ray of the brightest light flared in her mind, shooting to her chest and bursting with a warmth so pure and *safe*.

Faythe arched her back with a need to be impossibly closer, a want for this moment to be suspended in time. She felt herself become complete with that kiss. She felt him within as though her soul rejoiced. In the way their mouths moved together, the final barrier crumbled. The kiss was soft and searching, but it was also claiming, savoring every taste and feel, the desire all-consuming.

When they parted, Reylan rested his forehead on hers as they caught their breath. Faythe felt unexplainably weightless. Unburdened.

When her heart calmed enough to speak, she asked quietly, "Why did you wait so long?"

Reylan pulled back, one arm around her waist to hold her to him while the other caressed her cheek and neck while he looked over her face. As if he didn't believe she were real. "You were healing and needed time to adjust. We both had demons we had to face, and I didn't want you to think for one moment that this was a distraction." His eyes were pained, a look of terror filling them that pierced her chest. Every closely guarded emotion opened like a book before her, and she embraced each page of him. "You are not a distraction, Faythe. You are everything."

Her heart could have stopped at the declaration. At the fierce look in his eye that showed he meant every word.

"I don't know what the future holds or where the path may end, but I plan to follow you down whatever perilous, reckless, adventurous road you lead, Faythe Ashfyre." His lips curled in tender amusement. "I vow to stand by your side. I vow to protect you with my sword and my life. And I vow to bind my fate to yours, if you will have me. I've lived enough years in this world to know should you leave it, so too shall my desire to stay here without you."

Every word he spoke she felt down to the depths of her soul. Felt them and returned them. Reylan held still, waiting for her response with rare anticipation, as though she might reject him.

"Reylan," she said through a breath while emotion tightened her throat, "I can't let you give up your life for me. *Gods*, if anything were to happen to you because of me—"

He cut off her words with a kiss, and in her selfishness she couldn't pull away. Knowing it was his will to follow her to whatever end made her burst with a happiness she never thought she would be blessed with in her life. Never believed she *deserved*. Reylan accepted her with every darkness and danger that came alongside her twisted fate.

Faythe kissed him back with a needy desperation that had her straining on the tips of her toes in an attempt to be closer to him while she tangled her fingers in his soft silver hair. She felt the longing in him too when his hands trailed down the curve of her spine and around her waist. Faythe cursed the hour, cursed that this hadn't happened on one of those blissful mornings when she awoke beside him—the one who understood her from the beginning, saw every flaw and strength she never knew she harbored. She would forever long for every minute of those hours she had watched the sun rise over his face, and for how he welcomed her each morning with a smile that made her believe no matter what became of the day ahead, it would be okay.

Where his hands touched, she wished desperately to be in her nightgown. Or without clothes at all. Knowing they were about to venture into the unknown without any assurance they would get another carefree morning like those she treasured crushed her spirit like a physical pain in her chest. Reylan seemed to feel her dip of mood at the thought. The kiss slowed, and when they broke apart, his eyes were clouded with desire but fierce with determination.

"I've had a long time to think of every way I want to have you, Faythe." Her name on his tongue always sent sparks through her body, but in this tone dipped in gravel, infused with rising lust, heat formed insatiably between her legs. His arm tightened around her waist as though he sensed it, tugging her to him, impossibly close. He leaned his head down, and when his lips met the curve of her ear, her fingers curled tighter in his hair with a sharp breath. "Alone." His breath carried down her neck and turned her mind to incoherent nonsense. "Safe and warm." His lips pressed to her neck, and a small whimper left her. Her veins throbbed hard, and she felt his elongated canines. As they scraped lightly against her skin, Faythe might have buckled were it not for his strong arms that held her. "In that bed behind me, perhaps. But in many other places too. What might you say if you knew of the indulgent thoughts I've had about you on that piano?"

Gods above. She had to refrain from glancing to the games room, certain her imagination would be Nether-bent on sending her off on the desolate quest with the torment of that mental image. Her mind was haze of lust and desire, but she found the words to say, "Are you trying to entice me into staying alive?"

He pulled back to look at her with wicked smile. "Depends. Is it working?"

Faythe bit her lip, which flared a hunger in his eyes. "Definitely," she whispered, reaching up to kiss him once more, thinking she would never get enough of the feel of him.

They parted before it could become heated again so they wouldn't risk screwing the damn quest and the rest of the world to stay and fulfill Reylan's promise now rather than later. But she couldn't ignore the tick of the phantom clock in her mind that chimed with the dawning of a dire fate if they didn't leave.

"Until the end of days, Reylan Arrowood."

His smile—warm, genuine, and heartbreakingly rare—had become the light in her eternal shadow. "Maybe even longer, Faythe Ashfyre."

CHAPTER 35

Faythe

ARRIVING AT THE royal armory below the castle was an interesting sight. Kyleer and Izaiah were arguing over something, both holding various hunting knives they seemed to be comparing. Livia leaned casually on Izaiah's shoulder, twirling a dagger of her own and clearly teaming up with him against an increasingly irritated Kyleer. Reuben stood at the other end of the long room, awkwardly squinting at a crossbow he held pointed toward the fae, which, to Faythe's momentary terror, was locked and loaded.

Reylan beat her to it, striding over to her friend. "Put that down before you hurt yourself," he scolded, cautiously taking the crossbow from Reuben and disarming it.

Faythe held in her chuckle at Reuben's sheepish look. He was merely a curious sort, though she didn't think he had the slightest clue how to use any of the weapons aside from perhaps a small blade. Reylan then stormed the short distance to the other fae in the room, fully slipping into his general/commander persona. She couldn't deny she found it highly attractive when he asserted his authority, and it no longer flushed her with embarrassment to admit it.

"Kyleer's right—we've been over this." Reylan caught the ornate dagger Livia was toying with, its blade cut in a wave. "Nothing fancy, and the lightest you can find. We're not attending a display."

Livia scowled at his back as Reylan went over to the wall of lethal blades in all possible shapes and sizes. Faythe was awestruck as she looked over the unique ensemble. She walked over to it, picking up a small but razor-sharp dagger.

"We know, but Kyleer just makes it too easy to tease," Livia chirped as she came up to Faythe's side. She slid a glance over at him, highly amused by the disgruntled Kyleer who was shaking his head in annoyance at his brother. Livia reached for two separate blades, swiftly sliding them into different slots on her body, then twisted over to the wall of swords, and Faythe watched with admiration as she equipped twin swords at her back. They were thin and likely the combined weight of her single long sword, Lumarias. She'd never seen the commander fight with two, but Faythe was highly intrigued.

When she turned back, Reylan appeared immediately beside her. She looked him over, now coated in steel despite only having averted her attention for a mere few minutes. He was a glorious sight to behold, even more so with the added edge of danger.

"If you're done gawking, the weapons could also use some of your admiration so we can get going sometime this morning." He smirked.

She refrained from whacking him at the teasing remark, twisting to look back over the blades. There were so many she didn't know how she could choose, or if there was a right or wrong one to go for as Reylan had indicated. But he waited patiently for her to decide what she wanted to defend herself with. Faythe settled on one her eyes kept returning to, which she took gently from the wall, casting a sidelong glance at the general to gauge if it was a good choice. At his slight side-smile, she asked, "What?"

He shook his head. "Nothing."

Faythe stood defiantly, and he huffed a laugh.

"Lilianna didn't take much interest in any kind of weaponry, but she did favor one blade in particular whenever she insisted on lessons in self-defense."

Faythe's eyebrows rose, and she stared down at the simple black leather handle of the blade over her palms. A smile bloomed on her face as she thought of her mother's spirit in the blade. Faythe slipped it into the holster on her leg, trying not to imagine Reylan on his knees before her and his touch on her thigh. Meeting his sapphire eyes, she found they were filled with pride as he watched her.

"If you two are going to stand around staring at each other all morning, I'm going back to bed." Izaiah's voice carried across the room. He didn't shy away from calling them out to everyone.

Faythe's face burned as she looked over, finding their companions fully equipped and ready to go. Even Reuben now sported a couple of flashes of steel she had no doubt one of the fae had supplied him with.

"Agreed. We've already wasted enough time waiting for the two of you to come down here," Livia added, and no one missed the subtle suggestion in her tone that added to the smirk on her face.

"Well, it's about time at least. I was at my wit's end with Reylan's incessant—"

"We'll be in the reception hall," Kyleer called to stop Izaiah's next words.

Faythe wanted to thank him for putting an end to the playful jests. She turned away from them to the ensemble of steel, more to hide her flushed crimson face from their taunts. Reylan nodded in gratitude for her, and their companions mercifully shuffled from the hall to give Faythe a little more time to gather herself and equip for the journey.

"How long did you say it could take to get to the Isles?" she asked, sliding a look to Reylan.

He chuckled. "At least three weeks."

Faythe blew out a long breath, taking another slim, short knife and fitting it to her hip. "If some foul creature or death trap doesn't kill them, I very well might."

Reylan grinned, and it was uplifting to see him join in with the light-hearted mood considering what they faced. "I think I'll help." He reached for a final blade of his choosing, whose twin he sported at his side. His hand held her waist as he slid it into the remaining sheath on her hip. When his fingers lingered and his eyes locked on hers, it was all she could do to close the distance impulsively and meet his mouth knowing they didn't have an audience anymore.

Reylan pulled back first, far too fast, and she couldn't hide her disappointment. His smile stretched out to a grin at her response, and then his thumb traced her bottom lip before he planted one final kiss there.

"We won't get off to a great start if Livia storms back through here because we're taking too long again," he said against her mouth.

Faythe wanted to retort that they should damn the time anyway and delay their departure. But in taking a moment to think beyond Reylan's touch, she realized he was right. Now they had confessed their feelings and acceptance of each other, Faythe had never felt more complete, more...free. She had no suppressed feelings, and with the strength Reylan brought out in her, she was ready for the road ahead. Ready to face anything that dared try to stop them in their task.

Reluctantly, she stepped away from him. "Let's get this over with."

He nodded his agreement, giving her one last lingering look. His expression alone kickstarted her pulse, but she breathed deeply to ignore it, or they risked eating into the afternoon if they didn't refrain from temptation. Reylan's presence was both what would keep her going through their long journey and what would heighten her frustration with the other party members, whom they had to be mindful of when her desires were running wild.

Leaving the armory, they were silent while walking the halls to the reception. Faythe tunneled into her own thoughts, taming the storm to sedate her heartbeat that rattled knowing her time was up. This was it, and whatever was to happen on the path of the unknown...no one was safe anymore. It no longer frightened her. They had all made their choices, and she felt stronger than ever with Reylan by her side.

Faythe spotted their companions straight away. Livia sat on the ornate center table, face plastered with amusement as she swung her legs casually. Faythe followed her line of sight just in time to catch Kyleer disarming Izaiah and twisting him into a swift position to snap his neck. While the younger brother called his disgruntled complaints, Kyleer released him and went on to explain something to Reuben, who stood with arms crossed observing them. It was both highly amusing and warmly endearing that he was at least attempting to clue her human friend in on some methods of attack and defense.

Spotting Faythe and Reylan, they ceased their brief combat lesson, and Livia hopped off the table. They halted to form a circle. Everyone looked to her, but she didn't shy from their attention, raising her chin with a smile.

"Whatever we face out there doesn't stand a chance," Faythe commented, looking them over. Lethal, focused, determined. It lifted the stern expressions around the circle and lightened the mood. Perhaps there was joy and excitement to be found in the dangerous unknown.

"We have your horses ready, General." A young human man came in through the open castle doors.

He gave him a respectful nod in acknowledgment, and Kyleer, Izaiah, Reuben, and Livia headed for the portico. Reylan cast her a look, and his smile of encouragement tugged her mouth upward. With a deep inhale, she followed her companions outside.

Faythe's eyebrows rose to find Agalhor at the top of the steps. He twisted to them as they were the last to step out, his woeful smile holding suppressed worry.

When they all stood before the king, he straightened with hands clasped behind his back. "I thank you all for your bravery in accepting this quest, and in doing so, your vow to protect your heir with your life if need be will forever be valued." Agalhor addressed everyone but her in that moment, and Faythe looked to them all in accusation.

They all gave a firm nod to their king, faces hard and determined. It was then she realized it was not the first time they had all spoken of this quest when she was not present. Though she knew they were willing to accept the risks of their journey to the Isles, Faythe had never once expected their lives would be forfeited for her own. It didn't matter who she was nor what crown they saw upon her head—she wouldn't allow anyone to make such a sacrifice for her.

"It is their honorable duty, Faythe."

Reylan's internal words made her cast him the same accusatory frown, but his soft, pleading eyes smoothed out her expression, and she caught his lingering meaning. It would be an insult to decline or object to them.

"In your blood oath to me, and in your unwavering bravery, I know you will not fail."

Kyleer, Izaiah, and Livia bent in a low bow to Agalhor. Reuben, through no reason other than trying to blend in, also doubled over a delayed few seconds later. After they all straightened, they headed down the steps to the awaiting horses that were fully equipped for riding with provisions.

Agalhor turned to Reylan then, taking the few steps over to them. He held out a hand to the general, and Reylan looked pained as they embraced forearms. Faythe felt his pinch of pain in her chest at their exchanged look of concern.

"Take care of her, and both of you come home." Agalhor's words were hushed, for Reylan directly, though it tugged her heart to hear them.

Reylan didn't answer with words, only a fierce nod, before they let their joined arms drop. It twisted her gut to think his lack of verbal response was because Reylan was nothing if not honest and he couldn't agree to the final part of Agalhor's wish when he wasn't certain they both *would* return.

He stepped away from the king, eyes flashing to hers for a second, then over to the awaiting party. It was his silent communication that they would give her as much time as she needed to say goodbye to her father as he strolled toward them without a look back.

Alone with Agalhor, Faythe was conflicted in what she wanted to say. No sequence of words seemed right to explain the lattice of emotions she felt in that moment. To think of the bond she had cut short when they had only been reunited for so little time. It was unbearable for the girl who never thought she would have a single memory to cherish with her father in her lifetime. Simply getting to meet him was a gift, and if that was all she would have, it was enough.

Neither of them said a word straight away. A goodbye felt too permanent. A promise of return was a cruel dose of hope.

"I'm so proud of you." His voice was shallow like a wisp of wind. It wasn't what she expected, and she struggled to find a response to utter how much it meant to her. "I know your mother looks at us now and is smiling at what we've found against the odds."

"Thank you," Faythe choked out. "For everything." She didn't mean for it to sound like a goodbye she would not return from, but in the cloud of sorrow that shadowed his hazel eyes, Agalhor took it to mean something similar. He reached both arms out but halted just for a second to see if she would retreat. When Faythe stood firm, his large hands encased her upper arms.

"You are more than I could have wished for in this life, Faythe. And I know...I know you have it in you to change the world. Not with the power you wield or the crown that may befall you, but with that golden heart that sings in your chest. For what is good, for what is right, and for what is fair." Faythe was transfixed by his fierce eyes. They struck her to listen; to absorb every word as though it were the truth. "But sometimes you have to fight fire with fire. Watch the world burn and then rise from the ashes."

Faythe lost all tethers on restraint and fell into Agalhor's arms with the wave of emotion that flowed from his words and his expression. He believed in that better world, and somehow, though she didn't know what she had done to deserve it, he believed in *her*.

"Stay safe, my child," he whispered within their warm embrace. She savored every precious second of it, and he refused to be the one to break the hold, as if knowing how much she needed the father's courage and pride she soaked in as he held her.

Then she let go.

The last look they shared held so many silent words, so many mutual feelings. Faythe turned from him and descended the steps. She didn't feel sadness or regret. She didn't even feel guilt. Glancing over at her companions, all mounted on horses except for Reylan, Faythe raised her chin in pride and confidence. The sunrise cast them in blazing amber hues, and beyond, the Phoenix sigil branded into the center of the expansive courtyard became torched by the glorious sun, giving off the illusion that the bird was caught in flame.

Rise from the ashes.

Reylan's eyes were bright with a rare emotion as he tracked her every step to him. He followed her, admiration and awe blanking his expression, but she couldn't be sure what he saw in her in that moment for his eyes to glaze as if deep in his own thoughts. He stood waiting for her by two brown mares.

"No Kali?" Faythe asked when she was close enough.

He shook his head. "We'll be trading horses frequently."

"Pity. I think she was beginning to like me more than you." When she came to a halt in front of him, the firm grasp of his eyes didn't release her. Faythe swallowed hard, partially to subdue the new rage of desire she felt at being near him knowing he felt the same.

Reylan took a deep breath as if reading her thoughts and snapped out of whatever deep trance he'd reeled himself into. A small, warm curl of his mouth relaxed her tense shoulders, and he looked to the mare expectantly.

Faythe turned for the horse, realizing now why Reylan had yet to mount like the others when she slid one foot in the stirrup and his hands went to her waist. "You didn't show this kind of chivalry when you were teaching me." She flashed him a smirk. "No need to start now."

Reylan took a subtle step forward until their bodies were flush, the flash in his eye a challenge. The rush of heat to her core from the movement made her curse the bastard internally. He was simply taking the opportunity to touch her without any obvious intimacy given their company.

"You seem to respond better to...*firm* encouragement." The way he settled on the word "firm" while giving her waist a gentle squeeze was almost her undoing.

Spirits be damned, this is going to be a long trip. Too long. When all she could picture now was what their return would earn. Her warm bed, Reylan beside her, and endless blissful hours for him to fulfill the promise he'd made to her in those rooms.

Izaiah cleared his throat but followed with no words—a silent acknowledgment he knew exactly the tensions that were running between her and the general. Livia released a quiet giggle, and from the glimpse she caught of Kyleer atop his horse, even he didn't bother to suppress his amusement. Reuben, mercifully, appeared as vacant and clueless as ever.

Caught between scowling and succumbing to the wave of embarrassment, Faythe channeled her frustration that they weren't alone into the strain of mounting the damn horse. She had to use little effort, however, as Reylan's aid made it a swift glide up.

When everyone was mounted and looking at Reylan, he gave a short nod, and they all sent their horses launching forward. Faythe hesitated. Was it a sign of wavering courage if she looked back? Would it give away the small dose of terror that lived in the pit of her chest? Reylan read her pause and didn't press forward with the others. Faythe cursed everything and twisted her body back to glimpse the king one final time.

Even from a distance, she thought she caught the relaxing of his posture that accompanied the smile that bloomed on his face. As if he hoped she would look back. Faythe was glad she did, feeling the farewell smile sink that terror deeper, replacing it with the courage he saw in her.

Faythe savored that image, of the sun proudly illuminating the Phoenix King. Of her father staring at her with nothing but pride and joy. With that last picture clutched tightly to her chest, Faythe tore her eyes from Agalhor to glance confidently over the horizon and snapped her reins.

CHAPTER 36

Zaiana

Z AIANA'S BLOOD HUMMED with a feeling so long dormant it awoke every sense with glee. Excitement. Fully dressed in her black-and-silver leather armor and strapped with steel, she secured the chain of her cloak at her shoulder before straightening with a confidence and determination that put her in an unusually high mood. She was minutes away from freedom.

As much as she wanted to storm out of her room and not look back, the other presence with her was still one hurdle in the way. One that could ruin everything if she was seen before they got her out and far away from the mountain with them.

Zaiana spun to Nerida, who was packing up the last of her things. She didn't have much aside from some spare clothing and a small collection of serums and herbs. Amaya had made a full recovery and would be joining them on the expedition, much to the great protest of her companions. But her mind was set, and aside from Maverick, Tynan was the only other body Zaiana was taking with her.

Drya and Selain couldn't glamour their wings, so they were never an option to come along, and although she felt bad to refuse Acelin and Kellias, she needed them to stay on her authority to the Silverfairs while she was gone. That, and she couldn't afford to have so many bodies to consider when their mission depended on them being stealthy and unseen as they tracked their targets all the way to the Isles.

The plan to get Nerida out was simple: while the masters and Mordecai were seeing them off, Acelin and Kellias would lead her out through the same dark, unused passages Maverick had used to get her in. What the fae didn't know was that she was not to return home. Zaiana hadn't thought about the long-term. Once their existence was exposed to the world, she supposed she would let her go. It was a life debt she owed her for saving Amaya.

"Are you ready?" Zaiana asked.

Nerida straightened in response, hooking the satchel she had brought across her cloaked body. She turned to Zaiana with the genuine smile that always unnerved her.

"Remember what I told you. Head down, don't observe or speak, and we'll get you to a pass just outside the mountains soon. You can trust Acelin and Kellias."

"Thank you," Nerida said.

Zaiana was already regretting the decision to bring her along and not end her life, as would be the most convenient option. Gods above, her damning lapse of mercy was sure to fall back on her hard. She couldn't be bothered to tell the foolish fae thanking her captor was ludicrous.

Instead, she strolled for the door, so close to being free and feeling air beyond the dull neighboring towns near the mountains. Maverick was leaning idly on the wall outside. His cheeks dimpled with an insufferable grin as he straightened, hands sliding into his pockets. Nerida scooted out past her. Zaiana commended herself for holding back her scowl at Maverick.

She went to close her door, but strangely, she paused. She was never one for sentimental attachment, and still she wasn't, but she spared a last look around the space that was *hers*, that she had *earned*, as it was the one thing she might even admit she would miss. With a breath, she closed the door as though it were goodbye. To pave the path to a higher victory. When she turned, Maverick was watching her, grin vanished. He said nothing, but there was something of understanding beneath the coldness of his gaze.

In the warped stone corridors, Zaiana's senses were on high alert to detect any wandering dark fae. She didn't want the inconvenience of silencing them if they spotted the fae in her company. Aside from the lack of wings—which wasn't that unusual as many would glamour them to preserve space while wandering the caves—Nerida's fae scent was different enough within these confines for one who was even mildly observant to detect she was not one of them. She had to credit Maverick's rogues for getting her here in the first place. She thought going incognito would be far beyond their brute capabilities.

She felt Acelin and Kellias silently fall into step behind her. Before they made their way to the upper courtyard where Mordecai and the masters would be waiting, Maverick diverted them to the underpasses. The fae shuffled close behind, clutching her bag as though she were only just now experiencing the rightful sense of fear.

"Have you been down here before?" Nerida asked quietly, though Zaiana gauged it was more an attempt to distract herself from the eerie descent.

"I told you not to speak," she hissed. She felt the air thin and wondered just how far underground they were. It was no wonder no one used this section of the mountain; it wasn't sustainable as a living quarters, and the confinement started to tighten her throat.

Panic wasn't an emotion she'd yielded to in *many* years, yet her breaths hardened of their own accord. The walls closed in, and the roof dropped down so far she thought she would touch it if she reached up on her toes. It felt like…a tomb. A cage of stone, not metal. A familiarity. Without warning, a flash of memory made her halt. The steel guard she'd formed around her brutal past slipped just enough for the wicked feeling to seep over her. *Helplessness.*

A force collided with her back. Hands wrapped around her forearms while she jerked. Maverick said nothing, but his touch was slow to release her. They had glamoured their wings to fit through the space, and his whole body pressed to hers gave her a short moment of relief, *awareness,* that she was not alone in a stone cage. She was free.

The others halted to glance back, and Zaiana put all effort into brushing the quick flash of panic away.

"Are you okay?"

Zaiana snapped her eyes to Nerida at the unexpected question, but her airway felt too constricted to answer.

"We're creatures of the air and sky. Confinement is a particular form of torture," Maverick explained, a note of hard detachment in his voice that pressed everyone to continue without further question.

Zaiana couldn't be sure why he said it. While it was true, she wondered if he too had been subjected to such a cruel form of discipline. She shook the thought, not wanting to pay notice to the kernel of gratitude for his seemingly casual remark that took the attention from her.

She pressed ahead. After another long stretch of insufferable claustrophobia, the passageway finally opened into a large open space. She had been powering on, but in spying a door off to the side, Zaiana's curiosity halted her steps.

"What's in there?" she pondered out loud but didn't look to see if anyone held the answer.

Maverick drawled, "Does it matter? We don't have a lot of time before we're expected. Exploring can be for another day."

She didn't react to his subtle gibe, as though she were a child seeking adventure. She couldn't explain why she cared, but Zaiana brazenly walked right up to the door. She strained her hearing. Nothing. She tried the handle, but it was locked. Now she was definitely curious.

"Honestly, Zaiana, I think we have far more pressing matters, don't you?" Maverick drawled on, but he was close as he sauntered up behind her.

She ignored him. "What would be so important to lock all the way down here?" Zaiana said it in a way she knew would spark the playful challenge in Maverick's eyes. Though he did keep an edge of skeptic caution as he folded his arms.

"I'm not sure it's worth trying to find out. Wreck the door with your little lightning tricks and you've all but sentenced your own death."

Zaiana only smirked, casting a look at Acelin, who smiled deviously. Maverick slid his eyes to follow as she pulled a pin from the back of her head and came up to the door before dropping to a crouch. She mirrored Maverick's crossed arms with a smug curl of her lips. He only rolled his eyes.

"Unlike you, I don't choose my company out of brute strength and savagery," Zaiana remarked. "There are far more useful and cunning traits to be found."

Maverick said nothing. Hearing a series of clicks that sang with triumph, Acelin straightened before pacing back to Kellias with a suppressed look of confidence. Zaiana smiled in delight, going for the door. Maverick was already there, to her great annoyance, and was pulling down the handle with caution before he widened the gap so she could catch a glimpse.

It was pitch-black. Maverick summoned his fire at the same time she conjured her lightning to provide some luminance. She formed it into a sphere of jagged lines and expanded it with her first steps into the room.

It was small and almost bare, save for a chair, a table, and some scattered books, as if someone had been in the midst of reading. Zaiana detected they weren't alone seconds before anyone else did. Her orb turned into a brace of defense that had her reaching for her sword. But then she saw it. The bars.

At the end of the long room, bars lined the place from wall to wall. A cell.

Zaiana advanced with caution until her amethyst bolts or Maverick's cobalt flames could expose what was within.

Not what—*who*.

She couldn't hide her sharp inhale at the small form she spied huddled in the corner of a rickety bed with a worn mattress. Small… because there was hardly any flesh to the bones that protruded, and for a second, she stilled, thinking they were staring at a corpse.

Until she heard the heartbeat. A sound she was all too familiar with and fascinated by. Usually, it was a hard rhythm. Even the most miserable souls had a somewhat strong beat to their vital organ. But this one…sounded *broken*.

"Gods above," Maverick muttered.

She didn't expect the disturbance from him, figuring he'd seen far worse things and wouldn't care enough for a single life to give any reaction.

The person didn't move, but shuffling sounded from behind her.

"Oh Gods!" It was Nerida as the fae ushered past her.

Zaiana hooked her arm. She was unsure why, but it seemed foolish to get too close when they had no idea who it was; *what* it was. Then the person inside the cell shifted for the first time. Zaiana stiffened.

Slowly, a balding head that held little clumps of gray hair lifted. At the first thing she noticed, Zaiana went rigid. Human. This person was human. Their rounded ears confirmed that. No one spoke as they continued trying to lift their head as though it were a boulder atop their shoulders.

When they looked up at last, and somehow locked onto Zaiana's ghostly gaze out of all the others, she had never felt such a coldness embrace her. She knew why. It felt as though she were staring at the face of the living dead.

She could only just distinguish that this human was female, barely a skeleton, with gray, sagging skin covered by no more than an old rag. But what struck her the most were her eyes—the only inkling of color against the grim state of her. While they were dull, cold, and perhaps already dead, Zaiana imagined the faint amber to have once been an envious gold.

"Please," she rasped, a broken croak.

Zaiana didn't know why she felt the tightening in her chest. This woman, however she came about such a harrowing fate, was not of her concern. Yet even as that selfish thought crossed her mind, it chanted the lie. Zaiana had insisted they open the door; she had entered this room. Whether she wanted it or not, it had become her concern. She may be a creature of darkness and born without a heart, but even without knowing all the human could have possibly been through, she refused to believe anyone in the world deserved to be abandoned to such a long, strung-out end.

The woman was old, and she couldn't fathom how long she had been down here. What was worse was that her mind raced with the reason *why*. No conclusion she drew made sense. She was one human, when the dark fae who needed and wanted to feed had plenty on offer in the surrounding towns.

"We can't leave her here." Nerida's voice broke, and Zaiana scented the salt of her tears. For once, she didn't think the reaction was weak or unjustified. Nerida was a healer by nature—she was good—and she could at least understand her desire to help.

"No, we can't," Zaiana agreed vacantly.

"We have to," Maverick said.

She whipped her cold gaze to him. He tried to hide his own desire to do something behind hard detachment, but she could see through his cracks.

"We do something, it's only a matter of time before it comes back to bite us," he snapped.

"Then look away, Maverick. We can make it out of here, and I'll meet you in the courtyard with Mordecai. Don't implicate yourself." She said it with bitterness, and the only reaction he gave was a flex of his jaw. He didn't move, and Zaiana didn't wait to see if he would. She turned back to the desolate human.

The plea remained in her despairing eyes. A plea for only one thing. Death.

Zaiana turned her head to Nerida. "How do we do it in the most painless way possible?" While she had inflicted so much of it in the world, she wasn't a complete monster and knew the human had been though more pain than any being should in a lifetime. She didn't wish for her final moment to be painful too.

Nerida wiped her wet face, and then an idea must have come to her as she dropped to her knees. The fae began rummaging through her satchel. Zaiana dropped her hand with the orb of electric light for her to better find whatever it was she searched for.

Zaiana was swept with unease, and her whole body stood taut. Nothing about the room, the conditions, or the unfortunate captive was short of barbaric. Even for her kind. She couldn't begin to fathom what the human had been kept down here for, and it was a puzzle she may never get the answer to, as when they were done, had put the poor soul out of her misery, they could never speak of it again without risking the masters finding out. If they were the ones who had locked her down here.

Nerida started opening various small vials, concocting something with a few drops and herbs from each one in an empty container. Zaiana couldn't stop her eyes from wandering back up to the human. Eyes of one already dead stared back at her. Only her. A chill colder than ice filled her bones at that look.

"What is your name?" Zaiana tried, but she didn't hold out hope for much information as the single-worded plea from her had been uttered as if sand coated her throat.

Slowly, the human peeled her bony arms from her tucked-up legs. It was like watching the warped roots of a tree grow, the way she moved. Zaiana winced for her, but the human yielded no reaction to the pain. She could hear the brittle bones of her body groaning in protest.

As the human stood, hunched, she dragged her bare feet along the ground to make it to the bars. Fully illuminated in the orb of her light and Maverick's, Zaiana knew the image before her would haunt her for the rest of her days.

"Who did this to you?"

Those dull amber eyes were vacant, hopeless, and pleading.

Nerida stood then, holding a small glass bottle with whatever lethal dose would grant the human the mercy she deserved. The fae would have crafted something painless to send the human off into a peaceful eternal sleep.

The fae reached between the bars, going to take the human's chin while she raised the bottle to her lips. Then, faster than Zaiana thought was physically possible in her state, the human lashed out to grab her wrist.

Zaiana jolted, hand darting to her side to draw her blade.

"It's okay." Nerida's calm voice halted her.

The human's eyes slid to the fae. Her other gray, frail hand reached up, and she placed something in Nerida's palm as she spoke. "Give this to the one with eyes like mine." Her voice croaked. "To the one they call Faythe Ashfyre."

Zaiana stilled. The name chilled her even more than the first time she heard it. How this human knew of her was mystifying.

"Tell her...tell her I knew her mother. And tell her...that I'm sorry."

That was even more baffling. Zaiana's head began to spin. The coincidence was too much for her to be able to pass it off as chance. Hearing the name they had been sent to find, the one who held the key to open the temple, the human she had never even crossed paths with yet who was quickly becoming someone she wished she never would.

Nerida nodded, her face in mourning as her fingers closed around the item she was given. A parchment. Zaiana didn't know why the fae felt so deeply for a stranger. The suffering was reflected on her face as she held the human's broken eyes.

"You have my word," she promised.

The human's mouth twitched, but she was too weak to form a smile. Zaiana felt a twisting in her gut as though the promise they had made was already broken.

"We must go," she said, slipping back into a coldness she knew all too well. So detached and full of loathing. She couldn't stand to be in the room any longer and turned to walk away just as Nerida helped the woman to drink the contents of her liberation.

Zaiana kept walking back out into the open space, not caring who followed. Nerida would end the human's suffering, Acelin would lock the door, and if the Spirits had any mercy left, the masters would simply believe their pet had passed away from the abominable conditions they had left her to rot in.

Her fingers clenched to the point of pain, lightning humming and prickling to be released. Only, her anger wasn't just about what she had discovered. It wasn't just toward the masters and their High Lord. Zaiana resented herself, the world—everyone. She couldn't afford to care. Not for the human behind her, nor for the one she had been sent to find. They were merely collateral in a war far greater that any of them.

So Zaiana closed off her emotions once more, hating more than anything that she had decided to grow a streak of mercy when she needed her stone-cold heart to reflect in her actions now more than ever.

Zaiana felt nothing as she stared into the eyes of the High Lord. She stood poised, hands folded at her back, where the others in her company formed. Even her mild buzz of excitement had been subdued by the icy demeanor that had embraced her since their harrowing discovery in the depths of the very mountains they had lived in for centuries.

Nerida had assured she would pass away painlessly and quickly, before they'd even locked the door. Zaiana didn't care. Not in the numb state she'd reeled into to get past this final conversation with Mordecai.

"You have what I gave you?" Mordecai asked.

"I do."

He assessed her from head to toe, a twinkling in his eye that held both threat and admiration. "You know how important it is. Guard it with your life. It serves one purpose, and I do not need to remind you it is not a tool to be used at your leisure."

She gave a firm nod. "On my life, this quest will be fulfilled. Dakodas will ascend, and we will rise."

Mordecai's mouth curled with the glee of a serpent. "Excellent. I know you will not fail me, Zaiana."

She didn't voice that what she set out to do was not for him. Not for the wicked masters. Not even for her kin below.

He went on. "When you return triumphant, you will no longer bear the title of delegate." Though she anticipated his next words, they fell on her with no impact. She did not want it. "You will be known to all as Master Zaiana."

Murmurs carried over their surroundings as those gathered heard his announcement clearly, as if it were some grand spectacle. Mordecai wanted an audience, *witnesses*. To everyone watching, it was an honor. To Zaiana, she felt the weight of new shackles. She didn't want to be equal to the likes of Nephra and the others. She didn't want to have any more connection to them than she already did. Imagining returning to share a league with them made her want to flee, far and fast, and damn to the Nether what would become of her in the unknown.

372

With all the eyes that pinned her—some with awe, some with envy, some with pure, blazing hatred—she did what she knew would be expected of her. She bowed. In acceptance of his title.

"You have earned it, Zaiana. Not just from the battle. I have been watching you for a long time." Mordecai spoke more intimately, just for her. He took a few steps closer. "In darkness may you triumph."

Zaiana swallowed, but her as eyes locked onto the pitch-black depths of his, she echoed, "In darkness may we triumph."

With a nod from him, she needed no other signal to leave. She turned away from him, looking over those who would accompany her: Tynan, Amaya, and Maverick. Drya and Selain were not present; they would be below, keeping eyes everywhere to report back after her absence. Acelin and Kellias would be nearing the meeting point with Nerida.

Amaya stood poised, equipped with her own bow and quiver that had been chosen for her exact weight and height. A gift from the rest of them for her performance and to welcome her into their ranks. Tynan stood by her, and Zaiana hadn't failed to notice his tendency to linger close to her since the battle, as though they had formed the most unlikely of subtle combat teams since being forced to work together when she'd earned his difficult respect. It brought a small warmth to her otherwise icy chest.

Then her eyes settled on Maverick. He locked her gaze. Hard and focused. For a moment, she didn't despise the fact he was joining them. She couldn't be sure of what it was, but she had come to accept he might be an asset if he managed to keep a lid on his insufferable arrogance. Nothing about the way he stood or looked at her was in the least bit bad. In fact, he looked to her with the same respect as the rest of them. She chose to enjoy the moment, knowing it wasn't likely to last.

"Good luck to you, Zaiana."

Mordecai's last words meant nothing at her back. Luck had nothing to do with what they were setting off to do. Triumph would be hers with steel and will. As it had been throughout her whole life.

It didn't take them long to spy Acelin and Kellias on the outskirts of Dalrune, standing by the desolate-looking fae. Zaiana couldn't bring herself to feel anything for Nerida, for the sorrow that clearly laced her heart at their discovery of the human and assistance in her death. If she were honest, she would admit an air of disturbance still clung to her from the harrowing experience, but she had to seal it behind the vault of her emotions. She couldn't afford any weaknesses. Out here, she depended now more than ever on the cold ruthlessness the masters had beat and burned into her. She had to become their monster to see this through.

"We'll see you soon," Kellias promised, and it put a mild ache in her chest that his tone was dipped in concern. Acelin also slipped a hint of worry through the cracks of her steel exterior.

Any other day, Zaiana would have reprimanded them for it as it was foolish to waste such energy on something that couldn't be controlled, such as whatever fate was to befall her out there. But she understood. It was the longest she would be separated from them, and she hadn't failed to acknowledge that. Whatever happened, she would not abandon them. On her return or not, they would be reunited.

There was no embrace, no words of sadness or farewell. Acelin and Kellias took off to the skies to return to the mountain. Zaiana didn't watch them fly away. She had no reason to look anywhere but forward —for her sake and theirs.

Everyone looked to her, waiting for the first instruction even though their plan of action had been run through many times. Far more than it should have been thanks to Maverick and Tynan's need to counter everything the other said as if it were a competition of who could piss the other off the most in a single conversation.

Zaiana cast her eyes up. "The clouds should give us cover to make it past Dagdune in Olmstone by nightfall," she said, grateful for the dark, overcast sky she had been hoping for.

Nerida's face brightened just a little at the mention as it would bring them closer to Fenher. Zaiana had to avert her gaze from the small twist in her stomach at her hopefulness. The fae believed they would be returning her to the town she came from, but that was never part of the plan. Even if she believed their secret was safe with Nerida, it wasn't a chance she was willing to take when it could ruin everything. Zaiana said nothing and figured she could hold off on the drop of fate until after they had rested and were leaving Fenher. Conscious or unconscious would depend on her reaction to the news.

"Let's get going," Zaiana commanded.

Tynan and Amaya didn't hesitate to shoot to the skies, and she watched them before they disappeared above the fog. Maverick turned to the fae expectantly as he would be the one to carry her. Nerida's cheeks flushed a warm rose as she clutched her satchel and shuffled over to him. In one swift motion, Maverick scooped her into a cradle hold, and she let out a small breath in surprise, the rose tint darkening. He locked eyes with her for a mere second. Zaiana held her face cold and unbothered despite taking in every inch of their closeness. How Nerida hooked an arm around his neck, a hand to his chest…

Maverick splayed his large wings and shot skyward, disappearing like the others in a few powerful beats.

Zaiana took a long breath in solitude. Closing her eyes for a brief moment, she stilled her mind, relaxed her body, and focused on what was ahead. No room for error. No thoughts of mercy.

Flexing her wings wide, she eyed the clouds, saw her freedom beckoning, and soared for it.

CHAPTER 37

Faythe

NOTHING COULD HAVE prepared Faythe for the agony of her thighs after a week of traveling on horseback. She bit back her complaints. Most of the time. But it was hard to disguise her stiff walk and winces of discomfort every time they stopped to camp for the night.

She would never complain about the cold, uncomfortable nights on her rickety bed in her old hut ever again, finding it far harder to achieve any decent hours of rest on whatever forest floor they deemed the least stony and uneven. The fae, on the other hand, seemed to be dealing with the conditions far better. Faythe couldn't be sure if it was their unfairly advantaged bodies that could withstand and endure more than her, or if they were more accustomed to such sleeping and travel arrangements from their time at war. The thought stirred her curiosity, but not without a pang of sadness to imagine them in a time of desolation.

Faythe shifted in her saddle for what felt like the millionth time since they'd taken off again after camping many hours ago. She clenched her teeth against the ache of her muscles in her thighs and pushed her spine back from falling to a hunch in her tiredness.

"We'll be coming to the town of Desture soon." Reylan's voice floated next to her. Sliding a look to him, she found his face was hard and concerned. "We'll find an inn to rest for the night."

Before she got the chance to respond, a sigh of contentment carried from her other side. "Finally," Izaiah all but moaned. "I can't take another night of beasties in my bed roll."

Livia released a short giggle, and it lifted Faythe's grumpy mood from traveling so long in discomfort and silence.

She hadn't expected the journey to be pleasant. Far from it. The last time she traveled for so long was her trip south. The first time she ever ventured out of her home kingdom of High Farrow. That was far more leisurely. On this trip, they were following a strict schedule that had been meticulously planned out by the commanders long before they left.

Luckily, she had been informed they only had another week until they would trade in the horses and go by foot to cross the Fire Mountains. She was equal parts relieved and daunted by the prospect of venturing through the great mountain passes. Uncertainty lay within, and in her experience, it always came with something nightmarish.

Reuben had been mostly silent, seemingly content, and hadn't once complained or shown much of what he was feeling. She checked in on him and stayed by him since the others were still unfamiliar with her strange friend, but she welcomed his easy company nonetheless.

Kyleer was often equally quiet, but always the one to help keep fires burning and collect the wood when it ran sparse. His and Reylan's actions and movements were calculated, while Livia and Izaiah were key to keeping the morale high with their constant jesting, typically at the expense of the two overprotective fae males.

Reylan inched his horse closer, their legs almost touching. "How are you feeling?"

She smiled, and it was genuine. "I'm okay," she answered. His look told her he didn't believe her. "My legs hurt," she admitted, "a lot." She knew Reylan wouldn't relax until she gave him some reason for her constant fidgeting.

His face fell knowingly. "Maybe we should rest for a couple of days in Desture."

Faythe shook her head. "I'm fine. It's nothing I can't handle."

"I won't pass up a few extra days' rest," Izaiah chimed in.

Faythe whipped her head to him. Like her, he shifted his weight with a twisted expression. She had to wonder if he truly meant it since he hadn't shown an ounce of discomfort before.

Kyleer met eyes with Reylan, and it was often perplexing how they seemed to communicate through a mere look. She pictured Reylan's nod while she had her head turned from him as Kyleer dropped his gaze to her.

"We can spare another night. We'll lodge for two," he said. There was a warmth in his green eyes that eased her guilt. Perhaps they were all in need of extra time out of the saddle and on hard ground.

They rode on for a couple more hours. Idle chatter was exchanged, but as Faythe's exhaustion grew with the descent of the sun, she could barely absorb the words they spoke, never mind engage. Her thighs were now numb, though she welcomed that in place of the chafing ache, and her lids had fluttered against fatigue on more than one occasion. When she spotted the amber glow in the near distance over the hill they were climbing, her whole body sagged in relief.

That day was the longest they'd spent on constant horseback, and it took a further half hour after first spying the signs of civilization until they were finally on the main path leading into the small town. They entered under an archway, and Faythe could already hear the lively bustle of people enjoying life after dark. With summer blooming, the air was cool and welcoming, allowing the nights to be filled with activity rather than spent huddled indoors avoiding the winter bite.

Everyone they passed stole curious glances at the travelers invading their village. Some stopped to gawk and turned to whisper, and she wondered if it was the fae in her company. The humans acted a lot like those in Farrowhold who weren't used to seeing fae outside the city. That thought was crushed when she spied a couple of fae already in the town, littered outside a tavern or walking along casually. Even they paused to steal a look.

The attention was unnerving, but what did she expect as a seemingly random traveler passing in the middle of the night?

"That looks promising." Izaiah's voice sounded ahead.

Faythe followed his line of sight to an establishment near the end of the path, the sign by a floating fire basket reading, "The Twin Flame Inn." A few people, fae and human, loitered outside. Upon their approach, Faythe began to feel ridiculously nervous. Everyone's gaze pinned on them, some in a disgruntled reception, others too intoxicated to muster an expression. When they all came to a halt, Kyleer was first to dismount in a swift motion. She watched him with envy, knowing there was no way she was getting down from her horse with such dignity in her state.

He stalked over to some of the fae, who were quick to straighten warily. Faythe admired his cool demeanor, not at all fazed, while they rested their hands on the hilts of their swords as he walked to them. They only engaged for a minute, the strangers' eyes flashing to them many times without dropping their cold glaze. Then Kyleer strolled back, giving Reylan another of those nods that passed silent words.

Reylan was already down from his horse by the time she turned to look, and the shuffling to her other side told her the others following his lead. She suppressed a groan as she released her reins.

"I'm sorry." Reylan's voice so close took her by surprise. Snapping her gaze down to his, it pained her to see the upset on his face.

"What for?"

He gave her saddle a pointed look. "I didn't consider you weren't accustomed to riding for so long. We should have planned more frequent stops."

An awful guilt dropped in her stomach. *That's* what was troubling him? Faythe clenched her teeth as she forced her leg to swing around to one side. Reylan didn't hesitate, positioning to aid her. He did more than that, and she was utterly weightless for a second in his hold as he guided her down. He very slowly eased her feet to the ground, but he still held an arm around her to take most of her weight. She couldn't deny she might have buckled without his help, but in an attempt to ease his worries, she planted her feet despite the internal yelp of tenderness that shot through every muscle in her legs, and then she stepped away from him to bear her full weight.

"See? Just fine," she said, as perky as she could act while feeling the total opposite.

He seemed to know as much, face as hard as ever. It wasn't just her stiff limbs that soured her mood; they were all in need of a meal and proper rest after a full day of grueling travel. Faythe took a moment to stretch on the spot while Kyleer tied up his horse and came back to lead both of theirs over to the makeshift stable by the side of the inn.

She turned to the inn, where Izaiah, Livia, and Reuben stood by the door. Though the strangers didn't offer even a crack of a smile, they seemed harmless, but Faythe eyed the blade Livia had unsheathed as she stuck close to Izaiah and cast frequent glances at the males who paid her more attention than the rest. Faythe walked the short distance to them on weak knees, each step feeling as if her soles were made of stone. Kyleer reached them first, and Faythe observed his hand as it fell to Livia's back. Her stiff shoulders loosened.

Faythe and Reylan stepped into the inn behind them, and the scent of ale and bodies was potent enough to wrinkle her nose. The commotion of voices grew louder as they continued down a dark passage that was barely wide enough for two people to pass through. Reylan was at her back, but close enough that she felt a part of him brush her with every step. It was the only thing keeping her nerves at bay. The foreign lands were overwhelming, but it was second to the small taunt that made her mind believe every set of eyes that lingered on her knew who she was. It shouldn't have mattered, but she couldn't shake the unnerving feeling that locked her spine.

The establishment opened into a dimly lit front room. It was quaint and bustling with life as people drank and played cards. She saw men, women, and fae. It was odd. And she realized her shock at witnessing their coexisting species, and her wariness in the new territory, highlighted just how sheltered she had been from the vast world back in Farrowhold. It was both exhilarating and daunting to experience so many things that were the same but *different.* So very different.

Kyleer took the lead while Faythe was otherwise preoccupied taking in the place. He walked over to the barkeep with the others in tow. Many—in fact, *everyone*—looked at the new bodies who had entered their space of entertainment. Conversation hushed as they stole looks and exchanged glances, whispering about whatever they made of the invading force.

A familiar touch on Faythe's back jolted her senses. With Reylan's hand she also felt a soothing internal caress that relaxed some of her wild emotions at trying to deal with the attention. People played cards, women were draped over the laps of men, alcohol stung the air, and laughter echoed through the space. When the attention started to disperse from them, Faythe's posture began to ease. A gentle nudge had her walking to where Kyleer and the others were engaged with the barkeep.

"How many rooms?" the man grumbled, not in the least bit fazed about addressing a fae twice his size.

Kyleer cast a quick glance over them as if calculating. "Four."

Faythe curved a brow. She wouldn't admit she was glad it meant she wouldn't be alone in a room, but she figured the four others would want their own space. It wasn't her business, but she noted how close Livia kept to Kyleer. Though it was Izaiah who laid one hand subtly around her this time.

Reuben was gazing around the room in curiosity, a million different thoughts and wonderment crossing his expression. Faythe shuddered, and out of instinct, she couldn't stop her head from turning. When it did, she was met with eyes of a man across the room, already blatantly staring at her. Her rigid posture returned, which seemed to trigger Reylan to follow her line of sight. A hand casually moved to rest on the hilt of his short sword. Faythe's skin pimpled. She wasn't sure what it was about the roguish man that inspired such trepidation.

She couldn't stop herself and stole a second look. He was big for a mortal, aged and weathered, wearing heavy, unusual clothing and a cocked hat that reminded her of a three-pointed boat. He wasn't staring anymore, but he still looked frequently enough between turns of the card game he was playing that it was unnerving.

"We've only got three left."

The grumble of the barkeep stole her attention. Why did he ask then?

"Looks like I'm shuffling in with you two," Izaiah quipped, jostling Livia at his side.

"One twin and two doubles," the barkeep added.

Kyleer flashed his brother a smug look. "How convenient. You'll be shuffling in with Reuben."

Izaiah's face fell, and it was amusing to see irritation on his usually perky features.

With the sleeping arrangement sorted, they went about ordering whatever questionable hot meal was on offer before Reylan guided her around the place to find a table. It was near impossible with the place full to capacity, and she was about to suggest they eat in their rooms when a voice carried over the noise.

"Well, well." When she jerked and turned, it was the same man who had been eyeing them the entire time. Her heart leaped, though strangely, she expected him to say something from his far-from-subtle interest. "Never thought we'd be seeing the likes of you around these parts." The man stood, and upon hearing the thump, Faythe was quick to flash her eyes down to find he only had one leg. At least only one made of flesh. The other was fashioned out of a thick peg of wood and secured by metal. "General Reylan Arrowood, famous white lion of the south, to what do we owe the grace of your company?"

"You'd be wise to keep your voice down," Reylan warned, his voice sharp.

The man's smile bloomed into a grin. Faythe felt the close approach of Kyleer and Izaiah, whose faces were equally steeled as they stared down at the man. She shouldn't have been surprised that Reylan would be recognized, but perhaps she'd underestimated just how widely his reputation was known.

"Join me," the man said cheerfully, casting out a hand to the table he sat at that was fully occupied. The men exchanged seats between themselves. With a distasteful look over at the newcomers, they began to rise. Faythe might have felt bad, but her need to sit only surfaced relief at the spaces they'd given up.

Faythe was eager to accept the offer in her exhaustion that left little room to care about the company, but Reylan's hand curled around her abdomen, and she halted. The man was observant, eyes flashing briefly to that hold. He rumbled a chuckle, throwing himself back down with the decorum of a water hog.

"You do not wish to eat standing. Your journey has been long if you've come all the way from Ellium."

Faythe lifted her brow in surprise. Who was this man to know so much? A glance over at her companions revealed nothing but stern reservation. The man had clearly overestimated that his somewhat warm reception would be returned.

Reuben was the first to move, and no one seemed inclined to stop him as he took the far seat. Faythe couldn't understand their caution against the man and followed suit, slipping out of Reylan's grip. She shuffled onto the bench next to Reuben, directly opposite the strange man who kept his lingering blue eyes on her. Reylan folded in beside her, leaving the others no option but to shuffle in beside the stranger.

"Who are you?" Reylan wasted no time on pleasantries.

The man reclined back against the wall. "I am a sea merchant," he answered casually.

"A pirate," Kyleer corrected.

His grin curled at one side, revealing a flash of gold that replaced a tooth. "A traveler, a trader—"

"A thief, a trickster. We know your kind. Brave of you to invite us to sit with you," Izaiah said.

"I didn't ask what you are," Reylan cut in. His face was scarily calculating. A shiver encased her body as she realized she hadn't seen this side to him. He was protective and stern and had used his tone of authority before, but this was different. Who he was now was someone who wouldn't take a chance; who would eliminate any threat no matter what it cost him. Out here, she couldn't be sure what Reylan was capable of. "I'll only ask once more, old man. Who are you?"

"You need not fear anything from me, General." He swiped his tankard, taking a long swig with a dramatic exhale. "I'm merely curious as to what would bring you so far south of the kingdom. It's not often we see you city folk around here, especially not our esteemed army commanders."

"And how is it you know so much?" Kyleer asked.

"You may call me many things, but what kind of pirate would I be if I didn't make it my business to gather knowledge from the places I travel?" His gaze locked on Faythe, and her spine stiffened. "The world is vast and full of wonders."

Reylan's thigh pressed to hers. Then, as the man straightened, his arm went around her once more, hand resting on her hip. She couldn't deny his closeness was a security.

"My name is Augustine, but you may call me Gus. And what might yours be?"

"Fay—"

"It's none of your concern," Reylan cut her off.

Faythe bit down on her cheek to hold in her snap. Feeling silenced like a child flushed her with embarrassment and riled her irritation. She shifted a fraction away from him, feeling his eyes on her as she did. Faythe straightened with confidence.

The man observed everything, amusement twinkling in his gaze as it darted between her and the general. "What a peculiar set of eyes you have," Gus observed, leaning on his forearms over the table. "I have only come across such a likeness once before."

Now, her attention was grabbed, heart leaping and skipping at the information. "Where?"

Before he could answer, a maid balancing various bowls approached the table and started placing down the food. The scent of stew and bread filled Faythe's nostrils, and her stomach twisted with hunger, but she kept her focus on the man, her sudden need for the knowledge over-powering all else.

Gus nodded down at the bowl. "My stories will not vanish while you take the time to eat. I imagine the food is not so great out in the wilderness."

It pricked her skin the way he looked at her; the way he seemed to know things before they were spoken but asked nonetheless. It was a familiar unnerving sensation she couldn't place.

Seeing he wasn't about to continue, reluctantly, she picked up her spoon and dove it into the stew. She wasn't expecting much but was surprised at the explosion of flavor and meat that almost melted in her mouth. She had to suppress and small moan of blissful contentment as she went straight for a second scoop.

Gus chuckled then turned to the maid. "Ale for all my friends here, Katia."

Katia nodded, a faint blush creeping up her cheeks as she checked them over before shuffling off. Clearly, the man was a regular visitor.

"Bold of you to declare us as such," Izaiah commented.

Gus flashed him a crooked grin. "Izaiah Galentithe, Shapeshifter and third-in-command of Rhyenelle's great army. I would have expected you to be the least uptight, yet you closely rival your brother here."

She couldn't be sure where this man got his brazenness from, but his words had the opposite effect if he was trying to gain their trust. All the fae stopped eating, pinning him with several sets of threatening eyes.

Gus didn't waver. Partially twisting, he went on. "Kyleer Galentithe, Shadowporter and second-in-command of His Majesty's army. Commander Livia Arrowood—you certainly don't need magick to be seen as a force to be reckoned with."

A creeping sensation washed over Faythe and cooled her skin. He knew exactly who they were. But that could have been common knowledge with their esteemed reputations. It was when his sparkling eyes slid to lock her gaze that she flushed with dread.

"That could only make you one person. One whose name has traveled far and fast since you arrived in Rhyenelle." His blue irises twinkled, but there was nothing threatening in his demeanor. His voice was hushed as he said, "Faythe Ashfyre."

Faythe blinked in shock. If the man wasn't under threat from her companions before, now he certainly bore the weight of their alarm. It seemed foolish to expose that he knew so much, but he didn't seem in the least bit concerned when the four fae around him all straightened with a new threatening focus, hands hovering over various weapons as the air tensed around them.

"Or should I say…*Your Highness?*"

"You should say nothing more if you value your life," Reylan snarled.

Though she blanched, Faythe ignored Reylan, who was one word away from unsheathing the blade he gipped tighter. "How do you know my name?" she asked.

The man simply shrugged. "It is not hard to see the picture when the pieces of the puzzle arrive so closely put-together."

Gus was odd indeed. But something about him didn't even surface an inkling of fear. Wariness, yes. She took a second to observe him. Under his obscure hat she spied the curled locks of dirty blond hair that poked out, though she figured a long scrub in a bath might brighten them to a golden honey tone. His blue eyes were…almost familiar. His face was peppered with short hair, and he appeared not long past middle age. Faythe supposed he was attractive in a disheveled, roguish kind of way, and his personality wasn't shy to attract the attention of women.

"Though that's not all you are, is it?" His eyes danced with challenge.

Faythe's appetite left her completely. How could this man—this one *human* man—know so much? She was scared to question what he meant.

Gus's gaze flashed to Reuben, who didn't stop devouring his food but observed the rest of them in mild interest. The pirate's eyes narrowed a fraction on her friend, but the quick second of odd attention could have passed as curiosity.

"I think you've had too much ale tonight, old man," Kyleer commented in a way intended to excuse Gus's bold behavior.

Gus waved a nonchalant hand. "I can assure you, that is not the case."

Just then, the barmaid came back over, placing several tankards in front of them.

"Now it is." Reylan stood, and the others, except Reuben, were quick to follow his lead. Reylan pinned Faythe with a persistent but patient gaze when she remained seated, in a complete stupor over the strange conversation and still trying to process the man's claims. He knew things, and Faythe's curiosity about him drowned out the edge of caution the others maintained.

Gus reclined back once more, his smile amused since he knew as much.

"You said you've seen another set of eyes like mine before." Faythe doubled back. "Who?"

"Faythe—"

"In Rhyenelle?" she pressed, ignoring the grinding irritation of Reylan's overprotectiveness.

Gus eyed the fae general standing behind her, and something like understanding flashed across his look. "How long will you rest in Desture for?"

"Tonight and tomorrow night."

"Join me again tomorrow night then," he offered.

Faythe wanted to protest. Her eagerness to know more was all that danced at the forefront of her mind. But she caught the looks he spared her companions and realized it was for their benefit he didn't entice her to stay longer. This man was smart—and *very* observant.

She conceded with a slump of her shoulders. "Tomorrow night then," she agreed, locking eyes with him. It was perhaps a fool's move as she exposed her desperation that he wouldn't vanish before then.

All he gave was a curt nod, and Faythe finally rose from the bench. She cast an expectant look at Reuben, who quickly shoveled in a few more mouthfuls of stew, rose, and snatched a roll before he began to follow.

Reylan waited for Faythe to move first, and she tried to keep the discontentment from her face, not looking at him as she passed and followed behind Izaiah. She felt Gus's stare tracking them all the way until they dipped into an ascending stairwell.

CHAPTER 38

Faythe

IT SEEMED EVERYONE was in need of a long rest as they only exchanged a few words before dividing off into the available rooms to retire for the night.

Despite the irritation that swirled in her mind, it only now dawned on Faythe the small space she was to stay in with Reylan as her eyes landed on the rickety bed. She had shared one with him many times, but it felt *different* now. He hadn't kissed her then. She hadn't kissed him back. Her stomach fluttered as she quickly noted the bed was far smaller than what they were used to in Ellium.

The click of the door behind her heightened her awareness. After over a week since leaving the city…they were finally alone. The knowledge flipped in her gut. When Reylan didn't move at her back, she turned to him. Hesitation was clear on his face as he scanned the space as if he too was acknowledging the close confines and awaiting her reaction. The faint clamor from downstairs still carried through the walls, alerting them to the fact although they were alone out of sight, they were far from such luxury in sound.

Her scandalous thoughts surfaced and brought heat to her face. To disguise the sensation that tingled in her stomach and lower, Faythe walked over to the chest of drawers. Facing it, she began to unbuckle some of the sheaths strapped over her body. She heard Reylan shift and discard a pack somewhere, and then the faint clink of steel against wood as he disarmed himself of the hoard of weapons he carried.

When she was no longer wearing any steel, she removed her jacket. Standing in just her thin shirt and pants, she didn't make any further move to undress. Reylan was silent for a long moment, but then she felt him approach, stopping only a short distance behind her.

He broke the silence. "You're upset with me."

Faythe took a long breath. "I don't need you to speak for me."

"That was not my intention. But it would be best if people don't know who you are. The world is full of those who want to do you harm."

She turned to face him. "I am no one."

His eyes flashed at that, and he took a small step closer. "That is not true, and I don't mean in regard to your family name." His face softened. "But you *are* Faythe Ashfyre, daughter of Agalhor Ashfyre and rightful heir to the throne of Rhyenelle. You have no idea what that information in the wrong hands could do."

Faythe swallowed hard. As though evil Spirit descendants weren't enough. But Reylan was right, and even if it wasn't some crook wanting to gain whatever they thought they could from the crown, if word traveled of her whereabouts, it could whisper back to wherever Marvellas lay in wait, seeking her out.

Faythe ran a hand over her face. "You're right, I'm just—"

"I know." Reylan closed the distance between them, and her skin tingled when his rough palm met her soft cheek. Her frustration dissolved completely, fatigue drowned out by the awakening of his touch. He didn't move. Faythe's eyes fell to his mouth. Several times. Still, he didn't bring his face to hers. The feel of him was something she craved more than anything since that first time in her rooms in Ellium.

"Are you going to kiss me?" she whispered when she couldn't take the longing, searching stare any longer.

One side of his mouth curled right before he angled and dipped his head. Brushing his lips against hers, it was soft, slow, and not nearly enough. Faythe pushed up on her toes, fingers knotting through his silver hair. The change had him dropping his hands to her waist, pulling her flush to his body. Fire ignited over her skin, prickling, heating. It still wasn't enough—not to cure the ache that began to form between her thighs. After a week of being so close yet unable to share any intimate moment, she knew that ache had grown since they left the capital.

The kiss turned claiming, demanding, and before she knew it, his hand had hooked under her thighs to lift her. Her legs tightened around him, and the angle deepened their kiss. Between her legs, the hard feel of him made her stifle a moan that caressed her throat. Her blood sang and roared at knowing he was just as affected as she was. She moved against him and couldn't stop the soft sound that escaped her lips this time. His hold on her thighs tightened as a low growl vibrated in his chest. This wasn't like what they shared in Ellium; this was more. This was a need so demanding she thought she would come apart right then.

She barely felt the step he took until she was set upon the flat surface. On top of the dresser, Faythe kept her legs hooked around him, low enough that if she ground her hips she would feel his desire. In that moment, she didn't care who might hear. She didn't care about anything but her need for him.

His lips left hers only to trail a prickling heat along her jaw, drawing her attention to the pulsing veins in her neck that came alive when his mouth ventured there. When she felt the gentle scrape of his elongated canines, the sound that left her made her clamp her mouth shut with a painful bite of her lips. Her hand that wasn't tangled in his hair gripped the wood beneath her so hard it was near painful. She didn't realize she had moved against him again until Reylan stilled. His hands on her hips tightened to still *her*.

"If you don't stop that," he ground out through a husky breath that blew across her collarbone, "I'm seconds away from damning to the Nether where we are and who might hear, and I'm taking you right now." His lips traveled to the hollow spot below her ear, hands hooking under her thighs to recline her back a fraction as she braced her hands behind her. "And let me tell you...this dresser will not hold."

Faythe swallowed hard. A dormant thrill rejoiced to hear the deep gravel of restraint in his tone. His words had the opposite effect, a warning that translated to a sinful invitation. She shivered delightfully, and her legs tightened of their own accord. She clenched her teeth at the twinge of pain from horse riding, but when Reylan pulled his face back she almost bit out a protest. He smirked as her expression must have voiced it for her. His hands trailed to her knees, where he paused, looking up to catch her eye.

"May I?" he asked, eyes flashing to her aching thighs. "It should help relieve some of the tightness by morning."

She realized what he meant, and all she could respond with was a nod.

Reylan moved both his hands to one of her thighs first and began a slow massage of her tense muscles there. The first knead was a small burst of pain, and she clutched the dresser with a hiss. Reylan winced at her reaction, but as he continued to expertly work his palms and fingers, the pain lessened and became...pleasurable. So much so she had to refrain from squeezing her legs together.

To distract herself, Faythe decided on a topic of observation from the night. "Are Livia and Kyleer...? I mean, are they—?"

"Together?" he offered with a hooked brow of faint amusement.

Faythe's cheeks flamed at the conclusion she had jumped to in seeing the pair engage tonight. She nodded her confirmation, and Reylan gave a crooked smile.

"No. Ky is just fiercely protective of her. We all are, given her history." His eyes dropped from her, brow pinching as it seemed to drag up a dark memory.

"Her scar?" Faythe inquired. It wasn't for her to press, and she wouldn't be upset if he said nothing further on the subject.

But he nodded in answer. "She has been through more than I think any of us will ever truly know. Before we saved her. Fae heal faster than mortals, but we're not exempt from a scar if the wound is deep enough. What you see on her face is barely half the injury it was, and it almost claimed her life." Reylan switched his attention to her other leg, and again, Faythe bit back a hiss of pain against the initial discomfort. "While I'm more than confident Livia could take care of anyone who dared to lay a hand on her now, I don't think the fear ever goes away."

Faythe's heart ached for the fae commander along with a new burst of pride and admiration for what she had overcome. To have risen above her attackers and become far more than what they ever did to her… Faythe could only hope to have that kind of strength and resilience.

Then something soul-deep cried as he brought forth a murderous flash of memory: the map of scars that marred Reylan's body. Those wounds must have been worse than she could have imagined to have left permanent reminders—exactly what his uncle would have wanted. Her eyes burned with rage and grief, a desire to kill someone who was no longer still alive.

Reylan's quiet voice defused her moment of inner turmoil. "Ky does what I cannot. He acts as though they are together as a deterrent to anyone even thinking of approaching her when they're out and around uncertain company. It's a natural comfort they share that I don't think they even realize anymore. Sometimes Izaiah will step in too."

Faythe couldn't help but ask carefully, "They've never wanted it to be real?"

Reylan's amusement returned. "Livia prefers the company of females...romantically." His eyes flashed to hers to gauge her surprised reaction.

"Oh." Faythe was sure her face was as red as the crimson of their leathers. "I shouldn't have assumed."

Finishing his tender work, leaving her legs feeling tingly and loose, Reylan braced a hand on each of her thighs and gave a teasing squeeze. "I do believe they *have* engaged intimately before. Though I try not to remember that part."

They exchanged a look, and Faythe couldn't be sure why she felt the overwhelming urge to pull him to her. Gripping the front of his shirt, she guided his head back down to hers. The kiss was soft. Until it wasn't. Their mouths, teeth, and tongues clashed in a heated pulse of unexplainable need.

To be close. To be here and now. As though there might not be a tomorrow.

She was reminded of the sharp teeth he hadn't yet retracted when they nicked at her bottom lip. Faythe inhaled in surprise. When she lay a hand on his chest, he stopped. That was all it took, and he pulled back to meet her eye. His breathing was uneven, as was hers, but her eyes fixed on those teeth she'd only seen once before. Her hand moved up to his face, and he stilled as her palm rested on his angled jaw, allowing her thumb to slowly trace and feel the tips of those fangs. She sucked in a faint breath, finding them sharper than she expected. With a bit more pressure, she would cut through flesh.

"The first time you showed me these..." She trailed off in a whisper, swallowing hard. "Did you want to harm me?" Her mind flashed back to that moment in High Farrow when he'd closed her in against the wood of her own door and she'd caught a glimpse of what set them apart far more than the contours of their ears. She'd gauged it as a threat then, and perhaps it was, as there had been so much anguish and distrust between them.

His jaw ticked under her touch, and his blue eyes hardened at the mention. "I have never wanted to harm you, Faythe. *Never.*" Faythe winced a little in guilt, but his eyes softened. "Though you were very trying of my patience back then."

Her mouth curled in mischief.

"That was the first time I nearly lost control with you. Perhaps the first time I really realized—" Reylan stopped himself.

"What?" she pressed, her heart picking up tempo.

"How much I wanted you," he finished, though it felt like an amended answer. Regardless, it burst a warmth in her chest.

"*Gods*, I objected to being sent back to High Farrow—I really did. Only because I knew even then how dangerous it was for me to be close to you. To get to know you. I feared… More than anything, I feared I wouldn't be able to stop myself, to keep my distance from you beyond making sure you stayed alive." His smile was partially broken, cleaving her heart. "It was a futile fear because I knew from the moment I laid eyes on you I wouldn't be able to stay away. Even if you weren't who you are, if Agalhor didn't send me back, at some point…I would have gone back to High Farrow myself. Even just to check on you, maybe only from a distance, and you would never have known. In High Farrow, you might have been fed and sheltered, but you were not happy. How could you be? You were someone who had been led to believe you had all you deserved when you had nothing. Nothing was yours."

Faythe was stunned speechless, doused with so many emotions that caught in her throat. She never realized just how observant Reylan was.

"Now, I am yours. This kingdom is yours. Freedom is yours to take and do what you want with. On my life, you will always have that."

She felt his fierce words like the joining of a fractured existence. Reylan filled her with strength and purpose and an unwavering belief. She didn't know what she had done right in her life to deserve him.

"I am yours too, Reylan." Her words were quiet, her offering in return seeming feeble against everything he had done for her. But she didn't sulk at that fact. Instead, Faythe was dedicated and would give all she could, all she was, until one day, perhaps, she would be enough.

His smile, which seemed weighted with heartbreaking relief, brightened the room. Faythe's eyes were drawn to those sharp teeth again. Her heart raced at the thought that had swirled in her head many times, causing her blood to heat and race with desire once more.

"What would happen if you...bit me?" She knew what it should do. If they were true mates, it would create that everlasting, unbreakable, and unexplainable bond between their two destined souls that could be matched by nothing else in this world. Faythe's heart tumbled from her chest and withered in pain at the realization it would never be possible. Not with them. Not with her being mortal.

"I wouldn't risk it to find out," he said, bringing his mouth back down to kiss her jaw.

She knew what he was doing as he tried to distract her—perhaps himself too—from the horrible truth. While her breath began to leave her, she couldn't let it go. "What *could* happen?"

His lips trailed back down there, to her neck, and her hands fisted the back of his hair.

"It would hurt, and it wouldn't be pleasurable for either of us," he mumbled against her skin.

She doubted that was true. While it wouldn't create a mating bond, and perhaps it might hurt, she couldn't help but think it *would* be pleasurable for him. That the primal part of his fae heritage would enjoy the act in the throes of pleasure.

"I want you to." The words tumbled out of her as a reckless, lust-hazed whisper, one she couldn't believe she'd let out as Reylan went utterly rigid against her.

Then he moved, his hand curling around her neck. Faythe inhaled a breath, barely believing he would agree and allowing herself to fall blissfully to his mercy. Her body pressed to his tighter as she felt his mouth, his teeth, settle over her throat. Her pulse was wild, and his chest rose and fell deeply with restraint. She tipped her head back, anticipation coiling and twisting in her stomach, time suspending.

She wanted this.

She'd asked for this.

Reylan applied slight pressure with those teeth, and her lips parted in a shallow cry at the faint pinch.

Then the sharpness was replaced by something far softer. Teeth turned to lips that pressed with more force against her neck. Faythe's breaths came heavier as she released all her pent-up anticipation. Reylan's low laughter rumbled over her skin.

He pulled his head back once more, hand shifting to stroke her jaw. "You are going to be the end of me, Faythe Ashfyre."

Disappointment weighed heavy in her stomach, killing her desire. Another more shameful emotion dropped her mood. A frown formed on Reylan's face as he seemed to detect it.

"What's the matter?"

Faythe held those sapphire eyes—irises that had become the center of her orbit, and selfishly so. "Why me?" she choked out. "There's someone out there for you. A mate—one you're supposed to be with who could still cross your path in this lifetime."

Both his hands went to her face, and the shift in his expression reminded her of a male in battle—one who knew how to give a speech that struck the heart, to invoke the strength and courage needed to see them through hardship. "I have more than everything I could have asked for in this life. I should be a better male. I shouldn't be selfish and should let you go to find someone far more deserving of you," he said fiercely. Faythe opened her mouth with a string of protest, but Reylan powered on. "As it turns out, I am not that male. I choose you, Faythe. I will always choose you. And I will always hope, as selfish as it may be, that you will choose me too."

Faythe's hands curled over his at her face. "I know what a mate means to your people—"

He kissed her. So soft and barely-there. Against her lips, he said, "You are my people."

Faythe held him, fighting the wave of emotion that held her conflicted between wanting to protest and accept. Faythe would never understand what she had done to deserve him, his devotion, but she was grateful. *Gods*, she was grateful.

Pulling back, his thumb brushed her faintly swollen lips. "You must be tried." Instead of waiting for a response, with an arm around her waist he effortlessly lifted her down from the dresser. Faythe's feet met the ground, bearing her weight, her legs feeling far looser from his help.

"Thank you," she said.

His palm curled over her nape as he pressed his lips to her forehead. "Thank *you*, Faythe."

"What for?"

He looked to her with that treasured smile that gave a full, hard beat to her heart. That rare smile: the one that turned up equally on each side of his mouth and creased faint dimples that chased away the shadows of a dark past and troubled soul. It reflected in his eyes as much as on his mouth. "For choosing me too."

CHAPTER 39

Zaiana

A WEEK SINCE leaving the mountains and Zaiana was teetering on the edge of murderous. She couldn't be sure who she desired to kill more: Tynan or Maverick.

"Do your precious little wings need rest?"

Tynan whirled to Maverick at the gibe. They had been debating risking another day of flight or finding horses when they landed in the Silver Forests of Fenstead before crossing the border lake into Rhyenelle territory. Zaiana had let them battle it out, if anything to expend their energy as she had already made her decision. The clouds had parted to welcome the glorious summer sun, and it was too much of a risk to fly and be seen in Rhyenelle, the strongest of the ally kingdoms.

"Little?" Tynan seethed, wings flaring.

Zaiana rolled her eyes at the ego-flexing bullshit at her back.

"Barely bigger than a darkling's," Maverick continued coolly. He leaned with arms crossed against a tree, completely unfazed by the fury that emanated from her second-in-command. Tynan took a step toward him.

"Enough," Zaiana cut in, whirling to them both. "We'll go by foot until we get to the main town. We'll get horses, and that's how we'll travel from here."

Maverick pushed off the trunk. "You're adding days to our journey—"

"The weather changes, and we adapt. There's not nearly enough cloud cover for us to be hidden." Zaiana took a few steps until she was right in front of him. "Don't question me again."

While she saw the flash of anger and protest in his pitch-black eyes, he simply turned from her without another word.

"You're going to love Fenher," Nerida gushed over the tension.

Zaiana said nothing even though she knew she should have informed the fae they would not be passing through to visit anyone she knew or to let her return home. "Glamour your wings," she instructed the dark fae, ignoring Nerida completely. While the fae's face seemed to fall, Zaiana couldn't afford to feel sympathy for her.

"It will take us two days on foot without horses to reach the town and acquire them," Maverick grumbled.

"If I wanted you to state the obvious I would have asked," Zaiana countered, passing him. "It will take longer if you keep questioning my every judgment and bickering like children."

Amaya was quick to shuffle into step with Zaiana. Nerida kept to her other side. It seemed they had all grown tired of the petty squabbling of the two males in their company.

After a long stretch of silence, Amaya spoke quietly. "When we catch up to them, what will we do?"

Zaiana slid her eyes down to the dark fae. She stared at her own footsteps with a mild frown. "We follow them to the Isles, they open the temple, and we make sure Dakodas's ascension is completed. You know this."

There was a pause of hesitation before she asked, "What will happen to her?"

Zaiana knew what they didn't. Knew the moment Faythe's name was given to her that the die had been cast. She didn't know how to respond, wondering if she would taint Amaya's innocent heart with the truth of what they set out to do. She couldn't be sure why she found her ability to hold compassion…*admirable*. When she had been taught to find it a repulsive weakness that only served to get one killed.

Suddenly, Zaiana halted, arm raising to stop her companions in their tracks as well. She tuned in to the presence she felt and heard the faint cracking of branches from a distance not too far away. Zaiana inhaled deeply, hoping to catch a scent in the wind as it carried their way. When she did, she relaxed.

Humans.

Zaiana continued her walk. Humans were of no threat, and to them, Zaiana and her company would appear a simple band of ordinary fae trailing through the woods. But as she got closer, the more bodies she began to detect, along with—

"It seems the Spirit Dakodas is not so eager to waste precious days," Maverick commented with an edge of amusement.

Horses could now be detected in both sound and scent. She suppressed her scowl as Maverick came by her. A minute later, the humans came into view. Three of them. Casually strolling on horseback through the woodland toward them. It was almost too perfect, and she couldn't deny the Great Spirit *could* be helping them. As they got closer, Zaiana noted the bows they carried, arrows ready, as they appeared to be out hunting. Her caution set on high alert as she focused on the glittering dark tips. Niltain Steel.

Of course, it shouldn't have come as a surprise. She figured most weapons would be crafted of the material legendary to Rhyenelle. Zaiana had to wonder if it was some ancient defense the kingdom had adopted against her kind specifically during the Dark Age. Over time, as they believed the dark fae to be extinct, she supposed there wouldn't be many alive who would know of its lethal effects on them.

Zaiana side-stepped, not realizing what she'd done until her gaze briefly cast back to the darkling she covered. Amaya met her eyes with nothing but innocent wariness.

"Just as well," Maverick said, his voice low. "I'm parched."

Zaiana stiffened, having no plans to drink from the humans and wanting to avoid death if possible. She wasn't one for senseless killing. With every life she'd taken she believed she had cause. Albeit some far pettier than others.

What she failed to remember was that Maverick depended on a feed. She couldn't deny him that. And while he could feed without killing, that wasn't an option when they were still a secret to the world. The fae didn't draw blood from humans.

Zaiana stopped, and everyone followed her lead. She turned to Maverick before the humans came within earshot. "Are you sure you need it now?" It wasn't in protest, but she needed to confirm if they were killing these humans, or if they could move on and his thirst could wait until they found a single life instead of three.

Maverick deliberated with a cool expression, his eyes shifting to the approaching humans and back to her. A part of Zaiana might have believed he wanted to say no, but she could see the hunger in his pitch-black eyes. The darkest side to him that held no humanity—not anymore—just pure, insatiable bloodlust. Zaiana had to pity him, for his monsters within were unrelating. His thirst was never a choice.

His face blanked to a familiar icy coldness. "I was rather preoccupied finding a certain healer and listening to your meticulous plans to make time for a proper outing," he said, meaning it had been too long since his last feed. This was bound to happen soon, and better here in the middle of the forest than potentially unchecked in town if he didn't curb his thirst now.

Zaiana said nothing but gave a nod of understanding, believing she caught the wince in the voids of his eyes that he might hate what he was about to do. She turned, braced and equally as heartless, to face the humans. While she didn't indulge on human blood anymore, she was still just as much the dark fae as he. The temptation would be a test of her will.

She stood straight. Maverick and Tynan flanked her on each side, blocking the path of the oncoming humans. She could already scent their fear as wariness pinched their faces. Shifting in their saddles, their arrows remained nocked but lowered. The hint of a threat was enough for her to slip into her coldhearted detachment that held no mercy. A freeze over her mind she knew all too well from her merciless upbringing.

"You might want to look away, Nerida," Zaiana warned without removing her fixed stare on her targets. But she didn't care if the fae choose to watch the heinous event that was about to unfold.

"You're not…you're not going to kill them, are you?" she whispered in horror.

Zaiana's silence was confirmation, and she heard the fae whimper and send a pathetic plea to the Gods. Words that would always go unheard and uncared for. The Gods had abandoned them.

The humans came to a cautious stop a few paces away. "Good day," the center man said with a wavering voice, not realizing it was about to be his worst and last day. "We should only like to pass and be on our way."

"I'm afraid not," Zaiana said, not an ounce of emotion in her voice or her firm, unyielding stance. She slid her glance to Maverick, giving a subtle nod when he met her eye.

He didn't hesitate and was across to the man on the left in the space of a breath. The horses bucked and huffed when he was dragged from his own, and the man's shrill cry sent the birds above scattering through the foliage as Maverick sank his teeth into the man's neck. Zaiana scented the blood, and to distract herself, she darted for the middle man before his shock and horror even had the chance to take root as he watched what happened to his friend. Tynan was quick to follow suit and take care of the final man.

Zaiana approached her target, pulled him down from his horse, and spared a few seconds to hold the gaze of the life she was about to take. She listened to his erratic, uneven heartbeat, so fast she wondered if it would fail him before she could end it. He didn't even fight her, struck still and petrified. In the reflection of his moss-green eyes she saw what she truly was inside. A monster. She snapped his neck with one quick twist, and his body fell to the woodland floor, but she didn't spare a glance down.

Instead, Zaiana turned back around, instantly locking eyes with the pale and horrified fae. While Amaya wasn't exactly undisturbed by what they'd done, at least she had the sense to know why it was necessary. To know what they were.

For the first time, Nerida looked at her with what she expected to see from the beginning: disgust, shame, and terror. Zaiana ground her teeth, straightening as she dusted herself off nonchalantly. She walked forward a few paces, and Nerida backed up a step as she did. She was afraid. Zaiana was too detached from her humanity to care for her ghostly look of abhorrence.

"Dear Gods," Nerida whispered, eyes scanning the three bodies.

Zaiana twitched in ire at the judgment on her face. "Do not pray to the Gods who have left you at the mercy of monsters like us." She took a breath to calm herself, turning her back on the fae.

"You are right to fear, Nerida. I tried to warn you…" Zaiana's gaze drifted to Maverick just as he pulled away from the body he had nearly drained dry. "We are made only of nightmares."

They neared the town in one day rather than two. Slower than flying; quicker than walking. But now they had the horses they required, Zaiana didn't feel the need to add wasted hours to their journey by stopping. Even though Amaya had to double up with Tynan, and Nerida with Maverick, she didn't think it was worth the time to acquire more horses.

It had taken a harsh approach to get the fae on top of the horse at all. Since their brutal display in the woods with the unfortunate humans, Nerida had shed all her warmth toward them and been pale and silent since. She looked to Zaiana with a cold hatred now that was out of place on her delicate features. Good. It was better to be hated for what she was than liked for something she wasn't. Whatever redeemable traits the fae seemed to think she harbored were now all proven wrong. It was better this way.

When they didn't shift course to enter the civilian town of Fenher and kept to the forest tracks into Esmire instead, Nerida finally found her voice again.

"We're not heading in the right direction," she pointed out apprehensively, casting her gaze to where she thought they should be heading.

"Yes, we are," Zaiana responded flatly.

The fae's panic was sour in the air, and Zaiana heard her shifting behind. "No—Fenher is *that* way," she insisted, voice dropping a pitch in fear.

Zaiana anticipated her protest, but in her low mood, she had very little patience for it.

"Take me back," Nerida said, louder this time.

Zaiana reluctantly pulled her horse to a stop as she heard the fae begin to struggle against Maverick, who held her from toppling off the height. "You're going to hurt yourself," he grumbled, jostling her like a child.

"Take me back!" was all she chanted, the words beginning to grate on Zaiana's last nerve.

Take me back! Take me back! Take me back!

I won't stay with you monsters!

Something in Zaiana snapped, and with Nerida's last violent struggle against Maverick, he finally let her go out of exasperation. The fae instantly fell. Zaiana dismounted and caught her, whirling Nerida around. There was nothing kind or merciful on her face as she grabbed her by the folds of her cloak, eyes blazing.

"Listen to me. You are *not* going back. You're a damn fool to think we were ever letting you go," Zaiana seethed, breathing heavy. Nerida stopped struggling, staring back wide-eyed. "We should have killed you. It is what you expect of us. Yet we get to listen to your rambling about how hideous and terrible we are. Well, guess what? We know *exactly* what we are and what makes us the monsters you should fear. We never tried to hide that, and it was your own naivety that made the truth that was right in front of you such a shock to witness." Zaiana released her harshly.

Nerida didn't move; her fear and panic stunned her.

"We wear our evil for all to see, but *your* kind...? Evil lies within you too, behind the illusion of forced peace and false kindness. So tell me, what makes you so different?"

Nerida only stood, her face unreadable, but at least she wasn't flailing around and causing a throbbing in Zaiana's head.

"Now, get back on the *damned horse.*" Zaiana didn't wait to see if Nerida would do as she commanded before she spun back around and swiftly mounted her own. Just as she pressed on, she said to no one in particular, "Kill her if she doesn't cooperate." It was an order she wouldn't retract, but even as she said it, she imagined the look of hurt on the fae's kind face. Zaiana hardened herself against feeling any remorse or pity. She wouldn't let one insignificant fae harm her plans and delay their quest. She couldn't afford to have mercy.

Despite this, she couldn't ignore the dip of relief in her stomach at the faint shuffling she heard behind her, no sounds of a struggle or snapped neck. Zaiana concluded Maverick had helped Nerida back on top of the horse as she heard its hooves following her beside Tynan and Amaya.

"She won't become a problem," Tynan promised.

Zaiana cast him a glance and dipped her head in acknowledgment. It was as if he knew, should it become necessary…Zaiana might not be able to end the fae's life herself.

Silence fell between them for a long stretch of forest, and Zaiana's mind drifted to nothing in particular. She tuned in to the murmurs of the woodland, savoring the heat from the sun that filtered through the canopy, and was surprised by how it helped to defuse the darkness and hatred that had clouded her mind since they left the mountains. The moment of quiet allowed her to remember *why* she was here—or rather, what she had done to get here. To be able to live like this, in the moment, without a thought for the tether that would yank her right back to the dark, claustrophobic confines of the mountains.

"Why did you do it?" Nerida's voice was weak, a quiet question of defeat.

Zaiana dared to slide her a look as Maverick trotted up beside her. There was a faint twist in her stomach, a feeling she wasn't so familiar with, triggered by the look on the fae's face. Not because she felt bad, but because her hazel eyes held…pity. As though she'd spent her moments of quiet thought realizing there was no changing who Zaiana was—who they all were—and that their existence was a sorry one.

"We needed horses, and I needed to feed," Maverick answered plainly, but his jaw locked, and he looked to no one while his expression was hard.

Zaiana felt something akin to remorse. She would have countered to take some of the blame, but what he said was true. If they didn't have a Blackfair with them, they could have avoided the killings.

"Why is it only you who *feeds?*" Nerida questioned with a wince, and while it held a note of disturbance, it seemed she was attempting to understand them.

"We can feed. It makes us stronger, faster," Tynan chimed in, "but only the Transitioned—the Blackfairs—need human blood to survive."

"Why didn't you...?" Nerida spoke quietly, but her eyes locked on Zaiana's to ask, "Why didn't you *drink* too? If it makes you stronger."

Zaiana didn't answer straight away or look to Tynan even though she wondered why he wasn't taking the opportunity either. "I did before we left," she lied, and she felt Maverick's stare the loudest. "It's a drug. Too much human blood can drive us to savagery or make us lose our minds. Despite what you may think of us, we are not that. Not those of us who are warriors anyway. Though there are those beyond salvation in their bloodlust, both the Transitioned and the Born."

Nerida inhaled a shaky breath. "Do you need to drain them every time?"

Zaiana arched an eyebrow at her sudden inquisitiveness, though she supposed it was better than seeing her quiver in fear. Perhaps if she knew more facts, she would grow to at least understand, even if her fear would never allow her to accept.

"No," Maverick answered, and she supposed it was his area to explain. "It can be moderated. I can survive well and strong as a fae by feeding twice a week and not taking enough to harm the human. Weaken them for a few days, perhaps, but not kill."

"Then why did you almost drain him back there?"

"It has been well over a week since I last fed, and we need the extra strength for this task. We would have had to kill them anyway." Maverick explained it like plain fact, but then his face seemed to fall, the frown so slight it was near undetectable on his fierce exterior. "I'm sorry you had to witness that."

His apology took Zaiana by surprise—more so than Nerida. The sincerity was unexpected. She would have passed off his remorse as common decency, simply to put the fae at ease that she wasn't traveling with some emotionless, unhinged beast. But at seeing Maverick's face… Zaiana *believed* his remorse. For what he was, and what he was often forced to be. She often forgot that he never chose this life; never chose to be a dark fae even though he'd embraced and mastered it like any Born.

He was wicked, evil, and brilliant. Her enemy…but her equal.

CHAPTER 40

Faythe

FAYTHE WAS TRAPPED. A violent scream clawed at her throat while she tried to thrash free. It was futile. He had caught her. The captain. And she knew what came next while her body was bound and restrained. She had been seconds from killing him. Seconds from being free…

"Breathe, Faythe."

It was a command that snapped her eyes open, a voice that didn't match the wicked face at the forefront of her terrors. Her heartbeat was so erratic it failed to match her wild breaths. The voice was close, too close, and while her eyes met with only darkness, panic thrashed her bound limbs once again.

Then there was a hand at her face and a flicker of sapphire and silver as her pupils adjusted to welcome faint light. Enough to make out the face of…

Reylan.

It was Reylan who held her. Reylan's fingers smoothing over the sweat-dampened hair that clung to her forehead.

Once she'd stopped fighting and he gauged her awake enough not to cry out or struggle, his hand that held her wrists above her head loosened, and his other arm reached up to take something she had painfully clutched in her iron grip. She realized then why he'd had to restrain her when she glimpsed the steel dagger he set back on the nightstand.

"Oh Gods," she breathed, reeling back from the night terror she had emerged from. Faythe shot up straight, looking to him with wide-eyed horror. "Did I...?" She couldn't finish her sentence, already knowing the answer that curdled her blood.

She had tried to attack him. In her sleepy, hallucinating mind, she had seen Captain Varis. She had *felt* the captain. Nothing brought her more disgust than to know she had mistaken him for the safety that was Reylan.

Faythe whipped back the sheet and twisted, feeling herself start to retch. She spluttered through a few hard breaths, but nothing came up. Reylan's hand was on her back, silently stroking her spine while he let her calm. She embraced the cool air, pinching at the front of Reylan's spare shirt—it was all she wore aside from her underwear—to fan air around her. When her breaths came easier and she had processed the ordeal, she couldn't bear to look at him.

"I'm sorry," she croaked, hanging her head.

"You have nothing to be sorry for."

She heard Reylan shift on the bed and glanced to see him propped back against the feeble wooden headboard, one knee bent with an arm draped over it while the other lay flat and spread apart. It did nothing to help the heat of her body to see his bare, perfectly sculpted chest so effortlessly reclining. It was unfair how godly he looked.

He extended a hand to her. "Come here," he coaxed softly.

Faythe hesitated, a flush staining her cheeks. "I'm horribly sweaty."

A crooked, devious smile curled his mouth. "I'm only envious I'm not the one to have caused it." While her mouth popped open, Reylan gave a low chuckle. "Come," he tried again.

Faythe crawled over to him, and his arm curved around her middle, twisting her so fast and smoothly she almost yelped. She tried to leave a bit of space, but it seemed Reylan had other plans. With his hands on her hips, he gently shuffled her back until she was flush to his front. His touch on her shoulders guided her to recline against him. The position only ignited her body more. Not a slither of space remained between her back and his chest, but it felt so...*right*. Faythe relaxed, easing into his form while his hand began a tender stroke on her arm.

"Do you want to talk about it?" he asked after a quiet moment.

Faythe thought for a second. She had never spoken to anyone of what happened with Varis in the room of torture. Nik knew what he did in her mind, and she supposed Reylan did too. But the restraints, the helplessness when she wasn't sure what they would do to her physically or otherwise, had become a new focus of terror.

"He would..." Faythe swallowed the dark coils of fear to revisit the grim memory. "He would bind my wrists and ankles when he took me to invade my mind. I'd never been so helpless, so completely at some- one's physical mercy that I couldn't be certain if my mind was the only part of me he wanted to harm," she confessed. The truth felt like shame. Like an oily coat of disgust despite him never having gotten that far.

Reylan's hand stopped moving, ripples of his rage flowing through her, only adding to her growing guilt for depicting the dark image.

"He didn't do anything to me physically beyond the restraints," she added. "But the thought that he could have if he'd had more time after getting what he needed for Orlon..." She took a deep breath to calm her heart. "I don't ever want to be at anyone's mercy like that again."

"You won't be." Reylan's words were hard. A promise. "You won't ever fear another vile monster like him again."

Faythe reached out to touch his hand that dangled over his knee. He gave her a gentle squeeze before she let her palm fall to rest on his thigh.

"I thought they were gone," she went on quietly. "The nightmares. Agalhor said I need to forgive myself, that they're my mind's own way of tormenting me for my failures. I haven't had one since Nightwalking to Nik."

Reylan's fingers stilled, contemplating, then he continued with idle strokes that sent wondrous soothing tingles up her arm. As it warmed over her chest, his touch, while nowhere near, tightened at her core. Faythe subconsciously bent her leg to press it against his.

"Maybe it was something I said," he reflected, "about Livia or—"

"No, I don't think so," she cut in, hating that he thought for one moment he could be at fault. Faythe pondered. "The man downstairs, Augustine—he knows about me. More than that I'm an Ashfyre."

"We'll deal with him."

She shook her head against his chest. "I think he has answers I need. I can't explain it, but he knows something, and I...I think I'm afraid to know. I think it has to do with Marvellas and my connection to her."

"Whatever it is, I'm right here with you."

His assurance settled her rising anxiety—to discover what the odd sea merchant could possibly know about her having never crossed her path before. Faythe's eyes fell, catching onto the markings that beautifully decorated Reylan's skin, ending at his wrist. She felt compelled to reach out her fingers and trace some of the swirling lines she knew continued up over half his chest.

"What do they mean?" she asked quietly, a curiosity that had swirled her mind since the first time she laid eyes on them.

Reylan's hand reached out to cover hers. Faythe inhaled a breath, thinking he was about to remove her touch. Instead, he began to guide her fingers over the markings.

"This is the battle of Fenher," he answered, hushed, his words infused with the darkness of the memory. He continued guiding her hand higher, and her fingertips tingled over his inked skin. "Every name of those I fought beside, every place they died, every date on which those battles raged." It was not in any language Faythe had seen before. Perhaps it even predated the Old Language and he wanted it that way, a story only he could read. One only he could share. But still, it was right there for everyone to see. His pain, his heartache, his loss. It was all in plain sight, and it suddenly cleaved her heart to realize very few had ever gotten close enough to him to decipher it.

Faythe felt every powerful muscle in his forearm with his hand still guiding hers.

"These are some of the other battles we faced during those dark years." His skin was soft but faintly textured by the markings and prominent veins. A delightful shiver raced from her fingertips, up her own arm and flushed heat straight between her legs. Still, she remained transfixed while Reylan continued to show her the map of his past, making her *feel* every memory with him while he moved her hand. They reached over his large bicep, up to his shoulder, then his and her fingers trailed over Faythe's chest together. Behind her, she knew his was latticed with scars and ink, and the image of when she first saw it raged in her blood.

"These are the few memories I have of my parents," he admitted. Their hands stilled over her heart.

Faythe's face wrinkled, fighting against the burn in her eyes. For his grief, and with the overwhelming relief that he would want to share that knowledge with her.

Reylan's hand finally released hers, falling to rest back over his knee. His fingers grazed her thigh that was tucked up against his. She glanced at his other tattoo-covered arm.

"Those are of my darker days. Before I became a general. Every life I took in my uncle's name and every battle I fought not of political war. If you look closely enough, you'll notice Kyleer and Izaiah have some similar markings. We share a lot of those dark days before we found purpose through duty." Reylan's fingers at her knee began lazy, idle strokes up and down her bare thigh. It took everything in Faythe not to elicit a physical reaction as the heat between her legs intensified. Her heart picked up tempo, and she focused on regulating her breathing.

"How did you become a general?"

"Agalhor found me—found all of us—and recognized me by my father. He saw something worth saving, I suppose." His fingers trailed halfway down her thigh and back to her knee. Over and over. It was the sweetest torture that scattered her thoughts. She couldn't be sure if he knew what it was doing to her.

"You are—" His hand dipped lower than the previous time, and she couldn't hide her shallow inhale, having to refrain from the need to clench her thighs together. "You are worth saving," she got out.

He was quiet for a long few seconds but didn't stop his tender trail on her leg. Reylan shifted, and she felt his warmth at her shoulder as she instinctively inclined her head to the side. The knot in her stomach tightened; the heat slicking her skin rose with the quickening of her pulse.

"Saving needs salvation," he mumbled. "A reason to *live.*" Then his lips met her neck.

Faythe's hands reached out in surprise, and she found her fists curling into the flesh of his thighs through his pants on either side of her. "What was your reason?" she whispered through an unsteady breath.

Reylan's fingers stilled, giving her a few seconds to gather herself. Then they moved again, and Faythe loosened completely with his touch. "My reason was I was still searching. Always looking. Knowing, somehow, I wasn't done here."

"And when you find it...what you're looking for—what happens then?"

"I will protect it with everything I am." His lips pressed to her collarbone, and Faythe's head fell back against his shoulder. "I will give my sword and last breath to it." The words he spoke she felt within as if he entwined them as a promise around whatever invisible tether ran between them.

Faythe's grip on his thighs tightened when his fingers trailed to her stomach, and she tensed until they cast back up to her knee. It was utterly maddening.

"I can stop," he said, the words vibrating over her collar to pebble her breasts. The faint friction of her shirt when she moved was torturous. And not nearly enough.

Her mouth dried out completely while his hand continued exploring lower on her thigh then back to her knee. Slow, tormenting strokes that had her biting back her plea for him to reach her aching core.

"Faythe." Her name sounded sinful in his tone dipped in gravel.

"No," she answered, barely a rasp.

"You need to be clearer with your words, Faythe."

"I don't want you to stop."

His other hand gently trailed down her extended leg, fingers curling under her knee and lifting, guiding her thighs farther apart. Faythe was so consumed by lust her hips arched a fraction every time his fingers neared where she so desperately wanted to feel them. His mouth on her neck, his hand on her thigh—it took great restraint not to twist in his grasp and take matters into her own hands. With the next teasing stroke of his fingers, Faythe's hips ground against him. She couldn't hide her sharp inhale as she felt the hardness of him at her back. The *length* of him that plastered her tongue to the roof of her mouth.

Reylan let out a short hiss. She couldn't stop herself—she moved against him again, and his other hand gripped her hip to still her.

"This isn't about me," his husky voice mumbled. "Let me help you sleep." This time, the tips of his fingers reached the crease between her leg and her stomach. Reylan's arm that folded over her abdomen was the only thing keeping her from the impulse to move.

"Please." She didn't know what she meant by the word, only that she needed more. More of him, and all of him.

The hand that pinned her to him reached lower, only to slide under the hem of the shirt that had gathered around her hips. He trailed his fingers up, equally as teasing, until it almost had her begging. Then he cupped her breast.

Faythe's head fell into the crook of Reylan's neck with a soft moan.

"You are so perfect, Faythe," he groaned against her skin. "You have no idea how long I've waited for you."

Gods, she was close to coming completely and utterly undone.

"As much as I want to hear you, I should remind you of the fae sleeping nearby with barely soundproof walls." His hand massaged the globe of her breast before teasing over the most sensitive part, and she let out a shallow, suppressed cry. She could feel his smile against her shoulder where his lips lingered. "I will hear you ride your pleasure, unchecked and with my name on your tongue as you find your release, but tonight, you may want to be mindful of the others."

Oh Gods.

With the next descent of his torturous, wondrous fingers, they finally trailed and dipped over the softest part of her. Faythe bit down hard on her bottom lip, head arching back against his shoulder. A noise rumbled up Reylan's throat with his first stroke over her underwear.

"So responsive," he admired. He moved in teasing circles around the bundle of nerves that had her straining against his hold. "So damn perfect." His slow pace drove her insane as he shifted the material of her underwear to the side, baring her before working his fingers just as gently. The sound that escaped her came too suddenly to bite back. In response, Reylan's teeth pressed lightly down on her shoulder, the faint pinch adding a contrast that only tightened the sensations at her core. He hushed her with a breath that blew over her neck and under her ear before his teeth nipped her lobe.

Faythe's eyes rolled and closed.

Then Reylan shifted, his hold around her tightening as he passed the point of slow teasing. His fingers moved faster, with more pressure, and all she could do was writhe against him. A single long finger moved down over her before curving and dipping inside. A quiet cry of ecstasy left her at the sensation.

She thought she heard him mutter something that sounded like a plea or curse, but she could barely hear anything with the pleasure that roared in her ears, igniting every nerve ending in her body. Faythe rocked her hips as much as she could. Reylan removed his finger for just long enough to add a second, which began a smooth rhythm as he worked her to the edge. His thumb teased the bundle of nerves that made her strain to chase her own release. Her nails dug into his thighs so hard she was sure it was painful. He only picked up speed, driving into her harder, faster, until she was there, reaching the end of the sprint that she knew would explode the stars.

"That's it, Faythe," he whispered, feeling her tighten around him. His other hand left her breast, coming up to curl around her throat. He guided her mouth to his, swallowing her muffled cry of pure pleasure when release shattered her mercilessly. He kissed her feverishly as she trembled against him and he held her through it, chest heaving as though he were suppressing his own sounds of desire.

He continued his strokes, slowing as she rocked through the final wave of her end. When she fell limp, utterly spent, only then did he remove himself from her. She inhaled sharply, feeling cool air as he fixed her underwear back on, and a stiff tremor shook her body.

Faythe was breathless and exhausted. Never before had someone made her feel like that, and to think that was only with his *hand*. She shivered. She wanted to return the favor, feeling her core flush all over again at the thought of feeling him. She tried to peel herself from his chest, but he held her there.

Instead, Reylan shuffled effortlessly back, taking her with him until they were lying down fully. Faythe twisted around until her cheek rested on his chest and lay over him, their legs a perfectly comfortable entanglement. She was about to say something—what, she couldn't be sure—but her eyelids began to flutter, heavy in response to the warmth that tingled over her body. Drowsiness lapped at her.

"Sleep, Faythe," he mumbled, palm smoothing the hair over her nape.

And she did. With those last beautiful notes of his voice, Faythe fell into a blissful, dark slumber with her body at ease, her mind soothed, and her heart full.

CHAPTER 41

Zaiana

A s THEY MADE it past the capital city of Ellium, they didn't risk
stopping by the heart of the kingdom. Not for rest or provisions.
Zaiana was determined to catch up with Faythe and her company, not
yet knowing how much closer to the Isles they were in comparison.

They trotted through yet another forest. Zaiana didn't mind; she
enjoyed the woodland, the sounds and smells so unlike the damp stone
of the mountains that always reminded her of desolation and hopelessness. Yet her companions were not so subdued.

Maverick and Tynan had somehow made a game of who could piss
the other off the most times in the span of an hour. Amaya and Nerida
were full of wondrous questions and stories they passed between them.
If Zaiana wasn't so adept at tuning her hearing to cancel out what she
didn't want to hear, she might have snapped a hundred times over from
having not a single minute of peace.

Their voices were but another murmur as she focused on her own
thoughts. They were strange but freeing. She found herself thinking

of a future that would never come to pass. Daydreaming, she supposed. Some of them were of a life of liberty as she glanced at the cloudless skies and longed to soar through them freely. Some of them were of having a beating heart and wondering if it would change anything. Occasionally, she tuned in to the fluctuating tempo of Nerida's that had her wholly fascinated. It gave away so many of her thoughts and emotions. Then, as she looked around the still and beautiful forest, sometimes she even imagined a land of *peace*—a concept that seemed so impossible with the constant clash of species. One *had* to triumph.

"We should be nearing a village." Maverick's voice cut through her wandering thoughts.

Tynan huffed. "And how would you know that?"

"Fine hearing and impeccable scent. Something you clearly lack."

Before Tynan could bite back, Zaiana cut in. "The ground is becoming more turned and disturbed. It's clear these parts of the woods are used for regular hunting. They don't stray far for food if they can help it."

By "they," she meant the humans and fae. The dark fae didn't track and hunt like them; they were often messy and without strategy or pattern.

"Basic observational skills too," Maverick commented. "Honestly, Zaiana, you say they have *talents*, yet I'm failing to see what this one adds."

Tynan's low growl was felt over her skin at the insult. "I would show you, but we've been warned against killing each other."

"Indeed. I don't suppose our esteemed delegate would be best pleased with me if I cut short the life of a member of her precious *inner circle.*"

"You two bicker like children," Nerida grumbled, clearly at the end of her patience.

Zaiana would be too, except she'd tuned them all out for the past

421

couple of hours as she rode ahead. Now, she couldn't come to care for either of their empty threats.

"I've been around plenty of children. These two are worse," Amaya said with a flat tone.

Something caught Zaiana's eye—a flicker of color that may have been passed off as rustling foliage or a creature. But Zaiana had her senses on alert for a clue, any sign to guide them to the right path that would intercept them with the human and her companions. Dismounting, she vaguely heard them question her sudden action from behind, but she paid none of them any attention. Her eyes were fixed on the rippling movement caught in the breeze through the trees.

Upon approach, it was clear what it was, and her suspicions were confirmed when her finger grazed the strip of fabric. What she first noticed was that it had been tied there on purpose, not merely a snag of clothing. With a faint tug of her mouth, Zaiana knew they were no longer on an aimless, hopeful wander. The piece of cloth was a direction, a scent to follow, and in bringing the fabric to her nose she identified it straight away.

"What is it?" Tynan came up to her side.

Her mouth curled wider. "It is the path straight to them."

Desture. It was smart to travel this path rather than risk traveling by sea past the Southern Gulf that was teeming with Valgard soldiers. It was also a huge risk, and equally as perilous, to take the uncertain route through the Fire Mountains instead.

They had tracked the scent Zaiana found all the way here, finding several more scraps of tied fabric to keep them on the fastest course. It led them right to this town, where the scent grew strong and fresh. Zaiana was giddy with a hunter's thrill. There was a high probability they were still here, and if they were, it would be far easier to devise a plan after gauging what they were up against.

They abandoned the horses near the edge of the forest and did not wander into the town freely. No—Zaiana had plans to stay hidden, keep to the shadows, and observe them from afar if they could help it. They split up, covering various rooftops when she tracked that their scents lingered the strongest around a small inn. Zaiana and Maverick pressed over the slant of an adjacent building that had a decent enough view to peer in through the long front window. It was packed with bodies, hardly any space to maneuver between drunkards.

"I could go in myself," Maverick offered when they'd crouched in silence for a long few minutes.

Zaiana debated. If they were sitting somewhere beyond where they could be seen from the window, their observation point on the roof was useless. If they wandered, it was a risk one of the fae might detect something different about them. They just wouldn't suspect them to be the impossible, ruthless dark fae.

"I'll send Tynan," she decided.

Maverick's disgruntled objection wasn't subtle, but he wisely refrained from voicing it.

Just as she was about to adjust her position to keep balance and free her hands to signal him over, movement from the window caught her attention. It shouldn't have, as it was bustling, but from the slanted top-down view she observed a bunch of drunken humans rising from a table. One man stayed sitting, oddly dressed and not of any sort she could identify, and then a couple of others moved to take the vacant spaces.

Zaiana shifted to get a better view, and in her distraction, she foolishly misjudged her footing against the damp stone. A hand braced firmly at her hip before she could embarrassingly slip. Maverick's fingers brushed her bare skin where her leathers had lifted from her stretched-out position. Zaiana blamed the adrenaline of the near fall for the heat that shot through her stomach. She meant to cast him a glare over her shoulder, but her breath hitched in finding him far closer than she expected. Shifting a few inches back would press her flush against him.

"I'm fine," she muttered as his hand was yet to release her. She didn't want to acknowledge the building hum over her skin that slowly drove that heat *lower*.

Maverick huffed as he let go. "You're welcome."

Zaiana bit back her retort, turning her attention to the inn. Her moment of bewildered distraction dissolved completely in her observations.

They were fae. She couldn't see much of them from her frustrating viewpoint, but from their massive forms in comparison to the humans that had left, she knew that much. When they sat, all she caught was the rear view of a silver head of hair. But next to him...

"That's her, isn't it?" Maverick concluded.

Zaiana didn't respond, eyes fixed on the distorted view she caught of the human next to him with light brown hair. She needed to confirm it, but she was almost certain it was her. It was Faythe Ashfyre.

Suddenly, the long, grueling weeks of travel, the insufferable bickering of her companions, the rough sleeping arrangements—it was all completely worth it for the thrill that replaced her bitter mood.

The companions inside were brought a hot meal and spoke to the other strange human who clearly had some influence to have vacated the space for them. Zaiana observed everything, though there was little she could gather with no way of hearing and a very limited view of them. Faythe and the silver-haired fae weren't the only two travelers. Two fae males accompanied them, and for a second, Zaiana's breath stilled.

"What is it?" Maverick questioned.

Zaiana ignored him, and to distract herself she settled her eyes on the last fae member of their party. An exquisite blonde female. Zaiana quickly decided she was not one to be underestimated. It was in the weapons she wore, her poise, and her constant attention on her surroundings. She was ready to use any of them, and she would do so with deadly accuracy.

Then there was the human man with them.

"You know, a little insight into your thoughts would be appreciated."

Zaiana rolled her eyes. "The key to preparation is observation. And that requires silence. If you keep mumbling in my ear, we could miss something."

He was close enough that any words he spoke were felt like shallow vibrations she consciously tried to ignore. Their bodies almost touched side by side, but she'd done a good job of not paying his closeness any attention, too immersed in their targets below to care.

The fae stood having only consumed half their meal, wearing an edge of caution directed at the seemingly harmless human man. She couldn't be sure what he'd said to invoke such a reaction. Faythe stayed seated for a moment longer before she joined them, and they shuffled out of Zaiana's vague line of sight. It was logical to assume they were retiring for the night.

Zaiana twisted, lying on her back against the slant of the roof instead. She sent one quick hand motion that she knew would be seen by Tynan where he was with eyes on her. She didn't wait for Maverick and stealthily made her way back to the ground.

In the darkness of a narrow alley, the five of them reconvened.

"You should all get some rest. I'll take watch in case any of them leave the establishment," Zaiana said.

"I can take watch," Tynan offered.

Zaiana shook her head. She was far too awake and alert from finally catching up to them that she doubted sleep would embrace her anyway. "Take Nerida and Amaya and find camp in the woods. We'll meet here again by morning."

Tynan looked reluctant to agree but gave a single nod before turning away with the two females in tow. Realizing Maverick stayed still, she slid him an expectant glance.

"I don't need you to stay here."

Maverick shrugged casually. "If I'm not getting to go inside for a drink, your company is marginally better than your dog's."

Zaiana refrained from giving a reaction, knowing it would only lead to far more conversation than she cared for. She said nothing as she made her way down the alley to scout. It was the middle of the night, and the bustle of drunken bodies and cavalry had begun to dwindle. They wouldn't find out much tonight. She had to wait until morning.

Zaiana didn't sleep that night. Instead, she kept track of movements throughout the town. She listened, she watched, and while she really should have captured a few hours' rest at least, her mind was too alert.

She lay slanted against the wall of the same alley, idly picking her nails with a dagger while keeping her eyes on the inn, spying from the window should any of their targets make an appearance. When the door opened and she caught the glimmer of silver, Zaiana instantly straightened, dipping farther into the shadows and out of sight. Stepping back, she knocked into Maverick's extended legs as he'd dozed off sitting on a discarded crate.

He gave a disgruntled moan at being woken up, but Zaiana's hard look had him peeling himself from his lazy position. He came to stand behind her. His head over her shoulder was so close she could feel his warmth against her back. While she cursed that she was even paying his closeness any notice, she couldn't shake the conflict of wanting distance from him or to step back.

The silver-haired warrior was accompanied by another—a male with longer brown, wavy hair and striking green eyes. Something about him was more roguishly beautiful than his companion, dark and untamed beneath the surface.

"See something you like?"

Zaiana whipped her head around. Foolishly, as his proximity brought Maverick's face so dangerously close to hers that the angle he looked down at her with almost had them grazing lips. It seemed to stun him just as much, but he didn't immediately step back. His eyes held hers, and she felt the pull in those black eyes. A shiver trailed down her spine as though she risked tunneling into their depthless voids, never to see the light again. It was a harrowing thought, but there was an allurement in such darkness.

A devious curl of his mouth that creased around his eyes snapped her to her senses. Zaiana shoved him back with a single hand against his chest.

"Not even close," she muttered in answer to his question.

"Hmm," Maverick said. "It's just not like you to let your attention wander."

"We're tracking them," she snapped. Not wasting time, or perhaps just desperate to drop the subject, Zaiana began to move as the pair of fae strolled down the streets. She followed and didn't have to check to know Maverick was trailing her. Coming up to a pile of discarded crates and gauging the building had enough worn grooves for them to scale it, Zaiana took to the rooftops for a better viewpoint and ease of tracking.

The fae made a few stops, and Zaiana tuned her hearing to catch what they inquired about. It was mostly boring, mundane life discussions, and she found it odd that they would care to check in with the citizens as mere travelers. What she gathered was that a lot of the townsfolk wanted to bring to their attention that there was a problem with a group they called "Raiders." A band of ruthless fae with a vendetta against the crown, apparently. One name in particular seemed to be a recurring fear. *Rezar.*

Zaiana didn't know if any of it was relevant, but at mention of the

Raiders' grudge against their king, the two fae seemed set in rigid alert. While they always walked with an edge of caution, always ready to jump into action should any situation arise, with the knowledge they gathered she didn't think it was possible for two males to look *more* threatening.

She and Maverick trailed after them deliriously for close to an hour, though it was better than standing stationary. Back in the alley she'd spent the night spying them from, the two fae entered the inn just as she felt the approach of Tynan, Nerida, and Amaya at her back. She turned to them as they came to a stop in front of her.

Zaiana had ponded for a while over all the information she'd gleaned from the two fae's ventures, and through the otherwise dull and useless information, a cunning plan sprang to mind. A curl formed on her mouth as she said to Tynan, "I would like you to spend the day tracking someone down for me."

He matched her wicked gleam and listened carefully to her instruction, knowing he was the best person she could choose for the task even if all six of her companions stood before her. Tynan wasted no time setting into motion what she instructed.

Meanwhile, Zaiana decided to have a little fun in an attempt to feel out what they might be up against. Rustling through the pack Tynan had left them with, she produced what she was looking for.

Glancing through the window of the inn, she spied the human sitting with her fae companions for breakfast. For a moment she paused, not knowing why exactly, but simply observing them and their carefree demeanors, their laughter, their *friendship*. It was clear they held a duty to this human as the daughter of their king, but it was so much more than that. Zaiana was surprised to feel what she would never admit to anyone. Jealousy.

She shook her head as if it would banish the thoughts that offered nothing but pure torment. She tore her eyes from them to the item she held in an attempt to distract herself.

"Are you sure about this?" Maverick questioned warily.

Zaiana steeled her expression. "We need to know what she is capable of."

Maverick took a long breath as if to brace himself. "I hate that damned thing."

Me too, were the words her mind chanted but never voiced.

CHAPTER 42

Faythe

FAYTHE AWOKE FEELING light and content. She stretched out, expecting to make contact with another body she remembered falling asleep in the arms of, but she was met with only thin cotton sheets as she flexed her fingers. She fluttered her eyes open. Finding the bed empty, she propped herself up on her elbows from her stomach-down position.

She was completely alone in the room.

Faythe bit her lip, a creeping heat flushing to her cheeks as she recalled the previous night. Her nightmare and what she'd mistakenly tried to do in her terror was completely drowned out by remembering how Reylan had soothed her every nerve back into a deep, restful sleep. How he'd managed to scoot out from under her without Faythe stirring at all was a testament to just how well it had worked.

A soft knock at the door snapped her back to the present. Faythe startled, grabbing the blanket that had been draped over her lower half. She fixed it around her shoulders to answer.

Faythe was cautious as she cracked the door open a fraction and dipped her head out. It was a relief to see a plump brunette woman wearing a welcoming smile.

"I was requested to bring this up to you, lady."

Eyeing what the woman cradled, Faythe sighed in relief. She opened the door wider for the woman to bring in the steaming basin of water. She set it down on the dresser—another place that flashed in her mind with the events of last night and tingled her skin with desire. Folded over the woman's arm was a towel, and she placed a small container next to the water that Faythe assumed was some kind of soap.

"Thank you," Faythe said when she turned back to her.

She gave a curt dip of the head. "Is there anything else I can get for you, lady?"

Faythe shook her head. "This is perfect."

The woman moved to take her leave, pausing at the door to say, "I believe the rest of your companions are downstairs for breakfast when you are finished."

Grateful for the knowledge, Faythe uttered her gratitude once more before the woman left. Feeling bright, she couldn't wait to freshen up her body from last night—and the past week since the trip so far had only offered streams to stop and take a bitter-cold bath in.

It was wonderfully freeing to be clean of mud and debris, and her mind eased, feeling lighter. Fully dressed, Faythe left the room, noting the clamor that carried from downstairs was far more subdued now than during the night hours. In reflection, most of the tables were also empty, and Faythe was glad for it, relaxing her stiff shoulders that there wasn't so much attention to worry about this time.

Faythe heard Izaiah before her eyes found him. He was laughing at something with Livia next to him at a table across the room. Reuben sat with his back to her, and she was quick to scan the space and discover Reylan and Kyleer were missing.

When he spotted her, Izaiah flashed her a grin before beckoning her over with a jerk of his head. She returned the warmth, and it was uplifting to see them in high spirits.

Faythe couldn't help the glance she spared at the table they had occupied the night before. It was now empty, Augustine no longer in the front room of the inn. Her stomach clenched with a sense of nervous unease. Part of her hoped he wouldn't return, to save her the second confrontation, but a larger part, she realized, was anxious to find out exactly what he thought he knew about her.

The same woman who brought her the water and supplies set a bowl of porridge in front of Faythe as she folded herself under the bench. She smiled gratefully, the scent of honey and oats filling her nostrils, and eagerly picked up her spoon.

"Sleep well?" Izaiah asked, taking a sip from his cup. Faythe met his eye as she scooped her first mouthful to find his eyes were twinkling. "Seems like you did."

Faythe slid a glance to Livia, who was doing a horrible job of suppressing a knowing smile as she looked away. "I slept just fine, thanks," Faythe answered coolly.

"Hmm." Izaiah set down his cup. "I'll take that as mediocre feedback on our general's...talents."

Faythe choked on her next mouthful of oats.

Livia giggled while Izaiah tried to maintain an air of innocence that was betrayed by the half-curl of his mouth. Together, the pair were an insufferable tag team of jesting.

"You can take that as none of your damned business," Faythe grumbled, face boiling.

Izaiah smirked. "When you're wall-to-wall with such goings-on, it's hardly a choice."

Faythe was on fire, her whole body torched, but neither of them looked mildly disturbed or annoyed. Only pure, blazing amusement danced on their faces. Faythe spared a dreaded look at Reuben, but he was only half-tuned in to the conversation, preoccupied with his breakfast. She only hoped his human senses meant he hadn't heard anything.

"Such thin walls they are too," Livia chimed in.

"Yes, I thought so," Izaiah agreed.

"Okay, you've made your point. Do you want an apology?"

Izaiah cocked his head. "You can't apologize for something out of your control," he said. Faythe's brow pinched, and his smile turned feline. "Nightmares are such horrible demons. What did you think I was referring to?"

Faythe was surprised she didn't turn to ash where she sat. She wished she would, to save herself from being the center of Izaiah and Livia's morning entertainment. With a scowl, she didn't deign to respond. She turned her attention to her human friend.

"How are you finding the trip so far?"

He was cool in his expression, as he had been for most of the trip. He'd yielded very little emotion other than vacant wonder. "It's enjoyable," he said, finishing his last scoop of porridge.

It wasn't the response she expected as nothing about their arrangements on sodden ground and long hours on horseback was comfortable.

He seemed to notice her skepticism, adding, "It's enjoyable being free, out there. I like the open space and fresh air."

Faythe smiled, supposing that was that true. It *was* pleasant to be so lost in places they had never dreamed they would travel to before. As children, she and Reuben never believed they would ever leave their hometown of Farrowhold. People rarely did. It had always been a sense of doom for Faythe, the thought she was destined to live the same bland routine for however many mortal years she had. Now, everything was different. She wasn't that girl in Farrowhold anymore, and she never would be again. Reuben was no longer that boy either.

They exchanged a sad, reflective smile as though their thoughts aligned. Faythe was glad to have him here. Glad he had survived the odds, just as she did. She couldn't stop herself when she leaned into his side, treasuring his familiar soft warmth. Despite seeming stronger, with more muscle and sharper features now, she would always remember Reuben as the boy he was. She would always feel the need to protect him.

Just then, Faythe was encased with an awareness seconds before she straightened from Reuben and her head turned to spy silver hair entering the inn. Her heart flipped, giddy but...nervous. She had no regrets or reservations about the night before or what they'd done, but it still sat on the forefront of her mind, making her body ache with a sense of *need* at the most inappropriate time.

His dark blue eyes flicked up to meet hers although he was still engaged in conversation with a stern-looking Kyleer. Regardless, he gave a faint smile, and Faythe mirrored it in response.

Kyleer slid in next to Livia while Reylan came around to her.

"I was just asking Faythe how well her first night's sleep went," Izaiah said as they sat, eyes on Reylan. "It seems you're somewhat lacking in your ability to console our poor Faythe after a terrible dream."

Reylan gave her a glance over, leaving a featherlight impression with his eyes that enchanted her skin, not in the least bit reactive to Izaiah's comment. "I don't believe so," he responded. In his dancing sapphire eyes, she felt the acknowledgment. He knew exactly how well she'd slept with his *help*. "You know, there's no one at this table who would object if you took away his speech for a while."

It was Faythe's turn to giggle as Izaiah's face finally fell into the scowl that was always a triumph to see. She hadn't considered using her ability against him and didn't believe she ever would. It was invasive, and she wouldn't use it unless she was under threat. Though she couldn't deny the idea was tempting when he became relentless in his teasing.

"I'll keep that in mind," she said, casting the fae opposite her a smile in challenge.

"The town seems clear of any threats," Kyleer cut in, "in case anyone is concerned."

"What exactly is considered a threat?" Faythe asked.

Reylan's hand landed on her hip as his arm subtly went around her. She straightened in surprise, not used to his touch in company but finding it relaxed and strengthened her. "We just wanted to be sure there were no suspicious persons and make a few enquiries about the town and how it's running while we're here. Agalhor likes to keep check of the smaller villages in the kingdom."

"And all is well?" Faythe found herself interested and concerned. "The people are well?"

Reylan cast her a smile, but she wasn't sure what she read in it. Pride —but it seemed misplaced. "They're a little short on food supply. The harvest hasn't been great this year, and it seems carts from the city have often been raided and compromised. I'll report it to the king who will look into it further."

"Raided?" she inquired, brow curving. When Reylan's fingers began an idle caress at her hip, she tried not to let it waver her focus.

"There's been a rise of rebel groups throughout Rhyenelle recently. It's why we weren't so quick to trust in that pirate last night. We still shouldn't trust him no matter what he thinks he may or may not know about you or anything else," Kyleer explained.

Faythe furrowed her brow. "I should like to see the town. If there's nothing else we need to do today."

The fae exchanged looks with silent words, and she hated that it made her tense and stirred irritation that she wasn't sure what it meant.

"It's probably best if we stay here in case anyone happens to recognize you," Reylan said softly.

She knew why he used the gentle tone because immediately her defensive side flared. "How in the Gods would anyone recognize me? I've barely been in Rhyenelle five months and not ventured outside of Ellium!"

Izaiah said, "Your mother liked to travel the towns. The people knew who she was to the king—that she was their future queen. I think the events in the outer city show just how much you take after her. It would be a risk."

Her damn golden eyes. Quickly becoming her most hated feature for the beacon they seemed to be in Rhyenelle. "I'll go cloaked and hooded, and I won't make eye contact where I can help it," Faythe persisted, adamant she wasn't going to be stuffed into this small inn all day and night.

"Faythe," Reylan began, but the look she shot him seemed to halt what she knew he wanted to say.

"Everyone in this inn has seen me, and no one has said anything," she pointed out.

"The sea merchant did," Kyleer countered.

She bit back her argument that his knowledge seemed not to be common since her suspicions of him still baffled her. "One man out of the dozens of people who were here last night is pretty good odds."

"It only takes one," Reylan cut in, voice hard. "One of the wrong kind to notice who you are and place a target on your back."

"I don't understand," she powered on, anger rising with the sting that they weren't being entirely up-front with her. "Why are you all so afraid of someone finding out I'm an Ashfyre?"

"Keep your voice down," Livia scolded.

The condescending tone flashed a white rage so fast it seemed to come out of nowhere and was perhaps a wildly inappropriate reaction. Faythe couldn't understand herself in that moment, and worse, she couldn't stifle it. It struck a hard beat of her heart and slicked a growing heat over her body, as if a blanket of power had begun to crawl over the surface before seeping into her skin. Faythe twisted and stood from her chair. The sudden urge to distance herself from anyone she risked harming made her take wordless, hurried steps from the room, feeling she risked saying—*doing*—something she would most definitely regret.

Faythe barely heard the voice call after her, only faintly registering a presence behind. She entered her room, breathing heavily, and began a short pace back and forth as if it would calm her.

"Faythe, what's wrong?"

It was Reylan. Of course it was. Faythe clamped her eyes shut at the shallow fire that caught in her veins, her palms. "I don't know," she breathed. She started to tremble in panic. "I think you should leave." It was a familiar feeling. The feeling of being overwhelmed; overpowered. "I don't want to hurt you."

Her palms… Why did they tingle with a sweet burn? Flipping them over, Faythe gasped in horror at the twin glowing marks within them—faint, but she already knew what the symbol was.

The mark of Marvellas.

She stumbled back but was caught by a firm force.

"I've got you," Reylan said, his touch sliding under her arms until her hands upturned in his palms.

Slowly, she felt him, just like she did in High Farrow. Faythe felt his presence within like a cool wave over her blazing, untamed fire. It was his ability, taking some of the power that raged inside to allow her to calm herself and take back control. Faythe closed her eyes and leaned against him, using all her focus to reel back her power before it could spiral too far. He was saying something in her ear. She couldn't make out the words, but his voice and the soothing rumble against her back kept her grounded and present.

Her breaths came easier, and the fire dipped, her palms no longer tingling with the sensation of an insatiable essence. When she opened her eyes and dared a glance at her hands still within Reylan's, a whoosh of air left her that there were no glowing marks within her palms.

"I don't know what happened," she admitted, shocked at the short pulse of energy now she'd returned to her normal self. She twisted out of Reylan's hold.

He was perplexed with concern. "It was like—"

"High Farrow."

He nodded. Faythe's pulse was fast, her breath still reeling from the short surge of energy that clung to her.

"You didn't bring it with you, did you?" Reylan asked carefully. "The ruin?"

Faythe stared at him wide-eyed, mustering a shake of her head. "Of course not."

Reylan was wary and deeply worried. "Perhaps it has something to do with the upcoming solstice...the ascension. Maybe it's manifesting your power from your spiritual bloodline."

The solar eclipse that would allow Dakodas to ascend. A shudder rattled her body. Faythe was unsure why it would cause her power to stir without her calling, but she supposed it could make sense.

"Aurialis warned me that the ruins respond to chaos. That I would need to get a hold of my negative sentiments to be able to channel the power they offer, or they would consume me."

Reylan took a long breath in contemplation. "I suppose the others should be warned against pissing you off in the meantime."

She huffed out a laugh that turned to a chuckle then ceased to a dry sob of frustration. Her hands rubbed her face. Despite her perfectly long rest, the short surge of energy was enough to make her contemplate a nap.

Reylan moved, arms wordlessly going around her, and they stood like that for a long moment. She was beginning to believe he was right, and however ridiculous it seemed that they were concerned about her walking around a humble town, she didn't have it in her to fight them on it.

"I think I'll stay up here," she muttered. She should apologize for her abrupt, dramatic exit. She would, but right now, all she wanted was to lie in bed until nightfall, when she hoped the pirate Gus would be lounging in his usual spot as he'd promised.

"I think I will too."

Faythe couldn't be sure how long she dozed off for. This time when she awoke, she still lay against a familiar solid warmth. The scent that wrapped her made her want to lie in that blissful, comforting space for an eternity. She couldn't remember the last thing they talked about as she'd drifted off to the low murmur of Reylan's voice when his words began to blur.

She tilted her head back, and when he caught her eye, the small smile he offered momentarily stole her breath. "Hi," she whispered, finding her throat dry from sleep. Faythe rose into a sitting position, rubbing her tired eyes as she adjusted to the faint light in the room. A candle burned on the table, and twisting to glimpse out the small window she confirmed it was nightfall from glimpsing the bright moon.

"You've been out all day." Reylan spoke her blanched thought.

Faythe blinked. She didn't think she was *that* tired. Meeting his eyes, deep concern lay in his sapphire orbs, laced with a hint of fear.

"What's wrong?" she asked, seeing there was something disturbing on his mind.

He shook his head lightly. "I just don't understand it…why you harbor such a power that can barely be withstood by your body." Because she was human was what he didn't say. Reylan had voiced the biggest argument she had against Aurialis's claims she was the only one who could stop her sister Spirits. Faythe was weakened by an episode of unchecked power, and it rallied her anxiety like nothing else to think she didn't possibly stand a chance against Marvellas if she ever came face-to-face with the evil Spirit.

"Your new friend is downstairs," Reylan admitted quietly, diverting the topic, and she had to wonder if he could hear when her thoughts started dangerously spiraling. "I would rather we didn't engage with him at all, but if you think he might somehow have answers that could help you…" He trailed off, clearly troubled by the mystery of her very existence.

It twisted her gut to see him so concerned, and to know she was the cause. Somehow, she wished she could suppress it, could appear stronger, for his sake. She felt like a feeble failure, and the truth was near crushing.

"How do you know?"

"The others have been checking in. I explained what happened. They know everything, Faythe—before now—about High Farrow and what you told me about the Spirits and you. They had to know."

Faythe took his hand resting on her thigh as she sat on the edge of the bed and tucked it behind her. She offered a smile—the best she could muster in her somber mood. She understood and wasn't shy for the others to know everything. She imagined they still had a million questions about it all, as did she.

"They're down there with him just now. I believe they've actually had enough civil conversation to be in the midst of a game of cards."

Faythe chuckled, and she felt him loosen with a smile of amusement. With a deep breath, she stood and tried to wipe the short events of the day from her mind. She was stretching her dormant muscles when Reylan stood by her.

"Are you sure you're feeling okay?"

Faythe nodded, her smile genuine. She *was* fine, physically, though her nerves were rattled by the thought of facing everyone downstairs, sheepishly apologizing for her all-day absence, and speaking with the strange sea merchant who set a wave of unease in her. But Faythe put on a brave face. There was no time to be cowardly.

The excited, drunken clamor hit her just like the night before. Faythe wrung her hands together, and Reylan must have noticed because his hand went to her lower back as they entered the front room. It was bustling like the night before, with hardly any space to maneuver and hardly any spare tables or seats. Faythe winced at the noise, thinking she should have perhaps taken a few minutes longer after waking peacefully in Reylan's warmth.

He guided her through the crowd, mostly humans who parted willingly where there was space to do so at the sight of Reylan, who towered over them. Faythe spotted their friends through the gaps of bodies a few feet away. They were laughing, and the sight relaxed her tenseness. Even Reuben held onto a small fan of cards with his boyish dimpled smile she hadn't seen in too long. Kyleer, Izaiah, and Augustine were the other players while Livia perched in Kyleer's lap, idly twirling stands of his brown hair around her fingers.

Izaiah was the first to notice them. "Ah, there's our sleeping beauty."

Faythe flushed a shade of red but tucked herself into the bench he scooted along while Reylan sat by her. "Sorry," she felt the need to say. "Did I miss anything?"

Izaiah waved a hand, sluggish enough that she eyed the empty tankards around them. "Not at all, but you do have some catching up to do." As if reading her thoughts, he swiped one up, wiggling it to signal it was empty.

Faythe bit her lip in amusement. She had never seen any of them drunk and thought they were in for an interesting night. When she turned her head again, Gus was looking at her with the same twinkle of mischief folded with wonder that meant she could never be sure what he was thinking.

"I'm glad you didn't run off, or we wouldn't have gotten the chance to have a proper talk," he said, plucking a card from his deck and placing it down.

Kyleer groaned. Livia giggled, but she decided on a counter card from the deck Ky held, placing it down in the same manner. Gus raised a brow, giving her a short nod of approval.

Faythe knew the game. Actually, she believed she was somewhat good at it despite relying a lot on luck and the odds of the stack. It brought a smile of a mischief to mind at the memory as it was the same game she was in the midst of, clearly too drunk, when she got herself and Jakon banned from the inn in Farrowhold. It was bittersweet to reflect on the night as her heart pined for her dearest friend. What would they be doing in High Farrow without her? She only hoped he and Marlowe were happy, living out perfectly carefree and safe lives in her absence. The thought of seeing them again was what willed Faythe to see this trip through to the end and back.

"You grabbed my interest enough to want to hear you out," Faythe said casually.

A barmaid came over, swiftly maneuvering around the table to collect the empty tankards and replace them with full ones. Ale wasn't Faythe's drink of choice, but she eagerly grasped the tankard, grateful for anything to take off the edge of anxiety. She held in her wince at the first bitter gulp.

Gus chuckled deeply. "I get that a lot."

"I bet you do."

He eyed her over his cards, eyes trailing over her and down to her hip. "A fine blade you wield," he observed.

She felt Reylan stiffen, and she knew the sea merchant's attention on her would be alerting every overprotective nerve in his stupidly overcautious body. It was reflected in his hand that always seemed to find its way around her. That part she didn't mind—welcomed even.

"Thank you," Faythe replied, trying not to be rattled by his odd comment.

"The key," he muttered, so casual as he looked over his cards and shuffled the order while Izaiah took his turn.

Faythe's heart skipped a beat. "What do you know of it?"

A curl formed on his mouth, but he still didn't engage eye contact. "I know many things, Faythe."

Faythe clamped her fists shut in irritation that he was dancing around direct answers. Perhaps he sought to gain something from them. Coin? Weapons? She was waiting for the shoe to drop.

"You know what you are, correct?" he drawled.

She realized then the cards he held weren't the only game in play tonight. This man was crafty in his questions, as if waiting for her to spill too much. She wondered if that was how he collected such a trove of knowledge, by getting people to admit things they believed he already knew.

"I know exactly who I am," Faythe ground out.

Gus rumbled with laughter, eyes sliding to hers with a gleeful sparkle for just a second. "I don't believe that was what I asked."

"You'd best watch what you ask and how you ask it, *pirate*," Reylan warned.

Everyone had their play, and the turn spun back to Gus. He looked over his cards before his eyes locked on Faythe's. His smirk almost creased his blue eyes.

"Why don't you tell me which card to play, Faythe?"

Her brow pinched. Seconds passed. Then ice doused her all at once and she turned completely rigid, spine straightening. She held his look, and his smile broadened to the other side as he knew she'd figured it out. How could he know? It didn't make any sense. She was human, as was he. How could he know what impossibility dwelled within her when very few did?

Faythe's heart was wild but not afraid. Strangely, she felt exhilarated, as if she didn't need to explain it to this man. Didn't need to hide. Despite not knowing his intentions yet, Faythe was determined not to yield to his unusual knowledge and grant him the upper hand.

She decided to join the game.

Carefully, she tested Gus's mind for entry and found it wide-open. Her eyes dropped to the spread of cards in play on the table. She pondered for a few seconds, back and forth.

"Red queen diamond," she settled.

Everyone whipped their heads to her. Reylan shifted, knowing what she had done.

Gus's smile was feral as he plucked and placed the card she chose.

Livia turned a card from the spare stack. It filled a suit, buying him another turn.

"Black eight spade," she continued.

He obliged, and the next maneuver put him in a very comfortable position.

"Whose side are you on?" Izaiah complained, looking over his deck hopelessly. Either he was too drunk or miserable at cards as his face gave away that he was already a losing player. Kyleer remained stern, Livia bemused, and Reuben grinned in amusement.

"Impressive," Gus commented.

"Which part?"

"All of you."

Faythe smiled coyly and took a long drink of her ale. Setting it down, she leaned on the table on her forearms, her confidence rising, maybe thanks to the slight buzz of alcohol. As she shifted, Reylan's hand landed on her thigh. Instead of grazing, he subtly lifted it to hook it over his own under the table while his arm pulled her into his side so she was partially on his lap. If he leaned forward too, his chin could rest on her shoulder.

He didn't. Reylan reclined against the tall back of the booth, one hand idly circling the rim of his tankard while the other lightly stroked her inner thigh. She couldn't be sure why it surged strength and pride within her.

"Now," she said, "let's cut the bullshit and get to it, shall we?"

CHAPTER 43

Faythe

"How is it that you know about me?" Faythe questioned.

Gus reorganized his fan of cards. "You're not asking the right questions, Faythe. Try again," he said, not meeting her eye.

Her fingers tightened around the tankard she cupped in both palms. Every time her irritation flared, Reylan responded with a slow trail of his fingers along her inner thigh, either to soothe or distract—probably both, as heat formed at her apex every time he moved.

"Where have you seen eyes like mine before?" she tried.

Gus arched an eyebrow. "It was a long time ago," he answered. "A woman in need of passage to a particular Griffin kingdom. She figured sea would be safer than land. She was quite adamant to remain unseen."

Faythe's pulse was a hard beat. "Do you know her name?"

"I thought we were past playing. Why don't you ask what you suspect—was it your mother?"

Another stroke of Reylan's fingers. Faythe took a breath then another drink.

Gus answered anyway. "Yes, it was Lilianna Aklinsera I came across on the harbors of Rhyenelle's outskirt town, Tamrest, around two decades ago. I had lived in High Farrow a couple of years—longest I'd stayed in one place—and offered the passage she sought in exchange for my stories. She too was of a rather...*spirited* sort," he said in way that tried and failed not to be an insult.

"Black knight spade," Faythe cut in, dividing her attention between him and the game. "What did you both speak of?"

His blue eyes flicked to hers. Hesitantly, he pulled the card and placed it. "It would take far more nights than the one we have to recall everything. You need to be more specific."

"What do you know of our gift?"

"What I *know* is that you should not refer to hers and yours as one and the same."

"What do you mean?"

"I mean what I said."

Reylan's hand gave a gentle squeeze as he concluded, "Lilianna only had the Nightwalking ability. Faythe has will over a person's conscious mind too."

Gus gave a small nod. "Indeed. Have you ever wondered why that is?"

"I'm an Heir of Marvellas." Faythe spilled the knowledge, immediately cursing that she'd fallen for his verbal sleight.

Reylan's fingers halted on the rim as he waited for Gus's reaction. The twitch of a smile on the sea merchant's face gave away his triumph.

"That you are, as was she."

"Red four diamond."

"Are you sure?"

"Positive." Faythe reached over to reorganize the game. "Then why didn't she have conscious abilities like mine?"

Gus smirked and played her chosen card. "Now I believe you are asking the right questions."

Kyleer grumbled. "Seriously, Faythe, you could sabotage him instead of wiping the floor with us." He lazily picked his counter move.

Reylan chuckled lightly behind her, the movement of his hand a caress of pride, and Faythe couldn't fight her smile of amusement.

"Her allegiance seems to have strayed," Izaiah added, and then he folded all his cards, eyeing something—no, *someone*. Faythe followed his line of sight to find a beautiful fae male with dirty blond hair glancing in their direction. Beautiful but darkly alluring. Izaiah stood. "I'm in need of a refill."

Faythe smirked, and the others rolled their eyes as he picked up his full tankard before sauntering off. She turned her attention back to the sea merchant.

"It's because of my blood?" Faythe asked. "From both a bloodline-blessed and a direct descendant of Marvellas?"

He pointed a finger at her. "Exactly. Your mother only had the direct descendant line, as your grandmother would have, and so forth. But you are not the only line of descendants. Having your father of the bloodline-blessed merge with her direct line—do you know what that makes you?"

Faythe shook her head, and Gus leaned forward, eyes full of wonder. "A miracle, Faythe. Not just an heir, but a *true* heir of Marvellas. One of only two to ever exist since she ascended near a thousand years ago."

Faythe blanched, heart racing and mouth drying out completely. "There was another like me?"

Gus nodded. "I believe she lived near five hundred years ago. I cannot be certain what became of her. There are very few scriptures to still exist that mention anything to do with the Spirits, just as she intended, for it could work gravely against her plans if they fell into the wrong hands." He spoke of Marvellas with his first note of fear, and Faythe's body tingled with dread. "What you are means something great. To her and to the world. But you should not be afraid of her stopping you…"

Faythe shuddered involuntarily.

"You should be afraid of her *capturing* you."

Faythe trembled. Straightening, her shoulder pressed to Reylan's chest, and his arm circled around her instead. "What would she want with me?"

Gus was halfway to drawing a card.

"No."

He halted.

"Blackjack then red five heart."

He eyed her then the spread. Everyone else seemed to arrive at the same conclusion. It would be near impossible for him not to win in the next round or two. Kyleer folded with a groan. Reuben followed with a shallow chuckle. Faythe couldn't muster an ounce of triumph she was so on edge for answers.

With a chuckle, Gus placed the cards she'd chosen then folded the others as everyone had backed out. He took a long drink of his ale. "I cannot be certain, I'm afraid, but I do believe it has something to do with your blood and those you call *the dark fae.*"

Everyone stiffened at the mention, and she felt it like a blow to the gut.

Kyleer leaned in with Livia. "So, it's true then—the dark fae rise again?"

"That is what people whisper. They have been rising for thousands of years but have found a way to multiply the numbers of their race by creation rather than reproduction," he said, the knowledge not disturbing him nearly as much as it did her. "A new Dark Age may be coming."

A slow sheet of ice began to prick Faythe's skin as she recalled the brief mention of the history Nik and Reylan relayed in the cottage back in High Farrow. They feared it then, and it was clear in the way Reylan became taut against her that it was right to fear it now.

"What does that have to do with me?" Faythe was pale.

Gus's face was wary. "You won't like my answer to that."

Faythe almost swayed, feeling Reylan's arm tighten around her.

"Do you know the High Lord Mordecai lives again?"

Another haunting flash of memory. All Faythe could muster was a nod.

"To create the dark fae requires spiritual blood. There was a time when the gift of being an oracle wasn't as rare as it is now. I believe Marvellas has long been hunting them for use in the Spell of Transition."

Oh Gods. A vibrant, beautiful face flashed to the forefront of her mind. Marlowe. Nausea filled Faythe's stomach to know her dear friend was so far away, where she couldn't send warning of the unwitting heinous threat against her if Gus spoke the truth.

"Faythe is not an oracle." Reylan pressed for the answer to her question, his voice near threatening.

"No—she is something far more. The blood of a spirit is a potent, dangerous thing. And as a true Heir of Marvellas, you may just harbor enough of it to be perfect for the darkest form of Blood Magick. Not to transition a life, but to *create* a life, or even raise the dead."

Raise the dead.

"The last true heir?" Faythe whispered, realization like a sweep of shadows unfocusing her vision.

Gus didn't need to confirm what he'd already answered with his grim expression. Everyone was silent. Even the loud commotion of the inn was drowned out by the pulse that filled her ears. Dread slicked her skin with a sticky heat. Breathing became difficult.

"If Mordecai is already risen, what would Marvellas want with Faythe?" Kyleer asked.

"That is one question I do not hold the answer to, but certainly one you should keep asking."

For the first time since she met Gus, all amusement and warmth winked out of him. He looked at her now with ocean eyes that portrayed his sympathy.

Reylan's hand curled over her abdomen, drawing her subtly closer. She could hardly take comfort in his touch, knowing he would stand by her no matter what, and with that, the same deadly target would follow him too. It was a thought she couldn't bear.

Gus said low, "Marvellas uses magick of such a dark kind that the Gods beyond the Spirits forbade it."

"That doesn't seem to have had much of an impact if she has succeeded thus far," Kyleer interjected sarcastically.

Gus cut him a look. "There are far more realms than our own. More than you could possibly imagine. It is why such Spirits were placed to act on their will, to keep our balance. I don't think even they could have predicted the turn of events that unfolded a millennium ago," he explained. "The will of the heart is a powerful thing even to the high and mighty."

Faythe tried to recall what she knew of Marvellas and why she had gone against her Gods to ascend. What she did remember was the love tale that had struck her with foolish awe from the book *The Forgotten Goddess*. She unhooked her leg from Reylan's, feeling too hot to be close to anyone while the air in the room thickened to restrict her airway. Above everything she had learned, the unsettling feeling that had enveloped her since the moment she laid eyes on Augustine remained.

"How do you know all this?" Faythe asked, trying to study what she could to figure him out.

Gus cocked his head, the light catching in his eyes to reveal a striking ocean hue. He was so odd in his inquisitiveness. His knowledge was so...

Faythe sucked in a sharp breath as the mystery clicked into place. It was impossible. It should be. And yet…she couldn't erase the blaring conclusion that screamed in her mind.

"What's wrong?" Reylan pressed with alarm.

Faythe spared a glance at him. His face was alert and concerned.

"Does he look familiar to you?"

Reylan eyed the man who remained silent. She thought she saw the moment he realized what she did. The man's blond curls, his blue eyes, even several other attributes that were so *familiar*.

"You're an oracle," Faythe said through a breath of disbelief.

Gus said nothing, yielding no expression to confirm nor deny. He didn't need to. Aside from his obscure knowledge that no person should have or could gain from simple travel, despite how he spoke in riddles and questions, withholding answers…in his appearance, Augustine bore an unnerving resemblance to the one Faythe knew to harbor the gift.

The man before her shared uncanny physical attributes with Marlowe.

It shouldn't make sense, but it was right there and near foolish to deny. Faythe had always observed that Marlowe looked nothing like Dalton, her supposed father. Her mind raced to calculate the timeline: Gus had been in High Farrow years before her mother arrived; Marlowe was a couple of years older than Faythe.

Gods above.

"Can you check his scent?" Faythe asked Reylan without removing her eyes from Gus lest she rouse his suspicions.

"He reeks of sea and ale," she got back, and she tried not to chuckle. *"I would have to get a lot closer to detect the scent of kin."*

After a second, Faythe blushed, recalling the first night Reylan arrived in High Farrow so long ago. She knew now why he'd gotten so intimately close to her in their very first lone encounter. He was searching for Agalhor's scent.

Even without the confirmation, Faythe couldn't shake the truth that was right in front of her. Did he know he possibly had a daughter?

Perhaps that was why he'd left. It twisted her heart for her friend that she could have a biological father who was still alive but didn't want a child.

"Why did you leave High Farrow?" she asked, trying to pass it off as friendly curiosity.

Gus shrugged and leaned back. "Change of scenery," he said, but it sounded like a lie.

"You met a woman there, didn't you?" Faythe went on. She couldn't stop herself—she had to know for her friend's sake.

Gus arched a surprised brow. "I didn't invite you here to talk about me—"

"Didn't you?"

His eyes narrowed a fraction. Her heart beat wildly.

"I did."

"What happened?"

"She was married."

"And?"

"And she wanted nothing else from me."

He was withholding some truth, and though it felt wrong to pry into his personal life, she couldn't let it go for Marlowe's sake. "Do you know what you left behind?" Faythe couldn't stop the resentful question that slipped from her mouth.

Gus's usual cool expression turned surprisingly hard and cold, indicating she'd struck a nerve. He straightened from his lax position, leaning in. The fae around her also shifted.

"Not that it is any of your concern, girl—"

"Watch yourself," Reylan snarled at the harsh tone.

Gus didn't balk. "I left behind a woman who wasted years of my life on an affair, only to toss me aside when she was done with me. If you knew her, whatever woes she might have spun I can assure you were false."

Marlowe's mother. It made sense that she would cut things off with him to protect her marriage if she discovered she was pregnant, because the alternative… She would have been cast out for adultery, homeless, her only option to rely on a man who traveled the seas—an uncertain future for the child she carried. But to think Dalton might never have known Marlowe wasn't biologically his was both a mercy and a tragedy. And the man before her now—he didn't seem to know of Marlowe's existence.

Before Faythe could ask anything else, the door to the inn down the hall slammed open, hushing the establishment to low murmurs. Reylan and the others straightened in alert—even Izaiah across the room—all with hands over various weapons, but no one moved. Faythe's heart leaped into her throat at the intrusion that was yet to be identified.

Through the gap in the wall poured several large forms. Faythe was quick to notice they were fae. She couldn't be sure how many there were as several still filled the hallway behind the one who was clearly their leader from his cool arrogance as he sauntered into the space.

"We're full tonight, Rezar," the barkeep said, his voice audible as everyone ceased conversation altogether.

"Look away from them, Faythe," Reylan instructed.

She did as he asked, knowing better than to argue. Casting her eyes to Reylan instead, she saw he wasn't staring at them either, but his face had changed completely. Every line was cut and focused, ready to leap into immediate action. He was calculating and listening and had likely determined several different outcomes to the situation. It was clear these fae were not well-received by the locals.

"Ah, come on—I'm sure you can make space for a few more." The fae, Rezar, spoke, his voice like shadows, dark and smooth. "After all, word is you are entertaining royalty in your fine establishment."

Faythe went utterly rigid. Kyleer, Izaiah, and Reylan exchanged the most subtle of laser-focused looks. Livia had moved from Kyleer's lap and was equally poised around her various concealed weapons, ready to strike at any given moment.

Faythe looked to Gus, eyes wide and accusatory as he was the only one who had been open about knowing who she was. But his face, while not exactly alarmed, displayed mild concern and showed no indication that he expected the intruders' arrival.

"I think I would know if Agalhor or Malin Ashfyre were in my bar." The barkeep gave a mocking laugh.

One second, the fae was by the door; the next, shrieks followed a loud commotion. The fae had crossed to the bar and hauled the man over it. He now held him pinned to the wall by his collar.

Kyleer and Livia stood then. Izaiah inched in from the other side. Faythe's hand instinctively darted to her sword's hilt, about to turn to the threat, but Reylan's grip on her arm warned against it. Faythe ground her teeth, keeping her eyes and head down in cowardly submission while all she could do was listen.

"Haven't you heard?" the fae drawled playfully. "We have a new *princess* to honor." Whatever his reasons for wanting to seek her out, his spiteful tone rang with malicious intent. "Oh, Faythe," Rezar sang out over the crowd. She felt it like a taunting caress down each notch of her spine. Thankfully, the inn was busy enough that she was just another body from where he stood. "How rude of you not to introduce yourself to your beloved citizens. Come out, little princess."

Her fear started to ease under the anger he enticed with the belittling words. A damningly familiar heat coursed through her veins. She had to focus and breathe; she couldn't afford another episode. Not now.

Her silence didn't sit well with him. "Tell you what, Faythe," he carried on, "I'm feeling patient tonight. I shall give you three seconds to show yourself, or it will be this man's life."

Her heart stopped. He couldn't be serious.

"One."

Oh Gods, he was. Faythe snapped her head to Reylan in wild panic, but he gave his a subtle shake.

"Two."

Her heart was pounding. Perhaps they knew it was a bluff, that the fae wouldn't kill an innocent man to get to her. Faythe wasn't that valuable.

"Don't you people see? Your precious royals do not care for your pitiful existence."

Then there was the most sickening crack that curdled Faythe's blood. She didn't look, gripping the table in front of her so hard splinters caught in her fingers. A ringing filled her ears that muffled the screams and commotion as everyone clamored to find distance from the evil being.

She didn't feel Reylan hauling her from the bench, nor when she was pushed behind him as they all drew their weapons and she became trapped behind a wall of tall forms. A man was dead. On her name, his life had been taken, and for what? She wanted to scream, to demand why, but words thrashed and clawed in her chest like a wild storm, unable to form any coherent sound. Words couldn't serve justice, but her blade could.

The tingling in her arms worsened. Heat slicked her skin, and her breaths came harder. This time, she didn't force it back. Instead…she reached back to that power.

"You should all leave before this becomes very messy." The voice she vaguely distinguished was Kyleer's.

A dark chuckle seeped through the bodies, flaring her rage. "The mighty General Reylan Arrowood," the fae drawled in surprise with his laughter. "Now, if I'd spotted you, we might have avoided this unfortunate incident. I don't suppose you're guarding anything of value at your back?"

The way he spoke reminded her of a predator playing with his prey. Malicious, taunting. It reminded her of Captain Varis. Suddenly, it was as if what she'd done to him—*killed him*—was not enough retribution. She couldn't be sure if it was all her own feeling or if whatever evil power that coursed through her chanted the dark thoughts in her mind, but she saw a second chance…to get her revenge on the monster who plagued her nightmares still.

"I should very much like to meet you, Faythe Ashfyre," Rezar called out.

Every time he said her name, it added to the fire that blazed under her skin. Still, she focused. She couldn't allow it to overwhelm her like before. Not before she had the chance to use it.

Rezar sneered. "To show everyone what the daughter of a tyrant looks like."

Steel sang as Kyleer and Izaiah moved, creating an opening in the block of bodies in front of her. The two brothers pointed their blades at Rezar's throat from either side, but they were equally threatened by six others who came to the aid of their leader.

"I'm right here," Faythe said. A lethal calm steadied her voice, subduing all feelings of fear.

Realizing she wasn't directly behind him anymore, Reylan moved to block her again, but Faythe cast her eyes to him, and whatever he read in her hard look made him halt his near step. His reluctance to let her face off against the fae was etched on his face, but while she watched his jaw tick, he backed down, staying close and armed.

As Faythe slowly turned her head back to Rezar, she drew her blade.

The smile he wore was nothing short of feral. His eyes held hues of hazel, but the longer she stared into them, the more she saw his pupils expanding to swallow any flicker of color. Over his rough face was a long, raised scar.

Before her…she saw Captain Varis.

"But you're going to wish I weren't."

Faythe took a step forward. There was only him and her. A second chance for her to slay the monster who tormented her still and avenge the innocent life that was taken so senselessly. She thought she heard her name as she closed the distance to Rezar, but the dark coiling in her stomach, the thrumming in her veins, only channeled her to hone in on one target.

"There she is," Rezar observed, his eyes dancing with the same sadistic gleam that never left her in sleep. "Feeble and *human,*" he spat. His smile fell and eyes filled with powerful hatred. "This is what Agalhor wants to bestow the fate of the kingdom to."

Not who—*what.* As though she were no better than a cockroach on his sole. She realized then why he didn't bat an eye at ending the man's life. Faythe's rage was white-hot at the thought of how many others he had thoughtlessly killed in his wake. Humans were cattle to him. To one who despised the weaker race.

"You ought to be careful how you speak to her." Kyleer's voice was unrecognizable in its darkness. "Not that I care if she rips out your throat."

Rezar didn't even spare him a glance. "Does it speak, or does it need its dogs for that?"

Faythe huffed a laugh that was so far from humor. "Kyleer, Izaiah."

Their attention remained on the opponent, but their glances flashed to her.

Faythe dipped a single nod, a silent command to step out of her path. Like Reylan, the conflict of protest twitched their expressions, and they didn't immediately move. Faythe held firm, internally begging for them to obey while she grappled with the reins of the power still growing within her, dancing with her anger and loose emotions. It was a relief—a huge relief—when Kyleer and Izaiah finally lowered their blades and stepped back from Rezar. She couldn't be certain what she was capable of in the embrace of the power that canceled out all thoughts of mercy. She wasn't confident it would spare anyone if she lost control to it completely.

"Brave little girl," Rezar provoked, relishing in the confrontation. Even the tone he used was akin to the vicious captain. It stoked the darkest desire that lived within her—one that thrived on revenge in only one form. Blood. She knew if she glanced down, she would see those markings in her palms that felt like flame within her grasp as she rested them over the hilt of her sword.

"General Reylan, what is the punishment for the murder of an innocent?" Faythe asked, not taking her eyes off the fae in front of her.

There was a pause of silence, and she knew he was deliberating whether to intervene on her behalf or not. He didn't, but he stayed close and armed by her side. "Imprisonment or execution depending on the trial, Your Highness."

She almost smiled, feeling the corners of her mouth curl faintly. For once, Faythe enjoyed the caress of the title he bestowed upon her, or perhaps it was the power that sang in her veins in reaction to the crown of authority. It whispered in her ear, chanted for her to use her ability, called for her to serve justice in the name he tried to defile. Tonight, someone had lost a friend, a brother, a husband, and maybe even a father. She could see no other just sentence for the culprit of such a brutal, senseless murder.

"Well, let's hold trial, shall we?" Faythe sheathed her sword, hands trembling slightly from the magick coursing through her. "You have unlawfully taken a man's life tonight. My judgment is that you meet with the same fate. Are there any here who object to that?" Faythe cast her glance over the room.

The humans huddled and stared at her with pale faces. The other fae were less afraid but still wary. A few of Rezar's companions shifted, glancing between themselves, wondering if they should be fearful of her. But no one spoke out.

Faythe smiled coldly. "Good."

"I'm not afraid of a *human girl.*" Rezar seethed.

Kyleer advanced a step, but so did Rezar's cronies. The tension waiting for one side to break first was tangible. There was only one way for justice, and one way they were all leaving that inn without erupting chaos on the innocents who crowded as far into the corners away from the threats as possible.

Faythe clicked her tongue with a shake of the head. She listened to the loud whispers, an unearthly power that sang and rejoiced to be used. "I could tell you what happened to the last person who underestimated me."

Rezar pulled his blade free with a flash of savage rage. His companions followed his lead. Steel sang, bodies moved, and blades raised.

"But I'd rather show you."

His attempt to advance was halted with one foot forward. A choked sound left him. Those behind him shifted in confusion, at a complete loss for what to do. They were no more than mindless followers of hate and evil.

Faythe took slow, deliberate steps toward him, assessing every inch that flared his nostrils while she held him still. A suffocating heat coated her skin, slicking her with sweat. Her ability began to heighten beyond what she could harness, consuming her. Gasps and murmurs and whispers of fear—maybe awe—echoed around the room. Stopping in front of Rezar, she never broke his loathsome stare. His rage passed right over her while she studied every piece of him outwardly and within, needing to be sure there was nothing to salvage within such hatred.

She raised her chin, lifting her eyes from his and making her judgment. "Bring him."

She didn't wait and strode for the exit, but she heard his shuffling and the string of vulgar protests. Everyone stepped from her path, but she didn't take pride in their fear. Perhaps what she was about to do was reckless and selfish. She didn't care. The dark caress that rejoiced and thrived with her equally dark thoughts was all she could pay mind to. One-on-one combat. Faythe's second chance…to slay the demon of her past once and for all.

CHAPTER 44

Faythe

OUTSIDE, FAYTHE DREW Lumarias. Focused, charged. She took one deep breath to remember she was in control. She would own what she was about to do and not let her power take over.

Footsteps followed her into the open space beyond the inn. She heard Rezar as he was dragged out by Kyleer and Izaiah. Townsfolk started to creep out from the shadows, attention piqued at the commotion. Silhouettes peeked through windows, and a crowd murmured and gathered.

Faythe tuned them all out.

There was only her and the fae she stood to battle as she finally spun back to him. Kyleer and Izaiah shoved him to his knees, and he hissed his curses to them.

"Arm yourself," Faythe commanded, lacking any emotion.

His face snapped up to her with a feral rage. That face… Faythe had to blink a few times to shake the image of Captain Varis who glared at her with powerful malice. It was tormenting. Every time that scar sliced down his skin, every time hazel eyes were devoured by black, it struck her heart still.

"What are you doing?" Reylan's voice was low as he reached her.

Faythe slid her eyes up to his. "Exacting justice."

"This is not the way."

"And what is?"

His jaw ticked with protest, but Faythe didn't back down. She couldn't. Reylan's eyes searched hers, but she couldn't be sure what he was assessing.

"You're expending yourself. Let me take care of this."

Faythe turned to him fully. "You cannot pick and choose when to stake your belief in me. *I* cannot choose. If I am to be Rhyenelle's heir, this is it. Responsibility. No matter how harsh or burdensome it may be to accept."

Reylan's calculating look softened in understanding. He gave a single small nod, and Faythe's firm posture threatened to sag in relief that he wasn't fighting her on the matter. His concern remained, and while it tightened in her chest, she forced the pain back. She had to do this.

"Make it quick," was all he said, a hint of pride slipping into his voice.

Faythe let a slight smile form on her lips. "I plan to." Her gaze returned to Rezar, who had risen and now stood holding an impressive steel blade. His rage became focused, and he pinned her with it as though he thought he stood a chance at getting his own back.

The crowd around them grew significantly. Everyone piled out of the inn as though this were a grand spectacle. The thought turned her stomach, almost enough for her to abandon the confrontation. Her goal was not to make a mockery of Rezar, but to show justice. The humans of this town and every other would be protected under the Ashfyre name he tried to tear down. She could do this.

Yet there was also a darkly selfish part of her that stood to slay the fae in the hope it would gain her peace. Peace from another wicked evil who refused to let her go even in death.

"You think you can defeat me, *girl?*" Rezar spat, advancing a single step.

Faythe could *feel* Reylan's fury like ripples of shadow. His overwhelming want to intervene. Through the whisper of chaos and power within, Faythe found the calming wave to channel back to him, hoping it was enough to keep him sated until she achieved what she needed to.

"Let's find out," she answered, but she didn't move.

She waited. She watched. She listened. Rezar was too consumed by his anger to even feel her presence in his mind, so much hatred and malice Faythe had to focus not to tangle her own subdued feelings, or she risked turning into something she never wanted to be. Ruthless and unhinged.

Rezar moved fast, exactly as Faythe anticipated. She twisted around his attack, but he wasted no time in whirling around and cutting his blade horizontally. Faythe backed up a long stride to avoid that too. His speed couldn't be matched, but having the answer to his moves before he made them felt like a choreographed dance. There was enjoyment in the song, and she couldn't be sure how much time passed while she stepped and twirled like the wind, completely disconnected from the crowd of onlookers. Her dance of tranquility was paired with savagery as Rezar's fury grew that he was yet to strike her.

Her blade connected with his for the first time with a force that sent vibrations of angst crawling up her arms and over her chest, snapping her mind to match the indignation. Faythe wouldn't hold out against his fae strength, so while she enjoyed the melody of clanging steel, she didn't allow their blades to lock again.

She twisted around his next lunge forward. Using all her strength, she sent a powerful kick to the back of his knees before he could reposition himself. Rezar fell to the ground with a loud grunt. Faythe held her blade to his back. While he was at her weapon's mercy, she traced the lethal tip over his shoulder, over his chest, and circled around to look down on him once more.

The look he pinned her with was nothing short of murderous. A familiar dark gaze that conflicted her with anger and utter terror. Despite his face, which contorted with an inhuman rage, for the first time, Faythe felt his fear. Fear of *her*.

A few of Rezar's crew moved to aid him. Faythe seized control of all six without sparing them a glance. The pulse of so many minds around her almost made her sway. It was overwhelming, but the power within helped her filter out those it wasn't concerned with. It listened to her.

"What are you?" Rezar choked out in rage-fueled bewilderment.

Faythe raised a palm, and for a second, she was mesmerized by the symbol alive within in it—but that wasn't what she focused on. Slowly, she felt the building pressure, a sphere of the fae's very essence forming within her physical grasp, which she knew no one else could see. Faythe could see and feel and hear everything he was. So much like the wicked evil she thought she had rid the world of already.

"You call me feeble, but look at you," she said vacantly, head tilting at the sphere in her palm. "So small on the inside. You use fear to distract others from seeing your own. You are nothing but a coward." Faythe met his eyes then, and he was right to look vulnerable; to surface that fear as an unveiling of his true self before he met his end. "Do you have anything you would like to say?"

Rezar's eyes were back to blazing. "This kingdom will burn before you claim it."

"Then it's a shame you won't bear witness," Faythe said calmly, "when I sit upon a throne from the ashes."

"A human cannot rule, much less a *girl!*"

"I'm not human." Faythe's expression didn't flinch, didn't balk. "I am not fae." She glanced around at the gathered crowd, seeing both species fix their eyes on her. "I am both."

"You are nothing but a worthless, human bit—" Rezar choked on the word, cut off by the strike of an arrow piercing right through his chest from behind. The blood-coated iron tip protruded so close to his heart.

Faythe glanced up in surprise, finding Reylan still expertly poised with the bow he'd released the shot from. His eyes were hard, livid. His chest rose and fell with the anger that steeled his expression into something frightening, fixed on the fae in front of him.

Everything was still and silent, save for the choking and spluttering of Rezar on his knees. Faythe didn't tear her eyes from Reylan as he stared down at the fae with powerful loathing. As he finally lowered his bow, he cast his gaze up to lock on her.

Faythe felt the pulse of Rezar's life force swirling in her palm—felt him faltering from the fatal arrow shot. It was Reylan who broke their stare. He passed off the bow, and there was nothing of kindness or mercy on his face as he crossed the distance so fast all Faythe could do was watch.

"You were warned about how you should speak to her," Reylan said in the most chilling calm. There was no pause for hesitation when he ruthlessly grabbed the arrow he had dealt and pulled it from Rezar's chest with the most sickening sound that wasn't masked by the fae's cry of pain. Blood poured from the wound, but as Reylan tossed the arrow aside, one of his hands curled around Rezar's throat, forcing his head back awkwardly to stare at the fae general who towered over him.

Yet he was not the general in that moment. Not the gentle warrior she knew. Faythe saw what he had once tried to explain to her. She saw the merciless killer he once was—who he was made to be. But she held no fear. No disgust or judgment as Reylan took his own need for justice out on the fae.

"You can torment in the Nether knowing you died on your knees before your queen."

Rezar's mouth floundered open and shut, but between the choking and spluttering he got out, "Long live King Malin."

Faythe felt the sear of hot fury—Reylan's—knowing in that second what he was about to do. She clenched her fist tight, clamping her teeth against the pain that scorched in her gut as Reylan sharply snapped Rezar's neck. Faythe winced as the pain subsided in a few quick seconds.

Then she felt…nothing. Not even like a just sentence had been served when the wicked fae's body hit the ground. He deserved it, but it didn't change the fact he'd taken an innocent life down with him, and likely many more before.

Faythe's head throbbed, but she couldn't let go. Or rather, the power that raged and rejoiced within at her actions wouldn't let her go. Breathing air became like breathing flames. Her vision became foggy.

Something touched her. A hand on her forearm she had yet to drop, and one on her waist. She welcomed the touch for the cool wave that lapped within her at the contact and partially leaned into that force, tiredness sweeping through her mind as the power cried and dwindled in its presence. Reylan's presence. As he swept in to calm the storm and tame the chaos.

The power was letting her go. For now.

The hold she had on the other minds released, and they shuffled back, complete fear stripping their brutal faces back to those of frightened children.

"Unless you want to meet the same fate as your friend, go," Kyleer snarled.

Faythe was faltering, but she heard the shuffling and could make out the bodies that rushed to gain distance from them. While the coolness continued to filter through her and douse the fire, Faythe glanced over at the crowd still gathered—to be sure no one else was hurt. She blinked, unsure if what she was seeing was right. Her senses snapped awake in a surge of panic to see many of them had fallen, and others rapidly joined. In a split second of terror, Faythe believed she had mistakenly attacked them too.

But when her vision focused, the people weren't dead or harmed.

Far from it. They had fallen to one knee, heads bowed. Faythe couldn't believe what she was seeing. Was it out of fear and submission to the fae? Was it out of fear of *her?*

"Phoenix Queen," a woman breathed in what sounded like awe from the crowd. It was echoed intermittently until it hummed through the masses. "Thank you."

Faythe was stunned, and a rush of embarrassment and guilt flushed her tired mind and body. She couldn't stand to be there any longer. She didn't deserve their gratitude, had done nothing but show an evil side to herself no matter how deserving the fallen fae was of meeting his end. She hadn't saved them. She couldn't save the man who lost his life because of her.

Only when the power had ceased completely did she come back into her full self, and the sense of awareness struck her like a physical blow. She wanted to feel guilt, horror, but she didn't. Maybe she would after the exhaustion passed. She wanted to rest more than anything.

Reylan was at her back, still holding her after bringing her back once again. The only remorse she felt was for having to drag him into it once again; having him expend his own ability to save her from herself.

He coaxed her to walk, but Faythe snapped her head up, searching for one person in particular. She caught sight of Gus by the entrance to the inn, the only one who casually leaned back against the wall, sipping on the ale he'd brought out with him. He held no look of disgust, only mild intrigue and disbelief.

Reylan didn't release her as they made their way over to him.

"Is there ever a way I can find you again?" Faythe asked, needing to for Marlowe's sake.

Gus seemed hesitant to give her a way, but after a quick few seconds of contemplation, he answered, "Phoenixfyre."

Her brow furrowed. She was far too drained to play riddles with him.

He gave a low chuckle. "You will know what it means soon enough.

Good luck to you, Faythe Ashfyre. The beginning of the end is near." He raised his tankard to her with a small dip of his head.

Without another word, Reylan was steering her sideward, and she didn't fight it. She could barely take a step with the darkness that forced her to rest. Reaching the others, they talked among themselves, but she could only catch pieces of conversation while her head felt submerged underwater.

"We can't risk them coming back in larger numbers," Reylan said.

"It's nightfall—it's a risk to travel now," Kyleer countered.

"Not as much of a risk as it will be if word spreads. We're idle bait here."

They debated for a few minutes more before she was moving again —not back indoors. Just as well. She didn't think she could climb the steps.

Faythe barely registered what happened next. She was passed from one warm force to another. Then her feet left the ground, and she thought she was flying for a second until she was seated and something embraced her from behind. *Someone.* Faythe fell back against that form. The scent that wrapped her with home and safety. Reylan. His arm around her middle held her from falling as they moved.

Faythe muttered, "I killed him." She moved with the expanse of his chest.

"No, you didn't."

She nodded. Or she thought she did. Words eluded her; the world escaped her. She was in safe arms—*they were safe*—and the rest of the people at the inn were safe from that monster at least. With that thought, she let go and fell blissfully into beckoning oblivion.

CHAPTER 45

Zaiana

ZAIANA HAD NEVER seen anything like it in all her three hundred years. The power the human possessed, the ability that surrendered seven fae to her will and command... It was far more than she had been led to believe. Mordecai had warned her she was not to be underestimated, but even that felt like a damning understatement. Yet Faythe was fatally flawed, someone with great power and potential but not enough discipline to be able to harness it.

As Zaiana, Maverick, Amaya, and Nerida watched from the outside, Tynan gathered what he could from the bustle inside. Finding Rezar was an easy feat for Tynan, and she was interested to find out how Faythe and her companions would respond to a real threat.

It seemed Faythe had other plans. She didn't get to see them fight; didn't get the chance to see any of the fae in action as she took control of the situation, risking her own life in the process, it seemed. Zaiana felt the power she harnessed; felt the earthly vibrations she was all too familiar with but knew how to control. It was a dark triumph to witness her so consumed, undisciplined.

"I'll be damned," Maverick muttered.

They watched as Faythe reduced Rezar to his knees, halting the movements of any other who wanted to intervene. What was surprising was that she didn't get the chance to end his life before the silver-haired fae lost the final tether on his tangible rage. It was beautiful to observe the two of them with the most darkly twisted admiration. To know what they were capable of.

Zaiana was right: darkness spared no pure heart.

But that wasn't the most remarkable part. Zaiana was close to feeling a slither of dread that Faythe's life might be claimed by the magick that seized her. Then the most unexpected thing happened when the silver-haired warrior laid hands on her.

"A Mindseer," Nerida murmured.

Zaiana twisted her head at the wonder in her voice. "A what?"

"The one with silver hair—I believe he is a Mindseer. One with the ability to detect power in others and diminish it. Sometimes they can stifle one's whole ability; other times only dampen it. It depends on the strength of the Mindseer versus the strength of the ability of the beholder," the fae explained, not taking her eyes off the scene.

Well, shit. An ability like that could work gravely against her plans. While Zaiana had every control over her own mental barriers, she had never come across someone with such a talent before to know if she would hold out against him. He was an uncharted threat, as was Faythe. It should have instilled a little fear and wariness in her as it clearly did among the others, but Zaiana saw a thrill in the challenge, a thirst to discover the unknown even in a perhaps deadly confrontation.

She turned her attention back to them. She was stunned by what unfolded next, perhaps even in mild awe, as she watched the onlookers of Faythe's grand spectacle begin to bow down one by one. Admiration widened their expressions, not fear.

Faythe exchanged a few last words with the human man she'd been in conversation with all night. Near limp, she was helped onto a horse with the Mindseer, and they were all swift to abandon the scene they'd created. The human was hardly conscious, and while Zaiana felt a beam of triumph to see her so weakened by the surge of energy, she couldn't prevent the faint twinge in her chest. Almost like sympathy as she watched the concern laced with collective panic on her companions' faces.

"I take it we're following them," Tynan said.

Zaiana's eyes slid back to the window—to where the man they had been in conversation with took up his lazy seat once again. "Take Amaya and trail them," she instructed her second-in-command after short contemplation. "We'll catch up soon. I should like to find out if there's anything to be gained from the human they met with."

Tynan followed her line of sight. "I didn't find out much. The noise was loud even for my hearing. He's a sea merchant, but the human called him something else—an *oracle.*"

Nerida inhaled a breath. "Remarkable," she muttered.

Zaiana almost rolled her eyes at Nerida's thirst for wonder and new concepts, but she had so far proven useful with her intrigue. "What does that mean?" she asked the fae.

Nerida met her eye. "An oracle is someone with a connection to the Spirits. They often get knowledge and foresight from them in the form of visions and dreams."

Something about the concept coiled dread in her stomach. "Will he know about us?"

"I can't be sure. Their visions are subjective and often not complete. Riddles and usually more questions than answers. Sometimes they figure out what they have seen through events that happen, people they meet... It's all very variable, really." Nerida spoke with utter fascination while Zaiana felt cold in anticipation. It was so long since she had been allowed to venture from the mountains and surrounding villages.

Though she had been taught and trained, ruthlessly and mercilessly, she was quickly learning her knowledge was nothing compared to the vastness of the world. What she hated the most was that in a matter of weeks, she had gone from being one of the most powerful and highly regarded dark fae to feeling like a sheltered *darkling*. There was so much to be experienced, so much she had been robbed of in her life. It only grew her need for retribution against those who had shackled her to that mountain.

"I think we should find out," Zaiana decided. She would not cower, and if the man proved to be a threat with what he knew or figured out by meeting them, there was one thing she had been coldly crafted to do: kill a problem before it became one.

Zaiana finished calculating her plan. "Tynan and Amaya will track the fae. You have to go by foot and keep *hidden*. They are no doubt skilled trackers and will be able to detect you if you get even an inch too close. Don't get caught, or you forfeit your life."

Tynan nodded, understanding hard on his face. He knew, as they all did, that if they were ever to be caught or taken captive, rescue wouldn't come. It was harsh, brutal, but it was how it had to be.

"We will catch up with you when we are done here."

No one stood to question Zaiana—a relief as she didn't have the energy to enforce her leadership. She looked to Maverick in particular with that thought. He stood coolly, yielding no expression to give away what he thought of the plan or the fact they were about to expose themselves to an *oracle*.

Tynan and Amaya left swiftly, gauging enough time had passed for the fae to have made suitable headway to be tracked from a safe distance. Zaiana wasted no time in dipping out of the shadows of the alley and making her way across to the inn. A rare edge of anxiety weighed in her steps. She was eager to get the confrontation over with.

Entering the establishment, Zaiana found it was hushed, consumed by an air of terror mixed with…awe. It was odd, and as they rounded into the front room, a few pinned them with looks of fear, perhaps thinking they were of the band of Raiders returning for revenge. Zaiana paid them no attention as her eyes shifted to the man she sought. It was both unsurprising and unnerving that he was already looking at her, as though he were waiting for their gazes to meet.

She walked through the mass of people who eagerly stepped out of her way and spared a glance down at the fallen human whose life had been taken, surrounded by his friends or kin. Their sobs and heartbreak were suffocating.

Standing before the man with blond curls poking out of his strange hat, she said nothing as they simply looked at each other and he took another long swig of his ale. For some reason, it ground her irritation, but she slid onto the bench opposite him regardless.

"Please, do join me," he drawled.

This man had a bold nerve, and while his cool arrogance grated on her nerves, she couldn't help but wonder if he was expecting them. She hated that the feeble being had such an ease of power to instill the prickling wariness that coated her skin.

The man peeled himself from his reclined position, setting his tankard down on the table. Zaiana didn't flinch when he leaned in on his forearms, staring at her so intently it were as if the man *assessed* her and saw straight past her steel exterior without even trying. It rattled her awfully, but she would not give a reaction.

Finally, he spoke again. "You are not the first peculiar set of eyes I have met with tonight." His gaze shifted briefly to Maverick, then Nerida, before returning his focus to her. He was observant and a critical thinker.

"Did you know you sat with royalty tonight?" Zaiana tested.

Maverick tensed beside her but said nothing. Zaiana had nothing to lose with this man, and exposing they knew of Faythe and her companions would change nothing.

A slow, cunning smile curled the man's mouth. "Indeed. Though she is not the only royal highness I seem to have the esteemed pleasure of sitting with tonight." The man's eyes fell to each of them in turn with equal attention and an air of wonder.

Zaiana's temper flared recklessly, feeling the man's statement was a mockery.

Maverick stood, gliding around the table, and slid into the man's side instead. He twisted his body, blocking the view of any onlookers, and it was then she caught the glint of the blade he'd drawn. "You'll find we are far less patient than your previous *company,*" Maverick said calmly. As he angled the blade, it lit up with licks of blue flame while he smiled with playful sin. "I've never been a fan of riddles. You don't want to test them against her either—this blade will feel like a pinprick compared to what she might do."

The first sign of fear flickered in the man's expression, but he quickly regained his cool demeanor after tearing his gaze from the threat of the flaming blade. Zaiana didn't fight the hint of a victorious smile.

"Who are you?" Zaiana asked him.

The man reached for his tankard again, pausing as Maverick shifted with him and they exchanged a tense look. "I am but a simple sea merchant. You may call me Augustine. I am not your enemy." He picked up his ale regardless. "Care for a drink, Zaiana?"

A low snarl left Maverick's throat as he leaned in closer. The blade he held moved to the man's throat, close enough that he would feel the heat, but Maverick could defuse his fire's burn and call it at his command. "How do you know her name?"

Augustine slid his glance to him, taking a casual sip of his ale as though the flaming blade were a stick of wet wood. "I think you know how since planting your spy by the far corner earlier this evening."

Zaiana felt constantly one step behind this man, not ahead as she was used to being with everyone else. It was absurd. Outwardly, he was no more than a drunken pirate who reeked famously of the title. But he was far more cunning and insightful than any human she had come across before. This man held no allegiance, perhaps only to his duty as an oracle. Otherwise, she was sure he would have warned Faythe and her companions of them.

"Do you know what I am?" she questioned, keeping her tone level to avoid giving him the satisfaction of knowing he had the upper hand.

That gleam in his eye returned. The glee he found in playing his own games, toying with his subjects with knowledge he harbored but wanted them to sing for.

"If you mean, do I know should that blade come to tear your flesh instead, neither of you would bleed the expected color—then yes, I suppose you could say I do."

His careful wording gave away the fact he knew Nerida wasn't a dark fae. Zaiana decided to take an equally lax approach and reclined in her seat.

"You are not afraid?"

"Should I have reason to be?"

Zaiana scoffed. "Yes. No one should know of our existence; you are a fool to expose that you do."

"I have known many things about many people, and I live to tell such tales."

This man was impossible. She couldn't decide if she admired or despised his courage. Not arrogant; he simply spoke with a factual calm.

Augustine slid his glance through the window to where a couple of fae had finally arrived to haul off Rezar's body. "Huh," he muttered to himself, seeming to come to some internal conclusion. "I did wonder how they came to discover an Ashfyre was in town so quickly." He didn't look at all disturbed.

Then his focus was back on her with a glare of blame. She didn't bother trying to deny it.

"I would be fascinated to see your wings," he commented, eyes flashing over her shoulder as if he could imagine them there.

"I could show you," Maverick offered, "but the death of everyone in this room would be on your conscience to satisfy the curiosity."

Augustine gave a lighthearted chuckle. "I have a feeling the sight will be of the common eye sooner rather than later. I suppose I can wait a while longer."

Something in that comment held a kernel of foresight, and from his look, she knew he had purposely shared it with her. A giddy thrill laced her veins. The dark fae would come out of hiding, and it would happen soon.

Augustine shifted his focus to Nerida, who remained silent and anxious beside her. Zaiana didn't fail to notice her heart's tempo had picked up not long into their conversation. She couldn't be sure what had sparked the unease in the fae to make her purposely keep still, as if they might forget she was even present at all.

"I haven't come across one of your kind in a while," Augustine said with a twinkle of admiration. "A Lakelarian. Though one might mistake you as a Fenstead native."

Zaiana supposed he was right. With her beautiful golden-brown skin tone that contrasted mesmerizingly with her white hair, she held envious traits originating from both kingdoms. Nerida went even more taut, heart rate spiking. She said nothing, which Zaiana found odd for someone who was often led by her voice to collect and share wonders. She had anticipated she would have a lot of questions for an *oracle*.

Augustine's eyes twinkled, but he smirked at the fae, seeming to drop his attempt to engage with her.

"What did you speak of with Faythe?" Zaiana questioned.

The sea merchant leaned back once more, seemingly unfazed by Maverick, who still threatened him. "That is not what you truly want to ask, Zaiana."

Her eyes narrowed. "You may have the gift of foresight, but don't make the mistake of thinking you know me and what I'm capable of."

His smile only widened. "I wouldn't dream of it. I may know some things, but the essence of a person is something to be experienced, not simply seen. You're very intriguing, Zaiana. So much conflict in those amethyst-cored eyes."

Her nostrils flared, hating his assessment. She wasn't used to the deep attention, and she despised that it made her feel *vulnerable.* "I can assure you,"—she dropped to the lethal tone she had used many times to assert her threats—"I hold no conflict or hesitation."

Never before had someone continued to address her after she spoke in such a way. The only debate she harbored was whether she admired the human's boldness or wanted to kill him for it.

"Strange, the stillness in your chest. Have you ever wondered why that is?"

He had a masterful way of swaying a person's interest.

"I was born this way."

"Because that is what they told you?"

Her fists curled. "Because we are not *weak* to your human emotions of love and mercy. Both of which are often what get you killed."

Augustine released a breathy chuckle.

"Perhaps you'd like a demonstration." Maverick pressed his blade to the side of the man's throat, but his fire did not burn him.

"I know quite well what you are capable of. It is not me who needs convincing." His eyes flashed down to the blade then up to lock on Zaiana. "You might find there are secrets within truths; that one answer is not always the *only* answer."

Her temper was close to eruption. She shot to her feet, regretting ever having set foot in the establishment. It had been a waste of time to have a drunken human infuriate her with a single conversation. She blazed down at him. Still, Augustine was not in the least bit threatened.

"Can I kill him?" Maverick spoke the dark thought that flashed through her mind.

They should. The man knew too much. Yet it didn't seem worth it. Augustine was an oracle—one with spiritual blood.

"I'm sure he'll meet his end soon enough."

Marvellas would find him, just as she had found so many others to keep the Transitions going. To kill one with such power in their blood out of rage and spite would be foolish.

Zaiana straightened as she regained her composure, cooling every emotion to embrace an icy steel guard. "What a pitiful existence." She glanced at him from head to toe. Augustine only grinned, flashing a single gold tooth. "I'm sure you'll meet your maker soon enough." With that, she made to leave.

"What you mock in others is what you see in yourself, Zaiana."

She halted, and her rage may have been tangible in how hot she felt. Her jaw locked while she kept her back to him.

"Please let me kill him," Maverick muttered low.

She was so close to snapping. So close to agreeing. Until the sea merchant who tempted death spoke again.

"Your fascination is a question—one you've harbored your whole life. Don't stop looking for the answer."

CHAPTER 46

Faythe

DAYS BLURRED, BECOMING an indistinguishable motion that only switched from night to day when she managed to flutter a glance. The darkness that held no memory, no conscience, cradled her endlessly. Sometimes she feared it would never let her go. Part of her didn't mind, but a larger part knew there was something worth returning to.

No—not something. *Someone.*

His scent had battled the embrace of the darkness, his voice often cutting through the oblivion. His tether that ran through her was all she could grapple onto to keep from giving in completely.

Sound returned to her. More voices than one. Focusing on that sense, she began to hear woodland murmurs too. The faint chirp of birds. It must be daylight. Thinking of that, she felt the light caress of sun against her face, along with the featherlight touch of summer-kissed air. Light began to faintly pierce the dark.

Faythe flexed her fingers, feeling textured leather, soft. Something hard and warm was at her back, something equally unmoving wrapped around her front, and she was rocking and dipping.

Finally, she took a deep breath. The scent of wood and pine came second to the scent of *him*. Spice and leather and something light and cold like ice. Her lids fluttered open, but she winced at the sharp light. She tried to move her head but winced at that too from the pain that shot down her neck as she tried to straighten.

Suddenly, the jostling stopped, and she felt another hand go over hers while the arm that held her tight loosened. Faythe let her head fall to the side and tried to adjust her sight again. Through the glare of the sun, she saw him. Reylan. From the locks of silver to the glimmer of sapphire. She wanted to reach a hand up to be sure she wasn't dreaming, but even that felt like too much energy.

"Hi," she whispered, finding her throat dry and hoarse.

She heard his breath like a release of relief, but he said nothing. Instead, he spoke to someone else.

Her surroundings slowly came to her, along with her sense and awareness. Then memories started to catch up with her. The last she remembered was the inn…the fae. He was dead, but that recollection didn't strike her with the disgust she thought she should feel. Not in remembering what he'd done.

All at once, Faythe was falling. She let out a whoosh of air in a panic, trying to grapple onto something to stop her plummet from the high horse. She didn't get the chance to fall to a painful tumble when her feet met solid ground and she was cradled by a new solid form.

"I've got you, sleeping beauty."

Izaiah. Disorientated, it took her a moment and a few long blinks before she could bear her full weight and began to step out of his hold. As she did, an arm curled around her waist. Reylan.

Faythe looked around, seeing Kyleer tying horses, Livia helping, and Reuben crouching down by a tree rustling through a pack. Finally, Faythe found the will to speak.

"How long?" was all she could ask. When she twisted to look up at Reylan, his face was cold, detached, as though he'd spent weeks in desolation. *Did something else happen?*

"Three days," he answered, not an ounce of emotion in his voice.

Faythe might have swayed had he not been holding her. He moved, and she with him, over to where the others seemed to be making camp. It was the first Faythe noticed the hues of daylight were of a welcoming twilight.

Reylan led her over to where a bed roll was set out against a large trunk. He helped her down, even though her full mobility had returned enough for her to maneuver unaided. He left her to aid the others who were tending to the horses and stacking wood in the center to light later. Faythe wanted to help but figured she would only get in the way and stir the concern of the silver-haired warrior even more. She watched him, a coil tightening in her gut to see him so detached. Was it all her fault? Was it what she had done to the fae? The thought of him having any ill judgment of her was a slow suffocation filling her chest.

Faythe leaned back against the trunk. Tucking her knees up, she curled to the side, unable to bear the emotions that swarmed with her racing thoughts if she kept looking at him. She wasn't tired—far from it now she had fully come to from her days of long rest. She didn't know what to make of it, the power that clung to her. Where had it come from, and why now?

She didn't know how much time passed as the night drew in and she sat alone. Faythe tuned in to the crackle of the fire, her muscles turning stiff, and shifted her position to watch the tango of flames, feeling utterly useless. Reylan wasn't there. She sat upright, clenching her teeth and moving her dormant muscles.

"They're checking the perimeter." Livia's voice sounded from across the fire.

Landing eyes on her, she saw they were filled with...pity. It only added to her sinking gut. Faythe noticed then that Izaiah was missing too. Livia stood, coming around the fire, and settled down next to her. She extended a helping of bread and cheese.

"You were somewhat conscious long enough for him to force you to drink, but you haven't eaten in days," she said when Faythe didn't immediately take it.

Her somber mood didn't even flare her embarrassment that she'd been fussed over and catered to, half-conscious. She didn't have an appetite, but she took the food with a grateful smile, knowing she needed to rebuild her strength.

"Gave us all quite the scare there, Faythe," Kyleer said, approaching on her other side and taking up a seat on a thick log.

Faythe winced. "I don't know what happened," she admitted, and it was mostly the truth. "I think something is reacting to my ability—it heightens when I get angry or upset, and I can't always come back from it. Not alone."

"Reylan," Livia mused. "It's never made better sense."

Faythe didn't know what she meant by it, but it was true. She might not have survived all the times her ability had manifested beyond her control without him. "I thought it was only around the ruin, but now I'm not so sure," she told them. "Aurialis seems to think there's a way I can control it on my own, by learning discipline over my emotions and power combined. But it doesn't make sense if my body can barely withstand the surge of energy regardless whether I harness it or it harnesses me." She ranted her frustrations, rubbing her hands over her face.

Livia shook her with a gentle hand on her shoulder. "You'll get your answers. Summon this Great Spirit of Life once we get back from this ridiculous quest to stop her evil sister."

Faythe couldn't help the chuckle that left her, easing some of her somber mood. Livia smiled, and it was a great reassurance that there was no judgment from her or Kyleer for what she did or what she was capable of. Everything that made her existence dangerous and unexplainable.

Reuben shuffled over from where he was eating his own portion of bread and cheese. "I don't think I even believed you until I saw what you did at the table with the cards," he remarked with a teasing smirk.

A grin bloomed on her face, overjoyed that her friend didn't mention the other heinous side to what she could do.

"The bastard got what he deserved." Kyleer seemed to read her thoughts. "I would have gutted myself if Reylan didn't get to him first, and it would have left far more mess and destruction. He was of a notorious group of Raiders we found out about earlier that morning. He would have been caught and dealt with once we reported it back to the king regardless. You just saved us a lot of hassle."

It didn't help with her guilt, but she asked, "Why do they hold resentment toward the crown? What did he want with me?"

Kyleer blew out a breath. "They're of a minority of our kind who still hold themselves in higher regard than humans. They resent Agalhor for showing them equality when it wasn't always so. We live for a long time, and change can take centuries to be accepted by some. I don't know how he knew you were there. Reylan and I spent the whole morning checking for threats and scouting for these so-called 'Raiders.' Rezar was a recurring name. I guess however he found out there was an Ashfyre within his reach, he would have used you to send a message to Agalhor."

She couldn't believe there was such a radical movement in Rhyenelle when all she'd seen so far was peace and diversity. Though she supposed it was her foolish and naïve side that believed the kingdom could be spared from any form of maliciousness.

"Would he have killed me?" she dared to ask.

Kyleer's face was grim. "We'll never know. But he was bound to come to the fate he did with his crimes. You should know that what you did wasn't wrong, and the people of that town will sleep far better knowing there's no chance of his return. I doubt any of the other shriveling cowards will be back anytime soon without their leader."

It eased the darkness on her heart just a little to know the people might feel a small semblance of safety as Kyleer implied.

"The people at the inn—they said a name... I think I've heard it before," Faythe began. She had been unable to shake the unsettling feeling.

Kyleer smirked, picking at his bread. "Phoenix Queen."

Faythe only nodded.

"You stirred up an old fairy tale in your words and will likely have created a buzz in superstitious minds."

Faythe was puzzled and didn't voice that she wasn't entirely certain they *were* her words. She owned what she did, and that act was solely hers to bear. She wouldn't allow them to believe it was a result of the power that whispered through her like its own entity. It had given her the strength to carry it through, but she was conscious and aware.

Livia recited casually, "In Ungardia's darkest hour, when all shall burn and fall, only the Phoenix Queen can find a throne from the ashes, and rise it true for all."

A shudder swept through her body and tightened her muscles. Kyleer chuckled at her reaction.

"It's just an old Rhyenelle children's rhyme from the time of the Firebird. The kingdom has never fallen before."

Livia's eyes also sparkled with amusement at the notion anyone could read into such a short romantic tale. Then Faythe realized where she'd heard it before. It was often she forgot: her mother was a child of Rhyenelle. The short poem was familiar as her mother had recited it to her many times when she was younger, along with longer tales of the supposed savior, the *Phoenix Queen*. Her own child-self had found awe and wonder in the story, but now, she was swept with a sense of unease. She would never have known her mother was born a citizen of Rhyenelle all along.

Faythe was almost finished her feeble meal when branches cracked ahead. The sound didn't come from the fire. Her head snapped up in a brief flash of panic, but as soon as she spotted the silver hair that illuminated in the dark against the flames, she relaxed.

Reylan's expression was still distant, and he didn't meet her eye as he approached. It dropped a horrible weight in her stomach.

"We are safe from any large beast or being within a quarter-mile radius," Izaiah announced as he threw himself down on the nearest bed roll. "At least for now."

"I'll take first watch," Reylan announced. He didn't look to anyone before he was walking away to settle at a nearby post.

A lump formed in Faythe's throat. Only she could be the cause of his obvious detached mood. She just couldn't be sure what part of the events that unfolded had disturbed him so much he couldn't even look at her.

After a long quiet moment, Livia's voice was low as she broke the silence next to her. "He was about to turn us around, you know," she said.

Faythe turned to her.

"Over two days went by, and you still didn't wake—not properly—and he almost turned our course back to Ellium. Izaiah and Reuben were the ones who convinced him to keep going, mostly out of fear of you kicking their asses. But if you didn't wake when you did, that was the last day he was prepared to simply hope you would come around without a healer. It may not have been close to the power you harnessed in High Farrow from what I've heard, but at least you had a healer there to bring you back faster and with more certainty." Livia's eyes were near white against the flames. "He didn't care what was at stake if we didn't reach the Isles."

Faythe was riddled with guilt and shame. For the turmoil she'd caused in him that seemed to extend to the rest of them as they looked to her with the same wary expressions. She opened her mouth.

"Don't say you're sorry," Kyleer said, anticipating it before she could.

She had to bite her tongue not to apologize for wanting to apologize. "Is he angry with me?" she had to ask, feeling her gut knot as she waited for the answer.

Livia answered. "No, of course not. He's just…dealing."

"It's been a long time since he allowed himself to feel anything for anyone," Kyleer explained.

Faythe swallowed hard. She had been a fool not to think it, but she supposed she wasn't a match for what he had with Farrah from the way he spoke of her with such heartache.

"He blames himself for what happened to her. He always will," Izaiah added with sorrow. "But if something happened to you—"

"I understand," Faythe whispered because it was all she could muster.

"You don't," Livia said, voice picking up a harsh edge. "You don't understand how close we were to losing him—perhaps in every way since he didn't care if he lived or died. You don't understand—"

"Liv," Kyleer cut her off softly.

"She should know," Livia powered on. "I understand your need for revenge back at the inn, but consider the lives that could be wrecked in the wake of your death before you're so reckless next time."

Faythe blinked, stunned. Then she dropped her eyes from the commander in submission. Guilt doused her into silence, and she didn't look up again though she heard Livia stand. After a still moment of hesitation, she walked away to the other side of the camp.

Faythe kept her head bowed, succumbing to tired defeat. Kyleer said softly, "You should get some sleep." As he got up, he leaned over to give her arm a comforting squeeze.

She didn't voice that sleep was the last thing on her mind after three solid days of it. Faythe took the blanket that lay beside her and folded it over herself. She lay back and watched the flames ripple and weave, tuning in to the sound of splitting timber and small bursts of fire stars. She waited until she believed enough time had passed for the others to have fallen asleep. There was no chance of finding rest, and it had nothing to do with her long slumber.

Faythe slowly propped herself up, scanning the others who all lay as still as the dead. She was as silent as a ghost rising to her feet and threw the blanket over her shoulders against the night chill as she took tentative steps through the woodland. It wasn't long before she saw him with his back to her. The moon shone bright, highlighting his silhouette as he leaned against a tree, his body outlined in silver and the side strands of his hair turned to white.

Only his head turned to the side as he heard her approach. Her heart thundered, anticipating he would cast her away as the pain of the rejection formed in her chest.

"You should be sleeping," was all he said, not turning to look at her.

"I think I've had enough of that for a while."

Reylan twisted his head to look forward again, and it made her stomach drop. Faythe was conflicted about turning back to give him the solitude he sought. But she couldn't… She couldn't turn away from him. So, she kept walking until she passed him, until she turned and was standing right in front of him, clutching the blanket around herself. His eyes fell to her, but they were distant, guarded. Like she'd often seen back in High Farrow when they were little more than strangers.

"You should get all the rest you can—"

"I'm alive," she blurted, feeling a surge of desperation. "I'm alive, and I'm here, and I'm not going anywhere." A flicker of pain made him flinch. "When are you going to acknowledge that?"

Reylan straightened from against the tree, taking a step toward her. "If I didn't acknowledge that, Faythe, believe me, this is so gods-damned far from my reaction to the alternative."

"Then why can't you even stand to look at me?" she exasperated.

Reylan studied her with a fear that chilled her to her core. Maybe it was the moonlight reflecting off his perfect face, highlighting every contour of his expression, that turned it ghostly. But the haunted look in his sapphire depths that rivaled the starry night sky—that was something deeper. It was something formed from a pain so deep-rooted it had never stopped growing.

"Because you are my biggest weakness," he began in barely more than a whisper. Faythe blinked, stunned. "But you are also my greatest strength, Faythe. I lost everything once before, and I thought that was as close to dying painfully every day as a living person could come."

"You don't have to explain—"

"Do you want to know what I saw that day in the Eternal Woods?"

Faythe's heart skipped a beat at the flash of memory, a chill seeping into her pores in the way he fixed his stare on her, an uncanny likeness to the ghostly vacancy he held that day he passed through the wood's trials in High Farrow. A look that had never erased itself from her mind.

"I was prepared to relive so many horrors, *fears*, that I knew the woods could call upon. I thought I could narrow down the worst of them and brace myself to face it. What I never could have prepared for…was seeing you."

Her breath hitched, caught in a shallow inhale.

"The woods knew before I did that you would become my greatest fear. That every broken piece of what I am would shatter completely if the vision I saw came to pass. That everything I thought I'd felt about the pain of loss would be nothing compared to losing you.

"The first day after leaving that inn, your breath was as shallow as it was in that vision. Your heart was weak. You were pale, faltering. Day two wasn't much better, but at least you were somewhat conscious enough to drink. Four hours into the third day, I was this close to turning us back, horrified I had taken you farther and farther away from any real help. Then, by the fifth hour, you took a long breath, you looked at me, awake, and I could have gone to my knees in a relief so strong it weighs on me still."

Her heart might have stopped. She felt cold, so cold, as she stared into his glittering blue irises that were so heartbreakingly vulnerable.

Fear wasn't an emotion Reylan bore so openly, but now, terror filled the eyes of the battle-hardened warrior.

Faythe took a step. Then another. Her hand released the clutch she had on the blanket to rise to his face, almost not believing he was real or that she was awake. His smooth, angled jaw tingled her fingertips when she felt him. Her other hand trailed up to his chest that moved with deep breaths under her palm. She felt the faint thump of his heartbeat.

Real. This is real.

Though it still didn't make sense. How someone so raw and fierce, so protective and beautiful, could stand before her. Could *want* her as much as she so desperately wanted him.

"You brought me back," she whispered. "You always bring me back."

Reylan shook his head. "No, Faythe." Both his palms held her face. "You brought *me* back."

Faythe couldn't help it then—she strained on her toes, and when their lips met, it was like the first time. Completeness. His forehead came down to rest on hers, and Faythe closed her eyes as she folded into his warmth. They stood like that for a long, tender moment, savoring the embrace of each other and remembering this was real.

"I know why you did it." He broke the silence. "He took a life in your name, and it was your revenge to be had. I couldn't take that from you. But please, if it means expending yourself and risking your life, let me be your sword."

Faythe had never heard him plea for anything, and it sounded so broken coming from his lips. "Yes," was all she could respond.

Reylan pulled back, vulnerability etched on his face. "I spent this whole time wanting to apologize for what you saw. For what I became when I couldn't stand the way the vile beast looked at you, *spoke* to you."

Faythe's hands gripped his leathers tighter. "And now?"

"Now, I'm not afraid to tell you I'm not sorry. That I would do it again. That I would kill every single man or fae who dares to look at you the way he did. And I would not be sorry."

Faythe's heart was erratic. But the fierce devotion in his gaze wavered with faint uncertainty as if he believed she might find horror in his confession. She couldn't give in to her want to show him how much it meant to her…when she harbored a dark confession of her own.

"You didn't kill him, Reylan," Faythe whispered. He opened his mouth to counter. "I shattered his mind seconds before you snapped his neck. I *felt* it. You didn't kill him…because I did."

Reylan's expression blanked. For once, his eyes were completely unreadable. Faythe tuned in to the hard beat that felt angrily caged in her chest, waiting for his reaction. For him to say something, anything, while he looked over her face and processed the truth.

"Why?" There was a note of disbelief in his tone. That she would take that burden.

Faythe thought for a moment. "Because you're not the monster in this story, Reylan. We're all someone's villain." His brow pinched, and a dose of treasured wisdom from a dear lost friend echoed past her lips. "It's not the act but the intention that separates the good from the evil."

His hand cupped around her nape. "Where did you come from, Faythe Ashfyre?" The question was simply an airing of his wonder as he drank every inch of her face as though searching for an answer that didn't exist.

"From the twisted depths of the Nether, most likely," she muttered lightheartedly.

Reylan angled his head down to hers. The kiss was a claim. A sense of urgency wrapped them as though the events, the realization of the fear of ever being without one another, had been made *real*. It made the need to make every moment count all the more desperate.

Faythe's fingers locked in his hair, and a soft moan escaped her when his hand traveled from her waist to cup her behind. It wasn't enough. It wasn't nearly enough. He seemed to read her thoughts, and with a low groan, he swiftly hooked his hands under her thighs, and her legs locked around his waist, weightless. Their lips moved passionately, heat slicking her skin beneath her leathers, pooling at her core. Her back met with something hard.

Pressed against the trunk of a broad tree, Reylan's hips jerked against her, scattering all care for decency or caution. She wanted him to do it again—to take all of her right here against the elements. It was a consuming need that dipped her hand between them until she felt the hard length of him straining in his pants. His hips bucked again when the heel of her palm dragged down firmly.

"Faythe…" His voice was near unrecognizable.

She wanted to return the favor from the inn. She *needed* to watch him come undone for her. But just as she went to stroke him again, he gripped her tighter.

"I can't lose control with you. Not here."

It wasn't fair. Where they were, with their companions nearby, riled a surge of frustration in her lust-hazed mind. When awareness returned to her, she was grateful he had a tighter grip on his restraint as hers was prepared to damn what anyone heard and surrender everything to him.

He pulled out of the kiss, burying his face in the crook of her neck while he held her still. He was breathless, as was she, from the short surge of consuming passion. Because no amount of time was promised.

"I wish we were alone," she whispered through a caught breath.

Reylan's faint chuckle vibrated across her neck. His hands squeezed her thighs tight, but that did nothing to help the urge she felt building.

"Me too." His lips pressed to her neck, and her head tipped back at the contact. She muttered an internal plea for the return of some control as her eyes cast up to the stars through the canopy. *"Gods*, Faythe, me too."

CHAPTER 47

Faythe

FAYTHE WORE A bright grin of amusement, chewing on a biscuit from her lazy position on a bed roll propped up against a tree trunk. As she forced herself to eat the stale breakfast, she observed Izaiah attempting to teach Reuben some basic close contact dagger maneuvers. A burst of giggles left her as she watched her human friend sprawling on his ass for the third time. He was getting better though —slightly.

Reuben peeled himself off the forest floor with a dramatic groan, dusting off leaves and dirt as he straightened. Faythe tipped her head back against the tree trunk, popping the last bite of breakfast into her mouth. She closed her eyes, enjoying the soft caress of the sun's rays that filtered through the canopy where she sat. She savored the moment, knowing it was their last day before they ventured into the mountains that had all her fae companions wary. The *Fire Mountains*, as they were titled on maps, from their history of being home to the Phoenixes. Supposedly, a few small forests ran throughout, but mostly, they would be trading soil for stone. Her internal complaints about the hard ground of the woodland they camped in seemed wasted when she had yet to sample the solid stone floor in the mountains.

It had been four days since she surfaced from her short spell of depleted energy. She'd learned they passed off her horse in Desture, so she had ridden with Reylan. The only complaint she had was that it did nothing for the growing ache she had for him to be pressed against her for hours on end. Though it seemed she wasn't the only one who was suffering.

Sliding her gaze, she found Livia and Kyleer engaged in a far more technical and impressive level of combat, but it was often interwoven with playful attack and defense. Faythe was uplifted. A part of her wanted to join in, and she had trained with them over the past few days to rebuild her strength, but right now, she was content to bathe in the sunlight.

Faythe felt him near before he crouched down beside her. She peeled her eyes open and let her head fall to the side to lock eyes with Reylan. A flutter of her heart stole her breath at the brightness on his face as he looked at her. His usual sharp and steely features were softened, his hair fell lazily around his head, and each strand shone in the sunlight. He was back from supposedly collecting firewood for the night, but she was quick to notice his arms were empty, and in straightening her head, she found no logs had been deposited anywhere around the campsite.

His smile stretched to a grin at her observation, and he extended his palm. "I want to show you something," he said, voice low as he briefly glanced at the others.

She had no doubt they could hear him, but none of their fae companions paid them any note or diverted their attention from the combat lessons they were engaged in. A giddy thrill knotted her stomach as she slipped her palms into Reylan's and he pulled her to stand in a single swift motion. His fingers interlaced with hers, so casual and *right*, as he began to lead her away from the group.

The few minutes of silence against the murmurs of the woodland further coiled in her gut as she spared a glance back, noting how far they were retreating from the others. Faythe heard the water before she saw it. Still, she remained silent, letting him take her wherever he wanted, as far as he could ever wish.

When Faythe spied the waterfall she had been expecting, her breath caught. It was massive, glittering, and mesmerizing. She stopped walking for a moment, and the strain on their joined hands made him halt too. She took a second to admire the wild crash of the waves as the falling water met the broad lake below and gawked at the shimmering veil the falling water created. Gentle mist danced along the joining of stillness and wildness. She had seen a waterfall before in High Farrow and didn't think anything could come close to matching the ethereal purity of the Eternal Woods, but this waterfall was far larger, like a thunderstorm falling from the high cliff.

"Come." Reylan gently tugged on her hand. Her eyes snapped to his, her mouth open and stunned. "That's not the best part."

Without question, she followed him, knowing it wouldn't matter if she stared in the face of beauty or horror. She would always follow him.

He guided her right up to that waterfall, the sound amplifying as the vision of water fighting water became chaos in her ears. They walked along a stone fringe that narrowed as she caught a glimpse at where it led. She saw it then: the small gap between stone and the lethal flow. He was taking her *behind* the waterfall.

The loud crashing made her wince, and her eyes narrowed to slits as they passed through the slither of darkness. Then, behind the wild storm, it opened up into a large, cavernous space containing another far smaller lake that pooled as far back as the carved-out space in the mountainside. Faythe drank in the beautiful surroundings. The water was crystal-clear, shining with iridescent ripples.

"I don't know how you thought you'd find ample firewood in a place like this," Faythe commented, sliding her eyes to him.

He grinned, so bright and *rare*, before pulling her flush to him with the hand he held. "I wasn't looking for firewood," he said. Even with the thrash of water, she detected the drop in his tone as his arm went around her. Just as her heart began to thunder, he added casually, "I thought you might appreciate a place to bathe with more privacy." Innocent, he planted a kiss to her forehead before letting her go and stepping away.

Faythe eyed the water then him. She couldn't deny she was in need of a decent bath as she'd been without one since leaving the inn over a week ago. But standing there imagining bathing in front of *him*... A wave of anxiety flushed her body and stopped her still. Reylan held no smirk, nor did he tease her over her nerves as if he knew what churned in her stomach. He began to turn around to give her the privacy he thought she desired.

"Don't," she got out, heart skipping a beat with her own command.

Reylan halted, his whole body going taut. Faythe's breathing was even but hard. So slowly, he turned his head back to lock her gaze.

"Don't stop looking at me."

The words struck something in him as he turned back to her fully. Seconds felt like minutes as they stared at each other and the air thickened. Without taking her eyes off his, Faythe's trembling fingers slowly reached the fasteners of her leather jacket. His sapphire eyes flashed to them then back to hold her own. A flare of something primal crossed them. Faythe shivered under the hold of that gaze, claimed by it.

Unhooking every buckle and button, she peeled her arms from her jacket, eyes not leaving his. Removing her boots, Faythe's hands trailed to the buttons of her pants, undoing them before stepping out and letting the cool, misty air breeze over her bare legs. She shivered, unsure if it was the faint cold or Reylan's gaze trailing down her that felt like a light feather touch. Her breasts pebbled painfully against her undergarments. Still, she didn't look away from his face even as she gripped the hem of her shirt and folded out of it in one swift, confident motion. She watched him as he watched her. His reactions may not have yielded much to anyone else, but Faythe saw him. Every slight flicker and flinch that told her he needed her as much as she needed him.

Faythe stood in nothing but dainty undergarments. Not exactly the alluring lacy set she had once teased him about in the Sloan Market of Ellium, but in the darkening of his sapphire eyes, they seemed to strike a reaction that made her whole body tighten with need. Need for *him*.

"Faythe," he said through a breath. Her name was a plea, a beg.

She didn't stop. He didn't look away. Faythe's wobbling fingers gripped the seams of her cropped undershirt, and she glided it over her head as swiftly as her shirt. She stood bare-chested mere feet away from him. His gaze dropped to her exposed breasts for just a second until he met her eyes again with a desire that danced within like a tangible midnight flame. When he didn't move, she did. Slow steps to him that he tracked right until she stood within arm's reach.

"Are you going to join me?" she asked, thinking her words might be swallowed by the thrash of the waterfall.

He heard them clearly. His throat bobbed, and carefully, his hand raised to curl around her neck while his eyes never left hers. "Are you sure?" His voice grated delightfully over her skin.

Faythe's hands snaked over his chest, across his neck, and she pressed her naked body to his powerful, leather-clad form with a desire that was all-consuming. Reylan's other hand remained by his side. "I have never been more sure of anything in my life," she answered honestly.

He remained unmoving as though he didn't believe this was what she truly wanted—that desire was clouding her judgment when that was so far from the truth. Faythe took his face in her palms, hoping that in her hold, in her eyes, he would see she wanted this. Not just with her body, but with everything she was within.

"I don't want to wait, Reylan," she all but whimpered. "Please."

Perhaps it was the scare of mere days ago, the thought of ever leaving this world and knowing she would only have one regret: that she hadn't taken the chance to be with him. Wholly and completely. That he might never get to know and *feel* how she burned for him.

Something shifted in his gaze of desire, a flicker of pain that made her believe their thoughts aligned. Faythe's hands fell to grip the folds of his leather jacket just as he took her face and crashed his lips to hers.

There was nothing slow or tender about the way they moved. This was possessive, demanding, months of desire utterly unleashed while they were blissfully alone to surrender. Faythe's hands fumbled clumsily over his jacket, and it was a bout of luck that she managed to undo it for him to slide out. Their mouths broke apart long enough for him to hoist his shirt over his head when she wasted no time untucking it from his pants, desperate to feel his bare skin against hers.

Her hands roamed his powerful chest, every sculpted contour like softened steel under her fingertips. He was built to protect, honed to defend, and she would worship every scar and imperfection that he'd lived through to be here, with her, right now. She trailed over his hard abdomen—lower—a thrill coiling in her stomach. She dragged her palm along the length of him over his pants, and a soft sound came from her when his hips jerked and a groan vibrated into her mouth. Just before she could fumble for the buttons, his hands caught her wrists.

He pulled back from her, both of them lustful, breathless. The curls of his hair that she'd thoroughly disheveled fell over his forehead, his pupils so dark they almost swallowed the sapphire. His chest heaved, but he looked at her with something far deeper than desire.

Faythe's heart hammered in her chest while she held the stare that claimed her entirely, connecting to something soul-deep. His fingers brushed slowly from her wrists, up her arms, over her neck, until he held her face.

"We should wait," he began, and Faythe's mouth immediately fell open to protest. His mouth curled in amusement before he continued. "But I've come to realize tomorrow isn't my promise to give. What I can promise…is me. Until the last tomorrow comes. I want you to know every broken piece of me belongs to you."

Faythe held the hand at her face. A wave of emotion pinched her expression, unknowing of what she'd ever done right in this life to deserve him. "You're not broken, Reylan. Not to me," she whispered, knowing he would hear her. "You should know…" Faythe's mouth dried out, a lump choking the words she tried to speak. There would be no taking them back, no coming back from bearing her whole heart to him and hoping he would protect it. She didn't doubt him, nor did she really care if he shattered it, because she'd known for a long time…she belonged to him too.

His forehead pressed to hers, and his eyes fell closed. "Say it," he breathed. A longing plea.

Her heart swelled and thrummed so hard she began to feel light-headed. One of his hands left her face to curl around her waist, her chest pressed bare to his, and nothing in this world had ever felt so electrifying and perfect.

"I was going to say I love you…" She took a short pause. Pain swelled in her chest, stealing her breath. "But it's not enough. Not for what I feel for you." Faythe shook her head, unable to voice what this was between them because it was so much *more* than that single mundane word. *Love.*

Reylan breathed a long exhale, his thumb brushing her cheekbone while she felt that pain growing in him too. "You are my heart, Faythe Ashfyre. When you lose yourself to anger, when you are consumed by passion, when you risk yourself defending… *Gods,* do I love every impossible, reckless, and fierce part of you."

Faythe released a laugh mixed with a cry. Her eyes blurred, but elation kept her tears from falling.

"And I will spend the rest of my days *showing* you when words fail

that you are everything. In this life or the next, I will always find you."
He brought his lips back to hers, a kiss-turned-claim. A claim turned
into a forging—something so deep within her rejoicing as their souls
entwined with every movement they made.

Reylan didn't stop her when she went for the buttons of his pants
this time. Her core had heated so desperately for him she was clumsy in
her work. When every button and tie was finally loose, she dipped her
hand to feel him. A gasp left her as Reylan growled low, hips jerking into
her touch with a force that made her blanch with a wild thrill. His lips
left hers to plant over her neck, his hands cupped her behind, and
Faythe's breathing was so uneven she began to feel dizzy between the
shortness of air and her high of lust.

For a second, her mouth dried at the size of him. She wondered if
he would even fit her. A blush creeped along her cheeks, and she must
have stilled as Reylan immediately pulled back, taking her stiffness as a
hesitation.

"Are you okay?" he asked, ready to defuse the tension completely if
that was what she wished.

Faythe swallowed hard. "It's been a while since I... I mean, I haven't
been with..." She didn't know what sentence she was trying to form
exactly. Something to explain her lack of experience as she suddenly
came to the realization it was nothing compared to what he would know
from his four centuries. She had been with a few men before, but never
anyone who *mattered*. And above all, she never imagined she'd fall so
deeply in love with a fae. Reylan was powerful, immortal, and she...

Reylan searched her eyes, the assessing look he always wore when he
needed answers that were too difficult for her to voice. And just like
every other time, he seemed to know exactly what she was thinking.

His lips brushed hers. "I can assure you,"—he kissed her jaw—
"nothing matters but you and me. No past. Just now." That feather
touch of his grazing lips was the sweetest torture down her neck. "And
nothing has *ever* driven me as insane as you do, Faythe Ashfyre." His

mouth opened and closed around her neck, his elongated canines scraping there, and a shallow cry left her. "I plan to worship every inch of you. Again and again, until you believe it. My love and desire for you knows no limits."

Her knees were close to giving out, but his large, calloused hands gripped her waist tighter. A rumble left his throat to travel over her bare skin. Faythe let go of all reservations then, her hands finding their way back to below his pants of their own accord. She palmed the length of him, and without thinking, Faythe took control. Her head angled and dipped, lips meeting his chest and trailing downward. Her fingers gripped the waistband of his pants, and she tugged them down with her.

"Faythe." Her name was a sinful plea from his mouth. He didn't stop her as she kissed down past his navel and dropped to her knees. Their discarded items of clothing cushioned the hard stone, and Reylan stood gloriously bare before her. He was powerful, beautiful, and she planned to show him just how blazing her desire for him ran.

Faythe cast her eyes up to his, and they were wide and feral as he watched her. She took the length of him in her palm, fingers barely meeting. Her lips wrapped around him, and even with her human hearing, Reylan's hiss folded into a groan, a melody to her ears over the waves. His fingers gently pushed into her braids while his hips jerked, as if he were being careful not to hurt her. But Faythe was beyond wanting to be gentle. She took him in her mouth while working her hand in tandem, relishing in the sounds it brought from him and the ones she knew he was holding back. She had to refrain from reaching down to touch herself to relieve the building ache between her legs as she imagined him fully unleashed.

Before she could drive him to the brink, he pulled away.

Faythe didn't get the chance to complain that she was far from done when he too fell to his knees, one arm hooking around her waist. A breath of surprise left her at the quick, weightless maneuver that had her lying on her back over their fallen clothes. Reylan's fingers dipped under the last piece of material she wore, swiftly peeling away her underwear until they were both completely bare in the cool, misty air. He was wild and free, and she loved every part of this side of him. Loved every wicked, brilliant, fierce thing about the warrior above her.

Reylan kissed down her body, taking each of her breasts in his mouth with a slight graze of those torturous canines, emitting unchecked sounds from her. Lower, over her navel. Slow, as though he left each trail of his mouth so she could understand his intentions and have a chance to object. She said nothing. Her hips undulated of their own accord. She wanted this—all of this.

"Ever since I felt you," he groaned, seeming to drink in the scent of her, "I've wondered if you would taste as sweet as you sounded finding that release by my hand."

Dear Gods. His words, the deep gravel in which he spoke them, were felt as pressure against the nerves at her core. Then his mouth was *there.* A loud moan left her as her back arched into the first contact that exploded stars beneath her closed lids. To the world and beyond, any noise she made was swallowed by the tantrum of water. Reylan heard her though and turned ravenous, one arm folded over her stomach to stop her from writhing. His other hand met his mouth, and he slipped one finger into her before quickly adding another.

Faythe forgot where they were. Forgot time, worry, fear. Every sense of grounded humanity left her as his hand and mouth worked her so precisely, sending her to new heights of bliss she had never experienced before. Never thought *possible* before. Right toward that end point she didn't want to reach without him this time.

"Reylan," she rasped sharply.

Immediately, he interpreted it as a plea to stop rather than a coax to push on. Their eyes locked, and she almost came apart at the sight of him there between her legs, utterly surrendering to anything she would want or need. Whatever he read on her face made Reylan trail his lips back up her body until he was close enough her fingers fisted in his silken silver locks and she pulled his face to hers.

The kiss was explosive. Faythe tasted herself on him and loved every second of it. She felt the tip of him between her thighs, the ache of emptiness almost becoming painful.

"Please."

Reylan pulled back to lock eyes with her. Sapphire blazed into gold, fusing and forging, both breathless with insatiable desire. His hand reached between them to position himself at her entrance.

Faythe's breathing was hard, and a sharp inhale curved her spine at the first feel of him inching into her. He took it slow despite the burning need that made her want to plea for him all at once even though she knew the pain it would cause. She breathed slow and steady to adjust to him, and he trembled with restraint, arms braced above her. Faythe's eyes shut at the tightening pinch that grew but quickly soothed into the sweetest pleasure.

"Don't stop looking at me, Faythe."

It was a command, a plea she could never deny. Her eyes opened to hold his as he moved slow, both of them silent, sharing breath, and consumed by the feelings that burned in the joining of their bodies until he filled her completely.

"You were made for me." Reylan glanced down between them, watching where he pulled back and entered her anew with the release of a harsh breath that scattered down her stomach. Faythe whimpered in bliss. "*Gods,* you feel incredible."

His essence was a warmth within that entwined with hers as he began to move, slow and steady, until a rhythm built between them, their own perfect harmony that soon made their desire unchecked. Nothing had ever felt so right, and she knew nothing would ever compare to this. To them. Together without a single boundary or reservation. She wasn't an heir to anything; she wasn't fated to kingdoms or Spirits; all she was in that moment…was his. What they shared wasn't just lust or passion. It was power answering to power, his ability singing to hers, and she knew this feeling could never be matched by any other in the world.

Reylan hooked a hand under her thigh, lifting her to bury himself deeper, and Faythe's head fell back at the new angle. His mouth met her throat, the vibrations from his groans tingling over her chest, and she could have cried from the pleasure combined with his wild thrusts.

Faythe kept climbing that impossible height of bliss, thinking there might be no end, no limit, to what he could give her. She would never want anything as much as she wanted him. Pleasure rocked through every internal piece of her. His skin against hers trembled and awakened every nerve ending.

When his lips met hers, something between a moan and cry left her, mixing with the low vibration of something utterly primal and possessive that answered from his throat. Her hands roamed his sweat-slicked skin, heated as much as her own. Faythe savored every flex of his contoured body as it moved against her. Every raised imperfection of his battle-scarred form that she loved. Against the angled contours of his back, her nails dug into his skin and only seemed to heighten his pleasure, so unchecked now as he claimed her to her very bones. His hips slammed harder; his angle turned deeper.

She didn't know what she expected, but this was far more than her imagination could have conjured. Before, perhaps gentle would have sounded romantic, tender, but now he gave her everything she didn't know she craved. It was wild and free. It was so many days, weeks, months spent in longing released all at once.

"I can't," she breathed, not having any words to follow, only knowing that her end was so near.

Reylan's mouth was on her throat as he said, "Let go, Faythe." His mouth opened and his canines dragged along her collar. *Gods,* she wanted him to bite. The sharpness pinched harder than before as he fought with restraint, against his primal fae instinct to mark and claim.

It was utterly maddening, and that slight pain against pleasure shattered the stars. She forgot everything but his name as she cried it out while her release surged through her like the forming of a galaxy. Colors, stars, darkness—it exploded like a blissful end and a new beginning behind her eyes, which clamped shut as her body bowed off the ground.

Reylan went with her, one arm locked under her arched back as he weathered it. After a few final, powerful thrusts, he jerked and stilled as his own end barreled through him. She might have heard her name, but it was drowned out by the roars and crashes she couldn't be certain came from him, her, or the thrashing of water. His forehead pressed into the crook of her neck while his release shuddered through him— through *them*.

Seconds that could have been minutes that could have been hours passed in her moment of suspended ecstasy.

Reylan's arm slipped from under her as she fell back to lie flush against the ground, breathless and spent. He was panting and unmoving too as she as he lay over her. Their skin was flush, but he bore no weight on her. Faythe's fingers slid into his hair as she caught her breath, idly caressing the silken strands of silver while they both came down from their glorious, earth-shattering high.

"That was…" He trailed off in a short breath that blew across her sweat-slicked chest. She shuddered.

"Yes," was all she said, neither making coherent sense but somehow knowing exactly what they meant. Nothing could ever compare to what burned between them. At least, it couldn't for her.

Reylan shifted to lean on his forearm while looking over her. His fingers brushed a few strands of her hair that had matted around her face. "You are my Phoenix, Faythe." She couldn't be sure what he meant by it, but the adoration quieting his words surged her with strength. Then his tone dropped to a husky murmur. "This is only the beginning of what I plan to do with you."

She shivered in utter bliss. Her cheeks warmed as his fingers trailed over her jaw while he partially hovered above her. Over her neck and shoulder, down the curve of her side, stifling her breaths.

"You have never once let this body slow you down or stop you from trying. Never saw being human as a weakness when you were forced to live among fae who tried to see you as inferior." Those torturous, godly fingers began to trace the same path, tingling over every inch of her skin. "From that first day I met you, I saw the determination in your eyes when you dared to speak up for yourself against a *king*. I saw the courage on your face when you dared to pull a knife against *me.*"

A nervous chuckle left her, and Reylan grinned. It was a sight so precious, without title or burden. In this cave, Reylan was simply a fae, and she simply a human, and all that mattered was their love for one another.

His thumb traced her bottom lip. *"Gods,* I wanted you then, from that moment, as twisted as it may sound. I hated you for it, but I hated myself more. Only because I knew…you were everything I would never deserve. Everything that felt so right but seemed so wrong."

Her heart swelled, her eyes burned, and she wondered if it was possible to love someone so hard the pain was absolution.

"I realize now that *I* was wrong. Wrong to ever deny that you were meant to be mine, and I yours."

For a long time, Faythe thought she would never find where she truly belonged. In High Farrow, in Rhyenelle, in anywhere else on the map of Ungardia and beyond—never did she believe she would find it. *Feel it.* Now she knew why. It was not in any one place where she would be bound by duty over heart. It was by his side. No matter where they traveled or settled, if the kingdoms fell and the world burned to ash, by Reylan's side she would always belong, and she'd never expected to find her true home in a fae so raw and fierce.

A wave of emotion pushed out a single tear that fell to her ear. "You saw me. As more than just a twisted existence. And I saw *you,* Reylan. I saw that you deserved everything you thought you didn't." Her fingers traced over the marks on his bare chest, a painful lump of emotion constricting her words, reducing them to a whisper. "Everything and so much more."

A sadness swept her for the pain he had endured throughout the centuries and the torment he'd lived daily for a wicked past. She knew she would spend every day of her existence making him believe he deserved to be *loved*.

"I would have endured it all again." Reylan kissed where her feelings had spilled over. "For centuries over if it led me to you, Faythe." Then he kissed her mouth, the salt of her tears on his lips. His pain and hers. His joy and hers.

Despite where they were, she couldn't have imagined the moment to have been more perfect. But as she lay on their discarded clothes, and with the hardness of the ground returning her to her senses, her only wish was that they were in bed with enough space for him to settle beside her and lie there in the aftermath for blissful eternity.

Reylan seemed to realize the luxury they were lacking too. With a final kiss planted on her collarbone, he pulled away from her. In straightening, he took her hands, pulling her upward with him until she straddled his lap. A wave of dizziness would have had her collapsing right back if he didn't hold her to him. It shouldn't be possible, but as their bare skin drew flush, her desire sparked a shallow fire once again despite her exhaustion. In the darkening of his eyes and the *feel* of him beneath her, she knew she wasn't alone.

"How about that bath?" he said in a low, husky tone.

A giggle escaped her and turned to laugh that called on her want to rest. Her arms circled around his neck; her cheek met with his shoulder. Reylan stood, taking her with him. It almost felt like flying above clouds while her body felt warm and floaty inside. Faythe inhaled sharply, feeling the cool water lap around her legs and backside as Reylan walked into the pool from the shallow end.

Faythe was carried—by him, by water. She didn't release him, and he seemed in no hurry to unhook his powerful arms from her either. She kind of wanted to sleep and even felt her eyes flutter closed as her head lay against his chest. His hand smoothed over her hair, trailing down the length of her spine. Then a thought snapped her eyes open, and she peeled her head back.

"We didn't plan for this," she said, her face heated as she added to his look of confusion. "I have no contraceptive tonic."

Reylan's brow raised, but he was otherwise unconcerned.

Faythe's mouth popped open, about to ramble the obvious that this was not the time to consider bringing a *child* into the world. Even if it was highly rare, with him being fae and her mostly human, there was still a chance. She was living proof. Faythe's body heated at the thought. They were reckless not to have considered the consequences.

Oh Gods, does he even want children?

His rumbling laughter cut through her sprinting thoughts, and she stared at him, incredulous. When his chuckles ceased, his smile was still bright. "Liv knows of a tonic that can be made with plants found around these forests. She used to help females in the war camps who didn't have access to the towns regularly to buy it," he said, amusement still twinkling in his sapphire eyes at her flustered look. "I wouldn't have risked it without you having that choice, Faythe."

Choice. The way he said it almost made her believe he wouldn't object to her not taking the contraceptive. It coiled in her stomach, a new longing at the thought. It was far from her desire right now. With so much war and uncertainty surrounding her, she couldn't stand the thought of bringing a soul into the world before it was righted. But the thought, staring into the sapphires that had become her orbit…gave her hope.

She wanted to *live*—for him, and for the future they could have.

CHAPTER 48

Zaiana

THEY TRACKED FAYTHE and her companions for days after catching up to Tynan and Amaya. For the first few days, Zaiana almost believed their quest would be over when the human wouldn't surface from unconsciousness. She didn't tell anyone of the plan that swirled in her mind by the third day of watching Faythe ride limply against the silver-haired warrior who grew so distraught with each passing hour. If Faythe hadn't come around when she did, Zaiana might have let Nerida go to aid the human like she had pleaded to do so many times it had become an irritating whine.

After all, Faythe was no use to any of them dead. It would have spelled her failure. Still, Zaiana didn't let her immense relief show when the human finally took a conscious breath and opened her damn eyes.

Since then, the dark fae had hunted from far enough away that she was sure they couldn't detect them while they continued their journey to the Fire Mountains.

Zaiana perched on a high cliff, spying through the canopy as the close ensemble below seemed to be sparring casually for *fun*. She found a lot of their actions and interactions odd and intriguing. It passed her otherwise dull days to watch them engage. Their friendship she dared to believe was true and genuine—something she rarely saw in any of the towns around the Mortus Mountains where she would venture.

"Should we follow them?" Tynan asked from behind, dragging her from her wandering thoughts.

Flicking her eyes to who he meant, she saw the silver-haired warrior leading Faythe away from the others. Her eyes locked on their joined hands, and her head tilted curiously. Zaiana had noted their closeness before. It was clear the fae was highly protective and near possessive of Faythe. His concern when she'd fallen for days was far deeper than the others' despite their endless fuss over her. Now it was clear why. If she'd been told a powerful fae warrior had fallen for a feeble—albeit perhaps equally powerful—*human*...she would have mocked the notion. Yet not a single doubt arose in her mind about his intentions at seeing them together. She almost felt it in her chest as something akin to awe, their unspoken devotion to each other as though they didn't care what the world would think of such an impossible pairing.

Zaiana shook her head in answer to Tynan. "They won't go far alone." She would let them have their privacy knowing the human's days were numbered. It tightened a strange sensation in her gut to think of it. She shouldn't care, but it was becoming exhausting in her own mind to deny she did. Faythe had people who would mourn her. She had a place in the world as the Heir of Rhyenelle. Her life held meaning.

Zaiana couldn't be sure when or why her tormenting thoughts had somehow bounced back to her observations of the human's life to compare it to her own. To acknowledge how pitiful her existence really was. She was but a soldier in this life. From the day she was born until the day she would fade on. It was a suffocating realization that it was all she would be. Her position, her life, was a replaceable one. The masters never let her forget that.

Her eyes cast back to the lessons the fae were engaged in. They were laughing, fooling around, and it was something she found oddly refreshing to see when combat under the mountains reserved no room for such mockery of the skill.

Every now and then, the fae with longer dark hair stopped to scan his surroundings, even the skies. The first time she watched his alert, her body had stiffened and she'd almost darted farther out of range, but she had come to decide it was habit for him and that he would have spotted her by now if her position were a risk. She couldn't be sure why, but he intrigued her, and she found her eyes fixed on him—the way he moved, the way he taught combat. Zaiana thought it highly *inspiring*.

"If I didn't know you any better, I'd say you look mildly impressed," Maverick said as he joined her. Unlike the others, who left her to have the space her detached demeanor requested, the annoying bastard decided to settle down beside her on the cliff edge.

"Hardly," she mumbled, not in the mood for idle chat. "But we shouldn't underestimate any of them."

Maverick reclined back on his hands. "I'm not concerned about any of them. Not with what we have."

She had to agree. The fae below stood little chance against them despite their highly skilled and lethal warriors. When it came to a fight, Zaiana wasn't concerned about losing, but a part of her—a part she would never admit to anyone—really hoped it didn't have to come to one. It was a fool's hope, and what they had to do might very well require killing them all to get to Faythe. Zaiana had been in turmoil for days, constantly needing to cast out any regard for the lives below. They were simply collateral in war. Nothing more.

"So, we confront them—then what? Ask kindly for the human?"

Zaiana pondered for a moment, eyes scanning over the fae then over to where Faythe and the silver-haired one had disappeared from view.

She thought out loud, "We need to separate her from her Mindseer." Zaiana could feel Maverick's eyes on her. "They're powerful together. I need her to either submit to the power she demonstrated she has no discipline or strength to hold or refuse to take it. If he's with her, she may be able to harness it by sharing it between them." It had struck her with awe to witness the way his ability brought Faythe back when her heightened power should have consumed her without the proper restraint and control.

"You fear that if they do, they might prove to be an equal opponent."

"Yes," she admitted. "I'm not such an arrogant fool to think otherwise."

Maverick took a long breath. "In your height of power, Zaiana, you are quite the force to be reckoned with. One I don't think the world is ready for."

He wasn't referring to the ability she had used during their battle. This was more than that. It was the darkest, most dangerous part of what she was capable of. A monster sealed away inside her that she hoped never to use. Yet she'd been suffering the humming in her veins since leaving the mountains as if in preparation for when her hand would be forced.

"Perhaps. But I don't think I'm the *only* force to be reckoned with in this war."

CHAPTER 49

Faythe

T HEY TRADED IN the horses for far less coin than they were worth in the final small town near the edge of the Fire Mountains. It didn't matter—they wouldn't need currency where they were headed and had spent what little they brought making sure food, wears, and provisions were well-stocked for their weeklong journey through the mountains, over to the Isles, and then on their return trip.

Having preparations to make it back gave Faythe slight determination to make it so, but even she could tell everyone had dropped in spirits and uncertainty coated the air between them all. She looked up at the dauntingly tall mountain range that seemed to stretch on for far longer than they could possibly cross in the timeframe the fae had calculated. They planned to use a tunnel route rather than climb and risk the unforgiving terrain of peaks and fringes. The stone of which they were made was a dark gray, but toward their peaks, before some that disappeared beyond the cloud cover, they glistened a faint crimson red.

Faythe had seen the mesmerizing, unusual color before over the mountains surrounding Ellium.

"Fyrestone." Reylan answered her thoughts, his hand falling on her back as he returned from scouting the area with Kyleer. They wanted to be certain they weren't being followed and that there were no creatures lurking that could catch them by surprise. "They say it's forged in Phoenixfyre, which is what gives it its color."

Faythe eyed the sparkling stone in the distance with awe. "Does it have any special properties?"

"Mostly it's just mined for weapons or wears." Reylan twisted Faythe to pull her to him. His face was pinched in a worry that splintered her chest. "There is a reason no one ventures these mountains anymore. They say since the time of the Firebird, the mountains have been cursed. Believe me, I would pass it off as superstitious nonsense faster than anyone, except no one has made it through them and returned in a very long time." A hand went to her face, and Reylan spoke to her mind while the others were in earshot. *"I have every intention of seeing us return and fulfilling my promise to you. Many times."*

A shiver of desire crawled up her spine, and perhaps her scent shifted to tell him how much she wanted it as his arm tightened around her.

"I hate to break up a moment and all, but if we don't get moving it will be nightfall before we even reach the cave entrance," Izaiah called, and the distance of his voice made her realize the others had already begun to make their way into the mountains.

Faythe giggled, and Reylan pressed one firm kiss to her lips before releasing her. As they began to walk, their hands brushed, and her palm slipped effortlessly into his. It wasn't a conscious effort, and not something the others had even once speculated about.

Upon returning from the waterfall cave, no one said anything to them directly, but they didn't have to. Izaiah was a master of indirect comments, and Livia was his cunning accomplice. Kyleer found easy entertainment in it all but refrained from joining in with the not-so-subtle jesting. She supposed they would have scented exactly what happened between her and Reylan or assumed it from the long hours they'd spent in the waters, especially after he took her again. Twice. Faythe didn't feel even mildly embarrassed and certainly not regretful. Not with every uncertainty they were to face. Time, days, were too precious; she wouldn't waste them not seeking what was in her heart.

Stepping into the fold of the mountain range blocked the sun out entirely, and they were swallowed by shadow. It was still light enough to see clearly, but an eerie gloom settled in place of the bright summer sky they had walked under just seconds ago. Faythe subconsciously gripped Reylan's hand a little tighter, not releasing until she felt a soothing caress on her senses within. She responded with internal gratitude.

"There is only one moral that will see us through to the other side," Izaiah chirped up from the front.

"And what, dare I ask, is that?" Livia questioned.

"That we remember, no matter what, to always have Faythe." He turned to her with a beaming grin and shot a playful wink. It lifted her skittish mood, and she shook her head with a loose laugh.

"To live as if death is a game," Kyleer joined in lightheartedly.

"Love is a prize," Livia continued.

"And danger is desire," Izaiah finished.

They all shared in the laughter, partly at the ridiculousness of such a meaning, but also out of determination. Because regardless, it was exactly what they needed to see them home. Feeling lighter, Faythe looked through the mountain passage, cast her eyes to the impossible heights of their peaks, and muttered a silent prayer to Aurialis that they make it through alive—and together.

They arrived at the mouth of the cave her fae companions had been following a map toward just as the sun waved its last farewell. They decided they would camp outside for the night and gather as many provisions as they could find in the sparse foliage and otherwise barren landscape to keep the torches going inside. Despite their unique array of combined abilities, it would have been highly advantageous if one of them were a Firewielder. Then they could create an eternal flame so they wouldn't have to worry about dying.

Reylan had extended his ability in any towns they'd stopped by in the hope he'd come across one and borrow some of their power, even for at least half the journey, before he would have to let it go or risk burning himself out. Of course, they had been unlucky. Man-made fire was their only option.

Faythe sat cross-legged on a bed roll by the center fire they'd built, warming herself against the night chill. She couldn't help staring into the dark, depthless cave mouth they would enter tomorrow. A creeping chill that had nothing to do with the drop in temperature rose the hairs over her body. She shivered, her mind running wild at the thought of the confined space.

Faythe always avoided places that held the possibility of trapping her. Even when she was young, in a game of hide-and-seek, Faythe would always win by silently tracking the seeker rather than hiding until they gave up searching. Jakon was quick to catch onto her methods, but others were hilarious to watch attempting to find her while she stalked them.

The idea of being underground with no sure way out and no measure of time without the rise and fall of the sun... Faythe didn't realize the panic she was spiraling into with her eyes fixed on the cave entrance until someone loudly threw themselves down next to her.

"The tunnels have been mapped out by various travelers. There are several ways through, and we are confident in the route we've chosen." Kyleer spoke to her fears. How he knew what she worried over she couldn't be sure. He placed various sticks he'd gathered in front of him, along with some other foliage and cotton-looking material. Faythe watched as he began his work, and she deduced he was assembling some form of torch.

"I thought no one makes it out of these mountains alive," she countered. A little grim, but it was what they implied.

Kyleer chuckled lightly, beginning to wrap and roll expertly. "We didn't say *no one*, but not many do." He slid her a teasing look. "Don't look so horrified, Faythe. Do you really think we would have risked it if we didn't hold confident odds?"

"Or we're counting on simply being the luckiest bastards alive," Izaiah chimed in from across the fire.

"Everything has seemed ordinary," Faythe observed. "What exactly is so grim about these mountains?" She couldn't help but think there was nothing except beauty and intrigue so far with the glistening red peaks and calm fringes.

"Since the time of the Firebirds, after what happened here, it's said the mountains are cursed. That bodies of the damned who tried to slaughter the Phoenix birds haunt in gruesome forms known as Skailies." Kyleer shuddered. Actually *shuddered*. She had never seen him express an ounce of fear before. "Faceless corpses."

A chill settled in her bones, and Faythe subconsciously scanned around them. Izaiah chuckled, which spiked her heart rate as she became skittish at the grim tale.

"Our poor Faythe is bound to have nightmares now," he teased. When his eyes locked on her over the licks of flame, his smile turned feline. "Out here, Reylan won't be able to—"

"Finish that sentence," the general warned, and Faythe's eyes trailed up to where he'd returned with Livia from scouting the perimeter, "and Skailies will be the least of your worries."

Faythe met eyes with Izaiah, whose face fell as he muttered a disgruntled response. She refrained from childishly sticking her tongue out at him despite the heat that rose to her cheeks. Glancing behind Reylan and Livia, she quickly noticed, "Where's Reuben?"

Reylan settled down beside her, close enough their thighs grazed. "Nature's call, as he announced."

Faythe chuckled. They wouldn't know it was the way he had referred to his bathroom breaks since he was a child.

Izaiah began to pass around some bread and cold cuts they had picked up at the last town as he said, "If we're all to die out here—"

"Seriously?" Livia cut in with a dead look.

He dismissed her with a lazy smile. "I would simply like to know, if you got the chance, what would your famous last words be?"

Faythe smiled too, thinking it a fun game to take her mind off the dark night and discovery of the possible ghoulish threats that could be lurking around them.

Kyleer obliged. "Please, Gods above, make Izaiah mute in the next life."

Chuckles were exchanged around the circle, amplifying at his brother's short scowl.

Livia said, "If I fall today, I will rise stronger tomorrow."

"You won't be rising if you're dead," Izaiah countered.

She smirked. "I believe there are far more lives for us to live than this one."

He gave a fair, one-shouldered shrug. "Perhaps."

Shuffling snapped their attention to where Reuben's form emerged into the glow cast by the firelight. As he settled down and helped himself to the rations, Izaiah asked, "Famous last words, Reu—what'll it be?"

Reuben winced, but she wasn't sure what could have caused the disturbance from what Izaiah asked. She thought the short nickname somewhat heartwarming, a sign they were not only accepting of his presence, but they were beginning to welcome and include him.

Her friend took a long breath, seeming to contemplate. Then he settled on, "I don't mourn the time I'll miss; I rejoice in the time I had."

Kyleer whistled low. "This is getting deep. Can I amend my words?"

"Nope. They're last words for a reason, and you wasted them. There are countless other ways I can torment you without speech, brother," Izaiah said, and they shared a knowing chuckle.

Faythe sat silently on her words the whole time, perhaps because she didn't want to acknowledge she'd thought of them before.

"Come on, General—give us them." Izaiah continued around the circle as he lazily reclined back.

Reylan shifted, pushing an arm around Faythe's back to subtly draw her closer. "I plan to go out with a blade in my hands and hardly time for such a thought," he said casually.

Faythe knew he was lying straight away and turned her head to him. When his sapphire eyes met hers, they held a warmth latticed with a string of pain as if he'd thought of his last words before too.

"My last breath would be yours," she heard his truth. *"To make sure you knew…I will always find you."*

The wave of emotion that lapped her made it a struggle to maintain her outward composure.

Izaiah scoffed. "Oh, I see how it is. Internal conversation is rather selfish in company, you know."

Faythe turned her eyes to the flames. She wasn't afraid to voice her final words to the group. She took a deep breath. "My last words would be thank you. To the family I found who shaped me into who I am." She spared a look at each of them, letting them know she was referring to all of them as well as Jakon, Marlowe, Nik, and Tauria whom she'd left back in High Farrow. She couldn't meet his eye as she added to Reylan's thoughts, *"And thank you. Because I never knew how lost I was until you found me."*

His hand at her hip gave a gentle squeeze, and she leaned sideward into his casual embrace.

By dawn, everyone awoke and packed swiftly, not wanting to be outside on the mountaintops for longer than necessary. The tunnels would be quicker, and with the knowledge of her companions whom she had no choice but to trust, they would be safe from the creatures they would otherwise encounter if they went over the mountains. That, and the climbing and uncertain terrain would make for a perilous trek. As much as it daunted Faythe to be walking willingly into confinement where she knew of no sure exit, the alternative wasn't much more inviting.

Torches lit and provisions secured, Faythe's heart pounded with her first steps into the mouth of the cave. But she walked alone, forcing confidence to curve her spine and press her feet forward. She couldn't afford to be cowardly. Reylan was close by, his presence a safety net that subdued her fear just enough to see her through to the other side.

CHAPTER 50

Zaiana

FOR HOURS THEY followed Faythe and her companions. The dark fae were alert, each of them focused on covering every inch of the surrounding areas while Zaiana honed her focus to detect where the fae moved below. Extending her senses to reach so far underground took every drop of her attention, and she heard nothing but the faint motion below her feet, saw nothing except the upturning gravel under her boots, her eyes boring holes through the ground as if she could picture the six bodies below.

Zaiana had been forced to take the more perilous exposed route out in the open. It wasn't the often deadly terrain and steep ledges they had to climb that set the dark fae on edge; it was the fact they were not the only monsters lurking in these mountains. She knew of the legends, the cursed *Skailies* that showed up in even the wicked's nighttime horror stories, faceless cursed foes that devoured anything in their path. Yet even if she'd had a choice, Zaiana may well have chosen this path rather than underground confinement. She would never choose something that could enclose her.

"I take it they are still in high spirits and joined at the hip," Maverick drawled.

Zaiana jerked, unaware of his close proximity after spending so long in focused silence. She scowled at him from the fright. "For now."

Maverick groaned. "It's insufferable."

Her lips upturned. "Of course, you only delight in suffering and wretched things."

He smirked. "I only delight in dark and beautiful things."

Zaiana halted, finding Maverick far closer than she detected seconds ago as his voice dropped low. His smile was wickedly enticing. "Maverick Blackfair." She matched his sultry tone, and for a second there was a sparkle in his onyx orbs. Her face fell straight. "Come within a foot of me again, and the creatures of these mountains will be the last thing you fear."

He didn't balk; in fact, he delighted in the threat. Zaiana opened her mouth, but something stole her string of profanities. She glanced back at the ground she had studied over the hours, focusing every one of her senses once more until she confirmed what she suspected. Their window of opportunity had been granted. A devious smile spread across her cheeks.

Glancing up, she met eyes with Maverick, who seemed to detect what she saw as the mouse played his part down below. He matched her dark triumph. The others scattered around, and she glanced over at them as her lightning pricked her skin. She knew what she had to do.

Her vibrant bolts snapped across the guards on her fingers. She dove into her well carefully, collecting and building for the strike that would shake the mountain. Magick coursed through her veins, a fire that took every ounce of her control not to be consumed by as she harnessed far more than nature gave her at birth.

She had collected enough to address them all. "Maverick and I will follow Faythe."

Tynan's mouth opened with a swift protest, but her pinned glare warned against it.

"As my second-in-command, I trust you in leadership to guide the others through the only other route underground. By the time you catch up, we will have already captured her. But should they turn out to be swifter and more cunning than we predicted, I don't care what it takes for you to keep them back."

"What do you plan to do with her?" Nerida's voice was horror-filled and familiar, but Zaiana had no room to feel pity.

"Don't ask what you're not willing to accept the answer to," was all she responded, casting her gaze away to avoid the irritating drop she couldn't suppress at witnessing Nerida's weak heart.

Amaya's gaze was mildly disturbed but hard in determination and understanding. Tynan gave a nod of obedience, and then they were all stepping back, seeking distance from the impact of what she was about to unleash.

She didn't know why her eyes found Maverick, who looked to her with a dark hunger that caressed her spine as she tamed and honed her magick. There was life in his cold eyes as he smiled. His hands slid into his pockets, and he took long backward strides from her as he said with delight, "Make it storm, Zaiana."

CHAPTER 51

Faythe

I ZAIAH ENSURED THE first few hours went by without much peace. Faythe welcomed the distraction no matter what teasing or wild thoughts came from his mouth. He even managed to force laughter from her tense body on occasion.

Until silence settled.

Faythe believed the constant darkness would play with all their minds, tiring them out before the sun was likely to even set. Having no concept of time of day was what panicked Faythe the most. Either her companions were masterful at subduing their emotions or she was far more irrational than she believed. So far, there was no reason for her to be so on edge as their travel through the passages had gone as smoothly and without surprise as she could have hoped. With that thought, she felt her shoulders begin to loosen and let herself walk with more distance from Reylan so she wouldn't seem like a clingy child.

After a long while, she couldn't be sure how many hours had passed. She walked by Kyleer's side ahead of the others. He had been telling her of the winters in Ellium, specifically the annual carnival that came to the capital city, and it sounded truly wondrous. Even though she knew his idle chat was only in distraction, she was grateful that it worked.

She didn't hear when the others stopped, and she and Kyleer walked a good few meters ahead. Turning back, she found them lingering at a fork in the path where Reuben was crouched and sifting through his pack. She couldn't be sure what he was searching for as Reylan dipped his torch down to see better. Her friend was muttering something, and Izaiah was rattling off comments, likely not of any help.

"Listen," Livia hissed with an edge of trepidation that silenced everyone.

Instantly, all the fae were on high alert, each positioning to grab various weapons. Faythe braced and strained her hearing in an attempt to discover what they had picked up on. The fae exchanged furrowed looks of confusion, scanning down the passages.

Faythe heard it then. A faint rumble, like colliding stone or distant thunder. She slid her glance to Reylan, and the widening of his sapphire eyes was the last thing she saw before an arm hooked around her middle, winding her as she was yanked backward by a tall, muscular force. The movement barely had time to register in her mind when that faint rumble became a deafening blow that blasted through her ears. She fell to the hard stone ground, cushioned slightly by flesh.

It happened so quickly but seemed to last for so long. The vibrations were felt under her body. Rocks rolled past her. The clash of stone against stone boomed like thunder and echoed through the passage to channel back and ring in her mind repeatedly. Something shielded her from the loose debris flying past. She managed to twist enough to know it was Kyleer crouching over her, his teeth clenched as he took the impact of falling rocks.

Faythe's heart pounded like the stones, wild and frantic. Then everything seemed to still. A high-pitched ringing replaced the sound of boulders, dust clogged the air, and she coughed to clear her throat. Kyleer groaned and finally fell away from her. It snapped her straight back to her senses after being blindsided, and she shot to her knees, looking over at him.

"I'm okay," he rasped with a strain that told her he was far from it.

She glanced back at their companions, and horror threatened to undo her completely. She couldn't see any of them. Reylan, who she'd been staring at seconds ago, was replaced by a wall of fallen rocks.

"I'll get help," she said breathlessly from the sheer panic that gripped her.

Kyleer muttered something back that was partially a groan, but she didn't hear him. Stumbling to her feet, Faythe took the few short strides to the avalanche of rocks and began to fumble clumsily over the loose slope, tripping and sliding as she tried frantically to get closer. When she was met with the wall of fallen boulders, she began to claw at the sharp, jagged rocks. A few came loose, and she tossed them out the way— small, feeble rocks that did nothing to make a significant indent in the thick stone wall. It was all she could pry loose. Her heart was racing, breathing hard, and she thought she could hear voices above the clash of stone as she clawed and clawed, beginning to imagine she was making some progress. She couldn't stop, desperate to get to them and desperate not to be trapped.

"I'll get help," she kept repeating as if it would spur her determination to make it through. *I'll get help. I'll get help. I'll get help.*

Hands wrapped over her upper arms, stopping her from reaching to grapple another rock. Faythe cried out as she was physically restrained from her digging. *I'll get help.* She thrashed to get free.

"Stop, Faythe." Kyleer. He held her tightly to his chest. His arm wrapped around her rib cage to pin her arms to her sides, and as soon as the task was forcibly taken away from her, awareness returned all at once.

Her fingers throbbed and stung. Breathing became difficult. She was spiraling into a panic, one of her worst fears coming to pass as she stared at the block before her, a barricade from the only sure way out of the mountains.

"Just breathe," Kyleer soothed, and with her surroundings coming back into clarity Faythe was alerted to the pain in his voice.

She did as he commanded. She closed her eyes and made breathing her only focus. In through her nose, out through her mouth, repeating the motion until her pulse was no longer a reckless beat. After seconds, perhaps minutes, she heard faint voices weave through the stones. Snapping her eyes open, she strained to listen, knowing it was Reylan and the others attempting to call through.

"We're okay," Kyleer shouted back, and she figured he would be able to hear them far clearer than she.

"Are they…?"

"They're all fine too," Kyleer reassured her. His arm that held her relaxed, deeming her safe from another episode.

Faythe turned to him and winced at the sight. His forehead bled down one side, and his hand clutched his side. He'd saved her, and a wave of guilt and gratitude doused her.

"Ky—" She didn't know what to say, but he stopped her from trying by waving a lazy hand.

"I imagine it looks worse than it is." He passed her off, but she didn't believe him.

"Faythe."

At the echo of Reylan's voice in her mind, Faythe whirled back to the stone wall with a gasp. She stumbled over a few loose boulders until she was right in front of it again, bracing her palms and forehead against it with a loose breath of relief as it sounded like he was unharmed.

"I'm here, I'm okay. Ky…he's hurt." She tried not to let her fear and panic seep into her voice, but she couldn't shield it from him internally.

"He will be all right, Faythe, trust me."

She nodded, and even though he couldn't see her she knew he would feel it. *"How long?"* She clamped her eyes shut, and Reylan knew exactly what she meant.

"One week, the way you're heading. We'll have to divert and take another route that's a day longer."

Faythe's forehead creased as she fought the surge of anxiety.

"Faythe, I will see you soon."

With that last promise, she felt his embrace from within and had to bite back her desire to sob that it wasn't his arms. *"Soon,"* she whispered back.

Then she heard his voice out loud, barely more than a distant echo as he spoke to Kyleer. While some words were lost on her, Kyleer heard it all.

"On my life, Reylan, she'll be safe," he swore with such a fierce determination it only added to her sinking gut. Both for Reylan's worry and Kyleer's willingness to lay down his life for her.

Faythe pressed her palms to the uneven stone wall for a moment longer as if she thought they would meet with Reylan's should the wall disappear. "One week," she said out loud in a flare of hope and determination to herself. She couldn't afford to be weak.

Kyleer put a hand on her shoulder. "Let's not make it any longer," he said in a gentle coax to get her to back away from the rocks as he eyed them with alert and caution.

Faythe moved slowly, realizing how reckless she had been when the structure was still so uncertain. Getting taken out by falling rocks would be a tragic way to go considering everything. Kyleer helped her over the scattered rubble, partially shielding her as he kept an arm around her shoulders until they were a good distance away from the scene of collapse.

He retrieved his fallen torch, and when Faythe's eyes fell on it, realization dawned and threatened her tamed composure once more. She met his look with wide eyes, and he seemed to come to the same conclusion: all the supplies to keep the fire going and make new torches were with the others.

"Oh Gods," Faythe muttered, feeling pale with dread at the thought of venturing the passages in complete darkness when their one torch dwindled out.

"It should last at least another day, maybe two." Kyleer kept a level tone. He had fae sight, and perhaps it would be enough for him to guide them through the pitch-black with a slowed pace. It was having her own sight robbed that terrified her. "We should get moving. If we pick up pace now, we could cut a day off our route."

Faythe appreciated his attempt to stay positive, and she willed her feet to move when he placed a gentle hand on her back. Her steps quickened with her growing panic, keeping up with Kyleer's long strides as their time in firelight became a countdown.

I will not be weak. I will not cower.

CHAPTER 52

Faythe

FAYTHE STIRRED IN her sleep. Shifting, she groaned as her bones ached against the hard ground. Opening her eyes, she was met with pitch-blackness. She gasped, shooting upward in a surge of panic. She couldn't see, but she was sure she was awake, sure her eyes were open as she blinked rapidly, desperate for some flicker of light or for her sight to adjust to at least make out something—*anything*.

"Faythe."

She jolted at the voice that was so close, yet she couldn't figure out where it was. A hand fell on her shoulder, and she jerked again, her whole body turning rigid. Her instinct to fight kicked in, and she jumped to her feet but stumbled in the dark. Her hand shot to her side. Relief was a temporary triumph at feeling the hilt of her sword.

"It's me. It's just me." Kyleer's voice was a flood of comfort that made the air whoosh from her. Her hand halted an inch from pulling her blade free.

Faythe's heart thundered, but her memories caught up with her all at once, and her fear was soothed by remembering she wasn't captured or alone. She focused on controlling her hard breathing, but it was difficult to let go of her skittishness while she couldn't see a damn thing.

"I'm approaching you now," he continued carefully, and she appreciated the warning immensely, nodding her head in confirmation even though she wasn't certain he could see her. "I'm right here, and I'm going to touch you." His voice was right in front of her, and as soon as she felt him, she fell into his arms.

It was the only way her muscles loosened, knowing she was within the arms of safety and that Kyleer could guide her where her own senses failed.

"I can't see anything," she whispered in terror. Without her sight, everything seemed louder, and she tuned in to the slow, steady rhythm of his heart to calm her anxiety.

"I know," he said. "I can see enough to guide us out of here. I won't let you go."

Faythe nodded against him.

He took her by the shoulders, and she felt his hand fall down the length of her arm before he caught her hand. Faythe curled her fingers around his with more pressure than was necessary, but he said nothing as she gripped onto him as if he were her lifeline.

A strain on their joined hands urged her feet to move, and she kept close to his side, not letting a gap form between them. Only a short beat of silence was left to settle before Kyleer spoke softly again, always with an edge of quietness so as not to spook her.

"I'm terrified too, you know."

Faythe's chest lightened, and she even released a partial laugh. "I didn't think you were terrified of anything." Kyleer was perhaps the fiercest of them all. She had thought Reylan was the pinnacle of guarded and detached when she first met him, before she was able to slide in past his walls. Yet there was something more heartbreakingly sorrowful about Kyleer. He didn't close off his emotions and blank his feelings from the world; he hid them behind smiles and encouragement, as though helping and protecting others was how he coped with whatever dark turmoil he buried deep.

His low, rumbling chuckle flared a light in her mind that was exactly what she needed. "Everyone has fears. I can't Shadowport underground. Confinement has always been a fear of mine but I knew this was the safest venture through the mountains."

She hadn't known about the restriction to his ability. Her chest tightened for him, but it was also soothing to know she was not alone or irrational in her anxiety.

Faythe was grateful when Kyleer filled the eerie silence to distract them both. "Did Reylan ever tell you how we met?"

The question took her by surprise. "No. I know you helped to save Livia, but I know nothing of the events or timeframe." He was quiet for a long enough pause that she squeezed his hand and added, "You don't have to tell me." She listened to his breath that was staggered faintly.

"We met in a slaver's camp," he said at last.

Faythe sucked in a sharp breath, pain pinching her chest at the mention. She had known some of Reylan's brutal past, his upbringing by his merciless uncle—Livia's father—but he hadn't mentioned this in his story. She had no words and simply stayed silent, waiting for Kyleer to want to share but holding no judgment or disappointment if he stopped at any point.

"Before I go on, I need you to know I am not proud of what I did, and I will own it for the rest of my days. But I would also do it all again to spare my brother from a worse fate." His tone dropped with something like shame. Faythe gave his hand another squeeze, and he returned the gesture weakly. "My father was a lot like Reylan's uncle. In his twisted mind, he believed ruthlessness was love and pain was nurture. I was not long past my first century when Izaiah was born, and I knew I would do anything to ensure my father's cruel ways didn't harm him the way they did me.

"As we grew, my brother started to notice the punishments I would endure, both for his faults and my own. Nothing was ever right or enough for my father." Kyleer's hand tightened, and Faythe's limp hand came around to hold his upper arm, hoping he took that as her assurance she held no judgment. "Things got hard for us. My father lost his station as High Commander for undue brutality on several accounts." He chuckled with no humor. "But as we fell into poverty, things got worse. He took to drinking, which was like lint to his already blazing fire of hatred and violence. My mother was a frail woman—she couldn't protect us—and before I reached my second century she left us all. To this day, I do not know where she fled to or if she still lives."

Faythe felt his lasting pain through the melancholic notes of his voice.

"I shouldn't, but I think a part of me blames her. Not for failing us, but for not taking Izaiah with her when I would have helped her. If she had taken him with her, I would have helped her escape and disappear forever."

Her chest hollowed out at the story, at Kyleer's utter selfless and protective nature. She wasn't focused on her panic or how her feet powered on, guided by him, or how much time had passed. While she tuned in to the heartbreaking tale of the warrior she clung to, Faythe connected with him deeply.

"Long after she left, I arrived home one day after fighting in a notorious pit that offered the only income we had. Izaiah was gone, and only my drunken father lay half-conscious in his bed. When I finally got it out of him, what he had done…I snapped." Kyleer's voice dropped, darkening as his tale took a turn. "He'd sold him to a slave camp, and they'd come for him while I was out so I couldn't stop them. I beat my father, and to this day I can't explain the rage that consumed me. It blanks out some of the gruesome ways I inflicted pain on him to get him to tell me what camp they had taken him to. When I finally got the confession, I killed him. Snapped his neck right there and then, and my only regret is that I didn't do it sooner."

Kyleer paused, and she wondered if he was trying to gauge her reaction to the shocking revelation. But it was not harrowing in the ways he thought she would perceive it. All she could think of was his bravery and his will to sacrifice his humanity to save his brother, knowing despite his father's evil actions he would bear the tarnish on his soul for the murder. Just like Reylan. She'd often observed how similar and close the general was to his second—more so than Izaiah. They were like two sides of the same coin.

Faythe gave his hand a long squeeze, her voice hushed with emotion. "He got what he deserved."

"Perhaps," Kyleer said sadly, in a way that proved he didn't believe it was enough to be granted atonement. "I found out Izaiah was taken to a camp across Rhyenelle, and I made a plan. If I simply surrendered myself as a slave, I would have condemned us both. So I made a plan to become enlisted as an overseer. It took six torturous months to get through training, pass their tests, when all I could think about was the horrific conditions and hard labor they were putting Izaiah through. Back then, he wasn't the fierce warrior you know him as today. That came after, when he was determined never to be at anyone's mercy again."

"I didn't know Rhyenelle had slave camps."

"We don't anymore, but that is part of the story." Kyleer's voice lightened, and she could almost feel his slight smile that eased the sorrow. "I finally got assigned as an overseer, but the camps were divided into different networks. I was located in a particular camp that wasn't where Izaiah was, and I was too new to request a transfer—it would have only raised suspicions. So, as much as I wanted to slaughter every master and overseer watching the brutal and unlawful conditions the slaves were being kept in, I had to be patient.

"These camps were filled with both human and fae. The humans would do most of the work, but there were some things that were out of their physical capabilities or that could be done far more swiftly by a fae. Mining, shipping, building. All laborious tasks that claimed a lot of lives." Kyleer's hand tightened in hers, anger flaring at having to recall the grim memories. Faythe's other hand fell to encase his between hers. "I tried to help as many as I could, bringing extra water, letting them have longer rest when no one else was watching. It wasn't enough, not nearly enough, but these camps were run by very high and powerful people, and they were very well-guarded, warded, and monitored. Escape was near impossible.

"It took a further six months for me to finally get the opening I needed to be transferred to the camp I hoped they still held Izaiah in. A whole year he was enslaved. I did fear that perhaps he wasn't even still alive as I'd seen so many, fae and human, lose their lives in freak accidents or from sheer exhaustion when their basic needs weren't even in balance with their excessive labor. When I arrived, it didn't take long for me to scour the cavernous camp until I found him by some mercy of the Spirits."

Faythe's heart was a fluctuating mess. With her sight gone, all she had was a dark, free mind to unfold the visual of what he described. It was grim and horrific, but she felt it all as though she were living vicariously through his memory.

"All he wore were torn pants. No shirt, no shoes. His body was far more built than I remembered as he was hacking away in the mining cave. But he was also so scarred and beaten. The whip marks on his back especially almost made me damn everything and kill every overseer I could get to before they ultimately killed me. But I had to be smart when it was clear my brother had done the same. Izaiah had fought not only to survive, but to be considered among the strongest of the slaves who were granted a little more food and water to carry out the work for as long as they could exert them for. Next to him was another who it was clear had the will and determination to survive. I watched them for a long time, trying to plan some way to get us out of there. It seemed they had formed some kind of bond or friendship from how they took turns to rest while the other carried out the work, rationing their water between them. Small things that were essential to stay alive in such conditions."

A flash of memory burned Faythe's eyes, and she almost halted her steps. Her throat constricted, but she found the words to whisper, "It was Reylan."

Kyleer was silent for many long footsteps, and while the scene was so vivid in her mind, she'd unknowingly left her mind open to feel the ripples of what Kyleer felt at recalling the details. Wetness trailed down her cheeks as she thought of what they had all endured.

Kyleer didn't confirm it. He didn't need to. "I found out later they had arrived around the same time, but Reylan was there first, after his uncle sold him with the intention of buying him back once he'd *learned his lesson.* His uncle sold Livia, his own *daughter,* to a brothel just before, and Reylan snapped, almost killing him then until friends of his uncle arrived just in time and Reylan was hauled off to the mines."

Oh Gods. A pain pinched her chest at the mention of Livia's part in the story. A rage filled her that she knew would always remain insatiable —because the evil fae was dead, as Reylan had said, and she was near trembling with anger wanting to inflict her own violent retribution on his uncle and the slave camp overseers.

"How did you all escape?" Faythe asked tightly, desperate for his victorious resolution that saw them all here today.

Kyleer blew out a breath. "We almost didn't. I spent a few weeks noting every guard, every shift change, every possible opening, to get us all out of there alive. The camps were warded against magick. Izaiah couldn't Shapeshift. I couldn't Shadowport. There was only one small window of time to attempt to escape the mundane way.

"It took time. As an overseer, I wasn't supposed to engage with the slaves. I had to pass messages through to them craftily, often in their food or in passing. When our plan was set, we didn't hesitate. We killed a lot of fae and made it to where no slave had ever made it before: freedom. We tasted the air above those caves, and I'll never forget that first breath. But our victory was short-lived."

Faythe didn't realize the tightness of her own grip with the tension that built in his story until Kyleer's hand rested over hers and snapped her back to the present.

"They closed in on us with a force that was horribly damning. Outnumbered five to one. But we were also out of the ward that stifled magick. We'll never know if we could have taken them all out on our own. We still hold bets about it to this day."

Faythe's brow flexed. "They let you go?"

Kyleer's chuckle echoed down the passage, bouncing back with contagious humor that upturned her mouth with delight.

"Of course not. They were determined to cut us down on the spot. But then the most unexpected person arrived—one with the power to declare from that day, he would not rest until every slave camp had been snuffed out and disparaged upon the discovery of the one we emerged from."

Faythe's inhale was audible. "Agalhor," she concluded.

"Call it fate, destiny, or three bastards' damn good luck that the king was returning from a trip at a nearby war camp when he stumbled across our epic display. He ordered our release, and the Fenher slavers' underworld was the first camp to be destroyed and all slaves set free. I'd never been more grateful to have Reylan by our side as I was in that moment. Agalhor, by some miracle, recognized him, and once he came to know he was the son of a close friend, a leading general Agalhor still mourned for…well, I suppose you know how we all ended up in our current duty."

Pride beat the heart in her chest. For the fae warriors; for her father. To have the privilege of knowing them and being kin to the merciful great king. Faythe had never been prouder of her father.

"It was not without great trial and determination. Agalhor opened the door, but it was down to us to prove ourselves and rise to our current status. It gave us something to strive for, and once we were high enough in station, we were allowed to lead the bands to find and dismember all the slave camps we could. I'm unsure if there are any that remain, but it is highly outlawed and punishable by death to keep lives against their will.

"Izaiah and I were happy with what we had achieved, content to lead and fight and *live*. Reylan kept pushing, as if he thought he could never do enough, *be* enough. He rose all the way to General, but even so, I don't think he has ever felt worthy of the title his father once bore. He won't believe it…but he's the worthiest any of us have ever known."

Faythe wiped her eyes with the back of her hand, her emotional sniff embarrassing in the resonating silence. Then she chuckled. Laughed. Kyleer joined in until it filled the space and lifted their hearts. Her laughter was joyous because she held such a depth of adoration for everyone involved in Kyleer's tale. It was also sad for everything they had endured, and relieved for each of them who fought and *lived*.

When her laughter ceased, Faythe felt lighter, closer, to each of her companions. She leaned her head against Kyleer as they walked, grateful he had shared the story with her. She thought of each of them with new pride and love. Of her father and his heart to see his kingdom free. *Their* kingdom. But most of all, she thought of Reylan. Of how she craved his warmth and longed to spend every day, however many they would have, showing him he was worth everything he never believed he was.

CHAPTER 53

Zaiana

"SO YOU WON'T risk a fire because you're afraid of what, exactly?"

Maverick leaned lazily against the opposite wall of the shallow cave they took shelter in. Zaiana tried to block out his presence, but the intermittent hum of his irritating voice stopped her from being able to tune in to any still peace. She didn't respond and didn't turn to look at him either as her eyes fixed on the endless black void over the mountain fringe.

They'd stopped their trek for the night, picking up that Faythe and her companion had done the same down below. They'd scouted a deep enough carving in the mountainside to shield against the weather, and worse, the fabled lethal creatures said to be cursed to these mountains.

Maverick huffed a short laugh. "You should get some sleep. What use are you worn out?"

Her eyes slid to his then, lacking any expression. "Do I look worn out?"

"Yes."

She held in her snap of annoyance. He wasn't worth her energy. She wouldn't admit to him that she was running low from her lack of rest in the high of the hunt. The other more rational reason she refused rest was because she didn't trust him. Either to guard her life if she left herself vulnerable or not to go ahead on his own in an attempt to seek the glory of finishing the quest single-handed.

A shudder shook her body, but she tensed to avoid letting it show. She heard Maverick shift before her eyes and caught him standing.

"What are you doing?" she demanded as he advanced toward her.

With an arrogant smile, he crossed the short space. Zaiana fought the urge to instantly pounce to her feet when he came to sit beside her, far too close for comfort.

"What about a discreet personal fire?" Maverick raised an open palm, sparking a shallow cobalt flame. His crooked smile widened at her scowl. Though she would never confess, the ripples of warmth were enough to loosen her muscles despite the fire's small size, and she figured he was putting in effort to amplify its heat without creating a blazing beacon.

Having no emotion at all was often more effective with Maverick. He took great delight in being able to invoke any sort of reaction in her. Her displeasure was his sadistic enjoyment, so she chose not to respond. While she'd tried to sound convincing that she wasn't tired, in truth, she was exhausted—both physically and mentally. She didn't have it in her to protest.

Maverick shifted until he was comfortable, legs extended and ankles crossed while he leaned back casually. She could feel his eyes on her, but she didn't turn to meet them.

Zaiana closed her lids, tipping her head against the uneven stone wall to enjoy the silence. Though it was short-lived when his voice rumbled once again. Her fists balled.

"After all this is over, what will you do?"

Her eyes snapped open, and she took a moment to decide if she would bother with a reply. "I'm not going back to be shackled to that mountain."

She might be foolish to admit it to Maverick. After all, he was far more loyal to the masters than she. At least, in all their centuries, he'd led everyone to believe so as their ever-submissive lap dog. It was no secret he warmed the bed of Nephra, and she didn't blame her for choosing him. Zaiana couldn't help the glance she spared in his direction at the thought, repulsion over what he'd done momentarily clouded by the softness in his black eyes as he stared back. Beautiful. Under the arrogance and darkness, Maverick was undeniably beautiful. She shook her head at the thought.

"They won't let you go."

Zaiana was surprised when what she could only interpret as concern weaved through his voice.

"They don't have to. Look at where we are—we're already free."

"For a quest they chose for us. If we don't return, they'll hunt and kill us."

Zaiana stiffened at his word choice: *"us."* Not just her. She didn't believe it was intentional. Maverick was no fool, and he had no reason to risk his standing and safety with the masters.

"There is no 'us,'" she clarified. "And I don't plan to outrun them, but the time for hiding is over."

He took a pause of deliberation, long enough that she gave in to her curiosity to gauge his reaction. His eyes flashed to her back, but her wings were glamoured like his.

"You don't plan to hide your heritage when we catch up to them," he stated rather than asked.

A small, cunning smile tugged at her lips. "The time for hiding is over."

He chuckled, low but genuine, and she cursed that it made her own smile widen while they exchanged a rare look of agreement. She almost dared to believe he held a glimmer of pride in the depths of those black orbs. Not that she ever desired or needed his approval, but admittedly, she felt relieved he didn't mock her. If he did, they would be exchanging blows instead of laughter.

"I do admire you for one thing, Zaiana. You have never shied away from defying orders," he mused.

She subconsciously flexed her fingers at the mention. Her many steps out of line had earned her a visible permanent marking along with the lattice of disfigured skin that marred her back and hands. She didn't care. It was only flesh, and she'd earned every one of her scars, but not without giving something back. Her moments of defiance were victory.

"I'm not defying anything this time. I'm taking back what's rightfully mine."

Maverick's head straightened. "And what's that?"

"My freedom."

In the short silence that settled, she gazed up at the dancing stars as if they spoke back to her. As if they agreed.

"Do you remember what it was like...?" Zaiana paused, fighting against her internal curiosity. Giving in might give the dark bastard the impression she cared. What concerned her was that she wasn't entirely sure she *didn't*. "Before everything, before you were turned dark fae, do you remember what your life was like in Dalrune?"

His pause in answering was too long. She slid him a glance, finding him with his head tilted back against the rock, also staring at the stars her eyes had fallen from. A deep frown disturbed his perfect pale skin, quietly troubled by the topic while he looked lost in thought. The moonlight softened every sculptured angle of his face and offered light to one who had lost the will to search for it.

For a moment, Zaiana imagined him as fae. Not dark fae. Not what he was forced to become. She wondered how his heart would have beat, and if it would have been filled with love and hope and everything that had been robbed from him. They were taught such feelings were a burden and to take them away was a gift. Yet Zaiana couldn't prevent her mind from flashing to scenes of the human and her companions. Their laughter, their togetherness… Maybe there was a part of her that envied them for it. Maybe there was a part of her that mourned what Maverick might have once had too.

The foolish thought was expelled from her mind as quickly as it came. Zaiana looked away from Maverick, who still gazed at the sky. Perhaps their thoughts had aligned in that rare moment and he was trying to recall even the faintest detail of his former life from over a century ago. Zaiana almost pitied him.

Maverick's deep inhale snapped her back to her senses. "I don't remember anything past waking up in that dark room," he admitted. "Alone and feeling…different. I had wings when I knew I shouldn't, only I didn't know *why*. I don't remember anything about the transition."

Zaiana felt haunted by the flash of memory. She didn't look at him. She couldn't. She whispered to the wind instead, "I do."

She *felt* the impression of his stare on her. Like desperation and surprise. Zaiana didn't owe him anything, and he wouldn't ask her to go on. But something compelled her to give him the answer he silently begged for.

"I remember the day they brought you under the mountain. Over a century ago, yet I remember feeling so young. Not because I was in mind or body, but because I felt real *dread.*" Zaiana tensed completely knowing his full attention was on her and hearing him shift ever so slightly closer as if she might tell the story faster.

"It was the first time I ever witnessed the ritual and saw the transitions. There were ten of you, all fae captured from Dalrune, but that's as much as I know. I can't tell you exactly where you came from or who your parents might be. You were so scared, like all of them, and I didn't want to watch—didn't want to see what torture they were about to inflict on you. But I didn't have a choice. I was the only one made to watch. I guess they thought it would make me stronger, more ruthless, as they always claimed I was never enough." Zaiana picked at her fingernails. The skin around her thumb stung as she thought of her cruel upbringing and that harrowing night that would haunt her for eternity.

"The eclipse came, and one by one Mordecai made the fae drink spiritual blood from a chalice, killing a captured human at the same time. Take a life to create a life. He got to you, and just before he went to force you to drink, you looked at me. Your eyes were blue—almost as bright as your flames." As if it were that same night, she locked eyes with Maverick beside her, closer than she remembered. The flickers of cobalt from the dancing fire in his palm reflected against the onyx that now filled his irises, breathing life into that memory. "There was something about you that gave me slight hope you would make it. I don't know why I cared back then, considering the damn pain in my ass you became."

He huffed a short laugh to break up the somber tale, and Zaiana didn't fight the smile that appeared on her lips.

"You drank his blood, and then he snapped your neck. Out of the ten fae, only three survived. It took nearly a week for the transition. I wasn't allowed to, but I checked on you every day out of curiosity to see how it worked. But also because I wanted to be right. That the defiance I saw in your eyes would make you one of those who *lived*. And you did far more than that. You held onto your ability, and you came back stronger than ever —not just physically." She couldn't hide the admiration in her voice even though she might live to regret it later. She truly did commend the innocent Maverick for his bravery all those years ago. He wasn't born wicked. Zaiana would like to believe she was the same, that she was once different, but she *was* Born dark fae. Born with the cold heart that occupied her chest.

Maverick's quiet voice disturbed her pitiful thoughts. "We used to tolerate each other." He huffed a small laugh. "I think I might have even considered you an ally. What happened to us, Zaiana?"

Though the question gave off a faint sting in her chest, she said plainly, "We grew up. Be glad we ever got a chance to glimpse peace through our innocence and naivety. But we were always destined to be enemies with a common goal; a common purpose. We are weapons of war, nothing more."

"Only because the masters will it."

"Yes, and while I plan to have my revenge on them for their methods, they kept us alive, brought back our species. They stripped us of weakness and honed us to win the war that will grant us our freedom in this world."

"What if there was another way?"

Zaiana's head twisted to him. Her expression alone coaxed him to expand on it, but Maverick shook his head, seeming to drop whatever he wanted to offer. Her face smoothed when she concluded it on her own.

"The fae and humans wouldn't accept our kind. They did not in history, and they will not now."

"Do you truly believe that?"

"It doesn't matter what I believe."

"You've fought your whole life to rise to the top. What reward is it to follow as another foot soldier with a title after all that effort?"

Zaiana gave a single dry laugh. "If that is still what I am, then I am not at the top. I am not finished."

"No, I don't believe you are." His answer was quiet, distant, and laced with wonder. She heard Maverick's faint shift. Out of the corner of her eye, she caught his fingers inching toward her face.

Her hand darted to her side, pulling free her dagger, and she spun where she sat, angling the blade against his throat in the space of a breath. She straddled him, looking down at his face that twinkled in delight. There was nothing kind on hers as she glared back.

"I warned you if you dared to touch me with that hand, you'd best be prepared to lose it," she hissed menacingly. "Now, I think I'll go straight for your life."

"You won't kill me," he said, his voice low with a deep gravel she tried to ignore along with their closeness.

She pressed the dagger tighter to his skin. "Won't I?" she challenged. "No one is here. No one would be able to prove your death wasn't the result of some untimely accident or fatal confrontation. You could die here, by my hand, and no one would bat an eye." Though she sneered the words, they lacked the impact she'd hoped to unleash. They missed the promise she'd spent a century building upon picturing his execution.

Worst of all…he seemed to notice it too.

"Then kill me, Zaiana." His voice dropped even further, grin vanishing. He straightened while she hovered in his lap. Leaning into the blade she held firm against his neck, his teeth clenched as it broke the surface of his skin. "Do it."

He wasn't afraid, and in the hard way he looked at her, he didn't entirely believe she wouldn't. He offered his life as if it were a gift. It didn't make sense. Maverick owed her nothing. If she had a beating heart, she knew its tempo would be erratic, just as she struggled to tame her rugged breathing.

How many times had she imagined this moment?

Yet with his life at her mercy, with the perfect opportunity…she hesitated. It sent her mind into a turbulent spiral as she realized it had nothing to do with needing him for the rest of the quest or the repercussions if she were found responsible. Zaiana looked at him. *Saw* him. Behind those heartless eyes…there was a vulnerability.

"Why can't I kill you?" Zaiana didn't intend to voice the confusion of her mind, yet it slipped from her mouth like a traitorous confession.

Maverick's depthless irises searched hers. She couldn't be sure what he was seeing, but she didn't recoil from him, as if she *wanted* him to find the reasons she couldn't gather for herself. Reasons that halted her in the face of what she had spent a century holding out for.

"Have you ever thought,"—Maverick's voice was a soft, gravelly whisper—"that perhaps when you look at me, you see yourself?" His hands grazed her thighs, and she couldn't hide her sharp inhale at the contact. "Every despicable evil, every treacherous thing. We're not so different, Zaiana."

Her knees somehow slid farther apart until she felt him beneath her where air could no longer pass. Zaiana kept her blade poised, still one swipe away from being rid of the monster who had tormented her for so long.

"Then perhaps killing you will bring my salvation."

"No, it will not." Maverick seemed to straighten a fraction, enough that she began to feel the whisper of his warm breath against her jaw, and she stilled. "You look at me and you see everything they made you. Made us. But sometimes…sometimes you pause to look deeper, through the thick darkness, and you wonder if there *is* something in the depths of a wicked soul that can be saved. If there is a light."

"You think I won't kill you because you harbor *goodness?*" she breathed. Because his hands still lingered on her. Because she couldn't make sense of what she felt in that moment. The staccato of her breaths, the fluttering hollowness in her stomach—it was a strangeness that could quickly become addictive.

Maverick's face was strangely soft, searching, dropping her incredulity. "I think you won't kill me because if you do, all hope of finding that light dies with me."

They never broke eye contact. His palms trailed up from her knees that were spread over his thighs, a touch so igniting but barely there. Higher and higher, and she said nothing to stop him. The chill nip of the night disappeared as she could focus on nothing else. His touch at her hips caught her breath, but they didn't pause, traveling carefully to her waist and slowly pulling her flush to his chest. Her dagger cut shallow, enough that a bead of black blood rolled down his neck. She watched the slow trail, thinking it would be enough to snap her back to her senses—the blood that made them different. The color that made him her enemy.

"Tell me to stop." His warmth breezed across her collarbone, sending her thoughts scattering.

She should voice the rational reasoning that roared in her mind, but they were entangled with those so wrongfully longing. Every internal scream and protest to stop was gripped by desire in her throat, pulled back with lust, and torched with a burning need to *feel* something.

His hands continued to roam to her waist, and she wished the thick material of her leathers were not there. He leaned his head into her neck and inhaled a long, careful breath as if he could devour her whole. She knew he could sense the effect he was having on her, and it was almost enough for her to recoil, to not give him the gloating satisfaction he could use against her for eternity.

"It means nothing." His words vibrated over her skin. "Tell me to stop, Zaiana."

It was an opening, a second chance for her to stop something she might regret. Again, her response was choked as she realized...

She didn't *want* him to stop.

At her silence, one of his hands left her waist to slowly curl around her wrist that still held the blade weakly against his throat. She didn't know what she expected from Maverick in this situation, but his gentle touch was so unlike the male she thought she knew. He guided her hand away, and her fingers loosened of their own accord, the dagger slipping from her grasp to echo a chime of steel meeting stone.

Still, it was not enough to snap her from her lustful trance.

"What is your game?" she asked, words no more than a whisper in her bewilderment.

His mouth was at her neck, and when his lips made contact she tipped her head back as a quiet breath left her.

"No games."

Her skin rippled with delightful shallow fire between the softness of his lips and the traveling gravel of his voice. When he met the shell of her ear, his voice was thick as he whispered, "What do you want, Zaiana?"

Every time he spoke her name in that tone, it only added to the aching heat forming at her core. She didn't know if she could answer. It had been a long time since her thoughts were so clouded, her judgment driven solely by the responses of her body, not the chants of her harsh mind.

"I want," she breathed, taking a moment to collect a coherent response, "you. Just to feel, just for one night."

He stilled, but only for a few seconds. Then she felt his smile against her throat. "One night," he agreed.

Maverick pulled back, and Zaiana had to put effort into biting back her pining protest. But there was something in his look—something she didn't think she would ever see in such a cold and wicked soul.

Vulnerability.

For a second, she believed Maverick might have surfaced an emotion akin to *fear*. He didn't look at her with the victory she expected from winning her body. She wasn't a conquest in that moment, and it drowned her guilt for allowing herself to give over to her impulses.

Her hands met his chest, traveling up to feel the powerful contours of him, until they found the back of his neck and her fingers tangled in the softness of his midnight hair. "I hate you," she whispered. Though it held no meaning, no impact.

What she hated…was her *want* for him.

His eyes held hers, and a new life sparked within their cold, black depths. "Show me," he challenged, eyes dipping to her mouth. "Show me how much you hate me."

His breath blew over her lips. His nose brushed hers—then over her jaw, her neck. Zaiana's grip tightened in his hair while her head tipped back and her eyes fluttered closed. Her chest rose and fell in a deep, uneven rhythm with the need that knotted in her lower stomach.

"I want it all, Zaiana."

The way her name rolled off his tongue was a caress he trailed down her chest, past her breasts. Her mouth parted with a breath of desire, and her body arched into his touch as it slowly traced up her spine. Zaiana had never felt so...*alive*. For just one moment, one night, perhaps she could pretend that she was.

She should back away. She was still in a position of control. All it would take was the will to pull back. Yet *control* was a mockery in her mind, which had already submitted to everything she should have the sense to resist.

The only chant she listened to was, *Screw the damned consequences.*

As if he heard her thoughts, Maverick's hand curled over her neck, and he guided her mouth down to meet his. They collided like the moon and stars: a merger of darkness, triumphant. Gone were all feelings of reservation, every thought that screamed to shake sense into her for tangling herself with the enemy. She cast out everything as she surrendered.

His hands came between them, but his fingers were slow in their work to undo the fastenings of her leathers. As though he still thought she would change her mind with one wrong move.

She didn't want gentle, and she didn't want slow.

Her hands left his hair to unclasp his cloak, and then her fingers went to work on the buttons of his jacket before she tugged it off his shoulders. She wasted no time in untucking his shirt and lifting it, just as she felt the coolness of the air blow across her chest and stomach where he finally took her hint and acted faster to remove her layers.

Maverick's hands left her only to hoist his shirt over his head. Zaiana took the opportunity to explore the beautifully marked muscles of his torso, enjoying immensely the feel of his uneven skin—a texture just like her own. Then she felt him hook his fingers at her shoulders, peeling away the leather material. She didn't get the chance to shudder against the cold over her bare skin as he pulled her flush to him, her breasts pressing to his chest, glorious and warm. There was nothing soft or searching in the way they moved; it was anguish and hatred, so many long barricaded emotions unleashed like an angry storm.

It was raw, and it was furious.

His hands trailed over her back, unflinching at the tarnished surface. His long fingers traced exactly where her wings would expand if she released her glamour, but the sensation still shot straight to her core, and the sound that left her was something between a cry and moan of utter bliss. He knew exactly what he was doing as a groan answered from his own throat.

The heat between her legs was almost painful, begging for release. She moved against him, feeling him hard beneath her. He groaned into her mouth, and it was her turn to smile in satisfaction. She moved again, but his hands gripped her hips tighter to stop her. Before she could protest, his strong arm hooked around her back, and he twisted.

She met the softness of their discarded clothes. He pulled back, eyes glazed as they roamed over the half-naked sight of her.

"The depraved things I've dreamed of doing to you, Zaiana," he said huskily.

The impression of his eyes crawled her skin delightfully. His words were almost her undoing.

"Do them all."

His smile was devastatingly beautiful. And promising. As he moved to hover above her, his disheveled hair curled around his face, softening the cruelty often etched into his expression. Right now, he was as free and unburdened as the wind, and a surprising warmth passed through her chest.

"We would not have enough time in a single night to do them all."

Zaiana didn't want to defuse the mood by reminding him this night was all they had. That with the rise of the new dawn, their time of release and fantasy would be over.

"Then do your worst, Maverick."

A deep rumble of approval left his throat just before his lips met the skin between her breasts. She inhaled sharply, body arching in response. His hand trailed over the dip of her waist, coming to stroke lazy, teasing circles on her lower stomach while he continued his torturously slow descent with his lips over her chest. She squirmed beneath him, raising her hips in a silent plea for him to go lower.

A low chuckle vibrated over her breasts. "Demanding, as always," he commented in delight, his hand dipping to work on the buttons of her pants. He said nothing more as he pulled back, gripped the edges of the leather at her hips, and pulled the material away until her legs were finally free, her bare skin glorious against the elements. Maverick paused on his knees before her, looking over every inch of her body with a dark, claiming hunger.

Zaiana rose slowly until she was also on her knees. Her hands reached for his hair as the only thing she could grapple to pull him close to her again. She kissed him fiercely, with a passion so all-consuming, while he clutched her tight to him. As though releasing months, years, *decades* of fighting herself, denying a longing she refused to admit she harbored.

One of Zaiana's hands glided down his chest, past his navel, until she felt his hardness through his pants. The sound that ascended from his throat had her fumbling for the buttons, desperate to feel him bare. Her palm dipped down, and she almost gasped when her hand curled around the length of him.

"Zaiana," he pleaded against her lips.

She wanted him—all of him. But just as she was about to shift back, his hands caught her wrists. She locked eyes with him as his arm circled around her, pulling her to him before she could lean down to taste him.

"If you do that," he blew out tightly, "this will end before either of us is ready."

Zaiana's body gave off a tremble that curved her spine.

"Stand."

Any other time, a command from Maverick would have her flaring in lethal challenge. It was a completely new feeling to *want* to obey him. A dormant thrill awoke at the order. She rose carefully.

"Face the wall."

She did without hesitation.

Maverick didn't rise. Instead, he moved to fit into that space between her and the stone, still on his knees for her. She knew before she glanced down that the sight of him gazing up at her with those dark, dangerous orbs would weaken her completely.

"This is what you've always wanted, isn't it, Zaiana?" Without breaking eye contact, Maverick removed the last flimsy piece of clothing she wore, and she stepped out of the undergarment, completely exposed to him. "Me, on my knees before you." His hand curled behind her calf, lifting and guiding her leg to hook it over his shoulder. When his lips brushed the inside of her thigh, Zaiana had to brace a hand against the wall, a whimper leaving her lips while the ache grew between her legs. "So damn beautiful."

Then his mouth met the softest part of her, and she couldn't suppress her cry as she threw her head back at the contact. Maverick wasn't gentle. Not with his tongue or his fingers that soon joined to add heights to her pleasure she didn't know were possible. He devoured without mercy, and she didn't have the words to warn him before release shattered through every piece of her. Her fingers grew tight in his hair when he didn't stop. He continued to pleasure her through the tremors that left her light-headed. It came out of nowhere, and when the waves of a blissful climax began to tame, she was panting hard, blinking slowly to process what just happened.

It wasn't enough. She wanted—*needed*—more of him.

Maverick's fingers dragged a sharp breath from her as they left her body and his face pulled back, lips glistening with her mark. There was nothing but dark hunger dancing in those eyes.

"A damn Goddess."

A powerful thrill raced down her spine. Zaiana lowered herself deliberately slowly, and with a hand on his chest she guided him back until she was straddling his lap once more. He submitted himself to her willingly. What they were about to do she wouldn't be able to take back, but she held no fear or protest.

Tomorrow, they would go back to how things were, and how they always would be while blood divided their species. Tonight, she would allow herself to forget, and more importantly...forgive. Forgive herself for denying her mind and body any form of happiness. And forgive *him* for the wicked past they shared; the cruelty that was often forced between them.

He took her face in his hands with a delicate hold she didn't expect. She leaned down and kissed him, tasting herself on his lips—on his tongue as it clashed with hers. Feeling him between her legs, Zaiana sank her hips down fully. Both of them released a harsh breath as he filled her. His lips left hers to go to her neck, and she felt his sharp teeth grazing over her pulsing veins. They moved together, passion clouding any rational thought. She didn't have the words to warn him not to bite her. She didn't care. In that moment, perhaps she even *wanted* it.

Nothing mattered. Nothing but him and her. She felt the sparks of her lightning humming through her veins, answering to the heat of his fire as he trailed it over her skin everywhere he touched. They were both panting, breathless with desire. She felt herself climbing and climbing, reaching heights she had never glimpsed before. They were darkness on darkness. Fire on fire. Together, they could blissfully destroy each other and the world in their wake.

Another end began to form in her lower stomach. Tingling over her thighs, up over her breasts, until it coated every inch of her. Maverick massaged the globe of her breast while he brought his lips to her ear.

"Unleash yourself, Zaiana." His words blew like sand across her neck. "Take what you want. What you need."

Her hand fisted in his hair so tightly she knew it would be painful, but Maverick only answered with a primal noise of desire. Her nails dug into the skin of his chest, his shoulders, drawing dark blood as her hips rocked against him with abandon, aided by the vise grip of his hands on her.

She didn't think her release could hit her harder than the first, but she was wrong.

So wrong.

Maverick seemed to reach that end with her, and his loud groans only heightened her pleasure as he stilled while she trembled. He clutched her to him, forehead pressing to the hollow spot of her shoulder as they weathered each other. Where she reached, there was no limit, and for a moment she didn't care if she drifted into oblivion and didn't come back.

Then she fell—blissfully and all at once. Her tense body became weightless. Still, Maverick held her, the melody of their labored breaths the only sound against the night in the cave.

Slowly, her hand uncurled from his hair, and she pulled back enough that their gazes locked. "I still hate you," she panted, exhausted and spent.

Maverick had gotten what he wanted. As had she. Yet there was no triumph on his face.

"I would be concerned if you didn't."

Their lips collided once more. Something burst in her heartless chest. She didn't fight it and didn't feel his movement until her back met with something solid while their mouths connected.

Maverick lay her down, and when he broke from her, a final kiss met her shoulder as he said, "Sleep now, Zaiana."

Her utter exhaustion and dwindling lust answered to those words. Her eyes began to flutter closed.

She didn't care that he could kill her in her vulnerability if she gave in to the darkness.

Something warm and weighted covered her naked body.

She didn't care that he could abandon her in that shallow cave the moment she was asleep.

Her head gave in and fell limp.

She didn't care.

But more importantly, she didn't regret.

CHAPTER 54

Zaiana

ZAIANA AWOKE WITH a full breath that felt so free, in a body that felt so light. She remembered everything. Everything she had done with Maverick, and even when the sun replaced the moon, she did not regret.

It changed nothing between them. But she did not regret allowing herself one night to give in to reckless impulse. Even with the one she despised.

At the thought, her eyes fluttered open and met with the jagged dark stone of the cave roof. She heard…nothing. Not even the breaths of another that she expected. In a flash of anger and panic, Zaiana shot up straight, clutching the cloak that covered her naked body. Her quick scan of her surroundings confirmed what she already knew.

Maverick wasn't here.

Disbelief stunted her movement, in complete contrast to her rage that wanted her to storm from the hidden space and hunt him down. How could she believe for one second Maverick was any different to what he portrayed in every breath of his existence? Ruthless, self-serving, uncaring.

He'd left her. Maverick had gotten what he wanted, and he'd left her.

That wasn't what boiled her rage. It was the reaction her body gave that she couldn't fight. Zaiana's teeth clenched so tight she didn't care if they broke—anything to take away that *damn* foolish sting in her eyes that chanted a mockery in her mind that she *cared*. Not about what he took from her...but because it had been so easy for him to abandon her.

This wasn't her. These emotions, these feelings, that carved so deep she didn't know what to do with them. Zaiana tried to throw a blanket of resentment and detachment over everything so pitiful that threatened to undo her. This wasn't what she was. *Weak.*

Her distraction from the damning, horrid emotions that swirled in her mind, in her stomach, froze upon detecting a nearby presence. Zaiana was completely exposed and vulnerable. He'd *left* her like this. She could only blame herself as her mind fell into a cool calm to calculate her next move and adapt to whatever was lurking around the mouth of the cave.

She rose carefully, swiftly clasping the cloak around herself, and swiped up her dagger that lay exactly where it was discarded last night. She couldn't deny the memory emitted a faint pinch in her chest. Her fingers curled into her palm to redirect that pain. She braced and angled her blade, in no suitable position to fight but willing to do whatever it took.

A shadow formed and grew at the cave entrance, and she clutched her dagger tighter, just as they came into view...

Zaiana's grip slackened as her firm face relaxed in dumbfounded surprise. Then there was relief. A single strong wave that she forced back with a surge of anger. Her face dropped into a scowl instead.

Maverick halted at the cave opening, staring right back at her with raised eyebrows. His eyes fell to the weapon she gripped then back to her stone stare.

"You believed I left you?" There was a note to his voice she couldn't place. Pain perhaps, but that didn't seem appropriate.

Zaiana finally lowered her blade, dropping her gaze. "I wouldn't have been surprised." *Liar.* She ground her teeth at her own tormenting thoughts.

"I found a nearby lake, figuring you might want to bathe after—"

"Don't," she warned, her eyes cold as they lifted to his. "We don't speak of it."

The flinch of his brow was unexpected. He took slow steps toward her, and it took everything in her not to retreat like a flustered *darkling*. She raised her chin firmly. Maverick stopped a few paces away, but there was conflict etched on his brow. His lips parted, and her eyes flashed to them as they did. A short pulse of heat flushed her as she remembered what they felt like against her skin.

"I only want to say this once—"

"I have no regrets from last night, Maverick." She had to cut him off. Her voice came out shallow, unrecognizable, in her quiet plea. To halt him from saying something that could ruin it all. "Don't give me one."

It couldn't be more. They wouldn't ever be more than that: a night of release. Affection, love, promise—it would kill them quicker than any fae or mortal. It wasn't what either of them wanted, not truly. He would see that. He would *have* to see that.

A protest twitched around his eyes. Zaiana had never seen him look so…defeated. But the crestfallen look on his face was gone as quickly as it came. To defuse the tension that thickened between them, Zaiana said nothing and swiped up her discarded clothing, leaving him in the cave to seek out the lake.

She needed the solitude. She needed the fresh air to clear her mind.

Space from him. Because she needed to convince herself as much as he...

That they *weren't* capable of more.

Zaiana soaked in the waters for as much time as she thought she could spare. Though as she stormed back to the cave, she couldn't scrub the scent of Maverick off her. Perhaps it was her own tormenting mind that taunted he would always be permanently wrapped around her now.

What they had shared she was determined to leave behind the moment they set course on their quest that day. The only way she could accept it was to slip back into the cold, detached persona that made her who she was. Gained her all she had.

She glimpsed Maverick casually leaning outside the cave. He straightened upon her approach, tugging at his cuffs. Zaiana schooled her face but could barely stand to look into his eyes while something unexplainable and irritatingly distracting emitted a current between them. No longer lust or anything else she might have thought she felt in that cave. The tension between them was hard to place, and that only riled her further. Her murderous thoughts about him returned. Maybe in killing him once and for all, she would rid herself of the ghost of her past and the dagger of her present.

Zaiana marched past the cave, not sparing a glance within. What was done would stay there. There was a small glimmer in her fool's heart that thought of it as treasured and protected, and that was as much emotion as she would yield to the memory before she stored it behind a steel barrier in her mind where anything warm and alive was abandoned. Felt once and never again.

Maverick followed closely behind but stayed silent. Zaiana decided to target all her senses to catch something from those they were tracking below. The mountains were so still and silent she lightened her footsteps until they were near inaudible.

"They're about a half mile ahead since you took your precious time *bathing.*" Maverick's voice was back to its insufferable harshness that always made her hand itch to reach for a blade. She shot him a glare of warning. She was still his superior; still the one in command on this quest. Maverick had done well so far to abide by that, but now, there was a cold darkness that hardened his expression. A challenge that could become cataclysmic.

"I needed every second to erase the scent of you," she sneered back. "Even a bath in fire sounds inviting to be rid of it."

In the slight flinch of his eyes, she saw her words had hit. It was surprising as even in their most wicked moments Maverick was never one to give a reaction. It was so small, but so significant.

Then his face turned to icy steel. "I can gladly arrange that for you."

"I don't want anything from you."

"Yet those were not your words last night, Zaiana." Maverick's voice dropped low, threatening. He was *angry.* Good. It was the best language she knew with him. He took a step toward her as they halted their walk to face off. "You desired everything. And you took everything. You don't get to pretend you didn't want it."

"I *did* want it!" Her voice rose to match his indignation. "Is that what you want to hear? I *wanted* it, Maverick. But I was not a fool to believe it would be anything more than a single night of release. No attachment. No feelings." Her chest rose and fell deeply as they stood in a deadly stare-off. Her lightning sparked while his flames ignited.

Zaiana took a few calming seconds to avoid doing something reckless at the opposition that surfaced naturally, effortlessly, between them. They were an eruption of conflict and chaos. Deadly alone, but utterly fatal together.

"Remember who you are, Maverick. Remember *what* we are. Want is not a luxury we can afford. We had a moment of fantasy, that is all.

This?" She cast out a hand to the cruel world around them. "This is reality. And we are the monsters who don't get the happy ending even if we *want* it."

There was response twitching to be voiced in his expression, so hard to read she couldn't decipher what he felt or thought. Zaiana would never get to know as his parted lips pressed in a firm line, his gaze cast from hers, and without another word, Maverick backed down, spun on his heel, and left.

They walked in silence from then over the hours, the tension between them tangible. The air was clouded and so thick to breathe that she avoided inhaling as much as she could. Her body was painfully rigid as her ire forced her to walk in a harsh march that made her feet protest. Zaiana soon tunneled into a state of detachment. They had work to do, and it seemed their time of hunting was about to come to an end.

Because it was time for the strike.

The sun was beginning to descend when they came near to the cave mouth where Faythe and her companion would emerge. Zaiana cast away every foolish and ridiculous distraction and entered a cool, calculating calm.

"What is the plan then, delegate?" Maverick's voice was harsh, familiar, but she didn't react to it.

Zaiana took a deep breath. "Capture Faythe, whatever it takes."

"Her companion?"

Zaiana hesitated. Maverick seemed to notice, and his quiet scoff tightened her fists.

"Whatever it takes."

CHAPTER 55

Faythe

FAYTHE'S LEGS DROVE her focus. All she could think about was one foot in front of the other despite exhausting her pace to keep up with Kyleer who begged her to slow. All she wanted was to be out of the dark.

They had exchanged many stories, and Faythe had lost complete track of time. It was a welcoming distraction from her otherwise racing thoughts of fear and hopelessness in their confinement underground. She wasn't sure how long had passed since the stone caved and divided them from Reylan and the others. Her heart cried that it was too long. *Far* too long, but she didn't deign to ask Kyleer if he knew, or she risked losing her composure. She focused on her steps and his voice and willed her mind to calm from the panic of the closing-in walls that suffocated her.

Her head was dipped, looking at the ground as she listened to Kyleer tell a tale of his antics with Reylan and Izaiah when they came to Ellium as free fae. Her heart was full with the story, and she stored away pieces she would tease Reylan with later. Laughter was the brightest sound in the dark, and Kyleer was masterful at coaxing it out of her, leaving little time for her to dwell on their desolate situation.

They turned a corner. Faythe knew from the strain on his arm, which she all but clung to like a newborn. She often envied his sight. Though she imagined it was limited, it was better than the void of blackness Faythe had grown accustomed to.

She cast her gaze up, not expecting to see anything in comparison to when her head was bowed. But after a few seconds, Faythe blinked. Again. And again. Kyleer's words became a blur in her surge of hope. She moved her eyes sideward, thinking she caught a glisten. Her eyes began to dart around the space. Shapes. She could faintly see bulges in what she thought were the stone walls. A flicker of shine here, an angle there. Faythe couldn't stop her racing heart as she concluded what her mind screamed.

There was light.

"Ky," she whispered, cutting off whatever story she felt guilty for missing in her glee.

He stopped talking immediately and almost pulled her to a halt. Faythe couldn't stop moving—not if there was an exit ahead, almost within reach. She quickened her steps, not unhooking her arm from his as she dragged him along with effort while he fought to maintain his edge of caution.

The more her eyes squinted and scanned the distance as she closed in, the more she could make out the uneven surface of stone wall and the faint glittering dampness beneath her feet.

There was definitely light.

Faythe tore her arm from around Kyleer's and vaguely heard her echoing name, but she couldn't halt the jog she broke into, far too desperate to reach the opening her mind had convinced her was near. As she kept moving, more light filtered into her vision, reflecting off the grim stone that surrounded her. She was running. Until a scent other than dampness and stone, one of slow suffocation, filled her nostrils and breathed life and relief into her.

It wasn't long until Faythe saw it. She spied the piercing white light ahead. Her eyes burned with the change in luminance after so many days, but it didn't stop her from racing for it. Though as the light grew, Faythe was forced to clamp her eyes shut against the pain.

She didn't slow her pace until she was at last encompassed by freedom. Swallowed whole by light that cast out the darkness all at once.

Air. Pure, unrestricted air wrapped her in a cool embrace, and she halted her steps abruptly. Faythe kept her eyes clamped shut, but salty water still formed behind them, spilling over. Elated tears. Triumphant sunlight tried to penetrate her closed lids, and Faythe had to double over, breathing greedily as she braced her hands on her knees, even releasing a chuckle in her delirious state. She couldn't believe that they were out. They were free.

Faythe was drunk on the clean air, and after finally peeling her eyes open, it took many blinks through watering eyes to adjust to the brightness of the outdoors. A week in darkness. A week without Reylan.

At the thought of him, Faythe whirled as if expecting to find the silver-haired general waiting for her. She met Kyleer instead, basking gloriously in the descending sunlight. He felt her stare, and as his eyes peeled open to meet hers the brightness fell from his face. He seemed to read her disappointment.

"They might still be a day behind, but we can make camp where I expect they'll intercept our path," he said, scanning the area.

Faythe nodded even though he didn't see it. She simply breathed the clean air as though it were her first ever taste, knowing she would never take such a simple thing for granted again.

She said nothing as Kyleer began to walk, motioning for her to follow. Faythe had to refrain from instinctively reaching for his hand after relying on his closeness and claiming a vise grip on his fingers as her guide in the dark.

Judging by the pink hues that started to diffuse against an indigo sky, they didn't have much daylight left. Faythe quickened her steps to match with Kyleer's long strides despite the ache in her legs. They'd stopped for little rest over the past week, eager to get out of the caves as soon as possible. She could rest later, when they were reunited with the others. When she was reunited with Reylan. The thought powered her feet and made her fatigue subside.

They came out of a narrow fringe and stepped onto a larger mountainside, closed in by towering peaks that lit up a ruby red against the bowing sunshine. It was beautiful, mesmerizing, and Faythe walked with a craned neck to watch the glistening crimson peaks. In her distraction, she didn't realize Kyleer had stopped walking, but before she could crash painfully into his back he pivoted, an arm catching around her waist instead.

He didn't drop that arm when she was pulled to a stop beside him. She cast her eyes to his face to find it was steeled and alert. His green eyes weren't scanning in front or behind; they tracked along the tall stone walls that towered over them on either side. His obvious alarm immediately set the motion in her too. Her heart picked up a sprint as her eyes darted to find what could possibly have attracted his attention.

"What is it?" Her voice was quiet in trepidation.

Kyleer slowly unhooked his arm from her, hand inching to the hilt of his sword.

Faythe copied the movement.

"I've sensed it before," he muttered, almost to himself as he braced and scanned. "First at the inn, then in the woods weeks ago."

Faythe gripped Lumarias. "What?" Her heartbeat drummed in her ears against the silence of the mountains.

"I think we're being followed." Kyleer instead went for the bow on his back, and Faythe in turn drew her sword. "Stay close to me."

Every nerve was on a razor's edge in anticipation, every hair on her body standing on end, waiting. And waiting. Faythe looked back. Nothing. She whipped her head forward. Nothing. She cast her eyes up, but visibility was becoming weaker in the twilight, and she would be even further disadvantaged if they were attacked when night fell completely. Her mind raced with the possibilities. The first haunting conclusion her mind drew was that Rezar's companions had tracked and followed them, ready for their revenge. Her blood thrummed, a familiar sensation tingling in her veins. *Oh Gods.* She couldn't succumb to the power within that was awakening at the most damning time, fearing she wouldn't be able to come back from it.

Reylan wasn't here.

Faythe focused and closed off her access to the well of power that sang to something unexplainably dark within. She cast her eyes skyward and found a spot of darkness where a bird flew overhead. Otherwise, everything was still, and the only signs of life around were the two of them.

Faythe didn't take her eyes off the lone bird. The more she stared, the more peculiar she found it. Alone without a flock, not seeming to be headed in any direction. A chill coated her skin as she realized…the bird barely moved at all. There was not a species she knew of that would hover in the air like that.

"Ky," she whispered, unable to take her eyes off it, thinking it was growing.

The black silhouette expanded, and Faythe heard the groan of the string as Kyleer nocked an arrow and aimed for the unknown target.

The wings of the creature disappeared. It was diving straight for them.

Faythe angled her blade. Kyleer wasn't willing to wait to see if it was a threat; he released his arrow with perfect accuracy, but whatever it was saw it coming and spun to narrowly miss the spear.

The form became bigger, closing in. Kyleer had fired three arrows now, each with expert precision, but the creature still managed to dart from their flight. The building tension in Faythe's stomach grew, and her fist tightened around the hilt of Lumarias.

Whatever it was, it had a mind and was able to make Kyleer's dead shot look like an amateur's aim. It rattled her nerves awfully that it also seemed to be *enjoying* his attempt to strike it down with the way it glided and rolled in the sky when it could have landed by now.

Kyleer was quick to catch on and didn't bother to release his next arrow just to be made a mockery of. He nocked one in place and stood braced, tracking it with laser focus in his firm poise.

"Be ready, Faythe," Kyleer said, and the command struck her straight like a soldier in battle.

She twisted her blade in her wrist, braced and determined, her fear subdued by the calm that honed her focus. "Always am."

Kyleer smirked but didn't drop an ounce of attention while he watched the dark form close the distance. It tucked into a dive once more before large wings splayed, casting a dark shadow with its final descent.

Then it all happened so fast.

It landed in a graceful crouch, striking the land like a stroke of lightning that set every hair on edge. Not a creature…

A person.

To Faythe's absolute shock and horror. With hair as dark as midnight and gleaming onyx eyes to match, he tilted his head up to lock on them. The smile he wore was beautifully cruel. The tail blast of wind from his powerful wings blew past them like a haunting embrace. Kyleer didn't hesitate to fire the arrow he had ready, and it should have struck —yet the being was impossibly fast. His wings tucked in tight as he straightened, twisting his body where he stood and catching the arrow in flight. Faythe was stunned. She didn't even have time to take her next breath before his eyes locked on her. A wicked smirk curving one side of his mouth, he spun the arrow in his fingers. Everything about him—the way he looked and moved—was so elegantly lethal.

Faythe was too slow to process what he was about to do until it was too late. She caught the pull back of his arm that held the arrow, and then a tall, full form blocked her sight, and Kyleer's grunt echoed in her ears. She stared at his back—at the bloodied arrow tip protruding from his shoulder—and nearly came apart.

It shouldn't have been possible. That he could have thrown the arrow with such velocity without a bow. Kyleer had seen no other alternative than to take the strike of it as he moved in front of her.

Faythe's cry was smothered by her shock. She stared at the bloodied iron point that would have shot through her throat instead. He'd saved her.

She was shaken from her stupor when she heard the snap of wood as Kyleer broke off the fletching at his chest. Faythe knew the safest way to remove it would be to let it pass straight through. Without him needing to ask, as her adrenaline rose and coursed through her at the chance the *thing* could be preparing for a second attack, Faythe stepped forward and braced a hand on his back. She curled her trembling fingers around the length, and the slick warmth of his blood curdled her stomach.

"I'm sorry," she whispered, but she didn't hesitate to pull the arrow free.

Kyleer gritted his teeth, only emitting a short grunt of pain. Faythe dropped the arrow immediately and stepped up beside him with her blade angled, sparing a look to make sure he was still capable of wielding a sword. Her concern was answered when he drew the blade at his hip, flinching in pain as he clutched his wound and crimson trickled over his hand. He needed help, but she couldn't succumb to her panic when she didn't know how far behind their friends were.

Faythe cast out the thoughts that threatened to undo her into complete uselessness. She let her focus fall on the target, let her rage build that storm against the dangerous hum in her veins. If it would see Kyleer live, she would *have* to use it.

She gauged the threat, who had so far remained where he landed, curiously observing them with dark glee. He was evil in the most beautiful form. His wings raised over his long, broad shoulders and curled with sharp talons. Her heart was wild now, her mind sprinting to put images and knowledge together to make out what he was. She'd seen the likeness of such wings before. When her eyes fell to his ears, the delicate pointed tip of them, the last puzzle piece, slid into place. The impossible before her that her mind struggled to believe.

He was a dark fae.

She thought she heard Kyleer utter the name of his species as she thought it, but she was too struck by disbelief to register anything except the dark fae male whose smile curled further as they figured it out. He was an uncharted threat and clearly a force to be reckoned with even against a lethal warrior such as Kyleer.

While they stared off in tense silence, Faythe wasn't alerted to the other presence until they dropped down beside the dark fae. Her heart leaped into her throat, smothering her cry of fright. Another of his kind, and Faythe didn't think she could be struck stupid any more than she already was until the winged beauty turned. A female dark fae. One so devastatingly beautiful it was a conflict to be fearful. They were weapons of allurement and bore no resemblance to the mutilated, ghastly creature she encountered in the caves in the castle of High Farrow.

The female stood straight and poised, head tilting curiously, hands folded behind her. "Hello, Faythe." Her voice was melodic, inviting, but a hint of cruel amusement danced on her lips.

Faythe's spine locked with the ice that froze over every notch. She knew her name. A thousand questions battered her, impossibilities to explain how the dark fae could possibly know who she was. And there was only one blaring conclusion that almost buckled her knees.

Marvellas knew she was heading to stop Dakodas's ascension.

The raven-haired beauty's eyes flashed to Kyleer, narrowing on his wounded shoulder. "Maverick," she drawled coldly to her companion, "I thought I said not to harm them yet."

He simply shrugged. "My apologies, Zaiana. Though in my defense, I believed he would have the stealth to catch it."

It wasn't hard to note that Zaiana took leadership. It was in her confidence, her poise, her cool collectiveness. She was a honed leader and warrior even at first glance. Faythe tried not to balk.

"Who are you?" Faythe asked, glad when her firm voice didn't betray her terror.

The dark fae cantered her head, eyes assessing her with an air of wonder. The kind a predator held knowing they'd trapped their prey beyond escape. Her eyes…they were hypnotizing. A core of bright purple circled her pupil, an obscure color Faythe had never imagined or seen before, unlike the stark black of Maverick's. Those haunting onyx orbs she would never forget on anyone.

"I am everything you should fear, Faythe."

Instead of succumbing to horror, unknowing of the height of their power or capabilities, Faythe straightened and soothed her mind and body to fight, just as she always did in the face of threat or challenge. It wasn't just her own life that stood in the balance; she would protect Kyleer with everything she had. The power within her seemed to rejoice at that—at her willingness to surrender to its calling that grew the more she channeled into her ability. She tested the dark fae's mind for entry, finding a solid block unlike anything she'd met with before. Nik and Reylan's were as close to impenetrable as she'd encountered, but this—it was more. It was something she wouldn't be able to shatter with the well of power she harbored alone.

A hum raked over her skin, a gentle coax, as if there was an answering force willing to aid her—to add a height to her ability that could give her a fighting chance. Her fist tightened on the hilt of Lumarias, her other clenching over nothing while she strained against the unexplainable dark calling.

Zaiana watched her carefully as though fighting back her own amusement, knowing the restraint Faythe trembled with. "You feel it, don't you?" she asked, curious and wondrous. "The pressure…the chant of darkness. Power as an entity calling to merge with you."

Faythe stayed silent, but she couldn't deny her composure was rattled hearing the dark fae explain so accurately what she felt within.

"Truthfully, I thought you might have figured it out by now. Or at least had your suspicions, considering you have harnessed it before."

Seconds ticked by, measured by her heartbeats as she held that vibrant stare. What dawned on her was a weight that threatened to collapse her—not just to her knees, but maybe beyond, pulling the world from under her. The dark fae was right: Faythe *should* have known sooner. Maybe the conclusion had filtered through her mind at some point over the weeks, but she was ignorant to believe it. It didn't make sense. Yet now, the answer undeniably screamed at the forefront of her mind, and she swayed on the spot.

Faythe's lips parted. "The temple ruin."

The dark fae's slow curling mouth was a sharp dagger of confirmation. "You didn't think that power you wield was all of your own making, did you?" When Faythe said nothing, Zaiana huffed a mocking laugh. "You are powerful, it cannot be denied, but even you couldn't harness that amount of power without an amplifier. Even then, your body is too weak to withstand it."

Faythe wracked her brain. It was impossible for the dark fae to have it her possession. Unless…

Unless it wasn't Aurialis's ruin.

The only other's it could be…was Marvellas. Faythe was a fool. A damn fool not to have considered the Spirit of Souls might possess her own ruin. She had to take a moment to focus and not let her composure crumble completely at the perilous odds that became of her.

"I wonder, Faythe, if you will risk taking its power to defeat me like you did those fae at the inn. Without your Mindseer by your side to bring you back, that is."

Faythe couldn't believe it, how they all could have missed being tracked by the dark fae, and how nothing had been coincidence. So many revelations shifted into place, and it rattled her fighting stance. The cave-in…it wasn't a freak accident of nature. The dark fae had wanted her alone. Was Marvellas behind it all? Nausea waved through her.

"We won't need its power to defeat you, darkling," Kyleer snarled.

The dark fae, Maverick, advanced a step at the threat, but Zaiana raised a hand, and he halted at her silent command. Her head tilted curiously at Kyleer. A smile creased her perfect mouth, and Faythe's eyes darted to the hand she still held poised, two iron-clad fingers pointed elegantly, catching the spark of amethyst that emitted over them. Small, jagged lines at first, which grew and snapped over the metal of those fingers. Lightning. Vibrant purple bolts that danced mesmerizingly at her command.

Zaiana didn't drop eye contact with Kyleer. "You might want to reassess your strategies, commander."

The look they shared was with thick with tension, but Faythe couldn't place it down to a single form. Then the dark fae's gaze shifted to lock on Faythe, and she stiffened at the attention. Zaiana poised her other hand, and within seconds, lightning sparked and shot across the iron tips in a mirrored position.

"They feel it too, you know," she spoke to Faythe directly, privately. "But it calls to us more. Magick as a way of finding the strongest well to fill. But the difference between you and me, Faythe, is everything."

Her lightning grew, and she upturned her hands sideward as the lethal fireworks lit up the darkening night. Her companion stepped away from her. Faythe could feel the dark fae's power growing, manifesting, and knew then it was a display to mock her as Zaiana seized the ruin's power without so much as a flicker of sweat or a tremble at being consumed by it.

"Discipline, control—you lack it all. And it is why you will not win this fight. If you take its power, perhaps you might be able to break past my barriers. Maybe the fight could be matched. But you will not, because it would consume you entirely to defeat me when you don't have the slightest idea how to wield the power you are capable of."

Faythe's heart was thundering, her mind frantically trying to draw solutions to see her and Kyleer live. But the odds were damning the moment they unveiled their incomparable weapon—the one neither of them could harness or fight against. She watched and listened to the snap of Zaiana's mesmerizing lightning and in any other situation would have admired its beauty. It matched the hue of her eyes, the core of color around her pupils flaring brighter in reaction to the unearthly ruin energy.

"I will give you one chance to surrender and come with me willingly, Faythe."

Faythe looked to Kyleer, whose jaw locked, blade angled at the proposition, fully prepared to go down fighting. To protect her no matter the odds. Her heart clenched scanning his injured shoulder that dropped his weight slightly to one side in pain. Faythe cast her assessment back to the two dark fae. Zaiana was a lethal force on her own paired with the amplifier, and Maverick looked just as eager to kill without a second thought. There was nothing human in his depthless black eyes while he waited for Zaiana's signal.

Faythe knew what she had to do so Kyleer would live. She opened her mouth to voice her surrender, but Kyleer spoke first.

"Not a chance in rutting damn."

Zaiana's smile only brightened against the luminance of her lightning. "If I'm honest, I was hoping you would say that." Her next maneuver happened so fast Faythe didn't have the chance to register what was happening. She caught a glimpse of Zaiana's lightning joining in front of her, exploding into an impossibly thick bolt. Her hand cast skyward as the purple jagged line expelled from her fingertips. A deafening boom resonated in her ears, cracking over the sky and angering the clouds. Then, with her eyes locked on Faythe, she cast her hand down.

Watching that deadly strike of electricity barrel down from the sky toward her was the last thing Faythe saw before smoke and darkness engulfed her.

CHAPTER 56

Faythe

THE AIR DEPARTED her lungs. A sharp pull tugged her body. Faythe was doused in a second of wild panic until everything stilled as quickly as she moved. When she felt the ground beneath her feet and the darkness shifted, Faythe sucked in a long breath while her heart calmed to process.

Kyleer's hand left her waist as the clouds of darkness dissipated, and when Faythe glanced up, she found herself staring at the backs of the dark fae as Zaiana's deadly blow finished landing where she had been mere seconds ago.

Kyleer had Shadowported with her.

She didn't know what to expect, but her stomach knotted with a horrible wave of motion sickness when the unnatural movement settled in. From the blast of lightning to the sky, the clouds broke. Rain fell, a light shower turning to a pelting fall. The water was warm like the air that brewed the storm, rolling furious clouds overhead, covering them with darkness all at once. Faythe blinked the rain from her eyes, cursing that her vision was now impaired by water and dimness. It took effort, but she could still make out the silhouettes of the enemy.

The dark fae whirled to them, and Zaiana's eyes flashed in a frightening fury at the mockery. Faythe still clutched onto Lumarias, though her blade seemed feeble in the face of what her opponent was capable of. She looked down at her blade, the dark steel a blend of smooth slate. A flash of memory struck her mind like an awakening, a brilliant realization. Her sharp inhale—or perhaps her racing heart—alerted Kyleer, who scanned her from head to toe.

"Niltain Steel," she said, the words like a beacon of hope. A way to shift the odds, however small, in their favor.

Kyleer tore his gaze from her and angled his blade as the dark fae stalked them once more. "Care to elaborate?"

"Niltain steel," she repeated, louder over the hammering rain, hoping to the damned Spirits what she knew was true knowledge. At least, true for all dark fae. "I believe it harms them far greater than any other material." It was the only thing the mutant in the caves of High Farrow feared, and ultimately the only metal that caused it significant harm.

Kyleer's mighty sword glinted a beautiful slate gray. Just like his arrowheads and the many weapons in Rhyenelle that were all crafted of the legendary Niltain Steel. She had never been more glad to come from a kingdom that belonged to such brilliant and well-prepared ancestors.

"I do hope that's true," Kyleer muttered, bracing to advance.

She looked at him. Tendrils of his long hair clung to his face, and droplets dripped from the strands that fell past his jaw. He locked her gaze, green eyes focused, alert, but...afraid. Not for himself; his eyes held a desperate plea.

"Faythe, no matter what you see, do not seize that power to save me. But if it comes to saving your own life, you must try. Harness. Do not yield."

In his words of desperation, Faythe straightened her poise, bracing for a fight she knew was perhaps already lost against the uncharted threat that held far more strength combined. Faythe hoped he could see the forgiveness in her eyes—that no matter what came of the fight ahead, it was not his fault.

"Promise me you will not risk yourself for me," he pleaded, their time nearly up.

"I promise," she choked, knowing as soon as it left her lips...it was a lie.

Zaiana had already charged a frighteningly large bolt of lightning in one hand. Faythe tracked her, but something blue caught the corner of her vision right before it went hurling for Kyleer, who ducked out of its path in the nick of time, putting distance between them.

Dear Gods. As if luck couldn't be any more gods-damned out of their favor, Maverick had to be a *Firewielder.* The only small mercy she detected was that his fire wasn't immune to the rain. The blast dissipated slightly as it shot for Kyleer again. And again.

With him distracted, Zaiana took her opening, and Faythe darted out of the path of the strike she sent shooting straight to the ground this time. The stone floor shook violently beneath her feet, the force of her blow enough to cleave the mountain fringe. Faythe cried out as the ground began to loosen and crumble beneath her feet. She stumbled, racing over the debris, then leaped and rolled, narrowly avoiding being sucked into the deep crevice Zaiana had carved. With the amplifier of the temple ruin, her ability was beyond anything Faythe had ever seen or imagined before.

Shooting back to her feet, Faythe spared one glance over, relieved while also terrified to see Kyleer alive but in a nasty combat of shadow, fire, and steel with the dark fae. The pair were utterly ruthless as they honed in on each other. It took all her will to tear her eyes from him, praying with everything she had that he would be able to triumph.

But she couldn't afford to think of that right now as her eyes snapped to land on her own imminent threat.

Zaiana didn't attack again with her lightning. Instead, she drew a magnificent blade from her side: a dark steel that glittered with iridescent black. Faythe's blood ran cold, immediately flashing back to the last time she saw such a stone. It seemed the fae weren't the only ones who knew what material to efficiently defend themselves with. Zaiana's blade was partially crafted of Magestone. Faythe didn't fear for herself and had to focus not to turn and shout a warning to Kyleer should Maverick's blade be made of the same.

"I'm nothing if not fair, Faythe." The dark fae stalked toward her, footsteps rippling in the pools of rain over the uneven ground. Faythe braced and angled her blade. "No power, no wings." As she said it, the towering taloned wings disappeared from over her shoulders with a faint shimmer. "Just you, me, and steel."

Though, Zaiana seemed to forget her unfair advantage of immortal speed as she darted for Faythe, who brought her blade up in a flash of instinctual reaction. Or perhaps she didn't care for Faythe's cruel mortal weakness in comparison. The clang of their blades echoed painfully in her ears over the pounding of water, dangerously close to her face.

Faythe pushed with everything she had, the movement awakening every dormant sense that focused her mind for combat. She locked on those vibrant, amethyst-cored eyes and attacked. Stepping forward with a lunge, she switched her maneuver at the last second, anticipating the dark fae would see it coming. Lumarias was a hairbreadth from catching her thighs, emitting a hiss from Zaiana who didn't hold back. Twisting, Faythe deflected her sword, which swung sideward, falling into a crouch. She cast her foot out, but Zaiana was quick to detect it, moving out of range before advancing. Faythe was caught off-guard, and a foot heaved against her chest, painfully knocking the wind from her and sending her skidding against the harsh stone.

Adrenaline had her rolling, pushing to her feet and shifting into defense against the stabbing of her injured ribs. Zaiana was fast and far stronger, and she didn't hold back those traits. There was a part of Faythe that acknowledged she was utterly outmatched, but her fight to survive pushed her to go on despite the odds.

"Take the power, Faythe," Zaiana chanted.

Faythe swung to deflect her blow, not gaining a second to catch her breath when their steel connected over and over against the storm that battered her body just as ruthlessly. The weight of her drenched clothes was enough to stifle her agility somewhat, her grip on the hilt of her sword slipping on occasion, sending her heart leaping up her throat. Still, Faythe didn't stop pushing. She honed in on Zaiana, becoming spellbound to the amethyst of her irises as a moving target; a beacon of light against the dark.

Thunder rumbled overhead, adding anguish to their dance of storm and steel. Faythe thrust forward, spinning to catch the counterattack at her back. They spun and darted through the waterfall, and she had long disconnected herself from feeling the exertion in an attempt to keep up with Zaiana's speed. This dark fae was unlike any competitor she'd faced. The way she moved was like air, her swipes and steps so calculated it was as though she could predict one hundred of her opponent's maneuvers before they were made.

Faythe was expending herself for nothing as Zaiana humored her, getting a feel for her steps and style. The dark fae was taunting her, reducing every ounce of Faythe's training and skill to no more than an amateur's practice.

Fire tore from her shoulder to her elbow, and Faythe stumbled back, clutching the long wound Zaiana dealt. The warmth of her blood spilled over her hand. She clenched her teeth and once again shifted her stance into a defensive position. She couldn't give up.

She would never give up.

"You cannot contend with me," Zaiana called, glancing at the gash in her arm. "Not as you are."

Faythe rolled her shoulders back, ignoring the searing pain. "Maybe not. But I do enjoy a challenge." She moved first, and Zaiana effortlessly parried against her attacks.

"You have a strong will," Zaiana said loudly over the pelting of water and the clank of steel, dancing around her attacks as if they were child's play. "An admirable fight in you," she went on, and Faythe felt her fury rising as the dark fae continued to deflect with ease. "But you are no match for me, Faythe."

Without warning, Zaiana pushed off Faythe's blade. The vibrant purple of her lightning was bright against the dark, engulfing her steel right before she cast her sword hand out. That lethal flare shot for Faythe far too quickly for her to attempt to step out of range.

It struck her chest, and Faythe was suspended in air for a few seconds before her back and head collided with a solid, unforgiving force. The rain stopped; the world disappeared; a darkness so depthless engulfed her. Then she was falling forward, her senses returning just in time to brace her arms and splay her palms. They slapped against the wet stone ground, and her knees cracked painfully. She couldn't withstand her weight and collapsed, her cheek meeting the cold ground. Faythe's uneven, harsh breaths rippled over a thin sheet of water while it attempted to drown her from above.

She thought she heard someone calling her name. Maybe it was Kyleer, but she couldn't be sure as the storm mixed with the ringing that filled her ears.

Faythe felt the presence in front of her and mustered all her strength to drag and angle her arms, pushing up on trembling elbows. She glanced up. Zaiana crouched slowly, observing her with a look she couldn't decipher. Not triumph or wicked glee like she expected. Her face was devoid of any emotion.

"We all have a destiny, though it is not often kind to us." Zaiana's voice was cold, personal.

The humming in Faythe's veins heightened, as if instinct made her power stretch out to grasp the amplifier of the temple ruin that might give her a fighting chance against the dark fae. Faythe was wholly, utterly outmatched in everything without it. Human, weak, feeble. Her ability on its own was not enough to break through the impenetrable block of Zaiana's mind. Her fingers curled against the stone, collecting water that pooled around her. She cast her sight but could hardly make out the two figures engaged in quick combat. She doubted even with her full strength and consciousness she would be able to keep up with how fast Kyleer and Maverick moved.

But it was clear one was leading the fight, forcing the other on the defensive. She had a moment of fool's hope that it was Kyleer, knowing how absolutely lethal he was on the battlefield. Yet the towering shadow of wings told her it was not he who was winning. The dark fae was beyond even fae agility, and a flashback of brief memory set in the realization that Kyleer was damned too. He wouldn't defeat him.

With human blood in their system, they could defeat an army five-to-one.

The flash of knowledge hit her with desolate hopelessness for her friend. Faythe wondered if Zaiana was the same; if she fed on the life force of humans to heighten her strength and speed. Faythe would be wise to assume so. Paired with her ability to harness the ruin...Zaiana was unstoppable.

A dark chant encircled her, filling her mouth with a taste of ash. Drowning her ears with a soothing whisper. Touching her skin with a tingling heat.

Harness. Do not yield.

Faythe pulled her legs from under her, wincing as she got to her knees. The unearthly power sang to her loudly as if knowing what she intended to do. What she *had* to do. They wouldn't stop until they had her, and Kyleer wouldn't stop if they tried to take her. For him, she had to try. The only way she stood a chance...was to even the playing field.

Faythe tipped her head up and clenched her teeth as she silently began releasing the crumbling wall against the ruin's power that yearned to merge with her. The first wave pierced through, and while it struck her like Zaiana's lightning, Faythe fought back to keep control this time. She locked eyes with Zaiana, who slowly rose as Faythe tracked her. The dark fae backed up a long step, and Faythe wasn't sure what she saw in her expression that almost made her appear *cautious*.

Breathing steadily, the ruin's caress took away her pain. The stabbing in her chest eased; the throbbing of her back and head from the blow numbed. Faythe's head fell back, the rainfall on her face soothing against the heat that began to torch her veins. Then she pushed to her feet, clutching her sword...

And *became* the well of dark power that amplified within her.

"There she is," Zaiana said, a hushed breeze over the storm. Her eyes dipped to Faythe's palms, to the glowing symbols within. Even though they both harnessed the power of the ruin, Zaiana didn't don such marks.

Faythe took a long breath, feeling the surge of energy that hummed in her blood, heightened her senses, and calculated her thoughts in one instinct. Survival. Not just for her, but for the fae warrior whose faltering she could now feel from the pulse of his mind across the mountainside. In mild triumph, the dark fae Maverick was not leading without great opposition.

She locked eyes with Zaiana, fingers clenching around Lumarias. "Here I am." Faythe moved, clashing blades once again with the dark, surging a new strength of determination. The two of them cut through the rain that fell like sheets. Honing in on the black barrier of Zaiana's mind, Faythe pushed through it, but even with the heightened power of the ruin, it wasn't without great resistance that she broke through.

Her movements flashed through Faythe's mind, and the pair became a blur of steel and leather, amber and amethyst, against the dark night. Zaiana fought back from within and occasionally triumphed in blocking her from her thoughts. They merged in a push and pull of minds, a dance of swords, and a battle of wills.

Faythe opened herself to seize more of the ruin's power, feeling it rejoice within her as she did. Her head throbbed a dull ache in her focus to parry back. Her life hung in the balance between two unparalleled sources. But she would destroy herself before she surrendered to either, and she would damn well try to take both out with her.

Their blades locked, bringing their faces mere inches apart. Amber flame blazed into amethyst lightning, at risk of destroying the world in the wake of their rage and defiance.

Faythe shattered through the mental wall Zaiana had once again erected in an attempt to push her out. This time, she didn't hesitate to take control. Zaiana choked and fell, knees cracking against the stone ground at Faythe's command while she poised the tip of her blade to her chest. It wasn't as easy as the other times she had used her ability in such a way. Zaiana fought back valiantly, and Faythe's head pounded against the effort it took to hold her mind.

"You made a grave mistake coming after my friends," Faythe said, her chest heaving with exertion.

Zaiana smiled, panting too as she let out a breathy laugh that lacked humor. "I don't think so."

Very faintly, she thought she heard Maverick call out the name of his companion whose life balanced at the tip of her blade. Faythe applied pressure, and as soon as the sharp point broke through her leathers to contact skin, Zaiana let out a cry that solidified Faythe's assumption. Niltain steel *did* harm them far more than ordinary steel.

"*Zaiana!*"

The call of her name was heard over the pounding of water and the throb of her blood. Not for its velocity, but for the sheer terror and desperation that laced the single word.

Both of them snapped their attention to the fighting males just in time to see Maverick drop his focus from Kyleer and begin advancing to Zaiana's aid. It was a reckless, foolish move, and Kyleer was fast. One second he was behind the dark fae, and when smoke engulfed him, he reappeared in Maverick's path.

Kyleer's strike was swift and without hesitation. The dark fae cried loudly in pain, clutching the long gash that struck across his abdomen as he fell to his knees. Over his ghostly pale hand, *black* blood spilled. Faythe lost focus for a second with the dizzying flash of memory of the last time she saw blood of such a color. Even though the creature she'd encountered before was beyond human or fae recognition, there was no doubt now it was somehow their *kin.*

Kyleer braced, fully prepared to plunge his sword through Maverick's chest…

"You don't want to do that."

CHAPTER 57

Faythe

F AYTHE FELT THE cool breath of the metal against her throat as the
dark fae used her distraction to her advantage. Zaiana's voice
called over to halt Kyleer before he could claim Maverick's life. Faythe
might have cursed herself for the fatal error, except she felt the creeping
claim of darkness as the power within turned raging with no outlet. She
had to try let it go; she had to reel back on her own before it took over
and consumed her entirely. But its talons sank deep in reluctance to
part.

Kyleer shifted, not taking his eyes off Maverick until he too was
poised behind his target, standing off with Zaiana. They were mutually
compromised. Except it seemed the dark fae behind her forgot the
extent of Faythe's ability and didn't consider she could seize Maverick's
mind and shatter it from this distance with the amplifier of the ruin.

Just as she thought to use the one thing that could grant them
advantage, a pounding echoed across the stone, traveling like rolling
rocks

No—not rocks. What raced for them wasn't danger but salvation. Everyone's attention was grabbed by the invasion as it rattled through the rain that battered the mountain fringe. Faythe's weight slumped in a relief so strong it made her forget, just for a second, the many threats that surrounded her.

Figures ran for them—four of them—and when they got closer…

Reylan halted with the others, eyes fixed with calculating fury on the blade at her throat. Izaiah and Livia assessed both sides of the situation with lethal focus and consideration. Reuben was panting as he caught his breath, but he stood armed with two short daggers.

Gods, she was in pain. *On fire.* But he was here, and even if the power claimed her this time, Reylan was here, and she could tell him…

"Don't you dare." His voice was clear through the glare of light in her mind. Faythe held onto those sapphires while her life balanced between being claimed by steel or magick. *"Don't you give up, Faythe Ashfyre."*

Faythe breathed, closing her eyes to keep hold of the reins of control that began to slip from her grasp. Her vision swayed but was snapped back to alert when she caught the pulse of more minds joining them on the open mountain fringe. They came from the skies, two forms dropping elegantly to mirror Faythe's companions.

One dark fae, equally as striking as Maverick but with dark blond hair, was carrying someone else, whom he swiftly set on her feet. Faythe was stunned to notice she was without wings. She was fae. And while she didn't completely fear the dark fae she arrived with, her demeanor was tense and concerned, scanning over everyone in the clearing.

The final member to join Zaiana was surprisingly younger, clutching a bow with an arrow nocked and ready but not poised to release.

No one moved, and no one spoke for an agonizingly long moment, gauging each other as opponents. It seemed no one was quick to find an advantageous strategy or foolish enough to start attacking without formation while her life and Maverick's could end in a split second.

Faythe had one. One way she was confident she could see her

friends come out of this alive. Yet it was the signing of her own death. Power chanted in favor of what crossed her mind. Through it, she felt a strong protest. Reylan fought that power, knowing what she planned to do. He was too far to reel her back, and perhaps when she let go, the buildup of what had filtered through her since she first opened herself to the ruin would be too much for even him to save her this time.

It was the only way. And in turn, Marvellas would fail to get what she sought. Her friends could still make it to the Isles without her. Faythe closed her eyes and imagined the barrier she held firm against the explosion of energy that would blast through her if she let go of her guard completely. Only then would she be strong enough to seize the minds of all the dark fae.

"I'm sorry," she channeled to Reylan as she braced herself. Just as she clenched her teeth, feeling the waves of staggering light begin to pierce her being…

Sharp screeches over the rainfall snapped her eyes open.

The sound alerted everyone, and as Faythe glanced at their reactions to the shrill cries that echoed, most were wide-eyed with horror, knowing what the sound was. Even Zaiana stiffened behind her before uttering one word that shuddered right through and froze over the heat in her veins, just for a second.

"Skailies."

It was followed by a curse as the wailing echoed louder and louder. Two directions. Reylan, Izaiah, and Livia whirled back the way they came, while Zaiana's companions twisted and braced weapons down the opposite valley entrance. Faythe followed Reylan's line of sight, heart thundering, though it had nothing to do with the unearthly magick she held in her trembling grip.

Their fears came to fruition a moment later, and Faythe gasped. It tunneled in like a cloud of smoke at first, but as it raced for them on either side, she was struck by horror in realizing it was not smoke. It was a feral stampede of stark black bodies, so tightly crammed together they moved as one like a wave.

So. Many. Bodies.

Zaiana swore again, and the threat of her blade was removed from Faythe's neck. Faythe whirled to her, but the dark fae focused her attention like everyone else.

Just like that, enemies became allies.

Nothing would matter if they were all consumed by the masses of faceless foes.

"What a tragedy it would be," Zaiana mused, sheathing her sword, "to see us all go down now." The darkness closed in; Zaiana conjured her lightning over her hands. "The Gods really do have a wicked sense of humor."

Faythe almost laughed, but when the frontline met with Reylan and the others, Faythe angled her blade as some began to break through and sprint to them. "I don't believe the Gods are at fault here," she answered though her incredulous terror. "You all but summoned them with your epic display."

Zaiana met her eye, but Faythe couldn't read what crossed them as she said, "Harness the power, Faythe. It will only consume you if you yield, or your body will start to shut down if you attempt to depart with it all."

Faythe gave a single nod, refraining from voicing that it was far easier said than done while she felt as if she were on fire. But it was not all-consuming; it was alerting and focusing. At least for now. The sensation reminded Faythe of a time in her carefree childhood when she was determined to beat Jakon in a race across the town. She started in a sprint—a fool's error considering the distance—and it wasn't long before a burn coated her throat and speared her breaths. Her muscles ached and protested before she'd even reached halfway. But in her defiance, she didn't stop. She kept sprinting past the agony to win, and eventually, the pain became bearable, subsided to a numbness, to keep her going.

But as soon as she stopped running, everything she was spared from feeling caught up with her all at once. Jakon had refused to race her for a long time after. Witnessing her scary recovery immediately after had felt like embracing death.

Harnessing the ruin's power was like that sprint. Faythe knew she had to keep pushing.

The Skailies were so near to them Faythe brought her sword up to strike, but a blaring flare of lightning struck through their path, incinerating the first and second line of them as they broke through the defenses of Reylan and the others. She couldn't bear to think of him, knowing if she did, her panic upon seeing how many he fought and the odds stacked against them all would be her undoing.

Finally, one caught up to her, and she didn't give her fear a chance to surface at seeing the back void it held for a face. Only snapping teeth and long, lethal claws swiped for her. She cut down the first with little effort but barely got a second of breath before another was in front of her. Then another. Then another. Faythe was spinning and cutting with a precision that shouldn't be possible in her mortal body. The ruin didn't just amplify her ability; it gave her immeasurable strength and speed that had her moving on instinct, feeling her blade tear through rotting dark flesh to no end.

Her drenched hair whipped across her face as she protected herself from all angles, noting the ones who slipped past Zaiana's companions behind her too. It was overwhelming, but she didn't falter.

Too many. There were far too many of them, and she couldn't see a way out. It seemed hopeless, but all they could do was keep fighting. Zaiana took out many at a time, vibrant purple bolts illuminating the gruesome battlefield as the bodies mounted but didn't cease advancing. Maverick attacked with darts and sheets of blue flame that engulfed the masses. Catching a glimpse through the darkness, Faythe saw Izaiah had shifted into a brilliant black panther and tore through countless. It still wasn't enough.

She felt the sinking seed of hopelessness grow in the pit of her stomach. She didn't stop moving. Didn't stop fighting. But she could see no light.

Over the cries and snarls of the Skailies, something far louder, far more piercing, rang out over the skies. It made her wince, but a shiver crawled over her body like an awakening at the sound. Faythe couldn't help glancing up, feeling compelled to. It was a grave mistake when seconds later pain lashed across her back and she cried out, falling to the ground. She didn't have the focus to see the next attack as something sharp dug into her shoulder. Teeth. The pain was excruciating, but the creature wasn't latched on for long before vibrant purple illuminated around her and the Skailie was incinerated to dust.

She might have thanked Zaiana, but her consideration for her life was only to keep her alive for some greater, far more sinful purpose. Still, she twisted her head and hoped the dark fae saw her gratitude in her helpless look.

Faythe felt something grappling her from within, emitting a pulse of strength to keep her from drifting. It was Reylan. His lifeline within her kept her from letting go of the ruin's power, which would incapacitate her quicker than it did at the inn. Her damned mortal body had been used far beyond its limits.

A dark smoke surrounded her, and the presence that wrapped her was a force so pure and safe. For a second, Faythe was taken away from the carnage unfolding around her. The heaviness of her body from the rain that fell mercilessly became light. The pounding of her head numbed. Just for those few blissful seconds…because he was here. Reylan was before her. But she couldn't look up as she watched harsh droplets ripple the water around them. She felt his hand on her neck as her head bowed, but with his touch, he didn't soothe the storm that raged within like she hoped.

"I'm here." His smooth voice, his words, made a whimper escape her mouth. A faint flicker of happiness in the midst of hopelessness where she kneeled in the puddles of rain, ready to submit and admit defeat. Her blood roared; her wounds tore like flame; her head was so close to erupting. Reylan fell to his knees with her. "I see you, Faythe. I see you, and I hear you."

The words struck her like the peaceful verse of a song, a promise she would always hold so close to her heart. She wanted to echo that promise back to him, but her agony was quick to douse any short moment of hope.

"It hurts," was all she could say. Or at least she thought she said. Her throat was so tight, her mind a cloudy haze of rage and pain. "It hurts so much."

"I know." His voice lapped soothingly through her mind, a cooling breeze against the raging inferno. But not even he could tame the blaze this time. His hand cupped her nape, and he leaned his forehead to hers. His palm slid into her loose hand while her other remained clamped around her sword. *"You are far stronger than you know, Faythe. You need to get up."*

She was a coward. A weak, helpless coward. Faythe shook her head. Another of those loud, shrill cries rattled the stars—louder now. Faythe winced with a sob.

"Please," she barely whispered. *"Please make it stop."*

All of it. Whatever it took. She wanted more than anything for the pain and power to stop.

"I can't." Reylan's voice was utterly devastated. He pulled back, and his fingers curled under her chin, forcing her lifeless head up to stare into the familiar sapphires that were her anchor to this world.

The rain battered them mercilessly. Reylan's silver hair turned to a sad gray that slicked around his face. So beautiful. Droplets of water trailed along his fierce, sculptured features. Every now and then, a bright flare of white and purple illuminated his expression. Hardened for battle but softened with a fear so haunting.

"If I help you release that power, your body will fail. You need to keep fighting just a little longer. Fight through this night. Fight for everything I haven't had the chance to give you yet. For the life I promise to always stand by your side throughout." His eyes connected to something within her. Not his ability, but a striking will to survive. For him, for herself...for the time they deserved to have together. *"Until the end of days."*

Faythe felt her strength returning. Sheer desperation and will alone coursed through her to subside her desire to submit. She breathed slow and steady. She focused and found the strength to straighten her spine once more as she said, *"Maybe even longer."*

With her answer, a breath of relief rushed through Reylan's chest.

He hooked an arm around her, and she didn't protest as he helped her rise on weak knees. She had to go on.

When she was standing, Faythe spared a dreaded glance around, and the sight almost made her buckle once more. Everyone fought the dark creatures, and it was then she realized Zaiana alone had kept the Skailies back from them while Reylan helped her.

All was dark, desolate, and grim. Then a brilliant flare of red and amber torched the sky, illuminating everything across the mountain fringe. It was followed by another sharp cry as something was cast overhead. The Skailies, they balked. One by one they stopped attacking and began to back away. She didn't think a faceless monster could feel fear, yet it was there in the way their savage flailing turned to a curl of submission.

Another shrill cry. Faythe cast her eyes skyward, flinching at the harsh, piercing sound. Reylan's arm pulled her closer as if he was prepared to shield her with his entire body if necessary against whatever claimed the skies.

It took a few chilling, tense seconds as nothing but the darkness and rainwater blurred her vision no matter how fast she blinked. It wasn't until the creature wanted to reveal itself that they would see. And that moment came when a vibrant flash of red and amber tendrils scorched the night...

The air left Faythe completely at what she saw.

She blinked hard to release the water gathering in her eyes, uncertain if her obscured vision was mistaken. She tracked the red inferno as best she could, fire that rippled beautifully like a wave over them. Faythe forgot everything, struck utter still in her stupor. Her eyes followed it until it flew past them, right to the end of the mountain range. Then, when she thought it would keep going and she would never catch sight of its beauty again, it turned in an elegant glide, coming back toward them.

The closer it got, right in front of Faythe, the lower it seemed to fall. Closer and closer. Its wings caught fire, magnificent vines of flame licking along its dark feathers. Faythe didn't fear as it advanced fast and to a deadly proximity. She couldn't believe what she was seeing was real, and perhaps that was what held her still. It was gigantic and utterly mesmerizing.

Reylan's strong arm around her was the only thing that snapped her to her senses. Just as the flames darted from its wings in a deadly wave, shooting for them, she was hauled sideward and pulled behind a large boulder.

Fire shot past their cover. Enchanting. Unlike any flame that could be made by man, and not like the fire conjured by magick. This was far more alluring. With a faint shimmer, it was pure blood-red with white and glowing amber hues. Faythe was spellbound, having to physically restrain herself from reaching out a hand to touch it against all natural instincts.

Shrill cries emitted over the grounds. The fire tore through the masses of faceless foes, incinerating the entirety of the deadly force where they stood mere seconds ago. Faythe was overcome by a different kind of chant then. A beckoning, cutting through the ruin's whispers.

The fire ceased, and she dared a glance around the stone. Ash and smoke clogged the air, but the fire still blazed, parting the clouds enough that she saw it completely. Not her imagination, as all the hideous creatures that had been there moments before were turned to cinders by its power.

A great Phoenix stood blazing and triumphant. There was no mistaking it. Its wings, while still coated in flame, were lowered as if it were assessing the threat to its domain before striking again.

Faythe locked eyes with it and dared to believe it stared right back at her. Everyone else had taken cover behind various rocks and boulders. But then she heard the cry of a dear friend—*felt* his pain through the pulse of his open mind.

Her eyes didn't search for long to find Izaiah. He was gravely hurt. Faythe shifted, but Reylan halted her.

"We need to help him," Faythe gasped.

The dark fae with blond hair had his arms hooked under her friend as if he'd narrowly managed to drag Izaiah behind the large rock they both took shelter behind.

"We wouldn't make it to him without becoming ash ourselves. He'll be okay."

She locked eyes with Reylan and saw the agony in them too. He also fought against the helpless situation they were in. The strong need to go to his brother.

At the thought, Faythe's attention found Kyleer. The one who had guided her, saved her, and defended her. Her teeth clamped tight to force back her whimper at finding the fierce warrior on his knees, clutching his wounded shoulder beside the enemy he fought valiantly, the battle between them dormant while they took cover against the mutual, far deadlier threat. Both of them were weakened greatly.

Another sharp line of pain shot through Faythe while she left her ability, her senses, wide open. Her hand clutched her abdomen with the phantom fire that scorched there, and then her eyes found the source.

Livia also lay wounded and helpless while the fae who had arrived in the dark fae's company seemed to be aiding her, tending to her abdomen as it bled. Faythe was right to assume it was a blow dealt by the monstrous Skailies. The smaller dark fae crouched with them, her bow set aside and her focus solely on whatever the fae asked of her while she helped Livia.

Reuben. Where in the rutting damn was Reuben? Faythe didn't get long to scout for him when a cold snake of fear replaced the searing heat of Livia's pain.

Glancing to her side, she saw Zaiana could barely fit behind her cover, which had crumbled even smaller against the first blast. The luminance grew, and Faythe fixed her eyes on the bird once more. It straightened and puffed its huge black-and-red-feathered chest, the flames along its wings growing as it splayed them wide. *Gods,* it was brilliant.

With a gasp, Faythe tumbled back around to take full cover behind the rock. She felt heat, but it was the fire in her veins from the ruin that slicked her skin. Faythe felt nothing emitting from the flames that turned the Skailies to dust in seconds. She lifted her hand and gasped at the stone that shone like a bright ruby on her wrist.

The Eye of the Phoenix.

It was reacting...and as her hand neared the fire, Faythe swore it *moved.* The flames inched away from her touch while the stone pulsed brighter. A hand lashed out to her forearm, pulling her arm back before she could recklessly attempt to touch the lethal fire. Reylan looked at her as if she'd lost her sanity. She wasn't entirely certain she hadn't. Between the ruin's influence and the new surge of something...*else,* Faythe felt deliriously unstoppable.

"It doesn't burn," she thought out loud.

The Phoenix didn't relent, and a cry to her left snapped her attention to Zaiana, who was close to becoming no more than dust in the wind. It wouldn't stop until they were all smoke and ash. They were the enemy on its sacred ground.

"I can assure you, it does," Reylan panted.

Faythe felt warmth, but not *heat*. Not like what seemed to scorch the air and land around them.

Finally, the fire let up, but she didn't believe the Phoenix was finished. It wouldn't stop until they were all expelled from its domain. Faythe dared to glance around again, and as she expected, it was braced and frighteningly huge as it expanded its whole body to engulf the space. The rain still fell, but rather than having any extinguishing effect on the flames that soared over its splayed wings, the water turned to steam that warmed the air before it could land.

Gods above.

It was bracing to attack again, and Faythe didn't know why her gaze fell to Zaiana, who curled into herself. The rock she hid behind wouldn't stand another blast, and she wouldn't survive the impact of its fire. Faythe shouldn't concern herself with her life. In fact, letting her perish would ultimately save her from the hunter. As soon as the threat was defeated, they would return to mortal enemies.

But Zaiana had saved her—perhaps to her own ultimate gain, though Faythe refused to believe that was all.

She watched the dancing glow of the Eye of the Phoenix on her wrist, and an image came to mind. One she had seen depicted within a book in the great library of Rhyenelle's castle. It made her heart pound, just as it did when she stared at it as a still image, believing then that it was simply a fantasy; a painting from a wondrous imagination.

But what if it were history?

If only you dare—another memory flashed to mind, from her encounter with the Dresair in High Farrow—*to take the leap…*

What if it was a foretelling?

Faythe's eyes widened. She didn't have time to second-guess the completely insane, desperate, and deadly plan that challenged her to act. There was no other way, and the reaction of the fire to the amulet on her wrist—the same one she now believed she saw in that painting

—was a small slither of hope she had to grapple onto to find her bravery.

And trust you will fly with the Phoenix.

"Faythe, whatever you're thinking…" Reylan warned, perhaps sensing her rising adrenaline.

She locked eyes with him, and they were wide with fear. It was for him—for all of them—that she had to try. She was the only one who could.

His face fell, desolate. He shook his head. "No—"

"Reylan," Faythe choked, the pain on the warrior's face striking far deeper than the battle of power within her. "Always remember…you are my heart." Her eyes burned. "Please forgive me."

She despised what she had to do to him, knowing he would follow her if she didn't. He would always follow her. A strained cry left her as she fought against the pain of betraying him. His trust. But she *had* to do it.

With the heightened power of the ruin, Faythe shattered clean through Reylan's firm mental barrier. He fought her. *Gods,* he did. His eyes widened in shock, horror, and realization the moment she entered to halt his movements. The sheer terror in his eyes cleaved so deep.

"I'm so sorry," she whispered.

His painful silent protest stole her breath.

"I love you. Please forgive me."

It took all her will and physical resistance to tear her eyes from his wildly pleading look. To straighten from her position behind cover. To take that first step away from him.

Faythe twisted around the large rock in one fluid movement…

And came face-to-face with the creature of myth and legend.

The superior race of the Firebird. Flesh, fire, and ash before her. It was equal parts awe-inspiring and terrifying.

Faythe walked to it, and she swore it tracked her. Stopping, she braced, but the bird didn't ease its flames. She thought she saw the slight canter of its massive head—an elegant mane of fire-torched feathers crowning it and running down its neck. It was the single most breath-taking creature she had ever seen.

Fire blazed brighter from its wings as it flared them a fraction wider, preparing to strike again. Faythe's pulse was wild, but she was focused. And she was ready.

The inferno collected, near blinding, and the bird's chest heaved in a deep inhale. Bracing to send Phoenixfyre hurtling to claim her.

CHAPTER 58

Zaiana

I‌T WAS JUST her luck that she had been sent to retrieve a human with a complete disregard for her own life. Not killing her was a struggle, but it seemed keeping Faythe from killing herself was even more so.

Zaiana couldn't believe her eyes as Faythe stepped out from the rock she was hiding behind. The silver-haired warrior surprisingly stayed in place, but his face was set in a terror so deep as he watched the human slip away from him. Zaiana tensed at that look, and she found her eyes sliding forward. Not to Faythe, but to Maverick, who crouched with the fae Kyleer. Both of them were injured, and she might have felt something for the fae warrior too. A want for him to be *okay.* Zaiana expelled the weak thought. His life wasn't her concern.

Maverick met her eyes, his expression focused through his pain. Zaiana switched her gaze to scan for Tynan, finding him unharmed but as the savior of one of the enemies. She should have felt anger for what he had risked, but she was only filled with *relief.* Upon finding Amaya and Nerida also as safe as could be with the last fae of the opponent's ensemble, Zaiana relaxed in the knowledge everyone was accounted for. They all lived.

But her crumbling cover would not withstand another blast of Phoenixfyre. She planned to release the glamour on her wings and attempt a shot at the sky. What had prevented her so far was the likelihood the beast would incinerate her long before she could soar out of reach. Zaiana knew little of the Firebirds—they were believed to be a myth. She might have even admired the brilliance and beauty of the creature were it not trying to burn them all to cinders.

Zaiana settled her gaze on Faythe once more, in utter disbelief at the human's stupidity as she walked straight onto the open stone field of fire. It may be a creature of her kingdom, but it still pinned her as the enemy while its blazing red-and-white flames continued to grow and torch the dark sky.

While Zaiana remained connected to the ruin, she felt Faythe's power line too. It was strong—too strong—for the body she had. Zaiana had pushed her to use it, knowing it would drain her beyond use after she let go. But she had clearly underestimated how long the human could hold it for. What was intended to tire her out to make the capture easy had turned out to be a challenge like she'd never faced before. Faythe's ability to control a person's mind…it was unparalleled and absolutely lethal. Now, the ruin's power was the only thing keeping her alive, fighting, as long as she held it.

It was all about to be wasted energy.

Faythe stopped before the creature, and it seemed ludicrous to watch the standoff as they seemed to gauge each other. If the human was afraid, Zaiana had to admire her for her outward steeled expression and battle-firm stance in the face of the mighty threat.

It was all about to be over.

Both sides had lost to the great Firebird.

Its wings splayed, and Zaiana didn't bother curling down as small as she could get. The rock wouldn't shield her against the singe of its heat. If she was going to die, it would be without fear.

Zaiana stood confidently. She was the storm against the rolling clouds; the thunder in the silent air. She was darkness triumphant. She wouldn't go out standing idle.

Doing the most foolish thing she'd ever done in her miserable life, Zaiana raced to Faythe. Beside her, in a potentially final futile attempt to shield herself, Zaiana conjured her lightning. Her fingers came together, pulling apart abruptly to snap a long, suspended bolt, and with a clockwise twist of her poised fingers in front of her, an electric shield formed.

She didn't believe it would be able to withstand Phoenixfyre, having seen how easily it tore through rock and flesh. The shimmering veil she'd created almost seemed laughable.

Blazing red fire hurled for them, and Zaiana braced her legs to absorb the impact if the shield was to withstand even for a few seconds. Just before it could hit them, Zaiana twisted her head with a wince, eyes clamping shut. She held her arms firm to maintain the shield.

Seconds passed, and she felt the heat, but not in the flesh-incinerating way she expected. It was even less blaring than when she lay shriveled behind the boulder. And yet she felt nothing. No force battering the feeble shield she still harnessed.

Zaiana opened her eyes and was stunned by what she saw. She dropped her arms, her lightning winking out in the process.

It shouldn't be possible, yet there she was.

Faythe, by some damn inconceivable, unexplainable miracle, stood as if she harnessed the power of a God in the way she deflected the fire that flared around them. As though summoning an invisible curved wall before them, she cast out a hand, and Zaiana's eye caught sight of the flaring red stone that adorned her wrist.

Impossible. It should have been impossible that they stood there alive.

Seconds crawled like minutes as she watched the fire blaze around them. Faythe's hands trembled, and for a moment she feared the human wouldn't be able to hold it. It shocked her still that she had the strength at all.

Then, all at once, the fire ceased.

Faythe gasped, panting hard as she doubled over to brace on her knees. Zaiana subconsciously took a few steps toward her, still tracking the Firebird.

"It worked," Faythe rasped through a labored breath.

Zaiana snapped her head to the human, incredulous. "Good to know there was method to your madness."

Faythe let out a single breathy laugh. "There was luck to my insanity."

Zaiana might have smiled at that, but her attention—and everyone else's—was grabbed by the shrill cry that emitted from the Phoenix as it angled its giant head skyward. The ringing in her ears was painful, and she winced.

"I think you might have just pissed it off more."

Faythe straightened, and her exertion was clear: she wouldn't withstand that again. But she remained devoid of fear as she stared at the bird with a rare defiance. Stupidity or bravery—they often walked a thin line.

"This…is most definitely stupidity."

Zaiana blinked, taken aback that Faythe had heard that thought. And likely many others since her ability was loose and amplified and reinforcing her mental barrier wasn't exactly her main priority right now.

Faythe turned her head to lock Zaiana's gaze, every emotion steeled in a hard, threatening look. "If you harm a single one of them," she warned, "death won't stop me from coming for you."

Zaiana didn't get the chance to question her words as she was answered by Faythe twisting on her heel and abruptly taking off. Without hesitation, the Phoenix splayed its wings and shot to the sky in a single powerful heave that blasted a hard gust of wind, nearly knocking her off-balance. Zaiana shifted her stance and shielded her eyes. When the air stilled again, she watched the bird glide overhead, then her eyes fell on the human sprinting away from them, toward the ledge that only led to one place: down. A long, deadly way down for anyone without wings.

Zaiana might have tried to go after her, but she gauged it was already too late. Faythe had sealed her fate. Perhaps to be the pitiful, tragic hero and distract the bird so they could all flee.

They should, but no one moved.

The silver-haired fae cried her name. Repeatedly. Zaiana couldn't even look at him. The tone of his voice alone cleaved something inside her. It was odd to react to someone else's pain, but even on her worst enemy, she wouldn't wish any physical torture alike to what the fae seemed to be enduring in that moment. It was foolish to care for one life so much. Zaiana pitied him for his weak heart.

"Such a waste."

Maverick's voice beside her startled her while she was focused on Faythe's last moments. He wasn't wrong. It was such a tragic way for someone so gifted to leave the world. Zaiana couldn't even think of the selfish side to it all. They had failed their quest without Faythe where they needed her. Yet it was almost impossible to have predicted how difficult it was to keep the reckless human alive.

"Save her!" Nerida cried desperately. "You have wings!"

"It's too late," Zaiana snapped.

Faythe reached the end of the mountain fringe, no more than a small silhouette illuminated by the fire of the bird that caught up to her.

Nerida whimpered, and glancing at Amaya, she saw her face was also written with sorrow. Ridiculous. Zaiana should reprimand her for showing emotion for someone she didn't even know. The enemy. Zaiana's ticket to freedom.

Faythe leaped off the mountainside. The Phoenix spun and fell into a dive after her.

Then all was dark and silent.

The tension of enemies returned. Disbelief swirled between both sides. The heartbreak of Faythe's companions was palpable.

"Well, I guess that's that," Maverick commented casually as though witnessing the end of a disappointing show. It was brazen—even for him.

Zaiana looked to him, noting how he clutched his abdomen that still leaked black blood. His voice was pained, and Nerida seemed to snap out of her stupor while she kneeled to aid the injured fae, realizing Maverick needed help. He had been struck by Niltain Steel. It was a miracle he could still stand, but she figured the human blood coursing through him would help.

Before Nerida could make it to Maverick to attempt to heal him, the silver-haired fae snapped his head to him. A rage so raw and beyond humanity filtered his gaze as he drew his sword. He was frightening. Then he was upon Maverick in a flash of movement. The dark fae brought his own blade up in the nick of time, hissing through the pain.

Maverick and the silver-haired fae locked blades, their deadly glares so intense as they stared off that she wouldn't be surprised if they combusted.

"That thing could come back any minute," Zaiana hissed to them. "She's gone. Despite what you might think of us, we have no desire to kill you all for nothing."

"She's right."

Everyone's head snapped to Nerida where she kneeled over by Tynan, assessing the fae he had foolishly saved. The healer looked between the fae and the dark fae. Zaiana's gut twisted with something akin to betrayal, though it was stupid to even feel an inkling of the horrid emotion. Nerida was fae after all. After the many weeks they'd spent together, she was their captive, and now she had the chance to seek refuge with her own kind.

"You are not born enemies. Let them mourn," she said to the dark fae. Turning her attention to the fae, she continued, jerking her chin to the two males in a furious standoff. "And you must let me heal him before it is too late. We must not let the time Faythe bought us go in vain if the Phoenix is to return."

Everyone listened to her, struck by her peace-making and sense, but still reluctant in their mutual defiance.

"Reylan," a soft, pained voice said. The blonde female fae propped herself up on her elbows, wincing while she clutched a deep wound across her abdomen. "It won't bring her back."

Something in those words seemed to strike the warrior back into sense. Undiluted rage fell to utter misery. Reylan backed up a long step with a hard push of his blade against Maverick's that made the dark fae stumble back. His deep blue eyes cast to where Faythe last stood. Broken. She had never seen someone so fierce look so utterly *broken*.

Zaiana opened her mouth, not even sure what she wanted to say. Instead, she was halfway to turning around, about to command the others to retreat for now. Going after Faythe's body to discover if she still held the key to the temple was too grim and harrowing even for her in that moment.

The all too familiar shriek that rattled the stars made everyone flinch and turn toward it in horrid dread. *Shit.* Zaiana swore inwardly and repeatedly. They had wasted their advantage of time. They had wasted Faythe's...

"Gods above."

The distorted mutter of disbelief came from one of the fae—the one who looked kin to Kyleer, but far more elegant and poised. Zaiana followed his awed line of sight, and she saw it.

Saw *her*.

Saw the Phoenix soaring high.

Saw the small form it carried on its back.

Spirits be damned. The impossible human *lived*. By some miracle of the Gods, Faythe had been saved by the giant beast that just a moment ago was determined to reduce her to ash.

"What is she?" Tynan said, equally disbelieving as everyone stared after the duo of smoke and fire.

The bird soared away from them, heading south, raining fire stars in its wake. Before they flew too far out of sight, Zaiana could make out Faythe wasn't sitting upright. It dawned on her that without the ruin's power, the human would be descending into that plummet of darkness. It would kill her.

She couldn't be sure if Faythe had any influence on the bird's direction, but it was safe to assume nothing was out of the impossible with her. It took her farther from her companions, farther from the only healer who could possibly give her a chance of survival.

Faythe was heading…to the Niltain Isles.

The lunar eclipse was in a matter of hours, and if she grappled for her life long enough…it would be used at the exact moment Zaiana intended.

Kyleer rose from his knees and spoke quietly through their stupor. "She is Faythe Ashfyre of Rhyenelle. And she *is* the Phoenix Queen."

CHAPTER 59

Faythe

EVERYTHING HURT. THE wild pounding of her head. The tightening ache of her unmoving bones. The heat of fire coursing through her blood, a tangible force, as if she'd touched the core of the sun and become the blazing star. She wondered why her mind would surface to consciousness only to suffer such unrelenting agony.

But there was a small echo of bliss in her misery. Every now and then, a wave of coolness answered her desperate plea for the pain to set her free. Yet it was not enough to extinguish the inferno that raged.

Thoughts beyond her suffering started to return to her, faint flickers of who she was. *My name is Faythe Ashfyre. I am… I come from…High Farrow—no, Rhyenelle. I…* Her mind was a haze with loose strings of memory. Instead, she put all focus into returning to her physical senses.

Faythe heard a huff before a gust of wind blew over her completely. It was followed by a prod to her side that shifted her, nearly rolling her over.

She mustered the strength to flicker her eyes open. It was bright enough that she flinched to focus her blurred vision. Her head lolled to the side, but something large obstructed her view. A wall. Yet as her vision adjusted with a few long blinks, she became aware enough to notice the wall *moved*. It backed away from her. Faythe was struck still when she remembered.

Remembered what it was.

Her horrors were confirmed when its large beak straightened along with its neck, and Faythe had to cast her eyes up to behold the magnificent Firebird beside her.

She held utterly still. Not that she could muster much else, but she figured if it thought she was dead it would lose interest. Yet the Phoenix cantered its head—a head the length of her whole body—and Faythe watched her feeble form reflected in the glass of its red-hued eyes as it stared at her. *Studied* her.

It was odd to place human emotions in a beast, but as it silently watched her, head intermittently twitching, she could only decipher its stillness as curiosity. Faythe should feel fear, reservation at least, but she tentatively propped herself up on her elbows, teeth clenching tightly to suppress her cry of pain. Without taking her eyes off the bird, she was filled with wonder as her memories returned along with the presence of a new spark of life within her. Like a tiny kindling flame. The strength of it was a pulse of energy that was perhaps the only thing keeping her from tunneling into oblivion.

Faythe was too far from the ruin—severed from its power—and she felt the failure of her body that was now on a rapid countdown. In a flash of memory from the ordeal she had narrowly escaped with the ghastly Skailies, Faythe reached a hand back to her shoulder. While it was tender, the wounds she expected to find there, along with the brutal wounds and beatings she had sustained from the dark fae…

Faythe once again locked eyes with the Phoenix. It had healed her. At least her flesh. The exertion of her ability within—it seemed that was outside its healing capabilities. Magick was not so easily challenged without fatal consequence.

Faythe rolled over with a groan, taking a moment on her hands and knees to gather breath, though it felt like a small fan to the flames within, shallowing then heightening. Another wave of cold lapped her, and she let out a whimper of immense relief, however short the small blessing would last. Faythe found the strength to sit upright, and in turning her head to the Firebird, she realized what the coolness was. Somehow, incredulously, it was projecting whatever healing power it could to her, directly from within. The tiny kindle of flame in her chest flickered, and realization clicked into place as they held each other's eye. One word—one *name*—echoed through that impossible bond, and Faythe gasped when she heard it.

"Atherius," Faythe whispered in disbelief. It was made all the more dizzying when the Firebird reacted to the name. Its flames flickered and head dipped faintly. Wary, but…confirming. Faythe was almost ready to believe she was dreaming. Or perhaps she had truly fallen to her death over that cliff, and this was some twisted welcome to the Netherworld.

It was inconceivable. Yet it could not stand to be denied when it was right in front of her, blazing and glorious. She couldn't explain how she knew. It didn't speak—not with words or in her mind—but somehow, Faythe knew.

She took the moment of internal reprieve from the inferno to gauge where she was. The sun was rising, the sight over the horizon truly breathtaking. Pinks and oranges filtered through the dark night, putting the stars to sleep and awakening the dawn of a new day. She wanted to sit there and bask in its beauty. If this were to be her last day, she couldn't think of a more beautiful setting to witness before her end.

But she couldn't. She had one final task. She still had breath in her body and the will in her heart to see her duty fulfilled. Glancing behind her, Faythe spied the entrance to a cave—hauntingly black and darkly beckoning the longer she stared into its depthless void. A dark and silent pull emerged from it. A shudder rattled her aching body, and she winced.

The answer to her question filtered through her, not of any known language. Faythe twisted her tired gaze back to Atherius. She had taken Faythe right to where she needed to be, for behind her...

Faythe kneeled in front of the caves that would lead her to Dakodas's temple.

She pulled a weak leg from under herself. Atherius shifted at her movement. Neither was fearful, but each remained wary of the other. It was an odd notion, to be tentative and cautious around an enormous beast as though it were a horse she was attempting not to spook. There were so many ways Atherius could kill her before she could take a single breath.

Her legs trembled, close to buckling as she slowly rose to her feet. She stared off with the Firebird for a long, tense few seconds, not entirely confident it was past wanting to kill her. In an act of pure, reckless insanity, Faythe had taken the leap—a fool's desperation at recalling Agalhor's tales of a history that wasn't entirely proved to be true. When that memory settled, her mouth opened in admiration and disbelief. At the impossible reality that the great legend of a Firebird stood before her. Had *saved* her. Atherius—bonded of Matheus Ashfyre, the first King of Rhyenelle.

"What happened to you?" Faythe whispered, more as a release of internal awe.

Upon closer observation, it was clear the bird was too thin to be healthy. Its feathers were duller than Faythe imagined they should be— not nearly as vibrant as what was depicted in the painting. If legend were truth, Atherius might have been suffering alone and with little food for millennia in the Fire Mountains. Pain pinched her chest at the grim thought. She wondered how and why such a magnificent creature who could take flight to anywhere it dreamed would succumb to such a terrible, strung-out fate.

Cautiously, Faythe raised a hand, tensing with a wince when the giant beast flinched. The shallow flames that coated its wings and blazing mane flared slightly. Faythe didn't move at first. Then, as the flames dwindled once more and its head seemed to dip in curiosity, Faythe dared to take a step. Then another. And another. She halted, heart pounding wildly while she watched every flicker of the Firebird's reaction. So cautious Faythe couldn't believe her eyes when Atherius began to dip her head, inching forward as if to meet her touch.

Faythe stood still, utterly rigid in her anticipation, watching the distance close between them. A faint heat emitted from her palm when its head was mere inches away. And when they touched, Faythe gasped as a bright flare pulsed from between them. Images flashed in her mind —so many colors. Of battle and reign. Triumph and freedom. Memories of Atherius and Matheus. Faythe wasn't sure she was still breathing as decades' worth of tales filtered through her. But it was not overwhelming. It was exhilarating.

In her chest, that tiny kindle blazed to life, this one a flame of strength and courage. Magick and wonder. A line ran straight to the very core of what she was, and she could *feel* Atherius there. Faythe knew what the Firebird felt, what it thought, but not in any way she had ever experienced before. Not in a way that could be explained or understood by man, fae, or anyone.

When she came down from her high, she breathed, "Thank you."

Atherius echoed something akin to gratitude, but Faythe knew it would take time to decipher. To learn the odd push and pull that filtered between them. To be able to understand each other. But suddenly, Faythe was awash with the realization she wouldn't have that chance. Not as the fires of the Nether began to rage once more, signaling her precious time was draining fast, and she still had one last endeavor to complete. She had to remove Dakodas's ruin and prevent her from transitioning to their world. It was what she owed to those she would leave behind: the chance to *live*.

Faythe turned back to the path she had to take, overcome with a fear that made her want to succumb to defeat. She felt a gentle heat gather in her palm. It was not the tingling burn she felt when the ruin taunted her with its power; instead, it was a calm caress. Upturning her palm, Faythe's eyes widened as she watched the flame grow within, until it was an orb of white light encased by red Phoenixfyre that floated in her palm. She cast her eyes to Atherius and didn't need to voice her thanks as she felt the odd encouragement—a silent push to go. Time was running out.

Faythe absorbed the strength, the belief, she felt emanating at her back. She cast out all fear and let her determination rise and hold down the blaze that threatened to consume her before she could achieve her final task.

Stepping up to the mouth of the cave, Faythe took one final breath. Of defiance, determination. Then she took her first step into death's domain.

Within the belly of the cave, Faythe found she could control the flame that danced with an ethereal beauty in her hand. She watched it grow to illuminate a wider expanse of the distorted passage she ventured. Faythe couldn't be certain how she was doing it, only that it was connected to the tether that ran within her, and should she stray too far from Atherius she would soon lose the ability to hold it all together.

Silence encompassed her. Her feet barely caught on any debris. Her flame was soundless, and all she could tune into was the hard beat of her own heart and her breathing, which she focused on keeping steady as the fire of her burnout crawled over every inch of her skin. Urgency quickened her steps. There was nowhere but forward. Not a single junction or choice to make. The rock of the cave was stark, glistening black, not made of any natural stone she had seen before. Everything about the place radiated *death*.

Faythe halted when the narrow passage finally opened up into a larger space. In front of her was a door. A large circular door that took up the whole wall before her. Carved into the stone…was Dakodas's mark. Faythe drew Lumarias with her spare hand. Just as the blade sang free…

Her light was snuffed out.

Faythe's panic spiked as she was engulfed in complete darkness suddenly and all at once. She gripped Lumarias in both hands, angling it with no sure direction now her sight had been robbed from her. She strained her hearing. Silence. Until…

Something shuffled behind her—steps that ran for her. Faythe whirled and sliced sightlessly with her blade. She cut through only air, and a chilling chuckle bounded around the space, setting every hair on edge.

Faythe's terror gripped her speech, every sense set on high alert in cold anticipation of the presence that lingered like a ghost.

"A peculiar mind you have," a voice sang, sending a coat of ice down every notch of her spine. "So much conflict. You love so passionately but hate so precisely. You fear so truly but have a bravery so rare."

A glow broke the darkness, but her relief was quickly doused at the face that illuminated from it. Shock stunned her into place. She was unable to comprehend, unable to believe who she was seeing was real.

Across the room, walking toward her…was Marlowe.

"H-how—"

"You left me." Her friend cut her off in her bewilderment. Marlowe's delicate features were so foreign in their harshness as she looked to Faythe with such hatred.

Faythe's mouth parted, but she didn't get to voice the outpour of apology that constricted her chest painfully. Another figure stepped into the light beside her, an arm going around her waist. Jakon's glare was powerful and pinned her like a blow to her gut, taking the air from her completely.

"You left *us.*"

Again, Faythe attempted to speak, but she caught the glint of the steel dagger seconds before her longest and dearest friend sent it hurtling for her without hesitation. Instinct made her fall into a crouch to avoid its path despite feeling wholly deserving of it striking her down instead. Faythe sobbed as she curled into herself and clamped her eyes shut. But she didn't hear the sound of the blade meeting with the stone behind her. When she dared to open her eyes, pitch-blackness surrounded her once again.

Faythe blinked hard as if it would return the light, even though she dreaded to see the disgusted look of her best friends as they wished her dead. For all she had put them through, she deserved it. On her knees, Faythe was ready to lie down and let the darkness embrace her forever.

"You really are weak, Faythe." The voice that sounded beside her froze over every cell in her body. A painful vibration shook her rigid form. A touch so ghostly curled around her neck, but Faythe couldn't fight it in her terror. She couldn't see a thing, but she could *feel* the warmth of his breath at her ear. "Such a pity we didn't get more time to play together." The captain's words were chilling.

"I killed you," Faythe whispered hauntingly.

A dark chuckle seeped right through her. "Something tells me the ghosts of your past torment you far more than the enemies of your present."

"Are you afraid, little princess?" Rezar's voice was darkly taunting as it echoed a chill from her other side.

"Please," Faythe whimpered, unsure what she was asking for.

Both of them laughed. The sound grew and bounded around the dark space. She felt it over her skin, plaguing her mind. Faythe clamped her hands over her ears, but the sickening laughter was omnipresent. She found the will to unsheathe her dagger, but she couldn't be sure where her tormenters were while the voices distorted and struck from all angles.

She gripped the hilt of her dagger tightly, but her bravery dissipated completely in her helpless state. Varis and Rezar would get their revenge on her. They would kill her.

"There you are."

Faythe gasped, and the laughter cut off suddenly at the voice that joined her. Her eyes snapped open. A sob left her. A faint glow of light chased away the darkness holding her eternal tormentors, welcoming the sight of her salvation.

"Faythe." Reylan's voice was so gentle as he emerged into the open space. Faythe sobbed harder out of relief and joy that he was here. He dropped to a crouch in front of her. "I see you—"

"And I hear you," she finished in a croak.

Reylan smiled, and she mirrored it weakly. His arms opened. Faythe shuffled over to him on her knees and fell into his embrace. Her arms circled around him, and she closed her eyes. The scent that wrapped her was his, the feel of him so real. Faythe allowed herself one small moment to feel comfort. Just a few seconds to believe...

"I love you," she whispered, then she cried out as she plunged her dagger into his back.

"Faythe," Reylan choked her name.

She was trembling violently, and when he pulled away from her, they exchanged a wide-eyed look of horror. It looked like him in every perfect detail. It felt like him in every contour. It *smelled* like him. Like home.

For a second, Faythe's heart stopped dead. She looked down at the blade she held, now coated in a thick red crimson. Reylan's blood.

What had she done?

Reylan's face was torn with bewilderment and agony, but slowly, he raised his hand and curled his fist around her own, stifling her trembling hold on the dagger. He guided her hand, never breaking eye contact, and she let him, right until she felt the lethal tip press to her chest. Faythe's mouth parted with a silent cry when Reylan applied pressure through their hands. The blade broke past her leathers, pinching her skin. His eyes turned cold. So cold. No love or joy sparkled in the sapphire pools.

He wanted to kill her, and she was ready to accept it.

Faythe breathed hard at the piercing pain when the blade submerged a little deeper. Reylan's eyes were lifeless and unforgiving. Instead of plunging the dagger through her chest, he guided her hand down, cutting a deep wound as if to carve out her heart instead. Warmth pooled across her chest, over her leathers, and over her hand. Faythe glanced down, agony drowning out her need to cry out as she watched herself bleed. Watched droplets fall to the floor as her vision began to sway. Her hand fell; her body doubled over. The blade clanged to the ground while she pressed a hand to her wound.

"You are brave, Faythe."

At his words, she found the will to cast her eyes back up. But Reylan was gone.

Darkness fell around her once more, and in her utter exhaustion, there was a large part of her that didn't yearn for the light anymore.

She was tired. *So* tired. And in so much pain.

Then a glow was cast in front of her. It grew and chased away the darkness. Her weak gaze found it: the Phoenixfyre as the same mesmerizing orb. Her eyes fell to the door, realization striking.

"Blood is the key," Faythe recited through a weak breath. *Her* blood. Along with the acknowledgment that she deserved to shed it. She had passed the temple's trial.

Lumarias lay on the ground beside her. Faythe kept her eyes on the Riscillius that glowed like moonstone against the light of the fire. Her wound still bled, but the pain of it began to subside, drowned out by the clawing of a far darker oblivion intent on claiming her life.

With the dregs of her strength, Faythe gripped the hilt of her sword, her cries of pain echoing through the space as she used it to rise to her feet. Her breaths were hard and burned hot. It was a conflict of wanting to suffocate herself to douse the fire but needing the air to carry on.

Raising the Riscillius to her eye, she saw the glowing mark etched on the door through it. Faythe shuffled over to draw the first one, having enough blood on her hands already. Stepping back to glimpse the final symbol, Faythe clenched her teeth to suppress her cry as she pressed her fingers to her wound to gather enough blood to trace the second mark.

The doors groaned inward, and Faythe fell against them, using her whole body to sluggishly push them open enough to slip inside. The Phoenixfyre moved, and she couldn't be sure if it was by her subconscious will or something else entirely that it split off into four and latched onto the surrounding torches to fully illuminate the space.

Despite being underground and in a far more sinister location in appearance, inside was eerily similar to Aurialis's temple. Though it was Dakodas's mark that painted the center, and it was the moon, not the sun, that shone a glistening ray to encompass it.

Beyond the crest, Faythe spied the podium and whimpered in relief.

All she had to do was reach it, remove the ruin, and she would have succeeded. What became of her after that didn't matter.

She clutched her burning wound as she shuffled over, each step feeling like a ton weight, as though the talons of the Netherworld's claim gripped her ankles, determined to take her along with the failure that would torment her for eternity if she didn't reach that podium. Her skin was slick all over, her breaths like a battle of fire and ice.

Just a few more steps.

It seemed so far away. *Too* far away.

Just…a few…more.

Her limp hand reached out to grab the podium for stability. She paused to breathe and focus while her head fell forward. It took all her strength to straighten. When she did, Faythe's eyes were wide, her heart still, as she floated around it to stand in front.

Floated—because she couldn't be sure she was awake anymore. That this wasn't all some twisted vision or distorted reality. Faythe blinked, then again, unable to comprehend what she was seeing was real. The world crumbled from underneath her as she stared and stared…

At the hollow carving where the ruin should be.

It wasn't there.

"Missing something?"

Faythe's eyes snapped up to the voice that joined her. The figure fell sideways. No—it was Faythe who was falling. Her palms slapped the stone as her knees gave out completely. She didn't feel the pain. Faythe didn't feel anything in her state of shock.

"I do admire you." The voice grew closer as she fixed her blurry sight on the cold slate stone of the ground. Breathing was difficult. "Your fight to survive is truly remarkable. It is a tragedy to have your blood spill for this cause. Unkind is perhaps too soft a word to describe destiny's twisted humor."

A pair of black boots entered her vision, and then the dark fae crouched to her level. Faythe couldn't lift her eyes to Zaiana in her utter defeat and exhaustion. She caught a flicker of movement right before an item was brought into her line of sight. When Faythe's eyes focused enough to see clearly what she already anticipated it to be, she let out a short sob.

"What ruin did you think I had, Faythe?"

She had been tricked. All this time… Aurialis had guided her, *pushed her,* here for one purpose. Faythe wracked her brain, but she knew her recollection of Aurialis's instructions was right. Remove the temple ruin to stop the ascension.

Faythe would be a fool to believe for one moment that the Spirit of Life didn't know the ruin was already missing from Dakodas's temple. It didn't make sense. In that moment, nothing made sense, and Faythe was so far gone, so close to falling into darkness, that defeat was all she had.

She couldn't care anymore.

About the Spirits, about the realms. About kingdoms and kings. War and destiny. All Faythe cared about now…was *him.*

Acknowledging she had entered her final moments, the one who surfaced at the forefront of her mind was Reylan. For everything he was to her, everything he'd done for her, Faythe owed him her final thoughts. And in doing so, just for a moment, there was absolution.

Zaiana stood, stepping around Faythe to stand in front of the podium. Faythe couldn't fight her even if she could peel herself from her hopelessly weak state on the floor.

Faythe had lost.

"Don't see it as failure," Zaiana said as though she echoed her thoughts, uncaring if Faythe was still conscious enough to hear. "You will be used to better the world. It is an honor. Though it may not seem like it, know that your life was not a waste, Faythe Ashfyre."

She faintly heard the scrape of stone on stone and concluded what Zaiana was doing and the moment the ruin was returned to its place. Faythe sucked in a long, sharp breath.

Falling onto her back, the explosion of energy through her entire body took her from that room completely. She was suspended in a void of light. Her fire was cooled. Then she was falling. And falling. And falling.

That long inhale she held whooshed from her all at once as she plummeted back to the present. Her arched back fell to the cool stone once more. Light dispersed to bring the dark cave back into clarity.

Her next few breaths were painless bliss—but it was short-lived when the inferno began to creep over her once more.

"We don't have much time." Zaiana voiced her thoughts. "Get up."

Faythe didn't move, still processing the quick surge of unearthly energy that dispersed from her. She lay there at the complete mercy of darkness and death.

She was hauled up to a sitting position by a harsh grip on her jacket. Faythe's head fell back limply with the wave of dizziness. She didn't fight or protest. Zaiana gave a groan of irritation as though Faythe's lack of ability to withstand any of her weight was the worst of inconveniences. Faythe was prepared to be dragged to wherever Zaiana thought to move her to.

To her surprise, the dark fae hooked an arm behind her and strained as she pulled Faythe to her feet, taking her whole weight. Faythe tried to set one foot in front of the other when they moved—or rather, shuffled. Zaiana could have far easier dragged her disgracefully in her weak, delirious state.

They didn't go far, and Faythe was lowered to where she managed to stay upright on her knees, but her head bowed low. It was then she caught the black markings under her: a shimmering, dark iridescence against the moonlight as she bowed over Dakodas's symbol. Against the desire to fall forward, Faythe used every ounce of her shredded strength to tip her head back.

It was not the true moon she stared at. Just as it was not the true sun that shone in the Temple of Light. But it mimicked in reverse what would be unfolding outside. The solar eclipse. A dark sphere slowly edged closer to the glorious luminance of the moon, eager to swallow its beauty whole. It was magnificent.

Faythe felt the coolness of the metal that rested along her neck, but she didn't flinch or fear at the threat of Zaiana's blade. She even felt relief that her pain was about to end. She kept her eyes on the moon—a sight that always reminded her of Reylan. His silver hair and the night sky of his sapphire irises. Faythe thought of Jakon and Marlowe, how happy and full their lives would be for having each other. She thought of Nik and Tauria, knowing they would triumph in their roles as monarchs. She thought of her father and the short but precious memories she treasured. She thought of her mother in her early years of innocent bliss and freedom. But she always came back to him, to Reylan, as the single thing she wanted to be in this life…was his. Something he would always have when he thought he deserved nothing.

"I'm sorry it has to be this way." Zaiana's voice was quiet, a faint sadness woven into the words that made Faythe flick her gaze up to catch the amethyst cores looking down on her from behind. Her expression was not reflective of the sadness but held a crease of disturbance. Underneath the coldness and ruthlessness...Faythe believed the dark fae wasn't entirely devoid of remorse or regret.

Faythe's lips cracked open, her gaze switching to the eclipse as it began. "I forgive you."

"I didn't ask for your forgiveness."

"I know."

Faythe was on fire. Her blood was boiling, her skin slicked with sweat. Her eyes fell closed, and she was so close to *begging* for it to end. For Zaiana to use the blade poised to take her life. Her mind entered a state of calm. When bracing for a final breath, panic set her free. Blissful, painless oblivion opened welcoming arms. She was ready.

Faythe felt the pressure of the blade but not the pain as its sharp edge broke the surface of her skin. Darkness rolled over her, cancelling fractions of the moon's caress above.

"Zaiana!"

The dark fae's name was a call to stop wrapped in the promise of death.

A shiver shot up Faythe's spine at the voice, snapping her wide awake. The malice and lethal threat that coated the word set every hair on end. She had never heard such a tone from him. With all her dregs of strength, she forced her limp head to straighten, and when met with those eyes she expected to find...Faythe was struck with a cold-set horror.

She should have felt relief—joy even—but staring at Reylan, all that drowned her was dread and heartache. Faythe blinked. Long and hard. She wondered if he was real, or if this were another illusion. A trick and torment in her final moments.

Then she felt the gentle cool breeze within—his attempt to help her, grapple her, while she rapidly fell. But it was a short breath of air against a raging inferno.

He's real. He's here.

Reylan held a fury so raw. In his firm, rigid stance, he aimed an arrow at Zaiana. His breaths were calculated but hard. His eyes held no mercy as they pinned the dark fae with a mark of death.

"You shouldn't be here." Faythe couldn't be sure if the words left her parted lips aloud, but Reylan heard.

His eyes flashed to her for a second, but it was enough for her to glimpse his distress under the lethal mask he wore. It was why she wished with everything she was that he wasn't here, if only to spare him from watching her die. He didn't deserve to carry that burden in his days without her.

Reylan's eyes were back on Zaiana, and there was nothing merciful in his voice as he addressed her. "If you harm her—" He took a few calming breaths, his wrath a tangible force in the room. "There is no place you will be able to hide. No distance you can run. I will find you. And when I do, death is not what you will fear from me, though it is what you will beg for."

A shiver crawled over every inch of her skin. Faythe thought she felt the faint slackening of the knife at her throat. Reylan's promise was chilling. It shattered her heart…because she knew he would. If she died here by the dark fae's hand, he wouldn't rest until that promise was fulfilled. Maybe not even then.

Faythe couldn't find the words to plea with Zaiana or beg Reylan to leave and spare himself from witnessing her death. By Zaiana's blade or under the fiery grip of magick, she didn't have long.

The dagger pressed tightly to her throat once more, emitting a sharp sting. "Believe it or not, I have heard such words before," Zaiana answered. Though it was not through taunting or malice; her voice was so detached it was monotonous. "Yet I still live to mock the speakers."

"I'm sorry."

"Don't," Reylan begged. *"Don't say that like goodbye."*

621

"I'm not saying goodbye…" Gods, she was hurting, her heart close to erupting. *"Because in this life or the next, I will always find you."*

"Please," Reylan spoke aloud. Not to Faythe, as his tense grip on the bow slackened, fury dissolving into pure desperation. "Take my life instead."

"It has to be her," Zaiana said, a faint tone of remorse slipping through. "She is the only one with enough spiritual blood for the ascension." Then her voice angled down to Faythe. "You were marked the day you were born. Hunted before you ever took your first breath. Marvellas knew of your conception, knew you were the only one who would be able to repeat history. A true heir is what it took to raise Mordecai, and it is what it will take to raise Dakodas. Why did you come, Faythe? You could have stayed away, stayed silent and hidden, yet you walked right into the trap for slaughter that has been set since the dawn of your days."

I was guided here. Aurialis. *It was all a trick.* Faythe thought she was shaking her head with utter disbelief, but she couldn't be sure since she was barely present. "Just do what you have to, Zaiana."

She had lost.

"No!"

"Reylan," Faythe whimpered. "Please…" She begged him with her eyes; with everything she was through that unexplainable bond that strained and cried painfully between them, sending her toward breaking point. She begged him to leave. To look away. To accept that this was her fate, and it was not his fault.

They deserved the life they had glimpsed together. Yet she couldn't be sad or angry, nor resentful or vengeful. All she felt…was gratitude. Faythe was grateful even for the short time she'd had in this world. She was grateful for the love she was wrapped with even when she didn't deserve it. For Jakon and Marlowe. For Nik and Tauria. For everyone who had accepted her and followed her. But most of all…she was grateful for *him*. The love she felt from him, *for* him, was worth every moment of borrowed time.

Overhead, the glow that once encompassed her was eclipsed completely. Her time was up. She had failed.

Faythe kept her eyes on the sapphire pools that took her away. Reylan—the steel warrior, survivor, her strength—fell to his knees, mirroring her position in front of her. His lips moved, but she couldn't hear his words. She could no longer hear him within either. *Oh Gods*, she couldn't *feel* him anymore. Faythe held his desperate eyes without a blink, not registering the other movements around him that blurred to nothing but faint color. She saw nothing but the night sky, embracing the absolution it delivered.

A searing pain erupted in her chest, but it was second to the agony of witnessing Reylan's final, haunted look of devastation. Faythe chanted her apologies to him. Over and over. Right until the last breath exhaled from her body and darkness opened its arms to catch her as she fell…she held those sapphires with a promise.

Faythe would always, in every realm and every time, find her way home to them.

CHAPTER 60

Zaiana

Z AIANA WAS A creature of death and darkness. She was taught not to have mercy, led to believe there was nothing to be gained from the weak emotions human and fae allowed themselves to be consumed by.

Watching the fae warrior fall to his knees, bowing to a force that surrendered him to her absolute mercy, was the most foolish thing she had ever witnessed. Foolish…yet Zaiana dared to believe her still chest *wrenched* for him.

Love. It was an absurd concept. To attach one's feelings to another opened them up to endless forms of torture and manipulation. From each other; from outsiders. Love was damning. But it was also absolution.

She saw it right in front of her eyes: Faythe held onto her love for the warrior to find peace in her final moments. Reylan held onto his love for her as though it shattered his soul.

Zaiana felt something she never thought she could.

Heartache.

She might have even believed there was a movement in her chest, if that were possible, with how strongly she felt the current of their connection. A distant memory slipped cruelly past the steel barrier of her mind, a time she might have looked just as hopeless and pleading as the fierce warrior on his knees.

Then Zaiana did something she never thought she would.

She let go.

Removing her blade, she took a step back. It wouldn't save Faythe, who was seconds away from meeting her end by another deadly force for the magick she had consumed beyond her limits. Zaiana was a damn fool. She was sacrificing everything…for nothing. She owed them nothing. But in seeing the faint relief on Reylan's face, she didn't feel regret.

She would be killed for her failure, perhaps even by the High Lord's hand. But he would have to find her first. Zaiana could flee. A sudden rush of actions she might need to take once leaving this cave made her forget all else. There was an ache in her gut, only in imagining leaving Tynan and the others behind. This was her failure, her weakness, and she would bear the consequences of it alone.

The eclipse was almost over. Her window of opportunity—of freedom—closing so fast it was too late to go back on her decision now.

"If you're not going to kill her, I suppose I am."

Zaiana's head snapped to the entrance of the temple, but she barely caught a glimpse of Maverick before he moved so fast, passing Reylan, who didn't even have the time to release a breath with his wide-eyed look. Maverick was behind Faythe, blade drawn, and there was no pause of hesitation, no thought or mercy, before he plunged it through the human's chest.

Time was suspended while Zaiana tried to process the maneuver. She blinked once. Twice. Maverick removed the blade. Faythe didn't utter a single sound of pain before her body fell. Zaiana didn't hear the thump of her lifeless form hitting the ground as she stared at her in shock. Crimson blood pooled out from beneath her, the tangy-sweet scent filling the room. Zaiana didn't give a reaction to it as she tuned her hearing back in to the thick, ringing silence.

The only heartbeat that raced and stilled to such an uneven rhythm...was Reylan's.

Faythe was...

The cry of soul-splitting agony from the silver-haired warrior was enough to stiffen her spine but weaken her knees. He fell forward, palms splayed, as though death tore through him too. The air fell icy cold, and a faint sting creeped behind her eyes while every hair on her body stood on edge watching him.

Maverick yielded no reaction to it. He swiped up Faythe's sword. A beam of light shot out through the stone in the pommel. Tearing a strip of fabric, he quickly wrapped the blade before his hand curled around the length of Niltain Steel. Then he stepped out of the circle marking, holding the Riscillius extended within, and when the laser of light connected to the stone target above the entrance...

A white flare erupted around them.

Zaiana flinched, shielding her eyes against the piercing light. Waves of ethereal power shot out from the center where the light encompassed them. It was pain, and it was strength. Ripples of magick and wonder entwined with darkness and chaos. Zaiana wanted to bow to such a force—an entity with no true form.

Seconds felt like minutes. Zaiana squinted to glimpse her surroundings. All was ethereally bright, until a form started to emerge from the void of light. Stepping right through the veil between what lay beyond and their ordinary, mundane world, a figure of darkness and power, of death triumphant, emerged.

The Goddess of the Moon. The Spirit of Death herself.

Dakodas ascended to stand before her.

Zaiana fell to one knee, compelled to offer respect to such a high and mighty being. Maverick beside her did the same, both their heads bowed low. It had been so long since Zaiana felt *unworthy* of being before someone.

The compass of light didn't fall once Dakodas had stepped through. Faythe's body remained within it, and for a short second, Zaiana acknowledged the twist in her gut. Remorse. Would her friends even have her body to say their goodbyes? Even though Faythe was Zaiana's enemy, she would have granted them that wish.

"Zaiana Silverfair."

A chill swept her body in the most delightful way. Zaiana cast her eyes up, locking them on the most devastatingly magnificent being she had ever had the privilege of being before.

"Stand, my child." Her voice was symphonic, a caress of a shadow like those that faintly hovered around her. Moved with her.

Zaiana did as Dakodas commanded, coming face-to-face with the Great Spirit of myth and legend. The Goddess of her people. Dakodas walked to her—no, *floated* seemed more appropriate for the way she moved. The black waves of her gown made it look as if it were made of shadows. A darkness that could wink out the sun.

"You have done well." Dakodas cast her eyes down to where Maverick still knelt. "Both of you. I knew you would not fail me."

Zaiana swallowed hard. She *had* failed. In the one task she had been entrusted to carry out. If Maverick had not shown…

Dakodas stepped over to Maverick. A long, slender hand reached down to his face, curled under his jaw, and guided him to stand. Zaiana couldn't be sure why the touch bothered her. Maverick deserved the Spirit's praise; she did not.

"Even more alluring in person," she said, a loose thought spoken aloud as her eyes drank in every inch of his face and trailed down his tall body. It was infuriating, conflicting, that Zaiana's fists clenched of their own accord as Dakodas's desirous gaze lingered on him.

Movement behind them caught all their attention, followed by the quick whistle of cut air. The arrow that had fired didn't make its mark although none of the dark fae moved. It was suspended in the air, caught by a vine of shadow a mere foot away from Dakodas.

Reylan already had another arrow nocked into place, a breath away from attempting the shot again. Then shadows lashed out to encase his wrists, an arm of smoke circled his throat, and he choked as Dakodas took hold of him. His eyes didn't snap to the Spirit. Or to Zaiana, though it should have been her. Those blazing sapphire eyes that were beyond humanity pinned on Maverick. The one who had taken Faythe's life.

Her companion didn't react to it, not giving a flicker of remorse or regret while he accepted the mark the fae made on him. The promise of a chilling end that would never cease until it was fulfilled. Maverick accepted it, and then turned to Dakodas.

"His companions might be making their way here already." His tone was so detached, not a single emotion. Maverick didn't look to Zaiana at all.

Dakodas took a long, elegant breath of deliberation before she said, "You are right, and we have much to do." Turning back to him, the curl of her mouth was that of a masterful seductress. Maverick answered back to it, and the small drop in her gut at witnessing the subtle flirtation was surprising even to herself. "Bring my ruin."

Maverick moved to do as she commanded.

Zaiana couldn't stand the thought of holding the wicked thing, but even with the ascension completed, it was still a deadly weapon. One Zaiana had been forced to spend her life learning how to wield, master, coming close to having her life claimed by it many times.

Dakodas's shadows released the fae warrior all at once. He didn't try a second attack. He didn't look to the dark fae at all. His eyes were fixed on the compass of light that held Faythe's body within it, his face so detached it was like watching the living dead. He was a ghost as he deliberated following straight through that veil, uncaring if he met with the same final fate.

For a pitiful second, Zaiana wondered what it would be like to mean so much to one person. In life and in death.

The two darkest forces in the room glided to the exit as though their dose of mild entertainment was over and boredom had become them. Zaiana hesitated, unable to tear her eyes from the fae who made slow, vacant steps toward that veil.

Zaiana had witnessed death on more accounts than she could track. She had *caused* death to so many. Yet this was…different. It was a strange feeling, watching someone else's world shatter right in front of her. She couldn't place the emotions that chilled her whole and hollowed her stomach. It was an odd sight to see such a powerful and fierce fae reduced to absolutely nothing.

"Zaiana."

Her name traveled like a dark caress as Maverick spoke it. As she snapped her gaze to him, she wondered if the Spirit of Death detected the slight note of a plea wavering in his eyes. He coaxed her to follow as they paused in the doorway to the temple.

Zaiana straightened her spine and hardened her eyes. She took three calming breaths to tunnel into a place so dark and lonely. A place that knew no feeling or emotion. Zaiana became everything she was expected to be as she took her first steps to them. Maverick and Dakodas took their leave.

She couldn't be sure what compelled her to halt in the entrance with her back to the fae. She stood still, canceling out every sense but one. Tuned so precisely one final time. There was something broken in every beat of the warrior's heart. She tuned that out too, kept tunneling and waiting. Until…

It was impossible.

Time slowed to a crawl.

The light behind them fell all at once, and her hearing snapped back, inviting the surroundings in once more. The warrior shuffled over to where Faythe's limp body should be.

Slowly, Zaiana turned her head. She glanced at the unmoving form of the human. Stared and listened to be sure. Reylan cradled her ghostly form on his knees, and it was a morbid sight she knew would haunt her for eternity. Then his eyes flicked up to her, and the wide look they shared...

Zaiana turned from him, intending to abandon him in his desolate state. Yet just as she took her first step, her voice dropped to a hush so quiet only he would hear.

"Don't let go."

CHAPTER 61

Faythe

N O PAIN. NO SOUND. No feeling. No burden.

Death was kind to grant such numbness when passing through worlds.

Faythe was weightless. She was free.

Her eyes revealed nothing in the void she lay suspended in, waiting. She didn't know what for or what would come next when she wanted to remain in the realm of silence and peace a little longer. Yet somehow, she knew…

This place was not the Afterlife. Not yet.

When Faythe tried to figure out why she couldn't let go to get there, she felt it—a tether that latched onto her soul, straining so thin it was a miracle it didn't snap. It stopped her from projecting completely to the next realm, but Faythe wasn't sure she wanted to be saved.

In the distance, a faint silhouette started to emerge, and Faythe felt her first real emotion in the space of light. Wariness. She straightened and waited. If the Spirit of Death had abandoned her duty to plague the world Faythe left behind, she was curious as to who else would come to guide her through the realms.

It shouldn't have come as a surprise, yet Faythe was struck by the sight of who emerged. Aurialis wore no expression as she came into full clarity as if born of the light that surrounded them.

Suddenly, every memory and feeling came crashing down on her. Faythe didn't know what to think or feel. She was dead. Above every-thing, she felt...*guilt*.

Oh Gods.

Reylan had watched her die. It was an unfathomable pain, because she knew if it were him here and her back there...

Faythe's knees almost gave out. Her eyes were wide as she stared and stared at the Spirit of Life, unsure if she was staring into the eyes of her ultimate betrayer but having no room for anger.

"I failed." The whisper of utter disbelief was a tightening pain in her chest. But it was a small consolation—she could still *feel*. What it meant she couldn't be sure.

Yet Aurialis shook her head. "No, Faythe, you are exactly where you should be."

It was so twisted Faythe found her statement amusing. "It's over."

"It has only just begun—"

"I'm *dead!*"

"You are transitioning."

Faythe blinked and recoiled. "I'm—*what?*"

The Spirit was so calm, so collected—a stark contrast to every fluc-tuating emotion that frenzied in Faythe's mind. "Come, Faythe." Auri-alis motioned her to follow as she turned and walked away—toward nothing as the space seemed vast and endless.

She had no energy to protest. Nothing to lose and nothing to gain. Faythe's feet pressed after the Spirit, figuring if she was taking her past the veil to the Afterlife, it would be better than this eerie space of light.

"You are so much more than what you have lived your life believing you are," Aurialis began, but she didn't look to her as they walked side by side.

Faythe watched the Spirit's unflinching expression, but then the first flicker of color and movement caught her eye. A small gasp left her at what unfolded around them. Moving images. So many of them, and Faythe featured in every one. Memories. Yet they were not in her perspective as she watched herself. From days when she couldn't remember being so young, right up until now. Faythe saw memories of her with her mother in her early years. Of her and Reuben growing up together. Of many years by Jakon's side. Of her antics with Nik, friendships with Marlowe and Tauria. Of her training days and dark days. Faythe saw the few memories with her father and every newfound friend in Rhyenelle. Kyleer, Izaiah, even Livia. The battle with the dark fae Zaiana. Then she saw *him*. Faythe's brow pinched at the sight of Reylan.

"Every person to cross your path and forge and bond with you has had a role in shaping who you are. Knowledge, courage, wisdom, strength, resilience, darkness, and light—you are made of them all. And it is with each and every one of them that we still stand a chance in this war. The war against my sisters."

Faythe couldn't take her eyes off the memories, feeling her chest tighten thinking of each and every one she had left behind. "I don't understand," she barely whispered. "We lost. I—I died."

At the thought, one scene was brought to the forefront out of all the others. Faythe's hand covered her mouth as she bit back her cry. At the broken sight of Reylan. At herself...lifeless. Seeing the utter devastation she had left in her wake, suddenly, all her sorrow was engulfed by a flash of white rage.

She targeted the Spirit of Life with that furious gaze. "You knew the ruin wasn't there."

Aurialis said nothing, but the faint rise of her chin was confirmation. Faythe had no power or weapons in here, but her rage had never been so palpable that she feared what she could do without either.

"You lured me right here like a sheep to slaughter." She seethed. "Right to exactly where Marvellas wanted me all along!" Faythe didn't care about herself, only for the pain she had left behind. Aurialis's silence made her cry out, *"Why!"*

Something like remorse flickered in the Spirit's eyes as she continued to assess Faythe. "Dakodas broke laws of our kind when she transitioned," she began to explain. "They needed your blood to be sacrificed, but in consequence, do you remember what I told you? With every evil born—"

"A way to destroy it is conceived in turn."

Aurialis nodded. "Marvellas may believe she has stopped her own prophesy, but in sacrificing you, my sisters have only created what will have the strength to bring about the demise of them both. We stand a chance at turning the tide of this war."

Faythe stayed silent. She had nothing to say. Not as she tried to sort through her dizzying disbelief.

They began a slow walk through the passage of Faythe's life again. "Dakodas and Marvellas are powerful, but in transitioning they are limited. Bound in fae form, they forfeit great heights of power, but they are still no match for any other in your realm, and together, they will be unstoppable." Aurialis's cool blue eyes felt like daggers of ice that chilled her to her core. "Until you."

Faythe swallowed hard, riddled with a daunting sense of unease. "What am I supposed to do from here?"

Aurialis shook her head. "You must return, Faythe. But not as you once were."

"I don't understand."

The Spirit smiled. With warmth and sadness. "We don't have much longer. It was I who caught your soul before it could cast on to the next realm, but it is not without your mate's tether that you are both here... and there. Though be aware, even the strongest of bindings can be broken."

Faythe took a breath that felt suspended in time. A weight dropped in her stomach. A dawning. An awakening. A brilliant flare of realization and enlightenment. Her eyes were wide. Still. Fixed on Aurialis as though she might repeat it.

"What did you say?"

A single word. She needed to hear it again to be sure she didn't imagine it. Aurialis straightened, knowing exactly what she had caught.

"The Great General of Rhyenelle, the one they call the White Lion of the South, and the one who will be remembered in history within stories of battles and reign for millennia…is your soul-bonded mate, Faythe Ashfyre."

The word was a pulse of energy. Striking. Faythe turned from Aurialis, and her eyes met with clarity, awareness, when they fell on a memory, staring straight into the pull of Reylan's eyes. *Mate.* Her vision unfocused with an overwhelming dose of disbelief. It shouldn't be possible.

Yet now, it was undeniable.

"Power answers power. You are a child of the Spirits, Faythe. The general may believe he has met others like himself before, with the gift he harbors, but he is misled. He is not simply a Mindseer, as such an ability is only used to diminish another's power. No other can *take*. Reylan Arrowood has strong bloodline blessings from all three Spirits. He is a powerful rarity none of us could have predicted."

The pieces were there, but in her bewilderment and sense of dread, Faythe's mind was too scattered to form the full conclusion.

"You are two parts of the same sword. A blade without a hilt cannot be wielded. A hilt without a blade is forgotten potential. With the weapon you could become, together, you could change the world."

Faythe blinked hard, wondering if…perhaps she might have realized sooner. The pull to him; the unexplainable bond that ran between them, which her mind had been content to accept so many other outlandish possibilities for. Because the truth had been clouded by the crushing heartache of their mortal differences she refused to dwell on. To be mates—it was a notion so impossible her mind never once allowed the thought an ounce of merit.

Then the world came tumbling down on her when the concept settled.

It changed nothing.

Nothing except adding a suffocating weight of sorrow on the shoulders of the selfless warrior who deserved so much better. He had already lost what he didn't know he had gained. And she had lost him.

Faythe's thoughts doubled back to another key point in Aurialis's words. "What do you mean by 'return'?"

"The only way to send to you back in the form you need is by the Spell of Transition. Yet it demands a life for a life...and my plan all along has been to give up my own."

Something in her chest pained at the thought. Despite all Aurialis had put her through, she wouldn't accept the price she offered. Faythe was about to shake her head, but Aurialis continued.

"It is not wholly a sacrifice...as instead, you and I will become one, Faythe Ashfyre."

She blanched completely. "I won't become your vessel."

"You misunderstand. How you see me now is only a form for your mind to be able to conceive what I truly am. A source of energy; power. I have no true form, no face or body. In transitioning, my sisters have manifested their visual mundane forms, and in creating such forms of bone and flesh they forfeited great power. In those bodies, they cannot hold nor wield any of the Spiritual ruins as it is what they are made of. What will give us the advantage is that I will not sacrifice by fusing with you instead. I will live within you as a power to call upon, dormant unless brought forth by your command. It will take learning control and discipline. You need a teacher who can tame the storm, as without, you could destroy the world in your wake with what I will grant you. And it is in mastering that control that you will be able to wield the Tripartite

Ruin to open the spirit portal and send my sisters back. You will become something the world has never seen before. But with great power comes great responsibility, my child. You must never lose sight of your golden heart, as power can inspire the allurement to darkness even in the purest of souls."

Faythe mulled over her words. Over and over and over. She shook her head, unable to comprehend the inconceivable twist her fate had taken. Her eyes cast up, landing once again on the image that threatened to shatter every last piece of her composure: Reylan, so broken, on his knees, cradling her still body with quiet pleas that whispered through to her here.

"Come back to me."

Wetness trailed her cheeks, and she knew...she knew she would do anything, *give* anything, for the chance to raise the warrior from his knees. To feel him again. This couldn't be the end. They hadn't had the time they deserved. Even if it were filled with horror and uncertainty, she wanted to walk that dark path with him.

Without taking her eyes off Reylan, Faythe asked quietly, "What do I have to do?"

"You fight, Faythe Ashfyre."

She found the will to tear her gaze from Reylan, and when she turned to Aurialis, Faythe's panic surged.

"You live, and you fight, for the world of the dreamer." The Spirit's form glowed so bright Faythe flinched, shielding her eyes.

"Wait!"

But it was too late. A flare of light erupted, forcing her lids to clamp shut against the sting of luminance. When it dimmed, Faythe snapped them open again. Before her, right where Aurialis stood a moment ago, a brilliant sphere of light glowed—*moved*—as though the sun blazed triumphantly before her. Amber flowed over its surface like a river of molten ore. It was *alive*. It was...

"Will I be able to speak with you?" Faythe was awestruck by Aurialis's brilliant true form. Pure, undiluted energy and radiance. She wanted to fall before such a force.

"Not in your realm." Aurialis spoke in the same soothing melody, but as an omnipresent echo. "While you still live, so will I, within you. I will not have influence over your conscious thoughts, and when you call upon my essence to aid you, it will be you in control. But let it consume you, and we will both meet our permanent end."

Faythe's body rattled with a daunting chill, a sense of responsibility and power she didn't believe she was capable of bearing. But she would try—for him, and for everyone else she'd left behind. Against all that wanted to submit to defeat, Faythe took three calming breaths.

One of belief in herself.

One of determination to succeed.

One of strength to return.

On the final exhale, Faythe straightened her spine with a flare of defiance. "I'm ready."

"Yes, you are, golden-eyed child."

Aurialis floated to her, that brilliant sun closing in to devour her whole. A fear so all-consuming stilled every muscle in her body as she watched that unparalleled energy travel to her.

"Will it hurt?" Faythe braced, watching the ripples of fire across the orb's surface, a mesmerizing dance of danger and wonder. As it got closer, to her surprise, the sun began to condense, shrinking until it was close enough to touch, and she reached out a palm. Faythe was wholly entranced to have the essence of a Great Spirit hovering above her touch—power that was so enticing, so darkly alluring, it enraptured her completely.

"After this,"—fear labored her breaths—"what comes next?"

The light drifted to her, energy already pulsing and tangible around her. Filling her lungs; torching her blood.

The echo whispered, "We enter the beginning of the end."

Faythe didn't have a second to prepare, not a single forewarning, before that ball of light surged straight through her. When it met her chest and sank through…Faythe ignited from the inside out.

An immobilizing pain gripped her whole, but it didn't bring her to her knees. Faythe felt as if she were floating in an endless oblivion as fire tore and devoured every internal piece of her. Claiming, destroying, and reemerging.

Faythe thought of him. Only him. She chanted her promise over and over as she reached for the tether within; as she reached back to the only thing that kept her from casting into the final oblivion. Faythe Ashfyre recited her promise as if they were the last words she would ever speak again.

I see you, Reylan. I see you, and I hear you, and I'm coming home.

EPILOGUE

Reuben

S O MANY WERE injured, yet Reuben couldn't deny it brought him satisfaction to see pain and suffering in those he had been forced to live among while they treated him as no better than a simpleton. They were the fools. It brought him no greater pride and joy to be a key part of the plan to bring them all to their knees. They would bow before *her*. He would make sure of it.

The war between enemies returned the moment Faythe soared far and fast on the back of the Firebird. An awe-striking moment, he had to admit, despite his displeasure she hadn't fallen to her end instead. Once, he might have held admiration for her. Love, perhaps. Yet it was all an illusion behind her insufferable arrogance and naivety. Even she looked at him as though he were a boy who needed shielding; a coward who needed protecting.

He would show her. He would show them all.

After a short conflict, Zaiana managed to slip away, chasing after the duo of smoke and fire. To his pleasure. Though it grated his anger that the general was also able to take the ability of the weakened Shapeshifter and follow close behind.

The healer distributed her attention between the wounded: Izaiah, Livia, Kyleer, and Tynan. Reuben let a small smile form on his lips to see them incapacitated. While everyone's attention was occupied, he lingered in the shadows watching the carnage unfold. The wicked weakness that came with being human was damning. He wanted to be like them—like her: dark and immortal. The true savior species of the realm.

A hard hand fell on his shoulder, and Reuben winced at the impact.

"What a busy little rodent you've been."

The mocking tone flared his irritation, but he respected the dark fae Maverick. He, like all of them, answered to *her*, whether he was aware of it or not.

Glancing over him, Maverick clutched his wounded abdomen that poured black blood. The Niltain Steel had stifled his fast healing. The dark fae followed his gaze down to his stomach and met Reuben's eyes with a knowing smirk.

"Our healer is a little preoccupied, and I don't have time to spare." His onyx eyes fell to Reuben's throat, a frightening hunger filling them. Reuben's spine locked with fear, but he didn't get a second to brace before the dark fae lunged. The sudden movement swallowed his cry of pain when sharp teeth punctured his flesh. He was stunned into place.

The pain didn't last long. Minutes could have passed for all he could tell when a subdued feeling of numbness embraced him while Maverick drank. Reuben wouldn't have objected even if the dark fae had bothered to ask. He knew it would be his intention to go after Zaiana, and Faythe would meet her just end in the necessary way.

Maverick pulled away from him abruptly, panting hard. With great resistance, he distanced himself. Reuben lifted a hand and pressed it to the throbbing puncture wounds. The dark fae looked to be battling within himself, as if refraining from attacking again to bleed him dry. With his back to him, Maverick finally straightened, seeming to have triumphed in his grapple with whatever shreds of humanity lay within.

"Why do you do it?" he asked, and Reuben gauged the question as Maverick's attempt to distract himself from the bloodlust he battled. Hunger began to ease into curiosity as Maverick's depthless gaze fixed on him. "What did Faythe do to you to earn such betrayal?"

It wasn't that the dark fae cared, but the question blanked Reuben's mind.

What did Faythe do?

Did hatred require motive? Were his feelings toward Faythe not justified without reasonable cause? He wracked his brain. Faythe was arrogant, selfish, foolish… But that wasn't what Maverick asked.

What did Faythe do?

"You're a peculiar human," Maverick drawled, one eyebrow curved as Reuben stayed silent in his moment of inner turmoil.

She despised Faythe as the human sought to stop everything *she* had built. That was enough because her enemies were his.

"You'd better get back. Wouldn't want to arouse suspicion." Maverick's smirk was darkly amused. Then he splayed his impressive wings and shot to the sky in a powerful motion Reuben tracked until he was engulfed by the smoke and ash that choked the air.

Reuben made his way back, plastering fake horror and fear on his face and drilling an urgency into his run. He spotted them across the mountain fringe clogged with thick clouds, coughing as it caught in his throat and stung his eyes. Nerida was tending to Izaiah, who at first glance appeared the most injured with charred clothing and burned skin. Everyone else crouched around, ready to aid in whatever way she needed.

He watched in awe as Nerida's hands motioned around her,

collecting rainwater before it could fall. Tentatively, she lowered it toward the worst of Izaiah's wounds.

"This is going to sting, but it will help cool the skin before I can make and apply a salve." She didn't wait for his response before the water lay over his skin by her command, and the warrior cried out, held down by his brother and the dark fae Tynan.

He shouldn't be helping them. None of them should. But when he glanced at Amaya, he saw she was also aiding Livia by adding pressure to her scorched abdomen.

The water stayed in place as Nerida shot to her feet, crossing the distance to drop right back down by the auburn-haired fae who was faltering.

"I think the Skailies have some kind of poison in their flesh. This shouldn't still be bleeding." The healer's eyes snapped up to lock on his. "There's a plant in that pack called Tazenite. Red dried petals and long black stems. Find it—now!"

Her leadership and unfaltering courage in the situation was admirable. To seem as if he gave a damn whether the fae lived or died, Reuben dropped down, scrambling to find what she asked for.

"It's not here!" he called back.

Nerida swore. "The woods back there—I was sure I saw Hemedite. It's not as strong, but it will help. Dark green stems with purple spotted buds. They're small and tend to grow under ordinary green bush plants, so look carefully."

Reuben nodded. "We passed through those woods. I think I might have seen some." He didn't hesitate and took off running.

As soon as he was out of sight, his face dropped all emotion. *Foolish fae.* His feet sloshed through the drenched woodland, body shuddering as puddles gathered in his boots. His teeth bashed together, and he clamped his arms around himself in an attempt to stifle his violent shaking. From the cold or perhaps the skittish fear there could be more of those ghastly creatures lurking at any given turn. He hated to admit his own feebleness, but despite his ruthless training in Lakelaria, he didn't believe his newfound combat skills would be of any match against them.

His eyes darted over the forest. Every dark flicker triggered a hard skip of his erratic heart as he weaved through the trees. But his attention never once dropped to scan the foliage for what the healer had described.

Reuben felt her before he saw her. The presence that caressed his mind soothed months' worth of pent-up irritation and anger at being separated from her to be among the enemy. A hand snaked over his back, and as he turned…every second of misery was worth it to meet the blazing pride in those sparkling gold eyes.

Gods, she was magnificent. Her red lips curled in delight, and it was all he could do to angle his head down to meet them. What they shared was raw and passionate, just like everything else that radiated from the red-haired beauty.

"I've missed you," he breathed, holding her face.

"We won't be apart for much longer, Reu, I promise." She took his hands. "They suspect nothing?"

"Not at all. Faythe has welcomed and protected me as though I am a boy." He sneered.

Her chuckle was warmth against the cold that weighted his body from the rain that had finally relented. But she remained dry. Flawless. Sometimes, he wondered if she were real at all to be able to maintain such perfection.

"Don't worry—everything is going exactly to plan." Her hand lovingly caressed his face, and he leaned into that touch. Of triumph and conquer. She was brilliant. "Did you find what we've been looking for?"

Reuben's brow furrowed, hating more than anything that he had to disappoint her. "Not yet. Faythe is already suspicious of my knowing about her trip to the Isles and my insistence to come, but she's too driven by her bleeding heart to see her own doom lingering at her back."

Her chuckle was smooth and sensuous, the sound so entrancing he couldn't stop the need to kiss her again. The soft noises that came from her caressed and awoke every nerve in his body. His hands roamed her waist, her breasts. He didn't think he could ever get enough of the magnificent creature before him.

"Reu," she panted, pulling away from him. "I'm afraid we don't have much time."

His grip on her only tightened, and the lust swirling in her blazing gold eyes had him stifling a groan. "Let me come back with you," he pleaded.

"The work is not yet done. We will be together again soon, and you will help me change this world for the better, my little pet."

"Whatever you need from me."

He was hers. He would do anything for her.

"You know what I need from you."

Reuben nodded. "The Light Temple Ruin."

A slow curl disturbed her rouge-painted lips. "You promised to retrieve it for me."

"Because you cannot hold them yourself."

She nodded.

"Then who will shatter them if Faythe is gone?"

For the first time, there was a hesitation in her eyes. A flicker of doubt that twisted his gut. He almost fell to his knees in fealty. It was a weightless breath when she spoke, deeming the knowledge safe enough to be protected by him.

He would always protect her.

"There are only two in existence with enough power to shatter the ruins."

"Two?"

"Faythe is one of them, and for a long time I believed her to be the only one." Her face faltered, and it crushed him to watch her in turmoil. "But there is one other unexpected candidate capable of shattering them. One who can take considerable power—perhaps even from me if I yield it to him for the task."

Reuben's face smoothed with realization. "Reylan Arrowood." *That bastard.* He was equally as insufferable as Faythe. The way they moved together, spoke, touched—it was a perfect harmony, a balance he wanted to break, if only to watch them fall.

"What's my name, Reu?"

Her name.

His mind scrambled for the answer that should have come so easily. But the question drew a blank. Slowly, his arms fell from her as he thought it over. He loved her. He adored her. He should know her name.

Confusion struck his heart. No—fear.

What is her name?

Then something he should have questioned as he stared into those golden eyes rushed to the surface and froze his drenched body. "Why do you look like her?"

He didn't expect an answer because his mind was already flashing with pieces of memory that made him stumble in fast steps away from her. She answered every one of them, all the way until his back met the trunk of a thick tree and she pressed her body to him.

"She is my kin." Her head tilted, and Reuben stiffened entirely when her palm raised to his face. "What is my name, Reu?"

He clamped his eyes shut because her name was a key, unlocking the gates he wanted to force shut for all who stormed behind them. He didn't want to remember—not anymore.

Who he was.

What he'd done.

Faythe wasn't the enemy. She was his friend, and he was her ultimate betrayer.

Oh Gods.

"Say it," she hissed beautifully.

His lips parted, his body vibrating when he found it in the depths of his mind where the shadow talons sang and rejoiced to it. Their master.

"Marvellas."

Her gold eyes blazed at hearing it. The Spirit of Souls, Goddess of the Stars, had him at her complete mercy. But it wasn't just because of what he was to Faythe, the one she sought the most, fascinated and fixated by her. Faythe was everything she wanted and everything she despised. But Marvellas wasn't solely a beautiful monster… She had a history one could only sympathize with no matter the cruelty that turned in her heart. She had once loved. Once held joy. Once, she might have seemed as ordinary as the rest of them despite the powerful entity she was.

"Why me?" he whispered, terror weaving through her infiltration in his mind. She'd entranced him to follow her. Worship her. What was worse was that his feelings became entangled as he remembered all they had shared before. He wondered…maybe, if she wasn't the enemy, if her reign wasn't so filled with bloodshed and terror, would he have learned to love her truly?

"You look just like him," she said distantly, looking at him but seeing someone else entirely. One from her past. And for a second, there it was. Humanity. A glimpse of what she could have once been before every-thing was torn from her to blacken her heart.

As if a switch had flicked, a darkness that winked out the sun in an instant turned her stare to icy steel. "But you are nothing like him." Marvellas pushed away from him, and Reuben stifled his breath of relief.

"Why not put an end to it all? Why not just take her? Why use me?"

"You came to me, Reu. I have a hard time believing there isn't a God going against the others in seeing my vision for this world. I wanted you to fall for me. Of your own will. Believe it or not, I take no pleasure in doing what I need to do for you to see things my way. I'm not the villain, Reuben. I'm the savior."

He wanted to believe her. There was a pang in his chest that reacted with a desire to soothe the vulnerability she didn't even realize she had surfaced. Marvellas would never admit to her one tragic desire. That all she longed for in this life was someone to stick by her. Truly and wholly.

But he couldn't.

Not if saving meant killing. Annihilation. Betrayal. Submission.

He could never willingly stand by her. Or bow to her.

And it was as if she heard every wicked thought he had about her in that second. The sun in her eyes rippled like molten ore, but they pierced through him like spears of ice. Her hand lashed out to his throat, and he choked.

"Have it your way, Reu. But I will have what I want."

A dark, damningly familiar sensation crawled across his mind. Shadow talons hissed and clawed but froze him in place. His body, his mind, stilled with the agony as they devoured his thoughts and memories once more—everything that made him love and cherish and feel. But there was a part of him that welcomed the numbness they would offer once she'd relented her torture for his defiance.

In his next blink, Reuben opened his eyes to stare down at the beautiful creature.

"I'll see you again soon," she whispered against his lips before pressing down firmly. He wanted to reach for her, but she stepped away abruptly. "Run along for now, little pet."

His will to protest was strong, but the will to obey her stronger. This was what she needed him to do. Reuben didn't look back as he stormed his way to the group of unwitting fae who would welcome him like fools.

Reaching into his pocket, his fingers brushed something crisp and dry. He didn't stop walking as he pulled it out and eyed the plant. Red dried petals, long black stems. It was what the healer needed to save

Livia. Reubens palm enclosed it, grinding until the fragments caught in the wind behind him when he opened his hand.

Fools. All of them. He would get her what she needed, no matter what it cost or who he had to eliminate to find it.

Marvellas would have the Light Temple Ruin.

WHAT IF TO LOVE WAS TO CONDEMN?

As the sun made its final descent, Nik looked away from where she had vanished. He turned back to his castle knowing Tauria Stagknight had been willingly sacrificed as the opening gambit in their deadly game.

A Court... A Bond... A Darkness.

AN HEIR COMES TO RISE NOVEL

A CLASH
OF THREE
COURTS

C.C. PEÑARANDA

IV

LUMARIAS
PRESS

PRONUNCIATION GUIDE

NAMES

Faythe: faith
Reylan: ray-lan
Nik: nick
Jakon: jack-on
Marlowe: mar-low
Tauria: tor-ee-a
Kyleer: kai-leer
Izaiah: i-zai-ahh
Livia: liv-ee-a
Reuben: ru-ben
Zaiana: zai-anna
Maverick: mah-ver-ick
Mordecai: mor-de-kai
Tynan: tie-nan
Amaya: ah-mah-ya
Nerida: ner-i-dah
Lycus: lie-cuss
Tarly: tar-lay
Marvellas: mar-vell-as
Aurialis: orr-ee-al-iss
Dakodas: da-code-as
Augustine: au-guss-teen
Ashfyre: ash-fire
Arrowood: arrow-wood
Galentithe: gal-en-tithe
Zarrius: zar-ee-us

PLACES

Ungardia: un-gar-dee-a
Farrowhold: farrow-hold
Galmire: gal-my-er
High Farrow: high-farrow
Lakelaria: lake-la-ree-a
Rhyenelle: rye-en-elle
Olmstone: olm-stone
Fenstead: fen-stead
Dalrune: dal-rune
Fenher: fen-er
Ellium: elle-ee-um
Niltain: nill-tain

OTHER

Riscillius: risk-ill-ee-us
Lumarias: lou-ma-ree-as
Yucolites: you-co-lights
Dresair: dress-air
Magestone: mage-stone
Skailies: skay-lees
Fyrestone: fire-stone
Phoenixfyre: phoenix-fire

ACKNOWLEDGMENTS

My dear readers, how far we've come since the first book. I thank each and every one of you for spreading the love for this series. The ending of this book is not an answerless question of a cliffhanger; it's a promise. I can't wait to open this world further and dive into the turning point of Faythe's story. But first, I must take you back to a certain royal duo, whose story I couldn't do enough justice woven between Faythe and Zaiana's in this book. I'm excited for what's to come, and even more so to have you all along on the journey book by book.

To my mother, as always, I couldn't do this without you. You're my rock, my number one cheerleader, and I don't thank you enough for all your support.

To Eva, Marcus, and Jason, how can four siblings be so similar but different at the same time? I have each of you to thank for shaping me in different ways. I am rooting for you all to reach your dreams.

To my canine companions, Milo, Bonnie, and Minnie. Three tiny bundles of craze and love.

To Miranda, your friendship has been a true light to keep me guided and focused in this overwhelming sea we're in. I am rooting for you, my friend. Keep being incredible.

To a strong group of women, you know who are. We cheerlead for each other no matter what, and I can't tell you how grateful I am for you all.

To my street team who have been with me since book one, I can't thank you all enough for your enthusiasm for this story and excitement for everything I share with you first. You keep me thriving.

To my stellar editor, Bryony Leah. Once again I find myself so incredibly grateful to have you on my team. Over and above your brilliant edits, the friendship that came from it is so treasured. Thank you for your amazing work on this huge book. Here's to many more.

To Alice Maria Power, how is it possible these covers just keep getting better? You're truly magical. You capture Faythe's growth and strength so perfectly and effortlessly every time it's hard to believe we're not of the same mind.

As always, I come back to thank you again, my dear readers. Watching the audience grow and knowing how this world and characters are resonating with you is my life's joy. I'll never be able to express with words how truly stunned and thankful I am for your support. Here's to you. To us.